SAINT LEIBOWITZ
AND THE
WILD HORSE WOMAN

Also by Walter M. Miller, Jr.

A CANTICLE FOR LEIBOWITZ

SAINT LEIBOWITZ

and the

WILD HORSE
WOMAN

Walter M. Miller, Jr.

BANTAM BOOKS

*New York   Toronto   London
Sydney   Auckland*

SAINT LEIBOWITZ AND THE WILD HORSE WOMAN
A *Bantam Book* / *November 1997*

BOOK DESIGN BY GLEN M. EDELSTEIN

ISBN 0-553-10704-6

*Published simultaneously in the United States
and Canada*

Bantam Books are published by Bantam Books, a
division of Bantam Doubleday Dell Publishing
Group, Inc. Its trademark, consisting of the words
"Bantam Books" and the portrayal of a rooster, is
Registered in U.S. Patent and Trademark Office
and in other countries. Marca Registrada. Bantam
Books, 1540 Broadway, New York, New York 10036.

PRINTED IN THE UNITED STATES OF AMERICA

For David, and all those
who sailed against the Apocalypse

The estate of Walter M. Miller, Jr.,
would like to thank Terry Bisson
for his editorial contribution to
Saint Leibowitz and the Wild Horse Woman.

NOTE

The fictional Rule of Saint Leibowitz is an adaptation of the Benedictine Rule to life in the Southwest Desert after the collapse of the Great Civilization, but it is true that the fictional monks of Leibowitz Abbey do not always conform to it as perfectly as did the monks of St. Benedict.

Permission was kindly given by the Liturgical Press, Collegeville, Minnesota, to quote from the Leonard J. Doyle translation of *St. Benedict's Rule for Monasteries*, Copyright 1948, by The Order of Saint Benedict.

SAINT LEIBOWITZ
AND THE
WILD HORSE WOMAN

LANDS OF ⊕F ☉HE MARE

SAINT LEIBOWITZ
AND THE
WILD HORSE WOMAN

DANFER

VALANA
(Cathedral of St. John-in-Exile)

POBLA

WILDDOG

GRASSHOPPER

Misery

NEW ROME
(St. Peter's)

WILDDOG

Kensau

NEW JERUSALEM

ABBEY OF
ST. LEIBOWITZ

ARCH HOLLOW

GRASSHOPPER

TULSE

*WATCHIT-
OL'ZARKIA*

Nady Ann

YELLOW

JACKRABBIT

Valley of
the Misborn

SUCKAMINT MTNS

Great River

Red River

TIMBERLEN

Brave River

HANNEGAN
CITY

Bay Ghost

*HILL
COUNTRY*

© 1997 Jeffrey L. Ward

CHAPTER 1

"Listen, my son, to your master's precepts, and incline the ear of your heart."—The First Sentence of *The Rule*.

"Whoever you are, therefore, who are hastening to the heavenly homeland, fulfill with the help of Christ this minimum Rule which we have written for beginners; and then at length under God's protection, you will attain to the loftier heights of doctrine and virtue which we have mentioned above."—The Last Sentence of *The Rule*.

Between these two lines, written about 529 A.D. in a dark age, is Saint Benedict's homely prescription for a way of monastic life that has prevailed even in the shadow of the *Magna Civitas*.

 S HE SAT SHIVERING IN THE GLOOMY CORRIDOR outside the meeting hall and waited for the tribunal to finish deciding his punishment, Brother Blacktooth St. George, A.O.L., remembered the time his boss uncle had taken him to see the Wild Horse Woman at a Plains Nomad tribal ceremony, and how Deacon ("Half-Breed") Brownpony, who was on a diplomatic mission to the Plains at the time, had tried to exorcise her priests with holy water and drive her spirit from the council lodge. There had been a riot, and an assault on the person of the young deacon, not yet a cardinal, whose shaman ("witch doctor") attackers had been summarily executed by the newly baptized Nomad sharf. Blacktooth was seven at the time, and had not seen the Woman then, but his boss uncle insisted that she had been there in the smoke of the fire until the trouble began. He believed his boss uncle, as he might not have believed his father. Later, before he ran away from home, he

had seen her twice, once by day riding bareback and naked along the crest of a ridge, and once by dim firelight when she prowled as the Night Hag through the darkness outside the settlement enclosure. He definitely remembered seeing her. Now his ties to Christianity demanded that he remember them as childish hallucinations. One of the less plausible accusations against him was that he had confused her with the Mother of God.

The tribunal was taking its time. There was no clock in the hall, but at least an hour had passed since Blacktooth had testified in his own defense and been excused from the meeting hall, which was really the abbey's refectory. He tried not to speculate about the cause of the delay, or the meaning of the fact that pure chance had cast that deacon, now Cardinal ("Red Deacon") Brownpony, in the role of *amicus curiae* at the hearing. The cardinal had come to the monastery from the Holy See only a week ago, and it was well known, but most certainly not announced, that his purpose in being here was to discuss with the Abbot Cardinal Jarad the papal election (the third in four years) which would be called soon after the present Pope finished dying.

Blacktooth could not decide whether the eminent Half-Breed's participation in the trial was favorable or unfavorable to his cause. As he remembered the night of the exorcism, he also remembered that in those days Brownpony had not been friendly to the Plains Nomads, either the wild or the tamed. The cardinal had been raised by sisters in the territory conquered by Texark. It had been told to him that his mother, a Nomad, had been raped by a Texark cavalryman, then had abandoned her baby to the sisters. But in recent years, the cardinal had learned to speak the Nomad tongue, and spent much time and effort forging an alliance between the wild people of the Plains and the exiled papacy in its Rocky Mountain refuge at Valana. Blacktooth himself was of pure Nomad blood, although his late parents had been displaced to the farming settlements. His mother owned no mares, and thus he had no status whatever among the wild tribes. His ethnic background had been no handicap during his life as a monk; the brethren were tolerant to a fault, except in matters of faith. But in the so-called civilized world outside, being a Nomad would be hazardous unless he lived on the Plains.

He heard raised voices from the refectory, but could not make out words. One way or another, it was all over for him but the final break, and that was proving to be the hardest thing of all.

A few paces from the bench where he was supposed to wait was a shallow alcove in the corridor wall, and within it stood a statue of Saint Leibowitz. Brother Blacktooth left the bench and went there to pray, thus disobeying the last command given to him: Sit there, stay there. Breaking his vow of obedience was getting to be a habit. Even a dog will sit and stay, his devil reminded him.

Sancte Isaac Eduarde, ora pro me!

The kneeling rail was too close to the image for him to look up at the saint's face, so he prayed to the saint's bare feet, which stood on a pile of fagots. Anyway, by now he knew the wrinkled old countenance by heart.

He remembered when he first came to the abbey, the abbot of that time, Dom Gido Graneden, had already ordered the statue removed from his office, its traditional place of repose, to the corridor here where it now stood. Graneden's predecessor had committed the sacrilege of having the fine old wood carving painted in "living color," and Graneden, who loved it in its original condition, could neither bear to look at it, with its painted simper and impossibly upturned irises, nor put up with the smell and noise of having its restoration done in situ. Blacktooth had never seen the full paint job, for upon his arrival the head and shoulders of a man of wood emerged from what appeared to be the chest of a plaster saint. A small area at a time was being treated with a phosphate compound concocted by Brothers Pharmacist and Janitor. As soon as the paint began to blister, they painstakingly scraped it clean, trying to avoid any abrasion of the wood. The process was very slow, and he had lived a year at the abbey before the restoration was complete; by that time, a filing cabinet occupied its space in the abbot's office, so here it still stood.

The restoration was less than complete even now, at least in the sight of those who remembered its original condition. Occasionally Brother Carpenter stopped to frown disapprovingly at it, then to work on the creases around the eyes with a dental pick, or caress between the fingers with fine sandpaper. He worried about what the paint remover might have done to the wood, so he frequently rubbed it with oil and lovingly polished it. The carving had been done nearly six centuries ago by a sculptor named Fingo, to whom the Beatus Leibowitz—not yet canonized—had appeared in a vision. A close resemblance between the statue and a death mask which Fingo had never seen was used as an argument for his canonization, because it seemed to confirm the reality of Fingo's vision.

Saint Leibowitz was Blacktooth's favorite saint, after the Holy Virgin, but now it was time to go. He crossed himself, arose, and returned doglike to the bench to "sit and stay." No one had seen him at prayer except his devil, who called him a hypocrite.

Blacktooth remembered clearly the first time he had asked to be released from his final vows as a monk of the Order of Saint Leibo-

witz. Many things had happened that year. It was the year the news
came that his mother had died. It was also the year that the Abbot
Jarad had received the red hat from the Pope in Valana, and the year
Filpeo Harq had been crowned as the seventh Hannegan of Texark by
his uncle Urion, the archbishop of that imperial city. More to the
point, perhaps, it was the third year of Blacktooth's work (assigned to
him by Dom Jarad himself) of translating all seven volumes of the
Venerable Boedullus's *Liber Originum,* that scholarly but highly specu-
lative attempt to reconstruct from the evidence of later events a plausible history of the darkest of all centuries, the twenty-first—of
translating it from the old monastic author's quaint Neo-Latin into
the most improbable of languages, Brother Blacktooth's own native
tongue, the Grasshopper dialect of Plains Nomadic, for which not
even a suitable phonetic alphabet existed prior to the conquests (3174
and 3175 A.D.) of Hannegan II in what had once been called Texas.

Several times Blacktooth had asked to be relieved of this task
before he asked what he really dreaded, to be released from his vows,
but Dom Jarad found his attitude peculiarly stubborn, obtuse, and
ungrateful. The abbot had conceived of a small Nomadic library he
wanted created as a donation of high culture from the monastic Memorabilia of Christian civilization to the benighted tribes still wandering
the northern Plains, migrant herdsmen who would one day be persuaded into literacy by formerly edible missionaries, already busy
among them and no longer considered edible under the Treaty of the
Sacred Mare between the hordes and the adjacent agrarian states. As
the literacy rate among the free tribes of the Grasshopper and Wilddog Hordes who ranged with their long-haired cattle north of the
Nady Ann River was still less than five percent, the usefulness of such
a library was a thing only dimly foreseen, even by the Lord Abbot,
until Brother Blacktooth, in his initial eagerness to please his master
before the work began, explained to Dom Jarad that the three major
dialects of Nomadic differed less to the reader than to the listener,
and that by means of a hybrid orthography and the avoidance of special tribal idioms, the translation could be made understandable even
to a literate ex-Nomad subject of Hannegan VI in the South, where
the Jackrabbit dialect was still spoken in the shanties, the fields, and
the stables, while the Ol'zark tongue of the ruling class was spoken
in the mansions, the law courts, and the police barracks. There the
literacy rate for the malnourished new generation of the conquered
had risen to one in four, and when Dom Jarad imagined such moppets
receiving enlightenment from the likes of the great Boedullus
and other notables of the Order, there was no talking him out of the
project.

That the project was vain and futile was an opinion Brother Blacktooth dared not express, so for three years he protested the inadequacy of the talent he was applying to the task, and he assailed the intellectual poverty of his own work. He supposed the abbot had no way to test this claim, for, besides himself, only Brothers Wren St. Mary and Singing Cow St. Martha, his old companions, understood Nomadic well enough to read it, and he knew Dom Jarad would not ask them to. But Jarad had him make an extra copy of one chapter of the work, and he sent it to a friend in Valana, a member of the Sacred College who happened to speak excellent Jackrabbit. The friend was delighted, and he expressed a wish to read all seven volumes when the work was done. The friend was none other than the Red Deacon, Cardinal Brownpony. The abbot called the translator to his office and quoted from this letter of praise.

"And Cardinal Deacon Brownpony has been personally involved in the conversion of several prominent Nomad families to Christianity. And so, you see—" He paused as the translator began to cry. "Blacktooth, my son, I just don't understand. You're an educated man now, a scholar. Of course that's incidental to your vocation as a monk, but I didn't know you cared so little for what you've learned here."

Blacktooth dried his eyes on the sleeve of his robe and tried to protest his gratitude, but Dom Jarad went on.

"Remember what you were when you came here, son. All three of you, going on fifteen and you couldn't speak a civilized word. You couldn't write your name. You never heard of God, although you seemed to know enough about goblins and night hags. You thought the edge of the world was just south of here, didn't you?"

"Yes, Domne."

"All right, now think of the hundreds, think of the thousands, of wild young fellows just like you were then. Your relatives, your friends. Now, I want to know: what could possibly be more fulfilling to you, more satisfying, than to pass along to your people some of the religion, the civilization, the culture, that you've found for yourself here at San Leibowitz Abbey?"

"Perhaps Father Abbot forgets," said the monk, who had become a bony, sad-faced fellow of thirty years, and whose ferocious ancestry was in no way suggested by his mild appearance and self-conscious ways. "I was not born free, or wild. My parents were not born free or wild. My family hasn't owned horses since the time of my great-grandmothers. We spoke Nomadic, but we were farm workers, ex-Nomads. Real Nomads would call us grass-eaters and spit on us."

"That's not the story you told when you came here!" Jarad said accusingly. "Abbot Graneden thought you were wild Nomads."

Blacktooth lowered his gaze. Dom Graneden would have sent them home if he had known.

"So real Nomads would spit on you, would they?" Dom Jarad resumed thoughtfully. "Is that the reason? You'd rather not cast our pearls before such swine?"

Brother Blacktooth opened his mouth and closed it. He turned red, stiffened, crossed his arms, crossed his legs, uncrossed them rather deliberately, closed his eyes, began to frown, took a deep breath, and began to growl through his teeth. "Not pearls—"

Abbot Jarad cut him off to prevent an explosion. "You're pessimistic about the resettled tribes. You think they have no future anyway. Well, I think they do, and the work is going to be done, and you're the only one to do it. Remember obedience? Forget the purpose *of* the work, if you can't believe in that, and find your purpose *in* the work. You know the saying: 'Work is prayer.' Think of Saint Leibowitz, think of Saint Benedict. Think of your calling."

Blacktooth regained control of himself. "Yes, my calling," he said bitterly. "I once thought I was called to the work of prayer—contemplative prayer. Or so I was told, Father Abbot."

"Well, who told you contemplative monks don't work, eh?"

"Nobody. I didn't say—"

"Then you must think scholarship is the wrong kind of work for a contemplative, is that it? You think that scrubbing stone floors or shoveling shit from the privies would put you closer to God than translating the Venerable Boedullus? Listen, my son, if scholarship is incompatible with the contemplative way, what was the life of Saint Leibowitz all about? What have we been doing in the Southwest desert for twelve and a half centuries? What of the monks who have risen to sanctity in the very scriptorium where you're working now?"

"But it's not the same."

Blacktooth gave up. He was in the abbot's trap, and to get out of the abbot's trap, he would have to force Jarad to acknowledge a distinction he knew Jarad was deliberately avoiding. There was a kind of "scholarship" which had come to be a form of contemplative religious practice peculiar to the Order, but it was not the head-scratching work of translating the venerable historians. Jarad, he knew, was referring to the original labor, still practiced as ritual, of preserving the Leibowitzian Memorabilia, the fragmentary and rarely comprehensible records of the *Magna Civitas*, the Great Civilization, records saved from the bonfires of the Simplification by the earliest followers of Isaac Edward Leibowitz, Blacktooth's favorite saint after the Virgin. Leibowitz's later followers, children of a time of darkness, had taken up the selfless and relatively mindless task of copying and recopying, memorizing and even chanting in choir, these mysterious records. Such tedious work demanded a total and unthinking attention, lest the imagination add something which would make meaningful to the copyist a meaningless jungle of lines in a twentieth-century diagram of a lost idea. It demanded an immersion of the self in the work which was the prayer. When the man and the prayer were entirely merged, a sound, or a word, or the ringing of the monastery bell, might cause the man to look up in astonishment from the copy table to find that the everyday world around him was mysteriously transformed, and aglow with the divine immanence. Perhaps thousands of weary copyists had tiptoed into paradise through that illuminated sheepskin gate, but such work was not at all like the brain-racking business of bringing Boedullus to the Nomads. But Blacktooth decided not to argue.

"I want to go back to the world, Domne," he announced firmly.

Dead silence was his answer. The abbot's eyes became glittering slits. Blacktooth blinked and looked aside. A buzzing insect flew through the open window, circled the room twice, and alighted on Jarad's neck; it crawled there briefly, took wing again, and flew buzzing out by the same window.

Through the closed door of the adjoining room, the faint voice of a novice or postulant reciting his assigned Memorabilium penetrated the silence without really diminishing it:

"—and the curl of the magnetic field intensity vector equals the time-rate-of-change of the electric flux density vector, added to four pi times the current density vector. But the third law states the divergence of the electric flux density vector to be—" The voice was soft, almost feminine, and fast as a monk reciting rosary, his mind pondering one of the Mysteries. The voice was familiar, but Blacktooth could not quite place its owner.

Dom Jarad sighed at last and spoke. "No, Brother Blacktooth, you won't disown your vows. You're thirty years old, but outside these walls, what are you still? A fourteen-year-old runaway with nowhere to go. Pfft! The good simpletons of the world would pluck you like a chicken. Your parents are dead, yes? And the land they tilled was not their own, yes?"

"How can I be released, Father Abbot?"

"Stubborn, stubborn. What have you got against Boedullus?"

"Well, for one thing, he's contemptuous of the very Nomads—" Blacktooth stopped; he was in another trap. He had nothing against Boedullus. He liked Boedullus. For a dark-age saint, Boedullus was rational, inquisitive, inventive—and intolerant. It was the intolerance of the civilized for the barbarian, of the plantation owner for the migrant driver of herds, of Cain, indeed, for Abel. It was the same intol-

erance as Jarad's. But Boedullus's mild contempt for the Nomads was
beside the point. Blacktooth hated the whole project. But there across
the desk from him sat the project's originator, giving him pained
looks. Dom Jarad was as always Blacktooth's monastic superior, but
now he was more than that. Besides the abbot's ring, now, he wore the
red skullcap. As the Most Eminent Lord Jarad Cardinal Kendemin, a
prince of the Church, he might as well be titled "Winner of All Argu-
ments."

"Is there some way I can get out, m'Lord," he asked again.

Jarad winced. "No! Take three weeks off to clear your head, if you
want to. But don't ask that again. Don't try to blackmail me with
hints like that."

"No hints, no blackmail."

"Oh, no? If I don't reassign you, you'll go over the wall, right?"

"I didn't say that."

"Good! Then listen, my son. By your vow of obedience, you sacrifice your personal will. You promised to obey, and not just when you
feel like obeying. Your work is a cross to you, is it? Then thank God
and carry it. Offer it up, offer it up!"

Blacktooth sagged, looked at the floor, and slowly shook his head.
Dom Jarad sensed victory and went on.

"Now, I don't want to hear anything about this again, not before
you've finished all seven volumes." He stood up. Blacktooth stood up.
The abbot shooed the copyist out of his office then, laughing as if it
had been all in fun.

Brother Blacktooth passed Brother Singing Cow in the corridor
on his way to Vespers. The rule of silence was in force, and neither
spoke. Singing Cow grinned. Blacktooth scowled. Both of his fellow
runaways from the wheat plantations knew why he had gone to see
Dom Jarad, and both lacked sympathy. Both thought his job a cushy
one. Singing Cow worked in the new printing shop. Wren worked in
the kitchen as Brother Second Cook.

He saw Wren that night in the refectory. The second cook stood
on the serving line, apportioning mush to the platters with a large
wooden spoon. Each man in passing murmured, "*Deo gratias*," and
Wren nodded back as if to say, "You're welcome."

As Blacktooth approached, Wren already held a huge gob of
mush on the spoon. Blacktooth held his platter to his chest and signaled *too much* with his fingers, but Wren turned to speak "necessary"
instructions to a busboy. When Blacktooth relaxed his platter, Wren
piled it on.

"Half back!" Blacktooth whispered, breaking silence. "Headache!" Wren raised his forefinger to his lips, shook his head, pointed

to a sign—SANITARY RULES—behind the serving line, then pointed toward the sign at the exit, where a garbage monitor checked for waste.

Blacktooth laid the platter on the serving kettle. With his right hand he scooped up the heap of mush, with his left hand he seized the front of Wren's robe. He pushed the mush in Wren's face and massaged it until Wren bit his thumb.

The prior brought word directly to Blacktooth's cell: Dom Jarad had relieved him of his job in the scriptorium for three weeks, in order that he might pray the stone-floor-scrubbing prayer for the cooks in the kitchen and dining area. And so for twenty-one days Blacktooth endured Wren's smiling forgiveness while knee-skating on soapy stones. More than a year passed before he again raised the standing question of his work, his vocation, and his vows.

During this year, Blacktooth felt that the rest of the community had begun to watch him rather closely, and he sensed a change. Whether the change was really in the attitudes of others, or entirely within himself, its effect was loneliness. Occasionally he felt estranged. In choir, he choked on the words "One bread and one body, though many, are we." His unity with the congregation seemed no longer taken for granted. He had spoken the words "I want out," perhaps before he really meant them; but not only had he uttered such a thing to the abbot, he had allowed his friends to learn of the incident. Among the professed, among those who by solemn vows had committed themselves irrevocably to God and the Way of the Order, a monk with regrets was an anomaly, a source of uneasiness, a portent, a thing in need of pity. Some avoided him. Some looked at him strangely. Others were all too kind.

He found new friends among the younger members of the community, novices and postulants not yet fully committed to the Way. One of these was Torrildo, a youth of elfish charm whose first year at the abbey had already been marked many times by trouble. When Blacktooth was sent to the cooks for three weeks of floor-scrubbing penance, he found Torrildo already scrubbing there as punishment for some unannounced infraction, and he soon learned that Torrildo's had been the muffled voice reciting a Memorabilium in the room adjacent to Dom Jarad's during the professed monk's unhappy interview. They differed widely in their interests, origin, character, and age, but their common penance pushed them together long enough for a bond to form.

Torrildo was glad to find an older monk who was not impeccable. Blacktooth, while not quite admitting that he envied the postulant's relative freedom to leave, began imagining himself in Torrildo's sandals, with Torrildo's problems, Torrildo's charm, and Torrildo's talents (which evaded the notice of many). He found himself giving advice, and was flattered when Singing Cow told him sourly that Torrildo was copying his mannerisms and becoming his talk-alike. It became a brief case of father and son, but it further estranged him from the ranks of the professed, who seemed to frown on the relationship.

He was beginning to find it hard to distinguish the frown of the community from the frown of his conscience. One night he dreamed he knelt for communion in the chapel. "May the Body of Jesus Christ lead you to eternal life," the priest repeated to each communicant; but as he came closer, Blacktooth saw that it was Torrildo, who, as he placed the wafer on Blacktooth's tongue, leaned close and whispered, "One who eats bread with me here shall betray me."

Blacktooth awoke choking and gagging. He was trying to spit out a living toad.

CHAPTER 2

URING THE TIME OF BROTHER BLACKTOOTH'S
translation of the eleventh chapter of the
seventh and final volume of Boedullus,
and while he was working feverishly
toward the end, a special messenger
from Valana in the Denver Freestate arrived at the abbey with tragic news. Pope
Linus VI, shrewdest if not the saintliest
of recent popes, and the man most re-
sponsible for healing the postconquest schism, had fallen dead of
heart failure while he stood shin deep in an icy trout stream and shook
his fishing rod at a delegation from the Curia on shore. He was protesting to them that the Lord had never told Peter to stop fishing for
fish when he commissioned him to fish for men. Pope Peter had indeed taken five apostles boating with him right after the Resurrection,
Linus correctly pointed out. Then he paused, turned white, dropped
the rod, and clutched at his chest; almost defiantly he gasped, "I go

a-fishing," and collapsed into the frigid water. It was later noticed that these last words were from John 21:3.

As soon as the message came, the Most Eminent Lord Cardinal Abbot began packing his fine regalia. He notified the Papal Way Station in Sanly Bowitts that he would need armed escorts for the trip, and he arranged with Brother Liveryman to make ready the fastest pair of horses and the lightest carriage, as if he planned a quick trip. He mixed his tears with a nervous sweat, as he alternated between bursts of grief and flurries of excitement in making ready for the journey. It was the dead Pope who had made him a cardinal. It was going to be his first papal election. The community understood his mixed feelings and stayed out of the way.

After he had eulogized Linus and offered a Mass for the dead, he spoke to the assembled monks in the refectory after supper on the night before his departure.

"Prior Olshuen will carry out my duties as abbot while I am away. Will you promise to render him the same obedience in Christ which you give to me?"

There was a murmur of assent from the congregation.

"Does anyone withhold this promise?"

There was silence, but Blacktooth felt people looking at him.

"My dear sons, it does not behoove us in this monastery to discuss the business of the Sacred College, or the politics of Church and State." He paused, looking around at the small lake of faces by lamplight. "Nevertheless, you are entitled to know why my absence may be extended. You all know that one result of the schism was the appointment by two rival claimants to the papacy of an unprecedented number of cardinals. And that one of the terms of the settlement that ended the schism was that the new Pope, now of holy memory, would ratify the elevation of all these cardinals, no matter which claimant had made the appointments. This was done, and there are now six hundred eighteen cardinals on the continent, some of them not even bishops, a few not even priests. Since these are about equally divided between East and West, it may be very hard to arrive at the two-thirds-plus-one majority required to elect a pope. The conclave may last for some time. I hope not more than a few months, but there is no way I can predict.

"I fear you will hear gossip from time to time as travelers come and go. As long as the papal exile from New Rome continues, surrounded as it is by Texark forces, the enemies of the Valana papacy hope for a renewal of schism, and they keep all possible gossip alive. Listen to none of it, I beg of you.

"The force of the State has abated. The seventh Hannegan is not the same tyrant as the second Hannegan, who, as you know from history, used treachery and cattle plague to capture an empire from the Nomads, driving sick farm animals among the woolly Nomad herds. He sent his infantry as far west as the Bay Ghost, and his cavalry chased stragglers right past our gates. He killed the Pope's representative, and when Pope Benedict laid Texarkana under interdict, Hannegan seized all the churches and courts and schools. He occupied the lands adjacent to New Rome, forcing His Holiness to flee to asylum in the crumbling Denver Empire. He collected enough bishops from the east to elect an anti—or, I should say, a *rival* pope to sit in New Rome. And so we had sixty-five years of schism.

"But Filpeo Harq is the seventh Hannegan now. Indeed he is heir to the conqueror, but there is a difference. His predecessor was a cunning, illiterate semi-barbarian. The present ruler was raised and educated for power, and some of his teachers were educated by us. So have hope, my sons, and pray.

"If the right Hannegan sits down with the right pope, with God's help, surely they can come to terms and end the exile. Pray that the pope we elect may return to a New Rome free of Texark hegemony. Everywhere, people have strong feelings about the occupation, but it will do no good for us to argue within the Sacred College whether the Texark troops must be withdrawn before the Pope goes home. That will be a decision for the Pope himself, when he is elected.

"Pray for the election, but not for any candidacy. Pray for the Holy Spirit to guide our choice. The Church now needs a wise and saintly pope, not an eastern pope or a western pope, but a pope worthy of that old title 'Servant of the servants of God.' " In a lowered voice, Dom Jarad added, "Pray for me too, my brothers. What am I but an old country monk, to whom Pope Linus, in a weak moment perhaps, gave a red hat? If anybody in the College has a lower rank than I, it must be the woman—er, Her Eminence the Abbess of N'Ork, or else my young friend Deacon Brownpony, who's still a layman. Let your prayers help keep me from folly. Not that I'm going among wolves, eh?"

Barely audible snorts and giggles caused Jarad to frown.

"As a way of showing that I am not an enemy of the Empire, I shall cross the Bay Ghost and take the route through the Province. But I'm going to reschedule tomorrow's Mass. It's a ferial day anyway, so we'll sing the old Mass for the Removal of Schism before I go."

He spread his arms as if to embrace the throng, traced a great cross in the air over them, came down from the lectern, and left the hall.

Blacktooth became wildly anxious. He sought permission to

speak to Dom Jarad before the abbot's departure, but permission was denied. In near panic, he found Prior Olshuen before dawn in the cloister on his way to Matins, and he plucked at the sleeve of the prior's robe.

"Who is it?" Olshuen asked irritably. "We're already late." He stopped between the shadows cast from the columns by a single torch. "Oh, Brother Blacktooth, it's you. Speak up then, what is it?"

"Dom Jarad said he'd hear me when I finish Boedullus. I'm almost finished, but now he's leaving."

"He said he'd hear you? If you don't lower your voice, he'll hear you now. Hear you about what?"

"About changing jobs. Or about leaving the Order. And now he'll be gone for months and months."

"You don't know that. Anyway, what can I do about it? And what do you mean, leave the Order?"

"Before he goes, would you remind him about me?"

"Remind him of what about you?"

"I can't go on this way."

"I won't even ask. 'What way?' We're late." He began walking toward the church with Blacktooth tagging at his side. "If Dom Jarad has a free moment this morning, and if I mention your obvious agitation, will he know what it's all about?"

"Oh, I'm sure he will, I'm sure!"

"Now what was that about leaving the Order? Never mind, we're holding up Matins. Come by my office in a day or two, if you like. Or I'll send for you. Now calm down. He won't be gone for long."

Abbot Jarad, after he offered the Mass for the Removal of Schism, announced from the pulpit his wish that they sing a votive Mass for the election of a pope on the day appointed for the opening of the conclave, and another such Mass on the first day after any news came to the abbey from Valana, unless that news proclaimed a new pope. Afterward, he departed toward the Bay Ghost.

Two dozen or more monks, including Blacktooth and Torrildo, lined the parapet of the eastern wall and watched the plume of dust until it dwindled on the eastern horizon.

"To prove he's no enemy of the Empire, he's taking the way through the Province," Blacktooth sourly echoed his master's words. "But he takes armed guards. Why armed guards?"

"That makes you bitter?" asked Torrildo, who usually concerned himself with Blacktooth's feelings, rarely with his thoughts.

"If he *were* an enemy of the Empire, things might be different for me, Torrildo."

"How?"

"Things might be different for everybody, if nobody here had ever compromised. And he dared talk to me about pearls before swine."

"I don't understand you, Brother."

"I don't expect you would. If my own cousins Wren and Singing Cow don't understand, how could you?" He placed his hand reassuringly over Torrildo's where it lay on the parapet. "It's enough that you care."

"I care, I really do." The postulant was looking at him with those gray-green eyes that so reminded him of his mother's soft and searching gaze. There was something feminine about it. Embarrassed by the intensity of the moment, Blacktooth removed his hand.

"Of course you do. Let's forget it. How is it with you and that difficult Memorabilium?"

"Maxwell's equations, they're called. I can say them forward and backward, but I don't know what they are or what they mean."

"Neither do I, but you're not supposed to know. I can tell you this, though: their meaning has been penetrated during the past century. They're supposed to be among the notes Thon Taddeo Pfardentrott took back to Texark with him about seventy years ago. Maxwell's equations are among the very great Memorabilia, so I've heard."

"Pfardentrott? Didn't he invent the telegraph? And dynamite?"

"I think so."

"Well, if the meaning has already been penetrated, why do I have to keep it memorized?"

"Tradition, I guess. No, it's more than that. Just keep running the words through your mind, as a prayer. Keep it up long enough, and God will enlighten you, so the old-timers say."

"If somebody's penetrated the meaning, maybe I could find out."

"That might spoil it for you, Brother. But you can try, if you want to. You can read what Brother Kornhoer wrote about the subject after Pfardentrott left, but I don't think you'll understand him."

"Brother who?"

"Kornhoer. He invented that old electricity machine down in the vaults."

"Which doesn't work."

"Oh, it worked when he built it, but it wasn't very practical here; and for some reason, his abbot would never let him teach anyone to fix it. Have you ever seen an electric light?"

"No."

"Neither have I, but the Palace of the Hannegans in Texark is full of them. And they've got some at the university there. Brother Kornhoer and Pfardentrott became friends, as I recall, but the Abbot Jerome didn't approve. Say, why don't you read that placard that hangs over Kornhoer's machine?"

"I've seen it, but I never read it. The machine is a nuisance to keep clean. So many cracks and crannies for dust." Torrildo was an underground janitor and warehouse clerk. "You never told me about your Memorabilium, Blacktooth."

"Well, it's a religious one. I don't think it has any secret scientific value. They call it 'Saint Leibowitz's Grocery List.'" He tried to suppress the flush of pride he felt at being given the Founder's Memorabilium, but Torrildo did not notice.

"Does anything special happen when you say it?"

"I wouldn't say yes, I wouldn't say no. Maybe I never worked at it hard enough. As Saint Leibowitz himself used to say, 'What you see is what you get, Wysiwyg.'"

"Where is that saying recorded? What does it mean?"

Blacktooth, who loved the cryptic "Sayings of Saint Leibowitz," was spared answering as the bell rang the hour of Sext, marking the resumption of the rule of silence, which the abbot had suspended for the morning of his departure. The monks on the parapet wall began to leave.

"Come see me in the basement, if you get a chance," Torrildo whispered in violation of the rule.

Blacktooth's Nomadic ancestors had always placed a high value on ecstatic magical or religious experience, and this heritage, while pagan, was not incongruent with the traditional mystical quest which he had found so attractive and natural in the life of the monastery. But as his feeling of unity with his professed brethren gradually waned, he found himself less captivated by the formal worship of the community. Processions and the chanting of psalms no longer elevated his spirits and sent them soaring. Even the reception of the Eucharist during Mass failed to entrance his heart. He felt this as a distinct loss, in spite of his doubts about his vocation to the Order. He tried to recover by his solitary devotional practice what he was losing in the public worship.

A monk's time alone in his cell was limited to seven hours a night, of which at least an hour and a half was to be spent in meditative, affective, or contemplative prayer. Some of this prayer time was devoted to the reading of those parts of the divine office which his daily work at the abbey prevented him from singing in choir at the regular hours, but Blacktooth rarely needed more than twenty minutes to finish his breviary, and the rest of the time he gave to Jesus and Mary. In his sleep, however, his dreams were often colored by the myths of his childhood and of the Wild Horse Woman whom he had seen.

His confessor and spiritual adviser had sharply warned him, more than once, against taking seriously any seemingly supernatural manifestation that came to him during the contemplative work, such as a vision or a voice, for such things were usually either the work of the Devil or simply the spurious side effects of the intense concentration demanded by meditative or contemplative prayer. When the visions began coming to him one night in his cell, he attributed them to fever, for he had fallen ill the previous day, and was excused from the scriptorium.

He knelt on a thinly padded block of wood beside his cot and gazed unwaveringly at a small picture of the Immaculate Heart that hung on the wall. When his mind strayed, or a thought arose, he brought his attention back to the picture. The painting was undistinguished, lacking in detail, and hardly more than a symbol. The prayer was a wordless, thoughtless fixation of the mind on the image and the heart of the Virgin. He was a bit dizzy from fever, and a numbness came over him as he knelt there. Occasionally his field of vision darkened. The heart began to pulsate, and then expand. He could no longer focus his eyes on it. His mind seemed to be plunging into a dark corridor toward emptiness.

And then, there it was: a living heart suspended before him in the blackness of space, beating in cadence with his own pulse. It was complete in every detail. A puncture of the left ventricle leaked small spurts of blood. For a time he felt neither fear nor surprise, but continued to gaze in complete absorption. He knew, beyond words, that it was not the heart of Mary, but not until later reflection did this puzzle or perplex him. He simply accepted what came to him, at the time it happened.

A rap at the door dissolved the trance. His skin crawled at the sharp change in his consciousness.

"*Benedicamus domino,*" he answered after a moment.

"*Deo gratias,*" came a muffled voice from the corridor. It was Brother Jonan, arousing everyone for Matins. The footsteps receded.

He arose and made himself ready for his usual routine, but he carried the spell cast over him by the vision all that day and the next. It was very puzzling, even after his fever passed.

When Prior Olshuen had not summoned him by the third day of Dom Jarad's absence, Blacktooth sought him out. Olshuen was an old friend; he had been Blacktooth's teacher and confessor in the days before he was made prior, but just now the appearance of his old student at his office doorway evoked no smile of welcome.

"Oh, well, I did tell you to come see me, didn't I?" said Olshuen. "You might as well sit down." He returned to his chair, put his elbows on the desktop, pressed his fingertips together, and at last smiled thinly at Blacktooth. He waited.

Blacktooth sat on the edge of his chair, eyebrows raised. He also waited. The prior began flipping opposed fingertips apart, a pair at a time, and flipping them back together. Blacktooth always found this habit fascinating. His coordination was perfect.

"I came to ask—"

"Dom Jarad told me to throw you out if you came to ask for anything more than a blessing, unless you're through with Boedullus, and I know you're not. I don't throw you out, because I had already invited you." He punctuated each phrase with a pause and a flip of the fingertips. He did this only when nervous. "So what do you want, my son?"

"A blessing."

Easily disarmed, the gentle Olshuen lowered his hands, leaned forward, and laughed his relief.

"On my petition to be released from my vows."

The smile vanished. He leaned back, pressed fingertips together again, and said in a mild tone, "Blacktooth, my son. What a dirty rotten little Nomad kid you are!"

"You've obviously spoken to Dom Jarad about me, Father Prior." Blacktooth risked a rueful grin.

"He said nothing you'd want to hear, and he said a few things you're better off not hearing. He spent at least half a minute on the subject, talking fast. Then he told me to throw you out, and he left."

Blacktooth stood up. "Before I get thrown, would you mind telling me how I can find out about the procedure?"

"The procedure for what, to abandon your vows?" Olshuen waited for Blacktooth's nod, then went on: "Well, you turn right when you go out the door. You walk down the hall to the stairway, and then you take it down to the cloister. You go around to the main entrance, and on out into the courtyard. Across the courtyard is the main gate, and outside that, you go to the road. From there, you're on your own. The way to your new future lies open before you." He found it unnecessary to add that Blacktooth would be under excommunication, ineligible for employment in many places, deprived of all right to petition in ecclesiastical courts, cut off from the sacraments, shunned by the clergy and the pious among the laity, and readily victimized by anyone who realized that he was unable to sue in the courts.

"I meant to get out legally, of course."

"There are books on canon law in the library."

"Thank you, Father Prior." Blacktooth started to leave.

"Wait," said the prior, relenting. "Tell me, son—if, after you've finished Boedullus—this is hypothetical, understand?—if, then, you're given a choice of jobs, how would you feel about the other thing?"

The monk hesitated. "I would probably think about the other thing all over again."

"How close are you to being finished?"

"Ten chapters to go."

Olshuen sighed and said, "Sit down again." He rummaged through papers on his desk until he found a sealed envelope. Blacktooth could see his own name on it, written in Dom Jarad's hand. The prior slit it open, unfolded the enclosed note, read it slowly, and looked at Blacktooth. He put his fingertips together again and began tapping them by pairs as before.

"A choice of jobs?"

"Yes—he left you a choice. When you finish *The Book of Origins,* you can do the same author's *Footprints of Earlier Civilizations.* Unless you're sick and tired of the Venerable Boedullus."

"I'm sick and tired of the venerable one."

"Then you will be assigned to translate Yogen Duren's *Perennial Ideas of Regional Sects.*"

"Into Nomadic?"

"Of course."

"Thank you, Father Prior."

Blacktooth went down the hall to the stairway, descended to the cloister, left it by the main entrance, crossed the courtyard, and walked out to the road through the main gate. There he stood for a while, gazing uncertainly at the arid landscape. Down the trail lay the village of Sanly Bowitts, and several miles beyond the village arose the flat-topped hill called the Mesa of Last Resort. There were mountains in the distance, with a few hills in the foreground. The land was lightly covered by cactus and yucca, with sparse grass and mesquite growing in the low places. There were distant antelope, and he could see Brother Shepherd leading his flock through the pass, his dog snarling at the heels of a straggler.

A wagon drawn by a swayback mule pulled to a stop, engulfing Blacktooth in a thin cloud of dust. "Going to town, Brother?" asked its grizzled driver from his perch atop a pile of feed sacks.

Blacktooth was tempted to go past the village and climb Last Resort. It was said to be haunted, a place monks sometimes went alone (with permission) for a kind of spiritual ordeal in the wilderness. But after a brief pause he shook his head. "Many thanks, good simpleton."

He walked back through the main gate and headed for the basement vaults. When Saint Leibowitz had founded the Order, tradition said that there had been nothing here except an ancient military bunker or temporary ammunition dump, which he and his helpers had managed to disguise so that one might pass a stone's throw away and never notice its existence. It was in this place that the earliest Memorabilia were preserved. According to Boedullus, no living quarters were constructed on the site until the middle of the twenty-first century. The monks had lived in scattered hermitages and came here only to deposit books and records until the fury of the Simplification had abated and the danger to the precious documents from skinheads and simplifiers had waned. Here, still underground, the ancient Memorabilia and the latter-day Commentaries awaited a destiny which had, perhaps, already come and was swiftly receding.

CHAPTER 3

Let the monks sleep clothed and girded with belts or cords—but not with their knives at their sides lest they cut themselves in their sleep. . . . The younger brethren shall not have beds next to one another, but among those of the older ones.

—Saint Benedict's Rule, Chapter 22

AN OIL LAMP TOO DIM FOR READING HUNG IN each alcove where books were stored. A light held by hand was needed to locate a title on the shelves. Ordinarily one then carried the book up to the clerestory reading room, but Blacktooth scanned the abstract of Duren's *De Perennibus Sententiis Sectarum Rurum*, his next assigned project, by the light of a candle held close to the pages. He soon returned the book to the shelf and went to join Brother Torrildo, who was leaning against Kornhoer's old generator of electrical essence, a rusting hulk in an alcove where no light burned.

"Let's sit back here where nobody'll catch us," Torrildo muttered, and stepped into the deep shadows behind the machine. "Brother Obohl's gone out, but I'm not sure where."

Blacktooth hesitated. "I don't need to hide. I have reason for being here, even if I didn't ask permission."

"Shhh! You don't have to whisper, but keep it down. I'm only allowed to come in here to clean. Not that it matters much now."

"What's that door?" Blacktooth nodded toward the rear of the dark alcove.

"Just a closet full of junk. Parts of the machine, I think. Come on."

The monk hesitated. The machine somehow gave him the creeps. It reminded him of the special chair in the chapel, which was really a holy relic.

With the faster travel and communication made possible by the conquests of Hannegan II, invention had become contagious in a world that was beginning to recover twelve centuries after the *Magna Civitas* perished in the Flame Deluge. Most inventions, of course, were reinventions, suggested by the few surviving records of that great civilization, but new devices were nonetheless cunning and needed. What was needed at Hannegan City was an efficient and humane method of capital punishment. Thus, the building of a generator of electrical essences at the Abbey of Saint Leibowitz in 3175 A.D. was followed in a few years by the building of a chair of electrical essences at Hannegan City in the Empire of Texark. The first offender to be executed by the new method was a Leibowitzian monk whose crime was carrying a cardinal abbot's offer of sanctuary to a son of the late Thon Taddeo Pfardentrott, an enemy of the Texark state, whose work at Leibowitz Abbey had, nevertheless, made possible many new inventions that benefited the Empire, including the chair of electrical essences.

It was the first and only time the chair was used. Hannegan III had placed it on a platform in the public square, and while two teams of mules drove the electrical generator, the Mayor himself cut the ribbon that allowed a spring to close the switch. To the crowd's delight, the voltage was low and the monk died slowly and noisily. The method was abandoned until a better generator was built. Steam power came, but the chair was never brought out of storage, because a more recent Hannegan found the best executioner on this continent in the person of Wooshin, whose ancestors came from a different continent, and who used a hatchet with such artistry and ease that a whole afternoon of severing heads left him untired and tranquil, able to sit in deep meditation for two hours before dinner.

The chair of electrical essence was eventually disassembled and smuggled across the southern Plains, then out of the Empire at the Bay Ghost frontier. It reappeared at Leibowitz Abbey, where it was placed in the church over the crypt that contained the bones of the monk who died in it, and regularly on the day of his death, the chair was incensed, sprinkled with holy water, and venerated in his memory. Leibowitz Abbey became the only monastery on the continent with its own electric chair. Some thirty years later, the abbey inherited the now elderly executioner, Wooshin, who staggered out of a sandstorm asking for water and sanctuary. That was only three years ago.

"Are you going to stand out there until they catch me?" Torrildo asked impatiently.

Blacktooth sighed and squeezed into the dark cranny beside him. Someone had piled a number of worn sleeping pads, torn and stinking of mildew, in the shadows behind the machine. They sat in comfort.

"I never knew about this," said Blacktooth, amused.

"Blacktooth, are you going to run away?"

The older monk was silent for a time, considering. Earlier he just wanted to run as far as Last Resort, to make a decision, and then maybe come back. Torrildo felt his thigh, as if groping for an answer. He brushed the hand away and sighed. "I just read the abstract on the Duren book. It's a history of local cults and heresies that keep popping up and coming back in different places. God knows why Dom Jarad wants something like that translated into Nomadic. I can't even begin to guess, until I read the whole book."

"You aren't going to run away?"

"How can I? I took solemn vows."

Torrildo released a choking sob in the darkness. "I'm going to run away."

"That's silly. All you need to leave in good standing is Dom Jarad's permission, and for a postulant that's just formality."

"But Dom Jarad is gone. I have to leave now!" His sobbing intensified. Blacktooth put a comforting arm around his shoulders. Torrildo leaned against him and cried quietly into the hollow of his neck.

"Now, what is the matter with you?" asked the older monk.

Torrildo lifted his head and put his face close to Blacktooth's. All Blacktooth could see was an oval shadow with Torrildo's beautiful eyes peering out of it.

"Do you really like me, Blacktooth?"

"Of course I do, Torri. What a question!"

"You're the only reason I've been staying here these past months."

"I don't understand."

"Oh, you say you don't, but you do. Now I just can't stay here any longer. I'd just get you into trouble anyway. I'm impure. I haven't been faithful to you."

"What are you talking about? Faithful how?" Blacktooth shifted restlessly on the moldy mattresses.

"Oh, you're so smart, but you're so naive." He took Blacktooth's face in his soft thin hands. "I'm going. Will you kiss me goodbye?" He felt Blacktooth wince, and dropped his hands. "You won't, then."

"Well, sure I will, Torri." Carefully Blacktooth offered him the kiss of peace, first a peck on the right cheek, then—

"Ohhhh," the youth sighed, and caught him in a fierce embrace. Blacktooth felt lips pressing his own and a tongue trying to work its way between his teeth. He tossed his head aside and leaned back, gagging. Torri fell on top of him and groped under the hem of his robe, both hands sliding up his legs. Blacktooth was first frightened, then horrified by his own erection, which the inflamed Torrildo discovered with delight.

"Torri, no!"

"You know I was meant to be a girl. . . ."

The door of the closet burst open. A skinny arm thrust out a lantern above them. In the sudden light, Blacktooth caught a glimpse of four naked legs and two erect penes.

"Sodomites!" yelled the senior librarian, Brother Obohl. "I caught you at it. I finally caught you, you scum. Up to the prior's office with you!" He aimed a kick at Torrildo's bare rump, but missed. Obohl was nearsighted. Once he had owned the only pair of spectacles at the abbey, ground for him in Texark, but had given them up for religious reasons. Now he grabbed Torrildo's arm, and yelled at Blacktooth, who was scrambling over the machine.

"Elwen! Brother Elwen! Come back here, you filthy bugger!"

Blacktooth heard a scuffle behind him as he sprinted up the stairway. He paused on the landing to compose himself, then strode quietly through the reading room into the courtyard. Outside he paused in the blinding sunlight, dazed and confused. The myopic old man had mistaken him for Brother Elwen, a novice who worked for the groundskeeper. Blacktooth had seen Torrildo and Elwen together on several occasions, but thought nothing of it. Now he seemed caught in a trap the librarian had set for another. The mistake would not endure. Across the courtyard, in plain sight, Elwen was on his hands and knees, working manure into the soil under the rosebushes. There was no honorable escape. He started to report back to the copy room, but things might become embarrassing there, when the prior sent for him. He started again toward his cell, but the sound of running footsteps made him look around. It was Torrildo, sprinting toward the main gate. Blacktooth stood waiting for a commotion to follow, but nothing happened.

He waited a full minute. After a brief prayer to Saint Leibowitz, he made up his mind to return to the basement. At the bottom of the stairs, he met only silence in the dim light. He found the candle he had used earlier and looked behind the machine. The old librarian lay on his back. He clutched his head and rolled it side to side. There was blood on his forehead. Blacktooth bent over him.

"Who's there?" he rasped.

"Blacktooth St. George."

"God be praised, Brother. I need a little help."

Blacktooth picked the old man up, edged his way around the machine, and staggered with him toward the stairs.

"Put me down. I'm too heavy for you. I'll be all right in a moment."

They rested briefly against the wall. Then Blacktooth draped the librarian's arm around his neck and helped him up the stairs. Obohl was croaking and wheezing.

"It was Elwen and Torrildo. Those buggers. I knew. What they were up to back there. Just couldn't catch them. Until today. You know, so much semen. Gets spilled. Behind that machine. They call it the seminary. Now. Now. Where did they go?" Still wheezing, he blinked around at his blurred world.

Blacktooth set him carefully on the end of a table in the reading room and made him lie down on it. Monks at the reading desks got up and quickly gathered around. One brought a drinking jug and wiped the librarian's face. Another examined the cut on his scalp. Another asked, "What happened to you, Brother?"

"I caught them. I finally caught them. Brother Torrildo and Brother Elwen again, going at it behind the electric idol. Torrildo hit me—with something."

"Torrildo hit you all right," said Blacktooth. "But Elwen wasn't there. It was me, Blacktooth St. George."

He turned and walked away, not hurrying, and continued to his cell. He lay on his back and stared up at the picture of the Immaculate Heart of the Virgin until they came to get him.

Were it not for the fact that shoveling compost was defined as public punishment, Blacktooth might have preferred it as a career to the job of translating a monk's-eye view of history for Nomads too proud to read. Taking the raw shit out of the privies and transporting it by wheelbarrow to the first composting bin was the smelliest part of the task. There he mixed it with thrice its volume of garden weeds, corn husks, chopped cactus, and plate scrapings from the kitchen. Each day he shoveled the stinking mixture from one bin to the next in line, allowing air to penetrate and hasten the decay. When the mixture reached the final bin, it was crumbling and had lost most of its odor. From there, he loaded it into a clean wheelbarrow and moved it out to the great pile near the garden, where it awaited the pleasure of the cultivators.

On the third day, after an interview with the prior, Brother Elwen went over the wall. Blacktooth expected relief. None came. For three weeks in full he prayed the compost-shoveling prayer, offering up each stinking shovelful on behalf of the soul of poor, poor Torrildo. That he fry in hell—is not my wish, O Lord, he managed to pray.

No one snubbed or shunned him (after he bathed), but the shame of public penance made him isolate himself. In his loneliness, in his cell by night, he sought ever more fervently the indescribable emptying of himself that seemed to occur in a kind of union with the heart of the Virgin: a heart not filled with sorrow, but made empty by sorrow, made open by sorrow, made selfless by sorrow, a heart which was a pit of loving darkness, wherein, sometimes, he glimpsed fleetingly another wounded but still beating heart.

"The Devil too has his contemplatives, they say" was his confessor's harsh judgment upon the vision and upon Blacktooth's private devotional practice. "The focus of contemplation must be Our Lord. Devotion to Our Lady is splendid, but too many monks turn to her only when their vows fit too tight, when obedience is hard. They call her 'Refuge of Sinners,' and so she is!—but there are two ways of looking at this: the Lord's way, and the sinner's way. Pay attention in choir, my son, and stop chasing visions at night."

Thus Blacktooth learned not to mention the vision. He saw his confessor was made angry by it, for how could a professed monk who regretted his vows be granted any grace except that of contrition and repentance? He observed a similar attitude in Prior Olshuen, who, at the end of his three-week penance, sent him back to his regular work, but also ordered him to spend an hour a week with Brother Reconciliator for special counseling, to Blacktooth's utmost chagrin.

Brother Reconciliator, a monk named Levion, was part-time assistant to Brother Surgeon as well as a Keeper of Memorabilia from certain ancient healing arts. He handled cases of senility, fits, depression, delusion, and—contumacy. He had also been ordained an exorcist. Olshuen, without doubting Blacktooth's account of the incident in the basement, saw it as a manifestation of rebellious discontent, and saw the discontent as sin or madness.

Blacktooth's devotion to the Virgin, however, continued and grew in the face of this disapproval. His old hero, Saint Leibowitz, was at least temporarily pushed aside to make more room for the Virgin. He had chosen Duren's *Perennial Ideas of Regional Sects* for his next project, in preference to more Boedullus, partly because so many of

Duren's country religions were special cults of Mary, or of some local goddess who had borrowed Mary's identity and carried Mary's Babe on her arm. Duren even mentioned the Nomadic Day Maiden. It was a choice he would quickly regret, because of the extreme difficulty of translating theological ideas into Nomadic, but at first he was captivated by one section ("Apud Oregonenses") which dealt with remnants of what had been called the Northwest Heresy a few centuries before. The description of the cult's beliefs seemed to cast light on his own mystical vision.

"The Oregonians," wrote Duren, "considered the Mother of God to be the original uterine Silence into which the Word was spoken at the creation. She was the dark Void made pregnant with light and matter when God roared 'Fiat!' Word and Silence were coeval, they said, and each contained the other."

This reminded Blacktooth of the image of the darkening heart that became a pit of blackness containing another living heart. He was deeply moved.

"Thus is was impossible," Duren wrote in a later paragraph, "for the cultist to evade the Inquisitor's accusation that they made of the Virgin a fourth divine person, an incarnation of God's female wisdom."

Since no one at the abbey could read Nomadic except Wren and Singing Cow, Blacktooth felt safe in taking a few liberties with a work so resistant to understandable expression in that primitive tongue. In translating the word *eculeum* ("colt"), he could choose any of eleven Nomadic words that meant a young horse, and none of them were synonymous. But any one-word translation of the Latin "eternity" or "transubstantial" would only bewilder the reader. Theological terms, therefore, he left as Latin words in the Nomadic text, and tried to define them by lengthy footnotes of his own composition. But whenever he imagined himself trying to explain such matters to his late father or boss uncle, these footnotes became flavored with a facetiousness which he knew he would have to remove from the final version. Levity made the task less hateful, but strengthened his conviction that it was useless.

After an absence of two months, Abbot Jarad wrote to the prior from Valana and requested, among other things, that a votive Mass be offered weekly for the election of a pope, for he saw no quick end to a difficult election. Without a government, the Church was in confusion and turmoil. The city of Valana was too small to be a gracious host to hundreds of cardinals with their secretaries, servants, and alternates. Some were living in barns.

He wrote little about the conclave itself, except to note with obvious disgust that more than one cardinal had already gone home, leaving behind a special conclavist to cast his ballot. The practice was made possible by a canon which had been enacted for the convenience of foreign, not domestic, cardinals, but the latter took advantage of it during long periods of interregnum. The special conclavist in such cases must, if possible, be a member of the clergy of the cardinal's titular New Roman (or Valanan) church, and he was entitled to vote his own convictions under the guidance of the Holy Spirit, but such a proxy was always chosen for loyalty, and rarely deviated from his cardinal's wishes until an election became obvious and he switched his vote to back a winner. The practice made compromise more difficult, as the servant was always less flexible than the master. Jarad would make no prediction as to the date of his return. The messenger who brought the letter, however, got mildly drunk in Sanly Bowitts and expressed his own opinion of the affair: either the cardinals would all appoint conclavists and go home for the winter, leaving a hopeless deadlock, or would elect an ill old man who could be expected to die before settling any real problems.

Other news and gossip trickled to the abbey from Valana by way of travelers, guardians of the papal roads, and messengers who spent the night on their way to other destinations. Abbot Jarad Cardinal Kendemin was said to have received two votes on the thirty-eighth ballot—a dubious rumor which caused a flurry of excitement and joy at the abbey and a surge of panic in the heart of Blacktooth, who needed a pope's assent to be released from his vows, under the laws then in effect.

"You're not making sense," Brother Reconciliator told him at their weekly session after he listened to five minutes of Blacktooth's nervous chatter. "You think Dom Jarad has his foot on your neck. You think he'll never change his mind. If he comes home still the abbot, you can appeal to the Pope. But if he's the Pope, he'll have nothing better to do than keep his foot on your neck, eh? You'll spend your whole life translating the Memorabilia into Nomadic. Why do you suppose Dom Jarad hates you so much?"

"I didn't say he hated me. You're putting words in my mouth."

"Excuse me. He has his foot on your neck. Your father also had his foot on your neck, you said. I forgot. It was your father who hated you, yes?"

"No! I didn't say that either, exactly."

Levion shuffled through his notes. They were sitting in his cell, which served as his office; his role as a special counselor was not a full-time one.

"Three weeks ago, you said exactly: 'My father hated me.' I wrote it down."

Blacktooth sat slouched on Levion's cot, leaning back against the wall. Suddenly he leaned forward, rested his elbows on his knees, and began wringing his hands. He spoke to the floor. "If I said it, I meant when he hated me, he was drunk. He hated the responsibility. Raising me was supposed to be my boss uncle's job. Also, he was angry because my mother was teaching me to read a little." Blacktooth put his hand over his mouth, betrayed by this thoughtless revelation.

"Here are two things I don't understand, Brother St. George. First, you came here illiterate, did you not? Second, why should your uncle be responsible for you instead of your father?"

"That's the way it is on the Plains. The mother's brothers take responsibility for her children." Blacktooth was increasingly restless. He eyed the door.

"Oh yes, Nomads are matriarchal. Is that right?"

"Wrong! Inheritance is matrilineal. That's not the same."

"Well, whatever. So your father felt put-upon, because your mother had no brother?"

"Wrong again. She had four brothers. My boss uncle was the oldest. He taught me dances and songs, took me to tribal councils, and that's about all. I could not become a warrior. Mother owned no breeding pit, no broodmares, and we were outcasts."

"Broodmares? What have broodmares got to do with—" He left the question unfinished, waved his hand in the air as if trying to dispel echoes. "Never mind. Nomad customs. I'll never untangle that ball of worms. Let's get back to the problem. You felt your father's foot on your neck. You say your mother was teaching you to read? But you said you came here illiterate. Did you lie?"

Blacktooth rested his chin on his hands and stared at his feet; he wiggled his toes and said nothing.

"Whatever you tell me stays right here in this room, Brother."

The patient paused, then blurted, "I couldn't read very well, or speak Rockymount very well. Wren and Singing Cow couldn't read at all. I kept quiet because everyone thought we were real Nomads. If Abbot Graneden found out we came from the settlements, he would have sent us back."

"I see. So that's why you learned faster than Wren and Singing Cow. Your mother had already taught you. Where was she educated?"

"She learned what little she knew from a mission priest."

Levion was silent for a time as he studied his occasional disciple. "Whose idea was it to run away to join the wild Nomads?"

"Singing Cow's."

"And when the Nomads turned you away, whose idea was it to come here?"

"Mine."

"Tell me again. When did your mother die?"

"Year before last."

"When did you first tell Dom Jarad you wanted to quit the Order?"

Blacktooth said nothing.

"It was right after your mother died, wasn't it?"

"That had nothing to do with it," he growled.

"Didn't it? As a runaway, how did you feel when you got the news your mother had died?"

The bell rang. Blacktooth stood up with a sudden smile, unable to hide his relief.

"Well?"

"I felt very sorry, of course. Now I've got to go to work, Brother."

"Of course. Next week then, we'll talk more about this."

Blacktooth liked these sessions less and less. He had no wish to be reconciled by Brother Reconciliator, who seemed to treat his wish to depart as a symptom of illness, if not madness. As he hurried back to the copy room, he resolved to tell Levion no more about his parents or his childhood.

Because of the man's ignorance of Nomad life, his interviews with Brother Levion, instead of reconciling him with his calling, served instead to increase his nostalgia for that life which he had never quite inherited. He remembered his mother turning Christian, and his father, who sometimes tried to exercise an uncle's authority over him, insisting that he prepare himself for a manhood rite which he knew at the time would never be celebrated. The Church forbade the rite which turned adolescents into fully licensed mankillers of a war cult. But he had undergone training and understood something of the spirit of the Nomad warrior and his battle frenzy. It was hard to say anything true in answer to the question: What is Nomad religion like? Everything the wild Nomad did was religiously or magically hedged. It was hard to say what his religion was not. One might add up a list of ingredients for a religion: his ceremonies, his customs, his laws, his magic, his medicine, his oracles, his dances, his occasional ritual killing, his Empty Sky and his Wild Horse Woman, and call the list his religion, but this list would omit too much of daily living. There was even a ritual for defecation.

Bending over his worktable, he read again his favorite passage from Duren's *Perennial Ideas*, paused to think about his vision, and then penned a footnote to his translation of the paragraph:

> This conception of the Virgin as the uterine silence wherein the Word is uttered and heard seems to accord with the mystical experience of contemplatives who have encountered the living heart of Jesus within the dark and empty heart of Mary.

He hesitated over it, neglected to add the word *Translator*, and thought of tearing up the page. But Brother Copymaster was standing nearby, and whenever Blacktooth tore up a page, the copymaster remarked on the cost of paper. I'll come back to it later, he thought, for it was growing dark in the copy room, and he was not allowed more than one candle. Suppressing a sense of mortal sin, he cleaned up his table, and left the problem for tomorrow.

CHAPTER 4

 EARLY A YEAR AFTER THE HEART OF POPE LINUS VI failed him in the cold trout stream, a stormy conclave elected Olavlano Cardinal Fortos, an octogenarian from south of the Brave River, who was a stargazer, a scholar learned in the subject of witch detection, and a man believed to be neutral in the perennial East-West power struggle. He chose the name Pope Alabaster II and lived long enough to issue a bull ("for a perpetual memorial of the matter") which ordered Earth's prime meridian from which all longitudes are measured moved from its ancient (and until recently inaccessible) location. The line of zero longitude thereafter would pass through the center of the high altar of Saint Peter's Basilica in New Rome, and would perpetually remain there, free from the influence of what Alabaster called the Green Witch. Many representatives to the Curia from both coastlines of the continent had opposed

the decree, because in this century of rapid development, great wooden ships had begun again to sail the seas; Alabaster's bull would not only confuse navigation, but would hasten the time (previously expected to come in the fortieth century) when it would be necessary to drop a day from the calendar to keep it in step with the heavens. Both East and West suspected political motives behind the bull, somehow connecting it with the occupation of territory around New Rome by the armies of the Hannegan, and so Alabaster died of poison a few months after his election.

The subsequent interregnum lasted 211 days while hundreds of cardinals bickered, and the people of Valana threw stones at the carriages of the cardinals' servants. Divine Providence at last moved the conclave to elect Rupez Cardinal de Lonzor, also from south of the Brave River, and the oldest, sickest man in the Sacred College. He took the name of his predecessor of holy memory, becoming Alabaster III, but immediately repealed his predecessor's decree by a bull (also *ad perpetuam rei memoriam*) which restored the prime meridian to its ancient location, for scholars of the Order of Leibowitz had assured him that "Green Witch" had not been the habitation of a sorceress, but only the name of an ancient village on a distant island which had been depopulated by the Flame Deluge. Again political motives were suspected. Westerners opposed the change, and the old man died in his sleep after eating a dish of hare cooked in wine and vinegar, flavored with sautéed onions and laurel leaves.

Weary cardinals came again to Valana. This time the name of Abbot Jarad Cardinal Kendemin was placed in nomination very early in the conclave, and he, quite unwillingly, gathered the support of nearly fifteen percent of the electors before word was spread that Dom Jarad, if chosen, would utter the *"Non accepto!"* which had not been heard for nearly two thousand years, when Saint Petrus Murro Pope Celestin V futilely spoke them from his hermit's cave, only to be dragged to the throne by a desperate College.

The conclave sought this time in vain for one of its own members with no suspected loyalty either to the Empire or to the Valana bureaucracy and its western allies. The name of Elia Brownpony was proposed, for the Red Deacon was professionally a lawyer and diplomat, skilled in negotiation, but his relative youth, his reputation for being manipulative, and the fact that he would have to be ordained a priest and then anointed bishop before he could accept the papacy, all weighed against him. Only Dom Jarad, never a great judge of character, offered to support his friend, but Brownpony would not accept.

The only telegraph line on the continent stretched from Hannegan City in Texark to the very southeast corner of the Denver Republic. In order to obtain metal for its construction, the previous Hannegan had confiscated all copper coinage in the Empire, all copper pots, and many church bells. The line helped make the area of conquest in the south safer from incursion by the free Nomads of the north, but now it was being used to keep Filpeo Harq informed about the conclave, to send instructions from the capital to Archbishop Benefez and his allies in the Sacred College. Almost every day, a messenger from Benefez rode south to the terminal station to pick up the mail, while another messenger was taking mail in the other direction. No other cardinal bishop could stay in touch so easily with his home diocese.

The temper of the people of Valana grew ugly again. The Church was Valana's only industry, and the burghers themselves were dependent on the papal exile for their livelihood. Prayers against schism were fervent within the conclave, but unpopular in the local churches. Workers daily scrubbed the Cathedral Palace walls to remove graffiti of the previous night, painted there by the workers' kinsmen.

There were demonstrations. The people of the city and surrounding villages assembled to propose their own candidates to the inaccessible and unyielding cardinals. The name of one holy man of some local repute as a healer and rainmaker, one Amen Specklebird, was frequently heard in the streets. He was a retired priest of the Order of Our Lady of the Desert, and not unknown to the Bishop of Denver, who had forced him to choose between retirement and a heresy trial.

But driven by the Holy Spirit, a holy fear of the mob, and the onset of a bitter winter, the conclave at last elected the Bishop of Denver himself, the Most Reverend Mariono Scullite, not a member of the College, but a man who could be counted on to make matters no worse than they were. He took the name Linus VII, which suggested that he would return to the policies of the pope who had managed to terminate open schism before he went a-fishing.

But now Linus VII too was slowly dying of a wasting illness which could not be attributed to poison (unless his sisters and nephews who acted as tasters of the pontifical diet were part of the plot). After consulting the Pope's physician, Elia Cardinal Brownpony rented a private carriage without ecclesiastical insignia, hired a Nomad driver who apparently spoke no Rockymount ("I need to practice my Wilddog dialect," he explained to an aide), and quietly departed for the southwest desert to confer with Abbot Jarad Cardinal Kendemin. Actually, the Nomad driver was fluent in several languages, and they had much to talk about.

.   .   .

Brother Blacktooth had run away from the monastery again. He knew he would have to go back, but sometimes the wildness of his Nomad heritage took possession of him, and he abandoned his vows and his sanity for a few days, and he ran. He ran not from the bad food and the hard bed and the long tedious hours, but from an all-knowing, all-seeing, pride-consuming authority of his superiors. This time he had stolen coins from the prior's desk, bought bread and a wineskin in the village. The skin he filled with water, and went wandering northward. The first day he had moved across open country, just to avoid travelers on the road; but because of the wolves he had returned to the highway at sundown to spend the night in a monk pen. It was a roofless stone enclosure three paces square and just taller than a frenzied wolf could jump. Among the graffiti, a sign in Latin welcomed all visitors and bade them defecate *extra muros*. Monks of his own order had built such shelters along the way, but nobody kept them clean. A trickle of water from a spring on the mountainside ran across the floor. He built a small fire and boiled some of the water in his cup, adding some roasted mesquite beans for flavor. He ate some of his biscuits and a bit of dried mutton before the stars came out. In a few days, he would begin starving. He slept shivering in a corner, but before daylight revived his fire.

Traveling parallel—as he fallibly judged by the sun—to the direction of the highway from which he had fled at dawn after sighting a party of horsemen with long rifles, he had come to the canyon and there was no way in sight to cross it. It was already late afternoon and he had nowhere to spend the night. On the highway, there was the monk pen, where he could be safe, at least, from predators of the four-legged kind. But they would look for him there. It was soon after he doused the remains of his fire at dawn that he heard the horsemen coming beyond the hill, and he scrambled up a cut from the winding road and hid in the rocks until they came into view. They were soldiers. Papal guardsmen, or Texark? He could not be sure at that distance. He huddled lower in sudden fright. As a small boy, Brother Blacktooth had been raped by soldiers, and horror of it still haunted him.

The two-legged traffic on the highway was very light, and if a man was on foot he was either a monk or a frustrated horse thief. Today there were thieves. He had seen them from afar. It was a good hour and a half before twilight, but there was no sign of a way across the abyss below him. It was already a pit of darkness in the earth. He would have to walk. There was no law in this territory but the distant law of the Church. Turning back from the canyon, he decided to climb the Mesa of Last Resort.

It was from the Mesa that Blacktooth, missing from the abbey four days, had witnessed the Red Deacon's arrival without realizing that the passenger in the private carriage that emerged from the rooster tail of dust out of the north and hurried on through the village of Sanly Bowitts to the Abbey of Saint Leibowitz was the man who had shaped his unhappy past by admiring his translation of Boedullus and who would even more strongly influence his future.

When his water ran low, he searched Last Resort, looking for the mythical spring and the shanty once inhabited by an eremitic old Jew who had departed from the region at the time of the Texark conquest. He found the shanty in ruins, but no spring or other source of water, which could hardly have existed so far above the surrounding desert. Another myth said that the old Jew had been a rainmaker, and needed no such spring. It was a truth, he observed, that the Mesa was greener than the land below. There was a mystery here, but he sought no solution. For most of the time, until his waterskin ran dry, he prayed to the Virgin, or simply sat in the dry wind and seethed in his own evil under the sun. It was early spring, and by night he nearly froze. Having caught a terrible cold and run out of water, he knew at last that he would have to go back and plead insanity.

Now, three days after the passage of the carriage through the village, he sat shivering with a dripping nose in the gloomy hall and awaited judgment. Occasionally a monk or a novice walked quietly past, on his way to the library or workshop, but Blacktooth sat hunched over with his elbows on his knees and his face in his hands, knowing that no one would acknowledge his existence even by a nod. There was an exception. Someone strode quickly past him, then stopped at the door to the meeting room. Feeling himself being watched, Blacktooth looked up to see his former therapist, Levion the Reconciliator, gazing down at him. As their eyes met, Blacktooth inwardly cringed, but there was neither contempt nor pity in the monk's gaze. After a slight shake of his head, he entered the meeting hall, evidently summoned as a witness. What had passed between them in Levion's cell was supposed to be as confidential as confession, but Blacktooth trusted no one.

Cardinal Brownpony had learned almost immediately of Blacktooth's unsanctioned absence, for soon after his arrival he asked to see the work of the young monk who had been translating Boedullus into Nomadic, and Jarad had been forced to give an account of the copyist's growing rebellion. Worse, while admiring the Nomadic version of Boedullus, Brownpony read aloud to his Nomad driver, whose Nomad name meant Holy (Little Bear) Madness, and to his secretary, a white-bearded old priest named e'Laiden who fluently spoke Wilddog Nomadic, read to them some of Blacktooth's translation of Duren, and the three of them became openly contemptuous of it. "These theological ideas are completely alien to the Nomad mind," Brownpony explained to Jarad, thus lending unwitting support to the opinion of the copyist himself, against Jarad's view. Worse, while they were perusing the work, Dom Jarad's attention was called to the footnote in *Perennial Ideas*, which Blacktooth had neither deleted nor signed as his own: "This conception of the Virgin as the uterine silence wherein the Word is uttered and heard seems to accord with the mystical experience of contemplatives . . ."

Brownpony translated it back into Latin for him. No witness to the scene could remember a more furious Abbot Jarad.

Outside the refectory door, Blacktooth's fear became irrational terror when the old postulant named Wooshin came and sat quietly beside him on the bench. The man mumbled what might have been a greeting in Churchspeak with his thick Texark accent (although he refused actually to speak Texark, an Ol'zark dialect), and then he rolled a cigarette, an act requiring a special dispensation from the abbot or prior. But Wooshin was a very unusual man, one who made no claim to a religious vocation of any kind, but whose status as a political refugee from Texark, and whose consummate skill as a smithy, had made him welcome at the monastery, in spite of his gruesome past. He attended Mass and conformed to ritual, but never received the Eucharist, and nobody was sure that he was even Christian. He came originally from the west coast, and his skin was yellow, quite wrinkled now, the shape of his eyes strangely different. Behind his back, those who feared and disliked him called him Brother Axe. For six years he had been a headsman for the present Hannegan, and some years before that for the Hannegan's predecessor, before he fell from imperial favor and fled for his life to the West.

He had lost weight and seemed to age rapidly during his three years at the abbey, but his presence on the bench outside the judgment hall aroused irrational panic in the culprit who cringed beside him. Until that moment, Blacktooth's worst fear was excommunication, with all its civil penalties and disabilities. Now he thought of the superbly sharp cutlery for the kitchen, and the axes and scythes that

Wooshin made for the gardeners. Why, why, was this professional killer summoned to my trial? It was obvious to Blacktooth that Wooshin had been called by the tribunal, but not as a witness. I barely know the man! He had always wondered if the severed head retained a moment of confused consciousness as it fell into the basket.

Wooshin touched his arm. Blacktooth started up with a gasp, but the man was only offering him a large handful of clean, cottonlike waste from his shop.

"Leak the nose."

It took Blacktooth a moment to realize that the man was offering him a mop to wipe away the liquid snot that was running down to his chin.

"Horrid night cold on Mesa," said Brother Axe, betraying his knowledge of the runaway's whereabouts during the absence. So everybody knew.

Blacktooth hesitantly took the mop and used it, then formally nodded his thanks to the donor, as if he were actually observing a religious silence which, in present circumstances, seemed a bit hypocritical even to himself.

Wooshin smiled. Emboldened, Blacktooth asked, "Are you here because of me?"

"I not sure, but not probably. I think I leave here with Cardinal."

Mildly relieved, Blacktooth resumed his former posture. It seemed strange to him that the Axe, who could speak very good Ol'zark, refused to communicate in that tongue, which his accent in Churchspeak betrayed that he spoke. It was one of several languages, besides Churchspeak, which were used with some regularity at the abbey, but when Brother Axe heard it, he usually walked away. What use, he wondered, did Elia Cardinal Brownpony or the Curia have for an executioner who hated his former employer? Was the Church departing from its ancient refusal to shed the blood of its enemies?

An hour late, the bell rang for supper. The meeting hall became a refectory again, and the tribunal adjourned for the meal. As the stream of monks filed silently down the corridor, Wooshin got up to join them. "You not eat?" he asked the defendant.

Blacktooth shook his head and remained seated.

Before the meal was finished, Levion came to the door and spoke to him: "Brother Medic says you should eat."

"No. Too sick."

"Stupid," said Levion. "Stupid and lucky," he added, more to himself than Blacktooth, as he turned back into the refectory. *Lucky?*

The word lingered in his mind, but he could not find an application for it.

There was a faintly audible reading by the lector; then supper ended. Except for the members of the tribunal, the monks filed silently out of the refectory. This time Blacktooth made bold to watch them go, but nobody, not even Wren or Singing Cow, looked down at him in passing. The last man out closed the door. The proceedings resumed.

Soon the door opened again. Someone stepped outside and stood there. Blacktooth looked up, saw a freckled face, graying red hair, and a splash of scarlet. Blue-green eyes were staring at him. Blacktooth arose with a gasp and tried to genuflect with a leg that had gone to sleep. Elia Cardinal Brownpony caught his arm as he stumbled.

"Your Eminence!" he croaked, and tried again to bow.

"Sit down. You're not well yet. I want to talk to you for a moment."

"Certainly, m'Lord."

Blacktooth remained standing, so the cardinal himself sat on the bench and tugged at the monk's sleeve until he sank beside him.

"I understand you have trouble with obedience."

"That has been true, m'Lord."

"Has it always been thus?"

"I—I'm not sure. I suppose so, yes."

"You *did* begin by running away from home."

"I was thinking of that, m'Lord. But when I came here, I tried to obey. At first."

"But you tired of your assigned work."

"Yes. That is no excuse, but yes."

The cardinal shifted into Grasshopper dialect, with a Jackrabbit accent. "You speak and write well in several languages, I'm told."

"I seem to get along fairly well, Your Eminence, except I'm weak in ancient English," he answered in the same tongue.

"Well, you know, most of our present dialects are at least half old English," said the cardinal, lapsing into Rockymount. "It's just that the pronunciation has changed, and melted in with Spanish, and some think a bit of Mongolian, especially in Nomadic. Although I have my doubts about the myth of a Bayring Horde."

Silence fell while the cardinal seemed to muse.

"Do you suppose you could serve obediently as someone's interpreter? It would not involve hunching over a copy table for hours at a time, but you would have to translate on paper as well as interpret the spoken word."

Blacktooth mopped his face again with Wooshin's waste and began crying. The cardinal allowed him to sob quietly until he regained
control. Was this what Levion meant by "lucky"?

"Do you think you could obey me, for example?"

Blacktooth choked, "What good is a promise of mine? I broke all
my vows but one."

"Which one is that, if you don't mind saying?"

"I have never had a woman, or a man. When I was a boy, I was
had, though." Torrildo's accusing face came to mind as he said it, but
he rejected the self-accusation.

The Red Deacon laughed. "What about solitary unchastity?"
Seeing Blacktooth's face change, he hastily added, "Forgive the joke.
I'm asking you seriously whether you want to leave this place forever."

"Forever?"

"Well, at least for a very long time, with no reason to expect the
Order would take you back even if you wanted to come."

"I have nowhere to go, m'Lord. That's why I came back from the
Mesa."

"Your abbot will release you to come to Valana with me, but you
must promise to obey, and I must believe your promise. You cannot be
laicized yet. You will be my servant."

Once more, the copyist was overwhelmed by tears.

"Well, it's now or never," said the cardinal.

"I promise," he choked, "to do my best to obey you, m'Lord."

Brownpony stood up. "I'm sorry. What is 'your best'? You can't
be allowed to decide that for yourself. That makes it a crippled promise. No, it won't do." He started toward the refectory door. Blacktooth
fell to the floor, crawled after him, and clutched the hem of his cassock. "I swear before God," he gasped. "May the Holy Mother abandon me, may the saints all curse me, if I fail. I promise to obey you,
m'Lord. I promise!"

The cardinal studied him contemptuously for a moment.

"All right, get up then, and come with me, Brother Groveler.
Here, this way, give me your arm. Come on through the doorway. Face
them, Blacktooth. Now."

Feverish and dizzy, Blacktooth stepped into the refectory, walked
a few steps toward the abbot's table, looked at their faces, and fainted.

He was awakened by a voice saying, "Give him this when he
comes to, Father." It was Brother Surgeon.

"All right, go see your other patient," said Prior Olshuen.

"I'm awake," said Blacktooth, and sat up by candlelight as the only occupant of the three-bed infirmary. Brother Surgeon came back to his bedside, felt his forehead, and handed him a glass of milky green liquid.

"What is it?"

"Willow bark, tincture of hemp leaves, poppy juice, alcohol. You're not very sick. You can go back to your cell tomorrow if you want to."

"No," said the prior. "You've got to have him well enough to leave in three days. Otherwise, we'll be stuck with him until the next stage to Valana." He turned to Blacktooth, his voice turning cold. "You are confined. Your meals will be brought to you. You will not speak to anyone not in authority over you. If a sick brother needs one of the other beds here, then you will return to your cell. When you leave us, you will take your breviary, your beads, your toilet articles, sandals, and a blanket, but you will exchange your habit for that of a novice. You will remain indefinitely in the custody of your benefactor, Cardinal Brownpony, without whose intercession you would be under interdict and shunned. Is that clear?"

Blacktooth looked at the man who had been his teacher and protector in his youth, and nodded.

"Do you have anything else to say to us?"

"I would like to confess."

The prior frowned, almost shook his head, then said, "Wait until the medicine wears off. I'll ask Dom Jarad about it."

In a very weak voice: "May I have your blessing, then?"

Olshuen stood a moment in angry indecision, then whispered, "*Benedicat te, omnipotens Deus, Pater et Filius et Spiritus Sanctus,*" traced a tiny cross in the air, and departed.

CHAPTER 5

> But if he is not healed even in this way,
> then let the Abbot use the knife of amputa-
> tion, according to the Apostle's words, "Ex-
> pel the evil one from your midst . . . let
> him depart," lest one diseased sheep con-
> taminate the whole flock.
> —*Saint Benedict's Rule*, Chapter 28

NDER THE WITHERING GAZE OF HIS FORMER brethren, Blacktooth at last left his cell with his small bundle and made his way into the sunlit courtyard where the Red Deacon's coach was made ready for departure. While he was helping the driver lash his meager belongings to the top of the carriage, he overheard the voice of Singing Cow, just out of sight, talking to a newly arrived postulant who worked in the library.

"He tried persuasion at first, I'll grant that," his former comrade explained. "And when persuasion didn't get him out, he tried violence. And when violence didn't get him out, he tried sodomy. I heard *that* from a witness. But sodomy didn't get him out either, or stealing, or running away. So he inserted a gloss into a copy of the Venerable Boedullus."

"Without attribution?" gasped the assistant librarian.

"Despicable, isn't it," said Singing Cow.

"It wasn't Boedullus!" Blacktooth howled. "It was only Duren!"

Blacktooth rode with the driver as they bumped along the north road toward the mountain passes. He never once looked back at the abbey. The Axe was with them, sometimes driving when Holy Madness rode the cardinal's horse, sometimes riding inside the coach when the cardinal chose to be in the saddle. Both Wooshin and the Nomad treated the disgraced monk with courtesy, but he had as little intercourse as possible with Brownpony or his clerical companion.

One morning when they had been three days on the road, Wooshin said to him, "You hide from Cardinal. Why you shun? You know he saved you neck back there. Abbot wring like a chicken, except Cardinal save you. Why you afraid him?"

Blacktooth began to deny it, but heard an inner cock's crow. Wooshin was right. To him, Brownpony represented the authority of the Church, previously wielded by Dom Jarad, and he was tired of the obedience which he had been forced to swear again to save himself. But it was necessary to separate the office from the man. After Wooshin's remarks, he stopped shrinking from his rescuer, and exchanged polite greetings in the mornings. But the cardinal, sensing his discomfort, for the most part ignored his presence during much of the journey.

Sometimes Wooshin and the Nomad wrestled or fought for sport with staves. The Nomad called him Axe, which no one at the abbey had dared to do, and Wooshin seemed not to object to the nickname, as long as it was not prefixed by "Brother." In spite of his age and apparent frailty, the Axe was the inevitable winner of these bouts by firelight, and made the Nomad appear so clumsy that Blacktooth once accepted an offer to try fencing the driver with staves. The driver not-so-clumsily whacked him six times and left him sitting in hot ashes while Wooshin and the cardinal laughed.

"Let Wooshin teach you," said Brownpony. "In Valana, you may need to defend yourself. You've lived in a cloister, and you're soft. In turn, you help him work on his Rockymount accent."

Blacktooth protested politely, but the cardinal was insistent. So the fencing and language lessons began. "You ready die now?" the Brother Axe asked cheerfully at the beginning of each session, as if he had always asked it of his customers. Afterward, they talked a lot in Rockymount.

But it was with Holy (Little Bear) Madness, the driver, that

Blacktooth felt most comfortable, reckoning him to be a servant of no rank or status, and the two struck up an acquaintance. His name in Nomadic was Chür (Ösle) Høngan, and he called Blacktooth "Nimmy," which in Nomadic approximated the word "kid," meaning one who had not yet endured the rites of passage into manhood. Blacktooth was scarcely younger than Holy Madness, but he did not take offense. It's true, he thought; I am a thirty-five-year-old teenager. So the abbot had reminded him. As far as experience in the world was concerned, he might as well have been in prison since childhood. But frightened of an unknowable future, he was already homesick for that prison.

Life at the monastery had not really been equal parts prayer, hard labor, and groveling, as he had told himself. He had done things there he loved to do. He loved the formal prayer of the Church. He sang well, and while he tried to merge his voice in that of the choir, his was the clear tenor that defined itself by its absence when the choir divided into two groups singing the ancient psalms in a dialogue of verse and response. The group without Blacktooth missed him. And on three occasions when there were important guests at the abbey, Blacktooth, at the abbot's request, had sung alone for everyone—once in the church and twice at supper. In the refectory, he had sung Nomad songs with his own embellishments affiliated to childhood memories. He refused to take pride in this, but his Satan took it anyway. While at the abbey, he had made a stringed instrument much like the one his father had given him. He hedged its Nomad origin by naming it after King David's *chitara*, but pronouncing it "g'tara." It was among the few belongings he had brought with him, and he strummed it a little during the trip, when Brownpony was away on his horse. He was averse to doing anything which might make him seem ridiculous to Brownpony, and he wondered about this aversion.

Some of the territory claimed by right of conquest as part of the Texark Province was not well defined, and the ill-defined area between the sources of the Bay Ghost and Nady Ann Rivers and the mountains to the west was a kind of no-man's-land, where low-intensity warfare persisted at times among poor fugitive tribes of the Grasshopper who had refused to take up farming, Nomadic outlaws, also mostly Grasshopper refugees, and Texark cavalry sometimes joined by Wilddog war parties in pursuit of raiders. The cardinal's party carefully skirted the western edge of this area, for Brownpony claimed without much explanation that the mountains, especially the moist and fertile Suckamint

Range, were well defended by exiles from the east, of non-Nomadic origin. It was also true that Nomads were superstitious about mountains and stayed away from their heights. The trail led through the foothills, and the nights were cold. But there was much more life here than on the surrounding desert. From occasional horse-apple trees and scrub oak, the flora began proliferating and growing taller. Devoid of foliage at present, cottonwood, willow, and catalpa-bean trees flourished adjacent to creekbeds, while high upon the snowy mountainsides one could make out the trunks of mighty snow-clad conifers. There were a number of streams to ford, some flowing eastward, trickles of water edged by ice, and some were mere dry washes that would flow only during a flash flood in the foothills. The spring thaw had barely begun. All but the largest creeks would evaporate in the dry land to the east, where a small child could wade through a year's rainfall without wetting its knees.

As they gained altitude on their northward journey, it began to snow lightly. The Nomad took the stallion and began exploring side trails. Before evening, he returned with news of some abandoned buildings less than an hour from the main road. So they turned off the papal highway and drove a few miles along a rough trail until they came to a rickety village. Several spotted children and a dog with two tails fled to their homes. Brownpony looked questions at Chür Høngan, who said, "There was nobody here when I was here a while ago."

"They were hiding from an obvious Nomad," the Red Deacon said, smiling.

But then a woman with one large blue eye and one small red eye came out of a hut to meet them with a pike and bared teeth. A hunchback with a musket limped rapidly after her. Blacktooth knew that the cardinal had a pistol well hidden in the upholstery, but he let it alone. He looked around at half a dozen sickly-looking people.

"*Gennies!*" gasped Father e'Laiden, who had just awakened from a snooze in the carriage. There was no contempt in his voice, but it was the wrong word to utter at the moment.

This was obviously a small colony of genetically handicapped, gennies, fugitives from the overpopulated Valley of the Misborn, which was now called the Watchitah Nation since its boundaries were fixed by treaty. There were pockets of such fugitives throughout the land, and they were usually at defensive war with all strangers. The hunchback lifted his musket and aimed first at Chür Høngan, who was driving, then at Blacktooth.

"Both of you get down. And the others inside, get out!" The

woman's voice dog-whined the Valley version of the Ol'zark dialect, confirming their origins. She was as dangerous as a whipped cur, Blacktooth sensed. He could smell the fear.

Everyone obeyed except the Axe, who was freshly missing. The executioner had been riding Brownpony's horse only moments before. At the woman's call, a blond young girl came and searched them for weapons. She was lovely and golden, with no apparent defects, and Blacktooth blushed as her soft hands patted his body. She noticed his blush, grinned in his face, pushed close, seized and squeezed his member, then darted away with his rosary. The woman angrily called her back, but the girl was gone long enough to have hidden his beads. Blacktooth was almost certain the girl was a spook, that is, a Valley-born genny who passes for normal.

He remembered stories he had heard of ogres, perverts, homicidal maniacs among the gennies. Some of the stories were filthy jokes, and most of them were told by bigots. But, having heard the stories, he could feel the shame from them, but not forget in the face of these menacing figures that one or another of the stories came true from time to time. Anything was possible.

Brownpony stirred at last, stepped down from the carriage, and with some majesty put on his red cap. He said to them, "We are churchmen from Valana, my children. We have no weapons. We seek refuge from the weather, and we shall pay you well for shelter and a cooking fire."

The old woman seemed not to hear him. "Get all their belongings, from inside and on top," the woman told the girl in the same tone.

The cardinal turned to the girl. "You know who I am, and I know who you are," he said to her. "I am Elia Brownpony of the Secretariat."

She shook her head.

"You never met me, but you *do* know of me."

"I don't believe you," she said.

"Move!" said the old woman.

The girl climbed inside and began throwing out clothing and other belongings, including Blacktooth's *chitara*, then thrust out her head and asked, "Books?"

"Those too."

Brownpony's concealed pistol would be next, Blacktooth thought, as he wondered why Brownpony insisted that he was known to the girl. He was not self-important, not an egoist who expected to be recognized everywhere. For now the cardinal shrugged and stopped protesting. Apparently, the girl never found the pistol.

Suddenly a muffled cry came from the direction of the largest hut in the cluster. The deformed woman looked around. An old man with mottled skin and white hair appeared in the doorway. Behind him stood Wooshin with his forearm against the old man's throat. The Axe could almost make himself invisible. Having circled the village and approached from the rear, he held up his short sword for their edification. Evidently this was the chief of the village, for the woman and the hunchback immediately dropped their weapons.

"You must not rob them, Linura," the old man scolded. "It's one thing to take their weapons, but—" He broke off as Wooshin shook him and brandished the sword.

The woman fell to her knees. The girl ran. She came back with a pitchfork, darted behind Brownpony, and pressed the tines against his back. "My father for your priest," she yelled to the headsman.

"Put your knife away, Wooshin," Brownpony called, and turned to face the girl. She jabbed him lightly in the stomach and bared her gritted teeth in warning.

"Are you not the Pope's children?" asked the cardinal, using the ancient euphemism for the misborn. He turned about, his arms spread wide, facing each of them. "Would you harm the servants of Christ and your Pope?"

"For shame, Linura, for shame, Ædrea!" hooted the old man. "You will get us all killed or driven back to the Watchitah by acting this way." Then to the girl: "Ædrea, put that away. Also take care of their horses, then fetch us some beer. Now!"

The older woman lowered her head. "I only meant to search their baggage for arms."

"Put your knife away, 'Shin," the cardinal said again.

"I want my rosary and my g'tara back," said Blacktooth to the girl, who ignored him.

The old man advanced to kiss the Red Deacon's ring, found none, and kissed his hand instead. "I am called Shard. That is our family's name. You will be welcome to stay in my house until the snow stops. We have not much to eat just now, after the winter, but Ædrea can perhaps kill a deer." He turned to the old woman with his arm raised as if to cuff her. She gave the musket to the girl and hurried away.

"We carry corn, beans, and monks' cheese," said Brownpony. "We'll share with you. Tomorrow is Ash Wednesday, so we'll need no meat. Two of us can sleep in the carriage. We have tarpaulins to protect it from the cold wind. We thank you, and pray the weather lets us leave soon."

"Please forgive the rude welcome," said the mottled man. "We

are often visited by a small bands of Nomads, drunks or outlaws. Most
of them are superstitious, and fear the flag." He pointed to the yellow
and green banner that flew from the gable of his home. It bore the
papal keys, and a ring of seven hands. As a warning of papal protection, it had become the flag of the Watchitah Nation. "Even those
who don't fear it soon see we have nothing of value, except a girl, and
leave us in peace, but my sister trusts no one. But three days ago, we
were visited by Texark agents posing as priests. We knew they were
sent to spy on us, so we have been very suspicious."

"What happened?"

"They wanted to know how many of us lived in these hills. I told
them just one other family a quarter-hour walk up the trail. I advised
them not to go back there, that the bear boy was dangerous, but they
insisted. Only two of them came back an hour later, and they were in
a hurry to leave."

"Do you really think the Hannegan would chase Valley runaways
this far outside the Empire?"

"We know it. Others have been killed closer to the Province.
Filpeo Harq exploits people's hatred for gennies, and calls us criminals
because we fought our way out of the Valley. Some of his guards were
killed."

While they were unhitching the horses, Blacktooth noticed two
cows with shaggy coats in a pen next to the barn. They were not
ordinary farm animals, and appeared to be Nomad cattle. But Nomad
cows would have kicked and butted their way out through the boards
of the fence by now, so he decided they must be hybrids. Or genny
animals, like their genny owners. For that matter, the Nomad cattle
probably descended from a few successful freaks. Sometimes, rarely,
an apparent monster, whether man or beast, proved to have superior
survival value.

The gennies' hospitality improved sharply after the bad beginning. Apparently not of Shard's family, the hunchback had disappeared. Soon Ædrea had killed a fawn; she brought a cup of its blood
into the house and presented it to Chür Høngan, who looked at it in
frozen silence.

The cardinal was turning red as he choked back laughter. When
the Nomad looked at him, Brownpony hid his mouth. Høngan snorted
at him and took the deer blood from the girl. Growling at her, he
frowned mightily and downed it at a gulp. The girl stepped back as if
in awe. The Red Deacon's laughter exploded, and after a moment
they were all laughing except Ædrea.

"Well, Nomads drink blood, don't they?" she demanded. Blush-
ing at the laughter, she went to dress the fawn.

"Some do," said Holy Madness. "On ceremonial occasions."

After an evening meal of veal-tender venison, black bread, peas, and mugs of cloudy home brew, they talked again, crowding around the fire in Shard's house. Only the Nomad was missing; pretending to speak little Ol'zark, he had taken his blanket roll and gone to bed early in the carriage after losing a drawing of lots for a place in the house. The other loser was Blacktooth, who was glad to sleep away from a headsman, a cardinal, a crazy priest, and several portents, including a pretty female tease.

The common language among them was Ol'zark, but when Shard asked the Oriental a question, Wooshin replied in broken Churchspeak. After this had happened three times, Brownpony turned to him and said, "Wooshin, speak the language of our hosts. That language is Ol'zark Valleyspeak of the Watchitah Nation."

The Axe bristled and stared at Brownpony, who gazed at him evenly. "Valleyspeak is the language of our hosts," he repeated.

Wooshin looked down at the floor. The room was dead silent. He looked up, then, and said in flawless Texark, "Good simpleton, the answer to your question is that by profession I was a seaman and a warrior. But in my later years I cut off heads for the Mayor of Texark."

"And how did you sink to that, Ser?" asked a thin voice from Ædrea.

Wooshin looked at her without anger.

"Not sink, not rise," he said in bad Churchspeak, then returning to her tongue: "Death is the way of the warrior, girl. There is no honor in it, nor any dishonor, if one is just being oneself."

"But to do it for the Hannegan?"

Wooshin's normal expression was relaxed, alert, about-to-smile, wrinkled about the eyes, humorous, scrutinizing. But now it was as frozen as a corpse. Facing Ædrea, he arose slowly and bowed to her. Blacktooth felt his scalp crawl.

Then the Axe looked at the Red Deacon as if to say "See what you made me do!" and went to take a walk in the night. It was the last time the old manslayer ever resisted speaking Ol'zark, but Blacktooth noticed that when he did so, he always imitated Shard's accent, and he called it Valleyspeak. He treated Ædrea with extreme courtesy during their stay. There was no mistaking the bitterness of his regret, but regret for what? Blacktooth was unsure.

After two days of intermittent light snow, they stayed at Arch Hollow, as the Shards called it, for six days, while Chür Høngan spent most of his time riding out to investigate the conditions along the trail. Wooshin too was gone most of the time, but made no account of his activities, unless to the cardinal in secret. It seemed best to wait until other passing traffic began to shovel its way along in the near vicinity.

On the second night they sat around the fire in the center of Shard's lodge. Brownpony tried to elicit the family's story without asking too many questions. His skill in conversation soon led Shard into recounting his family's adventures since the famine and the exodus. There had been a mass escape attempt ten years ago. At least two hundred were hunted down and killed by Texark troops as they fled through forests and up streambeds across the crest of the ridge. At least twice as many escaped the troops that were there both to protect the Watchitah people against intruders and to prevent the escape of the gennies. The Valley was more than a valley; it was a small nation which had kept the name of its place of origin until the conquest. No one had counted the population, but Shard called it a quarter of a million, causing Brownpony to raise an eyebrow. Fifty thousand was closer to popular consensus.

"The approaches to the Watchitah are well guarded by the Hannegan, but the patrols could not catch so many at one time," said Shard. "Probably half of the dead were killed by Texark troops and the others lynched by farmers. Ædrea, of course, could have escaped by passing for normal, becoming a 'spook.' My daughter is very brave to remain with us. The spooks among us are the ones most hated and feared. They can marry unsuspecting normals and pass on the curse, give birth to monsters."

"How safe are you here from the natives?" Brownpony wondered. "I think of this as outlaw country."

"It was, and is, to some extent. The nearest town is two days away. They know we're here. The priest visits us every month, except in winter. He and the baron govern the town. There has been no trouble. Only 'Drea goes to town. Of course she wears the green headband. We're south of the Denver Republic, but the Church is respected here more than in the Empire. The papal highway is patrolled, of course. Still, there are occasional outlaws, but they are looking for traveling merchants. We have nothing here to invite robbery."

"Are there more of you living near here?"

"You saw the hunchback, Cortus. His family lives next door. But the only family behind us is the one with the bear boy."

"Shard, I am the Secretary for Extraordinary Ecclesiastical Concerns."

The old man looked at him with suspicion. "If you really are, then you don't need to ask such a question."

The monk could feel a tension bordering on hostility in the room, but it passed in silence. It seemed clear Shard was lying about the presence of other gennies in the region.

After the dishes had been washed outside in the snow, Linura entered and sat beside, but a little behind, her brother. Then Ædrea came in and dropped cross-legged on the floor beside Blacktooth, who stirred restlessly and almost stopped listening. He wanted his rosary back. Her girl-smell teased his nostrils. Her knees were shiny by fire-light. When she noticed his gaze, she pulled a blanket over her lap, but smiled briefly into his eyes before attending the conversation again. Remembering that this coy creature had grabbed his penis at their first encounter, he nudged her.

"Rosary back!" he whispered fiercely.

She giggled and nudged back, hard.

"I've often wondered about life in the Valley," the Red Deacon was saying.

"There is more death than life there, m'Lord Cardinal," Shard answered. "Few who live there want to risk giving birth. A normal birth is rare. Most die. Others are too feeble to want life. If it were not for the influx, the Watchitah would soon be empty."

"Influx? From where?"

"You must know, m'Lord."

Brownpony nodded. Many people in families of registered pedigree nonetheless had accursed offspring. Lest they lose their registration with the keepers of such records, families without fear of the Church killed their malformed babies. But often there were children whose deformities could be concealed for a time, and these were sent to the Valley at a later age by the pious. Monks and nuns often brought them. People who lived near the Watchitah hated and feared the inhabitants, especially the near-normal among them. Blacktooth noticed that everyone was glancing at Ædrea.

"Forgive me, daughter," Brownpony murmured when she met his eyes.

"I don't like admitting it," Shard was saying, "but the patrols who guard the passes were as much our protectors as our jailers. But they did nothing to help us when famine came."

"And the Church?" said the Red Deacon. "Too busy with its own schism to be of much help to anyone."

"Well, of course we were cut off from papal protection, but the Archbishop of Texark did send in some supplies. I think he is not a cruel man, perhaps only powerless."

"You cannot imagine how powerless is Cardinal Archbishop Benefez," Father e'Laiden sighed.

Blacktooth glanced quickly at the priest, certain that he was being sardonic and meant the opposite of what he said. Benefez had behind him the power of the Hannegans. And e'Laiden spoke Texark like a native, which he probably was, although his command of Wilddog Nomadic meant he had lived long on the High Plains.

"My rosary!" Blacktooth whispered angrily.

She winked at him and grinned. "I hid it in the barn. You can have it tomorrow."

The way she looked at him brought on an eruption of horniness, and he felt his face turning red. Blacktooth feared her. Many deformities recurred, and many were genetically connected. Various writers had made lists. There was one mutation in which great physical beauty was coupled with a defect in the brain, the most notable symptom of which was the onset of criminal insanity a few years after puberty. He stole a glance at her, but she caught him at it, and flicked her tongue and smirked. She might not be crazy, but she was a she-devil. He wanted to go to the carriage and to bed, but he was ashamed to stand up at the moment. At last he prayed his erection away and mumbled good night to the others. Ædrea followed him outside, but he fled into the latrine, then climbed out the back window. He was immediately seized by the hunchback and another creature and dragged away toward another house with a lighted doorway. Nearly fainting with fright, he heard the hunchback whisper hoarsely that someone needed absolution.

"But I am not a priest!" he protested. In vain. They dragged him into the house of Shard's neighbor.

The hunchback and his companion released Blacktooth after pushing him inside, and they stood blocking the door. The monk could only sit down on a stool pointed out to him, and from there await developments. There was firelight and a lantern. There was a wrinkled old man with a scraggly beard in the room, who said his name was Tempus. He pointed out the others. There was his wife, Irene, whose face was a permanent scar. There were Ululata, and Pustria, females both of portentous mein. The hunchback was called Cortus, and his companion Barlo. They were all siblings or cousins or half-siblings. Barlo had a terrible itch, especially in the genital area. Tempus shouted at him to stop masturbating, but the words had no effect on the creature.

God in His wisdom had given Ululata a deformed foot, although He had in all other ways given her the proportions of the divine image in His mind of God in mercy. But the foot was not something you would want to walk with. "God is thus," said the father.

The father had given her crutches. To him, God had given seven fingers, which he displayed to the monk, a third useless eye, and four testicles with two healthy penes, all of which he exhibited. Pustria was Ululata's half-sister, according to their faithful mother's best memory of their conceptions under the weight of the same sire. Pustria was deformed only by blindness, and Mother Irene was partial to Pustria because Pustria could not see her mother's face, a mask of scab of which Mother Irene was not proud. "God is thus, since the deluge of fire and ice," said the father.

Barlo was in need of absolution, Tempus explained, in order to make him stop masturbating. Blacktooth explained that he could not absolve anybody, and that absolution would not have the effect that Tempus desired. Tempus was adamant. Blacktooth would not be allowed to leave until he performed.

"Will you let me go then, immediately?" he demanded.

Tempus nodded gravely and crossed his heart. Nimmy closed his eyes for a moment and tried to summon a little Latin.

"*Labores semper tecum,*" he said in the softest voice he could muster. "*Igni etiam aqua interdictus tu. Semper super capitem tuum feces descendant avium.*"

"Amen," Tempus said in echo to this malediction.

Nimmy got up and left. At the moment, he was not particularly ashamed of wishing eternal suffering on the man, of pronouncing a dire sentence of exile, and calling down upon the head of Barlo a perpetual rain of birdshit; the glep who was still scratching his crotch followed him at a distance.

Chür Høngan was already asleep. Blacktooth had drawn lots with Wooshin and lost the third place indoors. He was relieved things had turned out so, especially after his escape from the clutches of the hunchback's family. If he must sleep in the cold carriage, he preferred to sleep with the Nomad. Although, during his waking hours, he had lost his fear of the killer of hundreds, the Brother Axe still haunted his dreams. Sometimes he dreamed he himself was the executioner, chopping heads for Hannegan with a mighty sword, but that night in the carriage, he dreamed he was Pontius Pilate, and Wooshin the headsman stood beside him as Marcus the Centurion, confronted by a pretender to the Kingdom of God among the Nomads.

Kings of the Nomads were common in those days. He crucified

not one but four of them during his lucrative career in south Texas-Judea. The first case was the hardest for him, and sad; Blacktooth-Pilate was like a boy killing his first deer. Because the pretender was harmless, the case was jinxed by the scruples of his wife. He had wanted to set the first one free. It was easier to kill the ones that followed, and certainly necessary to show that kings were made by Texark and not by tribal gods. He always asked them the same question. The first one could not or would not answer, and merely stood looking at him. The second to be crucified was more talkative.

"What is truth?" asked Blacktooth.

"Truth is the essence of all true statements," said the second King of the Nomads. "Falsehood is the essence of all false statements. Without saying anything, there is neither true nor false. I offer Your Majesty my silence."

"Crucify him," said Pilate, "with prejudice. And get it right this time. Wrap his arms and legs around the cross. That's the way it shows in the Texark Procurators' Handbook. Of course, that's not enough for you new recruits these days. You have to know why. Well, I'll tell you why.

"Nailing the hands to the back of the cross is sound engineering principle and sound governmental policy because when you nail the hands in front the weight of the body hangs on the nails, they tear, unless you also nail the forearm; but when you wrap the arms across the top of the cross and nail them from behind, the weight of the body hangs from the arm on the crossbar, and the nail does nothing but keep the arm in place. That way, you can smash his bones better when it's time to go home from work. Do it the Texark way, men; the Texark way is the eternal way. Let's carry out the sentence with some snap this time."

"Hail to the Hannegan!" said Marcus the Axe.

"Hail Texark! Next case."

Pontius felt better after that. Half-awake by now, he knew he was dreaming, but let the dream go on. The fellow's silly explanation of truth probably had nothing to do with the silence of the first King of the Nomads, but it noisily invoked silence as policy and thus took some of the sting out of Pilate's remembrance of the first one's half-smiling gaze, which had seemed to say to him at the time nothing philosophical at all but had expressed an utterly intimate, infinite regress of "I who look at you who look at me who look at you . . ." His wife Ædrea had been frightened by the same look. It was perhaps sexy, and for that very reason insulting to those whose duty it was to see such scum as loathsome.

"What is truth?" said Pilate to the third King of the Nomads.

"Root for pearls, Texark pig!"

Blacktooth-Pilate had no qualms at all with that one.

He woke up thinking about Ædrea instead—and their coming assignation in a hayloft. A prank. Drowsily, he remembered hearing Brother Gimpus argue that a detachment from sexual passion was the essence of chastity, and that detachment was possible without abstinence. Brother Gimpus was caught naked with an ugly widow in the village who claimed she paid him every Wednesday for the eighth sacrament. "Rest in peace," Blacktooth whispered against the pillow.

CHAPTER 6

 HÜR HØNGAN WAS STILL ASLEEP WHEN
Blacktooth started up, fully awakened by
hoofbeats, which stopped near the carriage. Then he heard voices speaking
softly in Grasshopper. They were talking
about Shard's cows in the pen next to
the barn, until something excited them
and there was another burst of hoofbeats, followed by the screams of Ædrea.
The monk pulled at the edge of the tarp and peered outside. A few
flakes of snow were still falling in the faint morning light. There were
three horsemen, obviously Nomads. Two of them held the kicking girl
suspended by her arms between them. Shard began yelling protests
from afar, and the hunchback ran out with his musket. Blacktooth
turned to awaken Høngan, but he was already up and moving, putting
on his wolfskins and the leather helmet with small horns and a metal
ornament. He usually wore the hat only when mounted. Blacktooth

thrust his hand deep into the upholstery and felt the Red Deacon's handgun. The girl had missed it.

Chür Høngan climbed out the other door and came into their view from behind the coach, yelling at the renegades in the Wilddog of the High Plains.

"In the name of the Wilddog sharf and his mother, put her down! I command you, motherless ones! Dismount!"

Blacktooth raised the cardinal's weapon, but his hand was shaking badly. The Nomad not involved with the girl lifted his musket, looked closely at Holy Madness, then dropped the weapon to the ground. The others eased the girl onto her feet, and she promptly ran away. The riders slowly dismounted, and the apparent leader fell to his knees before the advancing Høngan.

He spoke now in Høngan's dialect. "O Little Bear's kin, Sire of the Day Maiden, we meant her no harm. We saw those cows over there and thought they were ours. We were only teasing the girl."

"Only a teasing little rape, perhaps? Apologize and leave here at once. You know those tame cows are not yours. You are motherless. You ride unbranded horses. I heard you speaking Grasshopper, so you don't belong anywhere near here. Never bother these people; they are children of the Pope, with whom the free hordes have treaties."

The visitors complied immediately and were gone. The incident had lasted not more than five minutes, but Blacktooth was astounded. He climbed out of the carriage. Chür Ösle Høngan leaned against the coach and gazed absently after them as they rode away toward the main trail through a sprinkle of snow.

"They're Grasshopper outlaws, but they knew you! Who *are* you?" Blacktooth asked in awe.

The Nomad smiled at him. "You know my name."

"What was that they called you?"

" 'Sire of the Day Maiden'? Have you never heard that before?"

"Of course. It's what one calls one's sharf."

"Or even one's own uncle, on some occasions."

"But motherless ones recognized you? Last night I dreamed of a king of the Nomads."

Høngan laughed. "I'm no king, Nimmy. Not yet. It's not me they recognized. *Just this.*" He touched the metal ornament on the front of his helmet. "The clan of my mother." He smiled at Blacktooth. "Nimmy, my name is 'Holy Madness,' of the Little Bear motherline. Pronounce it in Jackrabbit."

"Cheer Honnyugan. But in Jackrabbit, it means Magic Madman."

"Just the last name. What does it sound like?"

"Honnyugan? *Hannegan?*"

"Just so. We're cousins," archly said the Nomad. "Don't tell any-body, and don't ever pronounce it in Jackrabbit again."

Cardinal Brownpony was approaching from the direction of Shard's house, and Chür Høngan went to meet him with a report of the incident. Blacktooth wondered if the Nomad was entirely teasing him. He had heard claims of the dynasty's ultimate Nomadic origin, but since Boedullus made no mention of it, that origin must have been in recent centuries. At least he knew now that Høngan was of a powerful motherline. His own family, displaced to the farms, had no insignia, and he had never studied the heraldry of the Plains. Some-thing else that piqued his curiosity about the Nomad was his apparent close friendship with Father e'Laiden, who called him Bearcub. The priest had often ridden beside the Nomad when he was driving, and their talks were plainly personal but private. They had known each other well on the Plains. From fragments overheard, he decided that e'Laiden was formerly the Nomad's teacher, but no longer dared to play that role unasked, lest a grown-up and somewhat wicked student laugh in his face.

Blacktooth went to look for his rosary and g'tara in the barn, which was half buried in the side of a hill. Ædrea was not visible, but he could hear the muffled sound of strings being plucked. The floor was swept stone, and a small stream of spring water ran in a channel from beneath a closed door in the rear and out to the cattle pen outside the wall. Above the door was a hayloft. He opened the door and found himself in a root cellar, with a number of nearly empty bins containing some withered turnips, a pumpkin, and a few sprouting potatoes: the remains of last year's crops. And there were jars of pre-served fruits—where could they have grown?—on the shelves. There were three barrels, some farm implements, and a pile of straw for layering vegetables. There was no one here. He turned to go, but Ædrea slipped down from the hayloft and confronted him as he started to leave. Nimmy looked at her and backed away. In spite of the weather, she was wearing nothing but a short leather skirt, a bright grin, and his rosary as a necklace.

He backed away. "Wh-where's the g'tara?"

"In the loft. It's more comfortable up there. You can snuggle down in the hay. Come on."

"The air's warmer in here than outside."

"All right." She came in and closed the door behind her, leaving them in pitch darkness.

"Haven't you a lamp or candle?"

She laughed, and he felt her hands exploring him. "Can't you see in the dark? I can."

"No. Please. How can you?"

Her hands withdrew. "How can I what?"

"See in the dark."

"I'm a genny, you know. Some of us can do that. It's not really seeing, though. I just know where I am. But I can see the halo around you. You're one of *us.*"

"Us who?"

"You're a genny with a halo."

"I'm not—" He broke off, hearing her rustling skirt in the darkness, then the scratch of flint on steel and a spark. After several sparks, she managed to kindle a bit of tinder and used it to light a tallow taper. Nimmy relaxed slightly. She took down two clay cups from a shelf and turned the spigot on one of the barrels.

"Let's drink a glass of berry wine."

"I'm not really thirsty."

"It's not for thirst, silly. It's for getting drunk."

"I'm not supposed to do that."

She handed him the cup and sat down in the straw.

"My g'tara—"

"Oh, all right. Wait here. I'll get it."

He nervously gulped the wine while she was gone. It was strong, sweet, tasted of resin, and was immediately relaxing. She came back in with his g'tara, but held it away when he reached for it.

"You have to play it for me."

He sighed. "All right. Just once. What shall I play?"

" 'Pour Me Another Before We Do It Brother.' "

Nimmy poured another cup of wine and handed it to her.

"That's the name of the song, silly."

"I don't know it."

"Well, play anything." She flopped down in the straw. Her skirt came up. By candlelight he could see under it. She wasn't wearing anything there. But something was unusual. He hadn't seen a girl that way since he was a child, but it wasn't the way he remembered. He looked at her, the g'tara, the cup of wine in his hand, and the candle. He gulped the wine, and poured another.

"Play a love song."

He gulped again, set the cup aside, and began plucking the strings. He didn't know any love songs, so he began singing the opening lines of Vergil's fourth eclogue to music he had composed himself.

When he got to the words *jam redit et Virgo*, she made a little puff of wind with her lips and blew out the candle from six feet away. He stopped in fright.

"Pour another cup of wine and come here."

Nimmy heard the liquid splashing into the cup, then realized he was doing it himself.

"You drink it," she said.

"How do I get out of here?"

"Well, you have to find the keyhole. It's not very big."

He fumbled in the area of the door.

"It's over here."

He felt her tugging at his sleeve, gulped the wine before he spilled it, and sprawled beside her in the darkness. "Where's the key?"

"Right here." She grabbed what she had grabbed when first they met. He didn't feel like resisting. They came together, but after a lot of fumbling, he said, "It won't fit!"

"I know. The surgeon fixed me so it won't, but it's fun anyway, isn't it?"

"Not much."

She sobbed. "You don't like me!"

"Yes I do, but it won't fit."

"That's all right," she sniffled, sliding lower in the straw. "Just come here."

He had not been so surprised since Torrildo's advances in the basement. Drunkenly, he feared at any moment Cardinal Brownpony would burst out of the broom closet and yell, "Aha! Caught you!" But nothing like that happened.

When he stumbled out of the barn with his virginity diminished, a smiling Ædrea (*semper virgo*) sat twirling his rosary, watched him from the hayloft until he crawled into the carriage and pulled down the tarp behind him. The term "against nature" insinuated itself into his tipsy consciousness. He had never been so drunk.

"Damn that witch!" he whispered when he awoke, but recoiled from the words at once. *I am my own witch!* quickly replaced them. Help me, Saint Isaac Edward Leibowitz. My Patron, I looked forward to entering that barn—pray for me. I was glad she stole my things. It gave me the excuse I needed to pursue her in pretended anger. The things she stole, I should have given her. I know this now. Why couldn't I have known it then? I wonder if I knew what I was doing with Torrildo too. I, or the devil in me. O Saint Leibowitz, intercede for me.

· · ·

Blacktooth had fallen angrily in love. His sexuality had always been a mystery to him. He had wondered about his once deep affection for Torrildo, among others who once had been his friends at the abbey. His erotic dreams had more often involved enormous buttocks than enormous breasts, but now he was suddenly smitten by a girl, and there was no doubt at all in his mind that it was the most powerful love he had ever felt except his love for the heart of the Virgin, a blasphemous comparison, but true. Or was that lust too?

In spite of their tryst in the root cellar, during the days that followed Ædrea responded to his enamored gaze with a self-satisfied smirk and a shake of her pretty head. He knew what she meant. She, as a bearer of the curse, was forbidden to fornicate with anyone outside the Valley. The penalty was mutilation or death. She had taken an awful chance in seducing him. But what they had done in the barn was only passionate play, not against the basic folklaw. Against his fractured vows, surely. She knew that. At the end, she teased him about how easily she overcame his vows. He knew he was still bound by the vows, and straying once was no excuse for straying again. But without more surgery, Ædrea was physically incapable of normal coitus. Her father had it done to her when she was a child, probably afraid that someone like Cortus or Barlo would rape her. O Holy Mother, pity us.

No one had seen them in the barn, but the pulsation of sexuality that happened whenever the girl and the monk came together did not escape the cardinal's attention. The Red Deacon caught him alone while Blacktooth was behind the coach lashing bundles in preparation for departure.

"It's time we talk, Nimmy. Excuse me, Blacktooth. I hear Høngan calling you Nimmy, and it seems to fit. How do you want to be called?"

Blacktooth shrugged. "I'm leaving an old life behind. I might as well leave my name behind. I don't mind."

"All right, Brother Nimmy. Just don't leave behind your promise of obedience. I remind you that Ædrea is a genny. Watch your step very closely here. I'll tell you, Shard's was not the first exodus here from the Valley. It's been happening for years. This place is more than it seems, and Ædrea is more than she seems."

"I had begun to suspect, m'Lord."

"You are not to intentionally see her again. If you ever see her again in Valana, avoid her." He commanded Blacktooth with his eyes. "This has nothing to do with your vow of chastity, but let this help you keep it. They are hiding a large genny colony back there in the

higher hills, but don't let them know that you know. They're frightened enough of us to be dangerous."

"Yes."

"And there's something else, Nimmy. Chür Ösle Høngan is an
important man among his people, as you found out from those outlaws, but you were not supposed to know, and it is not known in
Valana. Now I have to ask for your silence. There is a need for secrecy.
He is an envoy to me from the Plains, but you must not tell that to
anyone. He is just a driver I hired."

"I understand, m'Lord."

"Father e'Laiden is another matter. I had no need to read your
mind to see your curiosity about him. About him, you must also say
nothing. He grew his beard for this trip, to avoid recognition. I picked
him up forty miles south of Valana, and will let him off at the same
place, which will make you even more curious. Not even my friend
Dom Jarad knows who he is. I've told travelers he's just a passenger to
whom I gave a ride. You know I introduced him to Dom Jarad as my
temporary secretary. No more of that. You will not mention him to
anyone. If you meet him in Valana later without his beard, do not
allow yourself to recognize him. His name is not e'Laiden, anyway.
About these two men, you will be absolutely silent."

"I have had much practice at being silent, m'Lord."

"Yes, well, I took a big chance with you, Blacktooth. Nimmy. For
now, your job is just to keep your mouth shut. I may find other uses
for you in Valana."

"That would please me, m'Lord. I have felt useless for years."

Brownpony turned to look at him closely. "I am surprised to hear
it. Your abbot told me you are quite religious, and seemed called to
contemplation. Do you think that useless?"

"Not at all, but it's my turn to be surprised the abbot said I was
called to it. He was very angry with me."

"Well, of course he was angry, partly at himself. Nimmy, he's
sorry he made you do that silly Duren translation. He thought it
would be useful."

"I told him otherwise."

"I know. He thought you were ducking hard work. Now he
blames himself for your revolt. He's a good man, and he's really sorry
the Order lost you. I know how humiliating it was for you at the end,
but forgive him if you can."

"I do, but he didn't forgive me. I wasn't even allowed to confess."

"Not allowed by whom, Dom Jarad?"

"The prior said he would ask the abbot. I suppose he did."

"Nobody shrived you, eh? Well, Father e'Laiden can confess you if you can't wait until we get to Valana. I can imagine you need it by now."

Blacktooth blushed, wondering if the remark implied a reference to Ædrea. Of course it did!

He approached the old whitebeard priest later that day, but the cleric shook his head. "His Eminence forgets something. I'm not even supposed to say Mass. You have seen me do it, but I don't give the Eucharist, and I don't do confessions. Saying a private Mass is my own sin, if it is one—not involving others."

A wild and sorrowful look came over the old man's face, as if he were at war within himself. Blacktooth had seen the look before and shivered. Father e'Laiden was just a little crazy.

Strange traveling companions, he thought. A priest under interdict, a seaman-headsman-warrior, a wild but aristocratic Nomad, a disgraced monk, and a cardinal who was not more than a deacon. Brownpony, Blacktooth, and Høngan were all of Nomadic extraction, and e'Laiden obviously had lived among Nomads. Holy Madness, whose mother's family was called Little Bear, and e'Laiden seemed old friends, and often talked of Nomad families known to both of them. Only the executioner was unrelated to the people of the Plains. Blacktooth was more puzzled than ever about the Red Deacon's intentions. The cardinal, he had learned, was head of the Secretariat of Extraordinary Ecclesiastical Concerns, an obscure and minor office of the Curia which he had heard someone call "the bureau of trivial intrigues."

After two days of light snow the skies cleared. There was bright sun and a breeze from the south. Three days later, the thaw was well under way. Chür Høngan was gone for half a day, then returned with an opinion that the highway was not impassable, although they might have to shovel slushy snow in a few places. Brownpony paid Shard a fair sum in coins from the papal mint, and the travelers took their leave of the village. Only the children, Shard, and Tempus watched them go. The monk's eyes searched in vain for Ædrea. He was sure she was angry because of his mixed feelings and his avoidance of her. He wanted to let her know he blamed only himself, but there was no way. She was gone for good.

They were still closer to Leibowitz Abbey than to Valana when they left Arch Hollow, but progress was faster as the road improved. Several days later, everyone's breathing became labored as they approached the high passes. Something had happened to Earth's atmosphere since the catastrophic demise of the *Magna Civitas*. One could only gaze upward at, not climb to, ruins of ancient buildings on mountainsides far above the present tree line. Once the air had been more breathable. And of course Earth herself had changed, sickened by the wars that long ago brought the end of a world. A new world was rising, but it could not grow as fast as the old. Rich pockets of resources had been plundered and dispersed. Now ancient cities were mined for iron. Petroleum was always going to be scarce. Hannegan had needed to plunder his people for copper. Living creatures had become extinct or changed. The wolves of the desert and plains were known to be different breeds, even by those Nomads who wore "wolf-skins" but called their nation "the Wilddog Horde." There was less forest and more grass in the world than before, but not even in the records of Leibowitz Abbey could one learn much about biology before the Flame Deluge and the great freeze that followed. The curse pronounced by God in Genesis had been renewed; Earth and Man were doubly fallen.

On the twentieth evening of their journey, Holy Madness saw *Nunshân*, the Night Hag. They made camp early, and Høngan had ridden ahead in the late afternoon to check the condition of the passes, and he came back ashen and babbling after sundown.

"I looked up, and there she was standing on a crag against the early stars. Ugly! I have never seen a woman so huge and ugly. There was a kind of black light around her, and I could see stars through it. The sun was behind a mountain, but the sky was still light. Then she cried out to me—a great sobbing sound, wild as a cougar."

"Maybe it was a cougar," said Brownpony. "This thin air can make you dizzy."

"Cougar? No, no, a horse! She was there, and then she was a black horse and galloped away, into the very sky, it seemed!"

Brownpony was silent, busying himself with a plate of beans. Blacktooth studied Chür Høngan's expression and found it excited but sincere. He had learned that the Nomad was at least nominally a Christian, but Nomad myths were not dispelled by baptism.

It was Father e'Laiden at last who spoke. "If you saw the Night Hag, who is dying?"

"The Pope is dying," said the Red Deacon.

"Does the *Nunshân* appear for popes, m'Lord?" asked Blacktooth, almost amused.

"It could be my father dying," the Nomad said quietly.

"God forbid," said the cardinal. "Granduncle Brokenfoot must be elected Lord of the Three Hordes, and become the successor of the

War Sharf Høngan Ös." He looked quickly at Blacktooth. "This is
something else you must forget you heard, Nimmy."

"I shall obey, m'Lord."

For Blacktooth, things were falling into place. There had been no
Lord of the Three Hordes since the War Sharf Høngan Ös had led his
people to defeat against Hannegan the Conqueror seven decades ago,
and been sacrificed by his own shamans. The Jackrabbit Horde had
been completely subdued, as well as a few tribes, including
Blacktooth's, of the Grasshopper Horde, and the descendants of these
either lived within the Empire as small ranchers, or on the Denver
Freestate farmlands. Without the participation of electors from the
Jackrabbit Horde, the military and priestly office of the kingship could
not be filled. The Hannegans had prevented this from happening.
Blacktooth thought of his crazy dream in which he had been Pilate
crucifying would-be kings of the Nomads. He believed in the mean-
ingfulness of dreams; such was his Nomad heritage.

Now there were stirrings of rebellion from the conquered peoples, for whom the free Nomads had in Blacktooth's childhood years
displayed only contempt. Chür Ösle Høngan, then, was a relative of
Høngan Ös, and his motherline was qualified for the high kingship.
Brownpony was involved (meddling?) in Nomad politics, which was
the same as Nomad religion, for only the shaman class could be electors. The thought came to him now that the cardinal, the elderly
priest, and the Nomad with royal family connections in the Wilddog
Horde might have stopped to confer with Jackrabbit shamans before
they visited Leibowitz Abbey. Several half-overheard conversations
during the journey supported the idea.

He was ordered to silence, and he meant to obey. But to regard it
as a matter of no concern to him would be to turn his back on his late
parents and their heritage. He was grateful for Chür Høngan's kindness toward him. One day it might be possible to become proud of his
heritage, if pride were not one of the deadly sins his faith warned him
against. If the two northern Hordes, the Wilddog and the unvan-
quished tribes of the Grasshopper, stopped showing contempt for the
conquered tribes, Jackrabbit and Grasshopper, he might be able to
hold his head up in the world. But he knew the Jackrabbit Horde and
his own exiled people must again assert themselves before that could
happen. He knew he would be glad to help if he could.

Blacktooth saw her the following morning. She was a young girl,
much like Ædrea, but beyond Ædrea in beauty. Naked, she stood under a ledge washing herself and dancing in a little waterfall made of
new-melted ice. A stone's throw away, she looked once at Blacktooth,

who stopped and stood frozen, his scalp crawling. Her eyes left him to follow Holy Madness, himself unseeing, who rode the cardinal's stallion. They followed him until a big wad of loose wet snow fell over the ledge and made her dart back out of sight. Seconds later a delicate white mare galloped out from under the ledge and disappeared into a thicket of snow-dripping spruce. Blacktooth shook his head. The altitude made one quite dizzy.

Later, when the Nomad stopped and waited for all to catch up, Blacktooth walked past him and said, "I saw her this morning myself. As *Fujæ Go*, the Day Maiden."

"Was she young?" Chür Høngan asked.

"Very young, and beautiful."

"Whoever he was yesterday, today he's dead," said the warrior. "She wants a new husband."

"She was looking at you. Or the cardinal's horse."

Høngan frowned, shook his head, and laughed. "The horse. They say she copulates with stallions when there is no Lord of the Hordes. It's this thin air, Nimmy. Works on both of us."

Blacktooth continued to walk while the carriage caught up with the waiting Nomad. There was a trade-off somewhere behind him, and the same horse came back with a different rider.

"Why don't you ride beside the Axe?" asked the cardinal, for the first time referring to Wooshin by that name.

"Because I have a boil on my behind, Your Eminence, but also because I need to walk." Blacktooth had smoked some of the strong medicinal stuff the Nomad had brought down from Nebraska, and he was feeling more loquacious and less self-conscious than was his wont. Also, he had lost his fear of Brownpony, and begun to like the man.

"What's this I hear about you and the Wild Horse Woman, Nimmy? Do you change religions often?"

"I hope, m'Lord, that my religion of today is always just a little improved over my religion of yesterday, and a vision of a maiden in an icy waterfall does wonders for my religion of today, although tomorrow I might question the vision's reality. But did *I* say she was the *Høngin Fujæ Vurn?*"

Brownpony laughed. "You feel, then, that reality and religion might or might not have something to do with each other at this altitude?"

"At this altitude, yes and no, m'Lord."

"Keep me informed if she turns up again," Brownpony said lightly, and trotted on ahead.

It was a time of visions. Blacktooth had heard of miracles in the mountains, magic on the plains, and chariots in the sky. The Virgin was appearing simultaneously to small groups of her elect in three different locations on the continent. Furthermore, what her apparition said in the west, her voice in the east put to a severe test. It was almost as if she was arguing with herself. This, perhaps, was the best proof of her divinity, for in divinity opposites are always reconciled. *Nunshån* and *Fujæ Go*, Night Hag and Day Maiden, aspects of the *Høngin Fujæ Vurn*. There was a third aspect; at appropriate times, she became the War Buzzard, presiding over the field of battle, the feeding ground.

It's just the thin air, Blacktooth told himself. But why not a Wild Horse Woman? He had seen her on horseback when he was a child. He had seen her this morning under the waterfall, and she was the same young woman. The women of the Hordes own the breeding mares, and pass them to their daughters. Nomad women are wonderful breeders of horses. And no warrior rides a mare into battle. To ride a mare is to advertise one's unreadiness to fight. So Cardinal Brownpony's stallion is both a mount and a statement. Wild horses are forbidden, except to her betrothed, because they are hers. She is a natural projection of Nomad culture onto the Nomad consensual world, but to admit this is not to say she is wholly unreal. Christians make similar projections; so many apparitions of the Virgin! And she is an arbiter of power on the Plains; by choosing a husband, she chooses a king. It amused him to imagine her choosing a pope.

Blacktooth's departure from the abbey had not gained him a freedom to think for himself—he had always had that. But now he didn't have to feel guilty about it. His own religious practice was necessarily suffering because of the journey, and because of his sins, but he tried as often as he could to spend an hour silently reciting Saint Leibowitz's Grocery List while he rode or lay awake at night: *Can kraut, six bagels, bring home for Emma. Amen.* Short and sweet, it kept the mind from wandering toward Ædrea. He greatly preferred it to the Maxwell's Laws Memorabilium that had so confused Torrildo, and perhaps contributed to his delinquency.

But his anger at himself about Ædrea and his feelings kept seeking an outlet. When they camped that evening, the Axe as always asked, "You ready die now?" Blacktooth, without a negative comment, immediately kicked at the Axe's crotch. The headsman dodged, but the blow glanced off his hip; he laughed with delight. "You very mean man tonight," he said, and allowed Blacktooth to attack thrice more before he threw him on his face in the melting snow. It was the first time the student had ever touched the teacher, and Wooshin embraced him after helping him to his feet.

"This time you ready die, yes?"

That was the second night. They were gathering speed as they rode northward and downward. On the fourth night, a messenger with a lantern and a bodyguard trotting along behind delivered the news to Elia Cardinal Brownpony: the Pope was dead. He and the soldier stopped for refreshments with them, then continued southward with a summons for Abbot Jarad and other cardinals across the Brave River. More such messengers would be fanning out from Valana by all roads with the same summons for all cardinal bishops, cardinal priests, cardinal deacons, cardinal abbots and cardinal abbess (1), cardinal nephews and cronies across the continent, while the city of Valana prepared for another conclave.

That night the cardinal huddled in conference with the Nomad and the chaplain, while Blacktooth and the Axe sparred farther away from the fires. On the morrow, they availed themselves of the public baths in Pobla, the first real town they had visited. Father e'Laiden shaved his beard and was seen no more with the rest of them, although Blacktooth caught sight of him later in the company of a fair-haired man in Nomad clothing and with Nomad weapons but with manners that did not come from the Plains. Out of Pobla, Holy Madness rode eastward toward the Plains. Hence too, half an hour later, his Chaplain e'Laiden followed him, accompanied by the blond, urbane young warrior.

Brownpony hired a local driver and proceeded toward Valana with his new servants, a regular headsman and an irregular monk.

Blacktooth had been nursing an unasked question for a long time. Guilt from his encounter with Ædrea made him hesitate, but now he asked it. "M'Lord, back at Arch Hollow, when they were about to rob us, why did you expect the girl to recognize you?"

Brownpony frowned for a moment, then answered easily: "Oh, my office has had some dealings with a group of armed gennies in that general area. I assumed they were a member of the group. Apparently, I was wrong."

Blacktooth remained curious. Wooshin and Høngan had done quite a bit of exploring in the area, but had spoken only to the cardinal about what they found. He resolved to question Brother Axe.

By early afternoon, they were passing along muddy lanes full of dogs and children through brick and stone villages with log roofs with chimneys belching smoke. There was the sound of the smithy's forge and women's voices haggling with vendors over the price of potatoes and goat meat. These villages were now precincts of Valana, surrounding it, having grown up during the schism and the exile, brought by and bringing new commerce and industry to the foot of the mountains whose peaks Blacktooth had seen from the distance in his youth.

But they were too close now to see the peaks, and there was only the hulking presence of the massif to the west. It was all new and dirty, and bewildering to the monk who, although he had spent the first fifteen years of his life within a few days' ride of this place, had never been inside a city. And the city began to loom up around them as the cardinal's coach moved deeper into the more heavily populated area, where most of the buildings were, like the abbey, two and even three stories high. And all of it was dominated by the central fortified hill, looming ahead, the hill whose walls enclosed the Holy See, and from which rose the spires of the Cathedral of Saint John-in-Exile, where the vicar of Christ on Earth offered Mass to the Father. Blacktooth was in a daze and barely heard the cardinal, who turned to address him.

"Pardon, m'Lord?"

"Did you know that the plaza in front of Saint John's is paved with cobblestones brought here all the way across the Plains from New Rome?"

"I had been told, m'Lord, that the area around the Cathedral is New Roman territory. But all of the stones?"

"Well, not all, but Saint John-in-Exile stands on New Roman soil. Imported. That's why the natives here contend there is no need to go back. In fact, they remind everyone that New Rome itself was built on imported soil."

"From across the sea?"

"So the story goes."

"The Venerable Boedullus thought otherwise."

"Yes, I know. The theory of a schism at the time of the catastrophe. Who knows? How did it happen that Latin came back into use after it was abandoned?"

"That, m'Lord, was during the Simplification, according to Boedullus. The book burners did not destroy religious works. One way of saving precious material from the simpletons was to translate it into Latin and decorate it like a Bible, even if it was a textbook. It was also useful as a secret language. . . ."

"Now, that building ahead of us is the Secretariat," the cardinal interrupted. "That is where you and perhaps Wooshin will work from time to time. But first, we must find quarters for both of you."

He leaned forward and spoke to the driver. Moments later, they turned off the stone-paved thoroughfare and onto another muddy side street overarched by branches that were beginning to bud. It was not long until Holy Week, and time to begin choosing a pope.

CHAPTER 7

Now the sacred number of seven will be ful-
filled by us if we perform the Offices of our
service at the time of the Morning Office, of
Prime, of Terce, of Sext, of None, of Vespers
and of Compline, since it was of these day
Hours that he said, "Seven times in the day
I have rendered praise to You." For as to the
Night Office the same Prophet says, "In the
middle of the night I arose to glorify you."
Let us therefore bring our tribute of praise
to our Creator "for the judgments of His
justice" at these times . . . and in the
night let us arise to glorify Him.
—*Saint Benedict's Rule*, Chapter 16

HE WARM CHINOOK FROM THE MOUNTAINS HAD
breathed on the snow, and the snow vanished. Chür Høngan skirted the poor
farming communities along the bed of
the Kensau River as he rode toward the
northeast. In Pobla, he had armed himself with a heavy shortbow and quiver of
arrows. The cardinal had given him his
double-barreled handgun and bought
him an unshod stallion from a Nomad trader, but he wanted to avoid
trouble with Blacktooth's people, who in season tilled the irrigated
plots of potatoes, corn, wheat, and sunflowers, and who dwelled in
fortified lodges of stone and sod and worked the land for its owners,
among whom was the Bishop of Denver. They might mistake him for
a Nomad outlaw like the ones who had visited Arch Hollow. The soil
was poor here, but careful farming had enriched it. Now it was almost
planting time and there were men and mules in the fields, so he
avoided the rutted roads and kept to the high ground, while leaving a

trail that Father Ombroz e'Laiden and the Texark turncoat could easily follow.

There were always Texark agents traveling back and forth from the telegraph terminal southeast of Pobla, so Høngan rode alone until he was well into the short grass of Wilddog cattle country before he stopped to wait for the others. He waited in a draw, concealing his horse and himself some distance from the trail he had left until he heard them passing to the north. Still, he waited. When their voices died away, he left his horse, climbed out of the draw, and listened carefully to the wind from the southwest. He put his ear to the ground briefly, then arose and crept into the space between two boulders where he could not be seen except from the trail directly below. There were distant voices.

"Three horses have come this way, obviously."

"But not necessarily together. Only one horse is shod."

"That would be Captain Loyte's."

"Hereafter, do not call the renegade 'Captain'! He sold his rank and honor for the cunt of a Nomad spy."

The voices were Ol'zark. Høngan nocked an arrow and drew his bow. The first rider appeared, and fell from his horse with the arrow through his throat. Høngan leaped forth and shot the second rider while he was lifting his musket. With the second barrel, he exchanged shots with the third rider, but both men missed. The survivor turned and fled. This war between Nomad and Empire was more than seventy years old, but such battles were few and fought only when the imperial forces invaded the lands of the Mare.

Holy Madness reloaded the pistol and finished the job of killing the wounded, then went for his own mount and captured the other two horses. After searching the saddlebags and finding the proof he needed that the riders were agents, he released the animals and came back to search the bodies for more papers. He stared angrily at the tracks of the turncoat's horse. Knowing the destination, he had previously not noticed the hoofprints because he had not been tracking.

Mounting again, he rode on with a warm wind still at his back in pursuit of the priest and his guest. His own war with Texark had begun long ago and would never end. This he had sworn in the name of his ancestor, Mad Bear, calling to witness Empty Sky and the Holy Virgin. He followed the tracks through the afternoon and afterward by twilight. There would be no moon until morning. He ate a little jerky, and without building a fire prepared to spend the night listening to the howls and barks of the wilddogs which simpletons called wolves and greatly feared. After he had staked his horse and unfurled his bedroll, Høngan slowly walked a protective circle around the area at a distance of five or six paces and marked his sleeping territory with a trickle of his own urine every few steps. With his sleeping area thus protected, the animals would not usually molest a human sleeper unless they smelled blood or sickness about him. Only once during the night did he sense prowlers. Bursting from his blankets, he leaped to his feet and let out a roar of mock rage. There was a chorus of yelps, and several dark shapes fled by starlight from the downwind border of his realm. Having bellowed the sleep out of his head, he lay with sad thoughts about the corpses he had made that day.

Chür Høngan had killed his first man at twelve, a Texark border patrolman. Ombroz had absolved the boy at the time as he would have absolved any soldier in war, because the trooper had been on the wrong side of the river, in military uniform, and without a traveler's flag as required by the Treaty of the Sacred Mare. As far as the Wilddog was concerned—and the priest honored the sense of the horde— no treaty later than Sacred Mare had ever been signed with any secular powers including Texark, and the war against Texark had never become peace, it just had slowed down until it mostly stopped happening; it almost stopped because the only frontier across which the Wilddog faced the Empire was the Nady Ann River to the south, beyond which lay the occupied Jackrabbit country. There might be a time to fight there, but not until the Jackrabbit fought too. To the east, in the tall-grass country, the Grasshopper engaged the enemy when it saw fit, but it asked no help from the Wilddog while there was no Lord of the Three Hordes.

Ombroz had easily absolved him of that early killing, but gave him pure hell for honoring ancient custom as well. The boy had cut off the cavalryman's earlobe and ate it as an honor to the slain enemy, as his Bear Spirit uncle had explained was proper. The priest called it something else. He made the boy meditate for an hour a day on the meaning of the Eucharist, and put him through parts of catechism again before he would give him communion. Høngan remembered it in the night with a grin. He never told the priest that while he was eating the earlobe he was crying for his victim. About the men he had just killed today, he could not see what Wooshin had tried to teach him to see. Something about emptiness. The Axe tried and failed to relate it to the Nomad's Empty Sky. Something about emptiness becoming man. Or was that Christianity mixing in? There were too many ways of looking at things. A century ago, for his great-granduncles, there had been only the one way. Høngan thought that old way might be a little like Wooshin's way, but with more feeling and

vision. The right way, his own way, was not clear to Høngan, not quite
yet.

Before dawn he shook the frost from his blankets and rode on by
the faint light of an old crescent moon in the east. Knowing the route
the priest would take, he did not need to see their tracks to follow,
and within two hours he had found them. Ombroz had rekindled their
dung fire and they were drinking hot tea and eating jerky at sunrise.
The chaplain hailed him, and the turncoat to whom he had not yet
been introduced arose expectantly, but the Nomad went straight to
their hobbled horses. He petted one of them, spoke to it gently, then
cut the hobbling cord and lifted a front hoof to inspect it. Then he
turned to confront them.

"Father, you've brought a spy among us!"

"What are you talking about, my son? This is Captain Esitt
Loyte, the one Cardinal Brownpony suggested. He is married to a
granddaughter of Wetok Enar, your own kin."

"I don't care if he married the granddaughter of the devil's clan.
He's riding a shod horse to let them know he's here."

The priest frowned at the former trooper, then arose to stare
toward the west.

"Don't worry, Father. I killed two of them, and the other fled.
Here are the papers." He faced Loyte and drew his gun. The stranger
spat in the fire, and said, "You might look at both sides of the horse.
But thank you, if you killed my assassins."

Høngan aimed at his abdomen. "Your assassin is right here."

"Wait, Bearcub," barked the priest. "Do as he says. Look at the
brand."

Reluctantly, he lowered the pistol and inspected the stranger's
mount again. "One of Grandmother Wetok's horses," he said in surprise. "And you had it shod in Pobla? You damn fool!"

"If they were out to kill me, why should I leave tracks for them?"
Esitt Loyte began to explain, but Høngan ignored him, took tools
from his bag, and began prying a shoe from a forehoof. "Give me a
hand here," he said to Ombroz.

Soon the nails were pulled and the task was done. He put the
horseshoes in his saddlebag. "We'll have to show them to your
mother-in-law," he said to the stranger.

"I meant no . . ."

"Bearcub, he's an expert in Texark cavalry tactics, and he knows
their war plans. They came to kill him."

"But now he's useless to us, because they know he's here."

"From the tracks of one shod horse? It might be anybody. It might be a churchman. It might be a trader."

"Traitor, you mean. Before they died, they spoke his name."

"Well, it's done now, and the trail ends here. Loyte is right. They came to kill him. At least *they* must think he's useful to us, even if you don't." He turned to the young former officer. "Why did you have the pony shod?"

"Before I rode into the mountains, I talked to the liveryman in Pobla and he recommended it. And I have always ridden a shod horse. It's cavalry—"

"The trail ends here," the priest repeated. "Bearcub, there's nothing to worry about."

"Mount up," said the Nomad, and pointed toward the horizon. "Look at the dust. There's a migration trail just to the east of us. The herds are moving north. We'll wait there until drovers come. Then we'll ride ahead of their cattle for a few hours, and our tracks will vanish."

"If we do that," Loyte protested, "we won't be home before dark."

"Home?" snorted Høngan.

"The hogans of his wife and her grandmother," Ombroz said firmly. "But I agree, we'd better do as you say."

It was midafternoon before Holy Madness was satisfied that the woolly Nomad cattle that were following them in the distant cloud of dust would erase their tracks. They changed direction then, left the cattle trail, and resumed a northeastward course.

Ombroz was still trying to make peace. "If the cardinal's plan succeeds," he said, "the Hannegan will have to stop these incursions into Wilddog and Grasshopper lands, at least for many years. The hordes by then will be stronger under a single king."

Høngan was silent for a time. They both knew that the Grasshopper lands, the tall-grass prairie lands, lying to the east, would bear the brunt of any invasion. Those of Blacktooth's people who had remained herdsmen there had become the most warlike of the hordes, because they had to be. They faced Hannegan's armies, and the slow encroachment of farmers onto the more arable eastern fringe. And yet the Wilddog was closest to the Church in Valana, and to possible allies beyond the mountains. There was friction between the hordes, made worse by Nomadic outlaws who had departed from the matrilineal system and attracted young runaways from the conquered Jackrabbit south of the Nady Ann.

"There is the more immediate problem of paying for the goods," Høngan said to the priest at last.

"Don't worry about that," put in the trooper. "His Eminence controls considerable wealth."

"Yes, the Half-Breed owns many cattle," said Høngan acidly.

"There are other forms of wealth than cattle," said Captain Loyte, "and how dare you call him 'Half-Breed,' anyway? Aren't you a Christian, after all?"

The priest laughed. "Go easy, Loyte, my son. The Bearcub is just practicing his tribal accent, so to speak. After all, how would 'The Most Eminent Lord Elia Cardinal Brownpony, Deacon of Saint Masie's' sound in the mouth of the son of Granduncle Brokenfoot, Lord of the Three Hordes."

"My father is lord of nothing, yet," Chür Høngan grumbled, his sour mood persisting.

"See how churlish he turns as he gets closer to home?" said Ombroz.

"Not only is he lord of nothing," Holy Madness went on, "I'm only his son, not his nephew."

"You know that makes no difference," said the priest. "In no way can that old office be inherited, in the motherline or otherwise. The old women have their eye on you, Holy Madness. When the old women look for the *Qæsach dri Vørdar*, they look for a magical leader, not a somebody's nephew or son."

"I don't like this talk, teacher," said Høngan. "I love and respect my father. Talk of inheritance is talk of death. And there hasn't been a *Qæsach Vørdar* since Mad Bear. After seventy years, who knows how these modern women will think."

Ombroz chuckled at the word "modern."

"Granduncle Brokenfoot is going to live a long time," said the former Texark officer. "I saw him only three months ago when he came to visit my brothers-in-law."

"The turncoat has a degree in medicine too," said the Nomad.

The officer shot him a resentful look. "Wasn't it Magic Madman here who claimed he saw the Night Hag, Father?"

"Damn it, old priest! Did you have to tell him that?"

Father Ombroz glanced quickly at both of them. "Stop spoiling for a quarrel, you two. Or else give me your weapons, and get off your horses and fight. Right here, right now."

"Trial by combat?" Høngan snickered. "Yes, Blacktooth told me the Church used to do that. Why didn't you teach me that, Father? You neglected the part of the catechism about the Lord of Armies, but here you are now inviting us to submit to the judgment of God in a fistfight? And I was not looking for one. I just wanted to know, of our Texark adviser here, what other kind of wealth does the Half-Breed have besides cattle? If the turncoat says there is such a thing."

"God damn your mouth!" said the officer, and shifted his weight hard to the left stirrup, causing his horse to stop.

Chür Høngan looked at him for a moment, shrugged, and dismounted. Ombroz spoke quickly. "I have to warn you, Captain, Holy Madness has been practicing combat with an expert—a former headsman to the Hannegan. You may know of him."

"Do you mean that yellow-skinned genny? Woo Shin? Listen, if you fear traitors, fear him. I wouldn't wonder if Filpeo Harq didn't send him to kill the cardinal. He has a cadre of hired assassins, you know. They are all clever infiltrators."

"The Axe is not a genny, you citizen," said the Nomad, using the word "citizen" as an insult. "Where he comes from, *you* look like a genny. And he hates Filpeo Harq almost as much as I hate him, city boy."

"Bearcub, why do you do that? Captain Loyte's on our side. He knows his business. Try not to be an asshole, my son."

"All right, tell the bastard to stop patronizing me." Høngan turned to remount. Loyte was not appeased, and struck him across the back with his riding whip.

Høngan whirled, grabbed the wrist that came toward him with the whip a second time, and kicked the captain in the stomach with his pointed boot.

. For some minutes of semi-consciousness, it appeared that the blow might be fatal. But the priest at last revived him, and insisted that they spend the night on the spot to let Loyte recover. Ombroz prayed at them lengthily and angrily, praising God's mercy for allowing them an undeserved time to repent. Høngan groaned at him sleepily. Loyte whimpered and swore. On the following day, Chür Høngan pulled the officer out of his blanket by the front of his jacket and dragged him to his feet. "Now listen well, pigfucker. If you're a captain in our army, I'm your colonel. You say 'sir' and salute."

He pushed the former trooper down on his rump; the jolt brought forth a yelp of pain as Loyte grabbed his stomach again.

"No, you listen to me!" Ombroz grabbed his bearcub by the arm and pulled him quickly out of earshot. "I've never seen you this brutal! Why? Establishing your seniority is one thing, but you may have ruptured his gut. You've made an enemy for life out of pure bad temper."

"No I haven't. He's already everybody's enemy. A criminal to his own tribe is no friend to any man. He is what he is, and he must know his place."

"You don't mean that. His place is the same as yours, before God."

"Before God, of course. But his place in the ranks of a fighting force under a war sharf is what concerns me, and he has to know that his rank is low. He cannot be trusted."

"You know this because of your great insight into character," Ombroz said ironically. "Greater insight than that of the cardinal, who recommended him to us in the first place. I believe him when he says the agents that followed were sent not just to track him, but to kill him. And in any case, he would be living with the Wetok clan, whether he rode with us or not. They have accepted him. He wintered with them."

"Have you seen me quarrel with anybody else lately?"

"No, Holy Madness. And I hope you're wrong about this man. He knows too much about us for you to drive him away."

"No danger. He has nowhere to go. We leave him with his wife's people, no matter what the eminent cardinal said. I still want to know how he knows that Brownpony can find his part of the price of the weapons which he promised. And where do the weapons come from?"

"Elia worked hard for Pope Linus, Bearcub, and Pope Linus rewarded him well. I know that Elia owns estates on the west coast, and up in the Oregon country, but he may not need to use his own wealth. Trust him. If you pay the traders six hundred cattle, the cardinal will arrange for somebody to pay the other two-thirds of the price. As the most powerful state on the continent, Texark has many enemies and few allies. Many of those enemies would be glad to help arm the hordes. You are being ungrateful."

"Not at all. I like Brownpony. I know it's his influence more than his wealth that matters. And I trust his best intentions. That doesn't mean I trust the outcome of his intentions. If he's wealthy, fine. But how does Loyte know?"

"He probably doesn't. He *was* patronizing you. Nomad or citizen, each feels superior to the other. *Nomas et civis*—it's a story old as Genesis. But as for the money, there are states west of the divide which would like to see the Hannegans' empire stop where it is, or be driven back eastward. There is too much talk in Texark about uniting the continent, and their embassies report this talk home. One or more of them may be giving you the weapons for nothing."

"Six hundred cattle are not nothing."

"They are next to nothing. Cardinal Brownpony told me the real price of the merchandise. It's more like six thousand cattle."

"If we get the weapons at all. If the traders don't deliver defective junk."

"What puts you in this awful mood, Holy Madness? I half-expected you to call Loyte a grass-eater."

Høngan laughed. "In my mother's house, that word is still used. So at home, I might use it on him."

"You know, you have a certain political ugliness about you, Holy Madness, that you did not learn from me."

"Oh, but I did!"

"No, you didn't!"

"Are you going to try to whip me too, O Teacher?"

"I *have done* that."

"When I was ten and you were younger. You taught me not to hit clergy, but you're not—" The Nomad stopped. He saw the change in Ombroz's face, shook his head, *sorry*, and walked back to his horse.

By the time they had made camp for a second night under the stars, they met a messenger from the Wilddog Horde's royal tribe. He was riding south with bad news. Granduncle Brokenfoot had suffered a stroke, had lost the use of his left leg, and was composing his death song. It was therefore deemed wise for the grandmothers and shamans to begin considering other candidates for the ancient office of the one *Qœsach dri Vørdar*.

The following day, they arrived at the hogans of Grandmother Wetok Enar's clan. The old woman was weak and ailing, so it was Loyte's wife Potear Wetok who, unaccompanied by her grandmother, bade them welcome. Her husband dismounted and went to embrace her, but she pushed him away; his "learning about our horses," the Nomad euphemism for the breaking in of a new groom by the mothers of his new family, was not yet finished. She bowed to Father Ombroz and Chür Høngan, and invited them into the hogan of her grandmother. Out of politeness, they followed her, although both were in haste to return to Høngan's family.

"Chür, have you heard the bad news?" asked the lovely granddaughter. "I hope I'm not the one who has to tell you."

"We met a messenger. I know about my father." He handed her a leather pouch containing the horseshoes. "Your husband will explain these, but later." She looked at the pouch curiously, but left it inside the door-flap unopened as she ushered them into the hogan.

The old woman sat in a leather slingchair hung between two posts sunk in the hard dirt floor. She tried to rise, but Høngan waved her back. Nevertheless, she signed her respect for Høngan and Ombroz by making the *kokai*, striking her forehead with her knuckles, and bowing her head while placing her hand against her scalp palm outward toward each of them. This politeness seemed excessive, and she did not repeat it toward Esitt Loyte. Her son-in-law she ignored; whether this was normal groom-hazing ("teaching him about our horses") or real contempt was hard to say.

"What the Night Hag has foolishly done to your father grieves me greatly, Høngan Ösle Chür." The utterance was fraught with portent. Ombroz noticed that Høngan was actually fidgeting before her. To attribute Brokenfoot's illness to the Night Hag and call it foolish meant that he had been this Weejus woman's choice for *Qæsach Vørdar*, and her reversal of Chür's name, with the matronymic placed last, meant that the rank of Brokenfoot's son had risen in her eyes, for whatever reason. But *Høngan Ösle* was a diminutive for the historical Høngan Ös, who lost a war and half of his people to Hannegan II.

"Will you drink blood with us tonight?" the old woman asked. "We celebrate the birth of twin colts by Potear's best mare. And they are healthy, too—a rare and wonderful event."

"Toast the Virgin for us, Grandmother," said Father Ombroz. "My apologies for the haste, but Granduncle Brokenfoot needs us."

"Yes, he will want to see his son, and from you he will want last anointing. Go then with Christ and the Lady."

The two of them rode on, leaving Esitt Loyte behind with his bride and in-laws.

"The captain still has much to learn about the Wetok horses," Ombroz said wryly when they were out of earshot.

Høngan laughed. "He will learn quite a bit in a hurry when Potear shows that old Weejus the horseshoes."

The mountains had all but disappeared in a dust haze to the west when Holy Madness suddenly announced that Brokenfoot had become irascible in his illness, and that his old wife had found it necessary to appoint another as temporary head of the family.

"How do you know this?" the priest scoffed. "A vision?"

"That vision." Høngan pointed toward the east. Carefully he raised himself in the saddle, and soon was standing on the back of his horse.

"My old eyes can't see anything but emptiness. What is it?"

"There is someone there, I think my uncle. It's miles away, still! He moves its arms and dances a message. They see our dust."

"Ah, the Nomad semaphore language. I should have learned it when I was younger. It always amazes me."

"It gives us an advantage over their Texark warriors."

.   .   .

When the hogans of the Little Bear clan hove into view on the horizon, a small cloud of dust appeared and soon a rider approached them. It was Brokenfoot's wife's brother, Red Buzzard, who was the nominal leader of the clan, who nevertheless deferred to his sister's husband because she willed it so. Now during the husband's illness, the brother resumed his rightful role. He was a thin, serious man, nearly sixty, with livid patches of skin which might have marked him as a genny except among the Nomads, where the cosmetic defect was highly regarded as a mark of Empty Sky. He spoke seriously to Holy Madness about Brokenfoot's condition, which was disabling but apparently not getting worse at the moment.

"Some of our drovers are already back from the south," Red Buzzard said to Ombroz, "including our Bear Spirit men. They are with him now, Father. But of course he wants to see you."

Ombroz started to tell him about the Pope, but Red Buzzard already knew. Even in Cardinal Brownpony's absence from Valana, his Secretariat was constantly sending and receiving messengers from the people of the Plains. When they came to the Little Bear village, the children and younger women came out to greet and be hugged by Høngan and their priest.

"Will you stay with us after you see your father?" asked his mother. "Or must you ride on to Grasshopper country?"

Holy Madness hesitated. He had not told her before. "I think Kuhaly has divorced me." He glanced at Ombroz, who had married them, but the priest was looking away. "She said she would send for me if she wants me. Even if she does, I may not go."

His mother's face melted. "They blame you for having no daughters?"

"Perhaps. Also for being away too much of the time. Her brothers complain. I've done too little for the family. They say I am too attached to you. You know the word for that."

"I was afraid it would be so when you married Grasshopper. Our drovers told us they had to fight Grasshopper drovers again this winter, to get pasturage."

"Anyone killed?"

"Among ours, only wounded. Among theirs, I don't know. It was an exchange of shots and arrows. Now, come and see your father."

The Little Bear family shamans left the hogan while Father Ombroz administered the last anointing to his oldest convert. The priest knew they were embarrassed that some of their practices could not be reconciled with the religion he taught, and that they had accepted baptism themselves because Brokenfoot wished it so. When the old man died, their embarrassment (and envy?) might turn into hostility.

But the whole family knew that when he, Ombroz, had been forced to choose between them and his Order, when a new superior general of that Order, nominated by Archbishop Benefez, and therefore by Filpeo Harq, had called him back to New Rome, he had refused to go. He had been expelled and placed under interdict—measures which he ignored. Still, the punishment hurt him more than he cared to admit. He knew the Weejus women would be his allies in any quarrel with the Bear Spirit shamans, but he wanted to avoid the quarrel, and so far, so did they. Under his teaching, most of this Nomad family had become Christians, while he himself over the years had become a Nomad.

Ombroz was not the first teacher of the Order of Saint Ignatz to watch a favorite student whom he had taught to think for himself begin thinking otherwise than the priest had foreseen. That night he sighed heavily as he watched Chür Høngan dance the dance of the dying with the shamans in the dim and smoky light of the dung fire in front of Brokenfoot's hogan.

The drums seemed to say: "Gruesome go, gruesome go, gruesome Mama go. . . ."

The dance was to placate Black Wind, Empty Sky's frightful counterpart, and to fend off the Night Hag. For a time he went wandering through the village, visiting similar fires and speaking to old "parishioners." A minority were really Christian, but most he had baptized, and most accepted him as belonging to the shaman class. Among the unbaptized, his wisdom voice was still deemed worth hearing, when he sang in council.

Before the conquest, such villages had not existed. But more and more the Plains were dotted with hogans of stone and sod resembling those of the farmers, and located beside intermittent creeks and waterholes. Here the children and the elderly stayed for the winter, while the drovers moved their woolly cattle according to the seasons for best grazing and for protection from the worst of the howling blizzards which in the dead of winter swept down the Plains from the Arctic over the lands of the Great Mare and on into the conquered province which had belonged to the Jackrabbit Horde. Long ago the Jackrabbit had held the lightly forested land with deciduous trees to the southeast, land now claimed by the Texark Imperium. The Jackrabbit had rented pasturage there, partially sheltered from the icy blasts, to the Grasshopper and the Wilddog in the winter months, and they were well paid for this in cattle and horses. As a consequence, the Jackrabbit people were the least migratory of the hordes even before the war; and only a minority fled from the south after the conquest to form the Jackrabbit diaspora in the poor farming regions, neighbors to some of the impoverished ex-Grasshopper families who like Blacktooth's had fled toward the mountains across the short-grass country of the Wilddog.

He could not get away from the drums. Now they seemed to say, "Freedom come, freedom come, freedom maiden come. . . ."

After visiting nearly every dwelling, Father Ombroz went back to Brokenfoot's hogan. He stood near the fire watching the dance for a time; then, after a pause to catch the beat, he laughed aloud and joined the dance himself, bringing an amused cheer from his Bearcub.

CHAPTER 8

 HE SECRETARIAT OF EXTRAORDINARY
Ecclesiastical Concerns was located in
one of the few remaining buildings near
the center of the city which had been
there before the Pope came west. A two-
story building of stone with a basement,
it had once been a military barracks for a
few dozen sentries, and it stood alone
amid spruce trees on an acre of land fifteen minutes' walk from Saint John-in-Exile.

Although the monk and the old warrior spent the first night
shivering in their blankets on cots in the Secretariat basement, within
a day they were lodged with three seminary students named Aberlott,
Jæsis, and Crumily in a small house Brownpony found for them near
the western limit of the city. He had won the at-first-grudging consent
of the students by paying half the rent on behalf of his servants, and
by promising that they would share the housework and exercise no
seniority over the much younger students, one of whom—Jæsis—was

ill. Aberlott was a chubby, good-natured clown from the northwest, whom Blacktooth immediately liked. Crumily was a long-faced Easterner, who seemed morose at first, but who proved to have a wry wit that usually twisted the tail of Aberlott's jokes. The character of Jæsis was difficult to fathom because of his illness, but Aberlott called him a bit of a fanatic as a student for the priesthood, but did not dislike the boy, although he came from Hannegan City.

The house itself was adjacent to a brewery. A creek ran through the brewery and out behind the house. It came down the hill as pure mountain spring water in summer, but was now swollen by melted snow. Their outhouse and others in the vicinity were well above the level of the creek and probably drained into it during hard rains. Blacktooth had seen children drinking from the stream down at the ford, and he wondered about the illness of Jæsis, who, when he was not in bed, could be heard moaning in the outhouse. Blacktooth and Wooshin were to share a room in back, and come and go through a rear entrance, although they might use a common kitchen and share a space for study. So it was agreed. The newcomers had several days to inspect the city before going to work at the Secretariat.

They found the city itself rather filthy, except in local enclaves of power and wealth where street sweepers stayed busy and water arrived by aqueduct. Valana had grown up rapidly around an ancient hilltop fortress which had in earlier centuries been a bastion of defense by the mountain people against the more savage Nomads of an earlier age. Except for the ancient hilltop fortress itself, which now enclosed the center of a newer New Vatican, overshadowed in the afternoons by the spires and bell towers of the Cathedral of Saint John-in-Exile, the city was without walls. Before the exiled papacy had moved here, the city had become a sort of middle kingdom among the contiguous communities of the populated region, where merchants traded with miners for silver and pelts, with Nomads for hides and meat, and with farmers for wheat and corn. There had been two blacksmiths, a silversmith, two arrowsmiths, a fletcher, a miller, three merchants, one doctor of medicine, and one gunsmith, when the Pope had fled here from New Rome. Since then, the number of businesses had quadrupled, and there were now doctors, lawyers, and bankers. Half a dozen city governments in the region competed with Valana proper and each other for new business. It had been a growing economy, but with the coming of the head of the Church, the growth became explosive. Only one building in five was older than the beginning of the exile. Among them was the Secretariat building among the spruce trees, almost invisible from the road.

Blacktooth went to work almost immediately at the Secretariat,

replacing a volunteer lay translator who spoke Nomadic better than
Rockymount and who happened to be a Christian Wilddog cousin of
Chür Høngan and was glad to be relieved of the job and returned to
his family on the Plains. There were seventeen employees at the
agency, counting a janitor, but not counting the messengers that kept
coming and going between Brownpony and his many correspondents
around the continent, some secret, some official. There were five
translator-secretaries including Blacktooth, three copyists, three secu-
rity-guard receptionists, and five men who worked in a part of the
building sealed off from everyone else and accessible from the outside
only through a locked iron gate and from the inside only by way of a
corridor to the cardinal's own office. Blacktooth was quick to realize
that no one but the cardinal knew all the Secretariat's purposes, and
employees were isolated from each other as much as possible.

Blacktooth inherited the office space of his Nomad predecessor,
which was adjacent to Brownpony's office because the man had
needed more careful supervision than others. However secretive the
cardinal might be with his own employees, he was forced to confide in
a nun named Sister Julian from the Secretariat of State, who was there
to keep a close eye on those "extraordinary concerns" which also
might affect the official diplomatic relations of the Valanan papacy.
She seemed to have a certain nay-saying power, and she treated
Blacktooth and Brownpony's other people with suspicion and an attitude of superiority, although she seemed to be on good enough terms
with the master. She was, however, apparently not entitled to know
what went on in the sealed-off part of the building, and was denied
entry there.

There was a confluence of cardinals now, continually arriving for
the impending conclave. As soon as they found quarters, they changed
their garments from red to the purple of mourning for the dead Pope.
Anyway, purple was the color of penance, appropriate for Lent, now
drawing to a close. After the period of mourning was finished, the
color would change to saffron. They would not again wear cardinal red
until the election of a pope.

One of the first cardinals to arrive in the city came from the
most remote diocese of all Christendom, one who had, in fact, set out
by sea to attend not this but the previous conclave which had elected
the Bishop of Denver, now deceased. His name was Cardinal Ri, Archbishop of Hong, and he had sailed across the Pacific with a wife and
two lovely younger women said by some to be his concubines. These
were looked upon with horror by the local Society of Purity, but the
police were warned by the Cardinal High Chamberlain and former
Secretary of State, Hilan Bleze, to keep such people from harassing the

strange foreign archbishop, the existence of whose diocese had been unknown for centuries, until just three decades ago when a voyage of discovery had found Christian communities in islands far to the west. Pope Linus had been so delighted to learn there were still Oriental Christians that he made Bishop Ri a cardinal before fully investigating the traditions of his church. The Axe now too was delighted to learn of Cardinal Ri, for other reasons, and set out immediately to meet some of his staff. He returned to relate that it was possible for him to communicate with them, barely, in his native tongue, so similar were the two dialects of an ancient language. He was also impressed by the advanced weaponry of Ri's guards; when the Axe told Brownpony about the arms, the cardinal paid Ri a visit. He apparently asked that these weapons be kept out of sight, for the guards thereafter carried conventional cavalry pistols.

Wooshin made haste to explain to Blacktooth that the apparent concubines were nominal wives, extrasacramental, and that Ri kept them because it was expected of a man of the archbishop's rank in the society of his home island. Nevertheless, they apparently all bedded down together at times, according to the staff. While they were indeed looked upon with horror by the cardinals of the Society, there was hardly any conclavist who was not looked upon with horror by somebody. Cardinal Ri was very rich, but of course he had brought no more wealth with him than six soldiers could guard with their lives during the voyage, and he needed credit to keep his family and retinue living in comfort. Most merchants in Valana extended him credit, since Brownpony vouched for him orally (but declined to cosign his notes).

Sorley Cardinal Nauwhat from Oregon, himself a candidate, greeted the Oriental prelate most warmly, and Emmery Cardinal Buldyrk, the Abbess of N'Ork, immediately befriended Ri's extrasacramental wives and offered them the hospitality of her rented suite. This Ri reluctantly permitted, after he was told of the city's attitude toward his extra women. He was somewhat ill anyway—his personal physician spoke of dragon's breath from the mountains—and probably felt no need of his ladies. There were other married cardinals, of course, but most of them were laymen or deacons, and most left their wives at home.

Strangely, the most powerful prelate on the continent, Urion Cardinal Benefez, Archbishop of Texark, was late to come to the conclave, sending word by wire that he wished to celebrate Easter Mass in his own cathedral with his own people and his Hannegan.

·   ·   ·   ·

Brownpony and his new servants had been in Valana for a week when Blacktooth decided to go to confession. The cardinal, always charitably helpful to the little monk in such personal matters in this strange city, had gotten him an appointment with a priest whom he wanted Nimmy to meet.

The Reverend Amen Specklebird, O.D.D. (*Ordo Dominae Desertarum*), lived alone in what had once been a cave in the side of a hill. But somebody with rock-cutting tools had shaped the outer cavern, squared the tunnel, deepened it, filled the hole behind the living quarters with rubble and mortar, and added short walls of stone that protruded from the hill. Father Specklebird had partially reopened the hole where the cave narrowed. (It let the mountain spirits come and go through his kitchen, he explained.) A vaulted roof, also of stone, topped the walls that protruded from the hill so that the visible part of the dwelling reminded Blacktooth of the front of a Nomad hogan that had been half-swallowed by a mountain. Blacktooth learned that the wealthy owner of an ecclesiastical tailor shop had owned it a decade or more ago, and had used it as a root cellar until Cardinal Brownpony had bought it for Father Specklebird when the Bishop of Denver had forced the old priest's retirement. Strangely, after Bishop Scullite had become Linus VII of recent memory, he had summoned Father Specklebird to his private quarters on several occasions. If rumors were true, Blacktooth might be about to confess to a confessor of the late Pope. Another rumor, which had been traced to a papal chambermaid, had it that Linus VII, on the brink of death, had named the old man cardinal *in pectore*, pending the next consistory, but no one could substantiate the servant's tale.

The monk stood in the shadows under the trees, steeling himself to cross the trail and knock on the heavy pine door. A wisp of smoke arose from a chimney. Except for the light from fire that caused the smoke, it must be rather dark inside, for there were only two small windows, set high in the thick wall. Nimmy had been in a proper frame of mind and heart when he left the cottage, ready to make a good confession. But now that he was here, a kind of dread came over him.

He had left Leibowitz Abbey unshrived and stinking of guilt; moreover, on the trip to Valana from the desert he had done unspeakable deeds, and now he quaked at the prospect of confessing to a stranger, a thing he had never before done. The sacrament of penance had always been administered to him by a priest of the Order, and usually once a week. There was only so much mischief a monk could accomplish in a week, even an unruly monk such as Blacktooth St. George. Usually, it was a matter of whispering his self-accusations to his regular confessor, and hearing himself sentenced to, say, a few decades of the rosary, or at worst to make a public apology to a brother, or to flagellate himself three or five lashes with a not very painful piece of rope for solitary sins of impurity, resentful thoughts, and failures of charity or courage. Such penances always left him feeling cleansed and ready to receive the Holy Eucharist at Mass.

But now he had been sinning rather copiously for weeks on end, often neglecting his prayers, breaking his vows, and secretly disobeying his benefactor, the cardinal. It was to the cardinal, in fact, that he had mentioned his fear of confessing to a stranger; when the cardinal had suggested e'Laiden, and e'Laiden had declined, it was the cardinal again who had arranged for him to confess in Valana to a reputed holy man, none other than Amen Specklebird himself, whose name had been once or twice brought before a previous conclave as a candidate for the papacy! Blacktooth now wished he had never mentioned his problem to Brownpony. He would much rather confess anonymously to a faceless priest behind a grille at the seminary chapel than do it in the presence of a holy man, and he thought of sneaking away to do just that before the time came for his arranged interview. But Father Specklebird would ask how long since his last confession, as was customary, and would then realize that Blacktooth had circumvented him. Furthermore, he imagined, a seminary priest might be so horrified by what he heard that he would refuse to absolve him, and then he would have to tell Specklebird about that too. Even outside the abbey, being a Catholic was a very complicated business for a simple ex-Nomad recluse with little knowledge of the external world.

Suddenly the pine door was flung open, and an old black man with a cloud of white hair and great white eyebrows came out and walked straight toward him. His beard was white too, but close-cropped, as if he shaved it once a month or kept it trimmed with scissors. He wore a clean but ragged gray cassock, and sandals that appeared to be made of straw. He was gaunt, almost a skeleton with tight muscles strung along the bones, and hollow cheeks and hollow abdomen that hinted at much fasting. He walked with a lively limp, using a short cane heavy enough to be an effective club. When he came out the door, he was looking straight at Blacktooth in the shadows, and he came right toward him, wearing a thin smile and running his luminous gray-blue eyes over the small and timid figure before him.

"Deacon Brownpony has told me something about you, son. May I call you 'Nimmy'? You have left the monastery for good, is that so? Why?"

"Well, I began to feel I was wearing cangue and chains, Father. But in the end, they threw me out."

Amen Specklebird took his arm and led him across the trail toward his hermitage.

"And now you have lost your cangue and chains, yes?" They entered a room which with its bare stone walls reminded the monk of Leibowitz Abbey. There was a fire at one end and a private altar at the other.

Blacktooth thought about the priest's question. "No. If anything, they fit tighter than ever, Father."

"Who tightened them? Who chained you in the first place? Was it the abbot? Was it your brothers? Was it the Holy Church?"

"Of course not, Father! I know that I did it to myself."

"Ahh." He sat quietly. "And now you want to know how to free yourself?"

" 'Ye shall know the truth and . . .' " He shrugged. "One must know the truth to be free."

"So. And what is the truth that you already know?"

"The truth was made flesh, and dwelt among us. We must cling to him alone."

"*Cling* to him? Nimmy, Jesus came to be sacrificed for our sins. We offer him, immolated, on the altar. And still, you want to *cling* to him?" He laughed, and produced a stole. "Are you ready to confess now?"

Blacktooth delayed. "Could we talk awhile first?"

"Of course, but what would you talk about?"

He groped for a subject. Anything to postpone the moment. "Well, I don't understand what you mean about the sacrifice."

"To sacrifice Jesus is to give him up, of course."

The monk started. "But I gave up everything *for* Jesus!"

"Oh, did you! Except Jesus, perhaps, good simpleton?"

"If I give up Jesus, I will have nothing at all!"

"Well, that might be perfect poverty, but for one thing: that *nothing*—you should get rid of that too, Nimmy."

Blacktooth became bewildered. "How is it possible for a priest of Christ to talk like this?"

Specklebird pointed to his mouth and worked his jaw mockingly in silence. Then, without anger, he lightly slapped the monk's face. "Wake up!" he said.

Blacktooth sat down on a hard bench. He had been reciting formulas, trying to say the right thing for the old man, who was now laughing.

"You are a rich fellow," said Specklebird. "Your riches are your cangue and chains."

"I have nothing but the robe on my back; the g'tara which I made for myself was stolen," the monk protested with some irritation. "I don't even have a rosary, now. Also stolen. I eat other people's food, and sleep in other people's quarters. I don't even piss in my own pot. I promised to be poor for Christ. If I've broken that vow, I don't know how. I broke the others."

"Are you proud of this unbroken vow?"

"Yes! I mean no! Oh, I see, I'm rich in pride, is that it?" Amen Specklebird sat down across from him. They watched each other in the dim light. The old man's gaze was like that of a child, curious, open, pleasant, expectant. He snapped his fingers, unexpectedly loud. Blacktooth did not jump at the snap, but his gaze in turn was wary, and he looked away to the left. Specklebird continued to watch him in silence.

Still delaying, Blacktooth began to talk rapidly, about life at Leibowitz Abbey, not about his sins as sins, but about his frustrations, his loves and friendships, his devotion to the founder of his order and to the Mother of God, his vocation and how he lost it, and his homesickness for the very place he had tried so hard to escape. He kept pausing, hoping the hermit listening to his story would offer advice, but the old ordinary of Our Lady of the Desert only nodded his understanding from time to time. Blacktooth became embarrassed by his own self-pity and stopped talking. A long silence passed between them.

After a while, Specklebird began to speak softly.

"Nimmy, the only hard thing about following Christ is that you must throw away all values, even the value you place on following Christ. And to throw them away doesn't mean sell them, or sell them out. To be truly poor in spirit, discard your loves and your hates, your good and bad taste, your preferences. Your wish to be, or not be, a monk of Christ. Get rid of it. You can't even see the path, if you care where it goes. Free from values, you can see it plain as day. But if you have even one little wish, a wish to be sinless, or a wish to change your dirty clothes, the path vanishes. Did you ever think that maybe the cangue and chains you wear are your own precious values, Nimmy? Your vocation or lack of it? Good and evil? Ugliness and beauty? Pain and pleasure? These are values, and these are heavy weights. They make you stop and consider, and that's when you lose the way of the Lord."

Blacktooth listened patiently, fascinated at first, but drawing himself up, becoming distraught. He felt the old man was trying to undermine everything he knew and felt about religion. Was this kind of talk the reason the bishop had forced Amen Specklebird to retire?

"The Devil!" the monk said softly.

If Specklebird heard it as an accusation, he ignored it. "Him? Throw him away, dump him in the slit trench with the excrement, throw quicklime on him."

"Jesus!"

"Him too, oh yes, into the trench with that fucker! if he makes you rich."

Blacktooth gasped. "Jesus? Whom do I follow? Then why follow? It's blasphemy, what you say."

"You know, it's all right to pick up Christ's cross and carry it, Nimmy, but if you think you get anything special because of it, you're selling the cross, and you're a rich man. The path is without reason. Just follow."

"Without wanting to?"

"*Sine cupidine.*"

"Then why?"

"Your wish for a *why* is the cangue and chains."

"I just don't understand."

"Good. Remember it, Nimmy, but don't understand it. That spoils you."

Blacktooth felt dizzy. Was the old man quite sane?

Amen Specklebird laughed gently. "Now for your confession, if you still want me to hear it."

After confession, which he wanted to forget as quickly as possible, Blacktooth went home first, but the air was foul with recent vomit. Someone had washed the floor near Jæsis' bed, where the student lay moaning. He had lost a lot of weight. Once he opened his eyes and glared wildly at the monk, who asked if he wanted a doctor to come. "Here this morning," Jæsis croaked. "It does no good."

Blacktooth brought a cold wet towel for his head, then went back to the Secretariat, where he spent the afternoon and much of the evening translating the cardinal's mail to and from the Plains. He was very quickly learning about Nomad politics and the important personages among the hordes. He learned that Chür Høngan had now returned to the hogans and herds of his Little Bear grandmother, that Uncle Brokenfoot had been struck down by sudden illness, that an anti-Christian faction among the Bear Spirit men and the Weejus women of the Grasshopper Horde, some of whom feared Høngan's candidacy, had suddenly rallied to the name of one Hultor Bråm, a mankiller of undoubted prowess, as the most fit war sharf to reunite the Three Hordes. Bråm interested Blacktooth exactly (and only) because he was Grasshopper, and might even be a distant relative. His partisans translated his name as Kindly Light, but in Jackrabbit *hultor bråm* meant a bad sunburn. He also learned that his master was not entirely displeased by this development, for Bråm was possessed by a savagery that made Høngan's temperament seem mild in comparison, and the cardinal, although alarmed by the illness of Høngan's father, believed the majority of the grandmothers would never propose for the highest office and bridegroom of the *Fujæ Go* a hothead after the pattern of Mad Bear, whose reckless chieftainship had lost the Jackrabbit territory in the south to Hannegan II, and cost the Grasshopper dearly in men and cattle. The Wilddog on the High Plains had suffered the least from that old conquest.

Brownpony always left notes to help the monk avoid political pitfalls in his translations, when the wrong wording might offend certain groups, or compromise his plans if his correspondence fell into the wrong hands. The cardinal received more and longer letters than he wrote, and Blacktooth was surprised to learn that he had so many literate allies on the Plains. He knew, or had been told, that Nomad literacy was about five percent. The writers mostly belonged, he realized now, to the Christian minorities within the hordes, and most of them from powerful families. Brownpony was obviously trying to keep these three minorities in close contact with each other. With the help of certain Weejus women, he was even playing marriage broker to forge alliances between Wilddog, Grasshopper, and Jackrabbit families.

Blacktooth came to suspect that an unfortunate marriage of Chür Høngan to a Grasshopper girl was one result of such efforts. He had been doing this since the days of Pope Linus VI, with the blessing of subsequent pontiffs. While examining these files, he inadvertently encountered material from the Weejus women that related to the cardinal personally. For years his friends had been searching among the Wilddog people for some trace of the family of Brownpony's mother or for anyone who remembered her. The information from the Weejus was transmitted by e'Laiden Ombroz: "With the help of the Bearcub's family, I have come to the end of the search. I can only conclude, Your Eminence, that there is not, and never was, a Wilddog motherline using the name 'Brown Pony.' If your mother's people are among us, that is not their name. The sisters who told you the story must have been misinformed. Perhaps it is a Grasshopper or Jackrabbit name, or perhaps it was an assumed name. I regret that I have been of no help to you."

Embarrassed, the monk returned the file to its place without reading the rest of it, and never mentioned it to Brownpony.

Blacktooth was humbly grateful that his master trusted him enough to let him learn about these matters, even by accident, but he also knew that a few messages to and from the Plains were in code, and these were attended to by Brownpony personally. Something dangerous to Brownpony himself, or to the reputation of the Secretariat, was going on, but he found no clue in the nonsecret correspondence as to the nature of the intrigue. He was not allowed to see the cardinal's correspondence with Oregon and the west coast, but that, of course, was not written in Nomadic. A technical civilization rivaling that of Texark had been developing in the far west for nearly a century, although distance and the mountains kept them apart and not competitive.

The monk had been watching his master pore over his correspondence, wondering why the cardinal himself was rarely mentioned as a candidate for the papacy, when Brownpony whirled suddenly to confront him.

"Nimmy, I am weary of being the target of the corner of your eye, of being the addressee of all your unasked questions. What is it you want to know about me?"

"Nothing, my Lord! It is unseemly . . ."

"It is unseemly to lie to your patron. Ask me a question, an impertinent question, of course."

After a silence, Blacktooth found a small voice: "How is it that you are not a priest, m'Lord?"

"Yes, that would be first question. Explain yourself to the sometime monk, Elia Brownpony. Tell him how you were married once, and how Pope Linus was going to make you a priest before he made you cardinal, but you refused, saying that Seruna might still be alive, although you knew she was dead. She was kidnapped by outlaw Nomads like those at Arch Hollow. They don't keep kidnapped women alive long. Well, Blacktooth, there you have the waves. Do you want the ocean as well?"

"I'm ashamed that I presumed to ask."

"Don't grovel. I was called to be a lawyer, not a priest, and that's it. There are many priests who should have been lawyers instead, and even a few lawyers who should have been priests. I say I have been called to practice law and settle disputes. I'm not so sure where calls come from. Practicing law and negotiating disputes, this is what I do well. Plus politics and controversy. I would not be a good priest, regular or secular. I have neither the charity nor the piety for it. I can serve the Church best as the shepherd's dog, fighting for the flock, or snapping at the heels of the flock to keep the sheep together. There is no chance that Seruna is alive. I loved her in my way, but she was not happy. And if she were alive still, she would not come back to me. But I can't prove she's dead."

"You had no children?"

"I have a son in Saint Maisie's Seminary in New Rome."

"And you are the Cardinal Deacon of—" Blacktooth stopped and put his hand over his mouth.

Brownpony laughed. "Deacon of Saint Maisie's Church in New Rome, yes. Nepotism? Pope Linus made the appointment. Without asking me? Of course he asked me. Now what else do you want to know?"

"I'm sorry I pried."

"You didn't. Looking at me curiously behind my back is not prying. You are a good fellow, Nimmy. You know your place, and you work hard. I raise your salary by half."

"Fifty percent of—" Blacktooth stopped.

"—of nothing is nothing. All right, you may increase your living expenses by that much, and I'll tell Jaron to pay them. Now get on with these letters to the east. I'm so busy trying to keep track of who's here for the conclave and guess at their votes, I've no time for my proper affairs."

When he was not working, the monk fell into moods close to despair. It was not that the sin itself with Ædrea was so terrible, but that he was out of control. His life was reconsecrated to God every day, but if he had kept God in his heart, he would never have climbed into the hay with her. It did not matter to him that what they did together would not make a baby. That it might not even be a sin, if he were not promised to God, but to love her was to love God less, was it not? It was not the act that he despised, but the flaw in his character that permitted it.

Did I go to a monastery to make myself morally perfect?

No, not at all.

What, then?

The monk's ultimate goal is direct union with the Godhead. But to aim at that goal is to miss it altogether. His task is to rid himself of ego so that consciousness, once its usual discordant mental content is dumped out of it through ritual prayer and meditation, may experience *nonself* as a living formlessness and emptiness into which God may come, if it please Him to come. So Eckhart had spoken of it two thousand years ago: "God gives birth to His Son in the soul." Only in self-emptiness may it happen one day that Christ awaken within the monk, as I-to-I. But there was someone else awake there now, for Blacktooth, and he was very lonely, very lonely for her.

CHAPTER 9

The third degree of humility is that a person
for the love of God submits himself to his
Superior in all obedience, imitating the
Lord, of whom the Apostle says, "He be-
came obedient even unto death."
—*Saint Benedict's Rule*, Chapter 7

LEASED BY THE INCREASE IN HIS LIVING allowance, Blacktooth planned to change his residence as soon as the crowd left town after the election, but for the time being he was forced to continue living with the students. Wooshin would be leaving in a few days at the cardinal's bidding.

When he came home from work on the afternoon of Holy Tuesday, the student named Aberlott called "Catch!" and tossed something to him as soon as he came through the door. Blacktooth grabbed for it, missed, and turned to pick it up when it bounced off the wall. Looking down at the object, he froze in a half-crouch.

"What's wrong?" the student asked. "Isn't it yours? She said it belonged to you."

Blacktooth picked it up and turned to stare at Aberlott. "She?" he gasped.

"The nun. My God, what is the matter? You're white as snow."

"Nun?"

"Sure. One of the stricter orders, I believe. Brown habit, white coif. Barefoot. Isn't that your rosary? She said you left it in the cardinal's coach."

"Was she a genny?"

"A genny? Not that I could tell. She didn't wear the headband. Of course, celibate religious don't have to. You can't see much of a nun except her face and hands and feet. She *was* rather pretty for a nun though. She didn't look like a genny to me. You were expecting a genny?"

Blacktooth sat down on his bed and stared at the beads and the cross. The silver had been carefully cleaned of tarnish, and the beads seemed brighter than he remembered, well polished now.

"Did she say anything else?"

"No, not that I recall. We talked a little about the conclave. I was trying to flirt, I guess. She was kind, but she was distant. Oh, she did ask where you were, in an offhand way. That's all."

"What did you tell her?"

"I said you were usually at the Secretariat this time of day. I don't think she was actually looking for you though. She went off in the opposite direction. Just wanted to return the rosary, I think. I wondered what she was doing in the cardinal's carriage."

"Looting it," he whispered.

"What did you say?"

Blacktooth lay back on the bench and closed his eyes. After a long time, he said, "Thank you, Aberlott."

"Don't mention it." The student resumed his reading.

Perhaps the nun was really a nun. Ædrea had given the rosary to a nun, that's all. It was all right for a genny to be a nun and not wear the green headband, but for a genny to impersonate a religious in order to conceal ancestry was a crime under the laws of the Denver Republic, as everywhere. Persecution of the genetically diseased was nearly universal. They were protected only by the law of the Church, but not to the extent of allowing the impersonation of religious. And while the Church might protest against discriminatory legislation by the secular authority, she had never taken a firm stand against eugenic laws designed to prevent intermarriage between the healthy and the children of the Pope. Nor had she resisted laws defining the marriageability of citizens in terms of degrees of kinship to known freaks. The baptismal records of churches were used as evidence in secular courts, and priests were required to note the pedigrees of parents on certificates of baptism. Before any couple were given a license to marry by the secular arm, both had to undress and be tested by the medical inspectors of a civil magistrate. The Nomads, of course, had their own rules, but there was no tolerance among them for deformity, hereditary or otherwise. They simply killed the deformed at birth.

He fingered the beads of his rosary and decided that Ædrea must have given it to a nun in a party of religious traveling up the papal highway. He felt shame for the fear and hope that surged within him when he turned to pick it up. Surely, it must have been a nun. What the police would do to a genny impersonating a citizen was nothing compared to what a mob would do. And surely, Ædrea herself would not have polished the beads and cleaned the crucifix so. If she had sent it back sooner, he would have escaped that horrid moment in confession about bartering it for sex, as Specklebird construed it. But why had she returned it at all, even indirectly?

"What color was her hair?" he called to the student, who was immersed in a textbook.

"Whose hair?"

"The nun."

"Which—? Oh! Her coif hid it." He paused. "Probably blond. She was very fair."

Blacktooth stirred uneasily. Blondes were not plentiful, but there were probably dozens of them in Valana. The mixed ancestry of the continent's population produced skin colors in varying shades of brown, but fair skin and black skin were both rather rare, as were red and blond hair.

He arose from the bench and went outside. There was nobody in the street but an old man and two children. The rotten smell from the creek behind the house was particularly strong this afternoon. Several neighbors had become ill lately, probably from the creek or its vapors. He decided to take a walk up the hill, in the direction away from the Secretariat.

He walked for an hour. There were fewer and fewer houses as he moved along. At last he came to a guard post at the fenced limits of the city. Beyond it lay only forest and a few hermitages, including the home of Amen Specklebird. He stopped to speak to the sentry.

"How long have you been on duty, corporal?"

The young officer looked toward the sun, hanging low in the west. "About four hours, I guess. Why?"

"Did a young nun pass this way? Brown robe, white coif . . ."

The sentry immediately looked toward the woods, studied Blacktooth for a moment, and began to leer. "Oh, *ho!* I wondered why she was going out there alone."

Angered by the leer, the monk turned and hiked back down the

road for home. The anger turned to fear again. He knew it was fear for
Ædrea, but she was probably safe at home in Arch Hollow. The nun
was just a nun. And yet if nuns had a small convent farther up the
hillside, would the sentry have wondered about her destination?

He dreamed that night that he was wearing a green headband
and fleeing from a mob who wanted to castrate him for lying with
Torrildo, who had breasts as large as Ædrea's, or was it Ædrea with a
penis as large as Torrildo's? He was trapped in Shard's barn, which now
housed Brother Kornhoer's old generator and the chair of electricity
from the chapel. Someone was screaming. Rough hands were strap-
ping him into the chair when somebody shook him awake. The rough
hands belonged to Wooshin.

"Stop howling," said the Axe. "You'll wake up the whole neighborhood."

"He already has," Aberlott grumbled sleepily from the next
room. Crumily was swearing and pounding his pillow. Jæsis had never
stopped snoring and moaning.

When the others had subsided into sleep again, Blacktooth felt
under his hard pillow for the rosary. He fingered the crucifix and began whispering the creed, but stopped. Cleaned and polished or not, it
felt desecrated. In confession, he had tried to blame Ædrea for stealing it, but Father Specklebird had forced him to admit that he had *not*
taxed her again for the beads after a bout of pleasant but certainly
sinful sex in the hay.

"Don't mince words. You traded your rosary for a blow job," the
old man had said sourly, "and broke your vow of chastity. Now go on.
What else have you done?"

Blacktooth was still doing the penance which Father Specklebird
had assigned him. ("You shall make a list, an inventory of all your
wealth, my son.") At first he thought it a trivial penance, and that the
list would be quite short. But the more he worked at it the more
clearly he recognized that his riches were coextensive with, and not
different from, his sins. There was more (or less) to spiritual poverty
than owning nothing.

The city had not been well since the visitors had come. Down
from the mountains perhaps, a fetid chinook or chill miasma had
breathed upon it, sickening many of the young, the old, the frail. Food
was scarce. Wheat especially was in short supply, and rye of poor quality was imported at high prices. The inns were full to bulging, and
inadequate sewers overflowed to the streets in lower elevations. A quorum of cardinals had not yet arrived, but among those already in town,
several had fallen sick. The water was blamed at first. It happens every
time, the visitors said; none but the locals could safely drink it. But

this time was worse than before. There was sickness among the local population as well. The symptoms were various, and not always the same. There was vomiting and fever, as in the case of the student Jæsis. Others experienced dizziness, headache, depression, mania, delirium, or panic. One physician claimed there were two diseases at work and spreading. Only wealthy Valanans seemed immune, but the immunity was not due to wealth itself; visiting cardinals were not notably poor, but a number of them showed symptoms. There was an urgency to get the conclave started, and if possible, done with. Local people blamed the sickness on crowded conditions caused by visitors. Others cited the wrath of God, which would be appeased only by a swift election.

Because of the sickness and of impatience at lengthy conclaves, there were demonstrations and unrest in Valana that month. On Palm Sunday, what seemed to be a religious procession had moved toward the former fortress hilltop from the college of Saint Ston's. As it neared Saint John-in-Exile, its character changed. New banners were unfurled, and the procession became a political parade, whose half-serious purpose was to proclaim popular support of the students of Saint Ston's Seminary for Amen Specklebird as a candidate for the triple crown and the throne of Peter. Hearing about it, Father Specklebird did not wait to be summoned by the current Bishop of Denver, but came limping hastily into town to denounce the enterprise and scold the students. Leaders of the movement were arrested by the secular police—an action which Specklebird felt forced to condemn.

On the following day, students from the secular college staged a parody of the incident by demonstrating in favor of the candidacy of the trigamous Cardinal Ri of Hong, much to the delight of the Axe, who had made friends with Ri's six-man bodyguard, and had learned as much as he could from them about life beyond the western ocean. Again, leaders were arrested, but the jail was already full of drunken farmers, Nomads, and pickpockets who had come to exploit the presence of the growing crowds of petitioners and lobbyists who always converged on conclaves. The student leaders were lightly flogged, the others given probation. There were also ecclesiastical penalties for attempting to influence the election.

On Tuesday of Holy Week, the Dean of the Sacred College appeared on the balcony of Saint John-in-Exile and promised a turbulent mob of jeering people that the conclave would begin as soon as 398 cardinals were present. "Probably within ten days," he added. Since the death of Pope Linus VI, twenty-two cardinals had followed him to the grave, and the three subsequent popes had observed a moratorium

on the bestowal of red hats; but still under present law two-thirds plus
one of all eligible electors, excluding those who were certifiably infirm,
were necessary to elect. And when no more than the necessary 398 had
arrived, they would have to vote unanimously in order to elect a pope,
so the Dean's promise was an empty one and the crowd knew it. No
serious voting could begin until all but the senile, the sick, and the
lame had arrived in Valana.

Votes were being counted in advance, and the bookmakers of
Valana were already taking bets, an excommunicating offense. There
was no odds-on favorite, but one might bet two alabasters on Golopez
Cardinal Onyo from Old Mexico in hopes of winning three, while fans
of Urion Benefez could bet one to win three. There were somewhat
similar odds on Urion's talk-alike, Otto Cardinal e'Notto from the
Great River Delta, and Chuntar Hadala, a greatly respected missionary
bishop to the Valley of the Misborn, now the Watchitah Nation.
Sorely Nauwhat from Oregon was given at ten-to-one, because of the
persistent doctrinal problems in his territory. Abbot Jarad Kendemin
was rated fifteen-to-one, because of his reluctance. Only by betting on
such improbables as Elia Cardinal Brownpony or Amen Specklebird
could a poor porter or housewife hope to become rich.

Holy Week was celebrated with all the pomp possible in the absence of a reigning pontiff. Masses were concelebrated with all able
cardinals present, and many of the religious processions were real. But
the pageantry was not a distraction to a single-minded population who
wanted a pope, a western pope, and wanted him soon. Much anger
was directed at the absent Cardinal Archbishop of Texark for his deliberate delay, but his advance party of legists, servants, and conclavists
were already busy preparing for what would no doubt be his grand
entrance upon the scene at the appropriate moment.

A preliminary meeting of electors, their assistants and conclavists, legists, other prelates, diplomats, leaders of religious orders,
and eminent scholars, among them theologians, historians, and political theorists, was scheduled for the afternoon of Maundy Thursday.
The announced topic was to be the changing relationship between the
Church and the Secular Power in the first half of the thirty-third century. The informal and nonsacred nature of this convention was em-
phasized by holding it in the Great Hall of Saint Ston at the seminary,
and by admitting certain categories of nonparticipants as observers.

"Are you going to this fistfight, Blacktooth?" asked Aberlott, who
had put on his student's uniform.

"Who's doing the fighting?" asked the monk.

"Well, it's Benefez against any challenger. Who knows, your own
master might pick up the gauntlet for the west."

Jæsis rolled over on his cot and groaned.

"Cardinal Brownpony doesn't get into fights, and the Archbishop of Texark isn't even in town yet."

"Oh, but his whole staff is here. And thirteen cardinals from the Imperium. He's going to make his move, all right."

Jæsis yelped in his sleep, and muttered profanity.

"Mention Benefez, and Jæsis gets mad." Aberlott nodded toward the feverish sleeper. "Or maybe it's the Hannegan he hates."

"You think there'll be a squabble?"

"I know it. Father General Corvany of the Order of Saint Ignatz will be there, for one." This woke Jæsis up, and he began swearing more coherently.

Blacktooth reached for his robe. "I know a priest of Corvany's Order who defied him once."

"And he's still a priest?"

". . . 'forever, after the order of Melchisedech,' as they say. But he's under interdict. He wouldn't hear my confession."

"What's his name?"

Blacktooth hesitated, then shook his head, regretting that he had mentioned the Ignatzian. He had learned from his work as translator at the Secretariat that Father e'Laiden, with whom he had traveled to Pobla, and Father Ombroz, the tutor and chaplain of the Little Bear clan, were the one and the same man. "I get the name mixed up with somebody else," he said. "I must have forgotten."

"Well, are you coming?"

"As soon as I finish dressing."

The auditorium at Saint Ston's had seating for two thousand. A quarter of the seats near the front had been roped off for the cardinals, but was still half empty when the campus bell tolled three. Another fourth of the seats were reserved for the cardinals' first servants, and these were filled to capacity with priests and scribes who were obviously here to take notes and be bored. The other half of the seating was open to lesser prelates, faculty, priests, monks, and students, in that order of preference. The supply was greater than the demand. Blacktooth and Aberlott, who came early, took seats behind the cardinal's servants, and were not asked to move to the rear. A few people drifted onto the stage. He recognized the head of the seminary, then a man in a white tunic and scapular with black cappa who had to be a prominent Dominican, probably the head of the Order from the west coast. Blacktooth suddenly slid lower in his seat. The Lord Abbot Jarad Cardinal Kendemin had come from the wings and took a seat beside the Dominican. They beamed at each other, exchanged the kiss of peace, and began a lively whispered conversation over the empty seat between them.

"What's wrong?" asked Aberlott, looking down at Blacktooth. "Would you rather lie on the floor?"

When the clock somewhere above them dinged the quarter hour, Aberlott stood up with a straight face and said, "Here comes the judge." Several others in the vicinity climbed to their feet.

Blacktooth grabbed his sleeve. "Sit down, you clown!"

The man who had come to the podium was the president of the seminary. He spoke brief words of welcome, then invited cardinals who wished their servants to sit beside them to call them forward, and the rest of the audience to move forward to fill empty spaces. Aberlott hitched his corpulent self one seat to the left, told an interloper that the seat between them was taken, and when the audience was quiet again, he turned to beckon Wooshin, standing in the rear, to join them, but the Axe shook his head. His presence meant that Cardinal Brownpony was nearby. The warrior had become the Red Deacon's personal bodyguard, and expected to move soon into the servants' quarters at the cardinal's home.

The first speaker was the Dominican, introduced as Dom Fredain e'Gonian, Abbot of Gomar, Director General of the Order of Preachers in Oregon. "*Tu es Petrus*," he predictably began, and preached a sermon which began with a stirring summons to unity, but soon became a scathing denunciation of those partisans of exile or of return whose motives were economic. He would be seen later in the day with his robe spattered with slops dumped from second-story windows in the merchant section of the city.

The president of the seminary next introduced Father General Corvany of the Order of Saint Ignatz in New Rome, a man obviously in his seventies but still handsome and trim. His graceful carriage and sympathetic persona reminded Blacktooth, to his surprise, of his employer. Like Brownpony, Corvany's normal expression was a natural smile; when the smile disappeared, the effect was startling. He spoke only a few words of greeting to Their Eminences, then lost his smile. "Surely, there has been a mistake here," he said. "Please bear with me for a moment." He left the lectern then, descended the steps into the audience, and audaciously took the hand of Her Eminence, Cardinal Buldyrk, Abbess of N'Ork. "Please," he said to her. "You have a chair on the podium."

Her mouth agape, Buldyrk permitted herself to be escorted to the stage. There was a mutter of astonishment from the cardinals, and even a few muffled cries of outrage, for Corvany was not even a member of the Sacred College, and the expression on the face of the president of the seminary was one of complete surprise.

"See? What did I tell you," Aberlott whispered to the monk. "I'll bet a copper that seat was for Cardinal Ri."

The abbess was seated between Jarad and the Dominican, to the delight of neither, and Corvany thus established himself as the most liberal and gallant of all the prelates. He resumed his beaming smile and introduced to the audience a learned member of his own Order of Saint Ignatz to speak in his stead. This was Urik Thon Yordin, S.I., who was a clergyman but also a professor of history at the secular university at Texark. He was a lean, gray, bespectacled man in his fifties, and apparently another member of Archbishop Benefez's advance party. His manner of address was that of the lecture hall rather than the pulpit.

"What has not been well understood about the frequent condition of schism in the Church," he said, "is that it reflects a natural schism in the continent. There have always been two Churches, if I may say so, Eminent Lords: one Church in the East, the other in the West. While that pope inhabited New Rome near the Great River, he was living as far from this region and the far west as if New Rome were on the Atlantic. Since the papacy has come here to the foot of the mountains, there has been a great healing of the Church in the West, whose problems are now better understood. This has been made plain to us by events in the Oregon area."

Blacktooth saw two Western bishops leaning together to whisper. It was strange to hear one of Urion Benefez's men begin by admitting the truth of an argument some Westerners used in favor of continuing the Valanan papacy. The approach seemed conciliatory at first.

"And to understand the cause of the Western problem," Thon Yordin went on, "we have only to consider the route which messengers used to take before the establishment of peace in the Province. At the beginning of this millennium, a man foolish enough to travel alone from New Rome to the far West might take a route such as this: south through forest trails, skirting the Valley of the Misborn, then to the Gulf, and, paralleling the coast, on to the Brave River. Crossing the river, he would find the royal road leading west across the desert protected by soldiers of a king; arriving in the far West, he moved north again. A lone traveler coming eastward might make a similar detour. Why?"

He held up a sheaf of papers. "I have here a copy, dated one century and forty-eight years ago last month, of the military regulations for the Papal Guard in escorting the Pope's legates and other ambassadors directly across the High Plains by the most direct routes at that time. Do not be alarmed. I shall not read them to you, although anyone who wishes to examine them may do so. These rules call for forty heavily armed cavalrymen under the command of a captain, and a party of twenty archers in light armor with swords, and halberds to be packed with them and carried by mule. The regulations specify certain permissible routes, all riverbeds, and regularly scheduled crossings are forbidden. When a party was ready to leave, its departure was delayed until one man, the captain of the guard, decided to go. Can you guess why?

"Now, there were occasionally men in those days foolhardy enough to make such a trip alone, or in smaller armed groups. But this was like going to sea in a rowboat. Even if no one at all had lived on that great ocean of grass—tall grass at first, as one moves west, then short grass, then desert grass in the south until one reaches the mountains—if no one at all lived there, the journey would be dangerous enough. This continent itself exists in a natural state of schism, Eminent Lords. It is divided by nature. The open plain is a place of horrid winds and torrid or frigid weather, even today. There is nothing out there but earth, sky, grass, and wind. There is nowhere to hide. Everywhere he looks, a man is surrounded by a far horizon. The grass billows in the wind. That is the great grass ocean.

"In earlier days, there dwelt there upon that grassland those cruel, piratical herdsmen with their woolly wild cattle, and they took delight in torture, and they flayed messengers alive and ate their organ meats, or made them slaves. Some of you who have just crossed the Plains in coming here, in relative safety, I might add—although I sympathize with the hardships you still endured—you have seen the descendants of those cannibals. And unless you encountered an outlaw band, you were not molested. But the forebears of these people were the reason for these extraordinary regulations I hold in my hand.

"Wild they are still, these herdsmen, and cruel, but they let you pass now without harassment. While the Church in the West has, we all admit, rendered fealty to the one true vicar of Christ who traditionally resides east of the Plains, it has always gone its independent way in matters of faith, morals, and doctrine, as we learn from the history of the Oregonians. I refer you to the works of Duren, if you have any doubts about this."

Blacktooth looked suddenly at Abbot Jarad and regretted it immediately. His former ruler was watching him with a faint triumphant smile. Some cardinals in the abbot's vicinity were also murmuring among themselves.

Aberlott noticed Blacktooth's restlessness and turned toward him to whisper. "Nimmy, did you know the Oregonians used leavened bread at Easter Mass?"

"No, I didn't," Blacktooth whispered back. "Neither did Duren. Now hush."

"Oh, yes. Instead of 'Behold the Lamb of God,' when the priest held up the bread, he would say, 'Behold He is risen.'"

Blacktooth kicked his anklebone. His lips shaped an *ooo*.

"Transportation was simply too hard between the East and the West for the Pope to be in constant communication with all his flock and their bishops in those days," the professor continued. "But now we have relative peace on the High Plains and the Prairie, except for outlaw bands. And in the South, for most of your venerable lifetimes it has been possible for a man to travel alone, or in a small unarmed party as some of you from the Southeast have just done, to come from east of the Great River here to mountains with no more danger than you might encounter on the roads in your home diocese. Why? Because the southern horde has been pacified, and the Province is well governed, and those north of the Province are, if not pacified, then at least aware that robbery, rape, and murder of us 'grass-eaters' will bring swift retribution. Thus with travel and communication restored, the imagined advantages to the west of a papacy here in exile are no longer real."

Abbot Jarad had risen to his feet, but the speaker seemed not to notice at first.

"I am not a military man," the professor continued, "but—" He stopped because the audience was looking to his right, and he glanced around to see Jarad standing. "Yes? Your Eminence?—"

"Perhaps the advantages of exile are imaginary, as you say. I pray for a return to New Rome, under the right conditions, for the exile is a scandal and an abomination. But I would remind the learned speaker that the Treaty of the Sacred Mare predates the conquest, that the military regulations which the learned speaker quotes predated that treaty, and that the treaty was negotiated peacefully with the Church as mediator, and that while crossing the High Plains is never without danger, Church messengers have been doing it for at least a century, with no help from the Texark military." Jarad sat down, his face bright red, looking around for a murmur of approval. None came.

"Thank you. As I was saying, I am not a military man, but it has been explained to me that the mission of Texark troops which just happen to be in the vicinity of New Rome has nothing to do with New Rome or the papacy. They were sent there without any thought whatever of provoking or intimidating the Pope. The Hannegan of that

time was as astonished by the Pope's flight to Valana, as was the rest of
the country. The troops were sent not to outflank the Holy City, but
to protect the farmers settling in the timberlands between the Great
River and the treeless prairie. The farms were threatened from the
west and the north by the eastern horde, the one they call Grasshopper. The troops are there as a peacekeeping force only, as most inhabitants of New Rome now recognize. The herdsmen were penetrating
the farmlands, stealing the stock, and kidnapping little boys.

"Nomads give birth to more girls than boys, you know. Something hereditary, I'm told. Anyway, the return of the papacy to New
Rome would be protected, not threatened, by the troops in the—"

"Just a minute." Cardinal Brownpony's voice came over the
room loud and clear. Blacktooth looked around, as did many others,
but no one on the floor was standing. "Just a minute, if I may."

Eyes followed the voice upward and to the rear. Brownpony was
standing in the choir loft, with the Axe seated on one side and the
Reverend Amen Specklebird, O.D.D., on the other. Blacktooth and
Aberlott had been refused admittance to the gallery, but the guards
had evidently opened it to latecomers to avoid people wandering
down the main aisle after the meeting began.

"I am a descendant of these cannibals, as you call them. My
mother, I was told by the sisters who raised me, bore the family name
of 'the Brown Pony.' I never met her, but the family was Wilddog, the
sisters said, and she was the young widow of a Jackrabbit husband who
had escaped a Texark jail, but was killed by Texark bullets. She was
raped by one of your Texark peacekeepers when she went south to visit
her dead husband's people. I am the child of that violent union. The
sisters who raised me in your province let me keep the name she gave
them."

Blacktooth looked up at Wooshin with wide eyes, and his surprise was reflected by the warrior's. Neither of them ever mentioned
Brownpony's origins to others, judging it a taboo subject. Now the
Red Deacon was announcing his mysterious bastardy to the world,
which already knew of it in whispers. And yet he himself knew little or
nothing of it, according to the file the monk had seen at the Secretariat.

"And there is my secretary," said Brownpony, looking down at
Blacktooth. "His ancestors were Grasshopper refugees from your Texark pacification. They lost all their cattle to Hannegan's diseased animals. His parents died without horses, farming another's land. From
him, I know something of the Grasshopper people and their history.
For centuries they have pastured their animals on the land of which
you speak, among their other lands. That region was called 'Iowa' on

the ancient maps, I believe, but it is nearly treeless, and yet fertile
enough for the farmers to covet it. And the Grasshopper has always
gathered wood for poles, stakes, arrows, and spears from the thinly
forested lands north and south of that area. If the farmers are there
now, they've settled there since Hannegan's slaughter. You paint the
Texark forces as protectors. You want the Pope back in New Rome, in
the midst of his protectors. I too want the Pope back in New Rome, in
spite of his protectors, in the midst of his enemies, among whom you
have just counted yourself. You have been sent here to draw fire away
from your master. Now the Cardinal Archbishop of Texark, who we all
know has sent you, must either underwrite your views, or denounce
your slander against the people of the Plains."

There was an astonished silence, followed by brief applause and
cheering from two Westerners. Father General Corvany ominously lost
his smile again, and came to his feet. The applause quickly subsided.
Brownpony sat down smiling. Cardinals were looking over their shoulders at him. On the stage, Jarad's jaw dropped. Brownpony was known
as a diplomat, always courteous, a peacemaker who rarely took sides.
His tone had been calm, but he had just declared war, and it had to be
premeditated.

Before Corvany could speak, a sputtering archbishop from the
delta of the Great River, now part of the Texark Empire, arose in a
huff to defend the speaker's thesis concerning the protective role of
past Hannegans in the Midwest, and to deplore the interruptions. He
pointed a finger toward the balcony and began to say something about
Brownpony, but the Dean of the Sacred College arose and roared,
"God's peace! God's peace!"

The seminar was about to become a verbal melee, and few in the
audience noticed the student who wandered down the center aisle. He
was staggering slightly. Aberlott suddenly clutched Blacktooth's arm
and pointed. The man in the aisle was Jæsis, uncombed and un-
shaved, his face livid but with red blotches. He stopped in the middle
of the cardinals' section and pulled something out of his half-
buttoned cassock. He croaked Yordin's name and a curse. There was
an explosion and a burst of smoke. Thon Yordin put his hand to his
chest, looked down, but there was no blood. Instead, one of the men
seated behind the podium fell from his chair. It was the Father General of the Order of Saint Ignatz himself who lay bleeding. The assail-
ant in the aisle waved a Texark cavalry pistol aloft, yelled again at
Thon Yordin, fired the other barrel toward the ceiling, and collapsed in
the aisle. The audience was on its feet and roaring.

"Assassin! Texark assassin! Hannegan's agents!"

Blacktooth looked around for the source of this irrational voice, but saw only a fist waving in the surging crowd.

Men swarmed over the fallen student, and from the platform came cries for a physician. Blacktooth and Aberlott were seized by police as they hurried out of the building.

There followed eight hours of questioning at the Valana police barracks, but Cardinal Brownpony quickly appeared on their behalf. There had been no brutality. The police learned from the college that Jæsis was from Texark, had attended Thon Yordin's classes at the university there, had failed his tests and then transferred to Saint Ston's. A physician stated that even now he was delirious with fever. The police released Blacktooth and Aberlott just past midnight; they walked home by the light of the Pascal moon. Jæsis died that night in custody.

While the city slept, the Reverend Urik Thon Yordin sent a rider galloping toward the telegraph terminal at the final outpost on the road to the Province. The message he carried was addressed to Urion Cardinal Benefez and, with a copy to the Emperor, would reach Hannegan City by Good Friday's sunrise:

FATHER CORVANY WAS KILLED TODAY BY A STU-DENT ROOMMATE OF BROWNPONY'S NOMAD SEC-RETARY. THE SECRETARY WAS QUESTIONED BUT RELEASED AFTER BROWNPONY INTERVENED. KILLER DIED IN POLICE CUSTODY. DETAILS FOL-LOW. I AWAIT FURTHER INSTRUCTIONS.
YOUR OBEDIENT SERVANT IN CHRIST,
YORDIN.

CHAPTER 10

> Let a man consider that God is always look-
> ing at him from heaven, that his actions are
> everywhere visible to the divine eyes and are
> constantly being reported to God by the An-
> gels.
>
> —*Saint Benedict's Rule*, Chapter 7

 N VALANA ON SUNDAY THE 17TH OF APRIL
3244, Blacktooth arose before dawn and
watched the moon, now past full, settle
behind the mountains, then washed his
teeth with ashes and boiled water, relieved himself in the outhouse, got
dressed, and then spent in prayer the
short time it took for the sun to come
up. Without eating anything prior to re-
ceiving the Eucharist, he left the house. On the way to Mass in the
early-morning chill, he sensed someone following him. Turning, he
saw only a man talking to an open window a stone's throw away, and
someone wandering in the other direction. The window's occupant, if
any, was not visible. The man talking to the window was the same
man Blacktooth had seen begging on the same street the day before
Jæsis shot Corvany. Probably a denizen of the neighborhood. The feeling of being followed was an illusion caused by shame, the monk de-

cided. He kept walking toward the Cathedral of Saint John-in-Exile. It was Easter morning.

With hundreds of cardinals participating, the Mass of the Resurrection was spectacular in the Pope's own church, even without a pope. Blacktooth had come early enough to be assigned a spot to stand with room enough to kneel, but most latecomers waited in crowds outside the nave and outside the cathedral itself. Getting out of the building after Mass was worse than getting in, because many of those pouring outside paused to talk to acquaintances and blocked the way. It was a perfect situation for murder. Blacktooth felt the dagger pierce his side as the arm holding it darted between two other worshipers, who immediately fell back in dismay. Blacktooth clutched his side and faced his attacker. It was the man who talked to empty windows, the beggar. Feeling people moving back, he looked around. There were three of them, dirty and shabbily dressed, two with knives, one with a chain. They fought there on the great ascent of cathedral steps which had no landings, and two of them were thrown sprawling to the bottom by a victim with unexpected skills. Someone was screaming for the constable, others for the Papal Guard. The original attacker, the beggar, now cut the monk's face and might have gone on to kill him, but the blast of a constable's horn sent the three of them fleeing.

His wounds were cleaned and dressed at the police station, and he was interrogated by an irritable lieutenant who insisted on believing that he, Jæsis, Aberlott, and Crumily were conspirators in some larger scheme. Blacktooth's relationship with the cardinal provided him with a secure identity in which he dared feel immune to intimidation in the face of anything short of violence. He told the lieutenant what he needed to know and tried to ignore what he wanted to know, based on a wrong assumption.

"No common hoodlums would try to rob a poor monk."

"They weren't out to rob me, just kill me."

"Exactly! and why? They must have some reason to hate you."

"Well, they seemed to be common hoodlums, they had no reason to hate me, so they must have been hired."

"By whom, do you think?" asked the officer.

"By some fool who thinks Jæsis planned on killing Father Corvany, and that I was involved."

The lieutenant, who apparently thought the same thing, glowered at him and left the room for several minutes. Blacktooth prayed to Saint Leibowitz. When the lieutenant came back, his manner had changed.

"You will have to be on guard against another attempt. Stay with people you know. Stay home at night. Stay away from crowds like this morning's. Come outside my office and sit on the bench here. Your employer will be here soon."

"His Eminence? For me?"

"For himself. There was an attempt on his life too. Here, his own man can tell you."

Wooshin had emerged from another interrogation room. He sat beside Blacktooth and briefly described the attack on Brownpony by two strangers armed with handguns. Brownpony was unharmed, and the attackers were dead. The police found one beheaded corpse on the scene, and a severed arm with a gun still in hand. The armless assassin had been found bleeding to death in an alley. If he said anything before he died to the constable who found him, the police were keeping it to themselves. There was no need to ask how they died. Soon an officer brought Wooshin his swords. They had been wiped, but were not quite clean of dried blood. The Axe frowned but sheathed them without complaint. Soon Brownpony emerged, and after an inquiry about Blacktooth's wounds, they all walked together back to the Secretariat with two armed men following at a respectful distance.

"You have thought about what this means, Nimmy?"

"It means somebody made a mistake, connected me with Jæsis, for one thing. And you, m'Lord?"

"Same mistake. It is politically important to the Hannegan that gennies, Nomads, and citizens should live in mutual loathing and fear, that they might be more easily governed in their disunity. Did you know, Nimmy, did you know—Jæsis was a spook?"

"A hidden genny? Oh no, m'Lord! That's hard to believe. I've seen him undressed."

"There was an autopsy, and they found the signs. They've not made the fact public. There hasn't been a pogrom in decades, and we don't want one to start. Move your things immediately. Until the crowd leaves the city, you will live in the Secretariat's basement. In case they try again. We may never know who hired these men, but they were amateurs."

"Locally recruited," the monk added. "I saw one of them before."

"Yes, but the telegraph makes us a suburb of Texark, and words now travel faster than the sun moves over the earth. Fortunately, the conclave should begin by midweek. When Benefez, or even Corvany's replacement, gets here, he'll take command of their people. I don't think Cardinal Benefez hires assassins."

"His nephew does," grunted the monk.

"Professionals only, Nimmy, not amateurs," Wooshin said.

When they came to the Secretariat, a large but low building set well back among trees, Blacktooth found three basement rooms already furnished for use by occasional messengers or political fugitives, one of them now occupied by Axe. Blacktooth chose the room closer to the privy's exit, but Axe immediately warned him: "At night, use a slop jar. Never go out that door in the dark unless I go with you."

But no further attacks had occurred by the time the requisite number of cardinals had assembled on Wednesday of Easter week, and while people afflicted with Jæsis' disease ran amok in the streets, stripped naked in public, or just lay in bed and howled, the attempt at a conclave began. First the cardinals assembled in the great Cathedral to offer Mass together, then left the building in procession to cross the square and enter the palace where the election was to occur. An altar was set up at one end of the great throne room, and the palace was temporarily consecrated.

Cardinal Brownpony had chosen as his conclavists Brother Blacktooth St. George and Sister Julian of the Assumption; the rule that his conclavists be clergy from Saint Maisie's applied only in his absence, and he would not be absent. Nimmy recognized his master's choice of the sister as an exquisitely diplomatic one, but his own selection jolted him into surprise, until he noticed that Brownpony was having frequent conversations with Jarad, and that Jarad had brought with him as one of his conclavists Brother Singing Cow. Nimmy became vaguely uneasy. Perhaps Nomad politics were to be considered by the Holy Ghost in the choice of a pope. Well, why not? But he dreaded meeting with Singing Cow or the abbot face-to-face.

No sooner had the conclave convened, however, than a cardinal from Utah fell deathly ill and had to be excused, thus forcing an adjournment for lack of a quorum. Blacktooth returned to his new basement home. Police watched the building, but there was no further attack.

During the three days the Cardinal President of the Conclave allowed the adjournment to continue, seven more electors arrived from a far northeastern province. Word came from the telegraph terminal that the Archbishop of Texark would arrive within ten days. As soon as the conclave reconvened, Cardinal Brownpony, joined by one of Benefez's conclavists to show nonpartisanship, proposed a rule empowering the sergeant-at-arms to arrest any cardinal elector attempting to leave the city or even the building without permission from the conclave. A heated protest was made by cardinals fearing the epidemic, but Brownpony in his reply pointed grimly to the anger of the people in the streets, and what might happen to the cardinal electors if they failed to sustain the quorum. The rule was passed by a large majority, and was sent on to the Valana city government with a request for help in enforcement. The request was approved, and it became a crime for a cardinal to flee Valana. And so began the process of finding a candidate agreeable to the Holy Ghost and various earthly powers, began even before that most eminent of earthly powers, Lord Cardinal Archbishop Urion Benefez, had arrived.

The city continued to sicken.

The ancient custom of burning ballots with or without moist straw as a signal to lend white or dark color to the smoke from the chimney was observed, but the laws governing the election of a pope had changed according to the requirements of the age. In theory, the Bishop of Rome was elected by the clergy of Rome, locked in a closed building (con clave) until two-thirds reached agreement. For thousands of years, each new cardinal, wherever he might live, was assigned a Roman church whose upkeep was his responsibility, and whose name was part of his title: Elia Cardinal Brownpony, Deacon of Saint Maisie's in New Rome. Now there were more cardinals than there were churches in New Rome and Valana combined.

From time to time a protest group would march across the city to gather in Saint John's square and chant slogans before the palace. By the fifth day of the conclave, people were throwing occasional stones at the doors, and the Papal Guard, in mourning for the dead Pope, were sent out to keep order. Unwilling to shed blood, they were soon disarmed by the populace. The civil police were unable to control the crowd, short of using firearms. The crowds gathered and dispersed as they pleased. In fear, the cardinals voted for three days. When there was voting, the crowds drifted away, although there were always people who watched for white smoke.

An occasional cardinal, usually ill, tried to leave the city, was caught, and was hauled bodily back to the palace, where a room adjoining the great hall of the conclave was staffed as an infirmary. An elector in bed could vote, his ballot carried up to the altar by a conclavist helper who held it aloft so that everyone could see that no switching was done before he placed it in the chalice. While the early and indecisive balloting continued, however, citizens from outside the palace were sealing the great, bronze double doors by building wooden scaffolding against them. A blacksmith anchored the scaffolding by hammering long spikes into lead anchors set in holes drilled into the granite walls. Other men boarded up windows.

On the sixth day of confinement, a man climbed to the roof with a sledge and a crowbar and broke away clay tiles while another man, with an axe, chopped a hole in the roof deck beneath the tiles. Buckets of slops were drawn up to the roof, and a citizen cheerfully poured them through the hole. The ladies of the Valana Altar Society were prevented from bringing emergency food, since the kitchen had been closed by rioters. The water to the palace was shut off.

The cardinal with the loudest voice climbed to a broken window and yelled anathemas at the crowd, excommunicating everybody who remained in the plaza after five minutes. The crowd cheered and applauded as if he had been heard to announce good news. Actually, he was not heard at all above the din.

By late afternoon, a cardinal with diarrhea wailed that the privies were full to overflowing, for the Sanjoanini who worked outside were being prevented from emptying them. All requests from within for candles and lamp oil were refused. The palace began to smell like the local jail, with incense. The *conclave* was now indeed "with key." Also with nails and timbers. There were cots enough for the cardinals, but their conclavists slept on the floor.

Blacktooth sat against the wall, alert lest his master beckon, and watched and listened and smelled and tried not to be afraid. He had gained much self-confidence in Brownpony's employ. Also, that he could fight off attackers was a relaxing bit of knowledge to have with him in any situation. Blacktooth knew that he had not been changing, but unfolding in new dimensions. But he felt he was becoming worldly as he did so.

Brownpony waved him forward. "Talk to as many of the cardinals' conclavists as you can. Sound them out on Cardinal Nauwhat and Abbot Jarad, especially Nauwhat."

"Yes, m'Lord." He looked around at a particularly loud crash of a window breaking.

"I've been to four conclaves and never seen anything like this," Brownpony told him as he sent him on the vote-counting mission. "The sickness must be causing madness."

Blacktooth began moving from cardinal to cardinal, not approaching the electors directly, but consulting the prelates' assistants. But he came finally to Abbot Jarad. The self-confidence that had helped him with the police suddenly vanished. Brother Singing Cow was there as the abbot's conclavist, but Blacktooth fell to his knees and kissed the abbot's ring. Jarad pulled him gently to his feet and smiled but did not embrace him, and called him by name without calling him Brother. "You wanted to see me, my son?"

"Domne, my master asked me to solicit advice as to the possible nomination of Sorely Cardinal Nauwhat."

"From me, or everyone?"

"From everyone, Domne."

"Tell him that if the Holy Ghost is not against it, I'm for it." He smiled at Blacktooth and turned away again.

"What of the nomination of Jarad Cardinal Kendemin?"

"The Holy Ghost and I are both against it. Is that all?"

"Not quite."

"I was afraid not."

"I would like to ask the abbot's blessing on my release from the Order."

Jarad looked at him remotely. "I was the minister who conferred on you the sacrament of Holy Orders, remember?"

"Of course."

Jarad pressed his palms together, eyed the darkness above, and said to God, "Have you ever been known to take back Holy Orders?"

"Never," said Cardinal Brownpony, joining them. "What do we have, a problem here?"

"None whatever," exclaimed Jarad, clamping an arm around his shoulder.

"No problem with you, Nimmy?"

"Yes, a problem. When and how am I going to be laicized?"

"Well, that's partly up to the abbot here."

"And without his permission, it's up to the Pope?" Blacktooth shifted his gaze toward Jarad, noticed the anger, noticed the controlling of anger, and saw Jarad's lips move slightly in prayer while he breathed deeply and listened to Brownpony.

"Oh, it's up to the Pope in the end anyway, but his permission is almost automatic if the abbot has given his." Brownpony looked questioningly at Jarad. Jarad let go of his shoulder.

"And almost automatically refused if the abbot refuses?" Blacktooth also looked at Jarad.

"No," said the Red Deacon, "probably the Pope would want to talk to you personally. In your case, I'm sure he would."

Jarad faced Blacktooth squarely. "I suppose I owe you a hearing. Do you want to talk to me about it? Come to my quarters when all this is over."

"I thank you, Domne!"

When he turned away, Brownpony fell in step with him. "Do you want to be laicized, or do you just want to make the whole thing a quarrel with the abbot? He'll let you go, if you don't make him any madder than he is now. Let it alone, Nimmy. He's not happy with you. Don't make it worse."

The monk left the vicinity, his self-confidence drained. He missed the abbey. He yearned for Jarad's blessing, or at least some evidence of forgiveness. He continued canvassing, although he knew that all Brownpony really wanted was to spread the knowledge that he was considering Sorely Nauwhat. A deception, Nimmy thought. Or maybe not. The Northwest had probably been happier when the papacy was located across the Plains. There had been less interference in the Northwest Church's affairs from New Rome than from Valana. Nauwhat was leaning toward an immediate return, in spite of the hostility of Cardinal Benefez toward the Northwest's independence in matters of liturgy and of Catholic teaching. Brownpony was dragging in a red herring to lead the hounds away from politics toward theology, if Blacktooth correctly understood his master's hints. But on the other hand, Sorely Nauwhat would perhaps be a good man for the highest office.

From outside came the repeated roar: "Elect the Pope! Elect the Pope!" Occasionally, it became, "Elect the Amen! Elect the Amen!" Rumor came in from outside that Father Specklebird had left his cave and gone up the mountain, and a committee of citizens searched for his trail. Blacktooth prayed to Saint Leibowitz, and tried to keep up with his breviary, but could not pray well in the midst of havoc, as Abbot Jarad seemed able to do.

He was becoming very hungry.

Cardinal High Chamberlain Hilan Bleze tried to lead the frightened prelates in a *Veni Creator Spiritus*, but the hymn could scarcely be heard above the racket on the roof, the hammering of doors and windows, the splash of slop on the floor, and the babble of frightened conversation among the hundreds of electors and their conclavists.

Two hours later, perhaps in response to the invocation of the Holy Ghost, someone tossed a living bird down through the hole in the roof and covered the hole to prevent its escape. Not a dove but a vulture flapped around the Cathedral in terror and finally alighted atop the giant crucifix which hung suspended in midair by chains from a roof beam between the nave and the altar. Several cardinals were screaming about an omen, a warning from God.

Brownpony climbed up on the temporary altar itself and roared, "Silence! In the name of God, silence!"

Only the desecration of the altar could have caught their attention, and silence did at last prevail.

"What you see and hear is indeed the judgment of God on us! Now this congregation must invite Father Amen to address us. He should be one of us. We shall hear him, and hear him now. How say you?"

"Get down from there, Elia!" Abbot Jarad shouted.

"Not until you vote!"

There were dissenting murmurs among the cardinals, and a few cries of outrage, but after some muffled shouting outside the walls, the crowd fell suddenly silent. The crowd had posted reporters to listen at some of the broken windows.

"Quiet! Let the nays vote first," Brownpony called. "They'll be easier to count. Those who refuse to hear Father Amen, raise your hands."

Pointing here and there, counting aloud, Brownpony said, "Seventeen!" and stopped. "Amen Specklebird shall speak to us." He nodded and climbed down.

A face was looking in through a broken window above the choir loft. It was a Valana policeman. Brownpony and the Cardinal High Chamberlain disappeared through a doorway and soon were in the balcony talking to the officer. He shouted their words to the crowd. The hole in the roof was uncovered to allow the buzzard to escape, but the frightened bird took no notice and remained perched on the upright above the INRI sign. A roar of enthusiasm went up from the mob outside.

Soon some of the windows were uncovered, but nothing was done about the doors. Within two hours, shit was being shoveled from the privies. Baskets of sour rye bread with the black specks were lowered through the roof hole, and the water pumps began working again. Screaming reerupted, however, when the buzzard suddenly descended from the cross to the floor, attracted by a smelly lump of garbage on the tiles. Three Sanjoanini were finally allowed entrance through a loft window to shoo away the bird and clean up the slops from the floor.

Chaos subsided, order returned, and the only sound in the palace was the murmur of hiccups, moans, sighs, groans from the ill, a murmur which occluded any whispered conversations drifting past and echoing in the great and temporarily sacred cavern. The light was low, near sunset. Servants were beginning to light the candles, but only a few of the cardinals were up and about. The rye bread had been consumed, and most of the water, but hunger, thirst, and fear presided over the night.

Blacktooth overheard a Texark conclavist talking to one of the abbess's assistants:

"Everybody knows Cardinal Brownpony has taken off his gloves. Brownpony went to Leibowitz Abbey and hired himself a secretary and a bodyguard this spring. And who is this new bodyguard? A Texark runaway criminal, the former executioner Wooshin, now under a sentence of death for treason. And who is this secretary? A Texark-hating refugee from the Grasshopper Horde, brought up to despise imperial civilization but educated at the abbey, who was a friend of Corvany's assassin. The cardinal deacon stood up and denounced our learned

Thon Yordin and at the same time slandered Cardinal Benefez and all but declared war on the Texark Church. Now he wants a mountain-dwelling hermit, who barely speaks Latin and would be frightened to death by New Rome, to become the next Bishop of New Rome, in absentia again. Permanently in absentia, as Cardinal Brownpony would probably have it. However my master might otherwise have voted with respect to Amen Specklebird, Cardinal Brownpony's support of him will cause him to abstain, of that I am certain."

The necessary twenty votes were quietly gathered, however, and Amen Specklebird became a candidate for pope even before he appeared to speak.

CHAPTER 11

> Therefore, since the spirit of silence is so
> important, permission to speak should rarely
> be granted even to perfect disciples, even
> though it be for good, holy, edifying conver-
> sation.
>
> —*Saint Benedict's Rule*, Chapter 6

MEN SPECKLEBIRD WAS NOT STRONG ENOUGH
to resist the crowd that dragged him re-
luctant to the Papal Palace by midmorn-
ing. And so at last, to pacify the people
and the conclave, the black, old hermit
priest agreed to address the cardinals.
For this purpose, the dying Cardinal Ri
consented to appoint the old man as his
special conclavist, for Specklebird's
status as a cardinal *in pectore* of his former persecutor was doubted by
most. He was passed in through the broken window in the balcony, and
more baskets of bad bread and flagons of water were lowered
through the hole in the roof.

There were scribes who were appointed to record all speeches
during the conclave, subject to later editing or deletion by the speaker,
but some of the few who actually listened to the old hermit through-

out his seemingly interminable homily later swore that some of the scribes had been asleep, and none had accurately recorded the full speech. But at first, the electors listened with intense curiosity.

Strange stories were told of Amen Specklebird by the old people of the countryside. Some said he walked silently on the mountain paths by moonlight and spoke to the antelope, the mountain spirits, and the risen Christ. Some had seen him flying above the treetops at morning twilight, and in the hole in the back of his cave he kept serpents, the mummy of an old Jew, or a wonder-working genny girl. Sometimes he visited the farms of the settlers and made it rain for them. He was a man of subtle power. He had placed a spell on Pope Linus VII, the story went, who as the Bishop of Denver had forced his retirement, and the spell made Linus call him to the Papal Palace several times during his long illness, either to have the spell removed or to treat the sickness whose cause eluded the physicians. (Blacktooth had seen him change into a cat and back, but Blacktooth would be the first to admit that his distance vision could be sharpened by spectacles, but his reason for avoiding it was not so much poverty as the fear that sharpness would ruin the clarity of his occasional hallucinatory insights into people and things.)

Heretics and holy men made pilgrimages to Amen's cave. Children of irreligious parents threw stones at his door and called him a buggery man, and yet it was a fact that the Lord Cardinal Brownpony often came to see him, and he was confessor to prominent sinners from the city. Pregnant women came to have their bellies blessed by him, and for a small donation he would consult the mountain spirits, who controlled the weather even on the western Plains, and whom he addressed by saints' names, about the best time for sowing or reaping or breeding sheep.

But now this dark old man with the frizzy white cloud of hair began speaking to the cardinals in conclave, and his style of address was none other than Blacktooth himself had experienced as his penitent. He was an elderly confessor most tactfully admonishing sinners and less tactfully testing their minds with paradoxes, and sometimes tortured syntax.

He embraced the audience with his long bony arms. "Fathers of the Church, Eminent Lords, there is a simpleton among us who has no rank at all and sits in the midst of us as a spy in an enemy camp. It is to him this sermon is addressed."

The Archbishop of Appalotcha stood up and called out, "Point him out, Father. Call the sergeant-at-arms!"

"He is here without authorization, it's true," said Specklebird, waving the ushers back. "But please sit down, he was here among us from the beginning, and he always will be. He's here to spy for Jesus anyway. And this conclave is the enemy camp."

There was a murmur of righteous protest about the Holy Ghost and the apostolic succession, but it quickly died.

"The simpleton who sits in the midst of us as a spy is conscience. A conscience has no rank and no position. A conscience cannot be a cardinal's conscience or a beggar's conscience. It adheres to the naked man, wholly exposed. And to the naked woman." The Abbess of N'Ork flinched, but Specklebird avoided looking at her. "In him or her, the Father gives birth to His Son.

"To this naked simpleton I speak, regardless of his office. The offices have fought each other. Rank has quarreled with rank. Regional origin argues with regional origin. Does the simpleton want a one and only pope, an everybody's pope? Then let him put off his rank, his office, his regional origin and beg God's grace to vote as a simpleton, a pure man." From this rational opening, he began to wander.

At first he spoke mostly about the return of the papacy to New Rome, because he knew that this was the foremost issue, not the closest to his heart. And he made it clear from the beginning, to the complete astonishment of his Valanan supporters, the mob outside, that he favored an unconditional restoration of the New Roman Papacy in its ancient See. Brownpony, his friend, even looked shocked by this disclosure.

Only cardinals from the Denver Republic were in favor of making the exile permanent, and they too were truly shocked. They had refrained from calling the exile Exile, and proposed to change the name of Valana to "Rome." Their motives were well rationalized, but they agreed with the rabble in the streets that the end of exile would be the end of Valana. But the Valana faction was a tiny minority in the conclave. Everyone else wanted the papacy returned to New Rome. The sharp division of opinion concerned the circumstances of that return, and the demand for a demilitarization of the surrounding terrain by the Empire.

The conclave had dragged to a standstill.

In a general way, the far East and the West were aligned against the middle. The middle was Texark and its vassal states along the Great River. There were also single-issue electors for whom the Valanan exile was not of major importance. Emmery Cardinal Buldyrk was one example. From the far northeast, she had voted with the West in two previous conclaves, but was now apparently leaning toward Benefez because of a possible softening of his position against the ordination of women. Benefez, however, was not present to confirm the inclinations of his conclavists, so the lady's vote was not secure. Cardinal Brownpony was doing his charming best to reconvert her, and she her charming best to seduce his feminine side.

Blacktooth himself took notes occasionally, but the old man rambled on and on. He misquoted Scripture. He belched. He improved on Scripture. He broke wind. He apologized for his frailties. He talked about his boyhood in the Northwest. He talked about barnyard matters. He talked about the wisdom of a mindless God. One passage which was faithfully recorded, and later used against him, was this:

"All this talk about the Church, the State, and the causes of schism reminds me of a story. When the priests asked Jesus whether they should pay taxes to the Hannegan of that time, Jesus borrowed a coin from them, asked them whose head was on it. 'Hannegan's,' they said. So he told them, 'Render unto Hannegan what is Hannegan's, and to God what is God's.' Then he put the coin in his pocket and smiled. When the priest wanted his coin back, Jesus asked, 'Who do you think Hannegan belongs to?' When there was no answer, he reminded them, 'The Earth is the Father's and the fullness thereof, the world and they that dwell therein.' Of course that's just another way of saying, 'The foxes have their dens, but the Son of Man has nowhere to lay his head.'

"So he gave the priest his coin back and slept under one of Hannegan's bridges that night, along with Peter and Judas. The priest went home and paid his taxes and drew up an indictment."

Here, Specklebird began to wander wide of his topic of New Rome and Valana.

"Why, you may ask, did Judas and Peter and Jesus sleep under a bridge," he said, pursuing a tangent. "Judas had a good reason, you see: someone had stolen his horse, and he was too tired to walk to the inn. Peter also had a good reason: he had no money to stay at the inn. Jesus had no reason, no reason at all. Jesus was *free* to sleep under a bridge. Such is freedom. Such is reason. Such is rumination."

Another tormentation of Scripture that was later bound to be used against him was this:

" 'What does it profit a man if he gains the whole world but loses his own soul?' I spoke earlier about this world, and him to whom it belongs, but what, one might ask, is one's own soul, which can be lost? The soul, insofar as it exists or not-exists, is the seat of suffering. When Jesus was born, he looked around at the world and said to his mother, 'From the outermost to the innermost I alone am the suffering one.' Cardinal Ri, whose conclavist I am, told me that. And this is the first fact of religion: *I am* means 'I hurt.' Why is it that I hurt? Is it God's revenge on a son? No, I hurt because I, my soul, keep grasping at the world to gain it, and the world has sharp teeth. And thorns.

That is the second fact of religion. The world is slippery too, and it wiggles. Just when I think I have a grip on it, it stings me, and slips away, or part of it dies on me, and I am overcome with grief and a sense of loss—the consequence of sin. But there is a way to stop grasping at this slithery world, a way to stop hurting and hungering. That is the third fact of religion. That third fact, Venerable Fathers, can be called the 'way of the Cross.' It leads to Golgotha. For *you* among you who will be Pope, it leads to New Rome."

His return to the topic came with brutal abruptness.

"These are elemental things. The fourth elemental fact of religion is called the 'Stations of the Way of the Cross.' " He waved toward the paintings on the Cathedral walls.

"This, Venerable Lords, is what I say of New Rome: that the way of the Cross ends there. The last station. The Pope must go back to New Rome as to Golgotha, and be crucified. The Hannegan will have his coin of tribute, which belongs to God if you correctly understand the Lord's irony, and Peter will have his crucifixion. When Benedict fled from New Rome in the last century, Jesus appeared to him and asked 'Quo Vadis,' but Benedict mistook him for a Nomad, and said 'Ad Valanam' and did not turn around. This I heard from one of you." He smiled at the conclavists from Texark, whose expressions had changed throughout the speech from initial hostility, to astonishment, through outrage, to suspicious approval, for, although the premises by which he arrived at his conclusions were not flattering to their monarch, and his theology was outrageous, the conclusions were the same as their own. The papacy should go home without any concession of power from the Imperial Mayor of Texark.

Usually so silent, this bewildering man was now talking through the afternoon, and when the lamps were lit in the evening, he talked on by lamplight. Once, when Blacktooth himself nodded off, he reawakened to see a cougar in a ragged cassock change to a dark brown old man with wild white hair again.

Amen Specklebird made a speech that was to become famous in the history of the Church, as written by its severest critics. Such are the quotations and misquotations as written down by the scribes.

Amen on the Fall and its aftermath: "The fruit of the tree, Eminent Lords, was rumination. Out of rumination came good and evil. The devil is a cud-chewing animal with cloven hooves. The serpent Satan ate souls and chewed the cud, and he taught rumination to the female, who taught it to the male. Whatever you do, do not ruminate. The anointed one never ruminates. He marches straight on to Hell from the tomb—and ascends to Heaven if it befall him.

"But if you should ruminate, and thus sin through fornication or rage or greed, never be ashamed of your guilt. Shame is none other than pride, pride is none other than shame. Your pride is your shame, your shame is your pride. They look in opposite directions, shame and pride, because when pride looks directly into the eye of shame and shame looks directly into the eye of pride, both instantly die. They die to the accompaniment of laughter, the laughter of the man who has foolishly kept them in his heart and kept them apart. When he feels his shame as pride and his pride as shame, he is free of them, free forever from the sin of both. Guilt, however, is not a feeling.

"When you see that you have sinned, and you repent the sin, *do not* wish you had not sinned. Wish instead that God in His mysterious way will turn your sin to a good end, for your sin is now already a part of the history of His ongoing creation of the world. To wish it away is to resist His will."

Amen on truth: "The truth is God's subtle, abominable word, Eminent Lords, *subtile et enfandum* is His word."

Amen, repeating himself, on man's place in God's world: "Don't you know that Jesus Christ is alone and friendless in the universe? Don't you know that the Earth is the Creator's, and the fullness thereof? What does *that* mean, Eminent Lords, except that the foxes have their dens, but the Son of Man has nowhere to lay His head? He often sleeps under bridges.

"What is God that thou art mindful of Him, and the Son of God that thou shouldst visit Him?

"He who is close to God is in danger. It's possible to be so enlightened that blindness follows. The light was too bright for your eyes and you never see God again."

Amen on man, woman, and the Trinity, going on in a kind of rapture: "God lives at the center of the Son. Or Daughter." He nodded toward the Cardinal Abbess. "His throne—it's hotter than Hell there, you know. Even the Devil couldn't sit down in that throne. But you can. I can. We're in His lap, and we know what the Godhead's like—from inside. God-at-the-center-of-the-sun-I am bigger than I am. Jesus too, am. Saint Spirit also, am. And, oh my yes, the Virgin, am. One should be embarrassed to speak of God in the third person."

He went on openly to embrace what Blacktooth recognized as a tenet of the old Northwest Heresy, so called, although many in the audience seemed too sleepy to detect it.

"Whence came the Trinity and the Virgin? The unspeakable Godhead yawns and they emerge. The Virgin is the hymnal silence into which the Word is sung by the Father through the Holy Breath and begotten and made flesh within her flesh from the beginning. 'Before the creation, God is not God.' But behind this fearsome four-

fold God yawns the undifferentiated Godhead. To say so is false, however, Eminent Lords. To mention it at all is to lie. Godhead? To
presume to name it or even allude to it is to miss it entirely while
immersed in it. And yet it is to a union with this ultimate Godhead
that we dare aspire. In such a union the soul is like a glass of water
when poured into the great ocean. Its identity as a certain glass of
water is diffused into its identity as the ocean. It loses nothing. Nor
does it gain. It is home again.

"And the wages of death am sin," he added. It seemed an afterthought.

Brother Blacktooth realized early that the audience was briefly
captured by his pious enthusiasm and stopped listening carefully to
words. The man had a way about him. He could just be himself in
front of a crowd and the strength of his spirit prevailed upon them.
But after hours of it, the cardinals began to turn to one another and
even to get up and slip quietly about the throne room to whisper.

It was well into the following morning when he blessed his inat-
tentive audience and sat down. He had talked all night. That was the
first of the next Pope's miracles. He talked seventeen hours without a
glass of water and without becoming hoarse. He had talked them into
weariness. Only his friend Cardinal Brownpony voiced an "Amen," as
the morning sunlight broke through the eastern windows, but that was
because only a few had been listening toward the end, but among
these a handful had listened intently. Many were asleep. Others were
reading their breviaries, some were pairing off politically—actually
wandering from throne to throne—and seated bishops whispered and
giggled with neighbors, as innocent as girls in the early morning.
When Brownpony said "Amen" to the speech, Specklebird stood up
again and answered "Yes?"—and then, as if by a breath of the Holy
Spirit, the few intent listeners started erect and answered "Amen"
with such deep feeling that others were caught by it, and then there
was a chorus of guilty *amens* from the bewildered.

And that is really all there was to it. The speech was not famous
then. Like many of the great orations of human history, Specklebird's
speech seemed rather confusing to the conclave, which, in despera-
tion, finally elected him in spite of the strange homily. Only much
later would his words come alive, when men thoughtfully read the
transcriptions and random notes, and either damned it as foulest heresy, or praised it as divinely inspired, a new revelation. But to
Brownpony and all who knew him well, Amen Specklebird's talk was
like the twitter of birds who say in every language such things as "Bob
White," or "To Easter," or "Whip-poor-Will." The meaning is in the
ear of the listener.

They elected him that morning, the old man, before the crowd started throwing stones at the door. Cardinal Ri lay dead on his cot. Old Otto e'Notto had gone crazy as a loon. The corridors of the palace were places of vomit and shit. More than twenty-five cardinals were in the throes of the illness, and five were with difficulty restrained by their conclavists from becoming violent. They elected him without debate before noon.

To the surprise of many, including Blacktooth, the old man actually said, "*Accepto*," and called himself by his own name, Pope Amen, to the disapproval of many. It was a break with a most ancient tradition.

There were feeble protests preceding the election, of course.

"He said the anointed one marches straight into Hell!" a cardinal from the Southeast complained to the abbot.

" 'From the tomb' he descended into Hell," added Jarad. "And on the third day he arose again from the dead and ascended into Heaven. That's orthodox enough."

"If it befall him! And he called God's word abominable."

"A slip of the tongue," said Brownpony. "He meant admirable."

" 'Subtle and abominable' is what he said. Attributes of the Devil. The serpent was the subtlest of beasts. God's word is Satan?"

"Come, come!" said the abbot. "I think you misheard him. *Verbum subtile atque infandum.* It means finely woven but unutterable. Even elegant but unutterable. Truth so subtle it evades speech. The silence of Christ. And he was waving his arms around at the universe when he said it."

At the end, the conclave unanimously agreed on one thing. If any man could return to New Rome as the head of the Church and play Peter to the Mayor's Caesar without any compromise of fear, it was indeed this Amen (cardinal *in pectore* of Linus VII, as many were now willing to concede) Specklebird. But it was in compromise and fear that the conclave at last elected him, even permitting the conclavists of Archbishop Benefez to vote in his absence, which was not legal since he had not been present to instruct them. To their later chagrin, they voted for the gaunt and wild-eyed hermit.

"*Gaudium magnum do vobis. Habemus Papam. Sancte Spiritu volente, Amen Cardinal Specklebird . . .*"

The roar of the crowd drowned the rest of it, and the conclave turned within itself again as each cardinal came before the new Pope to kiss his slipper and be embraced by the new heir to Saint Peter's keys, and heir as well—if Brownpony the lawyer was correct—to both of Saint Peter's swords, meaning both the spiritual and the temporal power, the latter subordinate to the former. Brownpony the lawyer

who knew more about the history of canon law and the papacy than
anyone outside of Leibowitz Abbey had talked freely during the conclave about the ancient Theory of the Two Swords, to the dismay of
conclavists of the absent Archbishop of Texark. He quoted from an
ancient bull: *"Porro subesse Romano Pontifici . . . de necessitate
salutis . . ."* "And so to be eligible for salvation everybody must be
subject to the Roman Pontiff." According to Brownpony, this never-
popular decree had been aimed especially at monarchs, whether civil
or Nomadic, and the Hannegans and Caesars as well, but it passed the
test for infallibility defining a matter of faith and by backing it with a
stated penalty, the loss of salvation, for rejecting it. Perhaps what the
electors sympathetic to Texark feared most, Brownpony as Pope, was
now replaced by fear of Brownpony as gray eminence. That the cardinal had been the hermit's patron and cultivated his friendship and
managed to get him restored to favor with Linus VII was well known
to everyone. It had seemed a harmless relationship between a rich and
lordly churchman and a humble holy man. If one lacked a conscience,
one could always pay to support one, was the cynical view. But
Brownpony and Specklebird, though poles apart, had always seemed
genuinely fond of each other. There was that friendship to worry
about now.

There was jubilation in the streets at first, but then the people
heard with outrage that their hero had reversed his initial position,
which was thought to have been that the real Rome was wherever
the Pope decided to settle down. A further rebuff to the city was the
sentence of interdict which Pope Amen laid upon Valana until the
instigators of the violence against the conclave should be brought into
his presence. For three days, the population seethed. Under the interdict, Masses were forbidden to be said or confessions heard, and only
the last sacraments could be offered to the dying. The city was sick,
and the city knew that the punisher behind the interdict was Cardinal
Brownpony. But on the fourth day, the terrorists were brought bound
before the Pope. He ordered them untied, heard their common confession, and granted them absolution on condition that they repair all
damage to the building under the supervision of the Cardinal Penitentiary and satisfy any other claims against them before an arbitrator.
Having thus subdued the city, the Pope-elect again called together the
conclave and had himself reelected in the absence of mob violence.
This too was attributed to Brownpony's influence. A vote against the
Pope was a vote against an early departure from Valana; there were no
such votes, and only two abstentions.

It was true that Specklebird had once said that Rome was wherever the Pope settled down, but saying that the Pope was Pope wher-

ever he lived was not the same as saying he should live in Valana. Specklebird had never said he should, for he was Pope only by virtue of being Bishop of New Rome. The public ministry which informed and influenced popular opinion published an analysis of Specklebird's views, and it was posted on the doors or walls of every church in the city. Valanans, this essay concluded, had nothing to fear from Amen Specklebird's return to New Rome, for this was his home, and while he left as spiritual conqueror, he could be expected to return every summer to Valana for the rest of his life, and permanently to establish here many institutions of the Church which were now in New Rome, such as the Ignatzian Order, in order to free them from imperial influence. Nevertheless, the angry burghers seemed intent upon preventing Pope Amen from leaving Valana until Urion Cardinal Benefez had arrived and paid homage to His Holiness.

By this time the attendant electors, cardinals of the College, had knelt before, kissed the ring of, and been embraced by His Holiness Pope Amen. Only a handful refused to do so, claiming that the election was held under duress and therefore invalid. These few had obvious Texark affiliations and their attitude was not unexpected.

It was about noon on the fateful election day that the coach bearing the Most Eminent Lord Urion Cardinal Benefez, Archbishop of Texark, arrived in the sickened city with a party of cavalry. Blacktooth caught a glimpse of the fury on the portly archbishop's face when he learned of the forced election, and heard him rain abuse on his own conclavists for their votes, but the meaning of the fury and its portent faded almost instantly from his mind. Across the plaza from the palace stood a barefoot girl in a brown nun's habit. It was Ædrea, looking at him in apparent shock.

He took a step toward her; then Brownpony's voice echoed in his mind: *You are not to intentionally see her again. If you ever see her in Valana, avoid her.* He stopped. But she had already turned away and disappeared into the crowd.

CHAPTER 12

> Idleness is the enemy of the soul. Therefore
> the brethren should be occupied at certain
> times in manual labor, and again at fixed
> hours in sacred reading.
> —*Saint Benedict's Rule*, Chapter 48

S SOON AS ELIA BROWNPONY HEARD THAT HIS
old friend-enemy Urion Benefez was in
town, he began looking for an opportunity to escape from such ceremonies as
the vesting of the new Pontiff. When he
found the right moment, he insisted that
Blacktooth accompany him to see the
Archbishop of the Imperial City, but for
what purpose the monk could not quite
imagine. As they hurried to the address where Benefez had reserved a
residence, Blacktooth confessed that he had seen Ædrea. There was a
quaver in his voice, and the cardinal stopped smiling and looked at
him sharply.

"I told you to avoid her!"

"I did not disobey you, m'Lord"—*yet*, his internal demon added
silently.

Brownpony's smile dimly returned. "I know. She avoided you. I
talked to her myself."

"Where?"

"At the office, while you were out. I had asked Security to send her to me the next time she brought silver from the colony. When we stopped in Arch Hollow, I told you about the group of gennies in the Suckamint Mountains. They call it New Jerusalem. There's an old silver mine they work. She comes to town about once a month to the, uh, other wing of the building to exchange silver for currency. Their contacts are strictly with the covert wing, which keeps me informed. That's why she didn't know me before, although I was very surprised. We keep their secrets. They fear for their silver mine, among other things. You saw the papal flag over Shard's house.

"I'll tell you how our visit looked from their viewpoint, Nimmy. They're on the edge of lawless country. The last party of churchmen who stopped at Arch Hollow turned out to be Texark agents, and they were very suspicious of Shard's family. One of them penetrated behind their place to the cliff trail, and he saw too much, so the guards killed him quietly and dragged him away. When the other two realized he was missing, they wanted to go looking for him. Shard said there was danger of bear attacks. The guards would have killed them both. Ædrea went to search on their behalf, and brought back a piece of an arm with teeth and claw marks on it. So they prayed over it, buried it, and went back south the way they had come. But before they left, they let Shard know they were on Texark's side, and that all gennies should go back to the Watchitah Nation.

"Then, right after these false Texark priests left, there came a cardinal with no bishop's ring, a monk who plays a guitar, a Nomad in a magic hat, and a swordsman who admits he had worked for the Hannegan. Furthermore, if the cardinal was who he said he was, he should know all about them, but he didn't seem to."

"All they're hiding is a silver mine?"

"Not quite. The gennies in New Jerusalem are about ninety percent spooks, able to pass, relatively normal, like Ædrea. They began fleeing to those mountains generations ago. They put the gleps up front and call it Scarecrow Alley.

"Now, as for Ædrea—" He broke off and looked at the monk. "She sends her regrets."

"For what?"

"Probably for avoiding you in the square. For teasing you too, I suppose, back at her home. How do you feel about her?"

Nimmy groped for words, but none came.

"I see. The Secretariat can have no visible contact with anyone from New Jerusalem. Do you understand that?"

"No, m'Lord."

"Their aims are controversial. So are some of ours. They are refugees, and stand accused of killing Texark guards when they escaped the Watchitah Nation. They fear a raid from imperial forces from the Province. Stay away from the subject, and from her. She's trouble."

Don't I know! he thought miserably.

"She will no longer be accepted by us as their agent," the cardinal added sharply. "That should be the end of it."

The coaches from Texark were still loaded with baggage and both military and civilian personnel standing around as if waiting for orders. A monsignor politely blocked the cardinal's path and asked his name and business.

"Just tell him the Red Deacon is here."

"May I state the purpose—"

"Tell him I came to find out why he tried to have me and my secretary assassinated."

Shaking his head, the monsignor went through a door with the message. Half a minute later, the lecturer Urik Thon Yordin emerged, white as a sheet, looked in terror at both of them, and fled the room. The cardinal looked at Blacktooth and smiled. Nimmy now understood why he was here.

Brownpony was called inside. Blacktooth sat by the door, which was not quite shut. The Archbishop of Texark had not yet changed out of his traveling clothes. The Hannegan's uncle was pacing in fury.

"Elia, how dare you accuse me, even jokingly, in front of my servants and visitors?" he raged.

"I was not aware you had a visitor," the monk heard his master lie. "The fool seemed very upset. I apologize, Urion."

"Well, yes, Yordin is a fool. When he notified us about Corvany's killer, he associated the thing with you and one of your men. I'm sorry someone tried to kill you, but I resent your insinuation, Elia. As you no doubt resented Yordin's."

"I apologize again, Your Eminence. I do wonder if Yordin himself wasn't behind it. But we'll let this wound heal. And now, Urion, will you also heal the Church by paying homage to His Holiness? I know how you must feel, and while the election was very irregular, it's plainly valid. Be generous! The new Pope wants to go home to New Rome, unconditionally, where the Empire wants him, without demands. You have gotten what you wanted." There was such a stoppage of Brownpony's breath with the word "wanted" that Blacktooth could almost hear the *except the tiara* which did not follow. "He makes no demand for a withdrawal of Texark troops, Urion."

There was a long silence. "I shall consult with many other cardinals, Elia. Thank you for your advice," the big man said at last. "I don't like what I'm hearing, but let's not be enemies."

"What have you been hearing?"

"That you stirred up the city, that your agents caused the riots. Or that the, uh, hermit himself did."

"You have been lied to. The people had to drag that 'hermit' to the conclave. Talk to Jarad. Talk to Bleze. Then talk to His Holiness, that hermit, for love of the Church. A love we share."

"Oh, yes, Elia! I know you love the Church. It's what else you may love that I wonder about. We'll see, we'll see."

On his way out, Brownpony found that Blacktooth had been joined in the outer office by three frustrated electors who had come to Valana as Texark allies. One of them, however, had already knelt at the feet of Pope Amen and been embraced by His Holiness. Brownpony exchanged weather opinions with them and hurried on.

"Why did you want me to go with you there, m'Lord?" Blacktooth asked innocently.

"Because I knew Yordin was there, of course. I wanted him to fear we were going to accuse him. And frankly, I wanted to get him in trouble with the archbishop."

"You think he hired the men?"

"If not, he knows who did, but he knows it was a mistake. I think we'll be safe now. It just proves they're dangerous. Now we all need a rest after the worst conclave I've ever seen. Take two or three days off."

As Blacktooth was leaving the Secretariat, the receptionist guard at the entrance handed him two letters. One was a note from Ædrea. He glanced at the guard, who was watching him with an expression that made Blacktooth ask:

"Did the sender give this to you personally?"

"It was handed me by a young sister in a brown habit, Brother St. George. May it not displease Your Reverence that I did not ask her name, for she was silent herself and I did not wish to spoil it."

"Spoil what?"

"Her silence."

Nimmy studied him in surprise. He was a beefy man of mature years, and looked like a retired soldier. His name was Elkin. "You've been to a monastery, haven't you?"

"I was at your own abbey for three years in my youth, Brother, at the same time as the cardinal. Of course, he wasn't a cardinal then, or even a deacon. And I wasn't yet a soldier. But we left at the same time. He had been there to study, but I was there to—" He shrugged.

"Find a calling or not," Nimmy finished, and resolved to be amazed later by this information. "About the silent sister. Does she come here often?"

The guard's expression blurted a *yes* before he caught himself and said, "You should question His Eminence about things like that, Brother St. George."

"Of course, thank you." He turned to go. The other letter was a note from Abbot Jarad apologizing for being unable to meet with him as promised. *I am writing to His Holiness on your behalf, my son, and you may be sure I shall write only what will be favorable to your good intentions.*

Whatever that means.

The note from Ædrea said: *I shall leave your chitara in the crack in the ledge below the waterfall up the hill from the Pope's old place.* Blacktooth began walking in that direction. He wondered why she hadn't left his g'tara with the guard instead of the note. It was a five-mile hike to the falls, and the climb made him dizzy. When he arrived, a white horse was drinking at the pool under the falls, and he froze for a moment; but then he saw that it was a gelding rather than a mare, and wearing a bridle but no saddle; it snorted at the sight of him and trotted out of sight around a curve in the trail. The waterfall was hardly more than a shower, and it fluttered in the wind, producing an occasional flash of rainbow. He walked around the pool, fearing and half hoping to find her behind the falls. The g'tara was there as promised. It was slightly damp from the mist of the falls, causing him to grunt irritably and wipe it against his robe. Why had she made him walk so far?

He glanced at the hoofprints in the sand as he walked around the pool again. Then he stopped. The hoofprints of the horse crossed and partly overlaid a set of human footprints, smaller than his own. Both led in the same direction away from the pool. He wrestled with himself for a moment, then followed the trail.

Her footprints led him into a wooded ravine, then under a low ledge which overhung the sandy bank of the swollen creek. He had to duck low to walk, then dropped to his knees and crawled. Then he found her. He had heard of this place, but never seen it. The small cavern under the ledge was said to have been the home of Amen Specklebird before Cardinal Brownpony bought him the remodeled cavern closer to town.

Slanting sunlight filtered through the foliage and made delicate patterns on the stones and the bare thighs of Ædrea, who was no longer wearing the nun's robe but the leather skirt and a halter above her waist. She sat with bare flesh on bare sand. He had been following her trail on his hands and knees, and at the sight of her bare legs he paused to look. She laughed at him, and put away a handgun she had been holding in her lap.

"You might as well admire the rest of me." She pulled up her skirt and spread her legs to let the dappled light shine on her crotch, then closed her thighs quickly. He had seen it before, dimly, in a barn. Her vagina was small as a nail hole because of the stitches, but her clitoris was as big as Nimmy's thumb, and maybe because he loved her he could see nothing repulsive about her crotch, however embarrassing, and she could see that he was not repelled but sad and curious, and embarrassed. She smiled wickedly and patted his arm.

He sat in the soft sand beside her. "Why do you tease me?" he asked wistfully.

"Now or back home?"

"Then and now."

"I'm sorry. There was a runaway monk from your Order who stopped at our place once. He didn't like me, not at all. He was in love with another monk. I wondered if you were like him. And your gap was showing."

"Gap?"

"The gap between what you are and what you try to let show. I'm a genny, remember. I see gaps. Some call me a witch, even my own father when he's angry."

"So what did you see in this gap?"

"I knew you weren't just a runaway like the other, but something was wrong. You were some kind of fake. I wondered if you weren't the cardinal's prisoner."

Nimmy's laugh was remote. "Something like that. I was in disgrace."

"Are you still in disgrace?"

"As soon as the cardinal finds out I've seen you, I will be."

"I know. He ordered me out of town. That's why I didn't stay by the falls, so that you could go back the way you came."

"You left me a trail."

"You didn't have to follow it."

"Yes, I did." He eyed her accusingly.

"Come back here where we can't be seen." She rolled over and crawled back into the cavern entrance, taking the gun with her. Nimmy followed. The rock overhead was less than ceiling height, and he could not stand up, but in the dim light from the door he could see a mattress on the floor, a saddle, a low table with a candle on it, and several wooden boxes.

"You've been living here!"

"Only for three days. Your employer told the sisters to turn me out. I've made my last trip to Valana. I'm not welcome at the Secretariat anymore. Our people will have to get somebody else. I'm going back home alone. That's my horse you saw outside."

"But why? His Eminence told me you trade silver for scrip, but—"

"Scrip?" She laughed. "Yes, that's truth. Not the whole truth, but true. He doesn't want me to handle it anymore because of you and me, and because of Jæsis. Jæsis was one of ours. And now your cardinal thinks we have a spy among us. He may be right, but it's not me."

"Where did you get the gun?"

"I swiped it from one of the crates in our shipment."

"Shipment?"

"From the Secretariat to New Jerusalem, of course."

Nimmy was incredulous. "We are giving you guns?"

"Not giving. Selling us some, depending on us to store some for the Secretary's own arsenal. Didn't you know? We're bigger than you think, a nation almost. The mountains are easy to defend."

"I don't think I should have come here," he said in alarm.

She caught his arm as he backed toward the door. "We won't talk about it anymore. I thought you knew." Her hand moved up his arm under the sleeve of his robe, caressing. "You're nice and furry."

He sat down again. The gun was lying on one of the packing crates. He picked it up.

"Be careful, it's loaded. I was afraid, staying here alone. That's the smallest model, but it shoots five times. Here, I'll show you." She took the weapon from him, manipulated it, and five brass objects fell one at a time out of the gun into her lap.

"If those are the bullets, where is the powder?"

She handed one of them to him. "The lead part is the bullet. The brass part contains the powder. Now watch this." She cocked it and part of the gun rotated through a small angle. She pulled the trigger, and cocked it again, causing another rotation. "See? It shoots five times. And it's this easy to reload." She turned the cylinder one click at a time and dropped the cartridges back into their chambers.

"But how do you reload the cartridges?"

"You don't, in the field. You carry a lot of cartridges with you.

There's a loading press back at your base, if you don't lose the casings."

"I've never seen anything like it."

"Neither has the Texark cavalry. The guns come from the west coast. I think the design came from Cardinal Ri's country, but it was probably copied from the ancients." She put the gun away, and embraced him suddenly. "I'm not going to see you again. Let's make love—any way we can."

Resigned to what he had started, he did what he could to please her. They lay on the mattress, rubbing bodies and kissing. God, she is beautiful, he noticed in the faint light from the entrance. Spirit in the primordial ooze fucked the Earth, and the Earth gave birth to her, golden-haired as the new corn and laughing in the wind. O Day Maiden, thy name is Ædrea, and I love you.

"*Fujæ Go!*"

"What?" she whispered, squirming under him and grinning at her own pleasure.

"*Fujæ Go.* It is one of the names of—"

"What?"

He remained silent, watching her violet eyes search his own.

"Unspeakable?" she guessed.

"You, are, almost, awake," he groaned in sudden orgasm.

"Oh, let me take it. Like before!" She reached down with her hand and caught his discharge.

Spent, he nevertheless started up in total surprise. She was rubbing it into herself, into that tiny orifice no larger than a buzzard-quill pen. "What are you doing?" Nimmy gasped.

Still grinning, she said, "Getting pregnant. Like last time. I'm way late for my period since we did it."

Stunned, he sat up. It had been black as pitch in Shard's root cellar, and he had been too drunk to be certain what happened, and he could feel it but not see it, in spite of what he said in confession to an old onetime hermit.

"Nimmy, you're white as a sheet!"

"Why?"

"Shard had me stitched up by a surgeon, and he won't have it undone, and he's my father, and I love him, and I won't defy him, but this way I can let a baby tear it open, if he won't let a surgeon cut me."

"Oh, my God!" He rolled over with his face in his hands.

"Nimmy, please don't cry." She held his shoulders and tried to keep him from shaking so. "Oh, please!—I didn't mean to make you unhappy. I just picked you to have a baby with. You!"

Nimmy felt dizzy and sick. There seemed to be only a moment of blackness, but when he awoke and went outside, Ædrea and the white gelding were gone. He was alone in front of the tiny cavern. She had written in the sand: *Goodbye, Nimmy. You really are a monk.*

He saw her in town again, however, on his way home from the hills. Walking down the street, he looked over his shoulder at the sound of a horse and saw Ædrea slowly overtaking him. She shook her head quickly, but barely looked at him. He nodded understanding and kept going. She had stopped somewhere along the way, but had to come through town to go back home by the main road. Blacktooth, who was wearing his Leibowitzian novice's robe, turned a corner and just avoided running into another man, who was skipping rope. He wore a wood and leather harness which held a harmonica up to his mouth. He played a rapid but recognizable *Salve Regina* while he jumped the rope; a cup on the ground at his side asked for, and had collected, a few coins. Blacktooth suppressed a sharp gasp and tried to pass behind him as quietly as possible. For there wearing a Leibowitzian postulant's robe in the road was Torrildo playing the fool for coins. Blacktooth had gone about six paces when the music and the slapping of the rope suddenly stopped, so that he could hear the tread of hooves of his love's mount as she too passed the excommunicated musical mendicant.

"Hey, Blacktooth. *Darling!*" Torri called.

Blacktooth broke into a fast trot. Behind him, he could hear them. Ædrea stopped to exchange pleasantries with Torrildo, whom she had apparently met before.

"Oh, so he was the one!" he heard her say as he fled.

The sound came from the chapel, a *whish*ing slap followed by a moan. It was repeated every two or three seconds. His Eminence Cardinal Brownpony stopped to listen, then walked inside. After three days of absence without leave, his secretary for Nomad affairs was found at last. Blacktooth was kneeling before the altar of the Virgin in the Secretariat's private chapel; he was flagellating himself with a scourge of thongs.

"Stop it," the cardinal said quietly, but the sound went on. *Whish*, slap, moan. Pause. *Whish*, slap, moan. Pause.

The head of SEEC cleared his throat loudly. "Nimmy, stop it!"

Finding himself ignored, he turned toward his office, the Axe at his elbow. "Come see me as soon as you can," he called over his shoulder as the flogging continued. "We have an audience with His Holiness early tomorrow. It's about your petition."

. . .

The audience went badly. As they walked to the Papal Palace, Blacktooth, his back sore and his guilt making him sick, said nothing to his master and his master said nothing to him. There was an alienation between them that he had never felt before. Brownpony obviously knew he had disobeyed and seen Ædrea, but he could not know, or perhaps only suspected, that she had told Blacktooth about the smuggling of guns. If they had spoken as they walked, mutual accusation might arise, and Nimmy was grateful for the strained silence.

The Pope, still looking uncomfortable in his white cassock, greeted them warmly and without formality. As Blacktooth knelt to kiss his ring, Amen nodded to the cardinal, who then disappeared, leaving the surprised monk alone with the Supreme Pontiff.

"Please get up, Nimmy. Come let us sit over here."

Blacktooth moved as if in a dream. As he sat down, he felt as if he were resuming his role as a penitent in Specklebird's home cavern. Out of the corner of his eye, he saw Specklebird become a cougar.

"There seems to be a divine being among us," said the cougar, smiling a thin smile.

"The divine being should shut up," Nimmy heard himself say, and heard with pleasure the cougar's laugh. The being was playful.

"You are going to continue in Cardinal Brownpony's employ for some time, unless you object," said the cougar, dissolving into an old black man with a cloud of white hair and white skullcap.

"I am surprised he still wants me." (Nimmy again hearing himself.)

"Why do you think he chose you among his translators as a personal secretary?"

"I have wondered that myself, Holy Father. I can only think that he has become attached to the people of his unknown mother, through his frequent contacts with them. I am of the same blood."

"It's just ethnic nepotism? Do you really think so?"

"The alternative is to suppose that he thinks I have some particular quality or talent that he appraises rationally, and so chooses me, in spite of my disobedience, but I cannot, Holy Father, imagine what that could be. Whatever it is, it must be imaginary on his part."

"In other words, you're just a poor sinner who deeply loves God, but hasn't got much to offer in the way of talent."

Sarcasm? Blacktooth withered. He had unconsciously spoken through a mask of humility, and the cougar as Specklebird-Peter ruthlessly held up a mirror to the mask he was looking through.

Recovering after a moment, he said, reflecting the sarcasm, "All right, let's admit that I'm a genius in Nomadic languages, having invented the new alphabet myself, which even Saint Ston's uses, I'm told. Not only that, I've learned to defend myself, understand most of my master's affairs with the Nomads, and that's where we're going. So perhaps his choosing me is rational. Also, I've been taught how to kill a man."

"You are to abstain from deadly violence, my son," said the old mountain cat.

"Neither am I to covet my neighbor's ox, Holy Father."

The Pope laughed heartily. "You're awake sometimes, Nimmy. I do believe it: you are called to contemplation."

Blacktooth sighed and lowered his head. "I could be laicized and still work for the cardinal, Holy Father. And I don't have to be a monk to contemplate."

Specklebird returned to his subject: "In your case, I think you do. Cardinal Brownpony chose you because you *are* a monk, Nimmy, a real monk, and a contemplative. Why do you think he, a rich and powerful man, formed a friendship with me, a hermit and beggar, a bedraggled and much-reprimanded priest with no parish, denied access for several years to the altars of Valanan churches? Your master wants to learn more about people like us, Nimmy. There is hope for him, just because he perceives we are different, and the perception leads him to curiosity rather than contempt. If you were not truly a man of religion, why would he choose you?—who know less about the Secretariat's business than at least three of the others. I know him. He wonders what it is like to know God."

"If you are being infallible, I surrender. If not, I say he made a mistake, because I am, or was, a very bad monk."

"You bring in a load of donkey shit. That's yours to confess if you think so, but it's not yours to judge on the last day."

"I'm in love with a spook, a genny girl, Holy Father."

"Is that why you want to be laicized?"

"Not at first." He sighed. "Maybe that's part of it now."

"Maybe?"

"Because she too says I'm a monk. Everybody says I'm a monk but me."

"Smart girl. When you feel love for her, see God in her. Do not let this love lessen your love of the Lord. Passion is the other side of compassion, not its negation. You should be able to see and love God through any of His works, including a forbidden girl. But remember that you are a monk of Saint Leibowitz. Love is not a sin."

"But consummation is."

"For you. You yourself chose it to be so."

"As a runaway at age fifteen."

"Your solemn vows were taken much later, Brother St. George!"

"But I was still ignorant of the world I was undertaking to shun by my vows, from which only you can absolve me, Holy Father."

"You have learned so much about the world lately?"

"I am in love."

Pope Amen laughed. "Loving God through His creatures is admirable, if you know what you are doing. Now let me remind you of something. I have spoken to Abbot Jarad, and he reminded me. The Order of Saint Leibowitz was originally an order of hermits. It is possible for you to remain in the Order, but live apart from the monastery. You would live by the ancient rules of Saint Leibowitz, as he originally established them. This would be after your present employer releases you, of course. I ask you to consider the possibility, and postpone your request to be laicized until you decide."

Blacktooth sighed deeply. He looked at the old black man; the cougar was gone. He lowered his head in submission, but a question remained: *What if she is really pregnant?* he thought, walking away empty from the audience. Well, not quite empty: a poor monk had talked back to a Pope. Riches, riches.

Other employees of SEEC briefed him on events during his five-day absence. Valana was still in turmoil. The external violence and internal cowardice that tainted the Conclave of 3244 were acknowledged even by the new Pope, who had astonished everyone by placing the sickened city of Valana under a sentence of interdict. The security guard Elkin recited for Blacktooth the names of the leaders of the violence, who were brought forth to undertake to repair damages to the palace. "These seventeen thugs knelt there before Pope Amen, their hero. He got from them a promise to repair all damage. Then he imposed a penance of prayer and fasting, and then absolved them."

"But this did nothing to satisfy the Benefez people," Nimmy guessed. Elkin nodded.

It was immediately apparent that the election of an eccentric religious ascetic of dubious orthodoxy and religious impulsiveness caused a nervous shuddering to pass through the hierarchy and the institutions of power from coast to coast. It was either an unexpected attack by the Holy Ghost upon the conclave, or the work of the Devil and the Red Deacon.

The Archbishop of Texark interviewed nearly 170 cardinals who had participated in the election before he found enough electors who were willing to affirm that their votes for Amen Specklebird had been given under duress. He stayed only three days in the city, and, claiming illness, failed to come to pay homage to the elected Pope. He departed with his troops and quite a few Eastern cardinals who were healthy enough and eager to escape the sickened city. Some members of his faction announced that the Holy See was still vacant because the election was forced. They called upon the old man to admit the election was invalid, to announce another conclave to be held in New Rome, and then to step down from the throne he illegally occupied. Brownpony and others made the case for a valid election, and proposed that the faction recognize His Holiness or face ecclesiastical sanctions. Only one of the group changed his mind at this point, and the others left Valana for home. It seemed obvious that the old wound of schism had again burst its stitches.

By his will, locally drawn, Cardinal Ri left his servants to Cardinal Brownpony, an embarrassment which the Secretary for Extraordinary Ecclesiastical Concerns managed to share with His Holiness the Pope, to whom the Archbishop of Hong left his wife and lesser concubines. The lawyer who drew the will became angrily defensive when questioned about the possibility of a mix-up of the two bequests, with Brownpony supposed to get the women. The Red Deacon echoed his anger, and testified that Cardinal Ri before his death had asked him to take care of his servants afterward. He called it obvious that Ri had intended to leave the fate of his loved ones in the hands of none but the servant of the servants of God, Amen Papa Specklebird. Since the servants of Cardinal Ri were very happy to find a new master, Brownpony decided to keep all but one of them, not as bond servants, but on five-year contracts renewable only with mutual consent. The Pope granted SEEC an increase in funds to pay the expense of keeping them. They numbered six skilled warriors, two personal servants, and Ri's confessor. This priest he released to Saint Ston's, who wanted the former chaplain eventually to teach courses in the Oriental Rite as practiced in his land and in the language spoken there.

As for the Pope's inheritance of the three women, Amen gave them the gold which the prelate had willed to him, plus freedom, and, if desired, he offered a choice of school, a convent, or a marriage broker.

Wooshin for his part was delighted to be in command of a squad of well-trained fighters who shared a military tradition not unlike his own. The Axe was beginning to speak Rockymount like a native, and this fact alone made it natural that he assume command of Brownpony's private army, but he made them go through the formality of choosing him, and then swearing allegiance to him and to the Cardinal Secretary, their employer. Blacktooth wondered if Brownpony knew, as the Axe had once told him, that any one of the men of his tradition would kill anybody his employer designated, even the Pope, even themselves. Wooshin's comparison of these fighters to Hannegan's assassins revealed his contempt for even the professionals among the latter.

There was too much excitement in Valana for anyone yet to think of questioning what excuse the Secretariat might have for keeping an army of six professional killers on the payroll, although Blacktooth had been wondering the same thing ever since he left Leibowitz Abbey with the Axe under Brownpony's wing. He felt he was less privy to the cardinal's intentions than his inside job suggested. He now realized this more clearly since he had seen Ædrea's weapon. A whole wing of the Secretariat was closed to him. A whole range of SEEC activities were invisible to him. He tried not to be curious. He was temporarily sharing Brownpony's outer office with two other specialist secretaries, and they observed that at least once a day someone from the forbidden wing came to the office with a folder of documents, was admitted to Brownpony's private sanctum, and departed without the folders, which were never filed by the outer office. He had no files in his sanctum, but a stove for burning papers. Together, the other two secretaries had induced an opinion that the forbidden wing dealt with intelligence and operations, and with this Blacktooth did not disagree. He said nothing to them about weapons.

CHAPTER 13

The Abbot shall see to the size of the garments, that they be not too short for those
who wear them, but of proper fit.
  —*Saint Benedict's Rule*, Chapter 55

T SEEMED TO BLACKTOOTH THAT HIS MASTER
had become obsessed with Nomad poli-
tics during a time of trouble for both the
papacy in Valana and the Eastern
Church. While he might have been in
constant correspondence with Eastern
cardinals who had taken part in the election of Pope Amen, he was instead inviting Hultor Bråm of the Grasshopper to
enter Valana with all the guards he cared to bring in order to meet the
Pope. The purpose was obvious. The cardinal stood accused of favor-
ing the candidacy of Chür Ösle Høngan of the Wilddog Horde over
that of the Grasshopper war sharf. To establish a neutral posture,
Brownpony had invited Hultor Bråm to meet the Pope before he invited Høngan. He left the Pope's immediate vicinity to ride out onto
the Plains accompanied by only one meek-looking policeman instead
of his usual ferocious bodyguard to meet the Grasshopper war sharf,
although the Pope certainly needed him near at hand during such

troubled times. Blacktooth's admiration for his employer's courage had grown, even while he was entertaining suspicions laced with fantasy about the Secretary's loyalty to the Pope and his perceived guns-for-the-misborn activities. "This is the world, O Saint Isaac Edward Leibowitz, that I abandoned as your monk. And where am I now?"

He went early with Wooshin to the place Brownpony had set for their meeting upon his return from the Plains, and there they saw Ædrea's replacement as messenger from New Jerusalem already standing there in the street. Now that Blacktooth had learned both officially from the cardinal and directly from Ædrea something about the exchanges between New Jerusalem and the covert wing of SEEC, he and the Axe had both been introduced to Ulad from the colony. Blacktooth had assumed that all spooks were normal in appearance. Ulad looked normal, if one saw him at a distance with nothing nearby for comparison. But when he stood next to another man in a crowd, he stood about a man-and-a-third high and probably weighed about two men and a half. Thrice Blacktooth had watched the giant, whose hands seemed disproportionately slender, pick the pockets of passersby before he crossed the street to warn the giant, "If you do *that* again, I'll tell."

Ulad picked him up by the head with one of those long slender hands, the thumb so crushing his temple that he almost lost consciousness from pain. Wooshin slipped behind him and did something to his knee which made him release the monk with a howl and sit down on the pavement, clutching his leg. The Axe stepped in front of him and pressed a sword to his nose, flattening it. "If you do *that* again, I'll kill."

"I didn't recognize you at first," the giant sang out, his voice a surprising contralto, to the tiny old warrior.

"Do you like your job?" asked the Axe.

"It's good to be able to come to town, yes."

"Do your people know you're a thief?" the monk asked, picking himself up.

"It's part of my cover. People know me hereabout. It doesn't matter if I get arrested. The police know me. They think I'm local, and so I am, part-time. Sometimes they lock me up for a few days, but sometimes I work for them. I used to ride as a guard for Ædrea. This place is where we met before going home."

"Does His Eminence know all this?"

"I'm supposed to meet him here. He's coming in the Grasshopper Nomad's coach. I hate Nomads. You look like a Nomad to me, and you called me a spook."

Nimmy faced his glower. "Did you ever see a Nomad wearing a

monk's habit?" he scoffed. "Do you look like a spook?" He felt Wooshin touching his arm, trying to warn him, but it was too late.

Ulad growled and pulled a knife. Steel met steel, slid together, and then the edge of the short sword cut the giant's forearm, all in one sweep of motion from the thrust of the dagger through the cut to the fall of dagger and blood on the ground. They stood frozen for a moment; then Wooshin sheathed his blade and said, "Go do something for your arm. It's not a deep cut."

"I think he tried to stab me, Axe."

"You do?" Axe snickered. "Well! The cardinal warned me about Ulad, and he is very unhappy with him as Ædrea's replacement. The man has a habit of going berserk once in a while. He's only temporary, in my opinion; the New Jerusalemites were so infuriated by our master's rejection of Ædrea as persona non grata that they made Ulad her replacement. They can be arrogant."

"Why isn't he caged up?"

"Well, one, because the cardinal wants him to meet this Nomad he's bringing home, and two, because he's apparently a warrior of power and a high officer of a small army that's supposed to be on our side."

"Our side against *whom*, for the love of God? Do your one and your two make a three? Which is our side?"

"Why, our master's side!" Wooshin snapped, glaring at him. "Your loyalty is a question in my mind, Brother St. George. Do not think I would not cut your throat if you ever betray him!"

"Whoa, please! It's me, Blacktooth. I was just trying to understand his thinking."

"That is not your place."

"Are you the one to tell me my place and keep me in it, Axe? This is new."

"I can't tell you your place, but don't let me catch you out of it."

This is new—yes, and real. It was the first time he had felt real menace from the old warrior. Brownpony must be more angry than he realized. His fear of Wooshin at the abbey was founded on nervous imagination. But lately he had learned that Wooshin lived only to carry out his master's wishes and protect his person and his welfare; this was the warrior's highest good. Blacktooth, of a different persuasion in matters of loyalty, had disobeyed his master. Wooshin knew it, at least in a vague way, because the monk had been gone so long. Things were not the same between them, although Axe had just saved him from Ulad's dagger. Ædrea had changed everything about his life.

Just as Ulad came back with a bandaged forearm, a coach pulled by four beautiful gray stallions appeared from the east and stopped in front of the Venison House. The standard-bearer of the totemic Grass-hopper triumph pole rode up, dismounted, and stood at attention with his standard in front of the restaurant.

"Forth come the banners of the king of hell," Blacktooth said sourly, quoting an ancient poet.

Nimmy later learned that when Brownpony met Hultor Bråm, the latter was riding in his royal coach, probably of Eastern manufacture and stolen during a raid into the Eastern timberland, and he was accompanied by sixteen well-armed horsemen, while the Prince of the Church himself had left behind even his formidable bodyguard and brought along only a meek-looking Valana policeman. Bråm seemed embarrassed when he saw that the lone churchman was his host, and promptly sent all but two of his warriors home. Thus Brownpony rode back alone in the coach with a surprised but not yet friendly sharf. As the party dismounted, Ulad the giant strode toward the coach and presented himself to the cardinal, who frowned at him, spoke a few words, and waved him away.

"He will call you first," the giant said to Blacktooth, and to Axe, "You shall guard the entrance."

Ulad was plainly upset. "They should put all Nomads in jail when they come to town."

"Then how could they do any business?"

"Their only business is to steal!"

"I see. With you, it's a hobby, with them a business."

Ulad growled, and Wooshin nudged the monk again.

Next to the driver sat a Nomad with a long rifle and a mean mouth. Two mounted warriors rode guard. A policeman and a Nomad got out of the coach and then helped the prelate and another Nomad get out. The second Nomad was fancier than the first. Ulad was plainly disappointed to see that the Nomads were not in custody. Three Nomads and the policeman stayed with the carriage while the fancy Nomad and the prelate went inside to eat.

The coach was dirty from crossing the Plains but was of costly design and workmanship. The horses, while obviously tired, were elegant and well-bred animals that could be sold for at least a thousand pios as a team. The door of the coach was enameled blue and gold, with a touch of red on the crest that showed through the dust on the door. Someone was talking about the crest. They stood among a small group of people who, upon passing by or coming out of the inn, saw the Nomads and the police and the well-fitted coach with its spirited team, and lingered, becoming a crowd. Blacktooth kept a wary eye on Ulad.

"I tell you it can't be the Secretary's," the grocer from next door was saying. "Those aren't his arms, nor any churchman's." "What about the motto?" said a woman beside him. "It's Latin, isn't it?" When the grocer shrugged, she turned to a friar who had come out of the inn and was staring at the coach. "Isn't it Latin, Father?"

"As a matter of fact, it isn't."

"It can't be Nomadic!" she said.

"No, it's a Church language, all right. It's English."

"What does it say?"

"I've been out of school for twenty years," said the cleric. He turned to go, but paused to add, "It says something about fire, though. And that's Cardinal Brownpony inside, so you'd better leave."

"You leave, Father! I live here."

"Maybe the Pope's starting his own fire department," said a student from Saint Ston's who turned out to be Aberlott.

Blacktooth himself put them straight. "The motto says: 'I set fires.' It's the heraldry of a Grasshopper war sharf."

"See you later," he said to his ex-roommate, left the group, and went to stand near the window.

Inside the tavern, the cardinal shared a meal with the Nomad officials. The fare was chicken cooked with herbs served with a local beer. The hungry plainsmen were polite enough not to scorn the lack of beef, but they did scrape away every trace of greenery from the meat. Bråm was continuing a monologue he had begun on the road, but the cardinal saw his secretary at the window and beckoned him inside. Blacktooth entered and found his master being theologically harassed by an offensive sharf in the crudest of terms.

"The father of the mother of God is also her son and her lover," the Nomad was saying. He squinted toward the window and pretended not to be watching the cardinal. "That's the way our Weejus explain it."

The cardinal took another bite of chicken and chewed vigorously while he looked at Bråm.

"Did you hear what I said?"

"No," Brownpony lied. "Say it again." His Grasshopper dialect was adequate but he occasionally looked at Blacktooth for support.

"The father of the mother of God is also her son and her lover. This is the way the Grasshopper Bear Spirit sees it as well."

"Just so." Brownpony dipped the chicken leg in the sauce and took another bite. Hultor Bråm was trying to antagonize him in the most obvious possible way.

The sharf straightened and frowned. " 'Just so'! You agree?"

" 'Just so' means I heard what you said, Sharf. I'm a lawyer, not a theologian. Have a piece of chicken."

"He invites you to have a piece of chicken," said the monk, sensing a Wilddog usage.

"If you're a lawyer, then why don't you have me arrested?"

"Because I'm not a theologian's lawyer, and if I had you arrested, you would be of no use to anybody." He looked at Blacktooth, who nodded. Only occasionally did he need to clarify what was being said.

"You're the Pope's lawyer."

"Just so. The white meat is dry. Try the dark."

"Jesus is Mary's lover."

Cardinal Brownpony sighed with disgust and began using his drumstick to beat on the table.

"Why do you want to pick a quarrel with me? Do I say ugly things about Empty Sky, or your Wild Horse Woman?"

"You did so once. At a holy council fire. That's why I'm talking to you this way. You tried to drive her away, and your Christian puppet killed her priests."

Brownpony sighed. "So I haven't lived that down, eh? Sunovtash An was nobody's puppet. As for me, what I did was foolish. I know that now, and I regret it. But that happened in the farming areas, not on the eastern Plains."

"No matter, the tribe was formerly Grasshopper. You must remove the sacrilege."

"How can I do that?"

"We have discussed it. You must go to her."

"Where? Back to the farming area?"

"No. In the navel of the Earth, she lives: the breeding pit for her wild horses. It is a place of deadly fires, called Meldown."

"I have heard of it. Isn't that where Mad Bear became Lord of the Hordes before the conquest?"

"The same. Anyone nominated for the sacral kinship had to be chosen by her in that place. After election, each had to spend the night in that place by the light of the full moon. It will be so again. A new *Qæsach dri Vørdar* will be chosen. One of the three of us. It is also the place where we try men charged with crimes, a place of ordeal. Many never come out alive. Many come out sick, and lose their hair. Few emerge in full health. You committed a crime in the eyes of our Weejus and our Bear Spirit, Brownpony."

"And if I submit to the ordeal?"

"There will be an alliance, if you live. And peace with the Wilddog."

"No matter who is elected Lord?"

Bråm shook his head, seemed puzzled.

"As *Qæsach dri Vørdar*," Blacktooth put in.

"Ah, no doubt about that! The old women know best. And the *Høngin Fujæ Vurn.*"

The cardinal spoke to Nimmy in Rockymount. "Explain carefully and politely to the sharf that His Holiness is the high priest of all Christendom, and that diplomatic immunity, which he has been practicing on me, does not cover the *crimen laesae majestatis*, so tell him to curb his tongue before the Pope."

Hultor Bråm was a powerful Nomad about Chür Høngan's size, but perhaps leaner. His body language had few words. The predominant accent was force, a force prepared to spring at you, either for a hearty hug or to kill. All his muscles seemed drawn up that way.

Nervously, Blacktooth translated Brownpony's message.

For a moment, the sharf glowered at him. The body language said "kill the messenger," but then he turned to the cardinal and nodded curtly. At that moment Ulad stooped to enter the doorway and crossed, as a crouching mass of muscle, toward the table. Brownpony sent Blacktooth away in Ulad's wake. Ulad, the monk intuitively surmised, was to discuss matters not for his ears, for Brownpony needed an interpreter more than ever, because the genny giant spoke only Valley Ol'zark and a little Rockymount. Probably Ulad was there to discuss weapons with the Grasshopper sharf, and Brownpony would have to be interpreter for both of them. Temporarily dismissed, he headed home, accompanied by Aberlott, whom he had not seen since the election.

"Listen, I heard there is going to be schism, maybe even war. What about it?"

"Takes two to make a schism or a war. Who do you have in mind for the war? And why ask me?"

"You work for the Secretary."

"Who probably couldn't answer your question either. Why don't you ask a Weejus woman?"

"I don't know any, do you?"

"Not yet."

"When? I hear your cardinal is thinking of leaving for Nomad country."

Blacktooth shot him a suspicious look. Everybody seemed to know more about his employer's doings than he did. "Where did you hear that?"

"From a man who came out of the inn just before you did."

Blacktooth worried. Brownpony was careless enough to let his conversation with Hultor Bråm be overheard by another customer who understood Nomadic. But there had been no one else visible from their table.

"A secret's out?" asked Aberlott after a moment.

"I don't know. I have a feeling I'm going to be fired, sooner or later."

"By the cardinal? For what?"

"Remember the person who gave you my rosary back?"

Blacktooth said no more than that, but his friend watched his face, saw a blush, and asked no further questions. He turned away to cover a laugh with his hand, then asked, "What will happen to you then, Nimmy?"

"I don't know. I have a big debt to pay. What the hell are you doing out of school?"

"I take no courses during the summer. I like to travel."

"Where do you plan to go?"

"Where the horse takes me. No reins, you know. You just kick the animal when he stops to graze too often."

"Be sure and pick the right horse, you half-wit, or it will take you to its birthplace." He waved east toward the flatlands. Aberlott laughed and walked on alone.

It was two days before Hultor Bråm was admitted to an audience with His Holiness. During Cardinal Brownpony's absence from the Curia, the Pope announced a date for his return to New Rome. If the head of SEEC felt miffed about being left out of the decision process, he at least had an alibi for the bad decision. The Pope planned a very early departure. There had been no communication with Texark about the matter. The Pope used his interview with Hultor Bråm to send the Apostolic Benediction to the Grasshopper Weejus and Bear Spirit people, and to ask permission to cross Grasshopper lands on his way to New Rome. Graciously the war sharf promised that one hundred warriors would escort the Pope's party once it emerged from Wilddog country. Brownpony listened in silence to this, but made it clear to all that he would not accompany the expedition, having urgent business both on the Plains and in Texark itself.

"It is my wish to make you Vicar Apostolic to the Three Hordes," the old black Pope told the Red Deacon the next day.

Brownpony actually gasped, Nimmy noticed, and the few members of the Curia who were present exchanged frightened glances. There was a long silence, because what the Pope just said caused a mental avalanche. First thought: to make the territory of all three hordes a Vicariate Apostolic was to abolish the de facto status of the Jackrabbit Horde as missioners of the Texark Archdiocese. It would end the archbishop's authority in the Province, and would force him to recall his missionary priests there or let them submit to a new authority. Second thought: it would infuriate Benefez, no matter who was appointed. But Brownpony? Third thought: before Brownpony could be appointed a Vicar Apostolic, he would have to be ordained and then consecrated as bishop of an extinct ancient diocese, for he would be the equivalent of a bishop in a missionary area not yet a diocese. Blacktooth remembered the cardinal's own words: *I was called to be a lawyer, not a priest, and that's it.*

"Well, Elia? Will you do it?"

"Holy Father, I don't think I have a calling."

"*We* are calling you. Right now." It was the first time Blacktooth had ever heard Amen use the pontifical *we* except in formal Latin.

With great dignity, Brownpony prostrated himself before the old man, but still he said nothing. He stayed that way until the Pope interpreted it as consent, whereas it was, as it seemed to Blacktooth, merely submission.

"Get up, Elia. We'll have you ordained, consecrated, and on your way by next week. If we do it quietly, you can go to the convention on the Plains before Benefez hears about it."

Later, at the cardinal's request, Blacktooth explained the situation to Hultor Brâm before the sharf left town. "He will be the representative of the Pope to all of the hordes, and govern all churches and missions both north and south of the Nady Ann. However, you must not speak of it before it is accomplished."

The sharf shook his head. "He will not be accepted by the Grasshopper," Brâm growled, commenting on the appointment, "unless your master makes his peace with the *Høngin Fujæ Vurn*, as he has promised. And the Bear Spirit must be consulted."

"It seems," said Brownpony, when Blacktooth relayed the remark to his employer, "that ever since I made the mistake of denouncing Yordin's speech, I have been ambushed by unpleasant surprises, not all of them from my enemies. Aren't you astonished, Nimmy?"

"Not altogether, since I provided one unpleasant surprise myself." It was as close as he had come to an apology, but the cardinal just looked at him curiously.

The monk's attitude toward Brownpony had been tainted by suspicion, but not to the extent of doubting that the deeds of his friend, Pope Amen Specklebird, were entirely unexpected by the cardinal. Perhaps it had been Sorely Cardinal Nauwhat or Hilan Bleze who, during Brownpony's absence, had put Amen in mind of making all Nomadic territory an Apostolic Vicariate, to be ruled as a diocese would be, but by a bishop directly responsible to the Pope, clearly ending the de facto role of the Texark Archdiocese as missioner to the conquered

Province. The churches throughout that Province were now headed by missionaries appointed by Urion Cardinal Benefez, but in no way had the Province been added to the Texarkana diocese. Most of its first priests had been military chaplains. But to create a papally dominated Vicariate out of the whole domain of the Three Hordes was to deprive Benefez of power and revenue throughout half of his nephew's domain. Could a holy old hermit come up with such an idea without a sinister force at his elbow? The sinister force might indeed be the Holy Ghost, so far as Blacktooth could distinguish. The old man was, as Saint Leibowitz used to say, "Independent as a hog on ice." It was an idea just crazy enough to have come from either God or Specklebird. Or as Urion Benefez might say, from either Satan or Brownpony. The very fact that the Red Deacon became an overnight archbishop made it evident, to anyone who wished to think so, that the promotion was a coup, coaxed by cunning out of a crazy old pope-contender who began to rule before he was legally elected.

Elia Brownpony's ordination as a priest and consecration as Bishop of Palermo were conducted in secret ceremonies to which no one was admitted except the participants, nor did Blacktooth's master change his manner of dress or wear a bishop's ring until he was ready to leave the city for the Plains, somewhat in advance of the Pope's own departure for New Rome. It was clear that Filpeo Harq and Urion Benefez were to remain in ignorance of Brownpony's new rank and office until his acceptance by the Nomads of all three hordes as the spiritual leader of Christians on the Plains and in the Province had been established.

"There's no doubt they'll hear about it, Nimmy," the cardinal told him. "But only the Pope will inform them officially, and when he's ready to tell them. Now I have a new task for you. You will find your predecessor has taken over your office for the time being. I am going to visit first Chür Høngan, then Hultor Bråm.

"Deliver my written message to Mayor Dion in New Jerusalem; among other things, it introduces you. Tell them that Sorely Cardinal Nauwhat will, for the time being, be in charge of the Secretariat. Tell them that Ulad is out of control and must be replaced. If they insist on knowing why I refused to deal with Ædrea, I suppose you'll have to say she became too intimate with clergy."

"I am ashamed, m'Lord."

"How about contrite? Never mind. Do your best to mollify them. Learn as much as you need to know about New Jerusalem. Along the way, let Wooshin brief you on what is going to happen. These things are secret for the present, although they are becoming less secret every day. You may, or may not, continue working at the Secretariat—for

Cardinal Nauwhat. You *may* report back to him, if you wish. If he finds no use for you, he will tell you where to find me, or you *may* go back to your girlfriend in Arch Hollow and perhaps find a home in the colony. Or you *may* go beg them to take you back at the abbey, or become a hermit. I do not want to see you again unless and until this attachment is behind you."

"I expected to be dismissed, m'Lord. I did not obey."

"We'll see how it goes with you."

"And Axe is coming with me?"

"Along with all six of Cardinal Ri's men, and someone from the other wing—Elkin, I believe you know him."

"I didn't know he was from the other wing. I thought he was just a receptionist."

"Top security, and also a fighter almost in Wooshin's class. He was at Leibowitz Abbey once. You'll have a lot of expensive baggage with you, a twelve-mule train, but that will be Ulad's and Elkin's responsibility. When it's safe, they may let you and Ulad and Axe ride on ahead of the train and shorten your journey. Pack your habit and wear something else on the trail. You can put your habit back on when you arrive. Nimmy, I'm trusting you with new secrets."

"I'll be careful. And you, m'Lord?"

"I go to the convention of all the shamans of the hordes, all the Weejus and Bear Spirit people. I hope, with help from Holy Madness and Father e'Laiden, to be admitted as a Christian shaman observer and explain my new role."

"Hultor Bråm will try to keep you out."

"Of course, but the Jackrabbit will want to hear what I have to say, because they will be most affected by the transition. Bråm can't put together a majority. His grandmother might be able to do it, but she won't. Depending on what happens, I may go on to New Rome after the Pope, or even to Texark. Goodbye now, Nimmy. I would bless you, but you have heard me say I have no calling, yet here I am, a pretender."

"M'Lord, I know from history that once upon a time in a much earlier Church, a vocation to the priesthood meant a call from the bishop, not necessarily a call from God. And I heard the Bishop of Rome himself call you to be that which you have now become by ordination and consecration."

The cardinal smiled. "Thank you, Nimmy. Bless you, then, until tomorrow."

Blacktooth bent to kiss his ring, but the cardinal avoided his lips, squeezed his hand, said, "We'll say goodbye again tomorrow," and was gone.

Nimmy found himself near tears, and began to pray as he walked toward the nearest church. Brownpony had been to him like a kindly Nomad father who was never drunk, while Abbot Jarad had been like a sterner Nomad uncle, always judging and finding fault. But he had missed the latter; he knew he would miss the former more. He knew too that loving people was a way of loving God, but to be attached to the one loved was not proper for a poor monk, and evidence of worldliness or delusion. Not wrong to love, but wrong to be attached to the one loved, for always came the anguish of tearing loose from all impermanent things.

By the morrow, he had sufficiently recovered from his lapse of anxious worldliness to think of his former roommate and then confidently cajole his beloved (and possibly bedamned) cardinal into interviewing Aberlott, who as a friend of the late Jæsis could serve well as an emissary from SEEC to the dead student's family and help convince the ruling council that nobody had exposed Jæsis as a spook until the police learned of it after his death. There was suspicion at both ends, in the relationship between the colony and the Secretariat, which would now be managed temporarily by Sorely Cardinal Nauwhat, and Brownpony agreed that some gesture of reconciliation was advisable.

"But that would be one more person who knows about the armaments, Nimmy. So I think not." It was the first time Brownpony had mentioned the subject of the guns to him. And he would not have mentioned it now without a realization that the monk already knew through his forbidden contact with Ædrea.

"Do you really believe the secret is safe from Texark, m'Lord?"

"No, it's only possible to minimize their knowledge. They know the genny colony is there. They know it is well armed, and that I have been helping them. I hope that's all they know. I only pray the secret, as you call it, is temporarily safe from the Pope."

The remark caused the monk some surprise. In the first place, nothing was safe from Amen Specklebird, but his surprise was more due to a smell of betrayal about the words. The surprise was duly suppressed, and after some further discussion, the cardinal agreed to see the student, and so Blacktooth departed to seek him out before he began another journey.

"They say the mountains there are wonderfully cool in summer. You get to ride a free horse. You'll meet the family of Jæsis. You'll learn a brand-new skill."

"Like what?"

"Keeping your mouth shut?"

"What use is that?"

"You'll live longer as a secret agent."

Aberlott walked with him to the Secretariat. Brownpony was marching out the main entrance. He greeted his assistant, and his young friend by saying to Aberlott, "Student at the college, I'm told. And what do you think of our city and its young ladies?"

Aberlott answered fast, and the monk felt his face grow hot. "Well, when Blacktooth and I walked down past the police station last month, we saw a corpse hung there feet-in-your-face high, with a sign tied to his ankles. Blacktooth read the sign. 'For coitus interruptus' is what it said. I'm afraid of young ladies here."

Brownpony eyed him in mock dismay. "Do you think the Valana police force is a branch of the papacy?"

"Theology is not my strong point, Your Eminence."

"Or is the papacy a part of the police, perhaps?"

"Certainly I had no such idea in mind, m'Lord!" Aberlott was beginning to turn white.

"Of course you did, and you still do. In Texark, the mayorality is part of the police. The cities are quite different in that regard."

Aberlott had flirted with danger and was becoming scared. Brownpony had crowded him into a corner and was pressing him for comment. The joking student was, after all, talking to a Prince of the Church.

"Actually, I think the sign said, 'Hanged for impudence to a prelate.' I beg your pardon, m'Lord."

"I don't have your pardon. Get your own." Brownpony smiled a consoling smile at him, then shook his head at Blacktooth. "Do you really think this man can be trusted?"

"Of course, Your Eminence."

"Everything you need for the journey is ready at the stable. Pick up your papers at the office. Wear mufti until you get to the colony. After Ulad is replaced, and the council is satisfied, your ties to the Secretariat continue only if Cardinal Nauwhat needs you. I am going east to meet Chür Høngan, Hultor Bråm, and a Jackrabbit sharf who is still a stranger to me. No telling how long I'll be away."

"Then what, m'Lord?"

"You are free until you hear from me or Cardinal Nauwhat. *Or your abbot.* Goodbye, Nimmy. God love you."

Blacktooth thought about it later. He had expected to be fired. What astonished the monk most was not his master's tolerance of impudence, or even his offhand approval of Aberlott, but that Aberlott had looked at this one cardinal among cardinals and felt safe in being impudent. The student usually had a good instinct for audience. Aberlott had picked up the aura of Brownpony's nonhostile personality; his personality showed through the red cloth. Blacktooth had seen it before, and knew the aura was deceptive. Brownpony wasted no hostility when he struck. He was never hostile, except for show. He seemed to be anticipating the *now* of things just a moment before they happened, and anticipating with the best expectations. When he expected the best, many people hated not giving it to him.

Others who gave him the worst usually regretted it, without much effort on the cardinal's part. He moved easily among a herd of people, but he seemed more a friendly undercover sheepdog than one of the sheep, even among cardinals most of whom had far outranked him before his consecration. He made himself a safe man, approachable from above or below, or from straight and level.

"What a pope he would make!" was Aberlott's only comment. He looked at Nimmy for confirmation, but the monk was pointedly silent.

CHAPTER 14

Likewise those who have been sent on a journey shall not let the appointed Hours pass by, but shall say the Office by themselves as well as they can, and not neglect to render the task of their service.
—*Saint Benedict's Rule*, Chapter 50

HE WESTERN ROUTE TO NEW JERUSALEM FROM Valana was less clearly defined and proved more difficult to traverse with wheeled vehicles than was the Pope's road to the east, which Blacktooth and Wooshin had traveled with the cardinal in early spring. There were only four wagons, besides the pack mules, but their wheels had to be spoke-levered to help the animals at every draw, especially after a late summer rain. Annual rainfall was sparse, but this was the season for it, and flash floods often rushed through the desert's low places. The eastern road would have been so much easier and faster if the travelers had no reason to avoid other wayfarers. The reason was "security." While they forded a stream, one of the tarp-covered boxes fell from a wagon and broke open. Blacktooth watched Wooshin and Ri's guards scramble to retrieve rifles from the shallow water, while they furtively looked around as if for spies in the juniper scrub. Later, he was unable to avoid learning about handguns and ammunition in the mule packs. When he asked, Elkin told him it was a comparatively small shipment. The receptionist guard at SEEC seemed to be in charge of the expedition, and he let Nimmy know that he came from the covert wing. The party included several mule drivers, Wooshin, Aberlott, Ulad, and the six warriors from the party of late Cardinal Ri.

Ri's men were already skilled as weaponless warriors. By firelight they sparred with each other, and with Wooshin, who was hard-pressed to cope with the foreman among them, his junior by thirty years. They were speaking their own language among themselves, and Wooshin was laughing. "O Axe, please do remind them," Blacktooth called, "that they're supposed to be practicing either 'Mount or Church."

The Axe grunted at them, and they tried haltingly to continue their conversation in Churchspeak. Nimmy suddenly realized they had been talking about him, because he was an exception to what they saw to be the rule here, that monks don't fight, or can't, or won't. Whereas they themselves were Christians with vows, although one of them had a wife back home. When Wooshin explained this to Blacktooth, the monk was astonished.

Ri's guards were a puzzle to him at first. Wooshin had fallen right in with them, and they seemed to understand each other's language well enough when words were accompanied by frenetic gesticulation. On the third day, Blacktooth dared to remind Wooshin again that he was tasked with teaching Churchspeak to the "Yellow Guard," as they had begun to be called around Valana. Wooshin glowered at the reminder, but after a moment explained, not without embarrassment, that Cardinal Ri's men had been trying to convert him to Christianity.

The monk looked at him incredulously.

Axe laughed at his expression. "I don't think you want to hear that argument in Churchspeak. Have you forgotten that they were Cardinal Ri's men?"

"I assumed they were Christian, and I've heard them chanting, but—"

"But you wouldn't expect soldiers to be very religious?"

Nimmy thought about it for a while. His mind caught a chilling glimpse of remembered warriors, his boyhood rapists, in action. "I suppose I'm prejudiced, Axe. The soldiers I've met are often pious, but I never met any warrior except you who seemed to have a spiritual dimension."

"Except me? Do I have a spiritual dimension, Nimmy?"

"You may laugh, but I've thought so. All I really know about you is what you want me to know. Isn't it so, Axe?"

"Well, where these men come from, all monks, even Christians, have a weaponless warrior tradition."

"They're not weaponless now! Are you saying they are monks?"

"Yes, I think you can call them monks. As for the weapons, Ri dispensed them from that rule, and our master extended the dispensation. The order they belong to is Asiatic, and it isn't recognized here. When either Cardinal Brownpony or the Pope understands that they do have religious vows, they will lose their freedom until the Church can decide what to do with them. They are not anxious to go home, but their vows are similar to yours. They want to be free to form a community, but they've been afraid to ask. That's why they want and need to learn Churchspeak as soon as possible. You don't need to nag us about that. I suggested to the cardinal they stay awhile at Leibowitz Abbey. There, they could wear their habits and learn your liturgy. Would they be welcome?"

"I am not the one to speak for Abbot Jarad Cardinal Kendemin." He fought bitterness for a moment, but went on: "You've read the Rule of Saint Benedict, Axe. The Brothers of Leibowitz still honor most of that rule, which means that they must offer hospitality to anybody who comes to them, as if he were Christ wandering in from the desert. But I'm not suggesting that Ri's men take advantage of that rule."

"No, of course you wouldn't want the abbot to know you suggested it by suggesting against it," Wooshin said sourly. "But you're right about their learning Churchspeak. I'll drill them more. If they go to Leibowitz Abbey, it will not be at your suggestion, but the cardinal's which he already made."

"All right. I hereby forget it, although I would like to know about their Order."

"They know that I taught you to fight a little, and they want to know if other monks of your Order would be allowed to learn weaponless combat, or would it be against rules?"

"Well, there is no rule, as long as it's for sport or exercise. We have occasional ball games outside the walls, those of us whose jobs don't involve physical labor." He laughed. "But if you can imagine getting the Lord Abbot's permission to train fighters!"

"I know. It's too bad. Their Order has an interesting tradition. If they are to remain there, they would like to form a community, or merge with one."

Later he confessed to Blacktooth, "You know, Nimmy, my people out on the coast were refugees from these Asian Christians several generations ago. Cardinal Ri was a super-Benefez in his own country. These Christians were conquerors. My people were the losers, and crossed the ocean."

Nimmy looked at the executioner as if seeing him for the first time. "Mine were the losers too," he said. "We should be spiritual brothers."

A sharp glance from Axe told him this intimacy was getting too thick. He wheeled his mount around and rode back toward the guards and the wagon. Once again, Nimmy realized that Axe did not fully trust him since he had disobeyed the cardinal.

Wooshin had become strange to him again, but he knew the estrangement lay within himself. The news, conveyed by a possibly ironic Wooshin, that the Yellow Guard was trying to convert him to their Christianity—that news discomfited him. Why had he and his fellow monks ignored Wooshin's religion, if he had any? Axe had come to Mass habitually, but never received communion. His dedication and loyalty had a spiritual quality, as did his attitude toward death. He would have made a good monk, Nimmy thought. But the Albertian Order of Leibowitz was never devoted to the conversion of the heathen. That was why. It was against the rules. Monks were free to answer a guest's religious questions, but the Axe never asked any. Now these strange men wanted to bring him into their religious brotherhood. The Order of Leibowitz had missed its chance to have, besides its electric chair, a warrior monk and executioner.

Wooshin's new friends in the Yellow Guard had learned of his years as a headsman for the Hannegans, Filpeo Harq and his predecessor. Nimmy had heard them talking, understood very little of their mixed dialect except when they practiced Churchspeak, but could tell that the aliens were both sympathetic and amused, and he sensed that the Axe came away from the conversation both irritated and relieved. It seemed to Nimmy that Wooshin had succumbed to an attack of almost Christian guilt about his old job, and the warriors were apparently trying to cure him of it by conversion. The Axe obviously missed the cardinal as Blacktooth did; and the monk wondered who was now acting as Brownpony's bodyguard after the attempted assassination. Ri's men had all been loaned by the new Vicar Apostolic to SEEC's clandestine wing, once they had learned to communicate a little in Rockymount, but here they were: far from their new master, and as lost as Nimmy himself.

The monk tried to make religion his only concern again, at least for the duration of the trip, but the effort gradually failed, and the effect of the failure was that he became so irritable he went for three days without even attempting to pray, meditate, or read the canonical hours. His mind, affected by periods of heat exhaustion, kept reaching out to grasp at Jarad, Brownpony, Ædrea, Holy Madness, or the Pope, and to rehearse imaginary dialogues with them, to shake sense into them. Especially Ædrea. This was self-indulgence, self-absorption, vanity, and ego. Because he could not pacify his mind internally, he finally turned outward and tried to stay busy and available for conversation with even Aberlott.

The group of travelers had taken on an almost military structure of command under Elkin, with Wooshin and Ulad as lieutenants. By the route they were to take, there was danger neither from Texark agents nor from motherless Nomads, although drifting outlaws of every stripe occasionally wandered through the arid land, and there was always the possibility of hostile confrontation. The terrain was rougher than that which Blacktooth had encountered on his first visit to Valana. There was no fixed road; only passes through mountainous areas were clearly defined. The group carried conventional arms, besides those carried by pack mules and in the wagons, but they met no one except a wizened old man who joined them one night after sundown, having wandered in behind them from the direction of Valana. The advent of the old man was the occasion of an argument among those concerned with secrecy and security, but the old fellow seemed half dead, and he was headed toward New Jerusalem anyway. Ulad claimed that he had seen him before. "He's been to New Jerusalem," said the giant. "Magister Dion hired him once, so he knows about us."

"Hired him? For what?"

"He can make it rain, for silver."

"Is he any good?"

"It rained, but not much. Dion paid him, but not much."

"He knows the town, then, but does he know about our baggage?" Elkin wondered. "He's already seen us, so he must come with us. If he behaves himself, he's a guest. If he tries to leave, he's a prisoner, until we get where we're going."

Nevertheless, the old man refused to join them at first, and might have been arrested and bound to one of the wagons if he had not changed his mind upon learning that Blacktooth was a monk of Saint Leibowitz, a fact that seemed to amuse him greatly. He teased the monk about not wearing a habit while still wearing his rosary around his waist. Nimmy tried to avoid conversation with the old man, who seemed to know more about Leibowitz Abbey than seemed probable. The ancient stranger, after a few attempts to talk, shrugged at the monk's reticence, perhaps attributing it to religious silence, but he continued to snipe at him occasionally as if to keep in practice.

He called himself a pilgrim but not a Christian. He wore tattered garments of hemp, coarsely woven, and he carried his belongings in a bag tied to the end of his staff. He protected his pate from the sun with a curiously embroidered skullcap which he called a "yarmulke." Although defensive and suspicious at first, he seemed harmless enough and became talkative after the first day. Nimmy could not believe that Brownpony's enemies would send such a decrepit fellow as a spy. Elkin seemed to agree, for besides allowing him to ride an extra mule, the security man put him on one of the wagons after he complained of being saddle sore, even though he had to sit on a crate of weapons.

He told them he was a Jew and a tentmaker among other things. He was obviously one of those wanderers who peddled his skills as a rainmaker in areas of low rainfall. This old Jew had several useful skills and thus several sources of income. For fifteen pios, he would pull a tooth; for eight, he would scrape the incrustation from the rest of your teeth and scrub them well with talc. Root canals were negotiable. He contracted as a rainmaker, and if he made no rain in a week, he got no pay beyond his week's room and board; if rain came, he received whatever the petitioners could, in his opinion, afford. His advice in every imaginable matter was freely given to whoever would listen to him, and sometimes imposed upon whoever would not.

Blacktooth tried to use the journey for privacy and silence, insofar as his wish to be polite survived its many trials. But the old Jew would not let him be, and he asked all sorts of questions about an Abbot Jerome, who, to the best of Nimmy's recollection, had died seventy years ago at an advanced age, and yet this old man claimed he had been Jerome's friend, Benjamin.

"You must be nearly a hundred years old," Nimmy said skeptically. "Or maybe even more."

"Hmm-hnn! I would have to be, wouldn't I?"

Claims to extraordinary longevity arose in the Valley of the Misborn, but the old pilgrim was not an obvious glep. Still, he had been admitted to the secret nation in the Suckamints, had been allowed to leave again, and was not going back. Magister Dion must have looked into his background. But if he was a spook himself, Ulad should know. Ulad, however, seemed to regard the old Jew as disreputable, at least as a rainmaker. That the Suckamint Mountains were a refuge for the misborn was widely known within the Church, but the nature of the heart of the colony as a nation of spooks was obscured by the fact that gleps like Shard and his family inhabited the surrounding foothills, not admitted to full citizenship, but protected by the well-armed central colony from outlaws, loose Nomads, and Texark agents. Wanderers usually shied away from the area, as they shied away from Misborn Valley, and those who did try to enter were killed or driven away.

"And what business would a monk of Saint Leibowitz have in New Babel," the old man asked. "Especially a monk in disgrace."

"Who told you that?" Nimmy looked at him sharply, surprised that gossip had already passed on to this total stranger. Who in the party knew of his status? Well, they all did. Wooshin, Elkin, Aberlott, everybody. Nevertheless, he was embarrassed that his private life was open knowledge.

"I am merely the bearer of a message from a cardinal to the community. Why do you call it New Babel?"

"Why do you call it New Jerusalem?"

"It is theirs to name, and they named it so. Where did you come from on your way to New Babel?"

"From Valana, the same as you."

"And what were you doing in Valana, praying for rain?"

"I went to see my old friend Amen Specklebird, but they would not let me in, and besides—he's not the One."

"Which one is that?"

The old Jew shrugged. "Who knows?" was all that he said.

Ulad the giant, whom Blacktooth had first assessed as a dangerous brute and a lunatic, became almost a playful child during the expedition to the Suckamint Mountains. The ugly side of his character apparently arose from his initial mistrust of any human being except a genny, but the mistrust subsided as they all became better acquainted during the long ride south.

On the journey, Nimmy lost his temper once, but not with the old pilgrim. It was only Aberlott, thank God. But, then, he lost it again! with the Abbot Jarad Cardinal Kendemin, in absentia, and really in a daydream. There was something beautiful about the mental image of his own hands grasping Jarad's throat, thumbs against the windpipe, although he always stopped the strangulation before the old geezer lost consciousness. Evil could be lovely, just lovely. This he knew. It was hard to try to tell a confessor how good sin can feel; it made the priest angry, as if the penitent were trying to force him to enjoy such putrid blackguardy. He felt his mind was slipping away from reality of late, and Wooshin caught him muttering blasphemously to himself as they rode the trail. He almost started out of the saddle when Axe whacked him on the back to bring him out of it. So much had happened to him in so few months, and none of it seemed real, and sometimes he felt he was going mad. He daydreamed, when he should be praying, then swore at himself under his breath.

"Stay busy, Brother" was the Axe's advice.

Staying busy was not very hard. Making and breaking camp every day took time and work. The ideal day involved eleven hours of traveling through the pitiless lands in summer, then thirteen hours packing, unpacking, seeing to the animals, hunting, cooking, eating, cleaning up, mending, repairing, and finally sleeping. Eleven hours traveling, with luck. Most days it was only ten.

On the seventh day, Ulad, Wooshin, and Elkin conferred and decided that the train with its valuable cargo would be just as well protected without Blacktooth, Aberlott, Ulad, and Elkin, who could ride on ahead of the baggage and be in New Jerusalem in half the time. Wooshin and Ri's warriors would stay with the mule drivers to fight off any outlaws or desert drifters. The only question was about the safety of the party riding ahead, but Ulad and Elkin were soldiers, and Blacktooth had been taught to fight by Wooshin.

The old Jew was allowed to come with the advance riders, and so was Aberlott, for both were useless if a need arose to defend the ordnance against seizure by enemies or outlaws. Aberlott attributed Blacktooth's recent black moods to madness. "I think you're going crazy," the student said to him the first morning as they emerged from their bedrolls. "You talked all night in your sleep, although you won't talk to anybody else by daylight."

"What did I talk about?"

"A girl with a very small hole."

"What girl?"

"One with a very small hole. You called it a hole in the universe. You're going crazy, Nimmy."

"Holes? Did I call you an asshole, perhaps?" But he saw that Aberlott was serious, and he added, "Well, I was dreaming. But maybe I am going a little crazy. I've failed at two jobs. I guess I need somebody to tell me what to do. I don't know how to get along without an uncle or an abbot or a cardinal."

"Or a pope? Once you mentioned Amen Specklebird in your sleep."

At last the advance party of five came to the western slopes of the Suckamint Mountains. Elkin was convinced they had gained three days on the remainder of the party with the pack mules and wagons. The slopes were steeper here than on the east side of the range near Shard's place, and they had hardly begun to climb before a volley of arrows and stones struck the ground only a few paces ahead. They stopped immediately. Three gleps with bows and one with a musket stood atop the cliff, glaring down at them in the noonday sun. Ulad swore blasphemies at them and identified himself and their mission. The gleps withdrew.

"Scarecrow Alley," the old Jew scoffed. "They would be better off and safer back home in the Valley."

"Perhaps. There are people in the Valley who believe Christ will come again as one of them," Ulad told them as they rode up the rocky trail.

"You mean he will be born as one of them?" Blacktooth asked.

"Yes."

"But that's not the way it's supposed to happen," said Aberlott. "He will be seen coming on the clouds."

"But he has to be born again before he is seen coming."

"That's not what it says."

"Does it say otherwise?"

"I guess not."

Blacktooth remained silent. The old Jew laughed scornfully at them all.

When they came to a small plateau, Elkin asked Ulad how many hours' journey remained until they reached the heart of the community.

"At least eight hours," the giant said.

The road leading into the mountains at that place was flanked by a deep ravine on the north and on the south by a few flat acres at the foot of a mesa. As darkness was approaching, Elkin decided to make camp here, a decision which Ulad resisted first by describing the land as haunted, then as populated by cougars. A vote was taken, and the giant was overruled.

"Just stay away from those woods, then," Ulad insisted.

They passed a peaceful night, with each man taking his turn at being awake to keep the fire burning. There were neither cougars nor ghosts. It fell to Blacktooth to take the last shift, and the sky became luminous with dawn as the shift ended.

Before waking the others, he descended into the wooded ravine for a bucket of water. Beyond the trees, he found himself on a beach in a boneyard. There was a ten-pace width of sand beside the creek where floodwaters visited the place every spring, and the sand was full of small human bones washed here from some upstream disposal site. New Jerusalem produced its share of monsters, then, and its claim of returning such children to the Watchitah Nation was a lie. Not all the bones were those of newborns. One half-buried skull seemed that of a child of five. Dead kids, a blight inherited from the Great Civilization. There were places like that on the Plains. Nimmy was not shocked, but decided against filling his bucket. There was still drinking water in the canteens. Shaving and washing could wait.

Halfway up the slope, he met somebody coming down very fast. Ulad skidded to a stop, spraying the monk with dirt and gravel.

"What were you doing down there?" he demanded.

"Nothing, as it turns out." Nimmy patted the empty bucket. Ulad grabbed his arm.

"There was an epidemic two years ago," he said. "Many children died."

"I understand," Nimmy said evenly and managed to detach his arm from the other's grip. Ulad let him go. What Nimmy understood was that communities all over the continent fell victim to such epidemics every few years. Often all the victims died in the same week, and all were incredibly glep or worse. When Nimmy later mentioned it to the old Jew, the pilgrim named the epidemic disease "Genny Passover."

"So much for what you said about New Jerusalem and its policy of returning gleps to the Valley," said Aberlott.

Blacktooth shrugged. What he knew of New Jerusalem, he had heard from Ædrea. Dead babies downstream of a village was more of a rule than an exception. That was just it. New Jerusalem was supposed to be the exception.

The climb into the mountains carried them into long U-turns around the sides of a valley or a mountain, and in places the trail was obscured by landslides which the drivers of the mule train would have to remove to gain passage. Great conifers rose above them on the mountainsides. Soon there were new signs of habitation, but the people who came out to eye the travelers were apparently normal. The few glep families lived on the periphery of the sprawling colony, as Shard and Tempus lived on the eastern slope of the same mountain range. But here there were real farms, although the guardian gleps inhabited the less fertile land. The mountain peaks attracted rain and snow, and the streams flowed continuously after the thaw. In the passes and valleys, beside the streams grew orchards of apples, cherries, pears, and peaches. The crops were ripe now in late summer, and peddlers hawked their produce from donkey carts parked in the community centers, of which there were several. Whole carcasses of beef, mutton, and venison were hung from poles and were cut to order for women shopping. Dusty men with faces darkened by soot and blasting powder walked home from the mines in the late afternoon.

The capitol, so called, was a three-story building of stone and mortar with, on the ground floor, a kitchen and communal dining hall divided into a large room for dirty miners and a smaller one for government workers and guests. The second floor, Nimmy was told, housed Mayor Dion's office and a council room where a small body of legislators met weekly to approve or disapprove administrative decisions. There were only a dozen or so buildings in the center of town, while residences and barns—mostly log structures built on stone foundations—were scattered throughout the mountains.

Blacktooth's perception of the country was colored by what Ædrea had told him, but the baby boneyard had aroused his suspicions. He was relieved when Ulad, who had ridden ahead into the heart of the community, rejoined them to say that Mayor Dion was away in another part of the mountains, and would not return until the next afternoon. Aberlott's meeting with the family of Jæsis was also postponed until tomorrow. He, with Blacktooth, Elkin, and the old Jew, would spend the night in a guesthouse, which already housed one visitor from outside the colony, who came out to meet them with a wide smile. Blacktooth, who first gasped in surprise, knelt to kiss the ring of Chuntar Cardinal Hadala, Vicar Apostolic to the Watchitah Nation.

"And how is Cardinal Brownpony?" asked the Bishop of the Misborn.

"Well when I saw him last, Your Eminence. I believe he is with Chür Høngan and the other Nomad leaders on the Plains."

"Yes, I knew of his plans. I suppose you are quite surprised that I am here?"

"Yes, but I should have realized that you would have a special relationship with New Jerusalem, which was colonized from your diocese."

"Vicariate," Hadala corrected him. "Well, you have come just in time to unpack and wash up for dinner. I'll see you then."

They followed Ulad to their assigned quarters. Hadala's presence reawakened Nimmy's shame for his disobedience to his own cardinal, but he weighed it against his recent perception of Brownpony as subverting the papacy, as disloyal to Papa Specklebird, and if not the author of the conspiracy then a promoter of an earlier plan. The plan was obviously to assure the Valanan Church some military power independent of Nomad alliances. Blacktooth decided nothing was necessarily wrong with this, except that the plan involved concealment from

the Pope. Would Amen Specklebird necessarily disapprove the ownership by the Church of arms? Probably, was Nimmy's guess. Was it his
duty to tell? He tried to think of a way to determine whether Chuntar
Cardinal Hadala was already privy to the secret, but decided he had
only to watch the cardinal carefully when Axe and the Yellow Guard
arrived with the weapons.

That night at dinner, however, the cardinal invited Ulad and
Elkin to share his table, well across the room from where Blacktooth,
Aberlott, and the old Jew dined with several clerks from Mayor Dion's
office. Watching the cardinal carefully would be a waste of time. That
he used dinner for consultations with Ulad and SEEC's covert agent
told him enough. He decided to enjoy the venison, potatoes, and fresh
fruit, while trying to understand the colony better by listening to
Aberlott banter with the clerks. He learned little that he did not know.
They described how New Jerusalem had grown by immigration from
the Valley.

Watchit-Ol'zarkia, the name claimed by the mountainous region
which, north of Texark, had grown into a ghetto nation from the original Valley of the Misborn, was surrounded by frontier guards of both
Church and State, but the border was a sieve by night for escapees
traveling without baggage, and escape by spooks was commonplace.
Some escapes were mere escapades, and the fugitives returned to their
homes after a few days or weeks abroad, and of course they usually
came back richer than they left. Men left their mountain homes to
steal or work at temporary jobs in the city. Women left for the same
reasons, but also sometimes to get pregnant by farmboys with supposedly healthy genes. However, some escapees never came back, and
while there were a few small colonies of spooks in the east, the isolation of New Jerusalem in the Suckamint Range, its resources and natural defenses, made it the largest congregation of genetically dubious
persons outside the Valley, and most appealing as a sanctuary for permanent fugitives. Especially in the years since the conquest, the population had grown rapidly because under imperial dominance the
Jackrabbit Horde was no longer a threat to travelers through the Province, and it was only necessary to evade Texark outposts and local
militia.

"We can defend our mountains," the chief clerk explained after
dinner, when he walked Blacktooth back to his quarters, "but against
Texark we have no offensive weapon except terror. Spooks become
good at infiltration. We have people in the army and the Church in
Texark. We have people in Valana as well as New Rome. If they abuse
our people in Watchitah, we respond with terror."

Nimmy paused and looked around. No one was observing or listening, and the chief clerk seemed more inclined to talk outside the dining hall.

"Was it your men who tried to kill the cardinal and me?" the monk asked.

The official sighed. "I cannot be sure. The order did not come from here. Our people denied it, naturally. Rational men sometimes go crazy under cover.

"Jæsis was to become a priest, before he failed at the university. We have others. Terror is possible. When the time comes, we may use it, although the Church will condemn us, including our friend Brownpony, for all I know. I know no more about Cardinal Brownpony's plans than you do. Cardinal Hadala probably knows, but it may be that there is no long-range plan. I have watched Magister Dion play chess with your cardinal when Dion was in Valana. He won as many games as he lost. He looks ahead a few moves, but there can be no long-range plan in chess. He piles up arms here, for us and for others. We can't know who the others are, but we presume there will be Nomads. He makes alliances with all nations who fear Texark. He has allies east of the Great River and south of the Brave River. He seems to me like a man playing for territory in chess. He does not take any pieces yet. He piles up power."

Nimmy found the clerk's openness surprising. Perhaps Brownpony was not as well liked here as he had supposed. The colony had its agenda, and Brownpony had his own. The monk changed the subject: "Can you tell me the whereabouts of your former agent to Valana?"

"And who would that be?"

"Her name is Ædrea, daughter of Shard."

The clerk opened his mouth, then snapped it closed, frowned at Blacktooth, and replied in a hesitant voice, "I have said too much. Here are your quarters. I have to go now." He turned on his heels and walked back toward the stone building.

That night Blacktooth dreamed he was back at the monastery. No one looked at or spoke to him, and he wondered if this were part of excommunication, this being shunned. But "shunned" was not quite the word for it. He stood directly in Prior Olshuen's path, head slightly bowed, waiting. When the prior's sandals advanced rapidly into his vision, he leaped aside to evade a collision. Olshuen would have walked right into him. Or through him, as if he were a ghost. He went outside to the cemetery and stood by the open grave.

It was the same open grave, and in the same place, as when he left in early spring. There was always an open grave at the Monastery of Saint Leibowitz in the Desert, even if no one was ill. No one had died, then, since the saintly Brother Mulestar. It still awaited its next occupant. The lip of the hole was protected by thatch all around, pointing inward so that drops of rain would follow the straws and drip into the hole instead of eroding the lip. When necessary, a monk would descend into the grave with a shovel and remove any earth which had fallen since the last cleaning. There were seven penitential occasions every year when the Brothers formed a procession that led to the grave. There they stood looking down for some time while the sun moved westward into the shadows of that yellowish adobe hole. A not-thing was that hole, like the soul itself, a not-thing at the center of the all. Blacktooth did not like this hole or this ceremony of medita-tion, although some Brothers found it to leave the mind wonderfully focused for at least the rest of that day.

Now the straw thatch appeared damp. As he watched, the grave stopped looking like a grave. As he stared, he saw that the straw was pubic straw, and the hole was not a grave. He shook his head, and, thinking of Ædrea, started to go see the abbot, to tell him that the grave was now a cunt, but then he heard a baby crying. There was a baby in the hole, and he went to look. It was covered with patches of fur, and had no hands: obviously misborn. A genny. His own son?

He heard himself making strangling sounds, then felt a sharp slap on the back of his neck. He came out of the dream-trance and Aberlott was sitting beside him. The student had stayed quite aware of the change in Blacktooth's state of mind and body since the depar-ture from Valana. His daylight fantasies had begun to acquire the quality of nightmare. "The Devil is on my back," Nimmy said.

Blacktooth's sense that the world is a weird place was stirred again when he met a Nomad, Önmu Kun, who returned with Mayor Dion and his party the following day. It was not until he spoke Ol'zark with an accent that Nimmy recognized him as a Nomad. That he was Jackrabbit was apparent from his clothing, which was cloth, his legs, which were not bowed by growing up in the saddle, and his skin color, which was not much burned by the sun. Because of diet, the present generation of Jackrabbit Nomads were shorter than both their ances-tors and the wild Nomads of today. It was obvious Kun was present as an unofficial spokesman for his horde to this *Parva Civitas* of New Jerusalem, which was evidently becoming an arsenal for all the chil-dren of Empty Sky and the Wild Horse Woman. Nimmy approached him and spoke Nomadic, shifting to a Southern dialect. Kun grinned broadly and they exchanged pleasantries and bits of life histories. They discussed the meeting on the Plains of the Weejus and Bear Spirit people from all the hordes, and Nimmy surprised and delighted him with the news that Cardinal Brownpony was now Vicar Apostolic to the Plains, including the south, pervaded as it was by clergy from Texark. When the monk asked Önmu Kun about his business in New Jerusalem, the monk was gruffly told to mind his own. The Nomad shrugged off his apologies.

"Perhaps your position as the cardinal's former secretary entitles you to ask, but I am unable to answer." To soften the rejection, he then told a dirty Jackrabbit joke about a Weejus woman, the Bishop of Texark, and a long-sought erection.

Aberlott was sent to see the family of Jæsis, and Blacktooth did not see him again in New Jerusalem. No one would talk to him about Ædrea, or even admit an acquaintance with her. As for the Mayor, he did not send for the monk until the day after the party of warriors arrived with mules, wagons, and guns, and a transaction was completed between Elkin and the *Civitas*. Every night the monk dreamed wild dreams about the blond and blue-eyed imp with an impassable gateway. The dreams frightened him.

The dreams also prepared him for the first meeting with Mayor Dion, who came directly to the point. "We know why you are here, Brother St. George," he said gently. "We took insult when the Secretary refused to deal with the agents we designated. We suspected that the killing of our Jæsis was a betrayal, too. But then we were persuaded by Shard's Ædrea that we had been mistaken. She took full responsibility. You need not explain or apologize. A new representative will hereafter contact the Secretariat for us. You will meet him later today. Now do you have any other messages for us?"

Blacktooth looked down for a moment, then up into Dion's gray eyes. "Only my own apology, Magister. Ædrea is not at fault. The fault was mine. Even the cardinal knows that. Ædrea is innocent. Where is she, and may I see her?"

The gray eyes watched him closely. Finally the Magister said, "I must tell you that Shard's Ædrea is dead." He watched the monk again for a moment, then beckoned a guard. "You! Don't let him fall!" then said to another, "Get the monk some brandy, the peach is strongest."

Blacktooth lowered his face into his hands. "How did she die?" he asked at last.

"There was a miscarriage. Something went wrong. As you know, they live way down by the Pope's highway, and by the time our physician got there, she had lost too much blood. So I am told."

The Magister briefly watched his grief, then quietly left the room, after whispering to Elkin, "We'll meet again here tomorrow."

When he had gone through all the motions, and his duties as an emissary were ended, Blacktooth went to confession at the local church, and fasted for three days in constant prayer for his love and her lost child. To cherish grief was as bad as to cherish anything: lust, triumph, or, as Specklebird would say, as bad as cherishing Jesus. He then spent several days in the city's library. When grief overwhelmed him, he paused in his study of the history of the colony, and studied the grief, pressing it firmly down into his abdomen from the diaphragm, then continued to peruse some of the private correspondence between early colonists and their relatives in the Watchitah Nation. He was looking for anything that would tell him about Shard's people, or their ancestors. Evidently, they were latecomers, as they claimed to be, and of no historical interest to the beautiful inhabitants of these mountains, bristling with guns, and surrounded by their ugly first line of defense. Why did not the glep Helots of those scarecrow alleys rebel against the well-armed Spartan spooks? Perhaps because those Spartans were relatives of men like Shard, and Shard was proud of his Ædrea. There was segregation here, but no visible repression. Only the glep's genes were unwanted.

He found out that the penalty for sexual union between a citizen of the Res Publica Jerusalem Nova and a glep was death for the citizen and the offspring, if any. There were people in New Jerusalem with special talents. Marriages were made by contract between families, and ratified by the Magisterium. People were bred like animals, but people throughout recorded history had bred not only slaves, but sons and daughters like animals. The only thing new here was the criteria by which the genetic potential of such unions was judged, whereas the historical matchmaker was usually interested in combinations of wealth. Nimmy felt vaguely that the criteria were not very different from what the Mayor of Texark would have chosen. But here you grew up a healthy citizen, with special talents, or went to the boneyard of infants, the one they had passed the morning after that night in the foothills. Maybe some glep children of citizens were returned to the Watchitah Nation, as Ædrea had said, but it was a long dangerous trip back to the Valley.

Having given much thought to his doubtful future, he decided that upon completion of his rather unimportant mission here, he would return to the world through Leibowitz Abbey because Ri's yellow monastic warriors wanted to go there, while Wooshin himself had been ordered back to Valana. Nimmy had his own reasons for going as a guide for the warriors. First, he suspected Brownpony had sent him here to get rid of him, and he no longer trusted Cardinals Brownpony, Nauwhat, and Hadala. He wanted to stay clear of any conspiracy, and a conspiracy was anything to which Pope Amen was not privy. His conscience and his relations with God were in need of repair as well. He wanted to confess to Jarad, and Jarad owed him a hearing. He would not be thrown out, but he knew he would not be welcome to stay beyond necessity. He intended that nobody think he was there as a suppliant, but Jarad would try to make him feel like one.

When Blacktooth and the party of warriors were packing gear and saddling horses for the trip, they were joined by Önmu Kun, who was driving a wagon, obviously loaded with arms.

"You can't take that to the abbey," Nimmy told him.

"Who said I'm going to the abbey?" said the Jackrabbit Nomad, and followed the party of riders eastward. The old Jew who called himself Benjamin followed them for a short distance, but changed his mind. "Tell the abbot I shall visit him before winter."

Nimmy promised to deliver the message.

He badly wanted to visit Arch Hollow on the way out of the mountains, despite the Mayor's warning, but as soon as Shard saw him, he ran for a gun. The guards fired a warning shot over Shard's head; then one of them popped the rump of Blacktooth's mount with his crop, and yelled, pointing a direction of retreat. They galloped past the homestead and down the road which led east to the papal highway. Nimmy was not allowed to weep at her grave.

As soon as they came to the Pope's Highway, the Jackrabbit Nomad bade Blacktooth farewell, and announced his intention to leave the trail and travel cross-country to the southeast. This would take him into a kind of no-man's-land where the border of the imperial province was in dispute.

"Aren't you worried about Texark agents?" Nimmy asked.

"I'll be meeting my customers tonight," Önmu Kun said with a grin. "They will then go home, and I back to New Jerusalem."

They parted after exchanging the Jackrabbit peace sign. Nimmy decided that Kun was simply a gunrunner for his captive horde. But he had seen the weapons in the wagon and noticed that they were not of the most advanced design—a precaution against their possible seizure by imperial forces.

·   ·   ·

On the trip to the abbey, the Yellow Guard's Foreman, whose name was Jing-U-Wan, cautiously questioned Blacktooth about the Order of Leibowitz, and then explained his own.

"The Order of Saint Peter's Sword has two traditions. One is purely Christian. Our creed is not much different from yours. Our canonical prayers are not identical, but quite similar. We use less from the Psalms, and there is more silent meditation. In our work, people expected us to do what non-Christian monks had always done in that country. Outside the chapter house we work in the fields and we beg only when we travel. We maintain a weaponless warrior tradition, because the Tanters monks had always done so. It was a necessity. In our history, the unarmed victim of a robbery was considered negligent for going about without a gun, and he had to pay for any police action against the robber. Unarmed monks had to be skillful with feet and fist."

"But you carry arms now."

"The rule is dispensed when a monk's job requires it. When the master died, we talked about going unarmed, but the master is at the edge of war."

It took Blacktooth a moment to realize that second master the man referred to was Cardinal Brownpony. "What makes you say he is at the edge of war?" he asked.

The man paused. Being cautious. "In a sense, we are always at war." It was a generality to get rid of the subject.

Nimmy did not pursue it.

He had dreamed about the open grave at the abbey, and it was the first place they visited after exchanging greetings with the gatekeeper, because the gatekeeper pointed them toward it without breaking his silence. To Nimmy's surprise, the open grave had been moved. The old one was recently filled, and a new wooden cross bore the name of the grave's occupant:

HIC JACET JARADUS CARDINALIS KENDEMIN, ABBAS. The date of death was two weeks old.

"Brother St. George," a familiar voice called out to him.

He turned to see Prior Olshuen approaching. He was looking with astonishment at the Yellow Guard, which bristled with swords. The prior was in mourning. The whole monastery was in mourning. Blacktooth went to the chapel to pray sterile prayers for his mistakes, but it felt like self-indulgence. After a while, he went with mounting dread to seek a conference with the prior.

◆   ◆   ◆

*It was a truly massive hemorrhage. While offering Mass
on a Wednesday morning, Abbot Jarad, having consecrated
the bread and the wine, turned to his community in choir and
began to say the "Ecce agnus dei" when he turned white,
emitted a strangled yowl, and fell down the sanctuary steps
with a great crash and a ringing of brass chalice and paten on
the stone floor. "Body and blood all over the pavement," said
Brother Wren. The Cardinal Abbot of Saint Leibowitz died
without regaining consciousness.*

◆   ◆   ◆

CHAPTER 15

> And let the Abbot be sure that any lack of
> profit the master of the house may find in
> the sheep will be laid to the blame of the
> shepherd.
> —*Saint Benedict's Rule*. Chapter 2

 Y THE TIME NEWS OF ABBOT JARAD'S DEATH
reached Valana from the Texark tele-
graph terminal, the Holy See and most
of the Curia had already departed in the
direction of New Rome, while Cardinal
Brownpony had taken the more northerly
route to the sacred meeting place for the
Weejus and Bear Spirit shamans. The
message went first, of course, to the Sa-
cred Congregation for Religious, whose presiding cardinal had gone
with the Pope. His vicar promptly notified SEEC and the Secretariat
of State. Cardinal Nauwhat at SEEC was one of the few cardinals who
lingered in Valana, and he promptly sent messengers to chase after
Brownpony and the Pope, but they had been gone for some days and
would not be easy to find on trackless grasslands. Had Nauwhat sent
the message with a Nomad skilled in distance signaling, it might have
arrived before those to whom it was addressed, but Nauwhat had not

inherited Brownpony's Nomad connections with Brownpony's office, and the messengers would have to wander for a time.

The 6th of September 3244 was a Tuesday. The moon was five days beyond first quarter, and arose well before sundown. The Wilddog's lookouts who watched from the boundaries of the settlement at the "Navel of the World," the breeding pit of the *Høngin Fujæ Vurn*, saw at last a tiny plume of dust on the horizon. A lone rider waved his arms in a Nomad signal meaning "Church," and repeated it until he knew he had been seen, and was therefore recognized as the expected guest from Valana. But alone?

Father Ombroz was astonished, for he had expected the cardinal to be accompanied by his young secretary and at least one familiar bodyguard. He immediately sent for Oxsho, his young acolyte and most recent student, a warrior who was remotely related to Chür Høngan, and who had served at the priest's Masses for three years now.

"I can't go to meet him, because of the funeral," he told the young man. "I want you to stop him before he gets much closer, and warn him of the news. Treat him as you would treat a great uncle, with utmost respect. But you must tell him things he will not want to hear. Hurry, before he gets too close to camp. Try to stay on low ground, or behind a rise. Enemies will be watching. Remember to mention what is said of his mother, whether it is true or not."

"Certainly, Father," said Oxsho, and immediately rode out of the encampment. The youth was as surprised as his master to see that the new Vicar Apostolic had come alone, with a bedroll and a musket, wearing only a red skullcap—easily concealable—to distinguish himself from any other citizen trespassing on Nomad land. The young acolyte had too many things to say to give the cardinal an opening through an exchange of pleasantries. Still staring straight at Brownpony's apostolic ring after kissing it, he began listing the items in the Wilddog news. He seemed ill at ease, and did not directly meet the cardinal's curious gaze.

"Bearcub's father died last night. The sharf is dead. The Mare here is a widow again. The funeral is tonight. It was a ritual death." His glance flickered up to Brownpony's face to make sure he understood the word "ritual" in this context. A slight wince from the cardinal revealed his comprehension. "But there was much argument among the Bear Spirit and the Weejus. The slaughtering festival would be on Friday, when the moon is full."

"Would be? What does that mean?"

"They postponed it. It lasts several days, and it was about to begin. A postponement of so holy a celebration is without precedent, but it was inappropriate for the Great Uncle to be, uh, to *die*, while cattle are being slaughtered. And, uh, you know, the feast."

"I see. Go on."

"The funeral will be tonight. Much has happened, m'Lord. A representative from the Church in Texark is here: Monsignor Sanual. An observer from Benefez, but also a spokesman. He ordered Father Ombroz on behalf of the Archbishop to return to his order in New Rome . . ."

Brownpony laughed. "I can imagine how the good father responded. Well, as his new Vicar Apostolic, I shall order him to stay. I am very sorry to know that Granduncle Brokenfoot is dead. Your teacher gave him the last sacrament, of course?"

Ombroz's acolyte stared at him for a moment, as if not comprehending, and resumed his list. "The Lord Chür Høngan thinks he has located your mother. He said to tell you she is on her way to this place. He cannot be sure. For that and various other reasons, the desire of Kindly Light, the Grasshopper sharf, to see you spend the night in the devil-woman's breeding pit is probably going to be frustrated. His arrogance does not sit well with the Weejus."

"I may very well spend a night there anyway, whether Hultor Bråm wants it or not."

The young Nomad seemed alarmed. "It is a terrible place, m'Lord. Many have died there."

"Men do die, everywhere."

"She slays anyone she rejects."

"Are you not a Christian?"

"Yes, but she is not!"

"Perhaps I can convert her."

Oxsho showed great consternation. "The *Høngin Fujæ Vurn*—"

Brownpony cut him off. "Of course I would not try. But how else would I prove my right to rule over your churches? Monsignor Sanual may join me, if he pleases."

The young Nomad giggled. "I think he would wet his cassock."

"Tell me, what makes Holy Madness think my mother is alive?"

"I know only what Father Ombroz said—that the Sisters who raised you spoke only the Jackrabbit dialect, and wrongly translated her family name."

"So I am perhaps not a *brown pony*?"

"There is a Wilddog family name that means a 'sorrel colt.' But in Jackrabbit—" He shrugged.

"What do you know about her?"

"Only gossip, m'Lord. She has royal blood, but her small family is neither wealthy nor distinguished. She is old enough to be your mother, but she has never married. She lives with another woman as husband, and is said to hate men. Perhaps I should not tell you this. But it is not an uncommon thing among us."

Ombroz met them at the edge of camp, his shaved pate shining in the sun. It was dotted with scars where skin tumors had been removed. Looking at him, the cardinal realized that his name in Wild-dog sounded a lot like "shaved bear," although the priest claimed he used the razor to mark himself as different from the typical shaman. When the cardinal told him that Amen Specklebird had canceled his suspension from the Order of Saint Ignatz, and was considering his appointment as Father General of the Order, Ombroz laughed sadly.

"That will carry as much weight in New Rome as your recent promotion, m'Lord."

"Well, yes, but the Pope must assert all of his rights and prerogatives as if no one doubted the legitimacy of his election. He must act the Pope in every way."

"I understand that, but of course the Order will ignore my reinstatement. What about you, Eminence?"

"Well, at the very least, I shall invest you as a pastor of a church in my Vicariate."

Ombroz laughed again. "My church is in my saddlebags. Your couriers bring my wafers and my wine along with my mail."

"Even in saddlebags, a wandering church needs a name."

"It has a name. Our Lady of the Desert."

Brownpony smiled. "The same name as the Pope's old Order? *Ordo Dominae Desertarum.* Very well, and you would no doubt be happier if you changed orders?"

"If His Holiness consents. The Order of Saint Ignatz has been disloyal to the popes of the exile, and they haven't made a move to recognize Pope Amen. I am on their list of their God's enemies. So if His Holiness permits it?"

"Why not? He'll agree, I'm sure." The cardinal looked toward the crowded area. "Now, what's going on? Where is Holy Madness?"

"He is in mourning. As you know, Your Eminence has arrived just in time for his father's funeral."

"His death was expected, was it not?"

"Yes, even planned."

"Human sacrifice again?"

"It was a ritual killing, yes, but I prefer to think of it as euthanasia in his case. Still forbidden to Catholics, of course."

"Did Chür Høngan assent to this?"

"No, he was excluded by the Bear Spirit shamans, because of his religion."

"A religion his father shared."

"Brokenfoot was out of his mind. He did not understand."

"They are not going to—"

"Honor him? I'm afraid so. Tonight."

"I wish I had come a day later."

"I am amazed that you came alone! Where is Brother Blacktooth? Where is Wooshin and the Yellow Guard?"

"In New Jerusalem."

"With the guns?"

"With the guns. You must know that the Pope is crossing the Plains to the south of us, probably camped for the night by now."

"I know. I hope they let him pass. Eminence, there is a legate from Texark here. From Benefez. I would say you have arrived just in time."

"Your young man told me. Who is Monsignor Sanual, and what does he want?"

"He is simply here to meet with the Bear Spirit, the Weejus, and the sharfs. Benefez has never condescended to this before. I wonder if he'll be fool enough to proselytize. I dare say the Grasshopper sharf would have killed him as a spy, if he had tried to attend a meeting in the Grasshopper realm. But he is a guest of Chür Høngan's bereaved family. I counseled Bearcub to play host to the fellow, because otherwise the Jackrabbit delegates would have been forced to accommodate him."

"And thus either make him seem their protector or their ally. Very good, my friend. This will work out better than you could have known."

"No, I knew that all the Jackrabbit churches in the Province have been made subject to you. *If* you can win them over."

"I cannot take the churches or their pastors by force, but perhaps I can take their congregations away from them—with the help of enough priests loyal to the Pope. Of course, the priests have to speak Jackrabbit."

"There are many in the Province already, m'Lord, and they are just the ones who will be loyal to the Holy Father, even though they were taught by the Archbishop of Texark. The Nomadic-speaking priests are mostly converted Nomads. They embraced the Mayor's uncle's religion, but not the Mayor or his uncle."

"I'm glad to hear you affirm what I thought was true."

"I also know about Kindly Light's threat to have you atone to the Wild Mare Woman by spending the night in the Navel of the World, as they call it. Hultor Bråm will never be nominated, and he can't make you do it. However, the Bearcub and I have hatched a plan. May I tell you now, or later?"

"Later, please. We are being observed, are we not?"

"Yes, and it's a mistake not to be seen laughing together more than speaking seriously like this. Let me take you to the leading grandmothers and their spouses. Or do you need rest first?"

"Rest, please. And a bath, if that is possible."

The cardinal slept for a few hours. When he awoke, it was dark except for the flicker of many fires. The Nomads were already celebrating the royal funeral, and there was chanting and dancing. He could smell the cooked sacrament even from inside his tent. When he came out into the firelight he was immediately joined by Oxsho, who pointed and said, "There's your Father Ombroz."

"Mine?" Brownpony eyed him curiously. "Holy Madness told me you were baptized. Is he not your pastor?"

Sheepish, the warrior shrugged. "Sometimes, but he shaves."

"It sets him apart. It saves wearing his collar backward."

"Bear Spirit men do not shave, but sometimes he acts as a Bear Spirit man, as right now. I like him, as we all do, but I do not understand him very well. You want to talk to him now?"

"I should, but I hesitate to interrupt his, uh, meal. He seems to be, if you know the word, zonked."

"He has been smoking Nebraska *keneb* with the others."

Brownpony approached him. The unfrocked old priest of the Ignatz Order, whom Amen wanted to be its Father General, sat there on a heap of dried cow hides and gnawed with his good front teeth at the well-roasted remains of a human hand. He dropped the hand back in the bowl as Brownpony approached, but looked up at the cardinal brightly and without shame. Oxsho hung behind. Brownpony could see that he was not drunk but in an extraordinary state of mind from the Nomad sacramental mixture of potions he had consumed. After participating in tribal rites, he seemed a changed man to the cardinal, but Ombroz smiled at him lovingly. Brownpony met his smile with a gaze that seemed to come from a thousand miles away. *I do not know this man, this old friend.*

Ombroz was first to break the silence. "The old sharf willed me his right hand—an honor!—and an insult to refuse."

The Vicar Apostolic remained silent, watching him.

"Sometimes," Ombroz said, picking up the gristly hand of Granduncle Brokenfoot, "I take a piece of bread and consecrate it as the true body of Christ. And sometimes I take the true body of Christ and consecrate it as a piece of bread. Do you understand?"

"Ahh!" It was a surprised grunt from Oxsho. Brownpony looked at him curiously. Oxsho was smiling slightly, as if he *did* suddenly understand.

The cardinal, still from a thousand miles away, said, "You really do wish to join the Pope's old Order, Father?"

Ombroz e'Laiden, not so far gone as to miss the hint of sarcasm, answered, "Tell His Holiness that illness forces me to remain as I am, m'Lord. I cannot return to my Order, but I am too old to change."

"Very well. I'll tell him." Brownpony turned and walked away. Oxsho hesitated, and patted the old priest's shoulder before following. Ombroz grinned at the young man, and resumed his sacramental meal. Oxsho followed Brownpony.

"So much for the Order of Saint Ignatz," said the cardinal.

"Does it disappoint you that he is one of us now?" asked the warrior.

"No, I'm sorry for Ombroz e'Laiden, the man."

"Because he has become a Nomad himself?"

"No, but outside the Church there is no salvation," murmured the cardinal, quoting an ancient claim. The answer seemed to puzzle Oxsho; he had heard of the cardinal from Ombroz, who admired and called him liberal. It was an uncharacteristic remark for such a man to make. But he was a priest now, and a bishop too.

"M'Lord, who is to say who stands outside the Church?"

"Why, the Pope says, and the law itself says, Oxsho."

"Does not God decide?"

"Father Ombroz is an enlightened man," said Holy Madness, who had overtaken them. Both of them looked at him strangely, waiting for Høngan to continue, but he only yawned, shook his head. "The woman who may be your mother has come, m'Lord."

Brownpony looked at the moon and changed the subject. "The Pope is taking a walk tonight. He always walks under a bright moon and sings to the Virgin, her sister. The Pope that would give the Church away to the poor, if Nauwhat and I would let him." My God, what are we going to do?

"Your Eminence, do you not want to see the woman? She is of royal blood, a distant cousin of mine. Which would make you my cousin too." He laughed, perhaps with a trace of bitterness.

"The family name is Urdon Go, not Avdek Gole," he said, after the cardinal's silence. "Not a brown pony, but a sorrel colt."

"Oxsho told me. But my God!" Brownpony whispered, his face draining. "After all these years. The Sisters spoke Jackrabbit, of course."

"Your mother, if that's what she is, is there. She is that old woman sitting on the blankets by the door of the hogan there. I would be very careful. She can be as violent as the *Nunshån*."

"Of course. Thank you." Brownpony walked quickly toward her, then stopped a few paces away. The woman's eyes were white with cataracts. But she had perceived his approach with her ears, her wrinkled mask facing him. "You are Texark?" she asked suspiciously.

"Only half," he said in Wilddog. "Only half, Mother." Calling her "mother" was a polite form of address; she did not need to take it literally.

But she stood. She spat on his face and his cassock. She was chewing a quid of herbs. Perhaps her aim was bad. She was nearly blind. Surely it was unintentional? But they had told him about her. Had they told her nothing about him?

The cardinal retreated. It was no good. He could not tell her that the man she faced without eyes was what had been planted in her by force and ripped unwelcome from her thighs, and that his hair was red. He knew she would not want to know him. She was a simple woman, but bitter. He could see the family, while royal, was not wealthy. But now that it was known to Chür Høngan and the chieftains that he was her son, the news would come back to her that he was here, if she did not already know. Surely she was expecting it. There was nothing he could do about that but tell the Nomad sharfs that he was willing to come to her if she called. He felt certain she would never call. Though depressed, he was glad he had seen her, and glad to think she did not know for certain.

"Your Eminence, please!" The voice calling to him from the doorway of a tent was that of Monsignor Sanual, the Texark Archbishop's legate. The chubby diplomat seemed distraught. "Come in, please, Eminence, come in a moment."

Although Sanual had nearly snubbed him earlier in the day, Brownpony silently complied, stooping to enter a lantern-lighted space, stuffy with earth odors and the smell of spilled sacramental wine. The wine too was on Sanual's breath as he grasped the cardinal's arm.

"They're eating the old chief! I thought you would be staying in your tent tonight!"

"And miss the show?" He carefully recovered his arm from Sanual's grasp. "The Archbishop's legate may sulk in his tent if he chooses. The Pope's legate may not."

Sanual drew back. Both knew they were vying for the favor of the wild tribes and the new Christian chief who might soon unite the Three Hordes.

"You'd do anything!" said Sanual. "If His Holiness knew . . ."

"Look at it this way. My mother was a Nomad. The dead chief was a cousin of mine. The new chief is also a cousin. Remote, of course. But I'm not going to shun the last rites of my own people. Now what did you want to see me about?"

"Just that. Your relationship." Sanual was sneering. "Ombroz told me you've been chosen to be in the kingship ritual!"

"I just saw Ombroz. He said nothing to me about it. Besides, you always turn your back on the man. I don't believe you, Father. You've been drinking."

"He shouted it at me! And that cackling laugh of his. Of course, he's senile and quite mad, but I believe him. It's so, isn't it?"

"I have only been informed that, as a son of the royal mother-line, I am entitled to be honored during the celebration. The honor is personal, and has nothing to do with my office or my mission."

"Then for the honor of God, Your Eminence, take off the vestments of your office when the time comes."

"Are you here to express Texark's disapproval of the Nomads' pagan ritual, or are you here to honor the inauguration by them of a Christian chief?"

"I was hoping to do both, but I hadn't counted on your willingness to take the Devil to your bosom. We ought to be together on this. For the love of God, Cardinal, tolerance has to stop someplace."

"I was never a priest, Father, until just recently. I'm just a lawyer to whom my late lord the Pope Linus Sixth gave a red hat, and Pope Amen just made a bishop. Fine points of theology are not in my repertory."

"Cannibalism is a fine point, Your Eminence?"

"I take note of your objections, Messér. I'll mention them in my report to the Pope, as I am sure you'll mention them in your report to your Archbishop. Is that all you wanted to see me about?"

"Not quite. There is a rumor that you were sent to assert a pretended episcopal authority over churches in our missionary territory. Is this true?"

"Your missionary territory is not your missionary territory except by right of conquest, and no right of conquest exists except when a war is a just and defensive war. Pope Amen has made me Vicar Apostolic to the Three Hordes, if that's what you mean, and it has nothing to do with your masters, either of them."

"Damn! There is no pope! We agree on nothing! Not on common decency. Not even on saving the Church from schism!" Sanual turned his back. Brownpony left the legate's tent at once, strode toward the main bonfires, briefly observed the orgy, and then retired.

But that night the blind old woman came and tried to kill him in his sleep. At his outcry, Oxsho leaped from his sleeping bag, grappled with her briefly, forced the knife from her hand, and led her away.

"She cannot be your mother," the warrior said upon returning.

"She is. She just proved it."

Cardinal Brownpony spent the rest of the night staring at the drifting patch of stars framed by the smoke hole in the top of the tent. He thought of Seruna, his wife. He thought of the Sisters who raised him, of the Church and the Virgin, and the *Høngin Fujæ Vurn* to whom the nearby pit was sacred. He knew now that he must indeed accept the ordeal of courting the Wild Horse Woman in her place of ancient fire. If he was to become the highest Christian shaman in the eyes of the People, he must become a Nomad as fully as Father Ombroz. The drunken words came back to him: *Sometimes I take a piece of bread and consecrate it as the true body of Christ. Sometimes I take the true body of Christ and consecrate it as . . .*

Somehow it sounded like a thing Amen Specklebird might say.

The moon had almost set when a dark shadow filled the doorway. Not his mother again! Oxsho was snoring. But it was Holy Madness who called softly to him: "Dress quickly, m'Lord. I want to show you the pit."

Brownpony obeyed, but when they were outside, he asked, "Couldn't we see it better by day?"

"No. If you must face the test, you must face it at night. Even full moonlight obscures the glow of the poison."

They mounted the two horses Høngan had brought and rode quietly out of camp. The orange moon was just touching the horizon and there was little light, but the horses knew the terrain. The rim of the crater was a half hour's ride from the camp. A sentry gave them a sleepy challenge as they passed the outskirts, but he recognized a grunt from his sharf and sat down.

When they came near the edge of the pit, the moon was down and there was scarcely a hint of morning twilight in the east. The pit

was a lake of blackness, and they approached cautiously on foot. Holy
Madness grasped the cardinal's arm.

"Damn!" he said after a moment.

"What's wrong?"

"The fire comes and goes. Tonight I can't even see it."

"I don't even know where to look."

"Look at the sky. Find the brightest star in the Thief and then
bring your eyes straight down. There should be a tiny red spot near
the center."

"The Thief is a Nomad constellation."

Høngan pointed. Brownpony sighted along his arm. "I think we
call that Perseus. Yes, and that star must be Mirfak."

They both sat at the rim of the crater and watched in silence.
The only sound was the wind and the distant howling of the wilddogs.
Occasionally Chür Høngan swore under his breath.

"Does it really matter?" the cardinal asked. "Can't you show me
by daylight?" He glanced east. The sky was brightening.

"It does matter. You should see it glow. You must take note of
the wind, and stay out of its lee. Some nights you can see a trail of
vapor, as well as the hole it comes from."

"Isn't it better if the fire is inactive?"

"Yes, but the whole pit is somewhat contaminated. The only
vegetation in it is on the weather side of the average wind here. You
should stay where the weeds grow, except when the wind is wrong. You
can see what I mean in a few minutes."

Their vigil lasted until the sun cleared the hill. The pit did seem
lifeless, except for a little vegetation at the foot of a cliff. At the
moment, the breeze was blowing away from it.

On the following day, the leaders of the Bear Spirit and Weejus
met to consider Brownpony's wish to pay court to the *Høngin Fujæ
Vurn* in the Navel of the World and face the hidden fires of Meldown.
The cardinal himself was excluded, but twice Chür Høngan emerged
from the council lodge to ask a question.

The first question: "Will you treat the Great Mare with the same
reverence as the Holy Virgin?"

"Yes, if I may say my usual prayers to her."

An hour later came the second question: "You realize that if she
rejects you, you will not be accepted as having any authority over
Christian Nomads of any horde. Will you resign the office the Pope
gave you?"

"If I live long enough to resign, yes."

Høngan gave him a hard look and returned to the meeting. When it was over, the Wilddog sharf announced that the cardinal would spend Thursday night in the pit. Friday the Wilddog sharf Holy Madness would pay court to the Wild Horse Woman, and the Saturday's vigil was for the Grasshopper sharf Kindly Light. The Grasshopper's complaint was that of the three of them, only Høngan would have a full moon from dusk to dawn, but Holy Madness explained to him privately: "If you are familiar with the pit, so that you do not stumble into trouble in the dark, the moon is not your friend. You cannot see the hellfire by bright moonlight, and as you know, sometimes not even by dark. Clouds may cover the moon. Spend the day studying her breeding pit from every angle. When the wind changes, you will have to move."

The following night he spent in the pit. Oxsho led him to the place of descent. The moon, nearly full, was in the east at sundown. He carried a blanket but no bedroll. Sleep would be dangerous, but a chill would settle over the area after midnight.

"My teacher wishes me to spend the night on the clifftop and keep a fire burning," the young warrior told him. "I'll hold up a torch when the wind is changing. Watch for the torch. Sometimes a light breeze may be hard to feel down there."

"Is this permitted?"

Oxsho paused. "I won't start it until everyone's asleep, and behind this rock nobody'll see it. And only Sharf Bråm might object. God and the Mare keep you, m'Lord."

A wind that swooped down from the lip of the crater carried wisps of dust that dimmed the stars, but it was the dust of the prairie, not the pit. He chose a resting place in the sparse clump of vegetation where the dust of the devil's hole would blow away from him. He was still very sad because of the encounter with the bitter woman whose womb had borne him against her will. He had been a son of violence and hate before his adoption by the Sisters, but his memory of the Sisters was tinged with resentment, except for Sister Magdalen ("Cries-a-River"), a former Jackrabbit Nomad who told him stories and made his education her special concern. Seruna, when he married, had reminded him of Magdalen. Now both were dead. When he passed through Jackrabbit territory to visit some of his churches, would he visit the orphanage? And was it nostalgia or resentment that made him think of it? Better not, he decided. Neither emotion would benefit his ecclesiastical and political project.

After a while the cardinal began to pray, saying his rosary at first, and letting his eyes linger around the patch of darkness that marked the cave entrance under the moonlit ledge of rock. He spoke softly to the patch of darkness, but he still felt the sting of his real mother's spit like acid in his face. He spoke now to that other mother of myriad names: *Regina Mundi, Domina Rerum, Mater Dei, Høngin Fujœ Vurn,* even the War Buzzard. Her manifestations were always associated with a place: Bethlehem, Lourdes, Guadalupe, and here at the Navel of the World.

"I was born in the south end of your realm, Mother, and I know your paths. Even there, where the People are servants of those who took your land, I have seen your ways. Miriam, mother of Jesus, pray for me."

Oxsho held up his torch when a cloud covered the moon near the zenith. He could at last see a kind of luminosity above and about the hole at the center of the pit, and he moved a hundred paces away from the direction pointed out by the flame.

"Lord, have mercy. *Kyrie eleison.*"

Fortunately, the wind was at his back again.

"My mother was a woman of the Wilddog tribes, Mother; my father did evil to her, and to your people. Let him be dead, as she is now dead for me. Let me not find him, lest I kill him. Long ago, before I knew she was dead to me, her spirit told me to come here. I have not done as she wished. I have left the People. I have taken the religion the Sisters taught me. But at last I am before you, Mother."

The wind was shifting a lot that night. He kept moving.

"Christ, have mercy. *Christe eleison.*"

He moved again to keep the wind at his back, taking his cue from the occasional torchlight, but he went on talking softly in the direction of the cave.

"My hair is red. His was red, she told them. The Sisters who took her in. The Sisters raised me. Miriam, Mother of Jesus, pray for me. If he were living, I would kill him. *Ora pro me,* Wild Horse Woman. *Kyrie eleison.*"

Once during the night, he actually saw her: a woman's figure, black against the glow from the fire pit. Her arms were raised like wings. The *Nunshån?* No, the figure was young; the Night Hag was old. Because of the wings, she had to be the Burregun, the War Buzzard. But when he stood, she vanished.

Amen Specklebird spoke of her as if she were a fourth member of the Holy Trinity, and that was one of the excuses of the Benefez faction for refusing him recognition. A pope who could utter heresy was no pope. But he had not been pope when he said it. Would he say it still? No. Surprising to Brownpony was the ease with which the old man shifted into his papal role. A doubter would call it hypocrisy. A believer would call it the work of the Holy Ghost, protecting the flock against error.

How many popes were in Hell? he wondered. Dante had named a few, but the list was incomplete. The last pope before the Flame Deluge was surely one of them.

On that thought, he lapsed into slumber, for the moon had sunk below the rim of the pit. It was the brightness of the sky and the shouting of Oxsho that woke him. The wind had gone wrong. He grabbed the blanket and trotted as fast as he could toward the path leading upward. For better or worse, his trial was over.

"If you are sick within the week, you will die," was the matter-of-fact first prognosis of the Weejus who talked to him. "If you do not die soon, you can expect a shorter lifetime. They told you this beforehand?"

"Of course, Grandmother."

She questioned him closely. He told her about seeing the woman with upraised arms he had seen against the glow of the hellfire. She stared at him. After a long pause, she asked, "Do you know of the Buzzard of Battle?"

"I have heard of the Burregun."

"The Buzzard of Battle is red in the sky."

"She was not in the sky."

The old woman nodded, and that was the end of the interview. She took her opinions with her into the council lodge. Later that day, Chür Høngan came to tell him that the Bear Spirit accepted him conditionally as Christian shaman. The condition was that he not fall ill anytime soon.

Brownpony saw little cause to celebrate. A messenger came from Valana to report that Jarad Cardinal Kendemin, Abbot of Saint Leibowitz, had gone to meet the Judge. A report also came that the Pope and his party were encamped in the no-man's-land between Wilddog and Grasshopper domains. Holy Madness graciously offered to swap his appointment with the *Høngin Fujæ Vurn* for Kindly Light's, so that Hultor Bråm could leave with his escort party of warriors on Saturday morning to meet Amen Specklebird and lead him to the frontiers of the Empire.

Brownpony decided to ride south with the warriors. Bråm, fresh from his encounter with the Mare, offered no objection.

Early Saturday morning, an hour before their departure, Cardinal Brownpony borrowed bread, wine, a missal, and a portable altar from Father Ombroz. It was his wish to celebrate a pontifical High Mass; it would be good politics and showmanship, but he could not sing well, and had said no more than a dozen Masses since his ordination. Monsignor Sanual stiffly declined his request to serve either as co-celebrant or acolyte. The Red Deacon looked at Ombroz.

"Will you hear my confession first?" asked the old Ignatzian.

"You have something recent to confess?"

Ombroz took his meaning, and shook his head in annoyance. He called instead for Oxsho, his own altar boy. Between them, they rounded up all Christians and invited all the Weejus and Bear Spirit people who wished to attend. The Vicar Apostolic to the Three Hordes offered a simple Mass there on the high prairie with the smoke of dung fires in the breeze and a congregation of wild Nomads circling the altar at a safe distance. Probably more people came forward to receive the Eucharist than there were Christians in the encampment, but he questioned no one. Those who looked surprised at the bland flavor of the Body of Christ were probably pagan shamans. Neither Sanual nor Ombroz came forward to receive. After the *Ite, missa est,* a cheer arose from the crowd, but he could not be sure who incited it. Obviously, he was accepted as the Christian high shaman of the People.

Monsignor Sanual was drinking again. He came out to watch them ride away, and called out to the cardinal that he was following a loser, that the false Pope would never enter New Rome, and that grief for the whole Church would follow.

"Thanks for your blessings, Messér," the cardinal answered.

Hultor Bråm was not yet prepared to be a friend to a friend of his rival, but he had suffered a bad Friday night in the pit, and he knew that his report to the Bear Spirit council afterward had not been well received. Plainly, the Weejus had already made up their minds. He conceded to his warriors that unless Holy Madness experienced an even worse Saturday night in the Navel of the World, the office of *Qœsach dri Vørdar* would fall to the Wilddog sharf. At least the ancient office would be restored, reuniting the Three Hordes.

He noticed that Cardinal Brownpony had heard his remarks, and he gruffly asked the cardinal about his experience with the Mare.

"Were you accepted as her stallion the other night?" he wanted to know. "Did you see her at all?"

The cardinal hesitated. "I'm not sure what I saw. You spend hours staring at patches of darkness, you begin to see, but it isn't there."

"What is it that wasn't there?"

"There seemed to be a woman between me and the patch of dim light. I can't describe her. She faced me, and her arms were raised. Then she disappeared."

"Like the Buzzard of Battle?"

"They told you that's what I saw. I never said it."

Bråm nodded. "If I had seen it, I would be *Qœsach dri Vørdar* now. But I am going to die soon."

"Are you ill?"

"You saw the Buzzard of Battle. That is your future. They say I saw mine." Bråm laughed and rode away. Later one of the warriors told the cardinal that the Weejus had decided that the Grasshopper sharf had met the Night Hag in the pit, although, the man said, the Weejus had prejudged the contest in favor of Holy Madness, provided he survived the pit, and that he personally did not believe that Bråm would die as a result of the pit.

The warriors were feeling playful. Bråm had promised them they would be well paid by the Church for performing this escort duty. Brownpony grew more uneasy about the promise each time it was mentioned. He had not spoken of money to the Grasshopper sharf. Perhaps someone else in the Curia had made the offer, or even Papa Specklebird.

He watched the warriors gamboling on the grasslands under the September sun. A man stood up on horseback. Another stood up, and chased the first rider so closely that he had to sit down fast or fall. There was whooping laughter. One warrior could slide down his stallion's flank and crawl under his belly and up the other side. After he had done this three times, the horse began to have an erection. He crawled down a fourth time, took a look, and crawled back up. Somebody yelled a merry insult at him, and in a moment both were on the ground in a knife fight. Hultor Bråm came riding back, watched the deadly dance for a moment, then adjusted his tall leather helmet with his grandmother's crest and the badge of a war sharf.

There was a splatter of blood, not a deep cut, but it brought an order to drop the weapons. "Finish it with your hands and feet," Sharf Hultor barked, "or stop it right now. Hear me well! No killing! Not among ourselves. If you have a grudge against a comrade, save it until this war party gets back home."

"Why does he call it a war party?" Brownpony asked the man who rode beside him. "It was meant to be an honor guard."

"The Grasshopper is *always* at war," declared the rider, and spurred his horse to distance himself from this farmer and red-hat Christian.

CHAPTER 16

The beds, moreover, are to be examined frequently by the Abbot, to see if any private property be found in them. If anyone should be found to have something that he did not receive from the Abbot, let him undergo the most severe discipline.

—*Saint Benedict's Rule*, Chapter 55

T WAS A TROOP OF FOOLS, THOUGHT THE commander of the police guard. Thirty-seven cardinals rode horseback along with the Pope while another twenty-four bounced along in the beds of wagons dragged across the roadless grasslands by mules. Thirty Denver mounted police and thirty Wilddog warriors escorted the party, although this force would turn back when the party reached Grasshopper country and met the riders of Sharf Bråm.

When they reached the boundary, they pitched camp and waited for the warriors of the Grasshopper.

Amen Specklebird had waited more patiently than the others. The tents provided by their Wilddog escorts were comfortable enough, and the Pope insisted that the cardinals join him each day in singing Lauds, the Mass, and Vespers, and to pray the other canonical prayers in common. Most of them were accustomed to muttering the first few lines of each psalm; they called it reciting the breviary.

The camp of the itinerant Curia was surrounded by curious women and children of both Wilddog and Grasshopper families whose herds or breeding pits were located nearby, but the escorting warriors kept them at a distance to prevent thievery. Everyone was relieved, except perhaps the warriors themselves, when the Grasshopper riders appeared on the crest of the hill, not gamboling or quarreling now, but riding in a typical Grasshopper battle formation, a line of advance that surged alternately here and fell back there, making the order of battle difficult for the enemy to portray. The Wilddog scouts, outnumbered, grabbed their lances and sidearms and moved to mount their stallions, but Hultor Bråm called a halt and cried out, "Peace! In the name of the *Fujæ Go*."

The Curia watched as Cardinal Brownpony left their fierce ranks and rode forward. Amen Specklebird advanced to meet him, and raised him up when he fell to the ground to kiss the fisherman's ring.

"We have heard, Elia, that Jarad is with Christ, not yet risen."

That was a curious way of putting it, but the cardinal answered, "I knew that would be the first thing you mentioned, Holy Father. If you will excuse me from your presence, I should like to travel now to Leibowitz Abbey and join their mourning."

The old black panther seemed surprised. "I thought you would be going on south of the Nady Ann to visit your churches in the Province."

"That too, Holy Father. But the Texark forces will be expecting me to cross the Nady Ann, not the Bay Ghost. If I come in from the west, I may not be arrested. And it should only take a day or two to pay my respects at the abbey."

"We shall excommunicate anyone who dares lay a finger on you in the Province. I'll put that in writing. You are ordered to go to Leibowitz Abbey, and then east to Jackrabbit country."

"Thank you. I wish to go on to Hannegan City afterward, Holy Father."

"Then you go as my legate. The wax on your orders will be sealed by my ring. I'll send the papers by messenger to the abbey."

"Forgive me, but that may not impress the Archbishop or his nephew."

"You do not have my permission to be a martyr, Elia."

"Do I need it?"

Amen smiled and changed the subject. "How are our friends

among the Weejus and the Bear Spirit? And how was that cave of
theirs? You were in it one night?"

"Breeding pit, Holy Father. To be frank, I think its reputation is
highly exaggerated by myth and storytelling. It must have been a dangerous place centuries ago, but unless some ill befell Holy Madness, I
believe its devil has lost her cunning." He spoke these words three
weeks before an attack of nausea and lethargy came over him at Leibowitz Abbey.

When he parted from the Pope and the Curia, he went to thank
Hultor Bråm for his courtesy. Bråm complained that no money was
forthcoming. The cardinal merely denied any knowledge of the problem, and left it in the hands of the weary prelates of the Pope's company.

Pope Amen's last words to him were "See about Leibowitz Abbey, Elia. Tell them to elect their new abbot, and you impart to him
my confirmation. Cardinal Onyo here will be a witness that I so instructed you, if there is any later question."

A quick embrace ended it. He looked back at the Grasshopper
escort. The Wilddog warriors and the Valana police gave them wide
berth. The Wilddog mounted, and rode west-northwest, while the po-
licemen lingered for a time.

Later historians were to suggest that the war which destroyed the
papacy began when Amen Specklebird accepted the ninety-nine
Grasshopper warriors who had been recruited by Hultor Bråm, separated from their families by Hultor Bråm, trained, drilled, and indoc-
trinated by Hultor Bråm, but not paid by Hultor Bråm, because the
Grasshopper sharf was angry with Cardinal Brownpony, and extended
his anger to Brownpony's master. After the comptroller with the
Pope's party told him there was no gold with the train, the commander of the police guard explained the situation to the Pope.

The papacy in Valana had signed a contract with certain Wilddog
and Grasshopper families to furnish for hire fresh horses to Church
messengers at relay stations so that crossing the Plains from the Denver Republic to the marginal farmlands of the East could be accomplished in less than ten days. One enterprising Wilddog family and
one Grasshopper undertook to carry mail across the Plains, competing
with Church messenger service, but not with Hannegan's telegraph.
These families were given certain immunities in both written and
horde law. It was too early to say that a new class of Nomad entrepre-
neur was immediately coming into being, but certain grandmothers
were accumulating an embarrassment of riches from providing services

to the enemy: to civilization. Nomad society had always followed the wild, unfenced cattle, and a wealth of possessions made one's village less portable. But it was under the terms of this contract, as construed by Bråm, that payment was expected.

"Promise to pay them later" was all Pope Amen could say.

After a promise was made to Bråm, the Pope and the Curia proceeded east with these tutelary demons on horseback. Because of the weariness of old men, the journey took four days instead of two. The Pope was fond of chatting with ordinary people, and he spoke frequently to members of the Grasshopper escort along the way, whenever an opportunity arose.

"Our tribes are angry," one of them told him. "We are angry because the Wilddog has allowed churchmen to be guests at the sacred meeting of the hordes. Not only is Cardinal Brownpony there, but so is an emissary from Archbishop Benefez. And Brownpony favors Ösle Høngan Chür over Hultor Bråm."

The Pope took note of the warrior's polite reversal of Holy Madness' name. Angry or not, he accepted the grandmothers' political will, their favoritism for the Wilddog sharf, as legitimately governing the electoral situation on the Plains. But his resentment of Brownpony was extended to Brownpony's master, the Pope, and thus wages had been requested in advance.

Amen tried to reassure him that the men would be paid, but the list of complaints was not ended.

"Furthermore, the Wilddog offered Monsignor Sanual food and shelter."

"I would have thought Benefez's man would stay with the Jackrabbit delegates," Specklebird remarked.

"Oh, yes, he wanted to. There are Christian priests among the Jackrabbit Bear Spirit delegates. The Jackrabbit delegates are in danger of seeming to be puppets of the Texark Church."

"There is only one Church, my son."

And so went the journey.

According to the Treaty of the Sacred Mare, any farmer or soldier of the Empire who entered Grasshopper territory while bearing arms could expect attack, and any armed Nomad within musket range of the Empire's frontier could be fired upon. Thus, when the Pope's party crossed the hill overlooking the frontier checkpoint, Hultor Bråm and his men halted. The warriors were still grumbling to their sharf about not being paid, but the sharf was watching the confrontation at the border crossing.

"One way or another, you'll all be paid," he insisted, "maybe sooner than you think."

As the procession of prelates approached the gate, Amen Specklebird descended from his coach and brushed the dust of the Plains from his white cassock. He approached the officer who stood with folded arms in the center of the road. Flanking him were two soldiers with double-barreled weapons, probably loaded with buckshot.

"By orders of the Hannegan, you cannot pass," the officer announced. "If you try, you will be arrested."

"Do not bar the way, my son. Bow to God's will."

"Show me God's will."

"Pick up your right foot, and look."

The officer obeyed, and reddened.

"I see my right foot's shadow," he said, ignoring the horseshit with his footprint in it.

"His will is already done," said Specklebird. "Too bad."

"Such a smartass! They call it your 'wisdom,' don't they? Forgive me, but it is a pain in the butt to me, Your, uh, Holiness. I don't think the Lord Mayor will find it a pleasure, either. Why don't you say something new, in plain Ol'zark?"

Amen grinned at him and pointed to the sun while squinting. The colonel's eyes may have flickered, but he resisted looking and said, "Nice try, old man. There are good frauds and bad frauds, I guess. You're pretty good, aren't you?"

"I never thought of it that way, my son, but my office requires it of me, doesn't it?"

"I don't know whether to spit on you or kneel to you, old fool. But make it easy for yourself and go home."

"Colonel, why trap yourself in dualism that way?"

"What are you calling dualism?"

"Spitting God or kneeling God."

"I have my orders from the Hannegan himself. Get back in your coach, turn around, and go back to Valana, or you will find yourself in Hannegan City, facing a heresy trial. Say another word, and I'll testify to everything you say here."

"Bless you, my son, and thank you."

The colonel snorted, spoke in an aside to a captain, then mounted and rode away in a huff. The captain pointed a cavalry pistol at the Pope's thin black face. Two cardinals caught the Pope's arms and a third pushed him back toward the train.

Thus was the road to New Rome closed to New Rome's bishop.

The Grasshopper warriors parted to allow them to pass, but made no move to escort them back, even when Golopez Cardinal

Onyo beckoned to Bråm. Bråm frowned and shook his head. His warriors stood there watching until they became a patch of dust in the west. Wearily, Amen's party (a good part of the Sacred College) turned to remake the long journey. From far behind came the faint sound of shouting and gunfire, but there was nothing the prelates could do about it, and Pope Amen was a little hard of hearing. From the patches of forest at the east, through scrub and tall grass, through open grassland, through blistering days and chilly nights in the near-desert, some of it irrigated at last, and finally to the mountains they passed. Along the way, they accepted Nomad charity, and they were intercepted at one point by a delegation from the breeding pit.

Chür Ösle Høngan had married the *Fujæ Go*. The new *Qæsach dri Vørdar*, Lord of the Three Hordes, whose wife was the Day Maiden, knelt to kiss the Pope's ring and swore allegiance to His Holiness forever, in the name of God and His Virgin.

Before they parted, Golopez Cardinal Onyo called Holy Madness aside and told him about the behavior of Sharf Hultor Bråm after they had been turned back by the border guard. "They did not return with us, and I heard gunfire and shouting. I cannot be sure, but I think there was fighting."

The Lord of the Three Hordes sat astride his stallion and gathered a slow frown. "If he did what I'm afraid he did, I'll have his head."

"The Pope knows nothing," Onyo told him.

"I'll send to find something out immediately." He grunted an order to a subordinate, then rode away with his party back toward the breeding pit. The subordinate rode east.

There was something to find out. At the border that day, the Grasshopper escort, standing half a mile distant from all events at the gate, began to move. As soon as the dust of the Pope's party had dwindled beyond the hills, War Sharf Hultor Bråm ordered his ninety-nine elite fighters to take the road to Rome by a feat of arms. They circled south, and cut the road to Hannegan City toward which the colonel who had defied the Pope was riding homeward. He was among the first of many troops to die that day.

They turned north again. The road to Rome was swiftly taken, but only on a very temporary basis. These born-in-the-saddle man-animals cut through the Texark Light Horse, leaving other men and animals full of arrows and spear wounds on the ground. Slow firearms fell back before rapid and accurate bows. Many Grasshoppers used captured sidearms, but only as backup weapons. The Nomad horses

were faster and better, and together with their fighters they became
for the unseasoned troopers truly the riders of the Apocalypse, ninety-
nine of them and a leader with a demonic attitude. They had not
been paid, for nobody had brought the papal treasury. They cut the
troopers to pieces, killed 146 farmers, raped their wives, daughters,
sisters, mothers, sons, and then cut their way back to the frontier
through fresh but green reinforcements—cut their way back, yes, all
thirty-three of them, adrenaline-drunk, exhausted, including a leader
with a brooding attitude and a bad leg. But their saddlebags bulged,
and once on the Plains again, they made travois to carry some of the
loot. Now they had been paid.

The foray had been just a hell of a good party for the survivors,
who came back to their grateful and waiting wives, some of whose
hearts and crotches quivered with anxiety and hope, with mostly over-
worked and limp male members! It took amatory ingenuity on a warrior's part that night to convince a wife that he came home from
battle with a real lust for her sexual candy, but most pleaded combat
fatigue and went to bed alone.

Being at war was more fun—no doubt about that: even with the
odds at two to one you'd die before you got to rape, steal, and burn
barns full of newly baled hay.

There was both celebration and mourning that night in late September in the encampment of the sharf's own mother clan. The war
cries almost drowned the sound of women crying.

"I set fires! I set fires!"

It was the royal motto on the flag of Hultor Bråm. And no one
doubted that it was a deliberate slap in the face of the new Lord of
the Hordes, whose emissaries would arrive within two days. On the
morning after the celebration, several new widows brought their complaints to the Grasshopper Weejus and Bear Spirit. Bråm was summoned before the council. He listened to the accusations in silence
and made no defense.

The incursion to the very walls of High New Rome seemed of a
devilish inspiration, because it fractured the Treaty of the Sacred
Mare, and resumed a state of war between Texark and the Grasshopper. But everybody had fun except the dead, the raped, and the permanently maimed. In war, God is thus! old Tempus might have said.

Helped by telegraph, the news of Hultor Bråm's raid arrived in
Valana long before the Pope did, the Pope who knew nothing of what
was happening a few miles behind him, except that his Nomad escort
had vanished and some shouting and shooting was heard. At home, he
found himself facing accusations from Texark that he or the Secretariat of State had ordered the Nomad attack.

. . .

Subsequently in Valana the short, unhappy pontificate of Pope Amen Specklebird produced more important legislation for its duration than had the pontificate of any pope since the schism of the previous century. This was not surprising. The lack of participation by Texark's allies meant that the Curia could approach unanimous consent to proposals by the Pope's new advisers, who were led by Sorely Nauwhat, since Elia Brownpony was on the road. Sorely was in many ways Brownpony's talk-alike. In no way, however, was Amen Specklebird ruled by the Curia. He spoke of resigning, but first there would be legislation.

In a bull named *Unica ex Adam Orta Progenies*, after its opening words, the Pope again affirmed that no one of human ancestry should be regarded as less than human, and that the misborn must not be denied equal rights under the laws of the Church or of the nations. Nor were the Pope's children to be confined by law to a special domain, such as the Valley. He specifically outlawed their use as virtual slaves in the lumbering camps of the Ol'zarks. There was nothing new in the bull, except that the Pope denounced the practice within the Church of noting family pedigrees on baptismal certificates, since the lack of such documentation was used prejudicially by many states; a stranger might be required to prove that he was not a spook trying to pass as normal. "Rulers who, for political gain, exploit the people's fear of those with hereditary defects, and who sin against them through unjust laws and by stirring up mob violence, shall be held accountable for these evils. Sentences of ipso facto excommunication passed by Our Predecessors against any who, God forbid, do violence to the so-called Pope's children, are by these presents reaffirmed." The bull ended with a punitive clause, defining penalties for the violation of its letter and spirit, and extending the penalties to include violence done under the pretense of law. The language was that of a lawyer, but the message was clearly Amen Specklebird's.

With no help from the Curia, he originated a *Motu Proprio* (strictly by the Pope's own doing) in his own spidery calligraphy, deploring a drift in the Church away from proper liturgical reverence toward the *theotokos* (Mother of God). He did not need to mention which areas of the Church's spiritual domain needed reform in this area. The bishops of patriarchal societies were given to denouncing the Mariolatry of the Northwest, which Amen Specklebird had indirectly endorsed in a speech to the conclave before (emphasis by his supporters) his elevation to the papacy lent infallibility to his ex cathedra pronouncements. The *Motu Proprio*, however, lacked the defining and punitive clauses which were expected of infallible utterances by any pope; it was hardly more than a *tut tut* to his most vocal critics, and a poetic tribute to the Mother of All.

A law governing papal resignation, an event which had hitherto occurred about once per millennium, was ordered revised by the Pope. He decreed that such a resignation must come from the man himself, not from a Pope. A man who had been Pope would rise from the throne, remove all his vestments, and declare that *sede vacante* by saying, "The Pope is no more," and walk away as if the Holy Spirit had departed from him. He would not be admired for quitting, but he would not be punished for it either, unless he tried to change his mind. Specklebird insisted on this change in the existing law, and Hilan Cardinal Bleze tried to sell the others. It did seem to put an end to an ancient argument to the effect that papal resignation was impossible.

"He's planning his own departure," said Nauwhat, but still gave his assent to the law.

Kindly Light was marked for death. He had been so marked when the Weejus told him that what he had seen in the pit was the Night Hag. He had predicted his death to Cardinal Brownpony. Within two weeks of the ordeal at the Navel of the World, he fell ill. When the Wilddog shamans came to confer with their Grasshopper counterparts, he knew what the decision would be. He offered to submit voluntarily to a sacrificial death, provided that his younger brother, Eltür Bråm (Demon Light), be made Grasshopper war sharf in his place. Otherwise, he would take his own life. The Weejus of both hordes conferred, and all the grandmothers were consulted. Eltür was a warrior of considerable renown, but he had not been a member of the raiding party, and was known to be even-tempered, unlike his surly brother. The grandmothers in turn questioned their sons and nephews as to their willingness to follow Eltür. The battle frenzy had died out in the Grasshopper camp, and even the thirty-three warriors who survived the raid understood that Hultor Bråm had committed treason against the *Qæsach dri Vørdar*. They were commanded to purge themselves by ritual fasting for seven days, but were not otherwise punished for obeying their sharf.

It was decided that Hultor Bråm would not be honored by a ritual funeral such as had been conducted for Wilddog Granduncle Brokenfoot. Because of his heavy losses in battle, most of the grandmothers were quite angry with him. One of them said, "There is a wild stallion in my pit which I am about to release."

All of them looked at her, and the manner of Hultor's dying was immediately decided.

To prevent too much inbreeding the Weejus sometimes mated their mares with wild stallions, which men were forbidden to touch. The Weejus had her own way of stalking a wild stallion. Sometimes it took weeks, even months. A woman gradually introduced herself to a wild herd by staying far upwind. She worked her way closer, bit by bit, until the lead stallion first noticed her. Then she calmly but swiftly went away. The horses begin to tolerate her as a part of the terrain. One day a warrior of her family would bring the Weejus a jar of urine from a rutting mare of her own remuda. She smeared herself with it and approached as usual. When the lead stallion perked up and started to approach, she retreated again. This was repeated, with and without the scent, until the woman could actually walk in among the grazing mustangs. Eventually she would choose her animal, feed him tidbits, hang a rope on him, calm and cajole him, entice him, and lead him away to mate with her mares, and then be released. This was a way they had of keeping their own herds from too much inbreeding, but always, the wild ones were respected. When the Weejus seduced him, she did it without riding or breaking him. The only problem was that the stallion, no longer as wary of humans, might now be subject to capture by the motherless ones.

To make this stallion wild and wary again, the former war sharf of the Grasshopper Horde was sacrificed to the Owner of all wild horses, dragged to death by the released animal at the end of a long rope.

CHAPTER 17

Before all things and above all things, care
must be taken of the sick, so that they will
be served as if they were Christ in person;
for He Himself said, "I was sick, and you
visited me."

—*Saint Benedict's Rule*, Chapter 36

 BIQUIU OLSHUEN, ALTHOUGH HIS ELECTION AS
abbot after a decent period of mourning
was assumed by everyone, limited his decisions to small ones and exerted no
more than his usual authority as prior
until such elections might take place. He
therefore assigned both Blacktooth and
the Yellow Guard to visitors' quarters, invited them all to participate in the usual
four or five hours a day of manual labor, and told Nimmy himself to
join the other monks in choir in the liturgy, but not to receive the
Eucharist without specific permission from a confessor, meaning himself.

When Blacktooth told him that the alien guardsmen were not
only Christian but had taken religious vows, Olshuen was perplexed.
He called Levion the Reconciliator for advice, and with Blacktooth the
status of the foreigners was discussed at length. Olshuen and Levion
were both uncomfortable with the idea of professional killers with

religious vows, and Nimmy knew really very little about their creed and practice. He did know, and reminded Olshuen, that many centuries ago the monks of Saint Leibowitz had defended the monastery by force of arms, as evidenced by the parapet walls and the rusty iron weapons in a locked basement armory, to which only Olshuen now had the key.

Blacktooth found himself distracted by Levion's garments. The monk had become a priest. Although he did not dislike the man, Blacktooth imagined that having the Reconciliator as his confessor might be one of the pangs of his own personal hell, if both of them went there. Blacktooth had not changed a lot since leaving the abbey, but one minor change that had come from serving Cardinal Brownpony and studying warrior's arts under the Axe was a reduction of his fear of people such as these. It shocked him to realize that the ability to kill was a great tranquilizer, even among people he liked and respected.

"Why don't you talk to them instead of to me?" he said to Father Levion, his old shrink.

"I tried to, Brother St. George, but I can hardly understand them. Can't you?"

Not wishing to be stuck with the role of interpreter, Nimmy shook his head. "They are learning Churchspeak, Father. It would be kind of you to help them by communicating. I'm sure you are much better at it than I."

Afterward he tried not to indulge a temptation to feel smug. The alien Christians were soon invited to join the brethren of Saint Leibowitz at prayer; the reception of the Eucharist, however, would be delayed until their understanding of this continent's form of Catholic Christianity could be tested by catechists and confessors. Not elected abbot yet, Olshuen feared Valana's disapproval, and knew little about the character of either Amen Specklebird or the members of this yellow-skinned war band of the late Cardinal Ri.

He put Nimmy to work washing dishes and scrubbing floors in the kitchen. The errant monk was not respected by former friends, and he tried to avoid their charity. Apparently Abbot Jarad had told them little or nothing about his work for Cardinal Brownpony, and only Olshuen seemed aware of it but not much impressed. If Brother Singing Cow had told anyone that Blacktooth was one of Brownpony's conclavists when Pope Amen was elected, no one was interested. The business of the abbey was prayer and preservation of a heritage. Interest in the outside world was deliberately kept to a minimum. Nimmy was grateful that nobody sneered in his face or spoke of him loudly enough to be overheard.

. . .

Leibowitz Abbey had many visitors that season, and there were only a dozen furnished cells in the guesthouse. When Blacktooth came back from Vespers in the evening, he noticed a lamp burning in a cell which had been empty that morning. He glanced through the small door-window and froze at what he saw. Elia Cardinal Brownpony, looking pale and drawn, was lying in bed, propped up by pillows. Blacktooth pressed his forehead against the grille, the better to stare at the ailing prelate, his once and future master.

"Is that you, Nimmy? I wondered where you were hiding. Come in, come in."

"Nobody told me you were here, m'Lord." Blacktooth fell to his knees and kissed Brownpony's ring. He felt the cardinal flinch, and resolved not to kiss his ring again.

Two days later, Önmu Kun arrived at the abbey. Nimmy thought it a weird coincidence, but then saw that the Jackrabbit outlaw was taken directly to meet the ailing cardinal without even a visit to the prior. They had talked for several hours when Nimmy brought their dinners from the kitchen. Önmu was friendly, but their conversation stopped dead when Blacktooth entered, and did not resume until he departed. The Jackrabbit smuggler was on his way from the Province to New Jerusalem again, but he stayed until Brownpony was ready to depart, and then stayed some more.

There was no doubt from the beginning that Prior Olshuen would be elected abbot, spiritual father and ruler of the Order of Saint Leibowitz, but Brownpony let him worry about the power of confirmation which had been delegated to the cardinal by the Pope and it apparently came to Olshuen's mind that restoring the cardinal's health must be a paramount concern at the abbey.

For a time, the Red Deacon was afflicted by nausea and fatigue. He had no appetite. Attempts to vomit after picking at the cook's food usually resulted in the dry heaves. He was dizzy whenever he left his bed. He was short of breath, and his heartbeat quickened when he stood. Blacktooth asked to be relieved of his floor-scrubbing duties in the kitchen in order to consult the Venerable Boedullus again, for that respected author had written of Meldown, the breeding pit, and the illnesses that sometimes resulted from exposure to radiation there. He had even recorded a recipe called summonabisch stew, thought by the ancient Plains dwellers to be helpful in its treatment.

Prior Olshuen at first refused to release Blacktooth from the kitchen, for Brother Medic wanted no assistance from the likes of him. But when Brownpony learned that the prior had assigned the most menial of chores to the errant monk, he called the prior to his sickroom and showed symptoms of bad temper. The cardinal even raised the question of his approval of Olshuen's election, if he were so persistent in Jarad's error.

"What error is that, Your Eminence?"

"Keeping your foot on Nimmy's neck, you damn fool!"

"Why, we all do manual labor, and I thought . . ." He desisted, seeing that the Red Deacon was about to explode.

Brother Blacktooth was relieved of his kitchen assignment, and placed at the cardinal's disposal.

Nimmy read Boedullus again, and consulted with Brother Medic and the cooks. The cardinal allowed himself to be placed on a strict diet formulated by these consultants. Twice a day he must eat an apple into which iron nails had been driven and left for three days. The summonabisch recipe called for organ meats only. "Whatever the dogs won't eat," said a grouchy cook, quite incorrectly, according to the shepherds, whose dogs would eat every part of an animal but horns and hooves, if permitted to do so. The recipe called for wild onions and tiny wild peppers. The smelly wild onions grew only along riverbanks, and there were none near the abbey. The cook used onions from the garden, and although the shepherds found a few chiltepins while tending their flocks, hot peppers from the garden were deemed an acceptable substitute; the curative power was thought to reside mostly in the combination of tongue, liver, heart, brains, sweetbreads, kidneys, and tripe, all finely chopped. These were to be simmered in an iron pot with a splash of red wine or vinegar. The original recipe called for a calf, not a lamb, but none of the abbey's few milk cows had calved this year. Since about two young sheep a week were sacrificed for their organ meats, the monks were allowed, even encouraged, to eat mutton stew, although the Leibowitzian diet normally eschewed red meat. The very religious among them preferred to fast when it was served, but most novices ate it with relish (pepper and garlic relish) and in good conscience.

During the second week, the cardinal's appetite improved. "You know, Nimmy, this stew is actually quite delicious. Ask the cook what's in it, will you?"

"I doubt if you really want to know, m'Lord."

"No? And why are there holes and brown streaks in these apples? And why do they keep feeding me pumpkin seeds?"

"Iron nails in the apples. The Venerable Boedullus thought it's good for the blood. This is October and the pumpkins are ripe."

"But seeds only? Boedullus, eh? He's the one to whom you added a footnote, wasn't he? But not about pumpkin seeds."

"Apparently, I'll never live that down."

"Don't look so downcast. It's nothing to me. Tell me about your stay in New Jerusalem."

"She is dead, m'Lord."

"Ædrea? I'm very sorry to hear that. She was a bright young lady. A bundle of mischief, of course. Do you think you will recover from her?"

"I'll never forget."

"You learned something?"

"Yes."

"Then you have a choice of coming east with me, or staying here with your Order."

"I'll come, m'Lord. And thank you. This place has become an occasion of sin for me. I feel too much unjust anger here."

"Save your thanks. It's likely to be dangerous. And cold. It will be winter before we reach Hannegan City. Do you think you can induce one of Cardinal Ri's guard to come with us?"

"Induce? I don't understand. They regard you as their master, and even their owner."

"I know. That's why I won't tell them to do anything, until they get over that idea of ownership."

Nimmy had no trouble recruiting a bodyguard for the cardinal. They all wanted to come.

"We can't have that," he told them. "We'll be traveling with forged papers. Whoever comes will have to hide his weapons in a bedroll and wear a cassock."

Wooshin had told him Qum-Do was the best warrior among them, but he chose Weh-Geh, the smallest, whose skin was almost light brown. Only his eyes distinguished him from the local population.

By the time the cardinal's sealed papers and a letter from the Pope arrived, Brownpony was ready to leave the monastery and travel east to the Province and then to Hannegan City. The letter told him very little about Hultor's raid, except that it had happened and the Pope was being blamed. The cardinal penned a reply, begging the Pope not to think of abandoning the papacy until Brownpony returned from the Imperial Court. The message was posted in Sanly Bowitts, along with the abbey's mail, which was picked up by a messenger every ten days.

Then the three men, dressed as monks, left for the Province.

·　　·　　·

Soon after their departure, two more travelers arrived at Leibowitz Abbey. One was an old Jew on his way to the Mesa of Last Resort; he was leading two young nanny goats with blue heads, full udders, and swollen abdomens. Accompanying him was a young woman with bright blond hair, only a little less pregnant than the goats. The old Jew would accept no hospitality beyond a drink of water, a few biscuits, and some cold young mutton. The girl had escaped from captivity by her family, and demanded to see the father of her unborn child.

"They left two days ago. He told the cardinal you were dead," said Olshuen.

"He thinks I'm dead, but the cardinal knows better."

The abbot gritted his teeth and offered grudging hospitality, although the guesthouse was half full of alien warriors and a gunrunner; there were no separate facilities for women, and the monk she was seeking had departed.

"You can stay in a locked cell," he told her, "with a night pot. You'll be safe enough."

"Who keeps the key?"

Olshuen thought for a moment. Might she not come out and molest the men, as well as the other way around?

"Oh, well, I'll keep it myself," he said at last.

"Locked in by you?" She glanced up at three monks regarding her curiously from the top of the parapet wall. Grinning wickedly, she pulled up the front of her leather skirt to waist level. Under it she wore nothing. With her swollen abdomen and her bright blond beaver, she did a bump and grind just for a horrified abbot, dropped the skirt, turned on her heel, and marched away with a wiggling ass toward Sanly Bowitts. Someone cheered. The abbot glared up at the parapet, but the three monks had vanished. Soon a man with a mule and a wagonload of sheep manure stopped to give her a ride. Some minutes later he picked up the old Jew, and went on with the goats tied behind the tailgate.

"Blacktooth, Blacktooth," Olshuen muttered in disgust, and retired to the chapel, where he fell on his knees and tested his pulse before praying. A monk who began to pray, without first quieting heart and mind, prayed badly. He said a rapid paternoster with a rapid pulse and went back to his office.

The journey from Leibowitz Abbey to the eastern boundary of Jackrabbit territory would take nearly two months. Önmu Kun had provided the cardinal with a list of churches whose pastors and their flocks were of mostly Nomad ancestry, and to whom Kun had sold guns. Some of them were also on the cardinal's list of correspondents with SEEC. As long as they visited only such churches, their identity was secure. But the cardinal wanted to pass through settlements close to the telegraph line, so that he might pick up news from Valana and Hannegan City. They traveled far enough north so that the Bay Ghost River could be forded without swimming the horses, and also without passing an imperial checkpoint. Their journey thereafter was plotted on a map from church to church, settlement to settlement. It was grim dry land, for they traveled mostly to the north of fertile hill country.

It was at one such settlement at the old town of Yellow that Brownpony learned the extent of the offenses of War Sharf Brâm against the *Qœsach dri Vørdar*, and of the former's ritual death. He had never met Eltür Brâm (Demon Light), who was said to be Hultor's fraternal twin, younger by two hours. A Jackrabbit priest named Steps-on-Snake who knew the Grasshopper family told the cardinal that Eltür was less belligerent, less impulsive, but perhaps more cunning than his twin, whom he had worshiped. His election by the grandmothers surprised Steps-on-Snake, who said Eltür would certainly avenge his brother.

From the Grasshopper, Filpeo Harq had demanded the surrender as criminals of all warriors involved in the massacre, and the surrender too of fifty Grasshopper children to be held as hostages insuring against future raids, and the payment of half the Grasshopper's total wealth in cattle and horses. The alternative was said to be total war. But the Imperial Mayor's forces at present lacked logistics to support a dug-in infantry force on the open Plains, although Texark was working on it. Filpeo could only send out his cavalry to harass and be decimated. He would be ready to fight when he could occupy and hold territory. It was his continued occupation and holding of Grasshopper lands that left him little to spare for enlarging his lands in the west. If Texark's fighters had lost sixty-six out of ninety-nine men in a battle, the survivors would not celebrate. "It took dirty, heathen Nomads to act thus," the priest said wryly. For the foreseeable future the war against the Grasshopper was going to be fitful and opportunistic, but cruel.

The Province south of the Nady Ann was ruled by a proconsul commanding an army of police whose obvious and age-old job was to protect the property of the rich from the greed of the Jackrabbit poor. Blacktooth thought of the guns Önmu Kun was bringing into the territory. Lest some of them fall into Texark hands, they were not the

most advanced weapons in the New Jerusalem arsenal, and it seemed
to him doubtful that the Jackrabbit was yet capable of revolution,
although he had heard talk in Yellow of Jackrabbit bandits, motherless
ones, in the hill country far to the south. "Bandit" was a Texark political term.

One fact to Filpeo's advantage was that the Lord of the Three
Hordes, Holy Little Bear Madness, was pressing the new Grasshopper
sharf to avoid battle. The only permissible attack was a counterattack.
Whether Demon Light was more loyal to his lord, the Sharf of Sharfs,
than his brother had been was an open question. News of Brâm's raid
had caused exultation in the Province, coupled with rage at the Grasshopper grandmothers for his ritual death.

All these things Brownpony learned from the Jackrabbit priest at
Yellow, where there was an interesting crater nearly as large as
Meldown, but inhabited by living things. Steps-on-Snake was in close
touch with a Grasshopper Nomad who lived nearby with the family of
his Jackrabbit wife. News from his own family and the horde this husband picked up from a man who lived on the Nady Ann and watched
Grasshopper and Wilddog signalmen on hilltops beyond the river. The
signals were whole-body movements, many rhythmic, and the movements included those of his closely reined mount; such signals were
broad enough to be seen and understood at great distance. After such
a broadcast, Grasshopper news took several days to reach Yellow.

And so Brownpony's host, Father Steps-on-Snake, was in touch
with the Grasshopper, and also with a Texark sergeant who overheard
all the official news at a nearby telegraph terminal, and apparently
decided for himself as to the sensitivity of information.

"How can you trust the sergeant?" the cardinal wondered.

"His girlfriend is one of my parishioners, and she brings him to
my church every Sunday. I trust her because she likes him less than he
likes her. He is too simple to dissemble. But no, I am not prepared to
believe him always and every time."

"Is there any way you can get a message to the Pope in Valana?"

"No," said Steps-on-Snake, but hesitated. "It would be a dangerous thing to try."

"I need to try dangerous things."

"It would put a parishioner in danger."

"The girl?"

"Yes, and the corporal, and myself."

"But you know a way?"

"She sent a message once to a relative in the west by coding it
and getting the boyfriend to inject it anonymously into the stream of
traffic."

"And she could do it again?"

"Don't press me about it tonight," Father Steps-on-Snake answered crossly. "I'll see what can be done."

"The Pope must be persuaded not to resign."

"And a message from Your Eminence would persuade him?"

"I can't promise it."

"Neither can I, but I'll talk to her."

In three days, the message was sent. Although it said only, "Do nothing until I see Filpeo Harq," this tiny nugget was concealed somehow in a few hundred words of schoolgirl correspondence, and Brownpony had no idea how the addressee was identified or what the method of delivery would be.

"All I can say is that it's better than not trying" was all he could say.

He was reluctant to hurry away from the town of Yellow, because this was as close as their journey would take them to the Nady Ann River, across which came news of events on the Plains to the north. Father Steps-on-Snake was a man knowledgeable about the ongoing interaction between civilization and the Nomadic societies of the great grasslands. He had been born during the conquest, and remembered when his father had gone to join rebels in the hill country to the south. When his father was killed, he, like Brownpony more than a generation later, found himself in the custody of nuns for schooling. Later, as a young man, he had gone north with a Wilddog friend, but he lacked the talents of warrior and herdsman, and thus found no family willing to adopt him. He considered joining a band of the motherless ones, but the nuns had given him a sense of sin, so he returned to the Province and became a priest.

Now he was delighted to accept Cardinal Brownpony as his spiritual leader instead of Cardinal Benefez, and his sense of sin did not object to allowing his parishioners to acquire forbidden firearms from Önmu Kun. He even promised to encourage the development of a secret local militia among those he knew to be loyal both to the Church and to a Nomad heritage.

Probably he knew little more about Nomad culture than did Blacktooth and Brownpony, but he was seventy-five years old and saw things from a different viewpoint, which seemed global and almost detached from the passion of his Jackrabbit loyalty.

Father Steps-on-Snake had the most comprehensive view of the Nomad situation any of his three guests had ever heard. Much of it they already knew, in fragments. But the septuagenarian pastor put the fragments together in a larger picture. He was very disturbed by the raid of Hultor Bråm, and not just for the moral reasons of a priest.

The dead sharf was not stupid. He had believed in his own imminent death, for the Weejus had prophesied it to him after his ordeal in the pit. His raid, according to this Jackrabbit priest, was a message to none other than Cardinal Brownpony himself, right here in this rectory, to Brownpony whom Bråm had recognized as the significant figure of power in the Church at Valana.

The cardinal shook his head in apparent discomfort with the idea, but Nimmy noticed he made no denial. "The Grasshopper is always at war," he murmured instead.

"What do you mean by that?"

"It's just something one of his warriors said to me when we rode south from Meldown to meet the Pope."

Steps-on-Snake insisted that Bråm took the war party all the way to the gates of Rome to show the cardinal (and, of course, the Pope) that the brunt of any war would be borne by the Grasshopper, not the Wilddog, and that the Valana papacy was wasting its energy in courting Chür Ösle Høngan. The "success" of the raid was also a demonstration to Filpeo Harq that his opening to the west was more apparent than real, given certain advantages possessed by the Grasshopper. As he listened to this provincial Jackrabbit father, Blacktooth began to admire the late Grasshopper sharf for his bravery and steadfastness of purpose, in spite of his murderous bent. Again, Nimmy wondered if Bråm might be his remote relative.

Steps-on-Snake summarized the military, cultural, and historical situation as he saw it:

One advantage which the Nomad warrior had over the Texark cavalryman was that, as everyone knew, the warrior had grown up on horseback. It is commonplace that a tribe with no previous experience of horses, upon first seeing mounted warriors of an alien nation, see the horse and rider together as a single strange animal. Then they learn to see the phenomenon as two. But if the warriors of the alien nation happened to be Plains Nomads, the first impression would be the correct one. The Nomad horse and the Nomad rider together are one. When at work or at war, a mounted man is not called by his own name, but by the name of his horse, and on formal occasions by the name of his horse and the name of his horse's breeder, often the man's wife's mother. The man was, after all, only the controller of the horse, in war or at work with cattle.

Among the things one first noticed about a Nomad encampment, temporary or permanent, was that there were more females to be seen than males, unless one happened to come on a feast day when most of the warrior herdsmen returned from the open plains, where they usually lived with the half-wild cattle. When the herdsmen came home, they appeared almost as wild strangers in their own camp or village, where the old men, young boys, the maimed or disabled lived and sometimes worked with the women. At least the boys worked. Older boys became horse wranglers. Younger boys tended the remuda and tried to ride the partly broken horses. The old men tended to feel that their deeds of past glory entitled them to nonproductive retirement in comfort while the boys and women cooked, cleaned, carried water, mended, made clay pots, and tended the horses. Occasionally, a Weejus woman would use her supernatural powers to induce a retired old warrior to work, as long as the task was not demeaning, but the veterans were a lazy lot, usually protected in their retirement by multiple affiliations to the Bear Spirit. Sometimes they redeemed themselves by offering bursts of healing wisdom when the young men were split in angry controversy.

The average herdsman-warrior north of the Nady Ann was still illiterate, and spoke only the dialect of his horde, but his mother was Weejus, or his grandmother, and was probably learning to read herself, and might even be teaching his younger brothers and sisters. Although lacking in letters or a second language, the average Nomad now imagined in his mind a much larger world than his great-granduncle had imagined. He knew that the Earth did not drop off beyond the mountains, and that there were people who lived beyond the Great River to the east, and that they were just as dangerous and despicable as the human herbivores that lived on this side of the river. He even suspected that the great breeding pit of the Wild Horse Woman was not really the Navel of the World at all, and that his own grandmother's breeding pit, if she had one, was not necessarily lethal to a male human who dared enter it, although staying out of it was probably better for one's luck. He was not quite as much a Nomadic purist as his oldest uncles. He used the tools of citizens, wore citizen's cloth, drank citizen's liquor, and often ate the citizen's beans and corn if he didn't have to grow his own, as Steps-on-Snake remarked with a chuckle.

The Earth was made for growing grass, for cattle and deer and antelope and rabbits and prairie dogs and horses to live on, in turn to be lived on by men and wilddogs and several kinds of cats and buzzards. The animal hierarchy of the Plains was ruled by three overlords in a predatory partnership: men, horses, and dogs. Also by their women, mares, and bitches. Things were much simpler on the Plains than in the country of the growers of corn and beans. One might feel sorrow for farmers, as one felt sorrow for one's own prey, for the Nomad could see that the farmers were actually the prey of other men: soldiers, police, priests, and tax collectors. They were bound to one piece of land, while the Nomad owned the whole world beneath

Empty Sky. That indeed was one of the Nomad's ancient names for himself: the Nephew of the Empty Sky. Empty Sky, of course, was a person, but also he was just-look-up-at-it: empty sky. Nowhere but on the Plains from the back of a horse can a man see the Earth's vastness, unless it be from the masthead of an ocean schooner, but the Nomad was not sure he believed in oceans. He knew things came in opposites, so where he was surrounded by a semi-arid ocean of grass, to imagine an ocean of water was just a natural thought. But not all natural thoughts were real. Since his defeat of his great uncles by the second Hannegan's soldiers and the Hannegan's diseased cattle, this new Nomad had become a skeptic. He did not believe everything his uncles or his Weejus woman told him, unless he was getting ready to be a Bear Spirit man. But the average Nomad did not become a Bear Spirit man, and was skeptical of their powers. Among the Wilddog Horde, it was not a rare occurrence for a sick Nomad to visit a mountain town to find a doctor of a different tradition, especially for surgery. Usually the sick ones were young, but sometimes a half-willing older patient would be dragged to a mountain doctor by her younger kin. More than a few Bear Spirit men had worked for a time in the hospitals of the Church or the Empire, learning as much as they could of this different kind of healing. They learned to wash their hands. They learned which drugs to steal for use at home.

Then there were the myths of origin, of the birth of this grassy Earth and its true People, out of an ancient cataclysm.

During the primordial time of the great death, there was fire and ice. A few animals and a few men arose out of that terrible death. Then, after that primordial time, came the Old Time. In the Old Time, there arose a conspiracy among man, dog, and horse to rule the furry, ungoverned cattle that ranged freely on the Plains, that holy country of Empty Sky and the Sacred Mare. The alliance, the Man-Horse-Dog-Thing, controlled the furry herd to the herd's advantage, usually against the herd's will, driving them to where men knew the grass grew greener. The cattle got something from their predators in return for their flesh and hide and bone; they got Man-Horse-Dog's protection against wolves and large cats, but they remained Man-Horse-Dog's freely running prey, shot down from horseback, and the horses were superior horses.

"Today, the herds of cattle often no longer run," said Steps-on-Snake. All around the fringes of the Plains, fences were going up. These were attempts by some tribes to stay in one place year-round, building permanent houses, culling their herds (now flocks, even) in the fall, first picking out the breeding stock, then slaughtering what-ever animals could be used, eaten now or preserved for winter, and

finally selling the rest or trading with the farmers for grain. To the true
People's ultimate disgust, some of them even raised hogs.

The hordes at first considered these fence-line Nomads as outcasts, as despicable as ex-Nomads who farmed as Blacktooth's family
did, except that Blacktooth's kin farmed another man's land. But the
old women of the High Plains, these gaunt old grandmothers with
leather fists, grinning eyes, and Weejus powers, they took up the cause
of the fringe-area people, and they besieged the ears of husband,
brother, son, and father with warnings about the Night Hag, who
called to her dark bosom those chiefs who wronged their own realms
or hurt the beings that lived therein. Not only that, but if these settled
herdsmen were alienated by the roving herdsmen, they could only become allies of the farmers and of Texark.

When people began seeing the Hag, the nervous chieftains began to agree that Nomads who settled down behind fences should not
be pillaged and killed, but wooed back to the common life of the
horde if possible. This tolerance was reserved for haciendas adjacent to
existing fences, however. There were a few families on the Plains who
had dared to fence off choice areas for themselves, far from any other
fences. To these the leaders of the hordes sent warriors to tear the
fence down. They forced such people to choose between returning to
the common life or leaving the common land. Those foolish enough
to stay were killed by outlaws, who could be counted on to save the
tribes the trouble and the blood-guilt. The hordes of course joined
with the Church in condemning these murderous motherless ones.
Things had changed since the time of Høngan Ös, when Hannegan II
had spread cattle plague as a weapon of war by driving his infected
herds among those of the hordes.

The future was revealed to the tribal seers. It was foreseeable that
the open Plains would shrink, and the people and the cattle on it
would either perish or change. They had been changing continuously
through three generations since the Conquest, and what characterized
the present population was youth. The prolific grandmothers and
mothers had doubled the population in a very short time. Every Nomad warrior believed that his women's ability to produce babies fast,
running even to twins and triplets, rose and fell according to the nation's need. For whatever reason, the Great Plains were shrinking,
while their population had been growing fast of late. Was this not the
chief cause of war? It usually happened when men settled down in one
place with their women and had a lot of sex and babies, too many
children to fit into the local scheme of things. Teenage gangs become
the first warriors in this process, and because they start trouble with

other neighborhoods, it is necessary to put the gangs under the chief's command and give them violent things to do against people who are not enjoying the chief's favor. War is caused by agriculture, in the Nomad opinion. It was, after all, a herdsman killed by a farmer when Cain slew Abel, so Christians said.

The tribes were restless, anxious, angry. They all had compromised; even the wildest among them used the tools and the weapons that were manufactured in the towns and cities to the east and in the mountains. They brought their beef, hides, artwork, wolfskins, bear grease, and surplus ponies to a trading post, and then rode back to Grandmotherland leading a pack mule loaded with tools, gunpowder, musket balls, fabric, beans, and enough distilled spirits for at least the elders to get sloshed. They sang the old songs and danced the old rituals, honored the Wild People, and moved their dwellings and their herds according to the season. Each horde owned a sacred path, and sacred places along it to pitch camp for a season. They navigated the grasslands by the doings in the night sky as much as by landmarks. The sky told them when to move south. It was the middle of the thirty-third century, and Polaris traced a larger circle in the north sky than it did in the time of Leibowitz, but the hordes called themselves the people of the Polestar when they wandered. When they camped in summer, they were the people of Empty Sky and the Day Maiden. When they huddled down for winter, they were sons of the Wolf and the Hag.

Blacktooth knew much about the tradition, even though he had never lived it. But things were changing. He could see the change now; he had missed it as a boy. Power on the Plains among the warrior herdsmen was out of control, and the old women worried about it. Some leaders were chosen by men without due process of consultation with the grandmothers, the Weejus women, and the Bear Spirit men. War threatened the horses and the sacred bloodlines, and it killed grandsons. The women were usually against any war, except when necessary to curb intertribal horse theft.

When Empty Sky was dying in the presence of his Seventeen Crazy Warriors, he promised them he would come back from the dead in their time of need if each and all seventeen of them would in time of need utter his magic name of seventeen syllables. Empty Sky as part of his last will and testament taught the name to these warrior-priests who had served him best in battle, leaving to each man a different secret syllable which could be spoken only once—to speak it twice permanently paralyzed the tongue. A dying man could leave his syllable only to his eldest son, or if the son were unfit, to another chosen by the Bear Spirit shamans. Empty Sky promised to come whenever they spoke his name correctly, but to pronounce the name each man would have to utter his syllable in correct order.

What was the correct order?

They had been crowded around his couch at the time, and while most of them agreed as to who owned the first and last syllables, nobody had been counting the ones between; for example, there was a spearman who said Empty Sky had spoken in the ears of at least ten men before him, but not more than twelve. Inevitably, a skeptic who inherited his syllable from his father spoke it aloud, tried to speak it again, and was immediately struck dumb. Others heard him speak the syllable, but now doubt arose. Would it be effective if spoken in the correct order by a man other than its original custodian? And if a man spoke his own syllable, would he be able to repeat the orphan syllable as well, or would dumbness grasp his throat? But one day, about a century ago, they all got together, all except the speechless skeptic, and decided to try to call Empty Sky, because times were getting bad for the people.

When they spoke the syllables, nothing dramatic happened. They deemed it a failure, until they heard the cry of a newborn baby from the adjacent tent. The baby was the son of a mother of the royal tribe, and she was prevailed upon to name him Empty Sky, although at the time of his rite of passage to manhood, he was given the name of Høngan Ös, Mad Bear, who grew up to become the *Qæsach dri Vørdar* who led the hordes into horrible disaster. Obviously, the holy name had been misspoken.

They were fascinated by Step-on-Snake's storytelling. Nevertheless, it was necessary to go on, and to cross one branch of the Red River to the southeast, then make haste toward Hannegan City.

On the edge of town, following such a heading, they stopped at the rim of Yellow's crater. There was a small lake in the center, and the ground around it was fertile and green. Two wild horses were grazing, and somebody was fishing in the lake.

"I'm told," said Brownpony, "that this was a Jackrabbit breeding pit before the conquest."

"Is it like Meldown?" Blacktooth asked.

"No, it is not like the breeding pit of the Wild Horse Woman."

"I see there is a stone marker ahead. The place has a name."

"What is it called?"

"Lake Blessdassurance," Blacktooth read, and looked up at Brownpony, who was staring at the other side of the marker.

"Does it say something on the back side, m'Lord?"

"It says, 'Boedullus was here.'"

"Wh-a-at?" Nimmy took a look. "Paint! Recent paint. It's a joke. It has to be. Or else—" He paused. "Did you know, m'Lord, the Venerable Boedullus died in an explosion at an archaeological site he was investigating? There's a legend about a lake with a giant catfish named Bodolos that later came to live in the crater where the bomb went off."

"So it's a joke with a theory behind it. It has to be a Leibowitzian joke. Who outside your Order knows about the Venerable Boedullus?"

"Almost nobody, m'Lord, unless Nomads have been reading my translations."

"It seems to be signed with initials: BRT. I'd hate to lose time by going back to ask Father Steps-on-Snake about it."

"Let's ask that Jackrabbit farmer instead," Nimmy suggested, watching a man riding a mule toward them down the road.

The farmer laughed heartily. "My great-granduncle caught that old Bodolos nearly a century ago. He fed the whole village with it. Whoever painted the sign on the back last month couldn't spell. He was wearing the same robes as you, though."

Brownpony and Blacktooth exchanged glances. Nobody at the abbey had told them of a monk of the Order who had recently departed for the Province.

"Well, at least one Jackrabbit farmer learned to read," Brownpony later observed.

"There was a small church school at Yellow, you know."

"I'm sure there are many Nomads in the Province who can read a book but cannot ride a horse, especially in battle."

"How fast can they learn to march and shoot?" asked the usually silent Weh-Geh.

The question was considered by the monk and the prelate, but not answered.

They crossed the Red River and headed east across the grasslands. In all, they stopped at twenty-three churches, and secured the loyalty of seventeen Jackrabbit pastors, but many nights they slept in farmers' barns or found natural shelter along creekbeds. Twice they rented rooms from Texark landlords, but there were too many prying questions. The cardinal disliked lying and decided against doing it again, although it became a very cold winter during their trip; freezing rain did not usually come until January in these parts. The cardinal was still not quite well. He began to believe the Weejus' promise that he would have a shorter lifetime as a result of the ordeal. Blacktooth fed him a lot of apples into which nails had been pressed, but he seemed to be losing some of his graying red hair as well as his energy. Such was the curse of Meldown.

CHAPTER 18

The fourth kind of monks are those called Gyrovagues. These spend their whole lives tramping from province to province, staying as guests in different monasteries for three or four days at a time. . . . Of the miserable conduct of such men it is better to be silent than to speak.

—*Saint Benedict's Rule*, Chapter 1

 HEY REACHED THE OUTSKIRTS OF HANNEGAN City by early evening, and the cardinal decided to rent rooms and spend the night at an inn outside the city limits. There was the possibility of learning recent news from the innkeeper or fellow travelers; there was the inevitability of reading the government bulletin boards to learn of the response of the bureaucrats to the same recent news. There was a need to change from a monk's habit to red and black. Weh-Geh would need new clothes altogether, and could again wear his weapons as the cardinal's bodyguard. All Blacktooth needed was a bath and a change of habit. They had grown beards during the journey, but only Weh-Geh decided to shave. His whiskers were rather thin and added an alien touch to his appearance. Brownpony's beard was redder than his thinning hair. Blacktooth had more gray on his chin than on his pate, which badly needed reshaving. Weh-Geh barbered Nimmy's tonsure with a short

sword, grasping the blade with both hands and drawing it smoothly under the soapy hair. Blacktooth complained that the swordsman was leaning on him too hard.

"Only to hold you still. If you prefer, I could shave you just as easily standing back here," Weh-Geh said to the lathered monk. Blacktooth looked at him with affected fright. The guardsman held the sword drawn back past his right shoulder, as if to deliver a round-house cut to the scalp's long stubble.

"Stop boasting. Lean on me if you need to." He was surprised, because it was the first time Weh-Geh made a joke, a sinister joke besides, and one of the few times he spoke at all. In Jackrabbit coun-try, only once did a need arise to draw his long sword and Brownpony's pistol, when a group of young bullies had decided to pick on three itinerant mendicant monks for fun. Both Nimmy and the cardinal missed Wooshin. Blacktooth wondered if they had, without meaning to, resented Weh-Geh as a poor substitute for the Axe, on whose head there was a price in this realm. But Weh-Geh had no wish to be a substitute for anyone. Nimmy resolved to befriend him, if there was still time.

By midafternoon of a cold and sunny day, they were standing on the steps of the Cathedral of Holy Michael, the Angel of Battle, talk-ing to its Cardinal Archbishop. At the Archbishop's left and rear stood an attractive young acolyte wearing a long surplice with lacework and crocheted borders. Torrildo smiled happily at Blacktooth on first see-ing him, but then misinterpreted Nimmy's expression and cast his eyes on the ground. The monk was less shocked that Benefez had hired the pretty fugitive than surprised by a sudden realization that the letters BRT beneath the painted "Boedullus was here" legend at Yellow's crater lake stood for "Br. Torrildo," who had been traveling from Valana to Hannegan City.

Weh-Geh seemed ill-at-ease, for Benefez kept glancing at him, until finally the cardinal asked, "Young man, where have I seen you before?"

Brownpony answered for him, "In Valana, Urion. Weh-Geh was in Cardinal Ri's employ. Now he is in mine."

"Ah, yes, there were five or six of them, weren't there? Where are the others?"

Brownpony shook his head and shrugged. "I've been on the road for two months." The evasion was almost a lie, Blacktooth noticed.

"Of course," Benefez said, then returned to their previous con-versation: "Elia, mmm, Your Eminence, of canon law, I too have been a scholar. Before the Flame Deluge there had been only two papal resignations. One Pope, so-called, was a great sinner, one was a great saint. The former sold the papacy, the latter fled from it in holy terror. But the question arises whether either of these men was a legitimate pope. So can a real pope resign? I think not. If he resigns, he was never elected by the Holy Ghost in the first place. This may be against the majority opinion, but it is my opinion. A poet of his own time put him in Hell, but that poet was a bitter man. I think the old fellow was really hallowed, but I doubt the legitimacy of his election in the first place. If he were Pope, he would not and could not resign, and would not be talking about resignation."

"Are we talking about San Pietro of Mount Murrone, or Pope Amen Specklebird?" Brownpony asked.

"Aren't they two of a kind?"

"No, Urion, they are not." He hesitated. "Well, how can I say? Amen Specklebird I have known. I know San Pietro only from a book at Leibowitz Abbey. The writer thought he was a saintly clown."

"Doesn't this describe Amen Specklebird? In a charitable way?"

Brownpony paused. He seemed to be leaving himself open on all sides. Blacktooth tried to remember Wooshin's word for it. *Happu biraki*, he thought. In a fight, it was usually a deadly invitation to be foolhardy.

Brownpony closed in. "If so, then this saintly clown, Pope Amen, His Holiness, is disposed to absolve you, Urion, of any penalty of excommunication you may have incurred, *crimine ipso laesae majestatis facto*, or any other act of rebellion you may have committed in thought, word, or deed. I am here to announce this."

Blacktooth noticed that the purple in the face of Benefez was not merely reflected light from his purple vestments (it had been a day for burying the dead). He did not sputter, however, but purred, "How utterly wonderful of him, Elia. From so generous a man, I'll bet the penance I have to do is only kiss his ring."

"I doubt he would allow you to do that, Urion. He is an honest man. There are no conditions, and no penance unless I choose to impose one."

"You?"

"The Pope sent a plenipotentiary in this case. Me."

"You!"

"And I unbind you, Urion, without condition, *in nomine Patris Filiique Spiritusque Sancti*."

Blacktooth saw the Archbishop's right hand twitch toward mirroring the sign of the cross Brownpony made over him, but it was only the twitch of habit.

"Your credentials are as good as your Latin, Elia. Go home and stop being my gadfly."

"I am also empowered to offer you control over those churches in the Province where the parishioners are mostly settlers or soldiers whose native tongue is Ol'zark."

"Oh, I see. It's not a matter of geography, then."

"Geography is boundaries and fences. These don't mean much to a Nomad."

"Yes, we had a recent demonstration of that just west of New Rome. Human life doesn't mean much to them either, and they eat men's flesh."

"Only men they honor. It is a funeral rite, or a tribute to a brave dead enemy."

"You defend this evil thing!"

"No, I merely describe it."

Someone was yelling "Make way! Make way!" in the distance, and Cardinal Benefez looked up the street.

"Apparently my nephew is coming down the road," he said to Brownpony. "Do you want to step inside?"

"You mean do I want to hide? No, Urion, thank you. I must see him in order to deliver this." He showed Benefez the sealed papers which he had received at the abbey from Valana. "I must go to the palace to request an audience, unless he sees us and stops."

The Emperor was in a hurry as usual, and ordered his driver to wield the whip. He waved in a friendly way to his subjects in the streets who bowed or curtsied as the royal coach hurried on, preceded by two mounted guards whose costumes were more elegant than that of their ruler. Filpeo wanted to be seen as a man of frugal habits, generous to his subjects, and devoted to the economic interests of the Empire. He sought to distance himself in public from the ferocity of some of his predecessors, and had shortened the list of crimes for which the penalty was death. His own ferocity was carefully contained. He had secretly, on several occasions, insisted on administering the supreme penalty himself, but few men knew about this. One who had known it was named Wooshin, and it was the Hannegan's personal fascination with death by the art of the headsman which had, in fact, cost him his best executioner. The fellow had been repelled by his own art when practiced by his master. And Harq had let him get away! It was one of his few mistakes in judging men.

Filpeo Harq was a Hannegan only on his mother's side, and some considered this inheritance of the throne through the motherline su-

premely ironic, given the masculine, patrilineal, and certainly patriarchal cast of the Texark civilization, which in its origins was a reaction
to the matriline culture of the Plains. The original Hannegan (or
Høngan with a Jackrabbit pronunciation), the conqueror of the city,
had been leader of a band of Nomad "outlaws," and his acquisition of
the mayorality of the small town and trading post called Texark had
been by conquest. The term "outlaws" was a farmer's word; Nomads,
who despised them but feared them less, called them "motherless
ones," a term which was applied to those wanderers of the Prairie who
either evaded family ties because of hostility, or found themselves
unwanted by any woman of the horde, and these men formed homo-
sexual (not necessarily in the erotic sense) war bands, taking their
women by violence when they felt the urge and saw the chance, and
keeping them, if at all, as servants.

From the point of view of the *civis*, every *nomas* was an outlaw,
but in the Nomad view, the motherless ones had deviated so far from
the Nomad cultural norm that they were loathed by the people of the
Plains more than they were by the farmers along the eastern fringe
whom they sometimes plundered. As is usually the case, a completely
alien enemy is less to be despised than a deviant brother. The motherless ones who originally conquered Texark had been driven there by
the right-thinking orthodox Nomads of the several hordes. It was an
infusion of fresh blood and new ideas for the sleepy trading community and the surrounding farmers, and Texark began to grow and to be
fortified. It was located in a place where, exposed on both flanks, in
order to grow at all it was forced to conquer or perish. However, after
five generations the mutation of barbarian outlaw into civilized aristo-
crat was nearly complete, and Filpeo was a popular ruler except in the
conquered territories.

The town of Texark itself, or Texarkana improperly so-called in
the Latin of the Church, was not located at the site (now lost) of the
ancient city of that name. Now called Hannegan City, it did lie on the
Red River, and it grew up at the vague boundary between forest and
plain, where it was originally a minor center of commerce between the
two areas, the sown and the treeless wild. The relatively peaceful Jackrabbit people had come here to trade surplus cattle, horses, and hides
for wood, metal, spirits, medicinal herbs, products of the blacksmith's
art, and whatever trinkets the merchants could show that caught the
Nomad fancy. Among the merchants, however, there were a few
panderers who took advantage of the sexual hungers of the motherless
ones, and actually sold them brides, or rented them for a while. That
was the beginning of it. When the price of brides went up, the bandits
killed the merchants, took what they wanted, and settled down, but

they themselves, not their captive wives, kept and managed the horses—and every other kind of property. In one generation, a way of life was turned on its head.

Filpeo Harq himself was a student of this local and family history, which was not so well known to the residents of his realm. He had taken a personal interest in the writings of historians at the collegium, now a thriving university, and he who wanted tenure and royal favor wrote to please the monarch. He who wrote otherwise was rarely published, and failed to thrive. To put it mildly.

In passing his uncle's church, the Monarch suddenly signaled his driver to go slow. He pointed at a group of clergy, including his uncle Urion, standing on the steps in the morning sun. Cardinal Benefez seemed to be arguing warmly with another man in a red zucchetto whose back was toward the coach.

"Who is that man?" Filpeo asked sharply.

"Which one, Your Imperial Honor?"

The cardinal with his back toward the coach suddenly looked over his shoulder. The Mayor's head disappeared inside the window and he knocked for the driver to hurry on. Beside the second cardinal stood one man in the robes of the Albertian Order of Leibowitz, and another man-at-arms who was probably a bodyguard. He thought he knew who one of them might be. The armed man was too alien in appearance to be the cardinal's secretary. And Uncle Urion appeared to have acquired another pretty young man as acolyte.

"Drive on, drive on."

The manufacturer's representative had already arrived at the War College when the imperial coach discharged its royal passenger and his courtiers, but he and the officers in charge were not yet ready for the demonstration. Irritated by the delay, but determined to make use of every idle moment, Filpeo called an immediate meeting of staff to discuss long-term strategy on the Plains. It was disquieting to the officers to be quizzed by the Monarch on such an impromptu basis with no preparation, and Filpeo always enjoyed putting them in such a situation. He learned a lot from the practice, and it helped him weed out the fools. The commanders of Infantry and Corps of Engineers were out of the city on maneuvers, however, and their seconds were summarily yanked out of their offices and hauled to the conference room.

Admiral e'Fondolai was there in person, and so was General Goldæm, Chief of Staff, and Major General Alvasson of the Cavalry.

Infantry and Engineers were represented by Colonels Holofot and Blindermen. Not as a joke, but in a joking manner, Filpeo Harq himself collared Colonel Pottscar, S.I., in the corridor while the Ignatzian Chief Chaplain was returning from Mass and pulled him along to the meeting. "Someone may need your services here, Father," said the Monarch to the astonished Pottscar. "It may even be me. Did you know that Cardinal Brownpony and probably his troublesome monk-secretary are in town."

Colonel Father Pottscar nodded. "I just heard about it as I left the church. By now, he must have requested an audience with Your Honor, no?"

"No! Not that I have been told about."

"I'm sure he will, but naturally he would see the Archbishop first."

"By God, I should have him arrested. If Urion knew he was coming, he would have told me. What the hell is going on?"

"I would guess, Your Honor, that he has come to plead the cause of the man he calls Pope."

"Hah! The man who sent the Grasshopper Horde to smash its way to New Rome! By God, they killed two-thirds of the Nomads, and we chased that bastard Curia back to Valana with their Specklebird, all right. But they left a lot of dead men and raped women and burned buildings. There hasn't been an atrocity like that before the second Hannegan's conquest. And now we've got trouble with the Grasshopper all along the frontier, mainly because of him!"

"Who, Brownpony? Sire, you have been misinformed. He was not even with the Curia, so-called, at that time. He was with Monsignor Sanual at the Nomad election. Sanual told me that. He was quite shocked by Brownpony. Says the man is a pagan. But although he rode south with the Grasshopper to meet the Pope, he did not join the others but continued south. Your Honor, according to one of my chaplains in the area of conflict, the, uh, pretender Pope turned back with his whole retinue when the guards refused to let them cross the border. This priest says the Nomad escort attacked only after they were separated from the Valanan cardinals. It's not at all clear that they were acting under Valana's instruction. I know the Archbishop had received a message from this crazy Specklebird. It probably told him Brownpony was coming."

"I wonder that the guards let him cross the border!"

"I doubt that he came through the skirmishing zone, Sire. He probably crossed from the Province."

"By way of Leibowitz Abbey, I dare say, for he was with a monk of theirs. Right now, I want you to send one of your chaplains to bring Brownpony to me. Let a military policeman go with him. Let them not take no for an answer. Bring that monk along too."

Colonel Father Pottscar hurried away. The Hannegan glanced curiously at Admiral e'Fondolai and asked, "I don't remember calling you here. Do we need the Navy to fight Nomads on the Plains? Not that you aren't welcome—"

"I asked him to come," explained General Goldæm. "Brownpony inherited six alien warriors from a cardinal who died in conclave, and Carpy here knows something about their race and nation. We might need to know."

The admiral frowned. Carpios Robbery had been e'Fondolai's nom de guerre in his pirate days, when he had become the second man since antiquity to circumnavigate the globe, but he hated to be called "Carpy," especially in the presence of his Hannegan.

They entered the conference room. First, the Emperor asked about the status of the forces protecting new farming lands, and any further encounters with the Grasshopper people. Told they had drawn back defensively, Filpeo ordered there be no punitive raids by Texark forces until he so commanded. He then stated, "If I were a Grasshopper war sharf, I would make an alliance with the Wilddog to strike the Province. I would cut the telegraph line in several places. The Wilddog will cut the Province in half, while Grasshopper strikes toward Texark. What is your response?"

Colonel Father Pottscar entered the room and nodded to Filpeo.

Colonel Holofot spoke. "They can destroy, but they cannot hold. Such an invasion can be no more than a massive cavalry raid. Our forts would remain secure. They might massacre the Jackrabbit settlers and the colonists, but they would quickly exhaust themselves and be driven back, as in the Grasshopper raid."

General Goldæm looked levelly at his ruler and shook his head. "Your scenario is improbable, Sire. When they began establishing winter quarters after the war, they became vulnerable. If they attacked the south, they know our cavalry would strike in the north at their family settlements, which would not be well defended. When the hordes were entirely mobile, they could retreat forever. They could lead pursuers to exhaustion. Now they have fixed property. It's vulnerable. They have no infantry to take or hold ground."

"Suppose the Jackrabbit revolted and joined the invaders?"

"We have kept them disarmed," said the engineer, Colonel Holofot. "What will they fight with, pitchforks?"

"No, but if they could provide the invaders with food, water, shelter, and places to hide," said the general. "The question is: would they? The Jackrabbit has bitter memories of the Northerners, for the wild hordes were contemptuous of the Jacks. Frankly, to me it seems a tossup whether they hate us more, or the Northerners. But even with Jackrabbit support, Colonel Holofot is right. A mass cavalry attack would exhaust itself in the south, and the northern underbelly would be exposed. They would be more likely to strike the farmlands north of the Valley, uh, north of the Watchitah Nation, and that is what we are not well prepared for yet. But we are preparing fast, and the whole border will be fortified in two years. The surviving farmers there are well armed now, and since the raid, they have a lot of hate for Nomads. We have the troops to back them up, but not to attack prematurely, because we have the same problem in the north as they in the south."

"And that is?"

"We can attack and kill, but we don't have the men or the logistics to occupy Grasshopper territory. Unless, of course, we weaken our forces in the Province."

Filpeo became thoughtful. "I wonder," he said, "why is it that these farms on the eastern fringe, which get more rain, are not as productive as the refugee lands at the foot of the Rockies, where the land is said to be nearly a desert?"

There was a brief silence. The Hannegan's remarks seemed almost idle, having nothing to do with the Nomad as a military problem.

"Sire, that question is outside my field," said the commanding general. "But it may have something to do with discipline. As you know, ours are free peasants, and they work mostly for themselves. When you say 'productive,' you mean it in terms of commercial crops. The ex-Nomads are sharecroppers, working for landowners, especially the Bishop of Denver. They are forced to work, and they grow only a few crops."

"I think that is not an explanation," said Father Colonel Pottscar. "And it's not quite true. The ex-Nomads learned from the mountaineers, who have been dry-farming for centuries. And as for the rainfall—there is a monastery in the hills north of Valana where the monks keep records of events in the heavens, waiting for the coming of the Lord. One of the things they keep track of is rain, because they pray for the weather. They say the rainfall on the western side of the mountains is now nearly twice what it was eight hundred years ago. That, and that alone, is your miracle of the ex-Nomad farms. Of course, the monks think it's their miracle, answering eight centuries of prayer. But the runoff for irrigation is better than in ancient times, miracle or no."

"Well, doesn't the increase apply to the whole Plains?" asked the Monarch.

"Their records are local. I can't say. Thon Graycol points out that there are no very old trees in the edges of our forests where the prairie begins looking eastward. That suggests our tree line has been moving slowly westward for a few centuries, but nobody is sure. The Nomads may have cut the older trees for wood."

"Well," said General Goldæm, "if nature is closing in on them from the east and the west, they're going to lose their precious desert anyway. We'll just give nature a hand in their extinction."

"Extinction? I don't want to hear that word again, General," Filpeo Harq said sharply. "Pacification and containment are the goals, not extermination. We have achieved that in the south. The Jackrabbit population is stable."

"Except that their young men keep running away to join outlaw bands."

"The northern Nomads kill most of those. One way, maybe the only way, to secure the area between the forests and the western mountains is to colonize."

"How, Sire? Except along the eastern fringe, the land is poor, the water scarce, and the weather horrid. Who could, who would live there but wild herdsmen?"

"Tame herdsmen, and a tamer breed of cattle," said Filpeo Harq. "Fenced ranches, as in the south. Some places down there, they use yellowwood trees for fences. If you plant them a foot apart and keep them pruned, they make hedges dense enough and thorny enough to keep cattle in. There may not be enough water for agriculture, but wells can be dug to water stock. Some land can be fenced, farther north where the cold kills yellowwood. We hold much forested land in the east. Enough timber can be shipped to settlers, and they'll pay with beef and hides. And I'm not so sure agriculture is impossible either. The university is studying that problem. Until civilized men can live there, the Plains will remain an obstacle. The Pope might as well be living on the moon, and there is no way to unify the continent."

"But who in hell would want to live there?"

Harq the Hannegan thought for a moment. "The Jackrabbit itself has settled down in the south. That's why I won't stand for talk of extermination."

"But they were always half-settled anyway, Sire. The Wilddog and the Grasshopper would prefer to die in battle than give up their ways. To farm or to ranch is hard work. To the Nomad, work is slavery."

"The ex-Nomads learned to work when they lost their horses. You merely predict their choice. We must not allow them to have such a choice. There is no need to colonize the Plains if we can civilize the wild tribes themselves. I want Urion to send missions to the northern hordes."

"Cardinal Urion sent Monsignor Sanual to them, and he came back empty-handed, and I think empty-headed. The Christians among them are already tied to Valana, Sire, and there is a rumor this Pope in Valana means to take the Jackrabbit churches away from our Archbishop," said the chaplain.

"There is no Pope in Valana, and until there is a Pope in New Rome, they are tied to nobody. And Urion hopes to be the next Pope. If not, we'll see whether Urion or some antipope offers them sweeter salvation. Especially to the Grasshopper, after we punish them. The time is ripe for change. The papacy is up for grabs. The new Lord of the Hordes is a Wilddog, not a Grasshopper. We have to influence both.

"Please understand," continued the Hannegan, after a pause, "that what I ask of you is to tell me what you think would happen if we do this, or we do that, even if I would never do either. To show you what I mean, I ask General Goldæm what he thinks would happen if we undertook a war to simply wipe out the Nomad population of the northern Plains."

He spoke again after a silence. "Well, General?"

"Sire, I did not really mean to suggest—"

"Very well, I realize you were just making bellicose noises to exercise your military gland, but go ahead. Answer my question: What would happen if we undertook to wipe out the Grasshopper and the Wilddog?"

The general reddened, and after a few seconds said, "I think we would fail. We're stretched out. We occupy and police the Jackrabbit country below the Nady Ann. If we try to hit the Grasshopper hard, he can pull back until our supply wagons can't supply our forces."

"The Nomad can live on carrion and crickets. Why can't you?"

"I can, but we can't fight without powder and shot."

"Good enough. You have now taken charge of your military gland. However, you can put it to work again and organize a battalion of a special strike force. I want men trained to out-Nomad the Nomads. Take the biggest, toughest, meanest men you can find, both from our own ranks and from any motherless outlaws you can recruit. Teach them to live on the land, speak Nomadic, and learn their way of signaling."

"And what exactly is the battalion's mission, Sire? Not to hold ground, surely."

"Of course not. The mission is to surprise, kill, destroy, and run. Punitive strikes, in case there's another attack on the farmlands. As for weapons, be sure they have the new biologicals from the university. Draft Thon Hilbert, if you have to."

Goldæm looked at Carpios, made a sour mouth, and winked. He did not believe that biologicals were the wave of the military future and he hoped Carpy agreed; but the pirate admiral merely shrugged.

Filpeo turned to the chaplain.

"Colonel Pottscar, suppose my uncle the Archbishop had unlimited funds to spend on the conversion of the Grasshopper Horde. What would happen?"

"Well, if he didn't spend it on young boys, he would waste it sending people like Monsignor Sanual."

The Mayor seemed to suppress a giggle. "How would he spend it on young boys? Charitably?"

"Oh, of course. I was only thinking about how he just last week took in a refugee from Leibowitz Abbey. He hired a young Brother Torrildo as his assistant and acolyte. He's always thinking of the welfare of young boys."

"I'm acquainted with my uncle, Father Colonel Pottscar. My question is: do you think spending money to Christianize the Nomads would be a wise investment?"

"No."

"Why?"

"Because the Nomads would be baptized, take the money, ignore the priests, and do as they have always done."

"Just so. Well, look at the clock! Let us go inspect the wares of the gunsmiths, gentlemen."

"Wait a moment, Sire," said Goldæm. "I think Carp . . . uh, the admiral might have something to say first."

"Go right ahead, Carp," said the Hannegan.

The admiral winced slightly, but said, "The guns the alien warriors brought with them disappeared soon after they met Brownpony."

"How do you know that? And if true, what does it mean?"

"I heard it from Esitt Loyte, Sire. Their homeland has firearms superior to our own, and such guns are now being made on the west coast." He took out a small pistol, only to have it snatched from his hand by one of Filpeo's bodyguards. The guard seemed to have trouble determining if the gun was loaded. The admiral assured him that it was not.

"Where did you get that thing?" Filpeo asked.

"About fifty-eight hundred nautical miles from here, Sire. On a great circle course, almost northwest, I'd guess. Or sixty-three hundred miles, by rhumb line course, nearly due west. That's my best guess without looking at the charts."

"Across the ocean? Not our west coast?"

"No, but they're in production on our west coast by now."

"Show me how it works, Admiral," said Filpeo.

Carpios Robbery pulled five cartridges out of his pocket, loaded the revolver, walked to the nearest window, aimed at the sky, and shocked their eardrums by holding down the trigger and rapidly fanning the hammer five times with the edge of his hand. When he turned around, Filpeo looked pale.

"My God! Is that what's been piling up in the Suckamint Mountains?"

"I have no way of knowing that, Sire. But this special battalion you want Goldy to organize should have a lot of firepower."

"Give me the weapon. Let's go see the gunsmiths."

The admiral released the pistol with obvious reluctance.

According to the gunsmiths' salesmen, the prototype of a similar weapon was already on the drawing board and might be ready in two years, but they were alarmed to see a competitive firearm already in production.

"Would your possession of this gun hasten production?"

"That is very likely, Sire."

Carpios Robbery winced again.

"I'll let you have it before you leave the city," Filpeo said, then looked at his admiral's expression and added, "Of course, you must send it back to its owner here when you're done with it."

"Certainly, Sire."

Brownpony's interview with His Imperial Majesty Filpeo Harq, Mayor Hannegan VII, happened in City Hall, also called the Imperial Palace, on Thursday, the 5th of January, thus giving the lie to a Jackrabbit rumor extant in the Province which held that Filpeo Harq always had himself locked up in his private quarters for three days about the time of the full moon, and would see no one. That Thursday the moon was full, and after opening the sealed papers from Pope Amen, the Monarch flew into such a rage that Blacktooth wished the rumor were true. He and Weh-Geh were made to sit on a bench in the corridor outside the mayoral throne room, and they could hear only muffled shouting without being able to understand much of it. None of the shouting was done by the cardinal.

Presently a priest with a monsignor's bellyband came down the hall and spoke to the guards. One of them knocked hard, opened the door, and shouted, "Monsignor Sanual, in obedience to the Lord Mayor's summons," and pushed him inside, then followed him and closed the door. There was a lull in the shouting.

Blacktooth had never seen Sanual before, but had heard enough about him from both his master and Father Steps-on-Snake to know that he would be anything but a friendly witness, and that Brownpony's actions at the funeral festival on the Plains and his participation in the affair with the Wild Horse Woman were on the court's agenda. He exchanged a glance with Weh-Geh, and saw that both of them were aware of this.

The guard who took Sanual inside now opened the door and spoke to the other guard. "Seize them," he said, and again closed the door.

The guard had no way to seize them, but he pointed his gun at Weh-Geh and told him to throw his swords aside. Two seconds later, he was flat on his back with a sword point at his throat.

"Get his weapon, Brother?" It was a suggestion, not a command.

"No," said Blacktooth. "That was a mistake, Weh-Geh. Remember the cardinal."

Weh-Geh looked at the door. Then he booted the fallen guard in the stomach. Having taken the wind out of the man, he grabbed the gun and burst through the door. Nimmy observed the startled Monarch sitting on his throne. Brownpony had been forced to his knees, and the guard was holding a pistol to his head. Weh-Geh aimed at Filpeo Harq, and barked, "Let my master go!"

Nimmy leaped away from the door, for the Mayor was flanked by two more guards with raised muskets. The man gasping for breath crawled toward Nimmy, who leaped over him to avoid a fight.

There were three distinct explosions, then silence, followed by Filpeo Harq's voice: "Take him and the one in the hall away."

Blacktooth looked inside again. Weh-Geh lay in a growing pool of blood. One of the musketeers was down, but the Mayor himself was holding a pistol. It looked like the one Ædrea had showed to him in the cave. It was impossible to guess who had killed Weh-Geh. All weapons were still pointed at his body. When the Hannegan saw Nimmy standing white-faced in the door, he raised his pistol again, but the monk leaped aside. He made no attempt to escape. A frightened and humiliated Cardinal Brownpony was still kneeling there.

One of the jails at Hannegan City was part of the public zoo, where interesting prisoners were exhibited in cages not unlike those used for cougars, true wolves, and monkeys. On the way in, they passed an open area girded by a heavy fence on which there was a sign saying CAMELUS DROMEDARIUS, AFRICA, CONTRIB. ADMIRAL E'FONDOLAI.

"Guard, what are those things?" Brownpony asked.

"It says right there," snapped the jail guard. "Don't stop to gawk."

"They're domesticated!"

"How astute of you. Otherwise, the boy wouldn't be riding on the animal's back, eh?"

"Are they useful?"

"They can go for longer periods without water than horses. The admiral says they are used in desert warfare where he got them."

"Are there more of them?"

"Not as far as I know, but there soon will be." He pointed to a female with a large belly. "But they're the only camels in captivity on this continent, as far as I know. The admiral brought them in the hold of a giant schooner. Now move along, move along!"

They were escorted past cells full of lesser animals, and then cells full of human prisoners. On each cell was posted the name of the occupant species. The humans were mostly murderers: a *Homo sicarius*, a *Homo matricidus*, but two *Homines seditiosi*, and one child rapist. All of them jeered as the two clerics were locked into the third cell on the left. The jailer unwrapped a sign and posted it above the door of the cage, out of sight and out of reach. The man in the cell across the roofless corridor from theirs looked at it, entered a whispered conversation with the man in the adjacent cell, and fell silent, watching them as if in awe. His own cage was labeled not *Homo* but *Gryllus* (Grasshopper), and his crimes were war crimes. His jeering had been limited to Nomad grunts, so when the jailer was gone Blacktooth spoke to the man in his native tongue.

"What does our sign say?" he asked.

The man did not answer. He and Brownpony were staring at each other. "I know you," the cardinal said in Wilddog. "You were with Hultor Bråm."

The Nomad nodded. "Yes," he answered in his own dialect. "We took you south to meet your Pope. You asked me why the Lord Sharf called us a 'war party.' Now you know. I was the only captive, to my great shame. But Pforft here says that you tried to murder the Hannegan."

"Is that all our sign says?" Nimmy asked.

Evidently the Nomad could not read. He conversed again with

the man named Pforft, then shook his head. "I don't know what all those words mean."

Pforft, himself a pederast, spoke to them: "It says heresy, simony, the crime of wounding majesty, as well as attempted regicide."

Fortunately, the hour was late and the zoo was closed for the day. Although the other prisoners wore uniforms, none were furnished for the cardinal and his secretary. Each of them received three blankets against the January cold. The cage was open to the weather on the south side. At least they would get sun during part of the day.

The cardinal still had not fully recovered from the curse of Meldown. "My Lady of the Buzzards had a buzzard's breath, it seems," he told Blacktooth, when he was feeling almost hysterically cheerful. "When Urion's Angel of Battle fights my Buzzard of Battle, which do you bet on to win?"

"M'Lord, doesn't that old prayer go: 'Holy Michael Archangel, *deliver* us from battle'?"

"No, it doesn't, Brother Monk. It's '*defend* us *in* battle,' but 'deliver us *from* the snares of the devil.' As you well know. But what would you bet right now on either prayer being answered?"

"Nothing. If I remember the Nomad myth right, your Burregun, since you claim her, always mourns as she eats the fallen warriors, the children of her sister the Day Maiden. She doesn't want war either."

"You are right, we must pray for peace while girding for war. Of course you are right, Nimmy, you're always right."

Nimmy hung his head and frowned. But Brownpony was not being just sarcastic. To avoid being understood by other prisoners, they were speaking neo-Latin, and the cardinal's speech was unguarded.

"I mean it. You were right to leave the abbey, although you are a monk of Leibowitz. You were right to fall in love with a girl like Ædrea. You are right to disapprove of my importing and selling westcoast weapons without telling His Holiness." Blacktooth looked at him in surprise. Brownpony noticed the look and went on: "Pope Linus Six, who gave red hats to your late abbot and me, was the man who assigned me the task, in a letter which I still have in Valana. Linus told me not to show it to anyone unless I got caught, and then only to a pope. Frankly, Nimmy, I have almost wanted to get caught."

"Oh." Blacktooth thought it over. It was certainly true that Brownpony had not been cautious, allowing even Aberlott the Mouth to learn of his activities. But he would probably rather be caught by Amen Specklebird. Suddenly the cardinal seemed less sinister, an unwell man with a hump on his back and an uneasy conscience.

Fortunately, during visitor's hours, when children would spit at them through the bars of their cages, the human animals were fed raw beef and raw potatoes for the amusement of the crowd. No one was watching when they ate cornmeal mush for breakfast. Nimmy remembered from Boedullus that eating raw meat, or better still, drinking fresh blood as the Nomads sometimes did, was "good for the patient's own blood," and he persuaded Brownpony to eat some of the meat. Nimmy liked flesh raw, if fresh, but sometimes the jail meat tasted like coyote kill, and raw potatoes gave them both a stomachache. Filpeo's government did provide enough mush to keep the zoo's display specimens from looking starved. During their stay at the prison, three inmates were led from their death cells to the chopping block. From fellow prisoners, they learned that Wooshin had been replaced with a chopping machine, not another electric chair. The electric dynamo, an expensive affair, could be put to more productive use than frying felons.

The moon phase had waned from full to new. Then one afternoon past visitors' hours, a man in a lacy surplice came and stood looking in at them.

"Torrildo!"

The former brother winked at Nimmy but remained silent.

"What do you want, man?" Brownpony snapped.

"My Lord the Archbishop wonders if you would like the Eucharist brought to you here."

"I would like bread and wine with which to offer Mass myself."

"I'll ask," said Torrildo, and departed.

"Find out if the Pope knows we're in jail!" Blacktooth called after him.

"Nimmy!" hissed the cardinal.

But Torrildo had stopped. Without looking back, he said, "He knows," and resumed his departure.

"Damn! It's all over." Brownpony was angry and downcast.

Blacktooth decided to let him alone. He rolled up in his blankets and took a nap in the icy wind.

Three days later Torrildo came back. This time Blacktooth winked at him. Torrildo blushed. "I never saw a sarcastic wink before," he said.

"What about the bread and wine?" the cardinal asked.

"Your Eminence will not have time to say Mass." He produced a letter from a sleeve and a key from his pocket. "I am to let you go when you read this and promise to obey these instructions."

Brownpony accepted the papers and began reading, handing each page to Blacktooth as he finished.

"Damn! It's all over," the cardinal repeated, again downcast but without anger.

"I thought every cardinal had a church in New Rome," Nimmy remarked as soon as he read the first lines.

"There *is* a Saint Michael's in New Rome," Brownpony told him. "And it's Urion's church, but there he is not called the Angel of Battle."

They read in silence while Torrildo watched and impatiently drummed the key in his palm. The first page was thus.

> To His Eminence Elia Cardinal Brownpony, Deacon of Saint Maisie's.
> From Urion Cardinal Benefez, Archbishop of Saint Michael the Archangel.
> Inasmuch as the pretended Pope, one Amen Specklebird, has by trying to resign the papacy, admitted that he was never Pope, it has pleased His Imperial Grace the Mayor of Texark to pardon all of your crimes except attempted regicide, for which you and your servant Blacktooth St. George are under suspended sentences of death. You are to be expelled from the Empire as *personae non gratae*. By countersigning this letter in the place indicated below, you enter a plea to the remaining charge against you of *nolo contendere*, which His Grace is persuaded to accept, and you agree to be escorted under guard as swiftly as possible to a crossing point of your choosing on the Bay Ghost River, and promise never to return except by order of a reigning Pontiff, a General Council, or a Conclave, and only for the purpose of direct passage to or from New Rome from the nearest border crossing.

There was a place for their signatures below a statement acknowledging the charges with a plea of no contest, and agreeing to obey a decree of permanent banishment.

The other pages were a more or less personal plea from Benefez to Brownpony and other Valanan cardinals to accept New Rome as the proper place for an immediate conclave to elect a pope. When Brownpony finished reading, he looked up at Torrildo. The acolyte was holding a metal pen and a phial of ink out to him through the bars. They quickly signed, and the key turned in the lock.

Their trip back to the Bay Ghost by coach on the main military highway west was a fast, rough ride, taking less than ten days. Before they left the Province, the guards permitted Brownpony to buy two horses from a Jackrabbit farmer. The moon was full again, allowing them to ride sometimes by night. When they came at last to Leibowitz Abbey, an excited Abbot Olshuen knelt to kiss the cardinal's ring and tell him that he, Brownpony, was now Pope-Elect, chosen by an angry conclave of Valanan cardinals, called by Pope Amen before his resignation. The cardinals were eagerly awaiting his *accepto.*

"Who brought this crazy message?" Brownpony demanded.

"Why, it was an old guest of ours, who went to New Rome with you. Namely, Wooshin. Cardinal Nauwhat sent him with the letter from the Curia—it's in my office—and an oral message from Sorely."

"What was the oral message?"

"That he had opposed the conclave, but hoped you would accept the election anyway."

"He knows it isn't legal" was the Red Deacon's immediate comment. "Of course I won't accept."

"You have a more immediate problem," said Olshuen, recovering from his initial awe of the cardinal.

"And what is that, Dom Abiquiu?"

"Have you told Brother St. George about his young lady? She came for him while you were gone. He thought she had died. She said you knew she was alive."

Brownpony was suddenly nervous. "We'll talk about that. Let's go to your office. I need to read the letter from the Curia."

CHAPTER 19

Let all guests who arrive be received as
Christ, for He is going to say, "I came as a
guest, and you received me."
—*Saint Benedict's Rule*, Chapter 53

HEY HAD ARRIVED AT LEIBOWITZ ABBEY DURING
the recreational hour in the late afternoon of Ash Wednesday. The Yellow
Guard presided over several kick-boxing
matches between novices, and even the
professed Brothers Wren and Singing
Cow were sparring clumsily. Blacktooth
observed that the style of fighting differed in some respects from that of
Wooshin—although the Axe would never admit to having a "style."
However, Foreman Jing, who had fenced with Wooshin, called it the
"way of the homeless sword," and a "style of no-style."

Brownpony's first duty was to confer with Abbot Olshuen.

Blacktooth's was to bring bad news to the Yellow Guard. First he
established himself in the guest room.

"You're still here!" he exclaimed upon entering.

"No, no," said Önmu Kun, the Jackrabbit gun smuggler. "I'm
back for the second time since you left." He was full of wine and the

urge to talk. "The Jackrabbit Weejus and Bear Spirit have chosen me as sharf, did you know that?"

Nimmy doubted it, but didn't much care. By looking around at their war gear, Nimmy knew the comrades of the late Weh-Geh, although they were working hard around the abbey, participating in the liturgy, and teaching weaponless fighting to novices, were still staying in the guesthouse along with Önmu Kun. This to Nimmy meant that Olshuen was not about to take them on as postulants or novices without permission from on high.

They greeted him with smiles and handclasps as they returned from the bouts in the courtyard, but Önmu was still talking and laughing about his adventures in the Province, and the warriors were a polite lot. Only their eyes questioned him ("Weh-Geh? Where?"), but they waited for the smuggler to finish.

Brownpony's flirtations with churches in the Province had made it easier for Önmu to sell guns, he said. He had only to ask a pastor whether he had seen Cardinal Brownpony on his way toward Hannegan City. If the priest said that he had not, Önmu hurried away. If he had seen him, and showed the slightest enthusiasm, it meant there existed a group of local partisans wanting arms. One cadre which called itself the Knights of Empty Sky was a charity organization. He had supplied them not only with infantry weapons, but made a special trip to bring them three cannon that fired either a peach-size ball or a load of heavy buckshot, for those badly in need of charity. According to "Sharf" Önmu, the Knights anointed each cannon with oil, placed it in a well-caulked box, dug a shallow grave in the churchyard, and buried it by night.

Blacktooth murmured politely in reply, but finally turned his back toward the tipsy smuggler, and faced the five warriors who watched him expectantly with those dark eyes with uncreased lids. He was ashamed of his failure to befriend an alien in a strange land for no better reason than that he was not Wooshin.

"Brother Weh-Geh was killed while defending his master," he told them—rather loudly to silence Önmu. "I heard it happen, but I did not see it. There were three shots. There were four men holding guns pointed at him when I looked through the door, and he was already down. He had taken a gun he took from one of our guards. If he fired it, he must have missed. I am very sorry. Whether it was a mistake or not, he was living out his duty. He was a better monk than I."

"*Was* it a mistake?" asked Jing-U-Wan, the Foreman.

"Who were those four men?" Gai-See wanted to know.

"Did he have last rites?" asked Woosoh-Loh. "A proper funeral?"

"Dare we ask Abbot Olshuen to say a Mass for him?"

Nimmy tried to answer some of their questions and apologize for his inability to answer others. He finished his talk with them by promising to see Olshuen about a Mass for the repose of souls on behalf of Weh-Geh, and he went at once to the abbot's office. The door was open, and Brownpony was sitting at the abbot's desk and talking while Olshuen sat on a stool.

"It's a shame the Hannegan has a monopoly on the telegraph," the cardinal complained as he finished writing a letter which Nimmy was certain was addressed to the Valanan Curia. He turned sideways at the desk to look at the abbot who owned the desk and he saw Nimmy in the doorway, beckoned him in, and continued. "The Church has the money to hire Filpeo's technicians. We could build a line from here to Valana, and perhaps from Valana to the Oregonians."

The abbot said, "Money enough, yes. But what about the copper? I heard Hannegan had to confiscate coinage, pots, and church bells. Buy it, you might. But who has it to sell?"

"I'm told silver conducts electrical essence even better than copper. And I'm not sure it's practical, but we have a source of silver."

"Oh? Where is that?"

Brownpony changed the subject. He handed Olshuen a letter and asked, "What do you think of this? Come in, Nimmy, come in."

The abbot took it and studied for a bit, holding it so that Blacktooth might read it as well if he wanted to:

> To Sorely Cardinal Nauwhat, Secretary of Extraordinary Ecclesiastical Concerns.
>
> From Elia Cardinal Brownpony, Vicar Apostolic to the Hordes.
>
> *Non accepto!*
>
> You know it is not possible to hold a conclave without notification of every cardinal on the continent. The Curia must have recommended to His Holiness that he clarify the law on both resignations and conclaves, and I cannot believe that he made legal a conclave such as the one the Curia has apparently conducted. You know it, and I know it. You must have been a minority in an angry Sacred College.
>
> My imprisonment by the Hannegan forced His Holiness to offer his resignation. But I am free now, and I pray that he reconsider. He is not bound by anything he did under pressure of blackmail; let him renounce his resignation saying that it was forced. If he will not do that, then you must summon every cardinal (including me here at the

abbey) to Valana to choose another successor of Saint Peter, complying in every way with existing legislation.

Although I appreciate the irony of electing a Pope that Hannegan just released from jail in a trade-off of this kind, I have to say again, *non accepto*, as you, Sorely, knew I would.

I await instructions from my sovereign Pontiff, Pope Amen, and when they come, it would please me greatly if you can spare Wooshin to bring them here.

"You ask me what I think? How should I know?" Olshuen said while shaking his head. "In the name of God, m'Lord, I am only a monk of Leibowitz. I am not Abbot Jarad. My only vocation is here, my God is here, and although I am a servant of Holy Mother Church . . ."

"Oh, bother. Stop, stop, please! I'm sorry I showed it to you. Jarad should have refused the red hat, but the seventh Linus insisted. I know that, and you probably do too."

"I'm trying to remember if an abbot here ever refused a Pope's request, m'Lord."

"Maybe not, but if Amen Specklebird made you a cardinal, what would you say?"

Olshuen hesitated before he said, "No, not even from him." It was plain that even those who knew him only by hearsay adored the old priest-hermit-magician Pope. But among lovers of power, only Brownpony seemed to feel a deep affection for him.

Nimmy presented his petition on behalf of Jing-U-Wan's men and their deceased brother, and Olshuen promised a Mass. The next morning Brownpony sent Blacktooth to Sanly Bowitts with the message and gold enough to hire a courier with two horses to carry it quickly to Valana. The messenger promised to ride from dawn to dusk, and by night when the moon permitted, and to wait in Valana for a reply, unless Wooshin replaced him.

While he was returning to the abbey, he met Gai-See riding toward the village. They exchanged greetings and paused for a moment. Nimmy asked why he was going to town, and Gai-See said, "After you left, the cardinal decided to send another message. I have it with me."

"Another letter to Valana?"

"No. New Jerusalem." He frowned at himself. "You have a right to ask that?"

"Probably not. I'll try to forget it."

They went their opposite directions. Nimmy knew well what the cardinal had to say to Mayor Dion. Somehow a small weapon from their west-coast arsenal had found its way into the hand of Filpeo Harq. Both master and servant had seen it. There seemed to be no other possibility than that New Jerusalem had been infiltrated by the Hannegan's agent. But he would not ask Brownpony about it, lest he make trouble for Gai-See, who told him the letter's destination.

While Nimmy in October had found unfriendly attitudes in the atmosphere at the monastery, he now found them downright hostile in early March. He was being shunned again by the professed. On the other hand, some novices seemed to find him much more interesting than before. He tried to find out what had happened since, but "unexpected visitors" was the only mumbled answer he could get to his questions.

The three novices who were in the abbot's waiting room overheard a shouting match between the abbot and Cardinal Brownpony—or "Pope Brownpony," as one of them called him—and mentioned it to Nimmy. Very little of the shouting was understandable, but that it was about Blacktooth, they were certain.

Blacktooth decided to confront the cardinal, but upon finding him kneeling before the lady altar praying to the Virgin, he merely knelt beside him and waited. Brownpony stirred, and Nimmy sensed his discomfort. The Red Deacon crossed himself and arose. The monk waited a few seconds and did the same. Brownpony was pacing toward the door. Nimmy shuffled behind him. Hearing the shuffle, the Red Deacon turned.

"Do you want something, Brother St. George?"

"Only to know what's going on."

They walked outside and stopped.

"I knew she *might* be alive. But I did not want to arouse false hopes. Go climb the Mesa of Last Resort. The man who saw her last may be living there now." The cardinal started walking away.

"She? Who?" Nimmy called after him.

Brownpony looked back at him without answering.

"*Ædrea!*"

"Go to the Mesa. I'll tell the abbot I sent you. He wanted to send you himself. But it was my responsibility. I let you down."

Pale as a ghost, Nimmy hurried toward the kitchen to beg some hard biscuits and water for the journey. From the cook, who was in a good humor, he received the biscuits, some cheese, and a wineskin filled with a mixture of wine and water. Then he went to the guest-house to pack a bedroll; it was too late to leave that day, so he slept and left before daylight while his brethren were being called to Lauds. It was a long hike to Last Resort, and the first thing he saw when he arrived at the usual way of ascent was a recent grave with two sticks lashed together for a cross. Its meaning eluded him. After the slow climb, the sun was sinking behind distant mountains. He went straight to the ramshackle shelter he had discovered the previous year and found it rebuilt, but no one was home. He was reluctant to try the door.

After shouting a few times and hearing no answer, he sat on his bedroll to wait. The light was becoming too dim for reading Compline, so he said his rosary, sometimes contemplating the mystery of each decade and sometimes contemplating the beautiful waif who had stolen it from him. The grave at the foot of the Mesa kept coming to mind. He shook his head impatiently and resumed contemplation of the fifth glorious mystery, which was the coronation in Heaven of the Mother by the Son, after her bodily assumption. But there was no before or after, according to Amen Specklebird, for whom the coronation of the Virgin was an event belonging to eternity. The Virgin's face became Ædrea's, and he finished the last decade as quickly as possible. When he looked up, a gaunt silhouette with a club raised on high stood over him against the twilight sky.

It croaked: "Don't get up! Who are you? What are you doing here?"

"I am Brother Blacktooth St. George, and my master Cardinal Brownpony sent me."

"Oh, I remember you now," said the old Jew, squinting in the twilight. "On the road to New Jerusalem, you asked too many questions."

"Did you make rain for them?"

"Still asking too many questions. Your master sent you with a message? For me?"

"No, he sent me with a question. What can you tell me about Ædrea? You saw her. Where did she go?"

The old Jew was silent for several seconds. "I happened to be of some assistance to her when she fled from her father. She came here with me, after the abbey turned her away. She had her babies. She went away."

"Babies!"

"Twin boys. They were not alike, though. She left them with me, because they were not perfect. Her father would have killed them. And she had nowhere else to go but home. She knows too much about affairs in New Jerusalem to risk getting caught on the way east to the Valley."

"Where are the children?"

"The milk of my goat did not agree with them. I took them to
Sanly Bowitts. I left them with a woman who promised to take care of
them until they were sent for."

"By whom?"

"Hmm-nnn. How should I know? Someone from the Valley. Or
you, the father, probably."

"Ædrea told you that I am the father?"

"She is a talkative young woman. She was here for, hmm-nnn,
seven or eight weeks. She was always singing or talking. I miss her
singing, not her talking." He groped in his bag and handed Nimmy
pieces of flint and steel. "That's the hearth, there in the shadow. Light
the tinder. The wood is stacked."

"Was it a hard birth?"

"Very hard. I had to cut. She lost a lot of blood."

"Cut? You are a physician?"

"I am all things."

Nimmy got the fire started at last. Following the old hermit's
instructions, he found in the hut a box of crumbled dry meal, dumped
two double handfuls to a pot with a bail, and added water from a great
jug by the door.

"Hang it from the tripod. Stir it with a clean stick."

"What is that stuff?"

"Food, Father."

"Don't call me that. I'm no priest!"

"Did I say you were? You're a father, though. I could call you
'Dad.' "

Blacktooth felt himself reddening. "Why don't you call me
'Nimmy'?"

"Is that what they call you at the abbey?"

"No, but my master does."

"Is he not at the abbey?"

"Yes?"

"Well, it seems your master let you think she was dead, isn't it
so?"

"He said he couldn't be sure, didn't want to arouse false hope. I
think I believe him."

"Hah!" The old Jew began chuckling to himself.

Nimmy stirred the pot until the mush turned thick. The old
hermit brought out metal plates, spoons, and cups. Nimmy pulled his
biscuits out of the bedroll, poured the cups full of his watered wine.
They sat on a bench made of a flat stone supported by fat legs that
were sunk in the ground, and ate dinner by the firelight.

Blacktooth crossed himself and whispered the blessing. The old

Jew, holding his bowl, sang out a few words of prayer in a strange tongue which Nimmy supposed to be Hebrew.

The mush, Benjamin told him, was made of processed mesquite beans he had brought from Sanly Bowitts. Later in the year, he would pick and process his own. He had raised goats here before, and would try to acquire a herd again. He spoke of past ages as if he had been there personally. Several times he spoke of an "Abbot Jerome" as if he were still ruling the monastery, and referred to the conquests of Hannegan II as if they were still happening. For him, all ages seemed to coexist in his own private Now.

Nimmy spent the night inside the old man's hut. Again he dreamed the dream of the open grave at the abbey, the one with the baby in it, but he awoke in surprise from the dream, knowing that Jarad Kendemin was buried there. In the morning, he dared to ask Benjamin about the recent grave at the foot of the Mesa. The hermit denied any knowledge of it, then noticed Nimmy's doubt.

"If you think I buried her there, go try to dig her up."

"I believe you."

Nimmy was not in a hurry to leave. His anger toward the cardinal had been aroused, and he wanted to rid himself of it, or turn it into mere diminished trust. Brownpony had withheld the truth from him before, but he could not remember an outright lie. From what the old man said, he knew Ædrea thought he lied. But she had not heard his actual words to Blacktooth.

He stayed an extra day and night. The sky was overcast, and a cold wind had risen. The waterskin and the hermit's jug were empty.

"Where do you get water up here?"

Benjamin looked at him, pointed casually at the sky, then continued milking the goat.

Twenty seconds passed. A large, cold drop of water hit the monk in the face. Moments later, there was a brief cloudburst. Nimmy asked no more questions.

The old hermit complained that Nimmy was eating more food than he brought with him. So he left shortly after dawn on the third day. When gravel came rattling down the way behind him, he looked back up the path. The old Jew was following him down with a shovel.

Because of the dream, Nimmy had a brief vision of an open grave. And on the third day, she arose again—

But the grave was not open. Instead, they now found two graves at the foot of the Mesa. Obviously one had been dug only yesterday. The old Jew leaned on his shovel, and squinted at Nimmy.

"No, I won't dig," the monk said. "Goodbye and thank you." He hurried away toward Sanly Bowitts without looking back.

Benjamin had given him the old woman's name. He found her old adobe house without difficulty, and counted seven children playing in the yard. He suddenly realized this was the "orphanage" the abbey had always supported in the town. The woman was sullen. She seemed to know who he was and why he was here, but considered him an outcast and a scoundrel. "Why did you not come for them ten days ago? They have been taken away for adoption."

"By whom?"

"Three sisters."

"Where were they taken?"

"I'm not at liberty to say."

When Blacktooth showed signs of anger, she called him a scoundrel, a libertine, a false monk. She ordered him to leave at once, and retired to the old adobe building.

"Where did the mother go?" he yelled after her, to no effect. So he marched in gloom back to the abbey.

The shooting began while the monks were in the convent's refectory for lunch on the following day. Atop the parapet wall, Father Levion, now Prior, was fasting when the first distant *boom!* occurred. He was praying, as he often did, toward the grandeur of the broken desert horizon and to the God who made it. The first explosion scarcely distracted him from prayer, although his eyes scanned the open country for a sign of smoke. After the second *boom!* Önmu Kun came running out of the refectory and across the courtyard. He saw Levion on the wall and raced up the stairs to join him.

"Where?" he asked breathlessly.

"I don't know. I didn't see anything."

Boom! The interval between explosions was about a minute and a half.

"It sounds like it's coming from over there," said Levion, pointing down the valley.

"The crosswind makes it sound that way," Önmu replied, looking straight at the Mesa of Last Resort.

After the fourth *boom!*, he pointed at the Mesa. There was indeed a tiny wisp of smoke up there.

On the fifth *boom!*, a plume of dust shot up from a spot about two hundred paces from the abbey.

"Damn! He's getting our range!" cried the smuggler.

On the sixth *boom!*, a cannonball hit the center of the road in front of the abbey, bounced through the open gates, caromed off the stone curb around the rose bed, and went on bouncing directly into the convent and through the refectory doors. Screaming was heard, and monks came pouring out of the building.

"Take cover!" yelled the Jackrabbit. "He's got two balls left."

There were no more shots, and while the monks at their meager Lenten lunch were badly frightened, the only damage was in the kitchen; but Önmu had indicted himself by knowing too much. The cannonball was found, and although it had been deformed and somewhat flattened, there appeared to be a few characters in Hebrew scratched upon it. An expert was summoned. The legible part of the inscription said, ". . . maketh bread to spring forth from the Earth." It was a blessing over food. "Apt enough, considering the target," said the translator. There was an immediate conference in the abbot's office. Blacktooth was called in, and appointed interrogator, since he knew the man as well as anyone, and spoke his dialect best.

They met in the guesthouse.

"By what right are you staying here, good simpleton?"

"I was invited," said the Jackrabbit.

"By whom?"

"By Abbot Olshuen, who else?"

"At the cardinal's insistence?"

"Probably."

"The abbot knows what you do?"

"I don't know. But even if he knows, I would not, I could not, bring my merchandise here. I never have."

"So you bury it in the desert here until you're ready to travel again. Then you dig it up."

"This time, the old man dug it up. My bad luck. I thought he never came down, and never had visitors. It's the first time I used that spot. I didn't expect him to desecrate a grave."

"He's a little crazy, but not stupid. He knew it was no grave. So he dug up your cannon, and sent us a message with it."

"He must have exceeded the maximum load to reach this far. And pointed it up about forty degrees."

"And he's shooting from about five hundred feet above us."

"Was he trying to kill someone?"

"Old Benjamin? No. He was telling the abbot about you."

"I'd better leave."

"What was in the other grave?"

"Rifles."

"If you're going to try to reclaim your merchandise, someone is going to go with you. There are six of us. Any one of us can manage you."

"Even you?" The Jackrabbit laughed.

Blacktooth knocked the wind out of him and threw him in the corner. Önmu looked up in surprise, gasping for breath, but without anger.

"Why did you do that, Brother St. George?"

"To show you, if you get into a quarrel with the old man over your guns, you're going to lose."

"But they *are* my guns! They are for the Grasshopper, and I am Sharf."

"You know that's a lie. You told me yourself you get a commission."

"Sure, if I sell them. If I lose them, they're mine."

"I don't understand."

"I have to pay for them. Who do you think owns them, Cardinal Brownpony?"

"I don't know, but I doubt it. Mayor Dion, probably. But whoever sells them, you're only the broker."

"I am also Sharf! Secretly, of course."

Önmu Kun disappeared from the abbey that night, never to return. Being related to the royal tribe was prerequisite to election as sharf of a horde, and Nimmy doubted that any Nomad north of the Nady Ann would recognize his claim. Gai-See was sent galloping toward Last Resort on the abbot's horse to protect the old Jew, and if possible to negotiate the surrender of the weapons. He returned the following day dragging one cannon, and reported two empty graves, also reported that Benjamin had not opened the second grave. Evidently Kun had recovered his rifles and moved on. But so it was that Leibowitz Abbey came into possession of modern ordnance, but as yet no ammunition. Abiquiu Olshuen locked the cannon in the basement room with the rusty weapons from earlier centuries.

Novices reported another loud argument between the cardinal and the abbot behind closed doors. This time it was about guns. Brownpony emerged angry and humiliated; he told Blacktooth that Olshuen felt the abbey's hospitality had been abused.

"He knows now that the Jackrabbit is being armed," he told Nimmy. "He's afraid for the monastery, if the Hannegan suspects his monks are involved. He wants Jing's men to leave."

"But they have nothing to do with it!"

"No, but the concept of warrior monks is alien to Dom Abiquiu's idea of Christianity. To him it's a scandal. We should leave here soon."

"Did the Jackrabbit grandmothers really choose Önmu Kun as Sharf, as he claims?"

"Everything is secretive in Jackrabbit country, Nimmy. With

them, the test is not legal but practical. If the men follow him in battle, he is Sharf. If they don't, he is not, no matter what the Weejus say."

Well into Lent, a messenger from Hannegan City brought a petition addressed to all bishops and signed by Urion Benefez and seven other cardinals. It announced a General Council of the Church to be held in New Rome six weeks after Easter, and all bishops and abbots able to travel must attend. The purpose of the Council would be to draft new legislation concerning conclaves.

"Only a sovereign Pontiff can summon a General Council," said Brownpony, and refused to sign. Olshuen also refused. The messenger shrugged and rode on.

Wooshin arrived the following day with the expected summons to a conclave in Valana. He was warmly greeted by Brownpony, Blacktooth, and the Yellow Guard, but the summons he brought was rather strange. Apparently the Curia knew of the petition for a General Council, for the tone of the summons was angry, and the last paragraph threatened excommunication to any cardinal who attended a rump session in New Rome "where schismatics and heretics will try to install a known sodomite to sit on the throne of Peter the Apostle." The document was signed by *Amen, Episcopus Romae, servus servorum Dei*, but Brownpony was suspicious of the signature, and the language was certainly not Specklebird's.

"Things are getting ugly," said the Red Deacon. "We must leave here at once."

CHAPTER 20

OR MORE THAN A YEAR NOW, IT SEEMED TO Blacktooth that he was always on the road. This time there was no coach to Valana. Eight men with sixteen horses rode the papal highway north. Several miles south of the side road which led to Shard's place and on into the mountains of New Jerusalem, Cardinal Brownpony stopped, called Blacktooth and Wooshin to his side, and announced a detour around that whole area.

Blacktooth protested. "M'Lord, the only one who needs to take a detour ·is me. I can ride east out into the scrub, travel a few miles north, and then catch up with you on the road before dark."

"No," said the cardinal. "I want no more than one of us to be seen. Wooshin, pick a man to ride past the glep guards and take a message to Magister Dion. The message is really for Shard as much as for the Mayor, but Shard will accept orders only from Dion."

"Why not send me?" Axe offered.

"No. Shard remembers you."

Nimmy said, "He may remember any or all of us. He went for his gun and came out shooting when we were on our way to the abbey last fall."

Axe went to consult the warrior monks. When he came back, he said, "I suggest Gai-See. He's the smallest target and rides the fastest horse. If he can't find a way around, he can wait until dark and gallop right up Scarecrow Alley. There's moon enough."

Brownpony nodded and beckoned to Gai-See, then instructed him to avoid any contact with the families that guarded the passage. "Tell this to Dion: 'On the east, open gates to the Wilddog and to the Grasshopper. On the west, send gifts to the Curia.' Now repeat that, please."

"On the east, open gates to the Wilddog and to the Grasshopper. On the west, send gifts to the Curia."

"Good! Then remind him of what Nimmy and I saw in the hand of the Hannegan. I sent him a message about it from the abbey. If he got it, he will know what has to be done. Afterward, he will provide you with a well-laden pack mule. Leave New Jerusalem from the west and come on to Valana as fast as you can."

Gai-See dismounted, bowed to the cardinal, and sat down beside the trail. "He'll wait until dark," said Axe. "I too think it's safer that way."

Brownpony looked at Blacktooth. "Why so disappointed?" he asked.

"It's nothing, m'Lord."

"You were hoping someone would be able to find out if Ædrea is in her father's house?"

"I know it's not practical. It would be dangerous."

"Never mind. Gai-See can ask the Mayor about her."

"And get the same kind of truth about her as he gave to me?"

Brownpony shrugged. "I can't tell Dion what to say or do, except with my own property."

It was the first time the cardinal had spoken of the arsenal as his own property, but that was not Blacktooth's concern.

"M'Lord, I wish Gai-See would not mention Ædrea to Dion."

"Why not?"

"Because he will be wondering about a spy or a traitor when Gai-See tells him about the gun we saw in Filpeo's hand. And Ædrea ran away from home during that time. We know where she went, but the Mayor may not believe her."

The cardinal looked down at Gai-See. "Did you hear and understand that?"

"Yes, m'Lord Cardinal. I'll be discreet."

"We'll see you in Valana. Now, let's ride a mile or so back into the juniper scrub."

Three days later, they camped in the scrub half a mile east of the papal highway on the evening of Monday, April 3rd. It would be the night of the Paschal full moon of Holy Week, but the sun was not yet set, and because their food supply was running short, Nimmy went forth in search of roots and edible greens that might be beginning to sprout, while Wooshin took the party's only firearm and went to hunt small game while the cardinal's warriors gathered wood and tended the fire. Brownpony himself, clearly exhausted from the long journey and developing a nasty cough, wrapped himself in blankets and with his head on a saddle, fell asleep before dark.

Blacktooth dug up a few bulbs of last year's wild onions from the bank of a half-frozen creekbed; they had little value except as seasoning, in case the Axe came back with meat. Of course it was a day of Lenten abstinence, but it was also an emergency, especially for the cardinal, who had never fully recovered from his ordeal in the breeding pit. Nimmy tried to keep track of his direction from camp by watching the sunset, the stars of twilight, and finally the glow of the campfire in the distance. He found yucca, and uprooted some skinny tubers from the hard ground with a sharp stick.

He heard two gunshots, and decided that they came from Wooshin's pistol, but they were closely followed by a third—too closely for the Axe to have reloaded. A horse galloped past along a creekbank at the foot of the hill, and he caught a glimpse of a Nomad rider. There was a burst of shouting from the direction of the camp, accompanied by one more gunshot, but he could make out only the voices of Foreman Jing and Woosoh-Loh in their native tongue, until he heard Axe shout a death threat in poor but understandable Wilddog, and a weaker echo from the cardinal that the threat was real and enforceable.

Nimmy hurried back toward the firelight as quietly as possible. Two Nomad outlaws were sitting on the ground with their hands tied behind them, surrounded by Brownpony's guards. The cardinal himself was sitting up in his bedroll. A strange small horse was tied to a juniper, and two unfamiliar muskets were propped against a log.

"Nimmy, where are you?"

It was Brownpony's voice. Blacktooth hurried into the firelight and dumped the yucca and wild onions beside the body of a dead wilddog. The cardinal winced at the odor of the onions.

Wooshin explained. Three motherless ones with only one horse among them had tried to steal two horses from the cardinal. One had succeeded but the men who had dismounted to search and rob Brownpony had been surprised and captured by Axe and the others who had heard their approach.

The scruffy Nomads were looking around in terror at the strange warriors with their long blades.

"Nimmy, you tell them what the situation is," said Axe with a wink.

Blacktooth brushed the root dirt from his robe and went to stand behind his master. Facing them across the fire, he drew himself up, pointed at one of the men, and said in impeccable Grasshopper:

"I know you. You haunt this region. Now you have accosted the Vicar Apostolic to the hordes, to whom even the *Qæsach dri Vørdar* Ösle Høngan Chür comes for counsel, not to mention the Grasshopper sharf, Eltür Bråm. Your fellow bandit has just stolen the horse of the High Shaman of all Christendom, the next Sharf and Great Uncle of the Holy Roman Catholic Church. He has also been chosen by the Buzzard of Battle; the Weejus have announced it."

"Don't overdo it, Nimmy," said the cardinal in Churchspeak.

"Horse for horse!" said the bolder of the two. "You take this horse, Great Man. We even."

Nimmy ignored him and spoke again to the man he recognized. "You! It was Holy Madness himself, now Lord of the Hordes, that stopped you from raping Ædrea last year near Shard's place, not far from here."

The outlaw shrugged but seemed suddenly meek.

Brownpony picked himself up out of the bedroll and went to inspect the scruffy mustang. Having walked around the little mare, he faced them and said sternly in Wilddog, "She belongs to the *Høngin Fujæ Vurn.* You dare to violate a mare of the Wild Horse Woman! Lord Ösle Høngan Chür would have you eviscerated and fed to the dogs. Wooshin, release the animal at once."

The Axe flipped his sword twice, once to slice the hackamore that made her fast to the limb, the second time to swat her behind with the flat of the blade. The mustang snorted, kicked, and clattered away into the night. Since Gai-See had not taken an extra mount on his gallop through Scarecrow Alley, they still had an extra horse per man, but neither Brownpony nor his aides were ready to let the matter lie.

"Who is your master?" the cardinal asked.

"His name is Mounts-Everybody."

"How far is his camp from here?"

"Almost a day's ride, Great Man."

"How many men in your band?"

The outlaw seemed to be counting on mental fingers for a moment. "Thirty-seven, I think."

"And women? Children?"

"Yesterday there were five captives. Today maybe more, maybe less."

"And how many bands like yours?"

"I don't know. Sometimes we encounter other no-family people. Sometimes we fight, sometimes we join together. There are many bachelors along the fringes of the Wilddog range, and to the south along the Nady Ann."

"Do you ever fight or rob farmers?"

"It is not a wise policy."

"Does it happen?"

"Sometimes."

"Would you like to be paid for fighting farmers?"

The captives looked at each other and shifted uncomfortably. Brownpony elaborated:

"There is a war between the Grasshopper and the Hannegan's farmers."

"We know, but we are at war with both."

"But suppose the Grasshopper accepted you as allies?"

"That they would never do, Great Man."

"Did the monk here tell you that I am the Christian shaman to all the hordes?"

"We don't know what that means."

"It means," said Blacktooth, "that the word of His Eminence has power with all three hordes."

"Would you fight against the Hannegan under Demon Light?"

"There is no possibility."

"What about a Jackrabbit sharf?"

The idea of a Jackrabbit sharf brought roaring laughter from the bound men.

"Let the cowards go," Brownpony ordered. "You whimpering wild puppies go tell your Mounts-Everybody to come and see me in Valana, unless he's a coward, and bring back the horse you stole. Otherwise, you will be driven south of the Nady Ann and east of the Bay Ghost. The Hannegan will know what to do with you. Now go."

Easter arrived before they reached Valana. Brownpony concelebrated the Mass of the Resurrection in a wayside church with a circuit-riding mission priest who stumbled through the liturgy, too frightened by high rank to get anything quite right.

.   .   .

Some days later a fast rider from Pobla, where they had spent the night, brought word of their coming to Valana, and Sorely Cardinal Nauwhat and the SEEC guard Elkin were waiting for them at the Venison House Tavern, where the cardinal had entertained Kindly Light the previous year. It was close to sundown, so they ordered dinner. The two prelates with their assistants sat together, while Wooshin and the Yellow Guard took an adjacent table. Sorely Nauwhat was a fast talker, and he had a lot to explain.

Before submitting his resignation, which Nauwhat, like Brownpony, regarded as revocable if not wholly invalid, Pope Amen had broken with a recent tradition and created new cardinals, as many as forty-nine of them, and had been induced to take the almost unprecedented action of stripping forty-nine others of their cardinalates. This shocked Brownpony, but it made the attempt at a conclave understandable, if not legal.

Amen Specklebird, who insisted that his resignation had been duly submitted to the Curia, had retired to his former residence, the old building which seemed to grow out of the side of a mountain and which had been at one time a root cellar, and before that a cave whose deeper recesses had never been explored, and which the old man had reopened "to let the mountain spirits come and go." Here the cardinals of the Curia came to consult him, to scold and beseech him, to no avail.

And there was news from Texark. Although the text of what purported to be Pope Amen's resignation had appeared there, by telegraph, the original signed copy of the document, if it existed, could not be found in Valana or anywhere else. One enterprising forger in the Empire's capital sold a clever counterfeit of the original to the Archdiocese of Texark for ten thousand pios, a sum paid after a police expert affirmed that the handwriting was that of Amen the Antipope. But afterward, another expert showed that the document contained egregious errors of the kind often occurring during transmission of text by a telegraph operator, including several pure operating codes, such as ZMF, meaning "break, more follows." The forger escaped into Jackrabbit country and was never seen again.

"As I told you, the Pope refuses to live in the palace," said Nauwhat, "and he has returned to his old home. He said Easter Mass at home, not at John-in-Exile. He will see anyone who comes to him, and cheerfully submits to any indignity. He has signed blank bulls, perhaps by the dozen. He will press his seal of approval into the wax of almost anything. I don't know if he always reads it first. Did he really appoint all these new cardinals, or was it done for him? I should know, but I don't. Because he found out about some guns at SEEC, and he thinks I am responsible."

"Well, I must confess to him on that—"

"No, don't do it. I *am* responsible now. His actions are those of a man who has lost his bearings, if not his sanity, but not his good humor. You, Elia, he speaks of constantly, and he will rejoice that you have returned. You must go to see him tomorrow. You and Brother Blacktooth as well."

"Of course. But what are the agenda, if not weapons?"

"It was he who placed your name in nomination as Pope. His only agendum, probably, will be to submit to you as Pontiff."

"I must set him straight on that."

"Well, you can try. But besides the new cardinals, the College is coming into town again in numbers. And some from the East are bringing the military officers and envoys you invited. They pass for bodyguards."

"In response to the same summons I got? Who was it wrote that foul thing?"

"Domidomi Cardinal Hoydok."

"Do I know him?"

"No. He's one of the new ones. He's from Texark, but Benefez excommunicated him for supporting Pope Amen, so the Pope created him cardinal. He is a civil lawyer, not a priest."

"How are the Easterners getting here?" Brownpony asked.

"Mostly through the Iowa country. There, the farmers seem to get along better with the Grasshopper. They trade a lot. Only a few Texark patrols go north of the Misery River, and they wouldn't stop a cardinal there, even if they knew he was coming to conclave."

"Misery River?"

"The old name was 'Missouri,' m'Lord," Nimmy put in.

" 'Misery' better suits it now," said Sorely. "Before the occupation of the farmlands, it was a natural route to New Rome."

"Of course. My memory is slipping. The first thing I must do tomorrow is send a messenger to Holy Madness and Swimming Elk to come here for a conference, and to send a war party to New Jerusalem for the new weapons."

"Swimming Elk?"

"Sharf Eltür Bråm, Hultor's brother. The Grasshopper sharf."

Dinner was brought to them. This time there was venison and a good red wine. They were nearly starved after the long Lenten trip on light rations. Nimmy wondered absently if he should confess to eating barbecued wilddog on abstinence days, even though the cardinal had granted dispensation in an emergency situation.

"How are things in Texark, by the way?" asked Cardinal Nauwhat.

"Well, the Province is seething with revolt. And of course there is sporadic fighting with the Grasshopper. In Hannegan City, little has changed, except they are importing some desert animals from Africa for warfare in dry country. And they know about our guns."

"Two bad omens."

"And one other thing." He glanced at the adjoining table and tapped Wooshin on the shoulder. "Axe, I think I forgot to tell you of one small change."

"M'Lord?"

Brownpony looked at Blacktooth. "You tell him."

"His Imperial Majesty the Mayor has replaced you with a mechanical head chopper, Axe."

Wooshin shrugged. "A man without shadow and form, when he chops heads, becomes a chopping machine. No change."

This caused a murmur, apparently not of approval, but perhaps of recognition, from the rest of the warriors present.

"A remarkable man," Sorely said with a shiver in his voice as Wooshin turned away again.

"One without shadow and form," Brownpony mused aloud.

Four weeks had passed since they last saw Gai-See, and they had just begun to fear that he had been shot down in Scarecrow Alley when he arrived, not with the well-laden pack mule with "gifts for the Curia" as in Brownpony's message, but with Mayor Dion, Ulad, eight heavy wagons, and a whole brigade of light-horse infantry, bristling with new and superior arms. The secret of New Jerusalem was no longer secret. Brownpony showed no surprise, and Nimmy realized that the message to Dion had been code.

There was no way Valana could accommodate both the influx of cardinals and a whole brigade of light horse, of whom the citizens of the city were quite frightened as the word was quickly passed around that these armed men were spooks. But Magister Dion had no intention of imposing. His troops immediately set about building a fortified encampment on a hill well outside the city. As soon as the wagons were unloaded, they were returned to New Jerusalem for more supplies. Regular convoys were planned to supply his men with food, ammunition, and other necessities of military life. They would sleep in tents, at first, but within four days, a permanent log structure was built, with a basement beneath it, to store ammunition and to reload brass cartridges. The reloading machines were simple and portable, so that they might follow an army in battle.

Seeking information about Ædrea, Nimmy had approached the gate of the newly constructed fort in the hope of obtaining an interview with the Magister, who was now in the role of commanding general. He was told politely to wait, and a guard left for the armory. He struck up a conversation with the other guards.

Blacktooth noticed that their rifles were similar to the pistols in having revolving cylinders, with six chambers instead of five. A guard showed him that the ammunition was of the same caliber as the handguns, and used the same brass; only the weight of the bullets and the weight of the powder charge differed. The pistol ammunition might be fired with safety from the rifles, with a lesser range, but it was unsafe to shoot the more powerful loads from the handguns. With copper being so scarce, it was essential that empty brass be saved after firing, even in battle.

After three hours of waiting, the guard returned. Nimmy was given a polite excuse from Magister Dion and turned away. He returned to the Red Deacon's own private mansion outside the city, where all of them were temporarily living.

Brownpony had obtained a list of new cardinals created by Pope Amen during their absence. He gave a copy of it to Blacktooth for his own information, along with two copies of a summons for all incoming cardinals to register at the Papal Palace with a clerk of the Secretariat of State, which again had been placed in the hands of Hilan Cardinal Bleze by Pope Amen after the interregnum. He told Nimmy to post one copy of the summons in John-in-Exile Square, then to hire a town crier immediately to shout aloud the text of the second copy at every intersection in Valana.

When he had finished these chores, Nimmy returned to his old residence, where he was rather mournfully greeted by Aberlott, who had fallen in love with the younger sister of the late Jæsis.

"It seems to me," said Aberlott with unusual gravity, "that those people in those mountains are just as intolerant of outsiders, as the outsiders have always been of spooks. They actually look down on us."

"Ædrea never did."

"I know. And she's under arrest."

"Oh my God! Did you see her?"

"No, I was not allowed."

"What are the charges?"

"She left without permission some months ago. That's all I know."

Through his employer's intervention, Blacktooth obtained an interview with Magister Dion. Dion listened politely to Nimmy's account of Ædrea's trip to Leibowitz Abbey, and thence to the Mesa of Last Resort, where she had given birth.

"And then she went home to her father's place," he finished. "That's all she did."

"And her father beat her and brought her to me. We can't have people leaving without permission."

"But she always had permission to come to Valana!"

"No, she had orders."

"But her father would have killed her babies."

"Babies?"

"Twins, old Benjamin said."

"Well, what you think you know, you got by hearsay. I'll consider it, but she will remain in custody for the time being. Think of it as protection from her own family. You are never going to see her again. Neither your cardinal nor I will allow it."

Blacktooth left the camp, fuming with anger at both the Mayor and Brownpony. On the way home, he meant to stop at the hillside home of Amen Specklebird and ask for his intervention, but there were at least forty people in a queue outside the door, many of them cardinals, and the Red Deacon himself was tenth in line. So he pretended not to see him, and went instead to a nearby church to pray his anger away.

On the first day of May—normally a Nomad holy day—in response to Brownpony's call to a war council, Chür Høngan, his half-nephew Oxsho, Father Ombroz, and Demon Light with one of his lieutenants rode into town together. Brownpony was surprised to learn that Oxsho, in spite of his youth, had been chosen Wilddog sharf after Holy Madness was made judge and leader of all three hordes. The Wilddog leaders bowed and kissed the cardinal's ring. Eltür the Demon Light refrained, but offered a Nomad military salute.

From the south on the following day came Önmu Kun, cold sober, and wearing a leather helmet with his family badge. He introduced himself as Jackrabbit Sharf. Knowing of Önmu's reputation, the others demanded documentation. He presented a roll of soft deerskin with Weejus beadwork depicting a manlike figure with the ears of a jackrabbit. From his saddlebags, he produced a crest of buzzard feathers, also of obvious Weejus design; the sacred talisman was to be worn on the helmet of the sharf only in battle. After brief discussion, and some shaking of heads, his credentials were accepted by the others. Brownpony, who wished to honor them all, consulted with others of the Curia, then had the Nomad leadership housed in the Papal Palace, since the Pope had retired to his remodeled hillside cave and refused to return.

A military conference was scheduled for Thursday the 4th, at SEEC, and an invitation was sent to Commander Dion to come and bring his senior officers. Then a great embarrassment rode into town on the night of the third, and by the light of the full moon rode on through town and up to Brownpony's private estate, where he made a great clatter at the main entrance. Wooshin and Woosoh-Loh immediately rushed from the dining room to investigate the visitor, but then called for Blacktooth.

Nimmy stared out at the spectacle standing there in the moonlight. Three hundred pounds of muscle and black hair confronted them with folded arms and an angry glare. He uttered obscenities in bad Grasshopper and demanded to see "the Christian shaman who boasted to my men that he was married to the Burregun, and then called me a coward."

Blacktooth swallowed hard and went back to the dinner table. "There seems to be a motherless one at the door who wishes to speak to Your Eminence."

"Who?"

"I think they called him 'Mounts-Everybody.' Remember the outlaws you released? They spoke of their leader—"

The cardinal blotted gravy from his lips, got up, and strode to the entrance.

"Where is my horse?" he demanded of the burly outlaw.

"Tied to the gate, you damn grass-eater."

"Then come in and eat beef with us, you damn thief."

The man came in, surrounded by suspicious warriors with short swords in hand. Because of a foul odor about him, the cardinal had him seated at the foot of the table. Most of the others had finished eating. A servant carved him a few slices of roast beef and fetched him a hot baked potato and roasted onions from the kitchen. It was too early in the season for anything the Nomad would call "grass," but he grunted a few complaints about the lack of "inner meats" to go with the beef. Nimmy knew that Nomads usually ate virtually the whole animal, except for the hide, horns, hooves, and bones. It was the basis for the Venerable Boedullus's prescription for radiation sickness. The outlaw ate with his hands, wrapping slices of beef around bits of potato. The cardinal spoke.

"I thank you for returning my horse. But do you know that all the sharfs of the hordes and the *Qæsach dri Vørdar* himself are here in the city?"

Mounts-Everybody stopped eating and glowered. "You invited me here. They are enemies. You intend to have me killed?"

"No, all I wanted was my horse."

"You spoke to my men of fighting farmers. For money."

"I asked them questions."

"Which farmers are your enemies? Those nearby?"

"No, those are under the protection of the Bishop of Denver."

Blacktooth put in a word here. "His Eminence is trying to use your word for 'citizens,' and he means specifically the subjects of the Hannegan, and even more specifically the armed forces of Texark. He does not mean peaceful people who work the soil and grow crops. Many of them were formerly Nomads, including my own family."

"Thank you, Nimmy," said Brownpony with a trace of irritation, then to Mounts-Everybody: "Just how many fighting men could you muster, if you were inclined to do so."

Mounts-Everybody seemed to be doing mental arithmetic. "That depends on the pay. For gold, not many. We need good horses. The families kill us when we take wild ones. Offer us two good horses and a woman for every man, and you get a small army."

"Horses, yes, but no women. How small an army?"

"Maybe four hundred warriors. But the Grasshopper is at war against the farmers in the east. We cannot fight beside them."

"I realize that. What about the Jackrabbit?"

Mounts-Everybody was suddenly suspicious. "Wormy-Face told me you threatened to drive us south of the Nady Ann into Texark lands."

"Gai-See, fetch one of the new rifles."

The small warrior stepped into the adjacent room and returned with one of the west-coast weapons.

"Load it and take him outside for a demonstration."

Brownpony and Blacktooth remained sitting at the dinner table while a servant cleaned up after the meal. There were six loud shots in as many seconds, followed by a frightened whinny and hoofbeats in the roadway.

Wooshin came back inside with the outlaw, who was holding the empty rifle and staring at it in awe. "I'm sorry. Your horse ran away," said the Axe.

"When they find him, give him to the sharf of the outlaws here, and also the rifle."

The burly guest stared at Brownpony in amazement. "I made you no promises!"

"I know. And you won't get the gifts until you do."

"No promises!"

"Well, all I want you to do is stay here all night, and most of tomorrow. You can't come to the meeting tomorrow, because I'm afraid someone would kill you. On your way into town, did you observe the fortress on the hilltop?"

"Yes. It is new."

"Tomorrow night, you will go to the fort and talk to Magister Dion and the Jackrabbit Önmu Kun. Any men you recruit will be under their command, as will you, and you will not be driven south of the Nady Ann. You will go there well armed and with other forces."

"I will think about it."

The cardinal looked away. "Axe, see that he takes a bath, cuts his hair and beard, and dress him as a mountain man. He can stay here until moonrise tomorrow."

Mounts-Everybody growled angrily and started to his feet, but six half-drawn swords had a calming effect. He allowed himself to be led away.

Brownpony looked questioningly at Blacktooth.

"M'Lord, those men live by murder and plunder."

"And that is war, is it not?"

Nimmy prayed earnestly for peace that night, but he feared the Virgin would not listen. If the cardinal came to be elected Pope, he would make the Virgin a commanding general of the hordes.

CHAPTER 21

 IMMY SLEPT BADLY THAT NIGHT, AND AROSE twice from nightmares to pray before the crucifix. Once he had a visitor. Moonlight shining through the window fell on white bedsheets and he could see a dark figure in the doorway. By its bulk, he knew it could only be Mounts-Everybody. He came quickly to his feet, prepared to fight if the outlaw tried to live up to his name. But the hulk merely grunted and moved on. A few seconds later, another dark figure stole down the corridor behind the motherless one. That would be one of the Yellow Guard, shadowing him. Probably he was only looking for a place to urinate.

Nimmy went back to bed. He dreaded the morrow, for he saw clearly the direction of recent events, and how Brownpony was moving them. It was not as if the Red Deacon had drawn a map of the future, but he was bent toward one goal; whatever happened he examined it to see if it might be useful as a means toward that goal. Nimmy was not opposed to the destruction of the Empire, or the reduction of its power and the restoration of the New Roman papacy. That was Brownpony's end. The means, in part, he might deem legitimate. There was such a thing as a just war; he did not doubt the ancient teaching. But Leibowitz had been a man of peace, had he not?—after a warlike youth—and he was still the Saint's willing follower, although a half-unwilling member of the Saint's present Order under abbots like Jarad and Olshuen. He had renounced the world, just as the abbots and his brethren had renounced it, but now he was in the midst of the world, and the renunciation seemed meaningless. He lay awake most of the night, remembering his devotion to Leibowitz and the Holy Virgin. When he did fall briefly asleep, he dreamed of Ædrea, woke up with an erection, and fought an urge to masturbate because it was dawn and people were moving in the hallway.

Almost unwillingly he accompanied the cardinal to conference in the Palace with the leaders of the hordes and of New Jerusalem. It would surely last most of the day. His employer noticed his reluctance, and said, "I'm sorry, Nimmy, but I'm going to need you. So will the Grasshopper."

Only four members of the Sacred College attended: Sorely Nauwhat, Chuntar Hadala, Elia Brownpony, and a new cardinal, one Hawken Chief Irrikawa, who was said to be king of his northeast forest nation, and who wore a feather sewed to his red hat. He claimed to outrank all princes of the Church except the Pope. Besides the four cardinals, several military people of nationalities both east of the Great River and west of the continental divide were here, and they had come to town with their cardinal electors. There was a roll call, a counting of noses, and many introductions. Mayor Dion was obviously still irked by Nimmy's petition on behalf of Ædrea and at first objected to his and Wooshin's presence.

Brownpony turned to Eltür Bråm, winked, and said, "Would you please give the commander an account of the battles that have happened between the Grasshopper and Texark since the death of your brother?"

The sharf smiled wryly and began to speak. After half a minute of it, Dion held up his hand.

"What is he saying?"

"I understand most of it," said the cardinal, "but I'm only good at Jackrabbit, and fair in Wilddog. Grasshopper is Brother Blacktooth's native dialect."

Dion looked at Nimmy and nodded.

"And Wooshin commands the Yellow Guard, who offer training in very efficient methods of weaponless combat."

The Mayor acquiesced, but as if to prove his impartiality, told Ulad and another of his own officers to warm the bench outside the doors. Blacktooth translated Sharf Demon Light's account of recent skirmishing between his warriors and the Texark cavalry, but it had been low-intensity warfare with few casualties and fewer deaths. Because of orders given by Holy Madness, the Grasshopper forces had not made any further raids on the protected farmlands. Bråm noted with irony that the unprotected farmlands north of the Misery had been free from raids since trading between farmers and Nomads had begun a generation or more ago.

Most of the principals had their own interpreters, and local dialects were translated into Churchspeak. It made for slow going. The focus of attention was usually a wall map of that part of the continent between the Rocky and the Appalotchan Mountains. The map was a problem for all the Nomads except Holy Madness, but Father Ombroz tried to assist them with explanations of correspondences between the Earth and the paper.

Nimmy found himself becoming the ears and the voice of the Grasshopper sharf, and was soon rebuking the others, especially Brownpony and Dion, for communicating between themselves in Churchspeak or Ol'zark Valley dialect without waiting for his interpretation. Even Önmu Kun was trilingual, but if Demon Light understood anything but the Nomad dialects, he would not admit it; Nimmy noticed, however, that the sharf frowned when the monk interpreted "Red Beard" as "Your Eminence." His Eminence himself, though understanding a bit of Grasshopper, kept a straight face. Bråm acknowledged nothing spoken to him in the form of a request or an order unless it came from the Lord Høngan Ösle Chür. Only to the Qœsach dri Vørdar did he even appear to defer. He was polite, if only to hide a natural arrogance.

Nimmy found himself admiring the Grasshopper leader. True, it was like the admiration a man might have for grizzly bear or a cougar, but he might, after all, be a distant relative to Demon Light. The sharf was not condescending or rude to the monk, although he knew well enough that Blacktooth's ancestors had deserted the horde to farm on lands owned by the Denver Archdiocese.

At one point during the meeting, he noticed Holy Madness looking up at one of the high windows. Blacktooth followed his gaze, and it was the same balcony window through which Amen Specklebird had been passed into the building at the last conclave. The window was open. A policeman and the young Sharf Oxsho, who had been conspicuous by his absence, at least to Blacktooth, were both gesturing. The Lord of the Hordes came to his feet.

"M'Lord Cardinal, Your Eminence, I must excuse myself and find out what they want." He pointed.

Brownpony looked at the window, nodded, and said, "We will discuss matters which would not much concern your realm while you're gone. If something's amiss, please let us know."

Chür Høngan (Blacktooth tried to remember the deferential name reversal when speaking to the man, but sometimes failed to think it correctly) was gone for a quarter hour, during which the talk was mostly with suppliers of military equipment from the west coast. When the Lord of the Hordes returned, his face was a storm cloud.

"A Texark spy has been listening to every word spoken here," he growled, staring at Brownpony.

"They caught him up there?"

"Yes. Our Sharf Oxsho was on watch."

"Are you sure he's from Texark?"

"Of course. I know him. So does Your Eminence." He paused, and his stare at Brownpony became a glare. "He is, or was, the husband of Potear Wetok. He's your Texark cavalry-tactics expert. You sent him to us, remember? I always suspected him."

Father Ombroz who was sitting nearby dropped his head in his hands. "Esitt Loyte!" he groaned.

Brownpony turned pale. "He is in custody now?"

"Oh, yes, m'Lord. Oxsho bound his hands and has him tethered."

Nimmy winced. He knew what Holy Madness meant by "tethered." Holes were punched in the captive's cheeks and a loop of rope or rawhide was passed through the holes.

"Shall I bring him in for you to question? I'll cut the tether, so he can use his tongue."

"No, have them keep him in the local jail. Let him rot there, for all I care."

"NO! He belongs to me and the Wetok family. When I leave here, he goes with me, dead or alive."

Brownpony came to his feet and faced the angry Nomad lord. "Trusting him was my mistake," he said. "You are right to claim jurisdiction over him. But Lord Høngan Ösle Chür, as your Vicar Apostolic I forbid you in the name of God to kill him."

They stared at each other. The Nomad gave him a barely perceptible nod. The cardinal sat down.

Høngan left the room again. This time he was gone for nearly an hour. When he came back he faced Brownpony again.

"Is he in jail?"

"Most of him is in jail," said the *Qæsach dri Vørdar*. "The rest of him is here." On the table before his Vicar Apostolic, he emptied a bag of bloody parts. Nimmy could see a hand, two ears, the tip of a nose, and what was probably the captain's penis.

Sitting next to Blacktooth, Demon Light came to his feet with a deafening Grasshopper battle cry to announce his approval. Brownpony turned and vomited.

"You said not to kill him," Høngan said mildly.

The meeting was adjourned while servants cleaned the table and the floor. When they reconvened, Oxsho joined the other two sharfs in the meeting, and they sat with their Lord Høngan and Eltür's interpreter. Nimmy sat surrounded by four Nomads, and it seemed to him that the others took a different seating arrangement than before. No chair adjacent to a Nomad was occupied.

Magister Dion at first resisted the plan that Brownpony and the Nomads favored; he wanted to join forces with the Wilddog and the Grasshopper and move across the Plains north of the Nady Ann, then join forces with able-bodied gleps from the Watchitah Nation and attack Hannegan City from the north. Chuntar Cardinal Hadala, Vicar Apostolic to the Valley, was familiar with its military potential, once its people were armed, and he backed Dion in his plan for a combined army of spooks from the Suckamints and their glep relatives from Ol'zarkia. It was in expectation of this that the spook commander had brought his light-horse brigade here to Valana.

Brownpony, however, was opposed. Having made reconnaissance in the Province, he foresaw a war on three fronts. Present were military officers from four nation-states in the Appalotcha region, who were prepared to invade the Texark's puppet allies on the east bank of the Great River. Their aim would be less to conquer than to force Filpeo to send forces to the defense of the east-bank puppets, lest he lose control of the river. The plan would be to harass, skirmish, and retreat, and prevent these forces from returning until Hannegan City itself was directly endangered. The commander in chief of the armed forces of the King of the Tenesi was present, and he outlined the plans the eastern nations had made among themselves, with the participation of Hawken Irrikawa.

Most of the Nomads were pleased by this eastern plan. Lord Høngan Ösle Chür suggested that the Grasshopper sharf propose a temporary truce with Filpeo's forces, just before the attack on the east-bank states came.

"That way, he won't be so uneasy about sending forces across the river."

Sharf Demon Light smiled at his lord, and the smile said that the truce, if made, would be opportunely broken.

The role of the armies of New Jerusalem in this plan would be to join with the guerrilla forces of Önmu Kun, who were at present scattered throughout the hill country in the Province. The guerrillas would move in small groups into the disputed areas a few days' ride to the west of the town of Yellow, staying away at first from the well-patrolled, but narrow, telegraph right-of-way that led to the last station nearest Valana. Kun had taken a pointer to the map and used it to draw a circle around the country where the Bay Ghost and the Nady Ann were hardly more than creeks, except for small lakes where antiquity's crumbled dams left small waterfalls. It was outlaw country, to the east of the papal highway, and Blacktooth began to see why his employer wanted Mounts-Everybody among his allies, although the prospect for such a thing was not mentioned at all by the cardinal. The northern hordes would object to the motherless ones, but because of Texark protection, the Jackrabbit had been little bothered by these outlaw bands.

When the forces of Kun, Dion, and perhaps the outlaws themselves converged here under one command, the rearming of the Jackrabbit with the west-coast weaponry which Önmu had not previously been allowed to smuggle would quickly proceed. The complete destruction of the telegraph was contemplated; also the physical removal of the wire to New Jerusalem. Local Jackrabbit militias, already secretly armed, albeit with older weapons, would rise in revolt as Dion's and Kun's armies drove eastward, between the Red and Nady Ann Rivers.

While Texark's forces were thus engaged in the Province and beyond the Great River, the Wilddog and the Grasshopper would join forces and attack from the west, hoping to help arm any able-bodied gleps from the Watchitah Nation and mount a combined attack.

Eventually Magister Dion became convinced. He insisted that Valana should raise its own militia, and occupy the fort his men had built, where citizens might take sanctuary in case of raids by "infiltrators or outlaws," and the militia would be used to assist the police in apprehending disloyal citizens, especially those of Texark origin. He designated one of his two military aides, Major Elswitch J. Gleaver, a short keg of a man with a red face and long mustachios, as the right officer to command the militia. Blacktooth expected his master to resist this usurpation, but he said nothing. Chuntar Cardinal Hadala broke the silence and said to Brownpony with a wink, "I'll keep a close eye on the Major for you, Cardinal. I'm staying in the fort."

No one raised a question about Valana's possible response to putting an outsider and a spook in charge.

When the meeting finally ended, it was nearly dark outside. Brownpony told the Nomads that the Palace, where they were residing, would be needed tomorrow for the beginning of conclave, and asked them to pack their belongings and move to his estate for the night. "Blacktooth will show you the way."

Then he beckoned to the monk and whispered, "Make sure they don't get there before moonrise. I'll speak privately with Dion now and tell him to expect that outlaw leader."

Nimmy nodded his understanding. He prevailed upon the sharfs and Holy Madness to eat dinner at the cardinal's expense at the Venison House. By the time they arrived at the estate, Mounts-Everybody had gone, presumably to meet with Dion. They greeted their host with minimum cordiality, still angry about the spy, and went at once to their rooms.

The food was gone from the dinner table, but Brownpony asked Nimmy to sit with them over a glass of wine. He asked what he felt about the day's events.

"I felt myself in the service of the hordes instead of you, m'Lord."

"That's quite natural. You were Bråm's interpreter. What else?"

"I was both afraid and angry."

"Afraid of whom? Angry at whom?"

"You."

This brought a threatening grunt from Wooshin.

"I suppose that's natural too," said the cardinal. "Holy Madness and the sharfs were certainly angry at me, because of Esitt Loyte. And it rubbed off on you. Loyte was one of the few men I've ever completely misjudged. Well, tomorrow begins the conclave. You'll find that less rowdy than last year, and—" He broke off, noticing Blacktooth's expression. The Axe noticed it too, and was scowling, for his loyalty to his master was absolute.

"Oh, I can get along without you," the Red Deacon said. "I don't need a Grasshopper interpreter in conclave, and I can borrow a secretary from Cardinal Bleze or Nauwhat. Still angry?"

"No, m'Lord. Just very tired."

"It's been a tiring day. All right, then take a vacation until we have a new pope. The Nomads will be in town a few more days. They have things to talk over among themselves and with Dion's officers.

But remember Loyte, and remember last year's attack. Watch your back."

Early the next morning, while walking through the streets Blacktooth saw several cardinals and their servants on their way to conclave at the Palace. One of them was a woman, but she was not Cardinal Buldyrk. He had heard about her, but had not seen her before.

There was a small convent on the south bank of the Brave River where a community of barefoot nuns, Sisters of Amen Specklebird's *Ordo Dominae Desertarum Nostrae*, lived, worked, and prayed, and Mother Iridia Silentia had been created cardinal by Pope Amen, the second woman in the Sacred College. Blacktooth noticed that her conclavists wore the same religious garb that Ædrea had worn when she was serving as courier between SEEC and New Jerusalem. The same Order had last year held a temporary residence in Valana, and Nimmy had assumed that among these local nuns, Ædrea's friend, Sister Julian, had provided her with a habit for disguise. But the local nuns were gone now. He had a wild hunch, and it overcame his misgivings about approaching one of them in the street. He spoke to her in a low voice.

"Forgive me, Sister. I am a monk, not in very good standing, of Saint Leibowitz. A young woman wearing your habit used to come here sometimes from a mountain community. Her name was Ædrea. I was wondering if you might know . . ."

The Sister kept her eyes lowered and did not speak. Mother Iridia noticed her conclavist being accosted by a brash cleric of some sort, and she approached them wearing a frown. She and her nun exchanged murmurs in a foreign tongue. Mother Iridia inspected Blacktooth from head to toe, nodded, reached in her portfolio, and handed him a prayer card.

"God bless you, Brother Blacktooth," she said, making a tiny cross. "Pray for those in trouble." Then she gripped her helper's arm and led her fast away.

Blacktooth, amazed that she knew his name and therefore his sin, felt the heat of a blush in his face. He looked at the prayer card. It was thick, glossy, and heavily enameled, and probably blessed with holy water like many tiny sacramental placards sold by mendicant religious orders. Most were saccharine and sentimental, but this was not. On one side it bore a picture of a crucifix at the top, but the crucified one was a woman, and the name above it was Santa Librada. Beneath the cross was advice in ancient English, which he understood with small difficulty. The English said:

(Pray to Santa Librada in times of
trouble with the police, the courts,
and when freedom is not visible. She
will help you, if you believe.)

For Ædrea, freedom was certainly not visible!
He wanted to run after the nuns and ask more questions, but that would be highly improper, and they would not answer. Instead, he resolved to write them a note of inquiry, and get one of Brownpony's housekeepers to deliver it.

He looked at the other side of the card. There was printed a prayer or poem which he had difficulty understanding, for although the language reminded him of Latin, it was not Latin:

Santa Librada del Mundo,
Tengo ojos, no me miren;
Tengo manos, no me tapen;
Tengo pieses, no me alcansan.
Con los angeles del 43,
Con el manto de Maria estoy tapado.
Con los pechos de Maria estoy rosado.

He thought of Aberlott, who was back in school at Saint Ston's, and turned to walk toward their old shared residence. The student might know someone at the school who could translate.

A crowd was gathering in John-in-Exile Square, but this was no mob like last year's raging rabble. There was no sickness in the city, and more fear than anger, and what anger there was, was directed at Texark and cardinals absent from the city. The people wanted Specklebird to remain as Pope, but his refusal they now seemed to accept as a sad reality. Brownpony was well known and popular, but not well revered; if he was lacking in holiness, he was also lacking in haughtiness, and he seemed to feel affection for the common people of the city.

On his way to Aberlott's, Blacktooth paused to watch some of the cardinals recently created by Pope Amen as they arrived and entered the assembly. He stood beside a young priest, who told him their names.

There was Abbot Joyo Cardinal Watchingdown, from Watchingdown Abbey, far east of the Great River.

And Wolfer Cardinal Poilyf, from the North Country, came still wearing his furs, although it was not a cold day.

Domidomi Cardinal Hoydok of Texark was excommunicated by Benefez for supporting Pope Amen, who then appointed him to the College. He was the one who had penned the angry summons to conclave, and he seemed still angry as he stalked into the hall.

Then came Furi Cardinal Shirikane, quietly, almost slinking along; he was from the west coast, a priest who could also speak Wooshin's dialect, so the Axe had told him. His countenance also seemed to bear a trace of Asia in it.

And there was Abrahà Cardinal Linkono, a schoolteacher from New Jerusalem, the only known spook in the College.

"And there is Hawken Chief Irrikawa," said the young priest.

"I know. I saw him yesterday."

"Did you know that it was Cardinal Buldyrk who suggested him to Pope Amen in the first place? The Abbey of N'ork is adjacent to Irrikawa's forest kingdom."

"I'm surprised," Nimmy told his informant. "Last year, the lady seemed to be leaning toward Cardinal Benefez."

"Hah! That was before Pope Amen ordained two women, and made another one cardinal," the priest said—rather stiffly, it seemed to Blacktooth.

"Irrikawa makes strange claims, says his family is as old as the continent itself. And that eagle feather! He doesn't want to be called 'Cardinal.' His servants call him 'Sire' and 'Majesty.'"

Two humbler men then went in the door: Buzi Cardinal Fudsow, a local plumbing contractor who had added a flush toilet of his own invention to Amen Specklebird's hillside retreat, and Leevit Lord Cardinal Bæhovar, a merchant from the Utah country.

Then the new Bishop of Denver, Varley Cardinal Swineman, whose diocese included the whole of the Denver Freestate, except for Valana itself; his cathedral was two days' ride to the north at Danfer, a small community on the outskirts of an expanse of half-buried rubble which was once a city of Denver. Although a Bishop of Denver had mounted the throne of Peter a few years ago, the Denver diocesan chair was not traditionally occupied by a cardinal.

Blacktooth thanked the priest and picked his way through the crowd in the square again. The conclave, legitimate or illegitimate, was not yet officially locked and sealed. The doors and windows were all still open, and the crowd in the square was quiet because a loud voice could be heard from within addressing the prelates who had already arrived. It took a few moments for Nimmy to recognize the voice of his master, because there was anger in it:

"I am under a suspended sentence of death imposed by the Imperial Mayor. The Pope has been denounced as an impostor by the Hannegan, the Archbishop, and their allies. They are attempting to convene a General Council of the Church in New Rome, and this—as you know—cannot be done without the approval of the Pope, and if there is no Pope, it cannot be done at all. Texark has begun to wage an undeclared war against the Valanan papacy, and we are all in danger. While we all deplore the Grasshopper raid into the illegally occupied zone around New Rome, and the ensuing massacre of innocents, we find ourselves by necessity allied with the hordes against the Empire. You must protect yourselves. There are Texark spies in Valana. One was caught yesterday and severely mutilated, without my knowledge, by the Lord of the Three Hordes. He is receiving medical treatment in the local jail. As you must recall, assassins tried a year ago Easter to kill me and my secretary. There will be more attacks of this kind.

"Weapons are available—superior weapons—for the Papal Guard, and for any of you who wish them for yourselves or your servants. Valana is an open city. We do not have border guards, and you may be sure that the agents of the Hannegan come and go as they please. Sidearms for you and your servants will be provided . . ."

Perhaps the anger he heard in the voice was rhetorical. The monk shook his head in wonder and moved on. He did not regret that Brownpony had chosen other conclavists this time, although he hoped his obvious reluctance to serve as one of them would be forgiven.

Aberlott was not at home. Meaning to copy the strange prayer and leave it on his table with a note, he tried the door but found it locked. He shrugged to himself and started to retrace his steps when a thought struck him: he still had not been able to see Amen Specklebird because of the crowds waiting outside his door. But people who were not at work were now forming the crowd in John-in-Exile Square, and the cardinals were inside the Palace. So he turned around and started climbing the hill to Amen's home.

"I'll not translate it for you," said the old black Pope, holding Mother Iridia's card. They were sitting together alone in the hillside house of stone. The rocks were cold, but there was a small fire on the hearth, and the room was chilly but not uncomfortable.

"It's more poem than prayer. It is not written in the language the Sisters speak today, but their speech does have more classical Spanish in it than Rockymount or Ol'zark has. This is old Spanish with a word or two of country dialect perhaps. I have seen it before. I know what it means to the Sisters. They think the crucified woman does not depict an event of history, but an event in the mind of Mary when she allowed herself to feel the crucifixion of her son."

"She wishes herself in his place on the cross?"

"Wishes? In her own heart, she's already there. *Librada del mundo* means set free from the world. But the next three lines seem to be spoken by the crucified. She has eyes, but doesn't see herself. With her hands nailed to the cross, she can't touch herself. With her feet nailed there too, she can't walk about. The line after that—'with the angels of number forty-three'—its meaning is lost. The last two lines might be spoken by the Christ child: 'Mary's blanket covers me. Mary's breasts turn me rosy.' The child is nursing. This is the Sisters' interpretation."

"What is yours?"

"I'm not an interpreter. You are, Blacktooth. You have eyes, hands, and feet. Can you see yourself, touch yourself, walk about?"

"I never doubted it before, but—" He paused. "But what I see in a mirror is not me, is it? I can touch my body, but is that me? My feet move, but who is walking?"

"If you have the right questions, why do you need answers? The answers are in the questions." He smiled a cat's smile. "I like your questions."

"Is there anything you can do for Ædrea?"

Specklebird was silent. "Not that question," Nimmy was afraid he would say. After a time he purred a cougar's purr. "Stay awhile and pray with me. We'll pray the silent prayer."

They prayed without words. Occasionally, Blacktooth arose to feed the fire. At dusk, they ate a simple meal, and prayed some more. In the morning, Brother Blacktooth chopped more wood, and Amen Specklebird hung out a sign that said, I PRAY—GO AWAY.

Nimmy stayed with him and prayed with him. The silence was like what the silence at the Abbey of Leibowitz should have been. On the fifth day, someone came and yelled "*Habemus Papam!*" three times before he went away. Specklebird seemed not to notice. The silence was unbroken by the event.

Blacktooth stayed for nine days, a novena of sorts. He learned more about his own soul during those nine days than he had learned during all his years at Leibowitz Abbey. Amen Specklebird was a teacher in silence. The soul of the student somehow began to resemble the soul of the teacher in silence. There was no explanation for it, for to explain would break the silence.

He might have stayed longer than nine days, but when he came out to chop wood on the tenth morning, a great cloud of smoke was arising from Valana. Was the whole city on fire?

Amen followed him most of the way down the hill, until they could see that it was only the Papal Palace and the police barracks burning. *Only!* That was Specklebird's word.

They embraced in silence, and parted in silence. Nimmy was vaguely worried about the old man. He had tried to remove himself entirely from the scene of the ecclesiastical and political struggle for supremacy, but how could he be free from it while men continued to bicker and battle about his quitclaim on the Apostolic See? Was he ever Pope? Was he still Pope? Where was his resignation? If someone had burned the original, Blacktooth felt the old man was not safe. And yet he knew it would be useless presumption to advise him to seek protection.

The fires had been preceded by explosions, the guard at the gate told him. But Cardinal Brownpony, now Pope Amen II, was not dead. He had only fled the city along with most of the Curia. Gone where? The guard could not say. Most of Mayor Dion's brigade had ridden south on the papal highway, leaving a few men, with part of the Yellow Guard, to train the civilian militia in the fort the spooks had built. Several cardinals had taken refuge there. Perhaps the Holy Father had gone with Dion. The Texark spy had disappeared from the jail, and the guard reckoned there must have been as many as forty infiltrators to accomplish the jailbreak and blow up the Palace. "These bastards have been living among us for years—settlers from Texark. Most of them pretended to be fugitives."

The Nomads had returned to the Plains, he told Nimmy, and perhaps the Pope was with them, instead.

Blacktooth hurried first to Aberlott's. A note on the door said, "Gone to the fort. Help yourself." Blacktooth tried the latch. This time it was unlocked. Judging by the mess on the floor and the overturned furniture, someone had already helped himself, or else the student had been dragged to the fort after resisting.

He went to SEEC. The building was deserted, except for the covert wing. When he tried to enter there, he was quickly ejected. He went to Saint John-in-Exile. Only a curate was present. He told Blacktooth that the new Pope, after escaping from the burning building, had left the city in a coach belonging to the Grasshopper sharf, but they had indeed followed Dion south.

"Did the coach have 'I set fires' painted on the side?"

"Is that what it said? It was ancient English, I think."

Brâm was going to take charge of a shipment of guns, Nimmy thought. He started walking to the fort. On the way, he was grabbed by the scruff of the neck and dragged to the fort. It was Ulad, who would not believe that he was going there of his own free will.

"You know I am a servant of Cardinal, uh, Pope Amen Two," he protested.

"If you still were, you would be with him. You are a soldier now, piss-robe," the giant said. "You are going to fight for the Holy City."

Holy City? Did he mean New Rome or New Jerusalem?

"Will I get to see Ædrea?"

"Not likely," growled the hulk.

Nimmy stopped struggling, but Ulad kept his long slender hand around his neck as they walked.

CHAPTER 22

Let a good pound weight of bread suffice
for the day, whether there be only one meal
or both dinner and supper.
—*Saint Benedict's Rule*, Chapter 39

 LIA BROWNPONY—NOW POPE AMEN II—MISSED
his Grasshopper interpreter; no one had
seen Nimmy since the election. The new
Pope was reluctant to believe that
Blacktooth had deserted him; he had left
messages with cardinals who remained in
Valana. Now he rode with Sharfs Oxsho
and Demon Light Bråm in Bråm's coach,
while several cardinals came along be-
hind, some in coaches, some on horseback. Wooshin, who was not
fluent in any Nomad dialect, rode with the Pope's driver. Inside the
coach, the young Wilddog sharf fawned on his Pontiff, somewhat to
his Pontiff's annoyance, because Bråm was still calling him "Red
Beard," and every time Oxsho said "Your Holiness" or "Holy Father,"
the Grasshopper sharf grew surly. Bråm mentioned Esitt Loyte more
often than seemed polite. Oxsho argued that the spy had been caught
before he could learn much more than the identities of the participants in the war council.

"And that's too much," Eltür snapped. "Once the Hannegan knows we have allies in the east, he will be less likely to send forces across the Great River. Isn't that so, Red Beard?"

Brownpony had been staring out the window at the scenery as if in deep reverie. Eltür was forced to repeat the question. Oxsho rephrased it in the Wilddog dialect, but Brownpony's response was indirect.

"The attack on the Palace was a complete surprise to me. I was too confused to think clearly for an hour or two. The agents who broke Loyte out of jail must have taken him straight to the telegraph terminal. We should have thought of that immediately and sent forces to capture it before he could get a message out. Now it will be captured in due course, but too late."

"So the Hannegan's forces will *not* cross the Great River!"

"We can't know that until you try to arrange a cease-fire, Sharf Bråm."

"You expect me to play the coward, Red Beard?"

"Of course not! You can seem unwilling. Let him know that Holy Madness demands it of you, that you would be delighted to resume hostilities if Texark turns you down."

Brownpony had the uneasy feeling that Eltür blamed him for twin Hultor's self-destructive behavior, but this feeling probably arose out of Father Steps-on-Snake's opinion that Hultor's murderous raid was meant to send a message to the cardinal who pampered Wilddog Christians and left the Grasshopper out of his councils.

"Your tribes and your warriors, and you yourself, Sharf Bråm, are the most powerful force we have against the Hannegan."

Eltür had trouble understanding. Oxsho tried to shift the dialect to Grasshopper, but the result was less than satisfactory.

"We are not your force, Red Beard," said the sharf.

They passed a dozen armed men from New Jerusalem along the way. The papal highway had been seized by, and was being patrolled by, Dion's forces. The guard drew itself up into formation and saluted as the Pope passed by. Soon they came to their destination. The road to Shard's place was no longer just a path through the bushes leading to Scarecrow Alley. Magister Dion's men were fast builders. The brush had been cleared. Fifty yards from the papal highway, a log barricade had been erected, and twin guardhouses flanked the improved road. A cloud of dust raised by men and horses hovered over the area. The ramshackle houses of the gleps had been razed. Barracks and other log buildings replaced them. Two trains of wagons were loaded and stood ready to move out, while the dust of a third train heading south was still visible—Önmu Kun, Brownpony thought.

Amen II was quickly surrounded by his Curia when he descended from Eltür's coach, and his leave-taking from the Nomad sharfs was perfunctory and less than cordial. Each of them was met by a band of warriors from his horde, and they were ready to move out within the hour. The secrets of the Suckamints were no longer secret, and the colony now was clearly at war.

The Mayor strode up to the group of cardinals, genuflected with military precision to the figure in white, and brushed the Pope's ring with his lips. He answered questions before they were asked.

"The telegraph station has been captured. According to the prisoners we took, Loyte had already been there and gone. Outlaw forces ambushed a cavalry troop in the outlaw lands. The ruffian you sent me brought over a hundred men to us, and they took no prisoners. Our light horse are riding hard toward the second station, and they are passing Jackrabbit guerrillas on their way to join us. Now what of our allies in the East?"

"Well, word has not reached them yet about what's happening here." Brownpony shrugged. "So we'll not know for some time." He gestured toward the mountains. "Is the way open to us?"

"Of course, Holy Father. The buildings are all of logs, but new, and it is your third Rome as long as you wish it to be." He beckoned to a young man with such long legs and short arms that one might have considered him a glep, except that Dion introduced him as his son, and he was both well-mannered and handsome.

"Slojon will be your guide as long as you need one. He will be in charge of my office while I am with the army."

The young man bowed and squinted closely at the Pope's ring without actually kissing it.

Brownpony continued to peer out at the scenery as if in deep thought while they rode upward into the mountains in a coach formerly belonging to the Mayor, who had ordered the door panels repainted with the papal tiara and the keys. This time Wooshin rode with him inside the coach, along with Dion's Slojon, and Cardinals Hilan Bleze and Mother Iridia Silentia. With the latter, he had enjoyed a distant but enduring acquaintance, and she had thanked him for concurring in the first Amen's choosing her for the cardinalate. Brownpony admitted that he had in fact done no such thing, but he now applauded her appointment after the fact.

During the journey into the mountains, she brought up the subject of Ædrea's captivity, but Brownpony's respiratory weakness returned to him as they gained altitude, and he was unable to say anything to support her in her petition to Dion's Slojon, except to smile at her and gesture in the young man's direction. The gesture could have meant whatever each of them might want it to mean. Hilan Bleze changed the subject to curial matters.

By the time they arrived in the heart of the community, Pope Amen II needed to be carried by sedan chair to his new quarters. He asked the Secretary of State to send an urgent message to Blacktooth in Valana for a copy of a recipe by the Venerable Boedullus. Then he collapsed in a feather bed and slept for sixteen hours. Outside the building was a disappointed crowd of the faithful among these normal-looking "Children of the Pope," who had assembled in the hope of receiving the Apostolic Benediction from their special father. Secretary Hilan Cardinal Bleze blessed them himself, and told them to come back tomorrow.

Corporal Blacktooth St. George never received his Pontiff's urgent message, for when it arrived in Valana, it was routed to the fort and delivered to his commander, Major Elswitch J. Gleaver, who signed a receipt for it in Blacktooth's absence, but somehow forgot to give it to him later. He called Chuntar Cardinal Hadala's attention to the message. The cardinal opened and read it.

"Our new Holy Father must have become a gourmand since his election," said Hadala with a hint of contempt in his tone. "It's only a request for a recipe by a cook named Boedullus."

"Could it be a coded message?" suggested the florid major.

"I think not. If Corporal Blacktooth had any secret information, the Pope would just summon him directly."

"Well, I heard that His Holiness *had* sent for him."

"Where did you hear that?" the cardinal asked sharply.

"A rumor. He may have started it himself, but somebody said it came from Cardinal Nauwhat."

"Damn it! I'll have a talk with Sorely. You know Mayor Dion doesn't want that monk in New Jerusalem. There is his affair with that suspect girl, and the Pope, after all, is now too dependent on the Mayor to risk offending him. I'm sure that's why Elia hasn't summoned him. Besides, he won't need a Nomad interpreter in New Jerusalem, even if—" He broke off.

The Major looked at him and wondered if the distinction between interpreter and translator had stopped his line of thinking. As if to confirm this, Hadala continued:

"Besides, we are going to need someone to handle correspondence between ourselves and the Nomad sharfs. Sorely will surely need him too, for the same reason. That's why we proposed his promotion to corporal, and we want to keep him reasonably satisfied. I doubt any rumor about his going back into Brownpony's, uh, the Pope's service came from Nauwhat."

"Well, I can keep him busy until you need him," said Gleaver. "Right now, the police have him. And then he's on leave until after the funeral tomorrow."

"Better have him watched, lest he make a run for it. He can't be trusted. Brownpony learned that. And don't assign him duty in the city. He's probably too squeamish to shoot traitors."

A cleaning woman, who came on Mondays to scrub the former Pope's clothing, dishes, and floor, usually turned away when she saw his I PRAY—GO AWAY sign in place, but on the Monday in question, a brown stain from something that had leaked out under the door caught her attention. She knocked timidly, but there was no answer. She tried the latch, and the door swung inward. It was a quiet morning, and her scream echoed from the opposite hillside. A farmer and two shepherds responded. The decapitated body of Amen Specklebird had fallen sideways from the prie-dieu where he had obviously been kneeling before his altar when his killer struck. His head had bounced off the wall and rolled under a table. He had been dead at least two days.

The manner of his death—by a single horizontal stroke of a sword—caused immediate suspicion to fall on the Yellow Guard, but neither Gai-See nor Woosoh-Loh had left the fort during the week of the murder, and the others, including Wooshin, had accompanied Pope Amen II to New Jerusalem.

Blacktooth had been one of the last people to see Pope Amen Specklebird alive, and the police questioned him closely, but in the presence of his lawyer-advocate, a priest appointed by one of the cardinals to look out for his interests. As it turned out, the police did not suspect him, but his advocate was of some help in explaining the religious relationship that developed between the Leibowitzian monk and the retired Pope during their nine days of silent prayer in Amen's residence just days before his murder. Nimmy blamed himself. He had failed to act on his intuition at the time of their parting: the feeling which had come to him that Specklebird was in imminent danger. He was distracted from this worry when Ulad had grabbed him by the neck and drafted him into the militia, but he had felt certainty that Specklebird would ignore a warning anyway.

The police were unconcerned by his guilty feelings; they had as yet no suspects, although the population of the city was being carefully screened, and any citizen who could not offer proof of his place of birth was sent to a detention camp adjacent to the fort. Fifteen known participants in the terrorist uprising had already been shot. The death sword could as plausibly have been a well-sharpened cavalry saber as one of the beautiful blades of the Asian warriors. Nimmy was allowed to go in peace, and his leave was extended to include the time of the old man's funeral. He wanted to run away to New Jerusalem, but he would surely be caught, and Brownpony might not welcome him if he did escape.

Amen Specklebird lay in state, his body illuminated by many candles on the high catafalque in the Cathedral of Saint John-in-Exile, and all the faithful who remained in Valana after the insurgency, the purge, and the flight came now to pay their respects and to pass in a slow line to view the body. There was less pomp and grandeur than if he had died as a reigning pontiff, and a certain amount of chaos, but that was more a result of the exodus to New Jerusalem than it was of his resignation and the previous transfer of papal power to Cardinal Brownpony. Investigators found, for example, that no official had taken from the old man the signet of his fisherman's ring and the two seals (one for wax, one for lead) of office upon his resignation; these seals were normally seized and broken by the Cardinal High Chamberlain during the interregnum after the death of the Pope. Had they been used after Brownpony had ascended? The ring was removed from his finger after death, but militiamen searched his home and found no seals. Stolen by his killer? These and other irregularities cast doubt upon many documents that emerged from the Specklebird pontificate, especially in cases where living witnesses could not be located.

After joining the slow line and awaiting his turn, Blacktooth passed the catafalque. He noticed that the undertaker had done a good job of concealing the fact that the head had been severed from the body, but otherwise the corpse looked more like a pope than Specklebird had ever looked while alive. The wild white hair was carefully combed, the deeper creases in his face were caulked, and his black skin lightened somewhat with a brown powder. The stink of the corpse, however, had begun to penetrate the background odors of incense in the church. Nimmy choked with tears and hurried into the square.

There was a thin crowd. Many of Amen Specklebird's admirers had been fanatically devoted to the old holy man, and enough of them disputed the validity of his resignation, and therefore the validity of Brownpony's election, that some were heard to suggest that Brownpony himself had arranged the old man's murder in order to secure himself in office. Nimmy overheard two hill-dwellers giving voice to this theory, and he shouted at them, "You stupid oafs! That's exactly what Texark wants you to believe."

The men took umbrage, and Nimmy let himself be goaded into a fight. He won the fight, but lost self-respect, although he was now wearing the green uniform of a militiaman and not his brown monk's robe. He felt pats on the back, however, and heard cheers from Valanans who knew and liked the new Pope.

By the time of the funeral on the following day, Blacktooth smelled the stink of the corpse even through the haze of piñon pine incense that pervaded the cathedral; later witnesses for the cause of canonizing Pope Amen I would testify of the heavenly perfume exhaled by the body. He knew all about the olfactory miracles performed by saintly corpses; Saint Leibowitz had smelled like ambrosial barbecue, his followers said. He too now tried to smell the miraculous perfume of Amen Specklebird, but his piety perhaps had been diminished by his sins, for the rotten odor persisted.

Suddenly, however, the body of Amen Specklebird sat up on the catafalque and pointed straight at Blacktooth. The whiskers of the cougar twitched, and fangs were bared. Nimmy closed his eyes to squeeze the tears out of them. When he opened them again, the corpse lay back down and never moved during the high funeral Mass, concelebrated by the six cardinals who had stayed in the region.

The purge of Valana's people continued, even during the funeral. When Nimmy emerged from the church, he learned that the number of suspected conspirators who had been shot had risen to eighteen, and more than thirty citizens were imprisoned in the stockade next to the fort. Anyone unable to furnish proof of his place of birth, either by document or through testimony of witnesses, would, if no one appeared to testify of his participation in the terror, be sent into permanent exile. Any captive with an enemy or two in the city could expect a denunciation and testimony leading to his execution. Old scores were settled thus. The court trying the cases was neither civil nor ecclesiastical, but military. Nimmy guessed that most of the real villains had fled the city immediately after the crime, but the trials provided an outlet for revenge. In the murder of Amen Specklebird, however, the police had no suspects.

When Valana had been pacified and purged, there was no talk of disbanding the militia. That Chuntar Cardinal Hadala and his New

Jerusalem officers had their own plan of battle in the war became clear when orders were posted to prepare the combined forces to move out from the city by the first of the month, when the moon was full. Messengers had been sent out to the Wilddog, and Sharf Oxsho replied by sending three guides and more than a hundred horses for those citizen soldiers of Valana who had none of their own. The guides were assigned to Blacktooth for interpretation. He found them ignorant of the fact that they were directly following the orders of Chuntar Hadala, Sorely Nauwhat, and Elswitch Gleaver instead of the Pope. He was afraid to mention it, because Nauwhat had always been close to Brownpony. Valanans were skeptical and complained a lot about leaving the vicinity of the city for a move away from the mountains, but there was as yet no talk of rebellion.

Then, on the first of July, when the militia was preparing to ride east with fourteen wagonloads of arms, a messenger of the Papal Guard rode into Valana and posted on the door of the Cathedral and the wall of the Papal Palace an eight-page document with the papal seal, then proceeded to the fort and posted another copy on the orderly room wall.

Its heading was thus: *Amen II Episcopus Romae servus servorum dei, omnibus electis domini ipsis fidelibus in una Ecclesia vera Catholica atque Apostolica credentibus, qui subsunt nobis secundum Petrum unicum pastorem . . .*

Blacktooth knew historians would call it by the first words of the text, *Scitote Tyrannum,* which followed. Newly returned after dark to the fort from furlough, he read by torchlight the first few paragraphs on the wall:

> Amen II, Bishop of Rome, servant of the servants of God, to all the faithful believers in the one true Church, Catholic and Apostolic, to these chosen ones of the Lord, who are subject to Us as to Peter, the only shepherd appointed by Christ to become the head of His mystical body, sends greetings and the Apostolic Benediction.
>
> YOU SHALL KNOW THAT THE TYRANT Filpeo of Texark [Tyrannum Phillipum Texarkanae] together with his uncle, the former Cardinal Archbishop of the City of Hannegans [Civitatis Hanneganensis], having by their own acts [ipso facto] been excommunicated, as affirmed by Our predecessor of holy memory, Amen I, are hereby declared by Us to be enemies of God and His Holy Church, are cursed, condemned, cast out, cut off from the Body of Christ, apart from which there is no salvation. For crimes against human-

ity and the Church, including his own people and their clergy, We declare Filpeo Harq deposed from the office of Mayor; We absolve his former subjects from all oaths of obedience to him, We urge them to reconstitute a legitimate government in his place, and We enjoin all Christians against serving or obeying him. As long as the tyrant remains in power, We encourage all Christian rulers of peoples throughout the continent to take up arms against him. They shall receive through Our venerable Brethren, their own Bishops, Our blessing upon their armies and their arms.

Moreover, whosoever among the faithful is fit to bear arms shall, upon undertaking to wage righteous war against this heretical tyrant and his uncle, receive from Us through his confessor a plenary indulgence for all his sins and remission of all temporal punishment which may be due either in this world or in Purgatory. Upon confession, his only penance shall be to wage war against the forces of the imperial tyrant, and should he die in battle, We, who hold the keys of the kingdom of Heaven, shall unlock the gate thereof that he may enter into the holy Presence . . .

A crusade!
The word itself was not used, and had not been used since the twenty-third century, but all the characteristics were there. The Pope spoke of heroes marching behind a crucifer into battle. War was to be waged under the sign of the cross and the banner of the papacy. The church in Hannegan City was laid under interdict. Ecclesiastical courts were ordered closed. Priests were forbidden to say Mass. All sacraments except last rites were withheld. Clergy and laity who ignored the interdict were automatically excommunicated. The sentence did not extend to the Province, except to those parishes which had refused obedience to Brownpony's former Vicariate and remained tied to the Hannegan City Archdiocese.

Upon Urion Benefez himself the Pope pronounced a sentence of "Anathema, from which he can be absolved only by the Roman Pontiff and at the point of death."

There was more, but Blacktooth left the furious document and returned to the barracks by full moonlight. They would be moving out tomorrow. His astonishment was due to the fact that such language came from his former employer, a man slow to anger.

"Why astonished?" Aberlott asked him. "Haven't you heard of a crusade before?"

"Yes, but not since the twenty-third century, and that one of the least holy wars ever fought. The bull or whatever it's called just doesn't sound like Cardinal Brownpony."

"Well, it isn't Cardinal Brownpony. It's Pope Amen II. Maybe his voice changed when it dropped on him."

"It sounds more like Domidomi Cardinal Hoydok."

Aberlott pondered for a moment. "And why not? Hoydok wouldn't dare go back to Hannegan City. He's not here. So he must be with the Pope. And who could better write a letter to anger the Mayor and the Archbishop? He's probably the Pope's secretary for urban affairs by now."

Nimmy's urge to run away to New Jerusalem had not entirely disappeared, because of Ædrea, but it had been diminished in urgency by the tone of the bull *Scitote Tyrannum*. He was not sure that he wanted to work for its author.

Early the following morning, most of the remaining population of Valana turned out to watch its young men ride off toward the Plains and to war under command of the spooks of New Jerusalem. Minor clergy, who had read *Scitote Tyrannum*, had donned vestments and now fell in with the riders. A priest bearing a crucifix marched ahead of Major Gleaver's horse. Blacktooth suspected that the support of clergy had been arranged by one of the cardinals. The show of religion in support of the militia prevented a public display of hostility toward the alien commanders who were leading local soldiery.

The sun was approaching the zenith when Gleaver called a halt for food, water, and a brief rest. When the formation fell in again, Ulad sent Blacktooth to the head of the column as interpreter. Only now that they were safely out of civilian earshot was Gleaver prepared to disclose the planned route to his Nomad guides. Even so, the major ordered that the details be kept secret from the men and from Nomads of either horde they might encounter during the journey.

"From here we ride southeast until we reach the Kensau River. We'll follow the river until it turns northeast, then continue east-southeast until we pick it up again at some of the old dams near Tulse, and on until we're within half-a-day's ride from the Texark patrol road. At that point we reconnoiter, and send a patrol to infiltrate the Watchitah."

Blacktooth translated for the Nomad scouts, and Gleaver continued:

"The moon should be full again about the time we arrive. Our brothers beyond the border there can arrange incidents to distract the patrols while we try to drive the wagons past the border at night. With luck, we can arm the Valley people without a fight. If we have to fight to get them in, it will mean Hannegan has seen us coming. That means secrecy. Don't talk to any Nomads we meet about where we are going."

The Nomad warriors nodded their understanding, but Blacktooth heard them talking later about the troop being observed by motherless ones, who regularly sold news of Grasshopper movements to Texark agents. There would be a blue moon on the last day of July. By day or by night, a convoy of wagons escorted by light-horse infantry traveling east-southeast across the Plains toward Watchit-Ol'zarkia would not go unobserved. Nimmy and the Nomads expected a fight, but only Nimmy was committed to it, and his Ædrea was in jail.

The whole scheme seemed crazy. A week after the departure from Valana, Sorely Nauwhat caught up with them. He was weary from fast riding and immediately made a bed in one of the wagons. The horse he had been riding bore a brand which identified it as belonging to one of the Nomad messenger families, so it was clear that he had changed horses several times in catching up with them. Why Nauwhat? What was so important about this expedition that the head of SEEC joined the command? Previous to his appearance, Blacktooth had suspected that this feckless sortie of the Valanan militia was entirely Chuntar Hadala's project, and, impressed against his will, he wanted to desert. But Nauwhat had been Brownpony's closest friend and supporter in the Curia, and his presence seemed to confirm the legitimacy if not the sanity of the mission. Gai-See and Woosoh-Loh, now sergeants, had come with the expedition, and their loyalty to Brownpony was beyond suspicion. There would be no deserters with them looking on.

One morning early in mid-July, while passing the cardinals' tent, he overheard a murmur of conversation between these princes of the Church.

". . . peace, yes, but the peace of Christ!" Hadala was saying.

"Sure, Brownpony loves peace," Brownpony's friend answered. "He loves it so much he doesn't care who he kills to get it."

Blacktooth hurried away, but perhaps not before being seen; Sorely Nauwhat began avoiding him immediately afterward.

O Santa Librada! Freedom is not visible!

Pray for us!

That night he dreamed of a woman, a casualty of war. She was half buried in a hillside pocked by cannon fire.

Blood drained slowly in a thick stream from a hole at the edge of her breast. Half her body and her right arm was swallowed up by the landslide, while her left arm lay free and limp among the stones in sand. He touched her arm and felt for a pulse. He could find none, but the wound in her side continued to bleed. The flow of blood continued. It ran into the sand and between the stones and continued to run ten feet down the slide. He tore off a piece of his robe and tried to stanch the flow, but even after leaving it there while he counted to a thousand, the wound bled unchecked. He began trying to dig her out, but his work moved a critical stone, caused her body to shift, and caused several rocks to roll from above, as if the landslide had not finished its work.

Soon it became apparent that the flow of blood was increasing, until he saw that the blood could no longer be her blood but was coming through her from somewhere deep within the collapsed hill. But the blood was keeping her alive. After a while, she opened her eyes and looked at him.

For a moment, she was Ædrea. She raised her left hand toward his face, and he saw a torn palm with more blood.

"*Tengo ojos, no me miren.*

"*Tengo manos, no me tapen.*"

She was Santa Librada now, deposed from the cross.

He backed away in fear. She hissed and turned red and tried to bite him. She was the bride of Brownpony, the Buzzard of Battle. A shadow fell over him, and he looked up. There stood Elia Brownpony in white vestments and wearing the tiara. He sprinkled the woman with holy water, and she shrieked in agony.

Blacktooth always had trouble sleeping under the stars.

CHAPTER 23

> Indeed at all seasons let the hour, whether
> for supper or for dinner, be so arranged that
> everything will be done by daylight.
> —*Saint Benedict's Rule*, Chapter 41

 HE EMPEROR WAS A PART-TIME SCHOLAR.
With the help of a young political-sci-
ence professor who was also a popular
author, Filpeo Harq had written a book.
It was a book Brownpony not surprisingly
had sent to the Holy Office as soon as he
saw it. The Holy Office duly added it to
the *Index Librorum Prohibitorum*, although it bore the imprimatur of the
Cardinal Archbishop of Texark, and carried an introduction by a monk
of Saint Leibowitz, who, unfortunately for his career, happened to
agree with the Imperial Mayor that the restoration of the *Magna Civitas* could only be accomplished by secular science and industry under
the protection of a secular state against the resistance and hostility of
religion. It was such a self-evidently wicked book that the Holy Office
wrote neither an attack nor a commentary; the work was filed under
"Anticlericalism." Its author was already so thoroughly anathematized
that further curses from eternal Rome would seem petty.

But Filpeo was a scholar, and among other things, he had been able to restore several ancient pieces of music, including one of regional origin which seemed well suited to become the new national anthem for the Empire, and he published it in his book. The tune was now well known. Its ancient words were English, but the Ol'zark translation scanned well enough. It began: "The eyes of Texark are upon you." The Mayor wanted his subjects to feel well watched.

Every priest in the Empire who read the crusading bull *Scitote Tyrannum* aloud from the pulpit or who publicly observed the interdict imposed on the Texark Church by the Brownpony papacy—there were only thirteen of them—was arrested and charged with sedition. Two bishops who had suspended Masses and confessions in their dioceses in obedience to the bull joined the priests in jail. In six out of seven parishes throughout the Empire, however, the religious life went on as if Amen II had never spoken. After so many decades of a papacy in exile, the people of Hannegan City and even New Rome had lost sight of the Pope as a real player in their perceived world. He was distant, and his anger was like that of a player on the stage, except that the people only read the reviews without seeing the play. The communications media—mostly paper since the telegraph line to the west was down—kept them informed, but the media were deferentially kind to the relatively absolute ruler of the state.

Scitote Tyrannum, therefore—however binding it might be in Heaven—was the least of Filpeo's worries on Earth. The Antipope's forces were going to march, and the Antipope had used the treasures of the Church to arm the wild Nomads with superior weapons to be used against civilization. Filpeo always spoke of him as Antipope, although there was no competing Pope. Filpeo stood for the renewal of the *Magna Civitas*, and Brownpony the Antipope opposed it. It was that simple, from the Hannegan's point of view. Brownpony was the past waging war against the future. He armed the barbarians and would soon send them against civilization's holy places, if not against the City of Hannegans itself. Filpeo was confident he could defend the city until the new firearms were delivered, and after that his forces would be able to drive the spooks back to the Suckamints and herd the Jackrabbit into the southwest desert, push the Wilddog north of the Misery, and herd the Grasshopper into formerly Wilddog lands, so that the two northern hordes would be forced to fight each other for living space.

The Imperial Mayor hoped to win the Nomad outlaws over to his side, and he sent an ex-pirate to recruit them. Admiral e'Fondolai promised them Grasshopper lands in the aftermath of victory. Filpeo was amused to hear of it at first, but after giving the matter some thought, he decided that he would, if possible, honor the promise Carpy had so rashly made. If the motherless ones could marry farm women and be assigned enough land, they could raise fully domesticated cattle and live in fixed homes, and trade with the farmers and the cities. In such circumstances, they would not develop a society anything like the hordes. Very likely the taboo against capturing wild horses could not survive without the Weejus to enforce it, and the motherless ones, once they settled down, were not likely to restore the matrilineal inheritance of wild Nomads. They would acquire property and fight to defend it. In the Mayor's dream, in the wake of his certain victory, the Grasshopper and the Wilddog and the motherless ones would each be at war against the others, and the Jackrabbit would straggle back out of the desert to be arrested and put to work repairing war-damaged properties.

Filpeo was well pleased with his admiral, but not his general.

When General Goldæm went to the university and demanded Thon Hilbert's cooperation in teaching the troops how to contaminate wells in the Province and infect cattle with the new diseases, Thon Hilbert refused. General Goldæm went to the War Office and got him inducted into the Texark Army as a private. Then he ordered him to teach. Hilbert cursed the general personally, then cursed his Monarch. The general had the professor put in jail for sedition. The Hannegan summoned the general to his quarters, fired him, and retired him at half pay. He then put Admiral e'Fondolai, alias Carpios Robbery, in charge of the project. Because Hilbert's assistant at the university agreed to teach the military whatever was required, Hilbert remained in jail, pending an apology to the Hannegan. The apology was not immediately forthcoming.

Three months after he fired General Goldæm, Filpeo watched with delight as Admiral e'Fondalai's model strike force, led by Carpios himself on horseback, marched past his reviewing stand. The Imperial Mayor had never seen such a burly gang of cutthroats outside of a prison yard. They were armed with the several dozen repeating arms which had already been delivered by the gunsmiths, which was quite an investment, and one which Filpeo had been reluctant to make at first. Carpios made the point that for an effective assault force, firepower was everything, so the Emperor placed his most advanced weaponry in the hands of ruffians dressed in wolfskins and chewed leather. He watched them march under a banner that depicted a bird being roasted on a spit over a fire; the bird was branded with both the Weejus symbol for the Buzzard of Battle and with a pair of crossed keys. Filpeo laughed aloud at the sacrilege, called the old pirate back to the stand, and awarded him the ancient title of "Vaquero Supreme of the Plains," which had been claimed by the Hannegans since the time of their Nomad roots, but which dropped out of use after Hannegan IV fell off his horse.

Part of Filpeo's delight was at Carpios' expense, for the sight of the bearded pirate in admiral's white uniform riding at the head of three hundred bathless ruffians dressed in wilddog skins was hilarious. After the parade, Filpeo not only gave him the title of Vaquero but promoted him to field marshal—"so you can choose your own uniform" was the way the Emperor put it. But he made sure to let the old seaman know that when he finished the project, he would be made commander in chief of Texark forces. There was something oceanic about the Great Plains. The admiral sensed it too, and became enthusiastic about the wars that plainly lay ahead.

There was no clear Texark military doctrine for Nomad warfare, not since Hannegan IV fell off his horse, and the admiral's job was quickly to develop such a doctrine. The Plains resembled the ocean in that there was nowhere to hide, and no naturally defensive terrain in which to take refuge. Most land west of the last timber was equally accessible from all directions, and therefore as inhospitable as the storm-tossed sea. A cavalry battle there could be like an engagement between two ships of war—short, savage, and with only one surviving side.

The admiral thrice visited Thon Hilbert in jail. He informed his ruler of the visits, and affirmed their obvious purpose; he promised an account of the ultimate outcome, but declined to give a running report. The jailer told Filpeo that during the admiral's third visit, they played Old Zark chess and talked about nothing but the game. What came of the meetings was also nothing, but Carpy wanted the Mayor to let the professor go anyway. Filpeo refused. He had no use for an apology, but apology or no apology, Hilbert would stay in jail until the university's cooperation with the military was satisfactory and assured.

"Thon Hilbert's disease is hindering them in the South," a field commander told him. "A few cases have appeared among Brownpony's armies, but it is becoming endemic only in the Province. Because of it, the spooks and the Jackrabbit rebels are exhausting their military energy for the time being. We can soon launch a counterattack."

"And no cases of the disease have appeared among our troops?"

"No, as I told you, as long as they drink Hilbert's preventative every day. It tastes bad, and they don't like it. But there is a standing order than any trooper who catches Hilbert's disease shall be immediately shot. To prevent further contagion is the stated reason."

The Mayor shifted restlessly. "That sounds unnecessarily cruel."

"Well, if carried out, of course. The threat is necessary to prevent contagion; it is only meant to insure the men drink the preventative."

The War Dog was a constellation in the Nomad night, but he was also the mythical pet of the Lord Empty Sky. That ancient hero had led even wilddogs into battle against the army of the Farmer King. Nomads had always sent their dogs against the enemy whenever practical, but Empty Sky's battle was unique in that his dogs were wilddogs, and in that their elder Weejus bitches had elected Empty Sky to be sharf of the Horde of Wilddogs, while his sister thought the dogs were merely being loyal to the *Qæsach dri Vørdar* to whom all loyalty was due. The fact that the Horde of Wilddogs had elected him as its own rival to the human Wilddog sharf suggested that the office was usually held by a dog. That this dog had an equal claim on human Wilddog loyalty and young Wilddog women was a Grasshopper conceit. It was a conceit that sometimes led to fighting between rival bands of drovers of the northern hordes.

But the War Dog was still a Nomad mythic reality, and Swimming Elk had begun his reign as sharf by ordering a return to the old practice of keeping attack dogs trained to accompany horsemen into battle against an unmounted enemy, and he awarded a monopoly on the training of war dogs to the family of his brother's wife. Which is a Nomad way of saying that he gave the job to a brother-in-law, Goat-Wind by name, who happened to be good at it. Goat-Wind persuaded all the adolescents of his extended family to organize parties for raiding lairs of wild bitches and stealing their puppies. He turned the management of puppy collections over to his sister, with an injunction against killing bitches except in self-defense, and another against taking pups younger than six weeks.

A Weejus minority held that stealing wild puppies was an offense like stealing wild colts, but Eltür's sister asked them scornfully, "Who are we offending? The *Høngin Fujæ Vurn* is not the Wild Bitch Woman. The dogs belong to Empty Sky, for whom the sharf speaks. We don't even punish the motherless ones for roasting wild puppy."

Demon Light wanted results within two months, so Goat-Wind collected every available dog with any experience at all as a working companion to a horseman. Even now in late July results were apparent. Thirty-five willing warriors had been given thirty-five dogs to work with, and eighty-one younger dogs were already in school.

There was no way to test dogs in the occasional skirmishes with Texark cavalry, for dogs could never effectively join one side in an encounter between mutually mounted war bands. The dogs could participate in a cavalry attack on infantry, but since Nomad wars were usually ceremonial conflicts between hordes, there had been no reason since the time of Høngan Ös to bear the expense of feeding a large war pack—until Eltür began contemplating battle against the standing armies of the Hannegan. The spirit of the dog-man-horse war entity was still alive in the tribes, however, and Demon Light's attempt to awaken it was immediately popular. It added Empty Sky's blessing to his leadership. But any Nomad-speaking Texark agent—and there must have been at least one—who learned about the training of dogs for war would know that dogs were only for fighting unmounted armies like the defenders of Empire. They would be useful for incursions into Texark space.

His brother Kindly Light, when he broke through Texark border defenses and rode all the way to New Rome, had needed dogs. With dogs, Hultor might have lost only half as many men, even if it cost him all the dogs. A dog was a lethal loyal weapon, once the man and the dog and the horse became melded into a single spirit, which was then merged into a spirit of a pack. Man became more horselike and doglike. Dog and horse became more human, and more like each other. It was a spiritual unity, but probably the only outsider to notice it as such was that old Christian shaman of the Wilddog, Father Ombroz, a man Eltür much admired, although he begrudged his influence on the Wilddog shamans. The epiphany of the dog-horse-man unity was, when experienced, a Nomad sacrament—according to Ombroz. Monsignor Sanual had called it "a bestial form of diabolic possession," a remark which Eltür found flattering.

It was the issue of the War Dog that saved Chuntar Cardinal Hadala and his officers from death at the hands of a Grasshopper war party. The occasion of the issue being raised was a council called when the news of Hadala's invasion first came to the Grasshopper leadership. Demon Light became livid, and was quite ready to launch an immediate attack on the cardinal's forces. For negotiating purposes, it always behooved a Grasshopper sharf to take a harder line in council than he expected the grandmothers to approve. But it was his own sister who used the issue of the War Dog against him after Eltür proposed killing Hadala and anyone else who resisted a seizure of the militia's wagons.

"It is a complete betrayal, my sister," said Demon Light before he yielded. "Brownpony's plan was for the Suckamint spooks to attack in the Province, and the eastern allies to strike at the other shore of the Great River. The Grasshopper was to keep the peace until Hannegan took the forces which now face us to the defense of his allies. Now here comes this army of farmer clowns out of Valana tramping toward Glep Valley with guns! How is Filpeo Harq not to notice them coming? Every motherless one south of here has seen them and tried to sell the information to Texark. The first one who tried probably got paid."

"Yes, and I wonder," his sister said thoughtfully, "if the motherless one who told Texark about your war dogs was properly paid. And whether your dogs will affect Hannegan's temptation to weaken the forces that face us. No, I don't think Grasshopper justice demands killing the fools; it demands they turn back. You should let them choose: take their guns with them or surrender them to you. And that, my sharf, is the Weejus consensus."

Demon Light let his battle fury subside, as it usually did in the face of the Weejus consensus, if no Bear Spirit objection arose. After the council, Brâm assembled a force of eighty warriors and led them south by east to intercept this mounted militia of townsmen from the mountains. His men had armed themselves with new five-shooters as well as traditional lances, but Eltür ordered ten repeating rifles brought along for killing officers at a distance if they met resistance from the townsmen.

Then he took an action which changed the course of the war. He sent for Black Eyes, who had been captured during Hultor's raid. The man had been imprisoned by the Hannegan and had met Cardinal Brownpony in jail, but he was released months later to carry a message from Filpeo to his horde. Both Demon Light and the Emperor knew Black Eyes was a double agent, but as such he could be useful to both.

"Tell your contacts about Hadala's expedition," said the sharf, "so they can mount a defense in that area. And tell them I told you to tell them. If they want to know why I let them know, explain that I want hostilities to cease between the Grasshopper and Texark."

"The farmers will be glad to hear it," said Black Eyes with a snicker; he left camp immediately for the frontier.

Demon Light was not really turning on his allies, because he was not convinced of his own complaint of betrayal by the Pope, for while Brownpony alone might be foolish enough to launch such a venture, Brownpony had good advisers on Nomad affairs. Some were sent to him by Holy Madness, Lord of the Hordes. And Eltür thought highly of one of the Pope's secretaries, the Nomadic interpreter monk Nyinden, who spoke Grasshopper so well. None of these counselors would allow Brownpony to believe that Chuntar Hadala's incursion into Nomad country was acceptable to the Grasshopper, even were it not militarily stupid on the face of it. When his initial berserk reaction to the news of the advent subsided, Demon Light expected his war party to be confronted—not by a force of official crusaders launched by a Pope, but by a motley parade put in motion by the lunacy of lesser men.

When Brownpony first learned about Hadala's mission, he himself cried betrayal, and his anger was stirred against his successor in the Secretariat of Extraordinary Ecclesiastical Concerns. The Pope could think of no reason why Sorely Nauwhat would betray him or lend support to a harebrained scheme to arm and assist such dubious allies as Hadala's flock of gleps in the Valley, at the cost of probable hardening by Texark of its western frontier. Hadala had gone crazy in the service of his flock, the Pope decided. He would think thus: If Brownpony can arm the Nomads, I can arm the real Children of the Pope—not the spooks in the Suckamints, but the gleps in the Watchitah and Ol'zarks. The Pope could understand Hadala's passion for his own people, but not Sorely Nauwhat's duplicity in the ridiculous undertaking.

The possibility that his old friend Nauwhat had simply gone over to the enemy never occurred to Brownpony until it was put to him by Abrahà Cardinal Deacon Linkono, the New Jerusalemite schoolteacher who was invited to join the Curia because he knew everyone in this nation now playing host to the papacy.

"But what could Filpeo Harq possibly offer that would tempt Sorely Nauwhat to betray us?" Pope Amen II wanted to know.

"The papacy perhaps?" the schoolteacher guessed.

Stung by Linkono's speculation, Brownpony sent an immediate message to Valana ordering Cardinal Nauwhat and Brother St. George to appear before him. By including Blacktooth in his summons, the Pope hoped to alleviate suspicion in case Sorely really was guilty. Within two weeks, however, the messenger returned with the news that Blacktooth had gone with the Valanan Militia, and that Nauwhat had disappeared shortly after their departure. The news was very depressing to Brownpony. He called his Nomad messengers and instructed one of them to pursue Hadala's militia and order him to turn back. He deputized another as an Officer of the Curia to arrest Nauwhat on sight if found in Nomad country and to arrest Hadala if he disobeyed the order to retreat. He sent a third messenger to assure the Grasshopper sharf that Hadala's sortie was not authorized, for the Pope feared the wrath of Demon Light.

The Nomad messenger-service families, both Wilddog and Grasshopper, had for decades enjoyed a monopoly on a High Plains relay parcel delivery between Valana and New Rome. They kept fixed camps, and for this un-Nomadic practice they were not admired within their hordes. Sneering warriors would ask to see their "vegetable patches." But they had made money, and they used it to buy horses from outsiders, thus freeing themselves from family obligations incurred by both buyer and seller when the seller was a Nomad mare woman. Brownpony had always used the relay families for communicating with the sharfs and the tribal chiefs. Now he used them for keeping in touch with the *Qœsach dri Vørdar*, and he was encouraging the families to establish relay stations north of the Misery River and well beyond the reach of Texark patrols. He had already sent messages toward the King of the Tenesi and several other rulers beyond the Great River, and he was awaiting news from that front.

To New Jerusalem Brownpony had brought two Wilddog and two Grasshopper riders to open a branch office of the families' service. In the abrupt wake of Nauwhat's and Sorely's defection, he now found need for three of them. To one Grasshopper rider he gave a message for Demon Light. It "authorized" Bråm to exercise the papal warrant for the arrest of two princes of the Church in his territory with authorization to imprison them humanely. Forgetting for a moment that the Pope understood their dialect, this Grasshopper rider said to his kinsman, "Our sharf will surely appreciate these new powers in his own realm."

"Your family must send us someone less sarcastic," Pope Amen said to him in half-decent Grasshopper. "You can pass your message on to the next Wilddog relay rider tomorrow. Then you can start riding home to tall-grass country. Your family can send us your replacement when you get there."

He stopped looking at the man and spoke to the Wilddog rider. "You can be home tomorrow, and relay my message to Hadala from there. It will get to him quicker that way. We can't give arrest powers to a Wilddog in Grasshopper country. We do deputize you to arrest Nauwhat anywhere else you may find him. There will be a reward for him. Spread the word on that."

He turned to the second Grasshopper. "You must chase Hadala all the way to Ol'zarkia if you need to. Give him a copy of the same message. If he's not already obeying it and coming home by the time you catch up with him, you can read aloud to his men paragraph seven. It excommunicates all Hadala's followers who do not disband and desert at once. Arm yourself, but try to get help from your sharf in making the arrest." He then looked pointedly at the maker of the sarcastic remark.

"When you see a man you can't control about to take the law into his own hands, you might as well save yourself embarrassment and put the law in his hands yourself."

The man—having already been fired—answered back: "Nevertheless, Your Holiness will be embarrassed when I tell Sharf Eltür you said that."

Brownpony glared at him for a moment, then broke out laughing. "All right, you can come back here after you pass the message for Bråm to the relay. Someday we'll need an insolent rider with a gift for blackmail."

Grandmother Grasshopper raised insolent colts and children. "Maybe I'll come back, and maybe I won't," the relay rider said.

Chuntar Hadala's war party and ammunition train traveled faster than anyone expected. The moon was nearly full again in the late days of July, but when it left the world dark, setting before dawn, Blacktooth could see distant points of light on the eastern horizon. They looked like fires. Would farmers keep night fires burning? Nimmy knew that a relay messenger had come from the west with a message for Cardinal Hadala on the 28th. The messenger had seemed surprised to find Cardinal Nauwhat with the train. Of course, the Cardinal Secretary had left Valana two days late, and by night, so that no one in the city could be sure of his destination or whereabouts. The messenger left again, but the effect of the message on the cardinals was to command a forced march. The troop rode eastward until midnight.

The next morning, the sun arose above the distant hills where Nimmy had seen points of firelight in the night. Beyond those hills would lie the sprawling glep settlements of "the Valley." After a fast breakfast of biscuits and tea, the militia rode on toward them.

Two days later, near sundown, the Grasshopper sharf with a war band overtook them from the west. The militia had already camped for the night. After conferring with the cardinals, Major Gleaver ordered the wagons arranged in a defensive array and the men to take cover in expectation of an attack.

"This is crazy, Nimmy," Aberlott said. "They are allies."

"Just don't obey any order to shoot. I'll talk to them."

Blacktooth walked out of the defensive position and went to meet the Grasshopper warriors as they approached. He could hear Major Gleaver yelling at him to come back, and he stopped once when a Nomad raised a rifle at him; Demon Light spoke a word, and the rifle was lowered. He recognized the monk and beckoned him on.

A bullet struck the ground near Blacktooth's feet. The report came from behind him. The Nomad who had lifted the rifle lifted it again and returned fire. Nimmy looked back in time to see one of the lieutenants standing beside Gleaver drop his pistol and fall to the ground.

"For God's sake, stop shooting, you fools!" Nimmy yelled.

"I'll try you and hang you!" the major yelled back.

Behind Gleaver stood Chuntar Hadala, looking grim.

Sharf Bråm lingered just beyond gunshot range, and he sat there for several minutes while the monk came up to him.

"You remember me?" Blacktooth asked.

Bråm nodded. "But what is the Pope's servant doing with these men?"

"I'm not the Pope's servant now. My master left Valana without me."

"Yes, I knew that. I took him south to meet Dion. He thought you abandoned him. Did you?"

"Not intentionally. I was not in the city when the Palace exploded. When I came back, he was gone and I was drafted into the militia."

"You seem not to have been told the news."

"What news is that, Sharf Bråm?"

Demon Light, unable to read for himself, handed the monk a letter. Blacktooth read it with mounting dismay, looked at Eltür, then back at the cardinals.

"This must be the same message Cardinal Hadala got."

"You go tell him what it says, and ask him. Then tell him if he continues east, I shall not arrest him if he travels alone."

"Alone? I don't understand. What about Cardinal Nauwhat?"

It was Eltür's turn to be surprised. "Is he here? Then they can travel east together. The rest of you will stay here."

"I don't understand. They seem to be expecting you to attack."

"They expect me to arrest them. Doesn't the message say that? What they don't know is that I already sent a messenger to the Texark border guard. The enemy knows you're coming, and he knows why. The only way Hadala can keep the guns from the Hannegan is to give them to us. And the only way the cardinals can escape from me is to surrender to the Hannegan's border guard. Then the rest of you go home. Remind them what Høngan Ösle Chür did to Esitt Loyte. We can do as much for them, if we have to arrest them."

The letter Blacktooth had read said nothing about handing the cardinals over to the Hannegan, but he chose not to argue. When he returned to the camp, everyone was watching him and Ulad was waiting to seize him. At the last moment, he changed direction to put a group of recruits between himself and the spook sergeant. He spoke quickly to Aberlott:

"The sharf has orders from the Pope to arrest the cardinals. If we resist, we are all excommunicated. And the enemy is ready for us, because Bråm warned them we were coming. Tell the men, especially Sergeants Gai-See and Woosoh-Loh. Tell them to pray, and let Hadala see them praying."

He tried to get to the cardinals before Ulad got to him, but the giant was fast. He arrived in a headlock and was forced to his knees. Sorely Nauwhat since joining the expedition had seemed anxious to avoid Blacktooth, and he now hurried away. Chuntar Hadala bent over the monk. He was a glep himself, his skin dappled with various shades of brown—a common mutation—but he was a handsome man in spite of it, with a goatee and a long mustache that had once been golden.

"Well, Brother, tell us about your conversation with the Nomad warlord," said the Vicar Apostolic to the Watchitah Nation.

"Your Eminence won't shoot the messenger?"

"Nobody sent you as a messenger!" the cardinal snapped. "And the major may yet have you shot. Just tell us what you found out."

"Have you seen the fires in the east at night, m'Lord?"

"Yes, they are our people's beacons. They know we're here."

"So does Texark. The sharf warned them you were coming. The fires belong to the cavalry."

The lighter patches of the cardinal's skin drained of color. "They are supposed to be allies!" he gasped. "Why does he sell us out to the enemy?"

Blacktooth, under threat and afraid, decided not to mention the Pope's letter directly. Hadala already possessed a copy.

The monk resumed: "He says he will not arrest you and Cardinal Nauwhat if you surrender to the Texark troops. He orders the rest of us to surrender the weapons to him and get out of his country."

Hadala sputtered, and went in search of Nauwhat. Soon he came back with an order.

"Go see him again. Invite him here to parley. We will stay out in the open where his men can see us. If he comes alone, he may come armed. Do you think an oath by me that he will not be harmed or taken captive would help?"

Blacktooth thought about it for a moment. "No. He might find it insulting."

"Do the best you can without it, then."

The sharf was not reluctant. He borrowed a second pistol from a warrior, tied the leash of a heavily built war dog to his belt, grasped the monk by his uniform collar, and began walking toward Hadala's encampment with a gun to Nimmy's head.

"I'm not going to hurt you."

"I'm no good as a hostage, Sharf Bråm. They won't care if you kill me."

As they stopped before Hadala, Gleaver, and Hadala's Grasshopper guide, Eltür released Blacktooth, untied the dog's leash, and barked a single word at the animal, who began to growl and stare at the cardinal.

"If I'm shot, the dog kills you."

Hadala spat venom at Demon Light for trafficking with the enemy, and Blacktooth translated it.

The sharf ignored it. Bråm waved an arm toward the east and spoke in short sentences; between them Blacktooth translated:

"This eastward lane here will be kept open. It goes from your camp to the hills yonder and to sunrise. When an armed man steps into the lane, we shoot him. An unarmed man gets one warning shot. But you and the other Red Hat may pass, going east. Take with you any disarmed officers you wish. Red Beard ordered me to arrest and hold you. I am Sharf of the Grasshopper Horde. I give orders here. Empty Sky is my Pope. The Wild Horse Woman is my sister. Høngan Ösle is my Lord." Demon Light gestured broadly at the sky, at the earth, and again toward the northwest prairie where his Lord would be encamped. After a pause, he went on grandly. "I, the sharf of this country, offer you Grasshopper hospitality. You will be required to gather dry turds for the kitchen fires. And the women will make you shovel horseshit. They will tease you a lot, but you will not be hurt. When Red Beard sends for you, you must go to him. If you don't accept our hospitality, you just march east. Without arms and without men. The Hannegan's men will take you in. He may be glad to get you."

"Are you including Major Gleaver?" Hadala asked sourly.

Eltür grew impatient, and began talking in longer sentences. He knew nothing of Gleaver. He had already been told he could take unarmed officers. Bråm made scattered remarks about the cardinal's stupidity. Blacktooth waited for him to pause and then summarized.

"Let Major Gleaver cooperate in his own disarmament, he says. The sharf will leave him in command to hold the men together on the trek back home. He says the rabble will get out of his tall-grass country quicker if we are under command. But if Gleaver wants to surrender to Texark, Sharf Bråm will let him pass."

"He knows we outnumber his men nearly four to one. What makes him think . . ."

"He can stop us? Shall I ask?"

"Ask him if two of his men are equal to seven of ours."

The sharf chuckled as soon as Nimmy translated, then shared a few private jokes with his interpreter. Hadala became angry.

"What does he say? Stop having your own private conversation."

"He says seven-against-two would be fair, if you leave your wagons undefended. Your seven men with seven guns might chase his two men with two guns for several days, inconclusively, but you would lose the wagons. If we defend the wagons, we'll just be pinned down and starved out. And if you don't make up your minds soon, Texark will come out and get the wagons."

"Are those his words, or yours, Brother St. George? Be careful you don't go too far." After this admonition, Hadala began speaking slowly enough for Nimmy to translate simultaneously.

"Look, we are as worried as you are that the wagons will be intercepted by the patrol as we try to take them in. So why don't you help us? Your people have been well supplied with arms, and you don't need my wagons. The occupied territory ahead is just a narrow strip along the western frontier of the Watchitah Nation. It's hardly more than a double roadway. The outer road is patrolled by Texark troops; they look outward toward your country. The inner road is patrolled by the Valley Customs Service; they look inward at the Watchitah Nation, my people. I myself am on the Customs Service Board, for the Church. Their patrol will help us, once we're past the Texark troopers and the patrol sees who I am. If you could just help us hold back the Texark riders until we get the wagons through, we'll all cut and run afterward."

"You are another Christian war sharf? Another military genius in a red hat? There are so many of you." Blacktooth found himself unable to avoid echoing Bråm's sarcastic tone, although he could see that the cardinal was beginning to seethe. "But what will stop the Texark cavalry from riding right straight into the heart of the Valley of the Gleps to take the wagons away from you?"

"Why, we hoped to cross over by night, unknown to them. But you ruined that by warning them. And the treaty between . . ."

Hadala's explanation was cut off by a Grasshopper war cry. Someone shouted that a large dust cloud and a probable party of horsemen was seen in the east.

"They've decided to come and get you themselves, glep priest," said Bråm with a savage smile. "Now, we are going to get out of the way. Aren't you lucky? You can fight them instead of us."

All Nomads took immediately to horseback, and Blacktooth

watched them ride away toward the northwest. He was tempted to mount up and ride after them, but Ulad had threatened to shoot him in the back for desertion if he again broke ranks.

Hadala looked at him for a moment. "Do you have an opinion, Brother Corporal St. George?" he demanded sternly.

"Those riders will be here in a few minutes. That is my opinion, Your Eminence." Blacktooth turned and broke into a trot toward the wagons. Sorely Nauwhat and the major had been standing there watching the meeting between Brâm and Cardinal Hadala until the shouting started, but Nauwhat had faded from view.

"Cardinal Hadala's done with you, Private St. George!" Gleaver snapped at him. "Report to Sergeant Ulad. Get your arms buckled on, and get in the saddle."

Still wearing corporal's chevrons, Nimmy took note of his reduction in rank without openly acknowledging it. Earlier in the day, the major had been yelling at him about a court-martial and the gallows, so the demotion was a welcome commutation of sentence. When Ulad looked at him, however, he could still see a readiness to kill.

Having observed the Grasshopper withdrawal, the Texark commander halted his advance just beyond rifle range. The troopers dismounted. Some of them began digging.

Demon Light drew up his warriors in a half circle just out of range to the west of the Valanan brigade's position. Blacktooth had no doubt that they would fight to prevent the guns and ammunition from falling into the hands of the imperial forces, but they would not begin to fight until Hadala and his men were defeated by those forces. The Valanan light horse, untested troops and their spook commanders, were sandwiched between two superior war bands.

It was almost nightfall on Tuesday the 2nd of August. The moon rose an hour after sundown. During that hour, Sorely Nauwhat vanished, never to be seen again west of Texark frontiers.

"There is going to be a mutiny," Aberlott whispered to Blacktooth at the first opportunity, "unless the glep cardinal quits."

Nimmy shook his head. "These townsmen could mutiny in Valana, but not out here between two unfriendly armies."

Chuntar Hadala remained at the head of his command. Sergeant Ulad shot a deserter who made a break for Grasshopper lines during the night. When the body was dragged back to camp, it turned out to be the cardinal's Grasshopper guide, who was only quitting his job to return to his people.

Blacktooth told Aberlott: "He was the sharf's man, and here we all are in the sharf's jurisdiction—so look at the sergeant now." The monk was remembering how Ulad at their first meeting in Valana had expressed hate for all Nomads. But now that he had killed one, he showed in his face not satisfaction but an astonishing fright.

CHAPTER 24

> If a brother who through his own fault leaves the monastery should wish to return, let him first promise full reparation for his having gone away; and then let him be received in the lowest place, as a test of his humility.
>
> —*Saint Benedict's Rule*, Chapter 29

RIGHT, THE MOTHER OF HATRED, POSSESSED the whole militia, but there was nowhere to run. Behind them, the Grasshopper; in front of them, the Emperor. Prowling among them were Chuntar Hadala, and two willing killers of conscripts: the major and Ulad. The flanks were faced with fires, but it was an unusually windless day. The fires had been set in the night, and no one was sure who set them, but because of the calm air nobody worried about them much. Before dawn, Ulad and three husky townsmen unloaded two cannon from the wagons and dragged them forward to face the foe to the east. Then they unloaded two more and aimed them toward the Nomads. The sharf watched them do it, then broke his forces into two equal groups. He moved one group north and one south; they halted so as to face the Valanans from the southwest and northwest. Ulad rearranged the cannon accordingly, but the Nomad movement spoke of no need for cannon. The way west was wide open, by invitation of the sharf. In Blacktooth's opinion, acceptance was the only sane thing to do, but Chuntar Cardinal Hadala was adamant.

"All you who repent your sins, I absolve you," he announced to the assembled troops at dawn, "*in nomine patris, filii, et spiritus sancti.* And if you die in battle for God's glory and the Holy Father's righteous cause, you will attain Heaven without purgatory's purifying pain. I now bless you . . ."

"*This,*" Aberlott whispered, "from a man with the Holy Father's excommunication in his pocket."

Surprised that other conscripts were not jeering Hadala, Blacktooth asked, "Didn't you tell the others what I told you to?"

Aberlott was meekly silent. Nimmy looked him in the eye, then laughed bitterly. Everybody knew that Aberlott was an outrageous liar, not to be believed. Besides, where would he get the courage to accuse a cardinal behind the cardinal's back when every man would in the end point his finger right at Aberlott and say, "I heard it from him"? Well, Blacktooth would have to spread the word himself, or at least enlist one of the Yellow Guard. It was not easy to get close to them, however. They were close only to Cardinal Hadala, as they had always been to Brownpony.

Water was rationed. The supply of jerky was exhausted, and with no hunting possible, the men ate beans and biscuits. The enemy waited for Hadala to move. Hadala waited for gleps from the Valley to attack the enemy from the rear, but this seemed wishful thinking to Blacktooth. On the third day of the standoff, in plain view of the Valana forces, Sharf Brâm sent a messenger under a flag of truce to the Texark commander. This further traffic with the enemy increased the cardinal's fury. At Gleaver's orders, several townsmen shot at the messenger, but he was riding beyond range for accurate rifle fire.

That night before the moon rose, fourteen Grasshopper warriors stole into camp, killed two sentries, and stole or drove away most of the horses. After the rise of the gibbous moon, a detachment of Texark cavalry, which had approached noiselessly in total darkness, mounted and rode through the camp screaming and killing with sabers and horse pistols. Several attackers were killed in turn by the well-armed militiamen. After dawn, eighteen bodies were buried, five of them wearing Texark uniforms. There were seven nonfatal casualties as well. Aberlott had lost his right ear to a Texark saber.

"You never left your bedroll, you bastard," he said to Nimmy.

"I guess I slept through it," Blacktooth lied.

The loss of the horses drove the Hadala over the edge. He ordered an infantry attack on the now entrenched Texark position. The cardinal took a cross and proceeded to march proudly with it at the head of the army, his red cap and sash making him a conspicuous target. Major Gleaver shot three men who refused to move out. Three companies of green troops with bayonets fixed to their excellent rifles moved forward behind sporadic covering fire from three cannon. Ulad, furious as usual, led the way behind the cardinal crucifer, but kept looking back to see that the others stayed in line. Terror whitened men's faces as they came into range and some of them began to fall from a crackle of fire by the enemy. Nimmy kept his eyes half closed and prayed to the Virgin. He was astonished that there was no artillery fire directed at them from the Texark rear.

When they had covered half the distance to the enemy lines, he could see that berms of earth and sod had been thrown up. Imperial troops were firing at them from well-protected positions, and the effect was devastating. About a third of the men had fallen. Twice Ulad ordered the attackers to halt and fire, but each time the enemy's heads ducked behind the berms.

"Double-time march! Shoot while you run!"

In terms of accuracy, it was a waste of ammunition, but it kept the enemy's heads down. After five shots, it was necessary to slow to a walk in order to reload. Most men had brought two extra cylinders, already loaded, but while it was faster to change cylinders than to reload individual chambers, it was necessary to stop altogether to avoid dropping the pins. And to stop was to be shot by a spook officer.

"Look! They're clearing out. Run, damn it, run!"

Terror changed to a furious glee as the townsmen realized that the Texark rifle fire from the forward berm had ceased, although there was still shooting in the distance.

"*Pope's children! My people are there!*" Hadala was shouting back at them. He kept waving his cross like a club toward the foothills. "*They're attacking from the rear.*"

"That explains why cannonballs aren't raining down," Nimmy said toward Aberlott's bandaged ear. The message was not received above the sound of gunfire, but he added, "Maybe the gleps' cardinal is not as crazy as we thought."

The Texark army was not at all defeated. Forced by guerrillas from the Valley to defend their rear, they had retreated from the attack out of the west to defend their artillery from an attack out of the east. The retreat was limited. When militiamen climbed the first berm, three of them were shot down as they went over the top.

Gleaver called a halt. Obviously there were defenders of the second berm. But the attackers could use the enemy's first berm for their own shelter while they ate pocket rations and sipped from canteens.

Nimmy looked up to see Gai-See crawling toward him up a shallow gully. He was not hiding from the enemy, he was hiding from Hadala and the officers.

"Is it true?" asked the Asian warrior monk after taking a careful look around.

"Yes," Nimmy told him, "if you got it from Aberlott."

Gai-See nodded grimly and crawled away by the same route.

Now something would happen, he thought, but it did not happen immediately.

The sun was scorching in early August, but by midafternoon a light westerly breeze came up. Blacktooth noticed that the restless Grasshopper had moved again. The Nomads had re-formed and split into three groups, positioned to the north, west, and south of the wagons. They were still out of range, visible against a background of smoke, but the groups to the north and south were in place for a flanking attack against either the Hannegan or the cardinal.

The fires seemed to be moving slowly eastward. They marked the probable confines of the battleground and defined the possible lines of advance or retreat for the Nomad groups who had likely set them.

Soon afterward, during an assault on the second berm, while trying to shoot over a man's head Nimmy shot him down. Facing Blacktooth, the Texark trooper lay on his back on the sandbank just as he fell when shot. A glep, a glep in Texark uniform, with Hadala's dappled skin and the rather common hairy ears. He stared up at the former monk, trying to see him against the smoke-blurred orb of the sun. His hands were raised toward his face and they hung limply from the wrists; he looked like a puppy begging for a morsel. Why surrender with a ruined abdomen? He clenched his lids, waiting, hoping to be shot again. But Blacktooth dared not to waste ammunition on pity, or even take time to reload, because Ulad was watching him with deep suspicion. Every time he felt such tension, Wooshin's face and words came to his mind.

"Life is a dewdrop and a flash of lightning—that's the way to look at it, Nimmy."

Touching the point of the bayonet to the man's throat, Blacktooth severed the carotid artery. A blade of lightning, a drop of red dew. The drop became a spurting stream. He stepped back, looking around. His throat hurt and was dry; it was a hot day and the air was full of smoke from burning grass.

"Each man, each being is a world. There are innumerable worlds, my friend. Each world of this innumerable array contains and interpenetrates all the other worlds throughout the myriad cosmos, for there are no barriers between the worlds." Metaphysics from an executioner? For the Axe, religion was a martial art. He wanted to talk to Gai-See or Woosoh-Loh about it, but they were always with th cardinal and the officers, and he was made afraid by Gai-See's crawling to him in a ditch.

It's just that I have cut my own throat somehow, he thought, looking at the corpse. So murder feels like this to the murderer. Holy Mother of God, forgive me, but I don't feel very much.

Sergeant Ulad was still watching him from the left, shaking his head. He must be careful not to waver or hesitate. Ulad was suspicious of his piety. He could see two men beyond Ulad. Corporal Victros had climbed to the top of the berm. He motioned the attack party upward.

The sandbank flanked a scythed and well-hoed—but useless—firebreak. Blacktooth climbed the berm and cautiously peered beyond, but the patrol had fled. Why? It was the best place to stop and fight, unless they thought the Valanans' firepower overwhelming. Or, more likely, they might know that greater safety for them lay ahead, and that the glep guerrillas must be prevented from seizing their artillery. Standing atop the berm, he looked back toward the wagons. What had happened to the men guarding them? He could see Nomads in the distance, but no militiamen with the wagons. Without horses to draw them, they were lost anyway.

Somewhere to the north the tall grass was burning faster. They had been crosswind of the fire whose smoke veiled the foothills in the northeast, but they were almost downwind now and still the breeze was changing. He began to smell the smoke, and could see to the north distant horseback warriors moving west out of the fire's path. If the wind kept veering, the wagons would be in danger. He motioned to Ulad that the enemy had fled. They went over the sandbank and continued their cautious advance, camouflaged shadows flitting from knoll to knoll in the great ocean of grass.

Watching from a distance on a hillcrest south of the battle, the Grasshopper sharf could see some of the fight going on around the Texark artillery pieces. Texark was temporarily in trouble, and he was pleased. Demon Light hoped to influence the outcome of the battle by moving warriors about in a menacing way from time to time without actually exposing them to fire. His only intention at the moment was to keep the wagons from being captured by anyone except himself, although if he got them, the Grasshopper had no pressing need for extra ammunition, and the horde's arsenal was already wealthy in new guns. He was not opposed to giving the gleps guns, if it became possible. Now it seemed it might be possible. It was clear that the Texark force was being harassed from the rear. The fact surprised him as much as it did the Texarki.

Demon Light had warned them of Hadala's expedition, but they had trusted him only enough to send two companies of cavalry, two of light horse, and a few artillery pieces to the region where he told them the townsmen would try a border crossing. Surprising to Eltür was the fact that many of the Texark troops were gleps, drafted from the Valley. They had not expected a glep attack from the rear, and had not come well prepared. They would regret not having taken him seriously enough. Such regret might incline them to trust him more next time. When he sent them a message under a white flag, they had listened politely to the messenger as he laid claim to the contents of the wagons, and if this claim were honored, there would be no reason for hostilities. He had also warned the Texark commander that he was about to steal the townsmen's horses. About the wagons, the commander gave a polite but evasive answer, and he smiled on the horse-theft project. In this situation, Demon Light was reluctant to attack his hereditary enemies except to prevent seizure of munitions.

Nothing prevented his enjoyment of the conflict unfolding before him except a report by a scout from his southwest detachment that a band of motherless ones had approached but stopped a few minutes' ride away and occupied a hilltop there. To Bråm, they were a damn nuisance, and they too wanted the guns. He was aware that many of the motherless ones in the south part of the Wilddog lands had been armed by Dion and sent against the enemy in the Province, but these outlaws were far from that battle, and if they were able to get their hands on the new weapons, they were as likely to shoot at his people as at the Texarki, but they were even more likely to sell the fancy guns to the Hannegan, who had been slow in getting them.

Though it would spoil his view of the fight for a time, he decided to withdraw his detachment from the north where the fire was beginning to crowd his rear, then to skirt around the townsmen's position and join all his forces together again between the militia and the outlaws. It would give other commanders something to wonder about, and the fires had become the Grasshopper's allies, as the Grasshopper sharf knew they would when he practiced his family motto and set them. As he rode between the Valanans and a group of his own men to the west, he noticed with approval that the horses stolen from the wagoneers were being kept out of sight beyond a ridge. None of his warriors' mounts were broken as draft horses, so seizing and keeping the grass-eaters' animals was essential to his plans. He sent a messenger to tell his cousin to the west of him to post enough men to guard the horses and join the rest of the detachment with Eltür's main force.

Sundown was approaching when the enemy resumed fire, and Cardinal Hadala was among the first to fall. Elswitch Gleaver rushed to his side, inspected his wound, which he seemed to find in the back, and turned to look around at the men. This time Blacktooth saw Gai-See lift his pistol again and shoot Major Gleaver in the forehead. At the same time, a high-pitched scream came from the rear. Ulad's voice. The blade of Woosoh-Loh's sword rose bloody into the air and fell again. Junior officers were shouting angrily.

Brother Blacktooth St. George threw away his rifle, picked up a pistol from the body of a slain officer, and ran south for his life. A bullet struck the ground near his feet, but he was unsure which of three sides was shooting at him.

As he ran around the bend near the crest of the ridge, he noticed a wide tunnel under a rock where something made its home. It was just big enough for him to slip into, and he dived for it, feet first, praying earnestly that the owner was absent. The tunnel sloped downward as he slid into it and it was somewhat deeper than expected. He braked his slide and found his face two feet from the sunlit opening. Between the straps of his sandals, he felt wiggling fur with his feet; something bit his big toe, tiny fangs but sharp. He kicked it off. Other mouths were chewing on his sandal straps. My God, I'm in a cougar's den, and I am going to die!

Today is like any other day in being the day of death. Today a war is going on and I am not a Daniel in this den, O Saint Leibowitz. Still, it's the only day I've got. Last week it was a thunderstorm, and the wet body of a lightning-struck warrior. Year before last a cyclone killed seventeen Jackrabbit peasants. Then the locusts, the locusts, the locusts, and the emaciated corpses found frozen last winter. Just like any other day, he noted, as a bullet ricocheted off the rock above his head. The spent lump of lead fell into his waist and he picked it up to inspect in the dim light. It was no bullet from a Grasshopper or Valanan weapon, but a musket ball from a Texark or an outlaw piece. The fact gave him a general idea of the direction of the enemy.

He felt around with his feet, kicking kittens away. Their teeth were needles. What was keeping their mother? Afraid of the fires, perhaps. He too feared them. "In here, we'll choke to death," he told the kittens.

While he was thus indulging himself in more fear and self-pity than was usual before he had so recently killed a man, something came and darkened the light from the end of the tunnel. He prepared to die.

HailMaryfullofgracetheLordiswiththee . . .

"Ho! Who is down there?" The language was Rockymount, but the accent was from Asia. Nimmy looked up to see a rifle aimed at his face.

"Don't shoot, it's Blacktooth. Is is safe to come out?"

"It's not safe anywhere yet," said Gai-See, "and the fire is getting too close. Give me your hand."

Nimmy shook a playful kitten loose from one trouser leg and crawled upward into the smoky light of late afternoon. The din of battle had subsided, except to the east where Texark troops were still holding off gleps trying to get at the weapons. The warrior and the monk climbed the ridge and lay on the ground to look over the top. They could make out the bodies of Chuntar Hadala and Major Gleaver; both had been killed by Gai-See, who, like Wooshin, was prepared to execute anyone who betrayed his master.

"Where is Woosoh-Loh?"

"Ulad shot him when he saw me execute our master's enemies."

"But I saw—"

"My brother lived long enough to kill his killer."

Nimmy observed a detail of Grasshopper warriors hastily hitching three of the wagons to draft horses they had stolen, for the fire was coming closer. The wagons' defenders had scattered during the infantry skirmish. The Valana Militia had been destroyed, by death, desertion, and the absence of command. From the east, Texark cavalry was riding toward the scene, but warily, for behind the ridge to the south was the Demon Light's main force, and just to the north was the advancing wildfire. Half a mile from where they lay, a Texark trooper rode to the top of the ridge to observe the Grasshopper order of battle. Gai-See rolled over, lifted his rifle, aimed very high, and fired. The impossible shot fell close enough to frighten the trooper's horse, and alerted the Grasshopper, who joined Gai-See in firing on the scout. The scout retreated. Gai-See stood up and looked south. Eltür's warriors were watching. Evidently they were not shooting at militia uniforms.

"Look!" said Gai-See, pointing. "Somebody killed a big cat."

Blacktooth stood beside him, then went to investigate. The animal lay on the rocks twenty paces west of them. It was a female.

"Come on," he said to Gai-See, and went back down the ridge to

the cougar's den. Soon they had recovered the kittens, but three Nomads rode up with drawn guns and spoke in Grasshopper.

"Drop your weapons at once, citizens! Surrender."

They complied, but Nimmy smiled at the polite word "citizens,"
and replied in the same language. "The troopers are riding toward the
wagons, you know. We'll gladly surrender, but we'll need our weapons
to get home again."

One warrior rode to the top of the ridge. The other dismounted
and recovered the guns. As he unloaded them, he spoke to Blacktooth.

"You are the man who came out to parley with the sharf. He says
you are a servant of the highest Christian shaman. Is that so?"

"It used to be so."

The warrior handed him back his unloaded pistol, then returned
Gai-See's empty rifle.

"You are the man who killed the cardinal and the major, are you
not?"

Gai-See nodded. The other warrior came down from the ridge
and said, "We'd better tell Sharf Eltür it's time to attack. Let's go!"

They both rode away, leaving the two to follow on foot with
empty firearms. As soon as the warriors returned to their command,
the main party of Nomads split into two groups, one of which rode to
the bottom of the ridge, dismounted, and climbed it on foot; they
took prone positions on the crest as snipers. From the fact that heavy
smoke was blowing south over the ridge, and that the snipers did not
commence firing at once, Nimmy deduced that the fire was delaying
the movement of the cavalry toward the wagons. Every time a trooper
mounted the ridge to the east to reconnoiter, he was fired upon by the
main Nomad party. The Texark commander probably wished to cross
the ridge before riding west, but the Grasshopper made it impossible.
At least some of the wagons were being pulled west by Valanan draft
horses driven by Nomads. The rest would soon be caught by wildfire,
if not captured first by Texark.

By sundown, the rest of the wagons had been swept up in the
fire; some exploded, all burned. Burned too were the bodies of the
slain, but the wind subsided at twilight and the blaze did not cross
the ridge. Sharf Brâm had rounded up and fed all the militia survivors
who surrendered their arms. The few who refused to give them up,
mostly spook officers who feared revenge by Valanan conscripts, he
ordered killed. He ordered his warriors to treat the prisoners of war
with courtesy, but the Grasshopper fighters were too full of playful
malice toward farmers for the farmers' comfort. Food was shared, but
dipped in sand. One warrior lent Nimmy a leather pouch large enough

for three cougar kittens, then claimed the monk had stolen it. There were less than forty exhausted captives, but some other deserters had perhaps escaped capture by the Texarki or the Nomads.

When he saw Nimmy among the refugees, Demon Light called him to his side as interpreter. After laughing at the kittens, he returned the monk's pistol and ammunition. Nimmy immediately asked permission to turn the weapon over to Gai-See. "My eyes are too weak to hit anything. I killed a man by mistake, when I meant to miss him."

Eltür sent for Gai-See and after a brief conversation through Blacktooth concerning the warrior monk's continuing loyalty to Brownpony, the sharf gave him his weapons back. Then he looked at the smoky sky.

"Your Pope's wife has come. Look. The sister of the Day Maiden."

Overhead, a large bird was circling the battlefield. In the smoke and the light of the late sun, the buzzard appeared to be bright red. Other birds were gathering. They seemed small and dark by contrast, but perhaps they flew at higher altitude.

"It means the battle is over."

Nimmy and Gai-See were eerily silent.

"Tomorrow we leave for the tents of my tribe," Bråm said. "The wounded can stay there until they heal. The rest of you will be taken west to be judged by the *Qæsach dri Vørdar*, Høngan Ösle Chür. Then I imagine you will be escorted back to Valana, or in your case, Nyinden, to your Brownpony. Tell this to the others. Tell them they must travel with us, or they will fall into the hands of the motherless ones. We have recaptured enough of Hadala's horses for you to ride."

Demon Light seemed quite friendly, and Nimmy dared ask, "Are you satisfied with today's outcome, Sharf Bråm?"

"The Burregun will not eat Grasshopper bodies; I lost no men," said the Nomad leader. "We captured five wagonloads of rifles and pistols before the fire or the motherless got to them. The ammunition wagons exploded. The Texarki must have got about four loads of weapons that went through the fire. Those guns were ruined."

"Ruined as weapons, maybe, but not as patterns for Texark to copy," Nimmy said.

"You think so? And how long will that take?"

"I don't know. Months, probably."

"There is one other matter I do find troublesome, Nyinden," said Eltür. "Do you know that there were many gleps among the Texarki?"

Nimmy frowned. "The man I killed was a glep! That surprised me. It seems that the Emperor is either impressing able-bodied gleps from the Valley, or hiring them as mercenaries. It suggests he is short of manpower."

"Or, he is sending some of his main force to the east of the Great River, as we hoped. There was dissent in the Texark ranks. My messengers told me so. Do you understand why?"

"I think so. Cardinal Hadala was expecting a force from the Valley to strike the troopers' rear. When they did so, the glep troopers probably refused to fight. Maybe that's why they retreated from us."

Eltür snorted. "You townsmen make good corpses but not good killers. It had to be the reason. Now, tomorrow we must go to a messenger family and send today's news to the Lord of the Hordes and your Pope. You may, if you wish, write to Brownpony yourself, so long as you tell me what you say to him."

"Of course! You may read it."

Demon Light laughed scornfully and departed. Blacktooth's face burned. He had forgotten that the sharf was without letters.

Blacktooth was prepared to write his letter on cowhide with ink made of blood and soot, but the messenger family to which Bråm brought him the following afternoon kept paper and pens for such emergencies, although they themselves were barely literate. He wrote hurriedly, because the sharf was impatient to return to his family and tribe.

> I understand that Sharf Eltür Bråm is sending you an oral account of the battle fought here, and to his words I would add nothing. While most of the weapons were recaptured by the Grasshopper war party, Texark troops found a number of them that passed through fire and are probably unfit for use, but the Mayor's gunsmiths may learn much from studying the design.
>
> I am ashamed, Holy Father, that I was not present in your time of peril. I was staying with the late Pope when you departed from Valana, and then I fell into the hands of your betrayers. Sorely Cardinal Nauwhat has sought asylum in Texark. Chuntar Cardinal Hadala was executed by Brother Gai-See when he learned of his treason against Your Holiness. Many townsmen died in this futile battle. My body was unharmed, but my soul is a casualty, for I killed a man.
>
> I have been invited to stay with my distant Grasshopper relatives (yes, the Sharf knows who they are) of his tribe until I receive orders from Your Holiness, Abbot Olshuen, or

the Secretariat concerning my future duties and destination. Meanwhile, Sharf Bråm wants me to be tutor to his
nephews. I would find this work congenial, but with no
books and no proper writing materials it will be difficult.

Again, I beg your forgiveness for my absence without
leave in your time of need, and shall gratefully accept and
perform any penance it may please Your Holiness to impose.

Your unworthy servant,
Nyinden (Blacktooth) St. George,
A.O.L.

The relay horses of the messenger families were fast and frequently changed. In late August, the moon was waxing, permitting
them to ride by night. Still, Nimmy was astonished by the speed of
Brownpony's reply. It was very simple. "Honor the slaughtering festival, then come at once," said Amen II, only three weeks later.

His cousins had been teasing him unmercifully about joining the
fourteen-year-olds who would be undergoing the rites of passage to
manhood at the festival, which normally occurred during a period of
several days around the last full moon of summer, before the autum-
nal equinox. "They will stop calling you 'Nimmy,' if you endure the
rite," the great-granddaughter of his own great-great-grandmother told
him.

"Thank you, but the first man to call me 'Nimmy' was Holy
Madness, the Lord of the Hordes, and he intended no insult. I am not
a warrior, I am not a Nomad."

This was the same festival which had been declared a movable
feast last year when its usual time coincided with the funeral of
Granduncle Brokenfoot. The farmers celebrated a harvest festival at
about the same date, but for the Nomads it marked the beginning of
the time of killing off old cattle and weaklings who could not survive
the winter. Women culled out the horses not fit for war or breeding,
and sold them to farmers north of the Misery River, or had them
butchered and barbecued. Many of the slaughtered animals were converted into jerky for the time of deep snow when the wild herds were
hard to reach.

It was a time for dancing, for drums, for gluttony, smoking
keneb, drinking farmers' wine, for fighting by firelight, and for celebrating the ravishing by Empty Sky of the Wild Horse Woman. Young
men crawled into the tents of sweethearts, and Blacktooth was visited
in the night by the dark form of a woman who would not reveal her
name, but began removing his clothes. He was careful to do nothing
that might offend her, and it turned out to be a hot and sweaty night.

The following morning, one of his female cousins smiled whenever she caught his glance. Her name was Pretty Dances, and she was chubby as a pig, but cute and comely. He thought of Ædrea and avoided her glance as much as possible.

He had established his honor by fighting several young men his own size, and did well enough to avoid further teasing, but they still called him Nimmy more often than Nyinden.

On the day before his departure from the lands of his ancestors, the Grasshopper double agent Black Eyes brought him a book he had obtained in a transaction with Texark soldiers. Black Eyes had occupied the cage across the aisle when he and Brownpony were prisoners in the Emperor's zoo, and he still admired Blacktooth for an alleged attempt to kill Filpeo.

"The book cost me seven steers," he told the monk. "The sharf thinks it might help you teach his nephews, because the soldiers said it is written in our own tongue. I don't understand how a book can have a tongue."

Nimmy looked at the Nomadic title and felt a rush of grief and shame. *The Book of Beginnings: Volume One*, by Verus Sarquus Boedullus. The Texark publisher had done a good job of duplicating Blacktooth's pan-Nomadic orthography, with the new vowels which permitted any Nomad of any horde to hear the words as pronounced in his own dialect. In the front matter, there was an acknowledgment that the translation had come from Leibowitz Abbey, but there was of course no mention of the translator's name. Blacktooth had not included it in the original.

The face of the late Abbot Jarad loomed large in his mind, and Jarad's voice spoke to him as before, saying, "All right, Brother St. George, now think—think of the thousands of wild young Nomads, or ex-Nomads, just like you were then. Your relatives, your friends. Now, I want to know: what could possibly be more fulfilling to you than to pass along to your people some of the religion, the civilization, the culture, that you've found for yourself here at San Leibowitz Abbey?"

"Why are you crying, Nyinden?" asked Black Eyes. "Is it the wrong book for Nomads?"

CHAPTER 25

> If a pilgrim monk coming from a distant region wants to live as a guest of the monastery, let him be received for as long a time as he desires, provided he is content with the customs of the place as he finds them and does not disturb the monastery by superfluous demands, but is simply content with what he finds.
>
> —*Saint Benedict's Rule*, Chapter 61

 URING THE TWO MONTHS MOTHER IRIDIA Silentia spent at the court of Pope Amen II in New Jerusalem, one of the Pope's informants called it to his attention that this Princess of the Church and Bride of Christ visited Shard's Ædrea in her house of arrest three times a week, every week. He hesitated to inquire into this, for it was assumed by anybody who noticed or cared that Mother Iridia was either practicing spiritual therapy or teaching the girl the latest edition of the catechism as rewritten and promoted by Pope Amen I—the edition already condemned as heretical by several eastern bishops. Soon it became clear to her jailer that the girl wished to join Iridia's religious community. This caused no alarm, and only Brownpony stirred and became restless. Prisoners often converted to religion in jail.

Mayor Dion, as commander in chief of the insurgent forces in the Province, was gone most of the time, and Slojon's only interest in religion was as a tool to be used in the governance of men. When Ædrea took her simple vows as a nun of the Order of Our Lady of the Desert on Saturday the 12th of August, Mother Iridia visited the Pope and complained that the secular government of New Jerusalem was keeping one of her nuns in prison. Brownpony smiled and sent for Slojon.

"You are holding Sister Clare-of-Assisi in detention for unspecified offenses," said Amen II. "Messér, must I tell you that you have no jurisdiction over religious?"

"I don't even know a Sister Clare-of-Assisi, Holy Father!"

"You know her as Shard's Ædrea," said Brownpony. "She became a nun on the Feast of Saint Clare last week, and so Mother Iridia named her Clare, which is what she will be called in her cloister."

Slojon sputtered. "Her offenses are *not* unspecified. She violated the law by leaving the community without a permit from the Mayor's office. And she is suspected of espionage."

"She is innocent of espionage against this realm, to my certain knowledge," Brownpony growled. "As for your other complaint against her, the Church does teach obedience to legitimately constituted government, such as yours. Since she admits her guilt in disobeying the law while it was in force, I promise you she will be appropriately sentenced for that offense by me. I must take note, however, that you are no longer enforcing the law that she broke. That is your affair. Sister Clare is our affair. You shall release her immediately to an ecclesiastical court. You well know the sanctions incurred for usurping Church jurisdiction. My predecessor of beloved memory excommunicated the Emperor of Texark himself for jailing me and my secretary."

"So that's the trick! Well, it won't work with me." Slojon turned and walked away from the papal audience with minimum courtesy.

Brownpony immediately drafted a letter to all clergy throughout the Suckamints commanding that the sacraments be withheld from the Mayor's son until he obeyed the order to release Sister Ædrea St. Clare into the custody of the Curia. The Pope knew that Slojon would not give any weight to such a sanction, except for the humiliating effect of the bad publicity when the letter was prominently posted for all to read in every church in the mountains.

Still, Slojon would not budge until his father returned from battle a week later. Dion conferred with the Pope. First they discussed the war in the Province, which had stalled around the 98th meridian. Then they discussed Ædrea. Whatever he might believe privately, Dion was a public Catholic. After the conference, he released Sister Clare into the custody of Mother Iridia Silentia, O.D.D., who became her defense counsel. The sanctions against the Mayor's son were lifted. In an unusual move, the Pope permitted Slojon to assist the schoolteacher Abrahà Cardinal Linkono as inquisitor and prosecutor.

The outcome was inevitable, and the only point in dispute became the sentence to be imposed upon the nun by the Supreme Pontiff.

Brownpony noticed that the beauty of the barefoot Sister who stood before him had not been diminished by motherhood, or completely obscured by her coarse habit. She was radiant, smiling at him faintly, and her eyes were attentive and unafraid. That was bad. It implied that there was a conspiracy, and it had worked. Slojon already knew he had been duped, but—he noticed the faint smile.

Thus spoke Amen II, with some attempt at sternness: "Sister Ædrea St. Clare-of-Assisi, you are remanded into the permanent custody of Cardinal Silentia. For your offense against the laws of New Jerusalem, a legitimate secular authority, we sentence you to cross the Brave River and spend the rest of your life in exile there, or until your sentence is commuted by the Holy See. Should you cross the river again from south to north, you incur excommunication by the very act of doing so."

Ædrea's smile did not change. The sentence imposed was not different from that which her vows imposed. She came slowly forward and knelt to kiss her judge's ring. "Where is Blacktooth?" she whispered.

Brownpony suppressed a chuckle at her audacity, and whispered back, "I have no idea."

Thus it came to pass that the lady cardinal departed from New Jerusalem with Sister Ædrea St. Clare and the three nuns who had been her conclavists in Valana. A coach was provided, and four mounted soldiers were appointed to escort them all the way to the Brave River. At the last minute, Iridia paid the Pope another visit and sweetly asked his permission to make a rest stop at Leibowitz Abbey, a detour which would add no more than a few days to their journey.

Brownpony gazed at her in surprise. Cardinal Silentia was almost his own age, still gauntly beautiful and full of charm if not grace, but now he saw that she was being charmed by Ædrea.

"She wants to know if Blacktooth has gone back to the abbey," the Pontiff sighed.

"That had occurred to me, Holy Father. But the guesthouse there is adequate and secure. The Brothers and my Sisters will see each other only in church, if at all."

"Very well, but if you lose her, you are both in trouble," he told her. His permission was based on his belief that neither Blacktooth nor Abbot Olshuen wanted to see the other ever again. "However, if you meet Brother St. George anywhere, tell him I require his presence here immediately."

Iridia knelt and withdrew. That was three weeks before Nimmy's letter came to him from a battleground on the eastern Plains. Brownpony found the letter irritating, and said to the messenger, "Tell him to honor the butchering festival, and then deliver me his butt."

But as soon as he said it, there came to Pope Amen II a flash vision of Blacktooth's future—in shock upon learning of Ædrea's sudden calling to religion, and of the Pope's sentence passed upon her. Shock and maybe fury. He resolved not to see the monk immediately upon his arrival. Let him hear about it from Qum-Do, Jing-U-Wan, Wooshin, and the two Oriental secretaries he inherited from Cardinal Ri. They understood his motives and his necessity. Brother St. George would eventually apply his religious thing to his fury, and then it would be safe for the Pope to see him.

Late September came, and Blacktooth had still not arrived at Pope Amen II's log-cabin Vatican. His Holiness gulped the rest of his brandy, put his heels on the table, leaned back, and smiled at his elderly bodyguard. A single candle lighted Brownpony's private office in the Papal Palace with its log walls and fired-clay floor, but there was an exceptionally bright full moon shining through the big southern windows, and everything seemed to glow in its light, including the faces of the Pope and the warrior.

"Axe, do you know what tomorrow is?"

"Thursday, the twenty-ninth, 'Oliness."

"It is a feast of Saint Michael, the commander in chief of the heavenly hordes."

"I thought it was the 'heavenly hosts.' "

"No, no! All angels are Nomads and there are hordes of them."

"So what of it, 'Oliness?"

"Axe, the Cathedral of Saint Michael Angel-of-Battle is in Hannegan City, and belongs to Urion Benefez. For him tomorrow is a day of pomp and High Masses. And I shall offer the same Mass in a quiet way. The Gospel for the day is the first ten verses of Matthew Thirteen, and at first glance it seems unrelated to the Archangel Michael. In it, Jesus calls a little child to him, and tells how we must all become little children again before we can enter Heaven. Isn't that strange?"

"No, to the children the angel's sword gives life."

Brownpony paused. He knew what Axe meant, but what an odd way to say it.

"An old Jew once told me that this, our angel of battle, is the defender of the Synagogue, just as we see him as defender of the Church. And of course of her children. That explains the choice of the Gospel, I think. But do you know that a bunch of old Nomad women married me off to the Burregun, the Buzzard of Battle?"

"I believe you have mentioned it several times, 'Oliness. I hope it is a happy marriage."

"Oh, it is, it is! We're winning the war, I think." The Pope poured himself another glass of brandy. "But I feel strange praying to Michael now. I hope the commander of the angelic armies forgives me. It was a forced marriage. Must I apologize for imagining Benefez's Angel of Battle pitted against my supernatural bird-wife?"

"No."

"Oh, you have an opinion! It was a rhetorical question, Axe, but why do you say 'no'?"

"Because the angel and the buzzard are the same."

"I wish you had said they are on the same side. You'll never be a Christian, will you Wooshin? And yet you have certain shocking insights. Tell me about Mankiller again sometime."

"Again? I don't remember telling you about him a first time, 'Oliness."

"No, I just heard part of what you were telling Blacktooth one day. Who is Mankiller?"

"The Compassionate One." His capital letters were audible.

Brownpony stared at him by moonlight and wondered.

Wooshin added: "An ancient saying among my people goes: 'The sword that kills is the same sword that gives life.' "

"Have another glass of this good mountain brandy. But to whom has a sword ever given life?"

The Axe declined the brandy. "Whenever there is a fight, the sword gives death to one man and life to the other. And life to his family, his retainers, and lord."

"Yes, I suppose your sword has given me life once or twice. The saying is less than profound, though. Some things you say make a lot of people think you confuse God and the Devil, Wooshin."

"I hope Y'roliness is not among them."

"No, but what do you say to the charge?"

"I deny it. How can I confuse them? I see they are not two."

Brownpony laughed. "Axe, did you ever take paradox lessons from Pope Amen Specklebird?"

"No, but he kindly spoke to me a few times. You say I'll never be a Christian. Foreman Jing says the same. But if I could have been Saint Specklebird's student, I might have become one."

"You just canonized him. That's my job. Are you an atheist?"

"Oh no, I honor all the gods."

"How many belong to that *all?*"

"Countless. And *one.*"

"How meaningless!"

" 'Oliness, let me hear you count to one."

"One."

"Point at that *one.*"

Brownpony stirred restlessly. Finally he tapped his index finger against his temple.

Wooshin laughed quietly. "Wrong. You had to think about it too long. And you didn't count *to* one. You counted *from* one and stopped. The *one* is countless."

The Pope changed the subject. He was no mystic, but he seemed to attract mystics. Specklebird, Blacktooth, and Wooshin—they all had a streak of it, and they were all quite different. He was fascinated, but he did not understand.

In Hannegan City in mid-September, the Emperor called together his generals and waxed gleeful about the captured weapons; fire had not ruined them for study, only for use. Stocks and grips were burned, some cylinders had exploded, and some barrels were bent by the heat and by bursting kegs of powder. Filpeo handled them lovingly, and his hands were black with soot. According to his gunsmiths, it would be possible to begin duplicating this west-coast weapon as soon as they could tool up, produce the right kinds of steel, find copper for making brass for cartridges—if his forces could hold out that long.

Meanwhile Admiral e'Fondolai, Carpios Robbery, was already equipped with several dozen of the repeating weapons. Soon he and Esitt Loyte (he whom the troops called "Wooden-Nose") would begin their raids from north of the Misery. The wolf-skinned Texark forces, disguised as motherless outlaws, would wreak enough havoc on the Nomad women and horses left behind to draw off the left flank of the Antipope's crusade.

"Admiral?" protested General Goldæm. "I thought Carpy had been made a field marshal."

"Admiral for now," Filpeo answered. "An admiral is a pirate with a uniform, and a pirate doesn't think in terms of capturing territory. His method of warfare is perfectly suited to the ocean of grass that is the Nomad homeland."

Time as well as terror was on the Emperor's side. The opposing armies of Pope and Empire, Church and State, were dug in on opposite banks of the Washita, and it was easier for Filpeo to feed his men than for Amen II to feed his. Moreover, Brownpony was counting on forces he did not control.

"The Antipope thinks he holds the undying allegiance of the Wilddog Horde, but I am not so sure," Filpeo told his generals. "They say Sharf Oxsho licks the false Pope's footprints, but Høngan Ösle Chür seems to have risen above his Wilddog partisanship to become the Sharf of Sharfs, so to speak, of all three hordes. Even Sharf Demon Light pays respect to his lord, and we know how the Jackrabbit leaped into his arms and arose against us. No doubt, Eltür is as much our enemy as his brother Hultor, but he is cautious, he is clever, he is reasonable. And unlike Høngan, he is no Christian. We may be able to negotiate."

"I'm not sure you mean what you seem to be saying, Sire," said Father Colonel Pottscar. "You speak as if Christianity demands submission to a false pope."

"No, Pottsy. It just means Sharf Eltür, with no Christianity, cares nothing about disputes internal to the Church. Therefore he is free to negotiate."

A few days later, the glee of Filpeo Harq surpassed all bounds, and he danced a three-second jig in his private quarters when his uncle Urion came to him with the news that Sorely Cardinal Nauwhat had defected from the service of the false Pope. His jig-dancing stopped when he realized that he should have heard the news about Nauwhat before his uncle heard it.

"Why didn't the commander who accepted his defection report it to me?" he demanded.

"I made arrangement with Sorely while he was still in Valana, and I made the border guard honor it. I had advance knowledge he was coming, because he agreed to cross over only if my archdiocese granted him sanctuary."

"Bastards! You subvert my own military. Heads are going to roll. And he wants sanctuary from whom, *me*?" Filpeo barked.

"Of course. And I don't think you'll take Father Colonel Pottscar's head or mine."

"Damn! Why, with me the cardinal is completely safe. I'd give him a state dinner."

"That's what he's afraid of. And from you, he would be safe from harm, but not from interrogation."

"What has he got to hide?"

"Everything! He is here to separate himself from this maniac in the western mountains, not to betray him. He will give no aid and comfort to either side. He is neutral, but only under my protection."

The Emperor tugged at his nervous earlobe and paced for a time. "By God!" he said at last. "When this is all over and you elect a real pope, who to choose?—who better than a cardinal who remained principled but neutral?" He turned to watch the Archbishop's face, and immediately laughed. "Uncle Urion, you stand accused of too many bad habits to be the next Pope. I'm sure the accusations are false, but—" He shrugged.

"Yes," said Benefez. "I suppose Sorely has thought about Hoydok's slander."

"Treat him well, Uncle, even if you fear his ambition. And let me visit him in your palace. Invite us both to dine with you."

"Not unless he is comfortable with the idea. If he is comfortable with it, I'll invite you. Otherwise you won't even get an explanation."

The invitation to dine at the Archdiocesan Palace came to Filpeo after only three days. The Emperor eagerly accepted, and warmly welcomed the dissident Nauwhat to Hannegan City. But he began to question him as soon as his uncle briefly excused himself after a whispered message from the subdeacon Torrildo.

"Brownpony is under a suspended death sentence throughout the Empire," Filpeo told the Oregonian as soon as Benefez was out of earshot. "His election itself was an act of war by the Valanan Church against Texark. If he is caught, he will go to the chopping machine. He should not blame you for turning your back on him."

"No, Sire. But you call his election an act of war by the Valana clergy, and I helped elect him. I did not—we did not—think of it as declaring war on you, I can tell you that."

"The Valana *clergy* elected him, you say? Not the Sacred College?"

"Sire, in exile, the Valana clergy is the clergy of Rome. The Sacred College is the clergy of Rome only because each member maintains a Roman or Valanan church. But in an emergency situation, the clergy of the Roman diocese elects its own bishop. The College was a later development in Church history."

"Oh, I wondered how you justified that so-called conclave!"

"I believe it was justified. But afterward, it was Brownpony who abandoned the Curia. You may think of this war as his alone, although others *do* claim it and *do* pursue it. I was in Valana, and was not consulted before he proclaimed a crusade. I am not even sure his war is just, let alone holy."

"And yet I am told that there was a council of war before the election, and that you attended. And how is it that you joined Chuntar Hadala's attempt to bring arms to the Valley?"

"I merely accompanied him across the Plains, Sire. I left him before the battle started."

"Yes, well, tell me this. How long ago did Brownpony begin to pile up an arsenal in the Suckamint Range?"

"Did Cardinal Benefez not tell you that I would give no reply to questions about military matters? I am not a spy."

Archbishop Benefez returned to the table and, having heard the last exchange, began berating his nephew for breaking his promise not to badger the cardinal from Oregonia.

Nevertheless, the Emperor went away happy that night. The defection of Sorely Cardinal Nauwhat, now a guest in the episcopal palace of his uncle, added respectability to Filpeo's cause. Even though Nauwhat declined to be interviewed by intelligence, and made it plain that he considered himself the equal of his host, the Emperor was delighted at the prospect of establishing good relations with the Oregonians, who were Nauwhat's people. It was the odd move of a knight on the continental chessboard: two squares west and one north. Oregonia was not far from what the Emperor had concluded to be the west-coast source of Brownpony's arms. The man owned land there, and received revenue from it. Filpeo would bestow gifts upon the Oregonian ruler as soon after victory as possible, whoever that ruler by then might be.

To the east, while Hadala was preparing his expedition from Valana, before the time of harvest, the King of the Tenesi had taken advantage of the Mayor's problems with the Grasshopper and with Brownpony's army in the Province. He attacked the Texark puppet state of Timberlen on the east bank of the Great River. Filpeo Harq sent his regulars across the Great River to drive back the Tenesi from his burned and looted ally. But the Tenesi were expecting them; they retreated into impenetrable mountains, which the Texark general then decided to penetrate.

Brownpony in due course learned about these battalions, which constituted a regiment of cunning mountain fighters; the Pope sent a courier to express his wish that the Tenesi might encourage the Texark troops to extend their stay in the east until spring, by a minimum of necessary hostile engagements. The courier carried the message as a coded tattoo in his crotch, and he was too fat to lean over far enough even to see it himself without a mirror, and he did not have the key to the code anyway. Brownpony did not worry about him; there seemed to be no point in torturing the messenger. Nevertheless, agents from Imperial Intelligence caught and tormented him into revealing that the tattoo was a message to the Tenesi, and tormented him some more to establish his ignorance of the code. The I.I. men decided not to kill him, but they strapped him to an operating table and removed the message with a skinning knife. He was then free to go, but could not walk because of the pain between his legs. They salted the skin, tacked it to a board to dry, and sent it to Hannegan City for study. The skinning knife had not been sterilized, and the Pope's fat courier died of septicemia.

Upon learning of his messenger's fate, Brownpony could only heap more ecclesiastical sanctions upon an already excommunicated and anathematized Filpeo Harq Hannegan and his uncle, the apostle of Platonic friendship and other deviations from orthodoxy.

Wooshin did his best to console his master. "It seems to me, 'Oliness, that the Tenesi will be doing what you asked them to do anyway."

"So my message needlessly sacrificed the messenger?"

Wooshin was silent, remembering that his master, even if he did share the warrior's indifference to life and death, would never allow himself to realize it.

"How simpler it must have been to manage a war with the methods of communication of the *Magna Civitas*! Our generals receive our commands—if at all—weeks after we send them, and by then the situation has usually changed!"

"Yes, 'Oliness, and that is why, in my people's tradition, a general in the field is obliged to consider his Emperor's commands only as fatherly advice, unless he is fighting very close to the imperial court. As for the *Magna Civitas*, Brother St. George told me that generals in those days complained bitterly because commands from the rulers were so numerous and came so quickly that the war was mismanaged by politicians. Look what happened to the *Magna Civitas*!"

"I should not try to tell the Tenesi what to do?"

Wooshin was silent again, and Brownpony smiled. "Axe, if it were up to me, you would be the commander of the operation in the Province instead of Magister Dion."

"I have no ambition to command an army, 'Oliness."

.   .   .

It was November before Blacktooth came limping into the snowy mountains with a sore toe and in the company of Aberlott and a glep cougar kitten with one blue ear and a half-bald skull. He had been robbed of his mount by outlaws after his Wilddog escort left him on the papal highway, and then Aberlott—who had returned first to Valana and then taken the highway south in the hope of seeing the sister of Jæsis again—found him moaning and half-conscious, with a ravenous kitten sucking at his bloody big toe. When they arrived at the military checkpoint at Arch Hollow, Blacktooth's name was found to be on the guards' list of admissible persons, but Aberlott's name was not.

"He was here with me last year, and we were both here as emissaries from the Secretariat in Valana."

"There is no 'Aberlott' on the list. And I don't think he is one of us."

"Neither am I."

The guard stared oddly at the monk. "No? I could have sworn—"

Aberlott broke out laughing. "You're a spook, Nimmy. I've known it since Ædrea told Anala you were."

Blacktooth sputtered. To the guard, he said, "I'll vouch for the idiot."

The guard called an officer. Blacktooth was made to sign a guarantee as Aberlott's custodian.

"If he breaks any laws, you'll take his punishment."

"What a wonderful opportunity for me!" said Aberlott. "When I'm naughty, you'll get whacked!"

"And you'll get shot!" the officer snapped.

But as soon as they arrived at the new and temporary Holy City, they found themselves in the polite custody of Wooshin, Qum-Do, and Foreman Jing, and for the second time Nimmy had to inform them of the death of a comrade serving their common master. They expressed concern about Gai-See's continued absence.

"I think Sharf Demon Light is keeping him for a while as a teacher of his arts to young Jackrabbit warriors. He wanted to keep me to teach them to read. Now, when may I see His Holiness?"

He found himself looking at Aberlott and three—uh-oh!—expressionless yellow faces.

CHAPTER 26

 HEN THEY TOLD BLACKTOOTH WHAT HAD BEEN done to Ædrea, they were prepared to restrain him and tie him down until he listened to the whole story, including their master's promise to commute her sentence as soon as the Pope could leave New Jerusalem. Instead Nimmy listened in silence, wept a little, but in the end said, "Good! But what about Gai-See? Has he come back yet?"

"We have heard nothing," Axe told him.

Nimmy wanted an audience with the Pope, but Axe convinced him the time was not right. They waited five more days for the warrior's return. Then Blacktooth said to Foreman Jing, "Come with me to Arch Hollow."

"Why?"

"Because I am no longer the Pope's servant. Nor was Gai-See

when he started obeying Hadala and Nauwhat. The guards will not answer my questions. They may talk to you."

Jing agreed. They left the municipal area in the early morning and were back to their servants' quarters before sundown. Blacktooth allowed Jing to tell Wooshin the bad news.

"Gai-See arrived at Arch Hollow a few days after Blacktooth and Aberlott. The guards there seized him, charged him with murder, and escorted him straight up through the mountain passes. They took him to Slojon's court in the central square. There he was indicted, and thence he was sent to the cage. Slojon went directly to the Pope and informed him of the action. They met alone with no witnesses."

"I remember that meeting!" said Axe. "I did not know what it was about."

"Of course," said Qum-Do. "You were there too," he said to Jing.

"So, why aren't *you* looking angry, Axe?" Blacktooth asked.

"At whom?"

"At the Holy Father, of course! For approving Gai-See's arrest."

So unthinkable was the suggestion, so irreverent to their master, that they all glared at him.

"Well, false friends, I *am* going to see the Pope about Gai-See!" said Blacktooth.

"No you're not," said Wooshin, laying a hand on his arm. "His Holiness is not ready—"

Having called him a false friend without provoking him, Blacktooth slapped him. So unexpected was the event that Axe failed to evade the blow. Nimmy stepped back defensively.

"You'll have to kill me to stop me, Axe, and your master won't like that."

"But you're not supposed to crash in without—"

"That's not for you to say. I am going to see the Pope. Come along if you want, all of you." He glanced at Ri's warriors. Qum-Do and Foreman Jing were standing at hand-on-sword alert. Either of them would abandon Gai-See to his fate without protest, if their master so much as frowned at him. So would Axe.

Nimmy turned his back on them and walked out of the house. He could hear them coming behind him. He had recovered from the beating he had taken from the outlaws. The earth felt good under his feet again. However briefly, he had visited his ancestors. While with them he had seen something within himself as in a mirror. The earth, any earth, was his to walk on now. Moreover he had seen the Nomad wife of the Pontiff, red as the sunset, soaring over the corpse-strewn landscape. Gai-See was only the beginning of what he wanted to see the Pope about. Blacktooth was vaguely conscious of casting aside his vow of obedience, but felt no qualms about it this time. Ædrea was in his mind like a vision, but he had nothing to say about her.

At the entrance to the audience room, a member of the Papal Guard armed with a halberd blocked the doorway. Blacktooth stamped the guard's slipper with his heel, seized the halberd, and rammed his stomach with the butt of it to get inside the door. His Oriental companions watched the fight without comment. Once inside the doors, he was seized by Cardinal Linkono and the Grand Cardinal Penitentiary. Axe stepped in to assist them now, but Brownpony called out from the throne.

"Let him in. Let them all in."

Blacktooth strode up to the dais and fell to his knees before his Pontiff. The Pope reached down to lift him up, but the monk evaded his hands and stood erect. Brownpony regarded him with faint amusement.

"Is this so urgent, Brother St. George? We were discussing policy with our eminent brethren. About Ædrea—"

"It's not about Ædrea. Who do you see here besides your eminent brethren?"

"Why, I see an unhappy monk, and three of my personal guards."

"Why not *four* of your personal guards, Holy Father?"

"Oh. I did not know that you and Gai-See were close. It is unfortunate."

"We were not close at all, and your betrayal is worse than unfortunate."

Brownpony frowned as if not quite believing his ears.

"I see it is possible for a Pope to do evil."

Against these insulting words to the master, swords were drawn.

Nimmy turned his back on the Pope and faced his companions. "If your master wills my death, cowards, why do you hesitate? Hit!"

Immediately he turned to Brownpony again. "Can't you see what you've done? Right here before you, they're ready to do what Gai-See did. Except that Gai-See thought he was right and they know they are wrong. And Your Holiness accepts this kind of loyalty in good conscience?"

Brownpony was watching his former Nomadic secretary in apparent fascination. Blacktooth heard one sword return to its sheath. That would be Foreman Jing, he guessed. Wooshin would kill him without the Pope's nod if he thought the Pope's best interest would be served by the killing.

"Blacktooth, you were always a quick study, but this is a new role, isn't it?"

"Holy Father, as a Catholic, I have to believe that what you bind on Earth is bound also in Heaven, and I have to believe that when you are speaking about faith and morals, the Holy Ghost prevents you from speaking any error."

"You *have* to believe, but *do* you?"

"I have a question. Is a declaration of war an assertion about faith and morals? Ever? Even if you call it a holy war? Father Suarez taught—and he was extending Saint Augustine's teaching—that a war to convert the heathen can never be just. Can a war against heretical Christians be holy, if a war against the heathen is unjust?"

"The war is against neither heathens nor heretical Christians. It is against a tyrant who usurps the apostolic power and oppresses the whole world."

"But it's heathens and Christians who are killed, while the tyrant still lives and the apostle is still in power."

Brownpony seemed to swear under his breath for a moment, then recovered. "You wrote me that you killed a man in battle, Nimmy. Is that what's wrong with you now?"

Blacktooth nodded and spoke slowly. "The man in a Texark uniform was a child of yours, Holiness: a glep from the Valley. I meant to miss him. My aim was bad, and I hit him in the belly. What he wanted from me then was a bullet in the brain, but I cut his throat instead, because a sergeant was watching. Yes, I think that is what's wrong with me, Holy Father. Eltür Brâm, because I had already killed, would have made me a Nomad warrior with only the initiation, without the ordeal of battle. Then they would stop calling me 'Nimmy,' he said, and stop laughing about it. I don't mind the name or the laughter. I want never to kill again. But I don't want to see Gai-See punished. He saw Hadala as a fugitive from your commands. He couldn't arrest him or Gleaver; he did what he thought was necessary."

"He had no license from me."

"You accepted his services as a warrior. Did you really withhold from him the license that he assumed was his?"

Pope Amen frowned and called out for everyone but Blacktooth and one guard to leave the room. It was the guard with the sore stomach who stayed, and who sealed the doors after the others were outside.

"Go on, finish what you have to say."

Blacktooth looked around to make sure Cardinal Linkono was gone. "For one thing, Gai-See is a member of a religious order, and—"

"I see," Brownpony interrupted. "I claimed jurisdiction in Ædrea's case, why not in Gai-See's? Because no pope has yet recognized the Order to which Ri's men say they belong, that's why. I

meant to do it sooner or later, but I can't do it just to free Gai-See.
It's too transparent. But go on, if you have more to say."

"I cannot, Your Holiness, speak to the Vicar of Christ on Earth as
freely as I did to my former employer, the Secretary for Extraordinary
Ecclesiastic Concerns. I don't know the Vicar of Christ."

"It seems to me you've been speaking freely enough. But suppose
I just take off my zucchetto and tell you that the Vicar of Christ has
taken the day off. I am still Elia Brownpony—the bastard son of a
lesbian nomad and a Texark rapist. So, Nyinden, farmboy Nomad,
sometime monk, sometime lover, speak your mind. I may throw you
out, but I won't throw you in a dungeon."

"Then release Gai-See from a dungeon."

"I didn't imprison Gai-See. Cardinal Linkono did."

"Without your permission?"

"You don't understand the situation here, Blacktooth. We are the
guests of the city. I won't say we're captives here—until I try to return
to Valana and see if they let me go. Cardinal Linkono informed me of
Gai-See's arrest. Chuntar Hadala played bishop to these people, because he was bishop to the Valley whence they came. Slojon and everybody here knows that I sent men to arrest Hadala, and, well—"

"Oh. So when Gai-See killed him, they thought *you* ordered the
execution."

"Not yet, but they will certainly suspect it if I secure his release
now. He killed a bishop, and prince of the Church. Cardinal Hadala
was popular here."

"I was there when it happened, Holy Father. All along, Gleaver
and his officers had been shooting those of us who wavered or held
back. In that light, Gai-See shot in self-defense and the defense of us
all. But first he crawled up to me under fire. He asked if it was true
that Cardinal Hadala was defying your orders, and betraying you. I
told him it was so. I knew what he might do when I told him that, and
I hoped he would do it. So I am the one who sentenced the cardinal
to death. Have them arrest me too, Holy Father."

"I'll see what I can do," Brownpony said darkly, and beckoned to
the guard and breathed a quiet order. The guard with the sore stomach seized Blacktooth's arm, led him straight to jail, and put him in
Gai-See's cell. Gai-See embraced him. During the embrace, the guard
reached through the bars and punched Blacktooth hard in the kidney
with the butt of the halberd.

"I'll be back for you soon," he said with a sweet grin.

Gai-See was not alone in jail. Two men who claimed to be political refugees from the Empire and who now sought asylum in New
Jerusalem were imprisoned there until their claims were thoroughly

investigated. One was Urik Thon Yordin, S.I., the Ignatzian who was also a professor of history at the secular university at Texark, and whom Brownpony had suspected of hiring the thugs who tried to kill them on Easter before the last conclave. How desperate the man must be to escape Texark, that he should come here for asylum! He glanced at Blacktooth once, but neglected to recognize him.

The other man was Torrildo.

"Blacktooth, my God! You can't imagine what that beast Benefez did to me!"

Nimmy sat down on Gai-See's bed and fell to questioning the warrior. He tried to ignore Torrildo's confession of the intimately brutal sins the Archbishop of Texark had perpetrated upon his person.

According to Gai-See, Yordin and Torrildo were refugees, not from a terrible Emperor, but from a furious Archbishop who had suddenly been made to realize that he could never be Pope, even if his nephew conquered all of his enemies. At the university, Yordin had made the mistake of saying openly that Benefez was now *non papabilis*, and Torrildo himself was part of the Archbishop's problem which insured that he would never wear the tiara. In each fugitive's case, it was his own confessor who, after hearing the rumbles from the top of the mountain, advised his penitent to do his penance in some land far from the reach of the Imperium and the Diocesan Ordinary. So there they sat in a New Jerusalem jail, hoping to be of some value to a Pope who had the power to set them free. Blacktooth found this interesting and ironic, but decided not to concern himself with their fate.

After a while, the guard came back for him and they returned to the throne room. He asked Wooshin in a whisper if he knew about Yordin and Torrildo, but the Axe ignored him.

"Is Gai-See sick?" Brownpony wanted to know. "Is he mistreated or badly fed?"

"He is sick at heart. Keeping him caged is mistreatment, and so is the food."

"If you had not been hiding out with Amen Specklebird when they blew up the Palace, none of this would have happened," Brownpony told him. "You would have come here with me. Now you are furious, as if it were my intent that you fight or kill in battle."

"I was *not* 'hiding out' with the Pope."

"Just praying?"

"Not quite. We talked. One thing we spoke of was war, and I made the traditional mention of 'the Church Militant on Earth, the

Church Suffering in Purgatory, and the Church Triumphant in Heaven.' But the Pope said to me, 'There is no Church Triumphant in Heaven, although I have heard that foolishness before.' I asked him why he said that, in disagreement with all the elders, and he told me, 'John says it. Chapter Twenty-one, Apocalypse, "And I saw no temple therein." In the presence of God, the Church is a discarded crutch.'

"What I am saying to you, Holy Father, is that if the Church Militant on Earth does not produce members of a Church Triumphant in Heaven, then its militancy is not . . ."

"Stop. I bow to all the words of my predecessor, but not to *your* explanation of them. Especially not on the subject of war."

Nimmy fell silent, feeling stupid.

"It wasn't murder, when you accidentally shot that man. You don't need absolution for it—but I can shrive you if you like." The Pope stared at Blacktooth's face for a time, and began to frown. "I think you would *not accept* absolution from me if I gave it to you!"

"You have already given me a plenary indulgence and a passport to paradise in *Scitote Tyrannum*, Holy Father. What more could I ask?"

Brownpony reddened at the sarcasm, but Blacktooth persisted in standing there with his hands spread wide as if to receive gifts. In reality, he was frozen in fright by what he had said.

"Get out of here!" Brownpony erupted. "Go visit your patron saint at the priory. I don't want to hear this."

"May I be excused now?" Stupid again!

"Yes. Go."

Blacktooth glanced at the Pope's hand. Brownpony did not lift his ring, and Blacktooth did not reach. He made a fast genuflection and beat a faster retreat. He did not see Brownpony again during that winter.

He took residence at the Priory of Saint Leibowitz-in-the-Cottonwoods, where Prior Singing Cow St. Martha assigned him work in exchange for room and board. He was not required to assist in the Divine Office, but he was not forbidden either. So he added his voice to the choir, took dictation and penned letters for the prior, washed dishes and took his turn as cook. The brothers were kinder to him here than at the abbey, although they were the same monks; he had known them all at the monastery in the desert. They were all specialists. Brother Jonan, who used to wake Blacktooth every morning for Lauds, was a mathematician. Brother Elwen, who had been Torrildo's lover and went over the wall, had come back repentant and become skilled in his previous studies: mechanics and engineering. Old Brother Tudlen, whom Blacktooth had barely known because he had been on leave from the abbey for so many years at sea, was a naval architect, astronomer, and navigator; he seemed somehow out of place this far from the ocean, but Brownpony, like Filpeo, had ambitions. Tudlen had built a schooner in old Tampa Bay, and it was supposedly the property of the Order; here in the mountains where the air was thin and clear, he was grinding a telescope mirror. The others were specialists in Church history, in political and military history, and in the work of Boedullus among other authorities on the *Magna Civitas* and its catastrophic collapse.

Persuading Mayor Dion to permit the opening of the Leibowitzian priory in New Jerusalem had been no small undertaking. Singing Cow had only high praise for the Pope as a persuader and as a devotee of their patron saint. "His Holiness convinced Dion that we would be of educational value to the community here. But so far, no schools have called on us; Linkono runs them. These spooks don't want their superbabies growing up to be monks. There are two layers of religion here: Catholic above ground, and New Adventist below ground. They're out to save the world. Hadala was typical."

"The old Jew Benjamin told me about them," said Blacktooth, "but he kept mumbling, 'It's still not him, still not him,' and I don't know what he meant."

Singing Cow smiled as if he knew but said nothing.

He confessed to Father Prior "Mooo," as the Brethren sometimes called him. As one ex-Grasshopper farm kid to another, it proved a strange experience for them both.

"Were you taken into the Nomad war cult, my son?" Father St. Martha asked, in connection with Blacktooth's confession of killing a man in battle.

"No, Father. The Grasshopper people treated me with kindness, as they would a boy who had not yet passed through the ordeal. I did not intend to shoot the man."

"Of course not, but you intended to cut his throat, did you not?"

"I thought he was begging me to. I still think so."

Singing Cow, who sometimes liked to think of himself as a Nomad, mentioned that the Church frowned upon assisting a suicide, but that he would probably have done the same; still it was an act to be repented.

Nimmy failed to mention disobedience among his many sins. Singing Cow did not remind him. Absolution was forthcoming, and the penance was mild: pray five mysteries of the rosary and begin singing for his supper.

One cold night he and the Cow were walking home through the snow after singing Compline in the neighborhood church which they shared with the local pastor and his small flock. Compline was the night prayer of the Church, concerned with sleep and wakefulness, life and death, sinning and receiving grace. But it was no lullaby, and left him feeling lonely.

"I can tell you something I think you'll want to hear, Father."

"Tell away," said Singing Cow.

"Remember when we ran away and tried to join the Grasshopper? They fed us, let us rest two days, and then drove us out of the camp with whips in a snow like this. Were you as bitter as I was?"

"Those rope whips! Listen, I still don't know what we did to offend them. I used to think that you or Wren must have made a pass at a girl. Because our parents farmed? Was that why? Yes, I was bitter, and Grasshopper Nomads still make me uncomfortable."

"If we had fought back, we might have had a chance; instead, we just cringed and ran. There is a Grasshopper Weejus there who thinks she remembers three wandering orphans at about the time we visited their tents. She explained to me why they offered us no more than food, water, and two nights' sleep."

"Explaining cruelty doesn't absolve it."

"Perhaps not. But I'll try to repeat what she told me as best I remember. 'Who wants to adopt a teenage nimmy,' she said, 'no matter how he was raised? A Weejus spends four or five years feeding him, clothing him, and teaching him the horses. In exchange for what? Unskilled and lazy labor. He's horny and he gets in fights. He starts trouble with other families. Maybe she catches him coupling with one of her own daughters, but they can't be married under the breeding rules. Or worse, he runs off to marry a daughter of her horse-breeding rival! A family that mourns a dead son would be better off adopting a young cougar than another boy.' "

Singing Cow laughed. "She knew about your kitten?"

"I was carrying Librada when I visited her. She herself had adopted a pubescent orphan girl. But among Nomads, when a girl grows up she stays with her mother. A boy grows up and leaves her and her whole family when he marries. Motherless boys are as welcome as leprosy there, unless they can fight and join the war cult."

"Rope whips." Cow was ruminating on it.

"That was more than twenty years ago, Father. This year, the sharf himself wanted me to stay and tutor his nephews. I would have been adopted, at my age."

"Well, I'm glad you told me *why* they were cruel. Charity's rarely convenient; sometimes it's completely impractical." Singing Cow thought for a moment. "The sharf's grandmother probably believed your vow of chastity protected all of the daughters," he added.

Blacktooth looked away and blushed. "You're supposed to forget what I tell you in confession!" he complained as they entered the monks' dormitory.

At the small priory, each man took his turn at cooking or menial labor. Blacktooth had been told by the Axe that the Pope had wanted his recipe for summonabisch stew, and when his turn came to cook, he asked Father Mooo's permission to prepare the dish for all the Brothers, who needed permission to eat meat. When permission was granted, Blacktooth bought the ingredients from a local butcher, prepared the feast, and sent a quart of it to the Papal Palace. The lack of a response seemed an indicator of the Pope's disfavor. Librada consumed the leftovers with gusto. She had caught a mouse on her first day, thus insuring her room and board.

"Why did you name her Librada? What does it mean?" Cow asked.

"It was Spanish, and means 'set-free.' Because that's what she'll be, before she's much bigger and eats one of us."

The winter of '45–'46 was the mildest in memory. Most of the Wilddog Horde moved their cattle south as usual. Hannegan's agents among the motherless outlaw bands observed the migration, but saw nothing unusual to report until March, when all the warriors of the horde assembled as an army under Lord Høngan himself, with Oxsho second-in-command. They rode swiftly eastward for several days, then south to the river. Before Filpeo Harq learned about the movement, the Nomad horsemen had forded the Nady Ann and attacked from the rear those Texark forces dug-in along the east bank of the Washita. With them they brought three Grasshopper dog trainers and nearly a hundred dogs who would kill any unmounted man who did not smell like a Nomad. At least six of Sharf Oxsho's warriors were bitten for not having the usual Grasshopper aroma; by the light of the full Pascal moon the dogs tore out the throats of Texark soldiers in the trenches along with some of their reluctant Jackrabbit allies who ate too many onions to smell friendly. The dogs' attack on the night of Holy Saturday enabled the forces of Önmu Kun to cross the Washita without coming under fire until they charged the fortifications with fixed bayonets. By Easter's sunrise, the trainers had regained control of ravening dogs, and the battle was won without further Jackrabbit casualties, and Mayor Dion's well-rested men crossed the river to carry the war eastward on horseback.

After the fray, Høngan Ösle Chür met with Önmu Kun in the middle of a battlefield at dawn; he then rode with the Jackrabbit's forces without taking command. This was his reason for defying his shamans. The Jackrabbit were lacking in respect for Önmu the smuggler. Their respect for the Lord of the Hordes was enhanced by the fact that he was not Jackrabbit. Such was the self-contempt of a conquered people.

Father Steps-on-Snake had recently come to the vicinity and he now celebrated the Mass of the Resurrection at noon on March 25th—the earliest Easter in many years—and gave the Eucharist to Lord Høngan Ösle together with Sharfs Oxsho Xon and Önmu Kun in the sight of all the warriors and the Jackrabbit population of the region. Thus did the faithful rejoice in the victory of the Nomad over tyranny at the same time as the victory of the Christ over death. Never in the memory of old Steps-on-Snake had the subject people expressed such jubilation on this highest feast day.

Holy Madness spent nearly a week building up the Jackrabbit's esteem for the Jackrabbit sharf by accompanying him everywhere, listening to Önmu address the rebel fighters and civilian groups, then reinforcing the sharf's words with a few of his own, bringing on rousing cheers from the multitude.

There were about seven hundred unwounded prisoners. Jackrabbit warriors had begun to maim them until Holy Madness put a stop to it. That Nomad custom had been abandoned soon after the Texark conquest, except for captured spies and saboteurs, but the Jackrabbit was only trying to honor the custom, for they had been told by Önmu what Høngan had done to Esitt Loyte.

But the forces of the Hannegan were rushing westward to rejoin the battle against the Jackrabbit rebels, and Önmu's gathering army now marched to meet them following Dion's light horse. Having destroyed the enemy forces in the immediate vicinity and inspired the Jackrabbit fighters with a new enthusiasm for battle, Høngan and Oxsho withdrew the Wilddog horsemen from the area by crossing the Washita and riding westward to cross the Nady Ann at a point where their movement would not be observed by Texark scouts.

When the warriors rejoined the rest of the Wilddog Horde at their wintering grounds, Høngan Ösle first sent messengers with an account of the battle to Sharf Bråm and Pope Amen. Then he summoned Father Ombroz as well as his senior Bear Spirit shaman and his own Weejus mother; he told them to prepare immediately to accompany him to New Jerusalem and the Court of Amen II.

. . .

The Lord of the Hordes and his party arrived in New Jerusalem at the end of April. They were greeted by the Pope and the Mayor—Dion was briefly home from the wars—with high ceremony. The Major General Quigler Durod was already in town as plenipotentiary from the King of the Tenesi. Durod had taken the trouble to learn a Nomad dialect (Jackrabbit, because in his youth he had served in the Province as a Texark mercenary), and he made friends quickly with Høngan Östle. Besides Durod, armorers had come from the west coast, bringing samples of their latest model firearms.

Although Høngan Östle as *Qæsach dri Vørdar* spoke for all three hordes, Brownpony expressed regret that Sharfs Bråm and Önmu Kun were unable to attend the council of war. Three days later, an angry Grasshopper emissary rode up from Arch Hollow to confront the Pope.

The Grasshopper messenger was not a Christian. He stood defiantly before Amen II and six members of the Curia to voice the demands of his sharf. "Unless you release Nyinden and the swordsman Gai-See into my custody, the Grasshopper will make war not against your enemies, but against you!"

"Perhaps your sharf has been lied to by someone," the Pope said. "Nyinden is staying at the priory with the other monks. If he wants to go with you, there is nothing to stop him."

"And the yellow warrior? Where is he?"

"He's in the city's jail. I did not put him there. The only man in this room with any voice in city affairs is Cardinal Linkono, who grew up here. Your Eminence, would you please?" He beckoned to a short man with a white beard who looked like a gnome wearing a red skullcap. Then he said to the messenger, "I think your sharf would want his message to go to the right man. I am the wrong man, and His Eminence Abrahà is not the right man either, but he can take you to the right man."

"Are you not the most powerful man in this awful place—not Pope Redbeard, the Lord of the Christian Horde?" the Nomad demanded.

"Not really Lord as you understand it. You might think of my office as that of a high priest."

Linkono limped up to stand beside the Nomad, facing him, and spoke in a voice surprisingly deep for so small a man. His Nomadic was heavily accented but understandable.

"Young man, why is this an 'awful place'?"

Brownpony himself explained: "The Nomads say evil spirits come down from the mountains, especially the Old Zarks, and inhabit wombs. The belief explains why a Nomad woman sometimes gives birth to a glep baby."

"I see. Well, young man, compare our Pope to your oldest Bear Spirit shaman. Neither he nor your sharf has to obey the other. The sharf in this place is Mayor Dion. But he just left here to go back to the war. His son takes his place. This, the Church, is like the Bear Spirit Council. There is nothing we can do for you here, my nephew, except pray."

Linkono was smart enough not to say "my son" to a Nomad, but this Nomad did not like "nephew" either.

"My *only* uncle is Demon Light, gray runt. My name is Blue Lightning, and I am the *eldest* son of his eldest sister. We both witnessed Hadala's crimes."

"Surely you mean the crime against Cardinal Hadala!"

"I mean Hadala's crimes, for which he was executed."

The gnome's jaw fell. "Crimes under what law? Nomad law?"

"The Treaty of the Sacred Mare. He violated it by bringing an army into our lands. Hadala violated the law and defied our sharf. By his order, his officers killed his own men. If Nyinden and the yellow warrior hadn't put him to death, my uncle would have done it."

"I had not thought of it in that way before," Brownpony said. "He's right, you know, Abrà. Hadala clearly violated the Treaty."

"Holy Father, I can't believe what I'm hearing!"

Blue Lightning grabbed the small cardinal by the shoulders and shook him. "I can make war or peace, little man. My words are my uncle's words. Perhaps we cannot bring war to you here in your evil mountains, but we can join the war against your men who fight south of the Nady Ann. Take me to the man who jails the victim instead of the criminal."

Linkono limped toward the exit as fast as he could move, with the burly Nomad crowding his heels. When they were gone, Brownpony turned to his personal guard. "Axe, go with them, and take Jing and Qum-Do. Keep that Nomad out of trouble, and make sure Slojon has to look you in the face when he talks about Gai-See." Then, to the Cardinal Penitentiary who was also his personal confessor, he said, "Go to the guests' quarters, please, and tell Høngan Ösle Chür what has happened here. Blue Lightning does not realize that his *Qœsach dri Vørdar* is in town."

In the administration building, Slojon haughtily dismissed the Nomad's claim. The Nomad grabbed him by the ears and hauled him, squeaking in pain, across the desk. A sergeant drew a pistol, and instantly three swords were in the air.

"Drop it, or lose your head," said Axe. The sergeant dropped it.

Eltür's nephew now stood behind Slojon with his arm in a hammerlock and a knife held to his throat. He pushed him toward the door. "This fart is going to jail," said the Nomad.

Slojon screamed as he felt his own blood running down his chest. "Stop him, Wooshin! Stop him!"

"Only you can stop him, Messér. Take him to the jail in peace."

"Brownpony is behind this!"

"No, the Pope is not! The man behind it is also behind you, right now. You did violate the Treaty, Messér."

"All right, we'll go to the jail."

The trip to jail was halted by the sudden entrance of Høngan Ösle Chür and his two shamans. Blue Lightning took one look at him, gasped, and released the Mayor's son. He made a sweeping *kokai* to the chosen one of the Day Maiden, Husband of the Prairies, then fell silent to await orders.

The Lord of the Hordes asked for an explanation of the problem. Blue Lightning spoke first, then Slojon and Axe. Then the *Qœsach dri Vørdar* told the Mayor's son that he, Høngan Ösle Chür, ruled in favor of the Grasshopper claim and made the same threat to Slojon that Blue Lightning had made. The hordes would turn against New Jerusalem for breaking the Treaty, and might even carry the conflict into these feared mountains. The Jackrabbit would turn on the spooks in battle and kill Slojon's father as well.

Thus it came about that the charges were dropped and Gai-See was released into the protective custody of Blue Lightning. Because the Nomad claimed plenipotentiary power to speak for his uncle, Brownpony invited him to attend the council of war, which had all but ended upon the departure of Dion, but was now renewed in the presence of the Grasshopper. The Pope dispatched a message to Bråm through the Nomad relay network to assure the sharf that Gai-See and Nyinden were free. He also thanked him for sending Blue Lightning, who added to the document his initials—Blacktooth had taught him to draw them—and peace was restored among the allies.

After his harsh beginning, Blue Lightning proved a well-rounded diplomat. In spite of his initial threat to abandon the alliance and join the other side, he brought intelligence gathered from several sources. On balance, the news was good, but there were things to worry about. Filpeo had new repeating arms now, but not yet enough of them to turn the outcome of any foreseeable battle. The countryside surrounding New Rome was by no means demilitarized, but the occupation forces there were thinned out by the withdrawal of troops being sent to the Province to halt the eastward advance of the armies of Önmu Kun and Mayor Dion. Sharf Brâm estimated that no more than seven hundred men, Texark cavalry and glep mercenaries, remained to block access to the gates of New Rome.

And there was trouble in the Valley. Texark recruiters had been ambushed and killed. "I wonder who could be doing that?" Quigler Durod asked innocently, provoking laughter. Everyone present knew that Tenesi agents disguised as gleps had crossed the Great River and infiltrated the Watchitah-Ol'zark region. Further recruiting in the Valley of the Misborn was inhibited, if not halted.

"If we don't strike now," Høngan said, "the Emperor's firepower will increase rapidly. We will lose the advantage the Pope's weapons have given us."

Blue Lightning murmured assent. General Durod wanted to know if it was possible to use the Nomad relay network to contact his men in the Valley.

"If you have a secure cipher, maybe," said Blue Lightning. "There is a risk of a messenger being caught. He must not know what your message is."

Pope Amen came to a sudden decision. "We shall mount an expedition to capture New Rome, and do it as soon as possible, unless one of you disagrees."

Nobody objected. After so many decades in exile, the Holy See was going home.

Pentecost came on May 14th in 3246, and Blacktooth had known for a week that Holy Madness and other important guests were in town to consult with the Pope, but the consultations were private and he was as ignorant as any local citizen of what happened behind the closed doors. Prior Cow wanted all eight of them to attend the Pontifical High Mass in the Pope's log-and-stone cathedral, but Nimmy begged off. Instead, he attended Mass at their usual neighborhood church, sang the *Veni Creator Spiritus* with the small choir, and assisted the priest in distributing the Eucharist to local spooks and their beautiful children.

Singing Cow found him sitting in the garden, trying to extract a still fluttering pigeon from the jaws of his growling glep cougar. Librada slashed his hand and clamped down on the bird. Nimmy gave up. "I think it's about time for Librada to be *librada*," he said to the prior.

"We'll take care of it, Nimmy. You're going to be too busy."

"It's up to me, Father. I brought her here. She ought to be let go as far as possible from humans. She's not afraid of anybody. And why do you say I'll be too busy?"

"I think you will be. The Pope wants to see you right now. He's going away."

"Away?"

"To New Rome—as a conqueror, I believe. Now go bandage your hand and run over to the Palace."

As soon as he saw that Gai-See had been set free, Blacktooth felt shame for his earlier impudence toward his Pope, and he looked for an opportunity to apologize. But Axe had assigned him to a place in the baggage train in the rear, and the procession had been in motion for three days before he found an opportunity to approach his former employer. They were both on horseback.

"Don't thank me, thank God and the Grasshopper," said the Pope after waving aside Blacktooth's apology.

"I don't understand, Holy Father."

"You don't have to!" Brownpony snapped, and after a pause relented. "Somebody told Sharf Bråm that you and Gai-See were both in jail for killing Cardinal Hadala. Hadala was violating the Sacred Mare Treaty by bringing an army onto Nomad land. The sharf would have killed him if Gai-See hadn't. I don't know what made him think you helped kill him."

"I did help, Holy Father. I told Gai-See that Hadala was defying you, and I knew what I was doing when I told him. Eltür knew this."

"I see. Well, he became quite angry and sent his nephew with an oral message to Gai-See's jailer."

"Which nephew was this?"

"Stützil Bråm—Blue Lightning. He's up ahead with Høngan Ösle's party. At first he thought I was the jailer. He told everybody that unless you were released at once, he would make peace with the Hannegan and attack Dion's forces wherever he found them. Høngan Ösle stepped in at that point and took over; he even threatened to hit New Jerusalem. So you can thank the Nomads, not me. I'm only bringing you along to satisfy Eltür Bråm."

"So that's why!"

"That and your prowess as a soldier," said Brownpony, and spurred his horse to get away from the conversation.

CHAPTER 27

> Except the sick who are very weak, let all
> abstain entirely from eating the flesh of
> four-footed animals.
> —*Saint Benedict's Rule*, Chapter 39

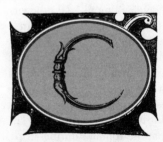HIEF HAWKEN CARDINAL IRRIKAWA, WHO HAD
departed Valana for his own country
some months ago, returned suddenly to
rejoin the Curia's wagon train. He explained that his road home north of the
Misery River was temporarily blocked by
the presence of Texark troops in the region. The lands beyond the Misery were
considered open range, and both Grass-
hopper and Wilddog peoples drove cattle there in season, although
the campsites were not permanent and there were no breeding pits. If
Texark troops were in the area, it was in violation of the Treaty of the
Sacred Mare. The Pope was alarmed at first. But those who questioned
the cardinal closely concluded that what he had encountered was a
band of well-dressed and well-armed outlaws, imitating Texark cavalry
maneuvers. It was strange, but only Sharf Oxsho seemed worried.
"Too many outlaws on the move," he said softly to Father Ombroz.
"Too many to believe."

The Pope's train gradually gathered a multitude as it moved east. Parties of ten or twenty warriors converged with the growing army every few hours. While passing through Wilddog country, the legion grew to sixteen hundred horsemen and their animals. Sometimes when the moon was bright in June, nocturnal riders thundered into camp with obscene war cries followed by laughter as sleepy men scrambled out of their bedrolls. There was talk of victory in the air, talk of spoils and of farmers' women. And rebuke for such talk from Sharf Oxsho's lieutenants.

Blacktooth rode in the back of the hoodlum wagon with Librada, his cougar. He had made a rawhide collar and kept her on a short leash. A sickness of the spirit had come over him. He was unable to pray except to God in his cat.

That was the summer of the Year of Our Lord 3246. On the eve of the solstice the moon was pink and full over the western horizon when dawn broke on the Plains. As Blacktooth crawled from under the hoodlum wagon, he could see that breakfast fires were already being extinguished here and there about the militant horizon. Groups of armed men, horses, cattle, and cannon as far as the eye could see: it was seething, but not yet boiling, this pot.

The Hannegan knows we are coming. When will he respond?

There was no haste to resume the journey, probably because today was a special day. Blacktooth could not be certain, for he was out of touch with those in command. A tripod with the remains of a slaughtered cow hung near the wagon. He scraped some raw meat from the bone with the hood's stolen bayonet. A monk of Leibowitz never ate such meat without the abbot's permission, which was rarely given, except on high holy days, or to the gravely ill. I am gravely ill, he said to Jarad breathing over his shoulder. The hood handed him a pancake, a cup of tea, and the usual morning insult. The hood was a Wilddog Nomad, whose name was Bitten Dog, drafted by the Pope's chef as cook's helper, and Blacktooth was supposed to be the Bitten Dog's helper, but diarrhea and deep sadness made him useless. His only work became the gathering of dry manure for fuel during stops, and the polishing of kitchen implements during days in the wagon.

As it turned out, the day was indeed a special day. The Nomads ordinarily celebrated the Nomad Feast of the Bonfires at the solstice; and the Church once had observed on the twentieth of June the Feast of Pope Saint Silverius, the son of Pope Hormisdas. Silverius had offended the Empress Theodora, and she exiled him—a punishment which led to his suffering and death in 538 A.D., and therefore to his being called a martyr. Pope Amen Specklebird had borrowed his feast day (which had been borrowed twice previously) for the observances of Our Lady of the Desert, patroness of his Order. But now it was not Specklebird's feast that Brownpony chose to celebrate, but the Mass of a Sovereign Pontiff, *Si diligis me;* for to consecrate a bishop was his aim, during an early Mass that day in the midst of his armies on the hot and arid plain.

Amen II gathered about him the eight cardinals who accompanied the train. He called it a consistory, and made the intended announcements. He and Wolfer Poilyf, Bishop from the North Country, together with Bishop Varley Swineman of Denver, consecrated Father Jopo e'Laiden Ombroz, S.I., as Archbishop of the ancient but moribund diocese of Canterbury, and then made him Vicar Apostolic to the Nomads—including of course the Jackrabbit Nomads, whose present clergy was now fleeing from the advancing Crusaders of the Western Church. The reluctant Bishop Ombroz was obedient to Brownpony, but less than elated by his own elevation. The Pope made him a cardinal as well, as announced in consistory. The elders of the Bear Spirit would, Ombroz said, laugh at his finery, and he would be called Cardinal Cannibal in Texark. Ombroz was now the ninth cardinal accompanying the main army of the crusade, and Brownpony confided in him and in Wooshin that he would be naming a tenth cardinal soon; he did not mention a name.

From what little Blacktooth saw of the Pope from a distance, it seemed to him that Brownpony looked more ethereal and spiritual than before. Maybe closeness had made him miss something in the man. The change, however, was not necessarily good. Brownpony looked at the sky a lot, other observers said. He always seemed to be looking for something in the clouds or on the horizon, and gave little attention to those around him.

Blacktooth wondered who had suggested to Brownpony the motto he had inscribed upon his new coat of arms as Amen II. It said LIKE HELL YOU WILL in ancient English, instead of the usual Latin. He understood it, but he wondered if the Pope really did. When Brownpony's coach overtook Eltür Brâm's coach one day, Jopo Cardinal Ombroz was the only member of the College who knew enough ancient English to laugh at the juxtaposition of their mottos.

It was to celebrate Ombroz's ascension to the Sacred College that Önmu Kun had traveled north with Father Steps-on-Snake and a party of thirty Jackrabbit warriors. They arrived well before the event, and brought with them disease, although none fell ill until days after their arrival. Blacktooth, already ill, was one of the first to get sick after Önmu came up from the south to meet the train; he heard talk of epidemic in the Province. At first they blamed the water, but a week later three of the warriors and several Grasshopper children fell ill, and then Blacktooth St. George, who already had the runs.

As Önmu explained it, the crusaders in the south at first attributed the affliction to poisoned wells left by retreating Texark forces, but the cattle that drank from the wells were not so afflicted. And the disease seemed to spread from the men who had drunk of the wells to men who had not. So far, the enemy was not affected by the plague, if such it was. The disease, whose symptoms were something like those suffered in Valana before the election of Pope Amen I, was not yet epidemic. To contain it, certain fighting units were quarantined.

Blacktooth did not attend the Mass of a Sovereign Pontiff or Father Ombroz's consecration, but watched from a distant hilltop while squatting in the grass, taking a long painful dump. Blacktooth had given himself over to the Devil. He had stopped praying the Divine Office, except when it came to him in snatches. He listened to himself fart and said amen. He had ceased to meditate, except for an occasional rosary in honor of the Virgin—but then his mind dwelled on Ædrea in the role of God's mother.

He assumed that he would never see her again, for she was now a nun. He had not, and would not, ask Brownpony for assurance that he had done what he had said he would do as soon as they were gone from New Jerusalem, that is, commute her sentence from permanent exile. He had no evidence for believing that the Pope had remembered or kept the promise, and he could not ask. He knew he was going mad; the origin of his cosmic madness was his inflamed bowel, which was caused by his guilt, which was driving him crazy during this summer of the Year of Our Lord 3246, the year of the Reconquest, not the previous year when he had killed a pitiful, drafted glep, for that had not been a year of diarrhea and fever.

His days of madness made him reclusive. Only the responsibility he felt for Librada, the duty to return her to the country of her birth, kept him from abandoning all hope and fleeing. Father Steps-on-Snake was available to him, but he did not confess. The idea of confession seemed to make his diarrhea worse. He had made himself a stranger to his master by his insolence. The journey was misery, and every few days he had a day of delirium and uncontrollable behavior.

But it was on such a bad day that the dead Pope Amen came to comfort him.

"Your Christ is the true man of no identity," Amen Specklebird told him while he took a dump at sundown, "the one not wearing a mask; he comes and goes through your face, where your mask is. He comes and goes as he likes, fore and aft, and your mask sees him not.

A mask sees self only in a mirror. But the true Jesus without a mask is alive and well; austere he sits in solitude under the bridge where the Christ sleeps, and takes a dump."

"Are not all sins, in themselves, their own punishment?" Blacktooth asked, impertinently. He thought he remembered Specklebird saying something like that during the nine days of prayer they had shared.

"Punishment like your congress with old Shard's daughter?" the Pope replied with a grin, and disappeared before Nimmy could say *that* was *not* a mortal sin.

Besides his illness of body and spirit, another factor discouraged flight. Just out of sight beyond the southern horizon another train was traveling eastward on a parallel course, and another might be coming behind it. There was too much chance of being caught. Dust from the other train was usually visible by day, and the glow of its wagoners' fires by night. A rare glimpse of the wagons and riders occurred when the train mounted a low hill in the distance. Some of the wagons flashed in the sunlight as if they were covered with metal, but with the heat and the distance even the hills seemed to be made of red-hot metal in the late light. The Nomad riders stayed clear of the mysterious train; they had been so ordered. No one to whom the monk talked knew much about it, except that it had departed from New Jerusalem after the Pope's train, and that someone who knew someone who knew Wooshin said that it carried secret weapons, and that it was under the command of Magister Dion.

A few days later, Blacktooth became aware that they had penetrated into tall-grass country. He knew it without looking up from where he lay on the feed sacks in the back of the bouncing hoodlum wagon. He knew because the bands of incoming warriors were beginning to speak the dialect of the Grasshopper, and their animals began to include dogs. The dogs were not immediately friendly to Wilddog Nomads, and were noisily hostile toward churchmen and New Jerusalemites. Because of the dogs, Blacktooth began sleeping inside the cramped hoodlum wagon instead of under it.

Pursued by a pack of the wolfish beasts, a screaming man leaped upon the tailgate of the hoodlum wagon one morning, and Blacktooth helped haul him inside. A snarling dog refused to let go of his shin. Librada shrieked. Cat and monk lunged for the dog at the same time. The man's shin was well wrapped in military leggings, but he kept

screaming until Blacktooth beat the dog off with a fagot and restrained the cat.

"Thank God! And thank you, Nimmy. I didn't know you were
with us."

"Aberlott! What in hell are you doing here?"

"I'm just here for the crusade. Wooshin let me join the team.
Damn, it's bleeding. Your cat did that."

"You've been on the train all along?"

"Sure, but this is the first day I've had free."

Blacktooth thought for a moment. When the Pope's party of
churchmen had left New Jerusalem, they brought with them seventeen wagons and an "elite" fighting team from the Suckamints, men
whose only loyalty to the Pope was guaranteed by their frightened
respect for Wooshin, their sergeant general—a rank created for the
occasion by the reigning Pontiff in a moment of whimsy. The wizened
old warrior wore gold chevrons and a star on his plaid tunic, which
Amen II had given him. That he had accepted Aberlott among his so-
called crack troops strained Nimmy's credulity, but the student swore
it was true. Blacktooth was glad for the company, at least for a day.

"Are you ready to run away again?" the student asked. "Like last
year?"

Nimmy snorted. "Last year, one mad cardinal was leading a
crowd of amateurs. This year, the Vicar of Christ is leading three
hordes of warriors and two small armies."

"Two? Where's army number two?"

"It's moving south of us."

"Oh, you mean the tanks. That's different. That's something I'm
not supposed to talk about, if I know anything, which I don't."

"Tanks? Secret weapons?"

"Water tanks for all I know. We'll need a lot of water."

While they marched across Grasshopper country and the Pope
watched the sky, the Burregun flew over the procession so often that it
became a Nomad joke. During this time, Pope Amen I appeared to
Blacktooth more than once, and warned him against continuing his
rebellion against his master. When he answered the old black cougar,
Bitten Dog the hood accused him of talking to himself, and he sent a
message to Wooshin saying that the monk needed a witch doctor. The
doctor who came turned out to be the Pope's personal physician, although the patient had never seen him before, and was unable to
guess to which of several schools of medicine the doctor belonged. He
wore Nomad leathers and he swore Nomad oaths under his breath, but

he carried a black bag full of pipes, needles, pincers, and charms, like a member of the ancient and mystical school of allopaths.

The doctor told him that the Pope was also not well, although he had not yet contracted the four-day fever, as it was being called. His symptoms reminded Blacktooth of Meldown. Blacktooth described the Venerable Boedullus's summonabisch stew. The doctor immediately claimed it was an old Nomad dish, and became enthusiastic when he learned that Brownpony had thrived on it. When he left Blacktooth, he went to see the cook. The reinstitution of summonabisch stew as a foundation of the papal diet was thus probably responsible for Blacktooth's elevation to the cardinalate when the Pope had another whimsical moment.

Because the movement of armies of horsemen was also a religious procession, each day must be begun with a sunrise Mass, and the Christians among the Nomads must be fed the bread of Heaven before the march resumed for the day. Out of deference to his Lord Høngan, Eltür Bråm put up with this sanctimony for a whole week before he went over his lord's head and asked the Pope's leave to lead his warriors on ahead as skirmishers. It was a bad idea only if one assumed the worst of the Grasshopper sharf. Brownpony had done his best to see the man without assumptions. The Pope took the sharf by the arm and led him into the tent of the Qœsach dri Vørdar.

Høngan Ösle Chür opposed the Grasshopper's request at first, but the Pope said, "There is merit in moving to separate a strong striking force from liturgical encumbrance, especially as we grow closer to the enemy. That enemy knows very well we are coming."

"That is true," said Holy Madness. "And what worries me most is that we don't see him doing anything about it. But I am not ready to relinquish my command to Sharf Bråm. With Holy Father's permission, I will take the sharf and as many of his warriors as he wants to bring, along with an equal number of Wilddog warriors under my command, and we shall advance as skirmishers toward the frontier."

The Pope turned to Wooshin, who quickly endorsed the plan, but added, "The Lord Høngan is right to worry. We must find out soon where the Texark force is massed, but skirmishers should avoid battle until our main force arrives."

"It is possible that they are embattled in the east," Brownpony suggested. "They dare not lose control of the Great River."

"If it is so," Axe said, "New Rome may not show much defense. Hannegan City will have the defense."

It was agreed then. At least six hundred warriors, part from each horde, stacked their arms for the Pope's later blessing and knelt beside the wagon tracks to pray at their last Mass before battle. Sharf Bråm and perhaps two hundred active disbelievers, both Grasshopper and Wilddog, waited on a distant hilltop for the Mass to end. The two forces then united and rode east.

Holding court in a field of sunflowers in the heart of Grasshopper country, the Pope mentioned the name of the next candidate for a papal battlefield promotion to the Sacred College, whereupon Wooshin went into a waking trance, while Jopo Cardinal Ombroz blinked and walked away uttering mysteries. The fall from grace by Blacktooth Brother St. George ended with a thud when the Pope—in a recurrence of the whimsy which had moved him to create the rank of sergeant general for his bodyguard—created Blacktooth St. George a Cardinal Deacon of Brownpony's old Roman Church, Saint Maisie's.

The monk was not immediately informed of this signal honor, for such announcements normally emerged from a full consistory, but he got wind of it in small whiffs, as when Aberlott first addressed him as "Your Eminence." Nimmy correctly attributed this to sarcasm. He therefore blamed Aberlott again when Wooshin rode back to the hoodlum wagon on the Pope's white stallion and used the same form of address.

"The Holy Father sends me to thank you for the special stew, and to ask about Your Eminence's health," said Axe.

Blacktooth glared quickly at Aberlott and responded, "I shit sixteen times a day, Axe. I'm weak. Every fourth day I have fits and Bitten Dog ties me up. Except for that, I'm very well, thank the Holy Father."

"I'll tell him you're dying," Wooshin grunted, and left. The physician returned that afternoon to check him over again.

"You have the Hannegan's science to thank for your illness," he told the monk. "Jackrabbit warriors brought the curse up to us from the south."

Sometimes the physician spoke Rockymount with a Grasshopper accent, and sometimes he spoke Grasshopper with a Rockymount accent. He made Nimmy eat bits of charcoal from a mostly dung fire and drink a slurry of its ashes. He put Blacktooth on a diet of meal boiled in milk, and gave him some bitter bark to chew. These measures could be either Nomad medicine or allopath remedy, but he blew *keneb* smoke toward the four quarters, mumbled a litany, and prescribed *keneb* to be smoked on Blacktooth's crazy days. The Pope apparently liked this medicine man, and Blacktooth was grateful to Brownpony for his care.

Before he left, the physician gave him a small package. "The Pope sent you this. I almost forgot."

Blacktooth neglected opening it. A gift from his former master would make him feel more guilt.

Sometimes he wanted to go to the Pope and prostrate himself as he had often done in his early years before Jarad and his brethren to obtain their forgiveness for putting a lizard in Singing Cow's bed, or for yodeling in choir; but that was within a brotherhood of equals under the Equalissimus. His present *laesae majestatis culpa* seemed much less forgivable. But that, of course, was before he opened the package and found the red hat. It was not the big red hat that was customarily nailed to the cathedral ceiling after the first wearing, but only an extra scarlet zucchetto borrowed from Chief Hawken Cardinal Irrikawa; it was identifiable by the hole in the brim through which the cardinal monarch inserted his feather.

"Now we shall have to ordain you deacon of Saint Maisie's," said Brownpony's note.

The Pope gave him three days to recover before summoning him to the head of the papal caravan. Blacktooth refused the honor. The Pope refused his refusal. "Put on the red cap," he said. "It means you get to vote for the next Pope. It is not a reward for holiness or good behavior."

"Then for the stew?"

"Not even for the stew of many blessings, Nimmy."

"A punishment for sin, then?" Blacktooth wondered.

"Ah! Symmetry. Either punishment or reward. You were always a symmetrical dualist, Nimmy."

"A symmetrical duelist?" asked the *Qæsach dri Vørdar*. "What is that, Holy Father?"

"Ambidextrous swordplay," the Axe told him in an aside.

Blacktooth was still holding the hat between thumb and forefinger as if it were dripping slime.

"Grab him, Axe," said the Pope.

Wooshin seized his shoulders. Brownpony took the zucchetto from his hand and centered it carefully upon his stubbly tonsure, then patted it down. When the sergeant general released him, his hand darted toward his head, but the Pope grabbed it and laughed.

"Do I have to wear it all the time?" asked Blacktooth Cardinal St. George, Deacon of Saint Maisie's.

.   .   .

When news of the war finally came, it came from the rear. Tex-ark cavalry had descended mysteriously out of nowhere to fall upon the Wilddog families in the west. They were dressed like motherless ones, and they made a great slaughter of the Weejus women and their breeding stock, the messenger said. At one family compound—that of Wetok Enar—there was a complete massacre, apparently to eliminate witnesses, but two daughters nevertheless survived, and one described a cavalry colonel with a wooden nose and long hair that covered his ears. The other, Potear Wetok, lived long enough to name her former husband, Colonel Esitt-of-Wetok Loyte, as the commander of the troop of Texark marauders. She had watched them shoot her whole family before he, full of hate, personally shot her in the lower spine so that her death was slow.

The Texarki seemed to know just which horses to kill among the breeding stock in order to ruin every Weejus as a breeder. Between murderous raids on family encampments the marauders were observed doing something to the Nomad cattle whenever they had made camp for the night.

When all this was reported to Brownpony, the Pope became sad but was not surprised. He looked at Hawken Irrikawa and said, "Your Majesty was right. They were Texarki you encountered in the north, although I'm surprised they made it that far west without encounter-ing the Wilddog."

He turned to Sharf Oxsho and said, "You'll have to take care of it." To Blacktooth, it sounded like neither a command nor a sugges-tion, but simply an observation about Oxsho's fate, or perhaps his own.

Sharf Oxsho called together the Wilddog warriors who had not ridden on ahead with the skirmishers. "There is a difference between being a shepherd to the Lord's sheep and a cowherd to Christ's wild cattle," Brownpony said mildly, as he watched a fourth of his army prepare to advance to the rear. He sent the Wilddog messenger on eastward to report the raids to the Lord Høngan Ösle.

Three days later Høngan returned to confer with the Pope and Wooshin. He brought no news from the east. No Texark patrols had been encountered, and even the motherless bandits were staying clear of the hordes as they advanced in battle array. The Grasshopper sharf had sent patrols toward Texark, but they had not yet returned when Høngin left the skirmish line to come here.

They took a census of the forces remaining to them after the homeward departure of Oxsho and his warriors. Their strength had diminished by a quarter. All leaders conferred, and were joined in conference by the spook commander from the secretive train to the south. There could be no change in the master plan. The strongest force would be directed southeast toward Hannegan City, as before, and only the force of the assault on the "protectors" of New Rome would be diminished.

But tonight the Pope determined that for a few hours, at least, there would be no more talk of war. Since leaving New Jerusalem, the same group of people always gathered around the Pope after supper on the trail. The summer nights were hot, and everyone sat well back from the fire, but close enough to hear and be heard. In the beginning the cardinals had wanted to say Compline at this time of evening, followed by religious silence. But the Pope objected to this as an imposition on non-Christian Nomad leaders who were part of his court, and he called this his "Curia Noctis," and encouraged the telling of stories. Tonight, he had determined that the subject would be saints and holy men, although anything but talk of war might be permitted.

Because Holy Madness was still with him, he sent for Cardinal Blacktooth to join them at the fire. The monk was too weak to walk alone. Axe gave him a shoulder to lean on, but at last carried him on his back to the Pope's vicinity.

"Where is your red hat?" Brownpony demanded.

"It was stolen by a holy man, Holy Father," said Blacktooth.

"Really? Who's the holy man, Your Eminence?"

"Your predecessor, Holy Father."

"You have been visited by Amen Specklebird, Brother St. George?"

"He comes to see me every fourth day."

"If so, he should have cured you. Tell him we need miracles to canonize."

"I don't think he wants to be made a saint."

"Why, Blacktooth! Nobody makes a saint. He is already a saint, or he isn't. And that is up to us to decide."

"Of course, Holy Father."

"Well, make him give you your hat back. Don't come back here without it."

Blacktooth confided in Wooshin. "Tomorrow is my crazy day. I already feel queer. Don't let me do anything disgraceful."

Some of the cardinals seemed to be dozing. There was a long silence at first. The Pope looked at Wooshin. The Axe cleared his throat, then offered a few words to open the session. "I admire the saints. You may not think so, Lords and Eminent Fathers, because I myself am not religious, but my people do honor holy men, and one of them was called Butsa. When he had squeezed his way out from his mother's gateway at birth, he stood erect. He pointed upward with one hand, down with the other, and said, 'Sky above, ground below, and I alone am the honored guest.' "

Ombroz laughed. "Every squealing baby says that before I baptize it. That's exactly what the kid's howling about. He is all too much the honored guest."

Sitting cross-legged, Axe smiled as if his point was made. He closed his eyes and became a sixteen-foot golden body, weighing seventeen tons. Then he vanished and became a blade of grass. Blacktooth noticed that Pope Amen I, having come earlier than expected, was standing in the fringes of the firelight. He had stopped there to piss. Having retucked his long black member into his robes, he slowly approached the fire—but he cautioned Nimmy by touching a finger to his quiet smile. It was plain that nobody else could see him. Blacktooth could even smell him, and he smelled like death.

Made nervous by the smiling Specklebird spirit, Blacktooth broke the silence.

"Saint Leibowitz spoke at birth too, you know," said the monk. "He stuck his head out of the birth canal and asked the midwife, 'Now what?'

"The midwife answered, 'For ninety-nine years, a great waste.' "

"Ag!" It was a low grunt from the Axe.

"Saint Isaac said, 'Begone!'

"She vanished. He lived ninety-nine years, you know."

The Pope smiled wryly. "Saint Leibowitz had the Devil for a midwife, then? Does this story come from the basement of Leibowitz Abbey?"

"You can find strange legends down there, Holy Father," Blacktooth admitted. "The earliest 'Life of Saint Leibowitz' was anonymous. A man could be hanged for writing a book. We have no bylines from those decades. But that's not the only story that connects Leibowitz with the Devil."

"Tell another," said the Pope.

"I can't, really. Did you ever hear of Faust, Holy Father?"

"I think not."

"It's about a pact with the Devil. We have only pieces of the story. I can't tell you why the Venerable Boedullus thought Faust was Leibowitz."

"Didn't the simpletons think he made a pact with the Devil?"

"Yes, but the Venerable Boedullus was no simpleton."

Amen II laughed. The word "simpleton" had come to be a polite form of address, and Nimmy had just asserted that Boedullus was no gentleman.

"I mean, he was not a Simplifier, who thought the Devil inspired all books except Scripture."

"And the Venerable Boedullus didn't think so?"

The questions were making Blacktooth dizzy. He watched Pope Amen II, who slowly and in a serpentine manner was becoming the sixteen-foot golden body of the idol Baal. Blacktooth after a moment of dizzy indecision lurched up to smash the Pope idol, until Wooshin objected. They took him to the hoodlum wagon bloody but unbowed, and they helped Bitten Dog tie him down. It was another day of the plague, and the war that disappeared only at the Curia Noctis.

During his dementia, the cougar Librada ran away.

CHAPTER 28

In time of famine, when the garden fails, when the brothers are eating yucca roots, cactus paddles, chaparral cocks, snakes, and the laying hens, and yet are near to starving, let the Abbot pray for Saint Benedict's blessing and allow them to eat the four-footed livestock, unless there be able hunters among them to stalk the wild blue-head goats.

Rule of Saint Leibowitz, Deviations 17

BBOTS WERE NOT ALL ALIKE. JEROME OF Pecos, abbot before the Conquest in the time of Pope Benedict XXII and Mayor Hannegan II, had thrown open the monastery gates to the world, and had allowed his sons to listen to natural philosophy lectures by practical atheists and play with electricity machines in the basement. What had happened to the religious vocation in that time, Abbot Olshuen could only wonder. The monks of Leibowitz Abbey under his guidance had kept themselves as unaware as possible of the changing world, including the controversial pontificates of the two Amens. Without offending the Pope, such isolation had not been possible under Abbot Jarad, who was also a cardinal, but Dom Abiquiu had discontinued Jarad's policy of letting the monks know about Church affairs outside the monastery. Always conservative in his interpretation of the *Rule of Saint Leibowitz*, the abbot withheld most news, including ecclesiastical news, of the outside world from his cloistered flock; the only monks he had told about the bull *Scitote Tyrannum* were the abbey's business manager and those Brothers native to Texark or the Province whose families were in the path of war, and these were told to keep silent.

But Amen II, when he marched out of New Jerusalem to conquer New Rome, sent Olshuen two letters. The first told him that he, the Servant of the Servants of God, was undertaking a Crusade to correct the errors of his beloved son, the Emperor, and that the S.o.S.o.G. needed the prayers of all the monks of Leibowitz to support this holy cause. The second letter ordered him to grant sanctuary at the abbey to a certain Sister Clare-of-Assisi in case she chose to avail herself of the Pope's clemency and return from her exile at the Monastery of the Nuns of Our Lady of San Pancho Villa of Cockroach Mountain south of the Brave River. Brownpony did not mention that Sister Clare was formerly Blacktooth's lover, but the abbot knew this anyway. Iridia Cardinal Silentia had visited Leibowitz Abbey on her way south. Olshuen had been startled to observe that the young Sister accompanying her was the same girl who had impudently flashed herself at him from the roadway the previous season before she followed the old Jew to the Mesa. He stirred unhappily at the memory, but the command to grant her a temporary refuge was the Pope's.

Olshuen was strict in matters of the rule, but he was neither a rebel nor an especially brave man. If he must lead his congregation in prayers for the Pope's intentions, he felt he must tell them about the Crusade. And if he must grant sanctuary anytime soon to a barefoot whore in an O.D.D. habit, he must begin construction immediately of a special extra cell.

The messenger who brought the Pope's letters to Olshuen had ridden as fast as possible to Leibowitz Abbey from New Jerusalem, and the next day he had to ride on south as fast as possible to San Pancho Villa Nunnery, evidently with a message of clemency for the girl.

Upon receipt of the Pope's letters, the abbot immediately sent a message of his own to New Jerusalem summoning Singing Cow home from his priory. This too was irregular. But the abbot needed to know how the departure of the Pope from his Suckamint Mountain sanctuary might affect the relations between the government of New Jerusalem and the monks of the Priory of Saint Leibowitz-in-the-Cottonwoods, a mission of the Order.

The special extra cell was a lean-to against the north wall of the guesthouse, but there was no door between them. Compared with the monks' cells, the whore-hut (as Olshuen thought of it) was luxurious, having its own running water, a charcoal stove for cooking or heating, a wooden tub for bathing, and an adjacent one-hole privy only three paces from a side door. Like the monks' cells, it had a cot with a straw mattress, one chair, one table for writing or eating, one prie-dieu for praying, and one crucifix before which to pray. A missal, a psalter, and a copy of the *Rule of Saint Leibowitz* were on the bookshelf. If the cook brought her food, the trollop would not need to leave the guest accommodations even for meals, unless she came to Mass, which the abbot considered unlikely.

The abbey had two guests already. One was Snow Ghost, a younger brother of Sharf Oxsho, who wanted to become a postulant. The other was Thon Elmofier Santalot, Sc.D., Vaq. Ord., who, besides being an associate professor at the Texark university, was a major in the Reserve Cavalry. His unit had been called to active duty, but he was on a leave to pursue his studies at the abbey, where he spent all his time in the vaults and the clerestory reading room, joining the monks only at meals and at Sunday's Mass. No one, not even the abbot, knew the purpose of his study at the abbey. Seventy-two years ago, Abbot Jerome would have begged him to tell them all. Now Dom Abiquiu begged him not to discuss anything with the monks.

Snow Ghost spoke no Ol'zark. Santalot spoke no Wilddog, although he had learned a little Jackrabbit while serving in the Province. Both of them knew a little Churchspeak. They had trouble communicating, but since they were enemies, this was just as well. Snow Ghost was already attending Mass and chanting the hours with the other monks in choir, although his habit was still being tailored for him. The abbot had warned him sternly against discussing politics with the Texark scholar, but the warning proved unnecessary. Snow Ghost seemed thoroughly afraid of the man.

Thon Santalot, whose life seemed to be driven by curiosity, became curious at this time as to why the extra cell was being built when the guesthouse was nearly empty. Snow Ghost could tell him nothing; Brother Carpenter said it was for a special visitor, and that was all he knew.

The expected trollop was never to occupy the extra cell, however. In late June, the old Jew who never died came out of the east and collapsed outside the gates. The abbot ordered him carried to the guesthouse, but when he began raving in Hebrew, Thon Santalot became frightened of him, and so Dom Abiquiu housed him in the whore-hut and fed him bread and boiled goat's milk.

Brother Medic was unable to diagnose the ancient hermit's illness, which seemed to abate on the day following his arrival. He insisted on going back to his mesa, but on the fourth day, before he got under way, he went wild again and had to be restrained. When he recovered temporarily from his fever, he insisted to Olshuen that he was a danger to the community, and exacted a promise of sanitary measures. He said he had caught the disease while traveling behind the lines in the Province, where he had sold military weather to both sides. He insisted that to prevent spreading the contagion, the doors and windows of his cell were to be covered with cloth to exclude insects. Knowing that old Benjamin had medical experience, the abbot readily consented.

When Elmofire Santalot heard of the nature of old Benjamin's illness, and where he caught it, the scholar went straight to the abbot's office. The abbot was out, so he gave the abbot's secretary a bottle of pills, explaining that he had needed them to avoid catching Hilbert's disease from the troops in the Province. The scholar was having a late breakfast in the refectory the following morning when Dom Abiquiu sat down beside him, placing the bottle of pills on the oak table.

"If you take one pill a day, it's a preventative," said the scholar. "Take twelve a day, for five days, it's a cure. You should have enough to give two pills to any monk who had contact with him."

"And you want me to give the rest to Benjamin?"

"If you want to save his life. It is not usually lethal, but he is so old and feeble . . ."

"Old yes, feeble no. But I don't understand how you happened to have these with you. You called it Hilbert's disease?"

Thon Santalot looked around the empty refectory. It was almost time for lunch. Beside the abbot, only Brother Cook and Brother Reconciliator were listening. "Thon Hilbert's disease is no longer a secret, really, I suppose. Our forces have prophylaxis—these pills—and the invaders don't."

"Go about your business," said the abbot to the other monks. When they were gone, he asked Santalot, "Are you saying that Hannegan's military is deliberately spreading the disease in the Province?"

"Certainly. Those who wage war have always used disease, Domne. Pestilence is one of the horsemen of the Apocalypse, is it not?"

Olshuen shook his head. "No. Well, there are various interpretations."

"You must remember that a sexual disease was one of the weapons used in the so-called Flame Deluge. A disease was used by Hannegan Two on the Plains back in the last century."

"But Hannegan's was a plague of cattle, not human beings."

"Well, yes, it is being used again on cattle. Horses too. That was part of Hilbert's work. He isolated the microorganisms. Today, we can infect the Nomad's animals directly, without driving diseased herds among them."

"How is that done?"

"I'm not sure. The cavalry carries it around in bottles. It can be sprayed from upwind, I think."

"You called it Hilbert's disease," murmured the abbot, who often became quiet when astonished. "Who is Hilbert?"

"Thon Brandio Hilbert is, or was, a brilliant epidemiologist, formerly occupying the Chair of Life Science at Hannegan University."

"Was? Formerly? Is he dead?"

"No, he's alive, but he's in jail. He conscientiously objected to the military use of his work. Well, here they come for lunch, Domne, and I must return to my research. Thank you, Brother Cook, for feeding me at this odd hour."

As they left the refectory, the abbot knelt to pray at the feet of the wooden figure of another conscientious objector who had founded the Order. Olshuen managed to pray for the Pope's soul and the Pope's beloved son errant, the Emperor, without mentioning victory in battle. He prayed only briefly, then returned to the refectory with his flock to consume his daily bread, red beans, and milk. Afterward, he took the pills to the old Jew.

The cure was effective. A week later, the patient returned to his mesa after leaving instructions for decontamination of the cell he had occupied. The procedure involved burning sulfur and leaving the cell vacant for several months, during which time it could not serve its designed purpose, if and when the need for a whore-hut arose.

If Singing Cow resented the abbot's midsummer summons, he kept it to himself, but his return from New Jerusalem did not seem a happy homecoming for him. Olshuen suppressed his eagerness for news of Brownpony's Crusade, for Cow seemed half-dead of heat exhaustion, and he let him rest for a day before interrogation. But on the following day, the prior of Saint Leibowitz-in-the-Cottonwoods claimed ignorance of the doings of the Papal Court. Further, said Father Moo, the relations between his priory and the government of Magister Dion could not be affected by the Crusade, because no such relations existed, by Brownpony's design. When Olshuen wanted to discuss Sister Clare-of-Assisi, Singing Cow knew her only as Blacktooth's Ædrea; and since this knowledge had come to him through the confessional he would say nothing about her, nor would he listen patiently to the abbot's gentle slanders.

The abbey had accepted seven Jackrabbit refugees as postulants that season, so Singing Cow's old cell was occupied. The abbot put him in the guesthouse with the Wilddog postulant and Thon Elmofier Santalot after telling him what Santalot had said about Hilbert's disease. Father Moo remained expressionless. Dom Abiquiu went away with a faint smile. He had not asked Singing Cow to question the scholar.

Three weeks elapsed, and no one else at the abbey became infected. Singing Cow requested permission to return to Leibowitz-in-the-Cottonwoods. Olshuen realized that it had been a minor mistake to summon him, but he was reluctant to let him go without putting him to good use first.

"I want you to go over all the work that Brother St. George left behind, not only the Boedullaria, but also the Duren manuscripts, and see if you can make a glossary. . . ."

A cloud of dust arose far to the south of Sanly Bowitts. At the time, three novices happened to be standing on the parapet wall, where they were recording the altitude and azimuth of the sun for comparison with an ephemeris; the purpose was to reset the monastery's clock. A coach escorted by two men on horseback emerged from the distant dust and entered the village, then reappeared a few minutes later on the road toward the monastery. The novices watched, transfixed, as the richly decorated coach stopped outside the gate and the two uniformed soldiers of the Laredan King opened the doors, whence emerged Sister Clare-of-Assisi, an unknown Sister, and the cardinal herself, Mother Iridia Silentia, O.D.D.

"Five for the guesthouse," someone called out.

It was after the evening meal and almost time for Compline. Iridia Silentia appeared at the abbot's office, but seemed reluctant at first to sit down. She seemed nervous but full of enthusiasm.

"Sister Clare is a vessel of the Holy Spirit, Domne. I am certain of it. The reason I am certain is that she cannot command this talent, and she will not pretend to heal when she can't. She is deeply sympathetic, and in some cases it might be helpful to pretend to be healing someone whose ailment is partly emotional. But she will not pretend."

"Does she attribute it to God?"

"I think it would not be prudent to ask her that," the cardinal said sharply, and Dom Abiquiu reddened. Iridia finally sat down. "If she said yes, she would become a problem for the Church. If she said no, she would become a problem for the Church. This is why we cannot accept such a treasure in our community. She has taken our vows, walked on our stones with her bare feet, prayed with us, eaten God's Body with us, and we quickly came to love her. But she is a treasure, and she has to be released."

"Did Brother St. George know about this talent?"

"She told me she had teased him. I think she meant she showed him her gift, in minor ways. You can see how we cannot have anyone special in our midst except the Lord."

"So you have brought her to me."

It was the cardinal's turn to blush. "Because the Pope told me to . . . No, not quite. The Pope told me to send her here if she wished to leave us. I decided she should go, and I helped her to wish it, and I brought her myself. If I sent her, I would not be able to tell you about her."

"You could have written a letter."

"I could not have written a letter, nor can you put anything at all about her in writing unless you want to destroy her. Don't you see?"

Dom Abiquiu was briefly silent. "Like asking her if her gift is from God or not?"

The cardinal smiled warmly, causing the abbot's heart to squirm.

"She needs to go home, if the Mayor's son will let her. You need keep her here only until the Holy Father can arrange it."

"You are aware that the Holy Father is otherwise occupied?"

Silentia ignored Olshuen's irony. "I'll tell Sister Clare that she must avoid talking to anyone outside the guesthouse."

"There is one of our postulants in the guesthouse."

"Then she must—"

"But I'll get him out. Who is the other Sister?"

"My assistant. She will return with me to San Pancho."

Brother Liveryman appeared in the doorway, caught the abbot's eye, and in response to the abbot's nod asked: "Domne, did you tell our guests to choose their own rooms?"

"Yes, of course. Is there a problem?"

"Only that one of the nuns chose the, uh, isolation cell."

"You must get her out of there! It's not safe yet."

"She said it was built for her. I don't know what she meant."

The cardinal studied the abbot's expression for a moment and said, "I think I know." She arose. "Well, Domne. I am very tired and would like to retire. If I may be excused, I shall say Compline alone in my room. I'll speak to my student. I do thank you for all."

Student? The word lingered in the abbot's office behind her.

. . .

That evening, Sister Clare abandoned the abbot's whore-hut for a cell in the guesthouse with the others, saying that she knew it had been meant for her originally, but that she had been unaware of the quarantine. Singing Cow suppressed his curiosity about her and said nothing.

Three nuns, two soldiers, a scholar from Texark, a Nomad who was a possible postulant, and Father Singing Cow now shared the guesthouse. Ædrea stayed in her cell except when they all went to the refectory or to Mass together. The cardinal, her assistant, and the Wilddog Nomad Snow Ghost were often absent from the building, presumably singing the Divine Office with the Brothers. Singing Cow was busy in the Scriptorium making a glossary from the work of Brother Blacktooth, and Thon Elmofier Santalot was usually busy searching the bookshelves in the basement, or reading and making notes in the clerestory. The Laredan soldiers were left alone most of the time, with Ædrea staying behind a closed door. One of the soldiers rode into Sanly Bowitts on the second day and brought back a jug of local hooch. When the soldiers were both solemnly drunk, the bolder of them knocked upon the pretty nun's door and offered her a drink.

Ædrea opened the door, took the proffered jug, tilted it, and swallowed mightily.

"Thank you, Corporal Browka," she said with a smile, then closed the door and clicked the latch.

Browka knocked again, but there was no answer. "You saw her smile at me?"

Father Moo and the Nomad youth returned from church, and soon after, Santalot came in. The soldiers offered everyone a drink, but there was little left in the jug and no one accepted. The cardinal came in and sat down in the reading room for a moment before retiring. The soldiers hid the jug and pretended to be sleeping.

"We shall leave here after Lauds in the morning," said Mother Iridia. "We must all thank the monks for their hospitality." She was speaking Churchspeak, which was the only common language among the monastery's guests. The soldiers spoke it poorly, but as soldiers they were very curious about the military campaigns of the present Pope, and had many questions, asked and unasked. In two days at the abbey, they had learned very little.

In the morning, after a last conference with the abbot, Mother Iridia bade her student a tearful goodbye and she and her servants departed. Ædrea cried in her cell for an hour after they were gone. She shared the guesthouse now with Singing Cow, Snow Ghost, and Elmofier Santalot the scholar. Abbot Olshuen told Snow Ghost he could now move to a cell in the dormitory, but Snow Ghost resisted, saying he was not yet quite ready for silence and solitude. Surprised, the abbot glanced quickly at Ædrea, as if he wondered whether the Nomad was not quite ready for chastity either, but he did not press it. Nomad vocations were rare, and except when Singing Cow was present, Brother Wren, the abbey's cook, had no one to talk to in his own tongue or a related dialect.

It was during the Feast of Saint Clare, one year after her taking her vows, from which she was now released, that Ædrea Sister Clare-of-Assisi performed a miracle in the guesthouse of Leibowitz Abbey.

In late August Brother Wren got permission to visit Singing Cow in the guesthouse, and Ædrea Sister Clare-of-Assisi became aware that Brother Cook had a cancer eating his throat. His voice had diminished to a hoarse whisper. He called his cancer Brother Crab, and joked about it. Ædrea came up behind him as he sat and talked with his old friend, Moo. He started up as she touched him, but then settled back in his chair with a smile and let her hands explore his throat. He started again when she pressed down hard with her fingertips below his Adam's apple.

"Relax, Brother. Does it hurt?"

"Not much," Wren whispered. "What have you done? Something popped."

She continued caressing his throat for a while, then left him and went to her cell. Father Moo crossed himself. Brother Wren noticed and followed suit.

"Better not tell anyone," Singing Cow said.

Within three days, Wren began to get his voice back. Word got around. Within a week, Sister Clare had healed infected blisters, a hernia, an abscessed tooth, and a probable case of gonorrhea of the eye. All this might have passed unnoticed, but when she cured the old librarian, Brother Obohl, of his myopia and he got a look at the beautiful woman who had laid hands on his eyes, his squawk of astonishment was followed by the joyful noise of his thanksgiving, and this fell upon the ears of Dom Abiquiu.

Singing Cow was present in the guesthouse when the abbot strode to the closed door of Ædrea's cell.

"I told you not to mix with the monks."

"I have not mixed with the monks."

"Cardinal Silentia forbade you to practice your healing tricks."

Sister Clare opened her door. "Beg pardon, Domne, but she did not. I do not have any healing tricks."

"You argue with me! Where is your religious training?"

"You prefer Brother Librarian half blind?"

"It was my fault, Domne," put in Father Moo. He ventured a lie: "I sent him to her."

"What?" Olshuen gasped and paused for self-control. "You are not to lay hands on anyone else while you are here. Do you understand?"

"Yes, Domne."

"Will you obey?"

"Yes, Domne."

The abbot glared at Singing Cow. "I think it is about time you returned home."

"Thank you, Domne." As soon as Dom Abiquiu was gone, he said, "Alleluia!"

Sister Clare smiled. "Will you carry a message to my family and the Mayor when you go?" she asked.

But Singing Cow had not yet departed when her wounds began to appear. When Ædrea went to Mass, she knelt in the back of the church behind a pillar where she was not visible to the monks in the choir. Thus she always left the church first. Following her back to the guesthouse, Singing Cow noticed dark spots in the prints of her bare feet in the sand. When she walked across the guesthouse floor, the blood was even more apparent. He called out to her, asking how she had hurt her feet.

The young nun stopped, pulled up the skirt of her habit, and looked down. She stared, then looked back at Father Moo. When she lifted her hand to her face, he saw that the palm was bloody. She seemed very confused.

"Who hurt you, Sister?"

Her voice trembled. "I don't know. It was dark. I think it was the Devil. He was wearing a robe like yours."

"What? Someone actually attacked you?"

"It's like a dream. There was a hammer—" She stopped, looked at him wildly, then bolted into her cell and latched the door. Singing Cow could hear her praying. He went to look for Dom Abiquiu, whom he found praying before the wooden Leibowitz in the corridor.

"She said it was like a dream," Father Moo told him. "But she thinks somebody with a hammer, maybe the Devil—"

"Was she raped?"

"She didn't say anything about it."

"Let's go. Did you tell Brother Pharmacist?"

"He is on his way."

The pharmacist had already arrived when they entered the guest-house. The door to Ædrea's cell was open, and she was lying on her cot. As they started to enter, the pharmacist pushed them back outside, joining them and closing the door behind him.

"Her wounds?" the abbot whispered.

"The wounds of Christ," the medic answered softly.

"What are you talking about?"

"The wounds of the nails. The wound of the spear."

"The stigmata? You're saying the female, the, uh, Sister, has the stigmata?"

"Yes, she does. The cut in her side is clean. The wounds in her hands and feet have bruised blue edges. She speaks of a hammer."

"Devil!" It was as close as Olshuen ever came to swearing. He turned and walked out of the guesthouse with Singing Cow at his heels.

"Retaliation!" he spat. "Retribution!"

"Excuse me? What do you mean, Domne?"

"I forbade her to use healing powers. This is her answer."

Singing Cow was silent for several moments as they walked toward the convent, then he shook his head. "Domne, I am leaving tomorrow for home."

Abbot Olshuen stopped. "Without asking permission?"

"You already gave it, remember?"

"Of course." The abbot turned on his heel and walked away, alone.

A few hours later, when Brother Wren St. Mary came to inquire about a change in the diet for the sick, he found Abiquiu Olshuen lying on the floor of his office. He could not move his right leg. When he tried to speak, he squawked.

Brother Pharmacist came directly to the infirmary where Wren had carried Olshuen.

"Is it a stroke, Brother?" Wren asked.

"Yes, I'm afraid it is."

The abbey had its own prior again, and Father Devendy was immediately summoned, along with Singing Cow. Wren went back to the kitchen.

Prior Devendy turned to Prior Singing Cow. "Can you get the Sister who heals to come?"

"You know about her?"

"Dom Abiquiu told me what Mother Iridia told him. I know he was alarmed, but—he may die, you know."

"I'll go ask her. She was, uh, injured, you know. Did Brother Medic tell you?"

"No," put in the pharmacist.

"Describe the wounds to Father Devendy," Father Moo told him, "but don't interpret them."

"I understand. Make sure she wears shoes of some kind and doesn't walk on the bandages."

Singing Cow glanced at the abbot. Dom Abiquiu was shaking his head from side to side with his eyes closed. It meant nothing, Moo decided.

Cow found a small pair of sandals in the storeroom. They were very old and might once have belonged to him or to some other adolescent Nomad whose feet had not finished growing. He took them to Sister Clare and told her they might once have been Blacktooth's. She said nothing to that, and put them on without protest.

"Where are we going, Father?"

"To see Dom Abiquiu. He needs you."

Ædrea had become accustomed to obedience, and came without asking why she was needed. When she limped into the infirmary and approached the bed, Dom Abiquiu groaned mightily and shrank back from her, his eyes wide and his face a mask of dread. He used his left hand to shield his eyes from her. Ædrea stopped and stared.

"Oh, pigs!" she said abruptly, and crossed herself with a bandaged hand. "There is nothing I can do for him."

"What do you mean?" asked Prior Devendy.

"I mean I can't do it tonight. And he told me not to do it again anyway." She turned and started to leave the room.

"Sister Clare, please, he may be dying," said Singing Cow.

She crossed herself again, but walked on down the corridor without looking back.

The next day, she was missing from the guesthouse, and her small traveling bag was not in her cell. No one had seen her leave, but there was a note on her bed: *I'm sorry about your abbot. Thank you for your hospitality. God bless.*

No one knew where she had gone. On his way back to New Jerusalem, Singing Cow stopped in the village of Sanly Bowitts to ask about her. She had been seen going toward the Mesa of Last Resort. He followed the trail to the foot of the cliff. Once he found a spot of blood on a stone, but no other sign of her. She was with Benjamin, then. Father Moo was certain the old Jew would cure her of the Lord's stigmata. Feeling a little guilty for abandoning her and Dom Abiquiu, he steered his mule toward the papal highway leading north. It was already September and he traveled by the dark of the moon.

CHAPTER 29

Just as there is an evil zeal of bitterness
which separates from God and leads to hell,
so there is a good zeal which separates from
vices and leads to God.
—*Saint Benedict's Rule*, Chapter 72

LACKTOOTH CARDINAL ST. GEORGE, DEACON OF
Saint Maisie's, was on the hillside taking
a long and painful dump, his first of
many for the day, when he heard the *pop
pop pop* of repeating guns. It was coming
from the main encampment, in the
wooded bend of a wide, shallow creek
back over the hill.

Blacktooth couldn't see the camp
from where he was standing, or rather, squatting. For his morning
ritual, which was the only one he found the leisure to perform in
privacy, he preferred the western slope of the little bluff, a hill so small
that it barely cleared the trees. Truth was, Blacktooth was homesick.
Not for a particular place; he had never had anything even approxi-
mating a home except for Leibowitz Abbey, and while he sometimes
(indeed, fairly often) missed the companionship of the Brothers and
the security of the routine and the Rule, he never missed the abbey

itself. He was homesick for the desert, the grasslands, the country of Empty Sky.

Even though he could see nothing to the west but more trees, Blacktooth knew there was open land beyond—rolling plains that went on and on, treeless and townless like Eternity itself. And the sky seemed definitely bigger to the west.

Unsmiling, unspeaking, unlimited.

From here I greet you, Empty Sky.

Pop pop pop.

Blacktooth stumbled as he stood up, hurriedly wiping himself with a wad of grass—then slowed, no longer alarmed, recognizing the sound. It was celebratory, ceremonial, not real; not a firefight. The Grasshopper sharf's warriors, disciplined for firing the precious brass cartridges but bored by the lack of military action, had perfected the art of imitating the sound of the new repeating "Pope rifles." As with everything the Nomads tried, they had quickly learned to do it well.

Blacktooth had first noticed it in the outriders returning from a scouting mission a few days before; he had remarked to his boss, Bitten Dog, that the warriors were mimicking the sound of the brass shell-firing guns from across the sea. "Imitate the sound of pots being scoured, Your Eminence," Bitten Dog had growled.

The *pop pop pop* was joined by the sound of dogs. It was not barking but the alarming half-howl, half-growl of war dogs being brought up on leash. All this was coming from the camp of the Pope's armies down at the edge of the trees, in the bend of the creek called Troublesome or Trouble Some. Attempting to shade his eyes from the early-morning, late-September sun, tying his habit back around him with his booklegger's cord, Blacktooth crossed the crest of the hill and started down toward the camp. He took off his sandals and carried them, so that he could walk barefoot in the pleasantly wet grass. Through the trees, he could see horses milling and stomping, warily watching the dogs that circled them like a dust devil.

The *pop pop pop* was punctuated by whoops and cries, and Blacktooth could see the Grasshoppers now, painted up, pumping their weapons into the air. More than a small party, too.

Something was afoot; or rather, a-horse.

Blacktooth was almost glad. For several weeks now, on the final approach to New Rome, the tension had been growing among the Nomad warriors that had attached themselves to the Pontiff's crusade. As the twelve-hundred-strong party, now fully a day's march long, crawled east, the arms of trees extending out into the prairies had become more numerous, longer and thicker, until it had changed—in a day, and Blacktooth remembered the day—into arms of prairie extending into trees. It was like an optical illusion; one thing turning, with a trick of the eye, into its opposite.

As they left the tall-grass country and began to penetrate the woodlands, the warriors had expected resistance from the Texark troops Hannegan II had—supposedly—left behind to guard the approaches to the Holy City. There had been none. The warriors had expected resistance from the semi-settled Grasshopper farmers, and the settlers Filpeo had sent to live among them. There had been none. Foraging horsemen had found nothing but abandoned farms, barns burned or burning, cattle killed or driven away, leaving behind only their footprints or their still-soft droppings. The log homesteads were burned or looted, sad-looking little homes bereft of even doors or window glass. The Grasshoppers in particular had looked forward to breaking glass, and this made them even more impatient. The contemptible grass-eaters had either broken or taken their windows with them.

The new cardinal was as firmly attached to the hood wagon as the old monk had been, but several times Blacktooth had deserted his pots and pans and explored one or two of the abandoned houses, hoping perhaps—although he never admitted this to himself—to find signs of Librada, his glep cougar that had freed herself before he could set her free. But Librada didn't eat carrion and the few farmers and farm families Blacktooth had found had been mostly carrion. Several times he had watched as parties of the Nomad horsemen, singing death songs and seated well forward on their ponies, had gone out into the trees—nervously at first and then with growing confidence, finally with boredom. The countryside around New Rome had been stripped of its people. There were no warriors to fight, no women to rape or even to be restrained from raping. Nothing but trees, dumber than horses and stiller than grass. The farmers—many of them of Grasshopper origin—had deserted their farms, and whatever troops Hannegan II had left in the region to defend the city were gone as well.

In fact, some said it was the troops that had driven the farmers away. An old man found wounded on his barn floor, and brought back to the camp to die, had told the Pope and his Curia that it was the Texark soldiers who had shattered his window glass and torched his fields, and his neighbors' as well, but Blacktooth thought he was lying. Or at least partially lying. Truth was as rare as beauty in wartime. It occurred by accident, in unexpected places; like the glint of sun off a button on a corpse.

Pop pop pop.

And now, some action at last. Blacktooth felt like two men: one who dreaded the excitement, and one who desired it; one Brother who slipped eagerly down the hillside toward the milling horses, and one who held back, heels digging into soft dirt. He valued the hilltop because it carried him above, or almost above, the trees. Descending into them was like descending into a prison.

Pop pop pop. One of the shots, at least, sounded real. Perhaps the Texark main force had been located by a scouting party, and a battle was planned for the day. It would have to be to the east. As he half slipped and half walked down the hill, Blacktooth squinted out across the sun-bright ranks of trees. Beyond them was New Rome, within a day's ride at most. And beyond the city, also unseen, was the Great River—the Misspee, the grass-eaters called it. Blacktooth had dreaded the Crusade's arrival for months but now he looked foward to it, even if it meant a battle. Much to his eternal regret, Blacktooth knew battle; and he knew that even worse than the fighting was the long waiting, the constant tension, and the heavy smells of men on the move.

The camp smelled like shit and smoke. It smelled like Hilbert's fever, the bowel-emptying sickness that Blacktooth shared with at least a third of the men, Nomad and Christian alike. The smell had thickened as the tall grass had turned to trees, as the world of Empty Sky had given way to a world folded in branches, hedged by trees. Darkness and mud and stumps and shit—in greater and greater profusion as the Pope's Crusade approached New Rome. The Mother Church was coming home.

Pop pop pop!

Down in the camp, the huge night fire had been rekindled. Logs as big as corpses smoldered and smoked, as reluctant as corpses to flame back into life. Everything here in the woodlands was damp. The edge of his habit wet from the long grass, Blacktooth joined the milling crowd around the fire pit at the center of the camp. Horses and people and dogs made an uneasy mix. More warriors came from the smaller Wilddog and Grasshopper campfires, joined by the *Qæsach dri Vørdar* and his personal guard. Nomad warriors were spitting into the fire and stomping, and firing their imaginary shots toward the impenetrable gray of the sky. It looked like rain again; it had threatened rain now for a week.

The Grasshopper sharf, Eltür Bråm, came out of the trees, holding up his repeating rifle, joined by a squat shaman in an intricate hat riding a white mule.

Pop pop pop.

Brownpony was conspicuously absent, but a small contingent of his Papal Guard joined the party, leading uncomfortable-looking horses. Their rifles were identical to the ones the Wilddog warriors carried. Blacktooth was surprised to see Aberlott among them.

"Don't look so sad, Your Eminence," said the pudgy Valana student, holding a repeating rifle anything but sheepishly.

"Where are you going?" Blacktooth asked, ignoring his old friend's sarcasm.

"To get a biscuit." Aberlott gestured toward the morning wagon, where there was a line, all Wilddog and Grasshopper; or rather, all men with guns. "Come."

Wooshin, the Axe, was in the morning-wagon line and he let Aberlott and Blacktooth in beside him. This was, Blacktooth knew, acceptable practice among the Nomads, who regarded every man as an extension of his friends and family. If a man was in line, his connections were in line as well.

"Morning, Axe."

"Good morning, Cardinal Nimmy. Why so sad?"

Do I really look so sad? Blacktooth wondered. He shrugged. Perhaps it was the sickness. It seemed he had been sick for years, although he knew by the marks he had made on the inside of the hood wagon that it was only two weeks.

"Maybe it is war," he said. "War makes men sad."

"Some men," said Aberlott. He reached up under his long hair and touched, as if for luck, the little knob of gristle where his right ear had been sliced off by Texark cavalry.

"All men," said Axe.

The line crept forward, feet sucking in the mud which seemed to be always laying in wait, even under what looked like dry grass.

"Perhaps His Eminence is mooning over his little lost cat," said Aberlott to Axe.

"She's not so little," said Blacktooth, "and I wish you would stop calling me His Eminence."

"Sorry, Cardinal," said Aberlott. It was his turn. He took two biscuits and gave one to Blacktooth. Apparently they were distributing extra biscuits only to the men with rifles. Blacktooth took it grudgingly. Life was difficult enough without Aberlott's continual sarcasm.

He followed Axe and Aberlott back to the fire, which was now blazing.

"It's a war party," said Aberlott. "The early patrols, Wilddog I think, entered the city yesterday. There was no resistance. Today we go in with Eltür Bråm and his shaman." He nodded toward the old man on the white mule. "Maybe we'll get to see the basilica of Saint Peter's."

"You're going?" Blacktooth asked.

"With permission. Along with most of the Pope's Guard," said Aberlott, glancing toward Wooshin, the Pope's sergeant general, who shrugged. Wooshin was staying behind with his master.

Aberlott held up his rifle, pumping it toward the sky as the Nomad warriors did. "Pop pop pop," he said, but not convincingly. He smiled, showing Blacktooth his bad teeth, and opened his hand, showing three brass shells. "His Greatness the Sharf didn't want to take us but His Holiness, Pope Amen II, insisted. We are his eyes and ears."

"And rifles," Blacktooth said.

"That too."

It was looking more and more like rain. Blacktooth secured his cardinal hat under the cover of the hood wagon—he was afraid the red would run if it did rain—and gathered up the morning pots and pans that had been left for him by Bitten Dog. His elevation as the Crusade's tenth cardinal had not released him from his duties as assistant to the assistant potscrubber. Nor had it reduced the intensity or frequency of the fevers that raged through his body.

A third of the camp, almost a thousand men, were sick. The rich smell of human excrement mixed with the usual camp smells of horse and smoke. The overall feeling was one of gloom. Maybe it will rain, Blacktooth thought, as loaded down with pots and pans he stepped over and around the ubiquitous dog turds. Better rain than threatening rain. Impermeable to almost every kind of adversity, the Nomads seemed to fold up in the rain.

He finished the pots, scrubbing them with sand in the feeder creek that ran from under a slab, out of a thousand-year-old drain. He took the long way back to the hood wagon, between the Pope's carriage ("LIKE HELL YOU WILL") and the gleaming metal wagons of Magister Dion's caravan, which had joined them two days before, where the long arms of the door prairies were merging into one narrower and narrower grassy swale, interrupted by pitches of shattered concrete and stone.

This morning was the first time Blacktooth had seen Dion's wagons up close, in the daylight. They looked like stoves on wheels. "Tanks," Aberlott had called them, but who would carry water from the dry plains to the rainy east? They were clearly weapons of some kind.

A glep was dozing on the seat of one of the wagons. When he saw Blacktooth he smiled an idiot smile and crossed himself, laughing. Blacktooth thought the man was mocking him, until he saw Brownpony standing with Dion, almost out of sight behind one of the metal wagons. They seemed to be arguing and Dion seemed to be getting the worst of it. Blacktooth couldn't see Brownpony's face but he recognized the slow hand movements of lawyerly persuasion passing into papal compulsion. The monk, now cardinal, turned away and hurried on toward the center of the campsite. He knew that he would be in trouble if Brownpony saw him without his zucchetto.

It was late afternoon before the rain finally came. The clouds that had been massing in the northwest all day, like riders on a hilltop, descended just when the Grasshopper sharf's party was returning. There was no *pop pop pop* this time, no strutting horses. The warriors looked gloomy and damp. One of the horses carried double, and the white mule carried a corpse tied on like a pack and left uncovered in the rain. The side of the mule was pink with rain and blood.

"The sharf's shaman," Aberlott said to Blacktooth, who was helping him dismount. He tried to hand the monk his rifle but Blacktooth wouldn't take it.

"Texark troops?"

Aberlott shrugged. "Snipers," he said. "They fired on us from the great houses."

"Great houses?"

"Piles of stone, really, although some of them still have windows. We have the better guns but we couldn't see them. We never saw any Texark troops."

Four women untied the shaman and carried him away. The dogs were howling, straining at their leashes and jumping up to sniff the side of the white mule that was smeared with blood.

"They must have been Texark troops," said Blacktooth.

"I don't think so. There was a lot of fire but they only hit two men, and we were all in the open. I was right behind the shaman when he fell. He was singing some Weejus song, and they shot him through the throat. I think it was a lucky shot."

"Lucky?" said Blacktooth.

"Lucky for someone; not so lucky for him." Aberlott showed Blacktooth three empty cartridges, nestled in his palm like little empty eggshells. "I fired all three of my shots, though. I liked that part. Not like you." He was referring to Blacktooth's depression after killing the glep warrior in the battle two days' march behind, at the edge of the grasslands, almost a year before. "I fired all three, pop pop pop."

It was Blacktooth's turn to shrug.

"I liked that part," Aberlott insisted.

Aberlott had been more impressed with the city than with the fighting. The city of New Rome wasn't a hole in the ground like Danfer, he said, or a collection of shacks like Valana. It was mostly stone, grown over with weeds and trees. "The center of the city is all great houses. They mine them for stone and steel. They don't care about defending them either. What is there to defend? What can you carry off? You can't fight men who won't fight."

"They fought you," said Blacktooth.

"That wasn't fighting," said Aberlott. "There wasn't that much firing, even. They are hiding in the city, taking pot shots at us."

"Did you find the cathedral?"

Aberlott shook his head. "We rode out behind the sharf. Who will burn them out, he says, and toss their livers to the dogs." He smiled sardonically, gesturing behind him to the center of the camp where the dismounted Nomads were milling angrily, confused, ashamed. A wail came up from the women tending the wounded man. The wounded man was dying. He had been shot in the side with a gun that fired stones.

Blacktooth left Aberlott for the medicine wagon where the wounded man was being bandaged. He was wondering if the Texarks had managed to duplicate the repeating weapons yet, and he imagined that he might be able to tell from the man's wound. But the wound was just a wound and not a sign; it did not speak. The ugly welt cut through the Nomad's flesh and hair like a road ripped heedlessly through grassland. In the back of the wagon the Grasshopper shaman's body was being prepared for burial. The old man's neck wound was already stuffed with clay the color of shaman skin.

Ashes to ashes, dirt to dirt. Both men would be carried out of the trees for burial under the haughty uncaring glare of Empty Sky. But not until the rain had ended.

The women and the medicine men shooed Cardinal Blacktooth away, even though he was wearing his zucchetto.

The next day a smaller party went out, while the Grasshopper war sharf met with the *Qœsach* and the Pontiff. As a member of the Curia, Blacktooth was invited to take part in the discussion, after he had finished the pots and pans, of course, and freed Bitten Dog for a day of drinking mare wine and playing bones. Brownpony's suspicion that the Emperor had withdrawn all his regular forces from the Holy City was confirmed when the rear guard of Eltür Brâm's war party came back with its only live captive, a farmer armed with a stone-firing musket. He had been dragged from one of the "great houses," along with two of his colleagues who had not survived the ten-mile trip back to the Crusade's war camp. Under questioning the grass-eater revealed that he and the other farmers had been driven from their homesteads into the city by the Texark regulars, then armed with leftover weapons and stationed in the tallest ruins. They had been told that if they surrendered they would be cruelly tortured by the Anti-pope's Wilddog, Grasshopper, and Jackrabbit fanatics; but that if they held out they would be rescued by returning Texark reinforcements from Hannegan City.

Brownpony doubted that the last part of this was true; so did the rest of his Curia. As for the torture, the farmer died before he could be convinced that it was propaganda.

Aberlott thought it was a trap. "But you think everything is a trap," Blacktooth reminded his friend. The two were sitting on the side of a wagon, in the unfamiliar sunshine, listening to the interminable martial speeches of the Nomads. Even though the speeches decided nothing, they had to be suffered by the Pope and his Curia.

"Everything *is*," whispered the former Valana student. His long hair was smeared with grease, and tied back to show his missing ear: a badge of honor. He held his repeating rifle between his legs. Though he was, technically at least, a member of the Papal Guard, he wore the bone earrings and hair bracelets of a Wilddog horseman. He looked, Blacktooth thought, like a man who had avoided the trap of the Mother Church only to fall into the trap of war.

"We can wait them out," Brownpony was saying. His Nomadic had gotten better and he no longer needed Blacktooth as translator. "If they were driven into the city, chances are they don't have enough food to last through the winter."

"The winter?" said the Grasshopper sharf. "The winter is far away. Our women are far behind, and like the Wilddogs they are threatened by the motherless ones who strike from above the Misery. Without the Weejus our medicine is weak but our war power is strong. We must strike now while we can. We can take them with just a few men. We can burn them out."

Grunts of pleasure and assent greeted these words. Wettened fingers were held up, as if to confirm that the prevailing winds were from the west. The fingers were also, for the Nomads, a signal of impending fire; of their willingness to watch the world burn.

Amen II stood, looking unusually ethereal and spiritual. When Blacktooth had seen him the day before, he had not realized how sick he looked. Brownpony's hair was mostly gone. His face looked like something drawn on an egg; a bad egg. "This is the Holy City of New

Rome," he said in measured Churchspeak. "It is sacred to the Mother Church. There will be no burning. We are here to take the city, not destroy it."

He sat back down. There was grumbling as his words were translated into Grasshopper and Wilddog. The grumbling fell silent as the *Qæsach dri Vørdar*, the War Sharf of the Three Hordes, stood to speak.

"We were going to feint south for Hannegan City," said Chür Høngan Ösle. "There is the heart of the Empire, not New Rome, which is nothing but a ruin. We will still head south. But now instead of feinting we can actually *strike* south. Now that we know there are few defenders in New Rome, we have more men to strike south at Hannegan City. The war will be over sooner. We can return to our women and our winter pastures." He spoke in Wilddog with only a few words of Rockymount and none of Churchspeak. Blacktooth thought it was ominous. The Crusade was becoming less of a crusade, and more a depredation of the Three Hordes.

There were grunts and clicks of approval from the Nomads as the *Qæsach* sat down. He had a boy behind him to arrange his robes when he sat; another watched the feathers on his headdress in case of wind. The numbers of the Nomads had increased, so that now men (and a few women and children as well) stood on all sides of the wagon on which Blacktooth was sitting. It had turned from a meeting of the Curia to a public meeting attended by warriors and drivers and hangers on. That, too, seemed ominous. Cardinal Blacktooth St. George was feeling trapped. His bowels were grumbling like the crowd, and he began to look for an avenue of escape.

"A few hundred men left here will be enough to drive the farmers out of New Rome!" said Eltür Bråm.

Wooshin was shaking his head but, as usual, remained silent. Brownpony stood up to answer the sharfs. He stumbled as he stood, and Blacktooth was surprised and a little shocked to see that he was wearing an empty shoulder holster over his cassock, under his robe.

Holding on to the side of a wagon, Pope Amen II made one last plea.

"We need the fighters here," he said. "With a show of strength we can force the farmers out of the city without much fighting." Blacktooth knew that Brownpony was trying to avoid a battle. He wondered if it were to save lives, or to avoid damage to the city and Saint Peter's. As soon as he asked himself the question, he knew the answer. Lives were cheap.

The Pope sat down, seemingly unnoticed. There was no grumbling; he was not even granted the honor of dissent. The power

Blacktooth had watched him exercise over the conclave in Valana was gone. Perhaps it was the Meldown, or perhaps his rhetoric was useless with the war sharfs and their warriors, who excelled at oratory when they wanted, but were not in the mood for talk these days.

Or perhaps it was the trees. They seemed almost evil, there were so many of them crowding in on every side. Blacktooth touched the cross that rode under his habit and called up, as he did when he was panicked, the image of Saint Leibowitz. But instead of the dubious smile of Saint Isaac Edward he saw the harsh glare of the desert sun, and he felt a sudden wave of homesickness so powerful it almost knocked him off the wagon bed.

"What's the matter?" whispered Aberlott. "Are you OK?"

"Are you?" answered Blacktooth. The warriors on the edge of the crowd were starting to make the *pop pop pop*. They were tired of waiting around for battle. Neither did they wish to ride into a city where the defenders were shooting at them from the windows of "great houses."

"They're going to burn them out, no matter what His Holiness says," said Aberlott. "Where you going?"

Eltür Bråm had risen to speak again. Blacktooth slipped away through the crowd toward the main trench, which was, even at this hour, even with all the excitement of the debate, busy with grunting men.

When he got back to the campfire, it was too crowded to get close. The Grasshopper sharf was still speaking. Blacktooth's fever was raging and he felt weak. He dragged himself off to the back of the hood wagon and rolled up in a blanket and went to sleep. In the distance he could hear drumming, and the martial, celebratory *pop pop pop*.

That night, while Blacktooth slept, Amen I came to visit him for the first time in over a week. The old man had the face of a cougar. Had he always had the face of a cougar? Blacktooth wondered in his dream; but of course! And Ædrea was there. She was sitting beside Specklebird, smiling, riding a white horse like the *Fujæ Go*; but no, her robe was open, and what he had thought was a white horse was the light coming from the gateway he had once—

Someone was shaking him, pulling his foot. It was Aberlott. "We are leaving," he said.

"Leaving? Who is leaving?" Blacktooth groaned and sat up. Aberlott was outside the wagon, leaning in. His face was painted. His greasy hair was pinned back. Beyond him Blacktooth could see the sky, a metal gray. He could hear horses stamping and men cursing and laughing. In the near distance, dogs.

"They've been up all night," said Aberlott. "After you went to bed there was another conference. But this was among the sharfs. The Pope was sent away."

"Sent away?"

"Wooshin was allowed to listen, but he was thrown out when he disagreed."

Blacktooth was amazed. No one threw Axe out of anything. "Thrown out?" Blacktooth was still woozy, half in and half out of his cougar dream. As he sat up, he realized with a sudden and unusual moment of clarity that his entire life since leaving the abbey, since he had met Brownpony in fact, had had the quality of a dream. So why was it that Specklebird, instead of Brownpony, came to him in his dreams? Brownpony was in the real dream.

Aberlott grinned and shrugged. "Not exactly thrown out, then, but asked to leave."

Blacktooth got out of the wagon. The rain clouds that had rode across the sky for days had disappeared, and the camp was almost as bright as day even though the sun hadn't yet risen.

"They are leaving only a few men from each horde, about three hundred in all," Aberlott said, too loudly. "The rest are heading south with the *Qœsach dri Vørdar* to take Hannegan City. I'm going with them!"

"But you are in the Papal Guard!"

"The Pope's Guard is going, all except Wooshin. Besides—the Pope didn't give me these!" Aberlott opened his hand. In his palm, where three empty shell casings had nested the night before, now there were six, and each was filled; each had a dark bullet peeping out of one end as though eager to be on its way.

"Goodbye then!" Blacktooth said angrily. Wrapping his robe around him against the morning chill, he half walked, half ran toward the latrine trench. As he squatted, through the bushes he could see hundreds of men stirring, grumbling, dressing, farting, laughing. *Pop pop pop!* Some were pulling at dogs, some at horses. The pall that had fallen over the camp in the last few days, the pall of rain and forest, was lifting even as the skies brightened toward the east. Almost a thousand warriors were crossing the creek, many of them slapping the sides of the metal wagons to hear them ring.

"He's taking all the healthy men," Blacktooth muttered to himself.

"There aren't that many healthy men," said the man at the

trench beside him, who sounded and smelled very unhealthy. "And I'm not that healthy and I'm going."

He spoke in Wilddog. Before Blacktooth could answer, he was off and running, barely wiping.

Through the shrubs that cloaked the latrine, Blacktooth watched the horses cross the creek, and then crawled back into his bed. It would be an hour or so before breakfast and he wanted to get some rest. He searched for Ædrea and Amen through his dream, but it was like prowling through an abandoned house, empty even of furniture. When he woke again his fever was back. He sat up, dazed. He could see by the sun on the wagon's hood that it was almost noon.

"Your Eminence," said Bitten Dog. "His Holiness and whatever, His Eminence the Pope wants to see you."

"Brownpony?"

"He wants your butt in his Pope wagon right away."

Brownpony had stopped shaving but it had hardly changed his appearance. There wasn't much left of his beard, just a few wisps of hair on his chin. Some were dark and some were light, giving him the look of a sketch that had been abandoned. He was finishing his breakfast of horsemeat jerky and plums when Blacktooth found him, at a small table that had been set in the shade of the papal wagon. "Nimmy," he said, "where is your zucchetto? I have a commission for you."

"As a soldier?" Blacktooth answered. He was ready to refuse.

"As an ambassador," Brownpony said, ignoring the novice cardinal's sarcasm. "As the papal legate to the farmers. They are all that is left in the city. Hannegan's troops have abandoned the place and left them there to fight. We could have avoided the fight altogether by peacefully slipping a thousand men into New Rome."

"A thousand Nomads are not peaceful, Your Holiness," replied Blacktooth. "And besides, the farmers have shown an inclination to fight."

"True. Perhaps you're right," Brownpony said. "Perhaps this is all for the best. We have only three hundred men anyway, mostly the Grasshopper." The Pope waved an astonishingly skinny arm around at the camp, which looked deserted in the harsh daylight, like a dream only half-remembered. Brownpony looked weaker than Blacktooth had ever seen him. Surely, he thought, it was the Meldown. *Nunshǎn* the Night Hag was claiming her husband, calling him to her cold bed.

"The War Sharf of the Three Hordes, the *Qæsach dri Vǿrdar*, our old friend and companion Chür Ösle Høngan, has taken almost a thousand of my crusaders south, to Hannegan City. Even Magister Dion and the New Jerusalemites have gone with him. They intend to join the Jackrabbit warriors and the gleps that are preparing to besiege the city, and instead of a siege we will have a battle." Brownpony sat down wearily. "Perhaps it is all for the best."

"Not so," said Wooshin.

"My sergeant general disapproves," said Brownpony. "But what does it matter? It is done." The Pope's hands fluttered in the air, like two birds. Blacktooth watched, intrigued; with that motion, this most worldly of men suddenly reminded him of Amen I.

"I'm sick anyway," Blacktooth said.

"We're all sick," said Brownpony. "Except for Wooshin, of course. Where is your hat, Nimmy?"

"Here." Blacktooth pulled his red cardinal's zucchetto from his robe. "I don't wear it around the camp. It might blow off my head and fall into the dogshit."

"No wind here," said Wooshin, who disapproved of Blacktooth's attitude toward his master.

"Oh yes, the dogs," said the Pope distractedly. "We get to keep the dogs. The *Qæsach* didn't want to take them on the campaign south. We have been left with three hundred men and almost as many dogs. And the Grasshopper sharf, of course. The farmers don't know this, not yet. What I want you to do is go into the city, Nimmy, and make them an offer of peace. Extend to them my offer of peace. The Pope's hand in peace."

"Before they discover your numbers have been reduced," Blacktooth said, scornfully.

"Why, yes. Wear your hat and your robes. I will give you a papal seal to carry."

"They will shoot me before they see it."

"Put it on a stick," said Wooshin. Blacktooth could see from the yellow warrior's eyes that he wasn't going to be allowed to refuse the mission. He resigned himself to it. He was curious to see the city anyway, and sick to death of pots and pans. So what if he got killed? Wasn't that bound to happen sooner or later anyway?

"You look very sick, Cardinal Nimmy," said Wooshin, his voice almost gentle. "Tell the farmers that we wish them no harm. We want to settle things peacefully. The Empire has deserted them but not the Vicar of Christ."

"And don't mention that the Vicar of Christ is down to three hundred men and as many dogs," Blacktooth said.

"I will overlook your insolence since it has never been an impediment to your vocation. Indeed, Nimmy, sometimes I think it is your staff. I hope for your sake it is not your crutch. Better get going, though. This has to be done today, or at least attempted."

"I have to walk?"

"Eltür Brâm has a white mule you can use," said Brownpony. "And God go with you, Nimmy."

He made the sign of the cross and allowed Blacktooth to kiss his ring.

The grassy swale had been a highway a thousand years before, and now it was a highway again. The muddy tracks of wagons crisscrossed in the grass. Who knew how many years this "door prairie" had pointed like an arrow from the plains into the forest and then to the city—or, Blacktooth thought, the other way? Though the monk had never thought much of the Pope's plans to return the papacy to New Rome, lately the Holy City had been appearing to him in his dreams. It had arrived with the fever. In the dreams it beckoned on the distant horizon, like small, steep mountains. How different was the reality! There was no horizon at all. The road ran straight between trees and low ruins that were just mounds of earth, some with openings where they were mined, others barricaded where some pitiful creature had chosen an intact basement or a mined-out room as a cave. The farmsteads were smaller here, close to the city, usually just a weedy vegetable patch and a ruined building or two; perhaps a shed emptied of pigs and chickens.

Just when Blacktooth had given up all hope of seeing New Rome, just when he least expected it, the road topped a small rise, and there it was—just as it had always been in his dream.

"Whoa." Blacktooth needn't have bothered; the white mule only moved when he got on and only stopped when he got off. He slid down and the mule stopped to nose at skunk cabbages beside the road. They were at a turn: the road went at an angle down the last hill before the valley of the Great River, or Misspee as it was called locally.

Blacktooth couldn't see the river but he could see the distant towers of what once had been a bridge; and he could see a low line of tree-covered bluffs on the other side, like a mirror image of the hill he was on. And in between, a few miles away, were steep brush-covered stumps of towers, like low steep mountains, just as he had seen them in his dream. New Rome.

But it was already afternoon, and there was no time to enjoy the view—even if it was the first horizon Blacktooth had seen in almost a month. He got back on the sharf's shaman's white mule and it started down the hill, and soon they were in the trees again.

There was more concrete and asphalt here, mixed with the grass. It would have made for treacherous passage on a horse, but the mule seemed unbothered. There were fewer farmsteads and more houses, even though the houses were just sheds attached to the sides of the ruins. Blacktooth even saw smoke coming from one or two, and shadowy shapes that could have been children playing or their parents hiding.

"Gee up," he said to the mule, just to hear his own voice and to let whoever might be watching know that he was in control and on a mission. He wished now he had bothered to learn the mule's name.

It was late afternoon before he passed the gates of the city, a low barricade now abandoned. A couple of corpses in the sentry box showed how the Nomads had avenged their murdered shaman, and how little the grass-eaters cared about their dead.

Of course, the corpses might have been Texark soldiers. Two pigs were rooting at the door, seemingly eager to find out.

"Gee up!" The white mule stepped over the rubble and Blacktooth rode on through, holding up Amen II's papal seal. It was made of parchment stretched over sticks like a kite, and held aloft on a spear decorated with feathers and the cryptic symbols of the Three Hordes. An amalgam of the sacred and the profane, the civilized and the barbaric. Like Brownpony's papacy itself.

There were more pigs on the street here, though there were no bodies. New Rome seemed deserted. The streets were straight and wide. The "great houses" Blacktooth had seen from the horizon were less impressive up close, but more oppressive somehow, dark ruins shot full of holes. There was no movement. Blacktooth knew he was being watched, though. He could feel it; he could feel more and more eyes on him as it got darker and darker.

"Whoa," he said, but the mule didn't stop.

Ahead Blacktooth saw a single figure in the center of the street. It was a man carrying a rifle.

"Gee up!" Blacktooth kicked his mule but the mule walked at the same slow pace, whether kicked or not.

"Wait," Blacktooth shouted at the man, but the man backed slowly into the shadows.

"I have a message . . ." Blacktooth shouted, just as the man knelt and fired.

Blacktooth slid off the mule, which was the only way to stop it.

He waited behind the mule for another shot. The silence was excruciating.

The man was gone.

The dialogue was too one-sided. His only chance, Blacktooth saw, was to push on toward the center of the city and hope that he came across someone with either some sense or some authority, and preferably both, before he got shot.

He got back on the mule.

"Gee up."

It was dark when they shot the mule out from under him. Blacktooth was almost in the center of the city, under the biggest of the "great houses." It must have been a long shot, because the animal went down before Blacktooth heard the shot; the *crack* came rolling through just as he was falling on his side, under the mule, which fell as heavily as an abbot having a stroke.

Blacktooth scrambled to his feet, looking for the papal seal-on-a-stick, which had snapped and was lying half under the mule. He was tensed through his shoulders, waiting for the next shot, which he knew he wouldn't hear and might not even feel. It never came.

With the papal seal, he ran back into the rubble of the "great house," where he hid under a stone slab. From here, he could see down the street both ways. It was almost dark; the sky was a salmon pink turning to rose in the west, and a darker blue ahead, in the east.

The mule was on its side, braying violently. It wasn't bleeding much, but clearly it was done for. Its front legs were kicking but the rear legs were still; maybe spine shot. Blacktooth felt his fever growing and then a fit of diarrhea hit him, and he squatted behind the stone slab. Should he hold the papal seal aloft, or did it just make him a better target? "Not now," he prayed aloud. "Not like this."

Finished, and still not shot, he decided to continue on with his mission. He had to find someone, and soon, before it got dark. Otherwise, he would be sleeping alone in the dark in one of these great piles of stone. Holding the papal seal aloft, he started walking. He knew he was still feverish, because he could sense Amen I beside him, his cougar face composed and quiet; free of concern as well as anxiety. Amen had nothing to say; lately he had had little to say.

The problem was, the mule wouldn't shut up. It kept braying louder and louder, the farther Blacktooth walked away from it.

"I have to go back," he said to Amen. He knew the old man

couldn't, wouldn't, answer, but he wanted to hear the sound of a human voice, even if it was just his own.

"I'll do for him what I did for the glep soldier," he said aloud. "It'll be a sin, too, just the same." A sin but he had to do it. Wasn't that what a sin was? Something you had to do?

No, that's duty, replied Specklebird, with his unquiet, ambiguous smile. *You have often confused them.*

It was a long way back to the white mule, and Blacktooth's legs were getting wobbly. He walked backward, holding the seal high, his shoulders tensed against the shot he expected. The mule was almost quiet by the time he got to it; the brays had turned to hoarse, honking moans. The front legs were still kicking rhythmically. The big eyes looked at Blacktooth with neither curiosity nor fear. Blacktooth knelt and said a prayer, a made-up one, as he put his knife to the creature's throat, and said a second prayer as he pulled it across.

It was like pulling a string and watching the grain flow out of a bag. The mule sank into a sudden quiet restfulness.

Blacktooth wiped his knife on the mule's coat. He was about to stand when he felt the knife on his own throat. "Stand," said a voice, and he did what he had been about to do anyway. He started to drop his knife when a hand took it from his.

Grass-eater, he thought, but perhaps he said it aloud, for someone hit him from behind, almost knocking him down. There was the smell; the grass-eater smell. There were too many hands—he thought perhaps it was a glep—and then realized that it was two men who held him, and a third who picked up his papal seal from the ground where he had laid it before taking out his knife to cut the mule's throat.

They marched him back down the street, the steps he had retraced to kill the mule. He felt a gun prodding him through his cassock. As he passed the corner where he had turned back, he thought, Why hadn't they taken him here? Had they been waiting for him to come back?

"I have a message for your leader," he said. "From His Holiness, Amen Two. I am his papal . . ."

"Shut up," said one of the men, in a tongue Blacktooth recognized as a variant of Grasshopper.

He was taken into a basement room that reminded him of the library at the abbey. It was lit by oil lamps, and several men were inside, armed with iron swords and old rifles. Most of them were dressed in rags but one wore the jacket of Hannegan's Texark cavalry. He spoke to Blacktooth in Churchspeak.

"Are you sick?" was his first question. "You smell bad."

"I come from His Holiness the Pope with a message for your

leader," said Blacktooth. "We are all sick. We all smell bad. There are thousands of sick, bad-smelling warriors, bloodthirsty Nomads, on the outlying reaches of the city, preparing to strike. I am here to give you a chance to . . ."

"Shut up," said the Texark soldier. He nodded at one of the other men, a farmer, who handed Blacktooth a cup of water and a handful of brown pills that looked like rabbit pellets. "Take one," the soldier said.

Blacktooth smelled the pills. He shook his head.

"Take one." A gun prodded him in his back.

Blacktooth took one.

"I am here to give you a chance to surrender the Holy City peacefully," he said. "The Empire is finished. The papacy is returning to New Rome. The Pope, His Holiness Amen Two, wants only to occupy his rightful place in the . . ."

"Shut up. I know who you are."

"I am the His Holiness Amen Two's—"

"We know who you are. The Archbishop sent us word to look for you," the Texark soldier said. He unrolled a scroll that had already been untied. "Are you not Blacktooth St. George, Secretary to the Antipope, and banished under sentence of death to the far reaches of the Bay Ghost and the Nady Ann?"

Blacktooth was at a loss for a reply.

A gun prodded him in his back. "Say 'I am.' And what's that hat? Military?"

"I am a cardinal," Blacktooth said. Suddenly the seriousness and the ridiculousness of it all struck him, simultaneously. The enterprise had been foolish. Perhaps even the Crusade. Now here he was, back in the Hannegans' zoo. "A joke, really. Cardinal. Pope. Soldier."

The pill was making him dizzy. He wondered if he should take another.

"We have orders to shoot you," said the Texark officer, rolling the scroll back up tightly and tying it with a ribbon. "But first you should get some rest. The pills will help you sleep. Take him to the death cells."

It was cool under the street. By standing on tiptoe, through a barred window, Blacktooth could see an alleyway and an occasional dog or pig, the pigs wearing medallions that identified, Blacktooth presumed, their owners. One pig was especially friendly; it kept coming back and sticking its nose into the bars, perhaps for the coolness of the iron.

As darkness fell, Blacktooth felt his fever subside, like a stream sinking into the sand. The chamber pot in the corner of his cell waited, empty, like the pig. The guard came just after midnight with a jug of water but no food. Blacktooth took another pill. This time they were going to shoot him, and he had little doubt that they would keep their promise. Somehow, the thought of it made him drowsy.

That night, again, he dreamed of Ædrea. She was waiting for him under the waterfall while his old friend, the white mule, grazed on the rocks outside. There was no grass but it sprung up as the mule ate. It had a hole in its throat like a wound, and Ædrea had wounds too; she showed her wounds to Blacktooth.

"Where have you been?" she asked in Churchspeak. "Where are you going?" Since he knew she didn't speak Churchspeak, he knew, in the dream, that he was dreaming.

CHAPTER 30

In the reception of the poor and of pilgrims
the greatest care and solicitude should be
shown, because it is especially in them that
Christ is received; for as far as the rich are
concerned, the very fear which they inspire
wins respect for them.

—*Saint Benedict's Rule*, Chapter 50

 HAT NIGHT WHILE BLACKTOOTH WAS
dreaming, a small party of farmers
mounted their horses, most of them
draft plugs, and rode toward the camp of
the Pope's Crusade. These were the
farmers who had survived after seeing
their families and livestock killed by the
Texark soldiers. Now they wanted revenge and the only one they could get it
on was the Antipope, whose armies their scouts had told them were
heading south, toward Hannegan City and the Red River. They knew
that Blacktooth was lying. They had seen only one party of raiders,
had wounded one and killed another. They wanted what the Grasshopper and Wilddog Nomads wanted: they wanted blood and revenge.

It was late September and there was no moon. They left, forty
riders in all, soon after dark, counting on the starlight and their knowledge of the road. It was after all the road they had ridden in on; it was
the road that led to their abandoned and ruined farms.

. . .

The Pope, meanwhile, was beginning to lose all hope for peace. The Grasshopper warriors were excited and eager for blood, after the long and loud funeral for the shaman. Many of them were drunk, and though the ceremony had been hidden from his eyes, Brownpony suspected many more had fed on the shaman's liver and lights.

"You must understand, my emissary has ridden into the city to make peace," he said to Eltür Bråm.

"You mean Nyinden. Nimmy."

"My cardinal," said Brownpony. "A member of my Curia."

"Cardinal Nimmy, then," said the Grasshopper sharf. He sat on the tailgate of the Pope's wagon beside His Holiness, watching the whooping, weeping warriors around the main campfire. It was a novelty to the Nomads, unlimited firewood, even if it was damp. The blaze grew bigger and bigger.

"They seek revenge," said Eltür Bråm. "Can you blame them? Can I deny them? They need it; it is like grass for ponies."

"The victory of the Church will be their revenge," said Brownpony, but even as he said it, he knew he didn't believe it himself. The muddy ground was crowded with moving shadows; the sky was scratched with trees. Brownpony yearned for the harsh outlines and open horizons of the grasslands and the desert. Here in the forest the noises and smells were too close.

Pop pop pop. The warriors pointed their rifles at the sky, barely visible as a smattering of stars behind the trees. The Grasshopper sharf had managed to keep only two shells apiece for them, but he knew that Brownpony had more, left with him as a concession from the stores in Magister Dion's wagon train.

"You must give the men the rest of the brass bullets—Your Holiness," Demon Light added, with a faint smile.

Amen II shook his head. "They must wait until my emissary comes back. Then your warriors can ride in, in triumph." In fact, Brownpony was already worried. He knew that if Blacktooth had not returned by morning it would mean he had probably been killed; perhaps even hanged under the interdict they had both signed when they had been released from the zoo in Hannegan City.

"Tomorrow, then," said Eltür Bråm. He looked up at the tree-hedged, moonless sky.

The Pope took the sharf's arm. "And you must control them!" he said. Across the clearing, in the firelight's gleam, he could see the sharf's carriage, with I SET FIRES painted on the door. "There will be no fires, Demon Light. The farmers will surrender when they see your force. They may have already surrendered to Nimmy."

"I think not—Your Holiness."

"I want no fires in New Rome. I am here to restore the city, not to destroy it." The Pope twisted the sharf's arm. It was like arm-wrestling; the point was not to defeat him but simply to show that he knew and understood Nomad ways. "No fires, understood?"

"Understood," said Eltür Bråm, pulling his arm loose and stalking off to join his warriors at the fire.

"I have unleashed a storm that I cannot control," said the Pope, retiring into the wagon and arranging his robes for sleep.

He was speaking to Wooshin, who stood in the shadows beside the wagon. The Yellow Warrior shrugged. That was, as far as he was concerned, the nature of all storms and all wars.

The Pope was asleep when the farmers came. They had dismounted and were leading their horses across the creek when the dogs awoke, and awoke the warriors who were sleeping it off around the dying campfires. The fighting was brief and vicious, and except for the screams and the splashing, almost silent. The Grasshoppers were reluctant to use their few bullets but eager to try the knives and clubs that slept by their sides, where women might have been.

When dawn came, the water was still bloody in the little pools along the shore. Death by the knife is a messy, lingering business; some of the farmers still flopped like fish. Four of them were captive, uninjured except for the rawhide cord passed through their cheeks. They sat tethered in the shade of the food wagon, one whimpering, the others waiting stolidly for whatever awaited them.

The Pontiff awakened to find his camp almost deserted. The Grasshopper warriors were gone; so were their horses and the dogs. "You said you were going to wait!" he complained, finding Eltür Bråm by his fire, eating breakfast.

"They gave us no choice." The war sharf shrugged. "They tried to steal our horses."

Brownpony kicked the fire. "They were only a few fools. You could have chased them off."

Eltür Bråm shrugged again. "The dogs followed them. My men had to follow the dogs. They are under orders not to burn the city, though."

Brownpony didn't believe him. And before noon the smoke was rising over the wall of trees to the east, from the city he had never seen.

·   ·   ·

The pig came in the morning, but the jailer didn't. She stuck her snout between the cool bars and sat, staring down at Blacktooth, who was trying unsuccessfully to pray.

As the morning dragged on, Blacktooth heard shots in the distance, shouts closer, the scuffling of feet in the narrow street outside. He still had six of the little pills but nothing to take them with. He was afraid of the warm water in the bucket by the door, so he took one with the last of his own spit. Toward noon, he drank the water.

Already hungry when he was locked in the cell, he grew hungrier. It was hard to tell time because there was no sun and it was raining, a gentle shower that spattered onto the alleyway all day, muddling the footsteps of the occasional passerby, always a dog, never a human.

The pig came again in the afternoon, or what seemed to be the afternoon.

Blacktooth kept the pills in his cardinal hat, which his captors had allowed him to keep, along with his cross and rosary. The zucchetto kept the little brown pills dry. They seemed to work. The fever was gone, and Blacktooth didn't miss the cramps and the runs that had kept him busy, especially in the mornings, for days. But he felt lonely without the visions of Ædrea and Amen, the companions who had walked by his side and accompanied him not only through his dreams but through the interminable waking dream that seemed, lately, to be his life.

Blacktooth had never felt so alone. He remembered with a certain affection Brownpony and the prison-zoo in Hannegan City, when they had been spied on by the Wilddog prisoner and observed by the amused citizens. He remembered brooding, taciturn Wooshin. He remembered the insolent, chubby Aberlott, failed contemplative and lover of cities. He missed them all; he missed even Singing Cow. From his solitary basement cell, Blacktooth looked back on the life at the Abbey of Saint Leibowitz and wondered at the cunning and perfect mix of solitude and companionship that was the monastic life. Some men were made for solitude, but not most; and certainly not he. Specklebird had loved his solitude because he filled it with spirit. He was never alone. Ædrea's solitude had been spook-solitude: accepted by none, scorned by all.

Desired by one.

The two of them in their solitude had kept Blacktooth company. But then, he thought, I don't require much in the way of company. "Right?" he asked the pig when she stuck her head between the bars again. And like Ædrea, like Amen, she returned no answer.

By afternoon no food had come and the rain had stopped. Was there to be no last meal? To die seemed bad enough, and to die hungry seemed the final, the ultimate insult. Would he then be hungry forever?

Shocked at his own impiety, Blacktooth fell to his knees and prayed for forgiveness.

The door was heavy wood, probably oak. It seemed more substantial than the black iron bars on the little high window. Blacktooth knocked on the door, then kicked it, timidly at first, then harder and harder. There was no response. He couldn't tell if anyone was out there or not. And what was out there—a hallway? He couldn't remember. It had been dark when he was brought in. That had been only a day ago—hadn't it? Blacktooth wished now that he had made marks on the whitewashed stone walls, as the previous occupants had done.

There was nothing in his little cell but the bed, which was two boards laid over stone blocks, a coarse wool blanket, a stool, and two buckets: one by the door and one in a corner. The bucket of warm water by the door was still almost full; the bucket in the corner was still empty. The room had apparently been used as a prison by the Texarki before; the walls were filled with intricate but illiterate scratchings—faces, smiles and frowns, a sun, various interpretations of the male and female body. The wall looked to Blacktooth like the surface of a monk's brain, the scratchings on the soul that a man learns to live with and, usually, hopefully, eventually, to ignore.

He sat on the bed. He lay on the bed. He stood at the window. He stood on the stool and looked out the window. He saw a narrow deserted alley with a ruined step against a wall where there was no door. There were bloodstains on the wall above the step. While Blacktooth watched a dog came and sniffed at the stain, then walked away. Was this the end of it, then? The killing place? The stairs that went nowhere, the wall without a door . . . He shivered. He was very hungry.

In the distance the street opened onto another, busier street, and Blacktooth could see people passing, carrying mysterious packages, or occasionally, guns. The ones with guns walked in twos and threes. Closer at hand, another dog sniffed at the stained steps in the alley, then trotted away.

"That's where they *execute*."

Blacktooth turned and saw that the door to his cell had opened silently; beyond it was an indeterminate darkness. For such a huge door it swung on silent hinges. An unfamiliar farmer/guard stood in the doorway with a bucket. Young, in his rude twenties; redheaded, a grass-eater. "You're not supposed to be up there," he said.

"I'm praying."

"What about your hat?" The zucchetto was on the bed.

"We don't wear the hat to pray."

The guard crossed to the corner and picked up the bucket; he set it down again when he felt that it was empty. He carefully avoided looking into it.

"I'm supposed to empty this," he said. It was a reproach.

"I suppose that means I'm supposed to fill it," Blacktooth said. "But aren't you supposed to bring me food? I had no supper, and now no breakfast."

The farmer/guard shrugged. He wore leather pants and a canvas vest, probably taken from some soldier's locker. Or body. His teeth were gone bad already. "They didn't tell me anything about food. They only told me to empty this. And bring the water."

"Are they going to—shoot me?" asked Blacktooth. He felt dizzy; he had to step down off the stool. When he looked up, feet on the cold stone floor, the guard was gone, almost as if he had been an apparition. The door closed, then a bolt slammed shut. Loudly.

"Bless you, my son," said Blacktooth, making the sign of the cross. "I'll go back to my prayers." He stood back up on the stool and looked out at the world, or what little of it he could see from his tiny window. Prayers indeed. But what else was prayer but an attempt to look out of the tiny window of the soul? Perhaps he would try to pray later, as it got closer to the time for his execution.

Would it hurt? he wondered. It seemed to be the wrong question, but he couldn't think of the right one.

Another dog came by and sniffed at the dark stain on the step—also praying? In the distance an old woman and a child poked through rubbish with a stick. When the woman turned up something, the child would lean down to get it. Blacktooth couldn't tell what they were collecting.

There were more shots in the distance, then a strange and yet familiar wild smell. Even before Blacktooth realized what it was, his heart was pounding.

Smoke.

"You told your men to set the fires," the Pope, Amen II, said to Eltür Bråm. Demon Light denied it but Brownpony knew better. *The Grasshopper is always at war . . . I set fires . . .* And what did it matter if he denied or affirmed it? It was done.

Brownpony and the sharf were sitting on the bed of a wagon,

watching the returning warriors thunder across the creek. It was beginning to rain again. Brownpony couldn't see the sky, but he knew from his Curia—half of whom were sick, and spent time at the secondary latrine halfway up the hill—that a curtain of smoke hung over the city a few hours' ride to the east.

"Fires just happen," said Eltür Bråm. "No man can prevent them. No man should."

Dogs barked. Horses neighed. The Nomads were straggling back in twos and threes, calling to the women to prepare bandages and food, and replenish the firewood stacks. They were shouting triumphantly, but in truth they had had few encounters with the mysterious enemy. The few wounded had been injured when their horses had stumbled in the unfamiliar streets, or had burned themselves setting fires.

None knew, still, how many defenders the city had, or even if it was being defended at all. And Blacktooth had never returned. It was almost sunset. "Perhaps he has found the peace you robed ones always say you are looking for," said Eltür Bråm.

"Perhaps," replied Brownpony, choosing to ignore the Nomad's sarcasm. But he doubted it.

Smoke. It was getting dark; or was it? The few people Blacktooth could see at the end of the street were running.

He got down from the window and banged on the oak door. He put his ear to the wood, but he couldn't hear footsteps or voices. It was a strange place, this room at the end of Blacktooth's life. It reversed normal life, which we go through always looking backward. Now it was the past that was the mystery. Blacktooth could see clearly into the future. Too clearly. He could smell it. It filled the air—like smoke.

He was afraid he would panic, and he did. It wasn't the fear of fire, or even the fear of dying. It was just panic, pure animal panic. It filled him, rushing in unbidden, with no thought or emotion intervening. As sudden and as irresistible as lust (which he had grown to know so well), it both comforted and terrified him with its intensity. Like the faith he had searched for but never found, it replaced all doubt with certainty.

Blacktooth let it rage, kicking and beating on the door, shouting first "Fire!" then "Help!"; then, "For the love of God!"

It brought no peace. The pain of his bruised fist and his own screams brought him back to a different reality; a more monklike reality. He stopped screaming, surprised at how easy it was to stop, and knelt by the bed with his rosary. The smoke was thicker, but the air was still breathable. Blacktooth was no longer hungry. The water in the water bucket was dancing, and in the distance he could hear dull booms—buildings falling or bombs going off. . . .

He must have fallen asleep. He sat up and saw that it was still dark outside the window. In the distance he could hear shooting. The farmer/guard was standing in the open door with the bucket. He wore a scarf over his face. For the smoke? It seemed to have diminished.

Blacktooth started coughing. "Excuse me," he said when he had stopped. The guard/farmer still stood in the doorway. "What's happening?" Blacktooth asked.

"They are fighting. Your Antipope is burning the city."

"Ah."

Then he was gone. He never returned. Whether he was killed or not, Blacktooth never knew. The shooting never got closer and it eventually faded away.

When dawn came it was a strange dawn that seemed to come from inside the cell, rather than outside, filling the tiny basement room with an eerie light. The city was on fire. The wind was scouring the alley, picking up bits of straw and grass and dust and scraps of ash and paper.

Blacktooth banged on the door, but he didn't scream this time. He didn't expect anyone to come and no one did. The fire seemed to be getting closer; the wind was hot, as if it were pulled through one fire on the way to feed another. Blacktooth stood as long as he could at the bars, and felt his face burning—then realized he had forgotten the pills. There were four left, folded in the hat. He took one and poured the last of his water over his head. Death by fire. He could smell fuel oil. He recognized the smell from when he was a novice, handling the abbey's relics for the first and last time. . . .

Beatus Leibowitz ora pro me!

He heard footsteps in the alley. "Help," he called out, but no one came. Not even the pig, who had probably been eaten. Blacktooth said his rosary, then put on his zucchetto and lay down on the narrow plank bed, on top of the jail blanket. Better to just wait, he thought. Sooner or later the end will come. "A dewdrop, a flash of lightning," Amen had said. "Ash, dust . . ."

He must have fallen asleep, for soon he was back at the waterfall with Ædrea. The water had stopped falling, though. It stood like a sheet in the sun. She was standing in it, in the sun, very wonderfully beautifully perfectly naked. "Hey," she was shouting.

"Hey!"

Blacktooth sat up. Someone was at the bars. He thought at first it was the pig, but it was a woman with a child.

"Are you a priest?"

"No."

"So what's the hat?" It was the old woman he had seen with the stick, going through the trash piles.

"I'm a cardinal," he said, taking it off.

"What's a carnidal?" she asked, reversing the syllables as simple people sometimes did. "Is that like a priest?"

"Sort of," Blacktooth said. "Help me out of here. I'm afraid I got myself trapped."

"I can't do that," the old woman said. "Will you baptize my son?"

She pushed a face to the window. The boy looked too young to be her son, and too old at the same time. He was bald and his wrinkled forehead was blue. A glep.

"I can't do that," Blacktooth said. "I'm not a real priest."

"He's not my real son," the old woman cackled. "I bought him."

"Bought me!" said the glep boy. "I commensurate the deception. Am."

"What?" A bell was ringing somewhere, faster and faster. Then Blacktooth heard the spray of shots. It was being rung with bullets.

"He's very strong," said the woman.

"Strong," said the glep. "Accurate am I the exception."

"He says all you have to do is move this brick."

"What brick?"

The woman stood up and made a scraping noise with her stick. With a fierce demented grin, the boy pulled a bar loose, then another. "Strong!" He threw both bars into the cell at Blacktooth, who ducked. They rang on the floor with the sound of bells.

"Hey!"

Blacktooth flattened himself against the wall. Had the bars been loose all along? The jail was like the abbey; all he had to do was walk out and he was free.

He waited until he was sure the old woman and the glep boy were gone; then he pushed his zucchetto and the jail blanket through the bars, and climbed after them into the alley.

The air was thick with smoke, and he held his sleeve over his nose. It had been easier to breathe in the basement jail. At one end of the street he saw the woman and the boy, poking through garbage unconcernedly, as if the world were not on fire. They seemed to have forgotten him. "Bless you, my son," he whispered—and walked quickly the other way.

CHAPTER 31

 LACKTOOTH HAD SEEN ONLY TWO CITIES IN HIS day: Valana, built of wood and stone, and Hannegan City, made of wood and mud. The Holy City, New Rome, was a city built of old pieces of old cities; it was a mixture of old and new, more like an abbey than a city, with piles of brick and stone built upon piles of brick and stone, all mixed and leavened with wood and grass and straw. All flammable, all tinder, and, it seemed to Blacktooth, all burning.

He was on a wide, straight street with mounds of rubble and stumps of towers, the "great houses," on both sides. At first he was alone, but as he walked farther east, into the rising sun and away from the fire, the street became more and more crowded with frightened, silent people. Blacktooth felt an unexpected, unwanted kinship with these frightened grass-eaters who were suddenly emerging from basements and the stumps of buildings (just as he had), dragging their pitiful rags and remnants and pots and animals and children with them. Everyone was leaving the city.

In the distance behind him, he heard shots, rare and ragged. If there were any fighting Nomads in the city, they didn't show themselves. No fighting horses, only mules and old nags. Only stray dogs.

The fleeing people were weirdly silent. Shouts or cries would have been welcome, but Blacktooth heard neither; it was as if the window from his basement cell had led him into a world where only children cried or complained. The adults were glumly silent, stumbling forward. Perhaps they thought their accents would give them away, or perhaps there was just nothing left to say.

New Rome was burning.

Blacktooth had prepared himself for execution, and now even his hunger was gone. A hand plucked at his sleeve—a child's hand—and he found himself, through some process he neither understood nor fully noted, part of a small group dragging a frightened mule up the steps from a basement room. How it had gotten there, who it belonged to, and who wanted it—these were questions that belonged to another reality. All that was present was the need to help coax the terrified, braying beast up the narrow steps.

Then it was gone into the gathering, streaming crowd, its owner—and the child—chasing it; and Blacktooth was half walking, half running after them. The wind had risen and now there was a wall of flame directly behind, to the west.

Four men and four women, all naked and holding hands, snaked through the crowd, singing hysterically. Blacktooth tried to look away from the women's breasts but couldn't. It wasn't desire he felt but some other, almost forgotten feeling: hunger, or hope. Two men in uniform with repeating rifles ran past, then two more, all running in step. It was almost comical. Blacktooth pulled off his zucchetto and hid it under his habit. A fallen mule in the traces of a cart was screaming pitifully, trying to rise. One haunch was smeared with blood.

The fire was either closer, or hotter, or both. At the end of the street it was a wall of flame, taller than the "great houses." Blacktooth now had two shadows, one that walked before him and one behind.

"*I set fires*," thought Blacktooth, remembering the blue and gold inscription on the Grasshopper sharf's carriage.

A farmer leaned over the injured mule and drew his knife. Blacktooth stopped him, with a hand on his arm. "Let him live," he said in Churchspeak.

"Huh?" The farmer stared at Blacktooth's robes, and then cut the traces. The mule limped off, whickering, and the farmer stuck the knife back into his belt.

"I will help with the wagon," said Blacktooth, in Grasshopper. He put his hat back on and pushed.

It was a two-wheeled cart of vaguely Grasshopper design, loaded with household goods and junk—including an ancient, tiny black-skinned old woman with two kittens, which she was kissing, first one and then the other. Blacktooth pushed and the farmer pulled, then two more men joined in, throwing their possessions in the back along with the old grandmother. They all spoke Grasshopper, mixed with a little Churchspeak and smatterings of Ol'zark. They fled on east, toward the Great River.

Blacktooth stayed with the farmer with the cart all day. Hair-Puller was his name; or it might have been a description, or even a confession. The man was bald. He was so solicitous, sharing his food and water, that Blacktooth assumed he was a Christian; until he realized that the farmer thought Blacktooth's red zucchetto meant that he was a soldier. Though he lived in the Holy City, he had never heard of the Church. To the farmer there were only two types of people, farmers and Texark soldiers. Though he was of them by blood, the Grasshopper Nomads, "the people," coming in from the plain "where the trees do not go," were less than human, or more, perhaps. An elemental like a herd or a storm.

Even after escaping from his basement jail, Blacktooth still felt imprisoned, between the fire to the west and the still unseen river to the east. By noon the smoke had eaten the sun itself, and a terrifying red darkness fell over the streets like a pall. The stream of refugees grew to a flood, all heading east. The streets grew wider, and at the same time more choked with refugees, all farmers. The "great houses" to the east were even greater, and there were no trees; Blacktooth had never imagined he would miss them.

It was late afternoon when they reached the river. Blacktooth didn't know what it was at first. The crowd piled up on itself, then started milling, turning. There was fire to the west, and fire to the north as well. There was a scuffle, a swift panic, and Hair-Puller was lost in the crowd. Once Blacktooth thought he heard the familiar creak of the wagon, then lost it again. Luckily he had managed to save his jail blanket.

It was getting dark. Except for a few children crying, the refugees were silent again, milling in place, making decisions through some sort of slow, visceral process, like a worm. The main stream turned south, following the bank of the river out of the city. Suspecting what it was that had turned them, Blacktooth climbed a low stone wall. A few others, like himself, stood on top, looking at the Great River.

Blacktooth had never seen, or even imagined, so much water before. It was a different substance than the water he had known in the mountains or on the Plains. It didn't dance, or swirl, or fall. It lay like a sheet of muddy glass, half brown and half silver. It was a plain of water. He thought he could walk across it, but he knew better.

Squeezing past the others, Blacktooth walked along the top of the wall to a fallen pier at the water's edge. Boats were standing off shore. He hadn't seen many boats before, just the flat-bottomed ferries on the Red, but he knew what they were. These were barges, some with sheds built with chimneys and window glass, and long sweeps that turned them and moved them on the water. People on the decks and roofs watched the city burn. The boats made small circles in the current, watching the fire, perhaps waiting to move in later to loot. A few farmer refugees tried to swim or wade out to the boats, but they were beaten away with the sweeps.

A few shots were fired. The people on the barges were dressed in rags, the same as the farmers, but Blacktooth assumed they were from the other shore.

The fire was getting closer. From the water, it was almost beautiful: fire, loveliest of the four elements of the world, and yet an element too in Hell. Blacktooth found a spot at the end of the pier, and wrapped himself in his jail blanket; paradoxically, it kept him cool. Beneath the wall of smoke and flame, he could see the stream of refugees heading south along the riverbank.

"So many," Blacktooth muttered. The man standing beside him grunted what sounded like assent. He was holding a long gun, but not a repeater. It was the type that fired stones through a thick iron barrel. For some reason, Blacktooth felt safe beside him. He had no desire to rejoin the refugees and head south.

"They could have defended the city," Blacktooth whispered, and the man grunted again. They could have, Blacktooth thought, but they hadn't wanted to. New Rome wasn't their city. They had been driven there by the Texark soldiers and then driven out by the flames. Few were armed, and those with very ancient weapons, of the kind that had killed the sharf's shaman.

Perhaps the man standing beside him had fired the shot.

The howling wind was whipping the water into whitecaps. It was blowing from the east, sucked into the city by the flames. As night fell the flood of refugees lessened to a stream, and then to a trickle, all turning south along the riverbank, heading toward Texarkana, as if drawn by some ancient, instinctive urge. Late that night their fires could be seen in the low line of wooded bluffs to the south. By then Blacktooth was asleep. He slept for hours, alone at the end of the pier. By daylight the fire had almost died away.

And the Holy City of New Rome was burned.

The smell of food awakened him. Blacktooth had slept wrapped in his jail blanket, propped against a wooden upright at the end of the pier. If the fire had kept coming it would have followed the pier to him, and consumed him along with the rest of the world. But he had been spared. He had taken off his boots and hidden them under his blanket; they were still there, as was his zucchetto, with three pills left. As soon as he sat up, he felt Hilbert's fever returning. But couldn't it be hunger? He hadn't eaten in days.

He smelled fish cooking. At the end of the pier, a boat was tied up on the muddy bank. A group of men were gathered around a small fire. Blacktooth stood up, pulling the blanket around him to hide his monk's robes. These boatmen were probably less Christianized even than the Grasshopper farmers, who were themselves barely Christian at all. And he remembered his jailer's remark, that the Antipope was burning the city.

Something in the shape of the group, their stance or the tone of their voices, told Blacktooth that he could join them safely. Still, he edged in cautiously, walking slowly along the edge of the wooden pier.

A body floated by, buoyed by its own gases. A woman's face smiled upward toward a scrim of smoke and sky. Blacktooth looked away and stepped onto the mud. Someone passed him a piece of fish, wrapped in big soft leaves. The smell of it was so overpowering, so delicious, that he had to sit down to eat it. No one paid any attention to him or asked him any questions. The men by the fire seemed united by a sort of rough charity; they were boatmen, and spoke a version of Ol'zark that Blacktooth could barely make out. The outsiders, two or three stragglers like himself, spoke not at all. Their silence seemed to be essential to the rough peace that prevailed.

After he had finished the fish, Blacktooth looked around. Now that the smoke had cleared he could see the big towers of the ancient bridge. He could make out low bluffs on the far side. The water was impossibly wide. The Great River, the Misspee, flowed into the sea; how big, then, must the sea be? Already this was more water than Blacktooth had ever imagined.

"The Nomads coming," said one of the boatmen. The word for

Nomad in their dialect was "horsepeople." The implication was, *so we ourselves must flee!*

There were no women among the boatmen; but even as Blacktooth was noticing this, several women walked down the bank, trudging from rock to rocky step, tracking ash and carrying armloads of what looked like rags onto the barge and into the shed/cabin. They were followed by other women with bags that clinked; perhaps crockery?

Someone passed Blacktooth another piece of fish, followed by a pot of warm water which seemed to be some kind of weak tea. "The Nomads are coming," said another woman, arriving at a run. The "horsepeople."

There was a shout, and Blacktooth and the other "guests" stood back while one of the boatmen scattered the fire with a stick. Before Blacktooth realized what was happening, the barge was spinning off in the current. The other "guests" by the dead fire quickly scattered— and Blacktooth found himself holding the boatmen's water pot, alone again. It was just as well. For the first time in days, he felt his bowels calling, so it was with pleasure that he found a hidden place by the water's edge under the pier and took a dump, and then cleansed himself and went into the city.

Blacktooth assumed that the Grasshopper warriors would arrive as soon as the fire burned out, and begin looting and raping, and with them would come Brownpony and the Curia. But it was noon and the streets were still empty. He had rolled up his jail blanket, and now he felt exposed and vulnerable in his habit and zucchetto as he walked the right angles of the streets waiting for the Nomads to find him and take him to Brownpony.

No one came. It was as if the Holy City had been cleansed. Even the corpses in the street, blackened like cinders, seemed cleansed somehow, as if the fire had swept away their corruptions leaving only a purified husk.

There wasn't much to loot. The fire had consumed everything but the brick and stone, reducing the city back to the rubble it must have been before the Harq-Hannegans had rebuilt it. How many times had these bricks fallen? Blacktooth wondered. How many conquerors had passed under this lintel, this stone? The Holy City with its grid of streets between blackened piles of rubble and shells of burned buildings was like a palimpsest of civilization and misery, all intermixed and intermingled, one age falling onto the other like leaves; like cottonwood trash, the debris of centuries good only for a twenty-minute or a twenty-hour fire.

No Nomads came—no howling barbarians to pick through the ruined and smoking center of all Christendom. No shots, no shouts, no neighing horses, no mad laughter or cries of delight or screams of dismay. A great fire brings with it a truce in the natural order of things, a still center; and there weren't even scavengers in the streets. The occasional corpses, one every block or so, lay in quiet dignity as Blacktooth walked around them. There were only the buzzards gathering high overhead, like fly ash.

Saint Peter's was not hard to find. The roof had burned and fallen, but the smoke-stained dome still stood over the ruins. Most of the interior was destroyed. Blacktooth sat in the back in one of the long pews that had survived the lottery of destruction. It was curious, he thought, what was left and what was consumed, by time as well as fire. There were a few memories left of his childhood—the hard months among the Nomads, the early days at the abbey. But whole years were gone, leaving nothing but ash, like the long rows of gray ash marking where the clean-burning oak pews had been. Where a pew was gone, its footstool might be left behind. It was like the remnants of the *Magna Civitas*, burned to the ground more than a thousand years ago. Parts of it stood almost intact, like the Church; other parts were not even remembered.

For the first time in months, Blacktooth closed his eyes and prayed; not under duress but because he wanted to. He stayed on his knees when he finished. He could feel Hilbert's fever returning, like an old friend. He welcomed it—for there was Ædrea again, in the waterfall that had no water where water did not fall. And there was Amen Specklebird.

Amen I with his cougar smile—

Amen was shaking him by the shoulder. But it was Amen II. "Nimmy, is it really you? We thought you were dead!"

"So here you see my church," said Brownpony. His hair was gone and his eyes stared out of dark hollows. Even the red beard of the Red Deacon was mostly white. All around the basilica, the great empty windows looked out on ruins. The deserted streets were quiet and only the howling of dogs could be heard, far off in the distance.

"Oh, God, the Grasshopper!" Brownpony knelt and blackened his hands in the ashes, and held them up toward the smoke-stained dome. "What a fool I have been, Nimmy. To trust the Grasshopper!"

"Holy Madness trusted them too, Holy Father," Blacktooth replied. "And so did Axe!"

"I trusted Bråm to fight well," said Wooshin. "He did that, before the desertions."

"It may be," said the Pope, "that he could not control his warriors, once they felt the battle fury—drawn down from Empty Sky, as they say." He wiped his hands on his dirty white cassock; over it he wore a repeating pistol in a shoulder holster. "And the Grasshopper warriors have no love for the Church hereabouts."

Wooshin stood by, still wearing the plaid tunic and sergeant general's stripes Brownpony had made for him. He seemed depressed. Blacktooth was not surprised. All Wooshin's friends, the Yellow Guard, were either dead or gone south with Magister Dion and the Qœsach dri Vørdar. His master, Brownpony, seemed weaker than ever; and ruined.

"Nimmy," Brownpony was saying. "Look what I have done to my church. It wasn't for myself that I wanted this throne. And now look at it."

"It wasn't you . . ." Blacktooth started. But he couldn't finish. Who else had done it? It was Brownpony who had assembled the Three Hordes, who had armed them with repeating weapons, who had set them in motion across the sea of grass toward New Rome—and who had then told them not to set fires.

I SET FIRES, Eltür Bråm's carriage was inscribed. He had made no secret of it. LIKE HELL YOU WILL, the Pope had answered.

Like Hell—and now, look around.

Brownpony laid his hand on Blacktooth's brow, leaving a smear of ash. "Your fever seems better, Nimmy," he said.

"I got over it," said Blacktooth. "They captured me and gave me some pills, the same pills the Texark are using south of the Nady Ann. But they are almost gone."

"You don't feel feverish."

"I can feel it," said Blacktooth. "I can see it coming. When I am feverish I see the girl, Ædrea. And the old Pope, Amen Specklebird. They were with me just now, before you came in." He saw no point in lying to Brownpony; not anymore. "I was glad to see them."

"Do you see them now?" Brownpony asked.

"No, of course not. The fever is not that bad."

"The fever is not that bad," repeated Brownpony. He seemed more distracted than ever. Then suddenly he drew the pistol from his shoulder holster. "Do you hear that, Nimmy?"

"Hear what, your—"

"Shhhh!—"

Wooshin drew his short sword from his belt; he left his long sword in its steel scabbard. Seconds later, Blacktooth heard what the old warrior and Brownpony had heard. Hooves on the paving stones, and then on steps, and then on wood—clattering "inside" the cathedral.

It was Black Eyes, the Nomad double agent who had briefly been imprisoned across from Brownpony and Blacktooth in the Hannegan City zoo. He was dressed in the full regalia of a Wilddog warrior, riding a sorrel pony. "Your Holiness," he said sarcastically. He nodded at Nimmy and avoided Wooshin's eye—and sword—altogether.

"Put it away," said Brownpony, softly—although he still held the repeating pistol in his hand. Wooshin put the short sword away, but kept his hand on the hilt of the long one.

"What are you doing here? I thought you were with the Emperor in Hannegan City." Brownpony stood straighter, tried to look regal. Black Eyes didn't seem impressed.

"As a spy," the Nomad said. "When the Lord of the Three Hordes came south, with the tanks and the glep army, I crossed the Red River to join them. But the battle is lost. The Hannegan's guns spoke too loudly, and too fast. The gleps have run back to their valley, the spooks are on their way back to the Suckamints, and the War Sharf of the Three Hordes is on his way home."

"Høngan Ösle?" Brownpony looked stricken. "The Qæsach dri Vørdar is going home?"

"The Weejus are calling," said the Nomad. His pony was dancing in and out of the pew ashes, ruining their straight lines. "The Texark Wooden-Nose is burning our lodges, killing our women, stealing our horses. We ride for the short grass. I am only here to make sure that none of the children of the Big Sky Woman are left in the city when the grass-eaters arrive. You should leave also. You are also her child and she is also your mother, begging your pardon, Holiness. The Texark cavalry is on its way."

"From the south?" The Pope pointed with the pistol. "From Hannegan City?"

"From the north as well. From the sea of grass. We will leave their city to them. Good luck, Your Holiness."

He rode off loudly, hooves clattering, and Brownpony fell to his knees, cursing his fate. "Vexilla regis inferni produent!"

"What's he saying?" Wooshin whispered.

"Forth come the banners of the King of Hell," said Blacktooth.

"It is not their city," Brownpony muttered. "They never wanted it!" He looked up toward the sky and saw only the blackened ruined dome. He tossed his pistol into the ashes.

. . .

In the center of the ruined sanctuary, the throne of Saint Peter's had been miraculously spared. Behind it was a painted wooden statue of the Holy Virgin, also spared. Blacktooth and Wooshin silently followed Brownpony as he crossed toward the throne, picking his way through the litter. Brownpony paused in front of the throne and studied it before smoothing his cassock and sitting down. His freckled skin was drawn and thin strands of gray hair showed at the edges of his dirty white skullcap. He still wore his empty shoulder holster.

"Here."

Wooshin tried to hand him the papal tiara, but Brownpony shook his head, so the Yellow Warrior placed it in the ashes at the foot of the throne. It was getting dark. Blacktooth had no difficulty finding a live ember with which to light a few candles. Set behind the throne, they hardly illuminated anything except the face of the Virgin, and that only barely.

Brownpony's eyes were shut as if in prayer, and Blacktooth was glad. Looking into them had been like looking in the window of a burning house.

Wooshin squatted beside the throne of Saint Peter, kneeling back on his heels, balanced on the scabbard of his long sword he still wore at his side. Though limber, he was also, Blacktooth saw, an old man. He moved without joy or ease.

The truce the fire had created was ended. Outside in the street Blacktooth saw a dog chase away a buzzard, to pull at a blackened body; then it was chased away in turn by a pig. His old friend? Another dog stopped at the huge open door and looked into the basilica in the dying light. It sniffed the smoky air, pissed on the bronze door, and trotted off into the gathering darkness.

A riderless horse wandered past, part of a severed human leg hanging from the stirrup.

"Glory to God in the highest." It was the weak, tired voice of Elia Amen II Papa Brownpony, speaking as if Job's wife had told him to curse God and die, and he was wearily complying. "I think I hear the Texark cavalry coming. Blacktooth, do be sensible and run for your life."

"It was only a riderless horse," Blacktooth said. But he cocked his ears and heard something in the distance. He could feel it as much as hear it: a low, indistinct rumbling that might have been faraway thunder.

"There's nothing to keep them out of the city now," Wooshin said.

"But you, m'Lord—" Blacktooth was confused. "Where will you go?"

If Brownpony heard him he gave no sign. Blacktooth looked at the statue of the Holy Virgin behind the throne of Saint Peter's. She stuck out her tongue. It was black, and forked.

The fever's coming back, Blacktooth thought. He looked around for Specklebird and Ædrea, the companions of his delirium, but they were nowhere to be seen.

Brownpony turned and looked up at the Virgin. His eyes grew bright. "So it's you, after all."

"Huh?" Blacktooth and Wooshin both asked at once.

"Mother, Mother of the night and the mares of night, the dreams."

"M'Lord?" Blacktooth took the Pope's arm.

"Look! Look at her!" Brownpony jerked his arm loose and pointed at the Virgin. The dark spot crawled out of her lower lip.

"A-a w-worm," Blacktooth stuttered.

"The Night Hag! My real Mother!" Brownpony said. "Blacktooth, escape while there's time. Loyalty to me stops here. Obey me: go!"

Blacktooth stepped back. "Why should I start keeping my vows by obeying you now?"

Brownpony laughed weakly, but repeated: "Go. Go be a hermit and teach those who come to you about God. Be yourself. That is His calling to you."

Faintly Blacktooth could hear distant hoofbeats, getting louder. "Go!"

Wooshin was still hunkered down beside the throne, his narrow eyes closed as if in prayer. Behind the throne the Virgin's face glowed in the flickering candlelight. Blacktooth walked under her, circling slowly toward the still-standing back wall of the cathedral. There was defintely a worm on her lip. Or a tongue that moved. Forked, black. Maybe it was a shadow from a candle. *Ora pro nobis nunc et in hora mortis nostrae!*

There was a door in the back. Halfway there, Blacktooth heard a sharp *hissssss* like an intake of breath. He recognized the sound of Wooshin's sword being drawn from its scabbard. Then he heard the murmur of Latin. To Blacktooth's surprise, this least orthodox of Popes was reciting the creed. In spite of himself, Blacktooth stopped and listened. It began as the creed of Nicaea: "I believe in one God, the almighty Father, maker of the earth and the sky, and of all things

seen and unseen, and in one Lord Christ Jesus . . ." but before
Brownpony was done, the creed of Athanasius crept in and took over,
saying, "and in One Holy Roman Catholic and Apostolic Church outside of which there is neither salvation nor remission of sins—*unam
sanctam Ecclesiam Romanum etiam Apostolicam, extra quam neque sa-
lus est neque remissio peccatorum*—"

"Now?" It was the voice of the Axe.

Blacktooth paused, afraid to look around, and heard the rustle of
silk. There was a faint affirmative grunt as Elia Brownpony, Amen II,
fell to his knees at the foot of the throne. The whisper of the sword
cutting the air ended in the chunk of flesh and bone, and the thump
of the head, and the splashing of gushing fluid on the littered floor.

Blacktooth ran toward the exit as fast as he could. He had almost
reached the doorway when Wooshin's quavering voice called after
him. "Help me, before you go, please!"

He stopped again, and turned this time. He saw Axe sitting on
the floor beside the corpse. Wooshin had taken out his other sword,
the short one, and held it pressed against his belly. While he pressed
slowly with one hand, with the other he picked up the bloodstained
long sword from the floor, and tossed it toward the monk. It fell short,
ringing like a bell on the stone floor.

Blacktooth stepped over it, shaking his head. With long steps he
strode to the warrior's side. "No!" he said fiercely. "Would you now
abandon your master?"

Wooshin looked at the heap of bloody silk beside him, glared up
at Blacktooth, and pressed the blade into his belly until the blood
came. He groaned and stopped and looked up at Blacktooth again,
pleading.

Nimmy picked up the long sword. But instead of lifting it for a
strike, he leaned on it as if it were a cane. "Your master's enemy still
lives," he said. "Cut open your belly if you want to, Wooshin, but I
want to hear you say 'Long live Filpeo Harq!' before I help you die."

Wooshin removed the blade from his flesh, and said something
in a strange tongue, clearly a curse. Blacktooth knelt down and looked
at the wound. It was bleeding profusely, but it seemed not to have
penetrated far, if at all, into the abdominal cavity. He helped the aged
warrior to his feet, then knelt down and tore off a piece of the Pope's
white silk cassock. He gave it to Axe to hold against his wound.

Wooshin picked up Brownpony's head and placed it next to his
body; then he covered both with the jail blanket, perhaps forgetting
that it was Blacktooth's.

"Shouldn't we bury him?"

Wooshin shook his head. "This was the way he wanted it. 'Leave me for the Burregan, the Buzzard of Battle.'"

"His bride," said Blacktooth. He looked for the Night Hag, but she was gone. The Virgin was back, with her glowing baby and gentle smile. Looking down at Brownpony, dead under the blanket, a still form, Blacktooth felt strangely unmoved. So much of his life since leaving the abbey had been in service to this worldly man. But who or what was Brownpony in service to? Do any of us know, ultimately, what it is we serve? Blacktooth wondered. Then he felt immediately ashamed. Was he not a brother of the Albertian Order of Saint Leibowitz? Why had he wanted so long to be released from his vows, if the vows meant nothing?

The hoofbeats were closer now, rattling in the square outside the front of the cathedral, then on the low, wide steps. For a moment Blacktooth thought of stepping out into the street and offering himself up for capture. Then would he be given the pills he needed; and perhaps the death.

But no. Wooshin recovered and sheathed his long sword. Blacktooth followed him out the back door of the cathedral. There was nothing more in Saint Peter's to do. The dogs were wandering back into the city, smelling new blood and death. Where was it written? *And the dogs ate Jezebel in the field of Jezrahel* . . .

As he followed Wooshin down the alley toward the river, Blacktooth could hear horses' hooves inside the cathedral of Saint Peter's; then raised voices over the dead body of Amen II.

CHAPTER 32

They are able now, with no help save from
God, to fight single-handed against the vices
of the flesh and their own evil thoughts.
—*Saint Benedict's Rule*, Chapter 1

T RAINED THE NEXT DAY, AND THE NEXT. THE
sky was close and heavy, not like the
bright Empty Sky of the grasslands, and
Blacktooth felt bent by it, even more
than by the rain, which was little more
than a persistent drizzle. He followed
Wooshin, and the Axe followed a small
train of wagons and livestock headed for
the Watchitah Nation. It was an infor-
mal attachment but it seemed better than traveling alone. The farmers spoke a degraded form of Grasshopper mixed with Ol'zark larded
with old English Churchspeak, a dialect Blacktooth assumed was confined to the environs of New Rome. He had trouble understanding it
at first but his talent for languages rescued him, and he was surprised
to find a dialect so rich in sources and influences, so poor in subtlety
and nuance, though it may have been his understanding that was
poor; or perhaps it was the farmers themselves.

There were few women among them. The apparent leader of the

train was a spook (Blacktooth suspected) named Pfarfen. He had a daughter, beautiful except for her huge glep ears, and her hands, which she kept mysteriously covered with rags. Pfarfen kept her in the wagon where she sewed and sang all day, and (Blacktooth was alarmed to discover) entertained her father sexually at night, when the wagon was pulled up with the others alongside the muddy road.

The Holy City was far behind them now, still burning, a smudge on the northeast horizon that was seen only when the low clouds broke. The army that had gone south with Høngan Östle had been routed, and the thinning stream of refugees heading south was mixed with a thickening stream of refugees heading north, giving the impression at the narrow stretches of highway of a great milling herd heading nowhere. At these points the traffic left the roads for the still-green fields, which were quickly churned into quagmires by wheels and hooves and feet. Though they all spoke versions of Grasshopper, it was not difficult to tell the Nomad warriors from the Hannegan's semi-civilized farmers: many of the refugees heading north were wounded, and most were still armed. A few had even kept their horses, and several times these looked at Blacktooth's clerical garb with an alarming anger.

"Come on, Nimmy," said Axe, whenever Blacktooth showed signs of wanting to ask about the Qæsach's campaign. He was in a hurry to reach Hannegan City. Since Blacktooth had refused to act as his keisaku and help disembowel him, the wizened old warrior had rediscovered his own purpose. Blacktooth suspected, but didn't want to ask, what it was. Axe had the peculiar ability to go for days without food and never look malnourished. This was not true for Blacktooth, who had a monk's love of dinner; but because he helped with the wagons when they were stuck, he was welcome at the meager dinner and breakfast fires.

The river was only a memory, somewhere to the east. Now there were the bottomland streams, at least two to cross every day, almost too deep to ford. At each crossing there were piles of abandoned, unburied bodies, stacked in grotesque positions as if they were in the process of composing themselves from the earth, rather than the reverse. The refugees walked by them pretending not to notice and commanding their children to look away. But children have always understood war better than adults. Death only mildly interests them; it holds neither the horror nor fascination it has for adults, who can almost hear the wings.

Overhead the sky was black with circling dots.

The faithful Burregun.

The spook-farmers with whom Blacktooth and Axe were traveling were tolerant of Blacktooth's tonsure and habit, even the zucchetto which he carried over his back without wearing. Still, he worried. He remained under the Hannegan's death sentence, as far as he knew. It was the death sentence that had given him Hilbert's pills, which were almost gone. Leaving New Rome with three, he had cut his dose to one a day, taken in the morning with his corn gruel. There were two left the day Blacktooth saw three brother monks, crucified by the side of the road, but whether by the Texark soldiers or by angry Nomads routed from their promised looting of Hannegan City, it was impossible to say. The Burregun had feasted and the bodies were too far gone.

"Come," said Axe, and after a hasty prayer, Blacktooth hurried to catch up with his companions. He wanted to bury the dead but he didn't want to join them yet. Above all, he didn't want to be alone.

The next day he took his next-to-last pill. That afternoon he came across a second group of two clerics, hung from poles by a muddy roadside. It appeared that they had been hung up and then stoned and shot with arrows, a merciful death overall. Their faces looked almost peaceful, as if they had only just entered the doorway into death. Blacktooth studied them for a long time. They looked familiar; it was not their faces, although in truth all men look alike, and looked increasingly alike to his Most Reverend Cardinal Blacktooth St. George, Deacon of Saint Maisie's, in these days in what he was beginning more and more to think of as the twilight of his life (even though it turned out to be a long twilight). They looked to him as monks all looked, hung on the cross of life. This was not their world. There was something almost inspiring in it.

"Come," said Axe.

"Go ahead," said Blacktooth. "I'll catch up." *Feed the hungry, clothe the naked, bury the dead.* He borrowed Wooshin's short sword and used it to bury the two by the side of the road, using stones and sticks to complete the work. When he finished, it was dark. Not wanting to travel alone at night, he slept in a shallow dirt cave by the side of the road, using his mud-stained zucchetto for a pillow.

The next morning he took his last pill, and under the clear sky he was almost overcome by terror. He hurried all day, hoping to catch up with the spook-farmers and the Axe. The few refugees he saw on the road eyed him curiously but left him alone. But he kept remembering the crucified churchmen, and he was afraid. He hid the red hat under a bush, and later that day saw a chance to get rid of his habit, trading it for the leggings and tunic of a farmer who had been laid out beside the road, almost tenderly, a corpse not too old. The monk buried him and took his clothes. *Bury the dead, clothe the naked.*

It had been easy to toss the zucchetto, but leaving behind the coarse brown Leibowitzian habit was not so easy. After a few moments of hesitation, Blacktooth rolled it up like a bindle and carried it with him. He felt like a pilgrim, or a booklegger again.

Under a clear sky speckled with buzzards, he pushed on south and west.

Hilbert's fever traveled with him. Blacktooth had no hunger, and after a few days no diarrhea, but no strength either. There were fewer and fewer travelers on the road, and those Blacktooth saw spoke in Ol'zark, or not at all. The stream of refugees had diminished to a trickle. Some had crossed the Great River, counting on the water to protect them from the depredations of Filpeo's soldiers and their Nomad adversaries, still thought of as the Antipope's army. Others had just disappeared into the forests to hide, to die, to wait for neighbor or kin.

Blacktooth never caught up with the wagons. He had lost Brownpony; now he lost Axe. When the road forked west he followed it, putting the morning sun at his back, even though he knew that Wooshin must be heading south for Hannegan City. Blacktooth was hungry for Empty Sky. The fever was like a companion, another consciousness. Often it took on a human form, as when he was crossing a small creek (the creeks got smaller and smaller, the farther west he went) and he saw Specklebird waiting on the far bank. Eagerly, Blacktooth waded across, but when he reached the bank the old black man with the cougar face was gone. Another time he saw Ædrea standing in the doorway of an abandoned hut. The illusion, if it was illusion, was so perfect that he could hear her singing as he climbed the hill toward her. But in the hut he found only an old man, dead, with a crying baby in his arms.

He waited for the baby to die before burying them both together. *Bury the dead.*

It would be dry and hot for days, and then the rain would come, announced by lightning, attended by thunder, falling in sheets and turning the roads to mud. Hilbert's fever was handy, enabling Blacktooth to go for miles without eating. The long feverish days reminded him of his Lenten fast as a novice, when he had been seeking his vocation and thought he had found it among the Albertian bookleggers of Saint Leibowitz. And hadn't he? He missed the abbey and the Brothers, now that he had the freedom he had sought. He had even been released from his vows by the Pope himself; or had he simply been bound in new chains?

Go, and be a hermit.

· · ·

The day Blacktooth saw Saint Leibowitz and the Wild Horse Woman, he had been traveling all morning over open grasslands between wooded draws. He was worried about outlaws because he had seen several campfires near the road, still smoldering, yet never saw anyone. He considered putting his habit back on, but decided against it. Even those who didn't hate the Church for what it had supposedly done to their world, often thought it was rich, and even a poor monk could be a target for highwaymen.

By midday he had the distinct feeling someone was following him. He looked back every time he crossed a high spot—the road was empty and he saw only buzzards, flyspecks to the south and east. Blacktooth was glad to see that he had crossed that shifting boundary where the forest begins to give way to the grass; but the feeling of being followed wouldn't go away. It became so real that when he crossed the next creek, he hid on the far bank behind the corpse-colored trunk of a fallen sycamore, to watch.

Sure enough, a white mule with red ears came through the trees and down the muddy bank. At first he thought the woman on the beast's back was Ædrea, with the twins she had gotten by him under the waterfall. But it was the *Fujæ Go*, the Day Maiden herself. Far beyond Ædrea in beauty, she carried an infant in each arm, one white and one black, both nursing at her full breasts. Even as she rode the mule down the muddy bank and into the water, they sucked on.

Then she dropped the reins. The mule stopped in the center of the sluggish stream. Its black eyes were looking straight at Blacktooth; no, *through* him.

He stood up, no longer trying to hide. As he stepped over the log, he realized that what he was seeing was not in his world and not for him to touch. He knew with certainty that if he spoke, she would not hear him, and that even if she looked straight at him, she would not see him. He felt that he had changed places with one of his own fever dreams, and that it was they, and not he, that were real.

That he was the dream.

It was then Saint Leibowitz stepped out of the bushes and took the rope halter. Blacktooth knew him from Brother Fingo's twenty-sixth-century wooden statue in the corridor outside the abbot's office; he recognized the curious smile and dubious eyes. That the Saint was no vision, Blacktooth knew from the faint, sweet fuel-oil smell that hung in the air as he passed. It was Blacktooth who was the dream.

As she rode past, the *Fujæ Go* gazed up toward the sky. Blacktooth hadn't noticed how majestic the little oaks could be, a filigree of branches against a pale sky. One baby was blinding, albino white; the other was as black as Specklebird. Both had their eyes squeezed shut like tiny fists fending off the world. The mule looked straight through Blacktooth, like the Day Maiden. Only Leibowitz, in his burlap robes with his rope over his shoulder, looked directly at the monk as if to say, like Axe, "Come."

Then he winked and walked on.

Sancte Isaac Eduarde, ora pro me!

Blacktooth followed; Blacktooth had always followed where Leibowitz had led. But now he was weak and he fell twice climbing the bank. By the time he got to the top, the two (the three? the five?) were far down the narrow trail, almost lost in the dappled shadows. He hurried after them but he was feverish, and even though they were not walking fast, he gradually fell behind. He had to stop again, and he must have fallen asleep, for when he woke it was almost dark and they were impossibly far away, like a speck in the eye, an iota shimmering in the distance.

But something was wrong.

The sun was setting behind his right shoulder. Saint Leibowitz and the Wild Horse Woman were not heading west into the sea of grass, but south, toward Hannegan City. The *Høngin Fujæ Vurn* always chose the victor as her Lord, and the Hannegan had won the war. By choosing a husband, she chooses a King, and she was Filpeo's now. Leibowitz was taking her to him.

Blacktooth wandered on, hoping to find Texark soldiers who would give him pills. The winter was coming; it was the winter of 3246. The Empire and its borders were being redrawn and the few travelers Blacktooth passed were wary. Every few days he buried a corpse as he walked west, no longer a cardinal, no longer even a monk. *Go and be a hermit.*

It no longer rained. The trees thinned out into shadows in the draws, and the road led higher and higher into a world all grass under a dome of sky. Blacktooth's fever had become a small fire that both weakened and sustained him. The morning he left the last of the trees behind, he saw a great bird circling far above. It was a Red Buzzard, the Pope's bird. Ahead by the road something or someone had fallen. Two smaller black buzzards pulled at it, but the meat was not yet ripe enough for their beaks. Nimmy stopped to watch as the Burregun, the Pope's bride (as he thought of it), swooped down. Awed by her size, the smaller buzzards stepped back, black heads bobbing; but she ignored them, and they soon joined her at the attempted feast. The Red Buzzard was stronger and had a little better luck, but still the carcass was too fresh for easy eating.

From where he sat on a hummock of grass, Blacktooth could not tell if the corpse was human. "Feed the hungry, nurse the sick, visit the prisoner," he said aloud, reciting the corporal works of mercy.

Bury the dead.

He tossed a rock. The birds stopped and eyed him with funereal solemnity, then strutted and preened and resumed eating. He tossed another rock and they ignored it. He still carried Wooshin's short sword, but he could not summon the resolve to quarrel with the queen of the buzzards.

Then he watched as a bald eagle came, driving them all away, even the Burregun, the Buzzard of Battle. The bald eagle was Filpeo's National Bird. It nosed at the corpse, then lost interest and left, riding a thermal straight up into the china blue sky.

Blacktooth St. George got to his feet and went to see what it was he had been left to bury. He hoped it was not another child.

CHAPTER 33

> Let all things be done with moderation,
> however, for the sake of the faint-hearted.
> —*Saint Benedict's Rule*, Chapter 48

T WAS A GOOD YEAR FOR THE BUZZARDS. THEY followed Blacktooth all the way back to the Abbey of Saint Leibowitz, little dots like eyespecks against the expanse of Empty Sky. Blacktooth gave up on finding Hilbert's pills, and the disease gradually gave up on him, burning down to embers. If he had a fever it was the same fever that had plagued him all his life, the burning that Amen and Brownpony had noticed, each from his own particular perspective.

There was no longer a safe route across the grasslands. One could no longer evade the Empire by traveling north of the Nady Ann, or avoid the hordes by traveling to the south. Both groups had interpenetrated, and the contended territories on both sides of the Nady Ann were passable, and yet uncertain. South of the Brave, the Kingdom of Laredo had collapsed in on itself.

The grass itself seemed to be shrinking back into the earth.

There were stretches of sand and dust that took half a day to cross. The Empty Sky seemed even more of an emptiness than before. Blacktooth wore his habit again, and said his rosary as he walked. But had he eaten? And where had he found water? The few people he saw were on horses, on the horizons.

One day there was rain. But it was a swift dry rain, the kind that comes to the high plains and barely reaches the ground, darkening the dust and throwing it up in great splotches, and then evaporating suddenly in the flashes of sun that showed, like slow lightning, after the clouds had ridden away on their long ponies.

Empty Sky.

There was no road, and then no trail. Blacktooth followed the setting sun. Wagon tracks braided across the dry rivercourses, running in every direction. The few people Blacktooth met were peaceful and shared their food; the bodies he found he buried, using the short sword he had borrowed from the Axe.

He walked alone most of the time, accompanied only by his shadow striding before him in the morning, and falling behind by evening. Only at noon, in the heat, would it desert him altogether. Reduced to its essentials, sky and earth, the world seemed more intricate and complex than ever.

Blacktooth missed the little glep cougar with its blue ears. He wondered what had become of Aberlott, who had so loved the little brass cartridges of war. Had he become one of the motherless ones? Or found his final home under the prairie soil?

Other such thoughts came, one with each step . . . arriving and departing without speaking, like birds. At other times Blacktooth walked with an empty mind, a gift, like Empty Sky, in which each step was a prayer.

It was a good year for the buzzards. Blacktooth could tell by how easily they were chased away. There were always other feasts waiting, just over the next hill.

Dom Abiquiu Olshuen had died after another stroke, and Prior Devendy was taking his place until a new abbot could be elected according to the time-honored Benedictine rule. Once he had arrived, Blacktooth had little desire to stay at the monastery, even though most of his good memories (as well as many of his bad ones) were set amid those ancient adobe walls. The stories of Ædrea's stay as Sister Clare had become almost legend, and Blacktooth heard several versions. They were linked with the apparition some of the Brothers claimed to have seen of the Holy Virgin in the eastern sky.

"That's the Night Hag," said Blacktooth. "She means war and death, not peace and hope." He could tell by the way Brother Wren and the others crossed themselves that they didn't want to hear it— even though they were preparing for war in their own way. They had sealed the holy relics in their original chamber and dusted off the Jackrabbit smuggler's cannon. Brother Carpenter was in the basement, planing boards for a heavier door. The defeat of Brownpony's plans for a new order signaled the beginning of a new age of darkness. Somehow Blacktooth no longer feared it, or even thought about it. Blood and screams were the water in which humankind swam.

Four children had been brought in from the village. Two of them had already died. It seemed there were new diseases abroad in the desert.

After visiting Jarad's grave, Blacktooth stood looking into the empty one that was always kept waiting. The straw around the open maw was hardly necessary, as there had been even less rain this year than usual, Prior Devendy explained. The grave was so deep that it seemed to Blacktooth that he could see all the way to the bottom of, of . . .

He swayed and almost fell. "Gerard's affliction," the Brothers called it after the beloved fainting monk of almost a thousand years ago.

"You seem a little woozy," said Prior Devendy. "Come."

He led Blacktooth through the crowded dayroom of the monastery, under the old familiar *vigas*, into Olshuen's office. Using a key that hung from a cord around his neck, Devendy opened a drawer, and took from it another key, with which he opened a cabinet of dusty bottles. He poured a glass of brandy. Blacktooth almost waved it away until he saw that Devendy was pouring one for himself as well.

"Oregon," he said. "It was left here as a gift for Brownpony when he became Pope Amen Two. He took the papacy to New Jerusalem and never drank it."

"And now he is dead," Blacktooth said. He had told no one about the scene in the basilica of Saint Peter's—only that the Pope was dead.

"He made you a cardinal," said Devendy. "Where is your hat?"

"My zucchetto. I put all that behind me. I suspect whoever is made Pope will undo all Brownpony's cardinals anyway."

"You don't need to be a cardinal here," said Devendy. He smiled tentatively. "Only a priest."

"Only a what?" Blacktooth looked at the old priest warily.

"The Brothers want to elect you Abbot. For that you will have to be ordained."

"That's not possible," said Blacktooth. "*Non accepto.*"

"My thoughts exactly," said Devendy, looking relieved. "But I promised I would ask."

"I have no vocation for it," said Blacktooth. "I was given my vocation by Pope Amen Two. I will stay a couple of nights and then go."

"To the Mesa of Last Resort?"

"I thought I might go that way."

"That's where she went," said Prior Devendy. "She was, uh, injured, you know, and she stayed with the old Jew after she left here. But I'm sure she must be gone."

Blacktooth looked out the window toward the Mesa. It shimmered in the distance like a mirage of rock.

"Is the old Jew still there?"

The old Jew was still there. Blacktooth left the abbey the next morning with the gifts of a blanket and breviary, a canteen and a loaf of bread. He was greeted with a rattle of stones halfway up the trail that led to the top of the Mesa. He ignored them; they were only pebbles. He wedged himself up through the last crack onto the top, and there was Benjamin Eleazar bar Joshua, looking no older than he had looked ten years before, or a hundred years before that for all Blacktooth knew.

"You," said the old man. "I suspected it might be you."

"Brownpony is dead," Blacktooth said.

"He was not the one" was all old Benjamin had replied. He told Blacktooth that Ædrea had stayed with him several months, until her sores had healed, and then had left without revealing her plans.

Had he found her much changed?

"Changed?" The old Jew only smiled and shook his head, apparently misunderstanding. "It never was any better, it never will be any better. It will only be richer or poorer, sadder but not wiser, until the very last day."

Irritated, weary of oracles and parables, Blacktooth wrapped himself in his blanket and went straight to sleep. He stayed with Benjamin two nights, sleeping in the tent where Ædrea had slept. The old tentmaker himself never stayed in a tent if he could help it. Blacktooth was awakened by rain on the tent every night, a few great splattering drops. Or was that a dream sent to advertise his tentmaking and rainmaking skills? There was dry lightning off to the east each night: the Wild Horse Woman, admonishing her children on the Plains.

He left on the third day. The old Jew filled his canteen from a pool hidden under a rock. The water was cold and clear, and Blacktooth was surprised to find that it lasted him all the way to New Jerusalem.

"Even if she had come," Prior Singing Cow told Blacktooth at Saint Leibowitz-in-the-Cottonwoods, "I would have turned her away. You heard what had happened to her."

"Yes."

Blacktooth had followed the papal road north, then cut off at Arch Hollow, into the Suckamints. The settlement at New Jerusalem was much diminished. Magister Dion had not made it back from the "Antipope's war" (as even the spooks were calling it), and no one knew of Shard's Ædrea, except that she had left for Laredo under interdiction. No one believed Blacktooth when he told them that the interdiction had been lifted by the Pope who was not a pope, at New Rome which was no longer New Rome.

Nor was she to be found in Valana.

But Aberlott was, working as a secular scribe in the square of Saint John's, under the walls of the Great Hall of Saint Ston's and next door to the old Papal Palace where Amen had delivered his now-legendary seventeen-hour acceptance speech. The air of Valana was rich with the familiar urban smells of horse dung, food, and smoke. The streets were bustling; after the Crusade's defeat, many of the Nomads had come to settle in the narrow strip of farmland watered by the mountains. They bought and sold horses and cattle, changing their ways to suit their world's changing ways.

"I got tired of being a soldier," Aberlott said. "Did you tire of being a cardinal, Your Excellency?"

"I'm not a cardinal anymore," Blacktooth said, finding his old companion's sarcasm as tiresome as ever. Aberlott had a long scar under one eye, which he said he had "earned" outside the gates of Hannegan City when the Texark troops had outflanked and ambushed Høngan Ösle's warriors. It went well with his missing ear.

"I almost bled to death," Aberlott said. "I ended up in Hannegan City. Once the fighting was over, the Empire just folded us in, like raisins into a cake. Many of the Qœsach dri Vørdar's Nomads are now part of the Emperor's guard. I wandered around for a few weeks, then got a spot as secretary to a N'Ork churchman who arrived for the conclave, and couldn't speak Ol'zark."

"Conclave?"

"Oh, yes," Aberlott said. "Sorely Nauwhat called a conclave and had himself made Pope, or perhaps we might say Filpeo had him made Pope. Urion Benefez was bitter; still is, I imagine. Without Brownpony to resist and stall and prevaricate, the bishops and archbishops drifted in, and Sorely nullified all the nullifications of the Amen Two, and then Wooshin nullified Filpeo."

"The Axe."

"Indeed," said Aberlott. "Stopped his carriage in the street. Sliced off his head when Filpeo stuck it out the window to see what was going on. The Hannegan's guard showered your yellow man with bullets but he welcomed them, he bared his throat and chest and belly to them. I saw it."

When Blacktooth closed his eyes he could see Wooshin's disapproving narrow eyes. "I would be dead now if it were not for him."

"Wouldn't we both? Anyway, you are no longer a cardinal. The papacy has been removed to Hannegan City, which is ruled by Benefez, as regent for several of Filpeo's sons, who will settle it among themselves, in typically bloody fashion, I imagine, when they come of age. In the meanwhile, a rough peace reigns."

Aberlott had married Anala, the sister of Jæsis, bringing her and two small children to Valana from New Jerusalem. He offered Blacktooth a place to stay, but the house was small and Blacktooth discovered he had no taste for domestic life. "I have been a monk too long," he told Aberlott, bidding him farewell and heading out toward the south.

It was a very good year for the buzzards. The younger generation waxed strong, soared high and far on black wings, waiting for the fruitful earth to yield up her bountiful carrion. One night, Blacktooth awakened in a cold sweat and thought that his fever was back. Then he looked north and saw the sky filled with Nunshãn, the Night Hag, huge and ugly. He could see stars through her upraised arms. "Who is dying?" he asked aloud; he found out later it was his old friend Chür Osle Høngan. Brownpony's plan had been a disaster for the Nomads. After the defeat, the Three Hordes had turned their backs on one another. The Treaty of the Sacred Mare no longer held, and the Plains were littered with bodies thrown down by drought, by famine, and by the motherless ones.

Blacktooth traveled south across the Nady Ann, the Bay Ghost, and at last the Brave. No longer a cardinal, he expected to be turned away at Mother Iridia's convent of San Pancho Villa of Cockroach Mountain, but she welcomed him almost as an old friend. She had no news, though, of Sister Clare-of-Assisi. She suspected Ædrea was somewhere with her own people.

"Her own people?" Blacktooth protested. "I was at New Jerusalem, and they knew nothing of her."

"The gleps," said Mother Iridia. "The spooks. The Valley of the Misborn."

The Jackrabbit country had always been harsh, but after two dry summers it had become even harsher. The wet years were over. Sand was taking the grass. Hannegan City was prospering, though. The Empire had turned east, and was looking toward the woodlands and the growing commerce up the Red from the Great River.

Blacktooth worked several days in the marketplace as a scribe before he was summoned to a papal audience. The summoner surprised him even more than the summons, for it was Torrildo, wearing a curate's gown, complete with feather.

"I told His Excellency you were here," the still handsome young man told Blacktooth. "You should be more careful; you are still under interdiction."

"I don't see why. If he took away my cardinalship, why couldn't he take away my interdiction?"

"It's Benefez," Torrildo said. "He thinks you had a hand in killing Filpeo."

I did, thought Blacktooth.

"He probably thanks you for it," said Torrildo. "But he doesn't particularly want you *around*."

Sorely Nauwhat was most respectful and even curious to hear of Blacktooth's adventures. He was especially interested in the situation on the Plains, but he knew more than Blacktooth. The apparition of the Night Hag had been seen all over the High Plains. The Weejus women were not pleased. When the *Qœsach dri Vφrdar* returned from the South, he was called before them and put to death. After the funeral feast his bones were buried in three widely separated locations, decided by each of the three hordes.

"Why is he telling me this?" Blacktooth wondered as the plump, grave Pope rattled on, seemingly unconcerned about the time. *He is burying Brownpony's dreams.* Filpeo's were buried next: the Pope, who had been in the Emperor's carriage, described in gruesome detail how Wooshin had done his work. Filpeo's guard were equipped with the first copies of the repeaters, and several misfired. Axe had removed the head of the seventh Hannegan in a single stroke, then laid down his sword and knelt to receive the bullets chasing into his chest like bees into a hive.

Dominus ex deu.

The audience lasted all afternoon, and was exhausting. After the lengthy and bloody assassination, Pope Sorely described the imperial situation in great detail. The repeating weapons were decisive. With them, Texarkana at last controlled the Plains. The old way of life was dying, and those who could not see the end coming could hear it keening in the wind. Even the grass was going. Crescent-shaped hills of sand marched slowly from west to east. The Empire that had secured its western frontiers now looked more and more to the east. New Rome smoldered for years but was never rebuilt. . . .

"My son—"

Blacktooth had fallen asleep. The Pope didn't seem insulted. When he left the log Papal Palace, Blacktooth was given a small sack of gold coins at the door. Pay for listening, he thought; and then on reflection realized it was travel money. He was to make himself scarce.

That had been his intention all along. Hannegan City, like Valana, was in turmoil. The streets were crowded with horses and men. The army was being decommissioned, new legates were piling out for the west, and the Grasshopper lands to the north were being opened up to the motherless ones and also to those among the Hannegan's former enemies who wanted to celebrate the new peace by raising cattle and grass.

Leaving was easy. Blacktooth was weary of cities and old friends and enemies. He was weary of mankind, so using the Pope's money he bought himself an ass, or to be precise, a mule, and headed north along the ragged edge where the forest meets the plains.

Grass. It stretched unbroken to one horizon, and meandered among the low, dark trees on the other. The little mountains called Winding Stare were lit with fires, whether of celebration or mourning, Blacktooth couldn't tell.

He rode unchallenged past the first log outposts of the gleps. He hoped the Valley of the Misborn would take him in, and it did. The Valley, or the Watchitah Nation as it was now called, had grown to be a network of valleys, up and down the low mountains called the Old Zarks. Blacktooth wandered until he found a little community of bookleggers and memorizers, called Post Cedar. He traded his mule for a g'tara much like the one his father had given him, and lived on the mountainside above the abbey, swapping his services as a scribe and a tutor for food.

He found shelter in a rockhouse cave, very like the cave where Amen had lived, except that these eastern caves were broad and open, like a mouth. They provide protection against the rain, and some against the cold; but none against the years.

And so, Blacktooth St. George grew old, reciting the Divine Office and meditating on *The Rule of Saint Leibowitz*, which enjoined him to the humility he was surprised to discover had been waiting for him all along. It was a sister to the deep loneliness he treasured, a loneliness he no longer wished filled. It was an emptiness as tangible as love. Some nights, though, he found himself praying to whatever might answer such a prayer that Ædrea would come to him. He had heard that a blond spook who wore a nun's robe practiced medicine in the next valley. The local priest called her a witch; sometimes she healed minds the priest had cursed, and because of this, the priest feared her.

Blacktooth needed his mind healed, but that was not what he feared in her. He feared the gateway beneath the clitoris, torn open by the black god and the white god he had seen riding with the Day Maiden her rubriauricular white mule. Or had the old Jew done that to her? It was just over the hill waiting for him, the world gateway of the Lord Jesus and of all the saints, and he was a coward. Sometimes he stroked himself into a moment's ecstasy thinking about it, and he did not hide his shame from the Holy Mother Day Maiden *Fujæ Go* who watched him from the corner of the hut of his mind. Neither did he mention it in his annual confession to the Leibowitzian priest who visited him every Maundy Thursday. The priest always wanted to wash Nimmy's feet on behalf of the abbot on that occasion, but the hermit refused.

"You won't acknowledge your poverty? Isn't that your pride?"

Blacktooth signed and let the man wash his feet and give him communion.

He had given up Jesus several times, as Amen Specklebird had advised, when the Savior became an occasion of sin for him: but he always came back, and so, it seemed to him, did the Savior. *Well, how have you been doing lately, Lord?*

For three hours every weekday, he taught thirteen children of various ages how to read and write their own dialect; he also taught them a little music, and taught them—sometimes to their parents' disbelief—a few things about the geography of the continent, and as much as he knew about the history of the world and the fall of the *Magna Civitas*. Some of the children believed him, and others believed their parents; but the laughing parents brought him food in payment for their urchins' literacy, and they mended his clothes, furnished him blankets, and occasionally brought him a hemina of wine for his weakness.

When he was alone, he opened himself. Sometimes the ecstasy of God came through the opening, but more often it did not. He decided to stop leaving an opening for God. That was what Meister Eckhart advised: to be so poor that he had no place for God to come into. When God had no place to come into, He was in every place. There was nothing else.

But Blacktooth did not consider himself a religious man. He did not know if God was the Father, or the maker of Heaven and Earth, and of all things visible and invisible. He couldn't see that it mattered, since God Himself, when He became manifest as a whirlwind bush, never bothered to tell him; never said, "Blacktooth, I am your Almighty Father, and I made this Earth you're kneeling on and the sky you are kneeling under."

CHAPTER 34

Let those who recieve new clothes always
give back the old ones at once, to be put
away in the wardrobe for the poor.
—*Saint Benedict's Rule,* Chapter 55

 UST OVER THE MOUNTAIN FROM POST CEDAR
was a convent, where there lived a nun
known as Sister Clare. She awakened one
morning with one of her "feelings," and
knew that the hermit who lived in the
next valley was dead. She had known of
him for years but had elected to leave
him in peace, knowing the difficulty of
the journey he was on. No one told her
he was dead; no one besides herself knew it yet, and she only knew
because of the feeling, not unlike joy and yet not unlike sorrow either,
that wouldn't leave her. She welcomed the feeling. The hermit had
few enough left in this world to miss him.

With the abbess's permission, Sister Clare packed a loaf of bread,
a little cheese, and then, as an afterthought, a freshly dead mouse
from the trap in the kitchen. She walked over the steep and little-used
trail to Post Cedar. On the far side of the valley, across from the

monastery, she found the narrow path to the dry cave, just where she knew it would be.

The old man hadn't been dead long. It was not his death but his age that filled Sister Clare's eyes with tears. She had expected some-how to find a handsome young man, even though she was herself an old woman, bent and spotted with years.

Blacktooth was sitting against a stone with the head of a small cougar in his lap. The animal lifted its blue head when she ap-proached. It was Librada. Ædrea waited but the cougar wouldn't leave, and finally had to be coaxed away with the mouse so that she could bury Blacktooth and place at the head of his grave the little cross she had carried with her all these years.

The rosary that was clutched in his hand, and the crude g'tara he had left leaning against the back wall of the cave, she took with her.

ABOUT THE AUTHOR

Walter M. Miller, Jr., grew up in the American South and enlisted in the Army Air Corps a month after Pearl Harbor. He spent most of World War II as a radio operator and tail gunner, participating in more than fifty-five combat sorties, among them the controversial destruction of the Benedictine abbey at Monte Cassino, the oldest monastery in the Western world. Fifteen years later he wrote A Canticle for Leibowitz. The sequel, Saint Leibowitz and the Wild Horse Woman, followed after nearly forty years.